THE
EVENING
NEWS

ARTHUR HAILEY

THE

EVENING

NEWS

DOUBLEDAY

New York   London   Toronto   Sydney   Auckland

This Large-Print Edition contains the complete, unabridged text of the original Doubleday edition.

PUBLISHED BY DOUBLEDAY

a division of Bantam Doubleday Dell Publishing Group, Inc.
666 Fifth Avenue, New York, New York 10103

DOUBLEDAY and the portrayal of an anchor with a dolphin are trademarks of Doubleday, a division of Bantam Doubleday Dell Publishing Group, Inc.

The Production Review Committee of N.A.V.H.* has found this book to meet its criteria for large type publications.

Library of Congress Cataloging-in-Publication Data

Hailey, Arthur.
The evening news / Arthur Hailey.—1st ed.
p.   cm.
I. Title.
PR9199.3.H3E9   1990
813'.54—dc20   89-27629
CIP
ISBN 0-385-41335-1

FIRST EDITION
BVG

To Sheila and Diane
with special gratitude
and to
my many friends in the media
who trusted me
with off-the-record information.

Author's Note: In Frederick Forsyth's novel *The Day of the Jackal,* published 1971, an assassin obtains a fraudulent British passport. In *The Evening News,* a terrorist obtains such a passport—in a differing way, the description the result of my own research.

However, I acknowledge that in this matter, Mr. Forsyth's footprints were there first. —A.H.

T H E
EVENING
NEWS

PART
ONE

1

At CBA Television News headquarters in New York, the initial report of a stricken Airbus A300, on fire and approaching Dallas–Fort Worth Airport, came only minutes before the network's first feed of the National Evening News.

It was 6:21 P.M. Eastern daylight time when CBA's bureau chief at Dallas told a producer on the New York Horseshoe through a speakerphone, "We're expecting a big aircraft crash at DFW any moment. There's been a midair collision—a small plane and an Airbus with a full passenger load. The small plane went down. The Airbus is on fire and trying to make it in. The police and ambulance radios are going wild."

"Jesus!" another Horseshoe producer said. "What's our chance of getting pictures?"

The Horseshoe, an outsize desk with seating

for twelve people, was where the network's flag-
ship news broadcast was planned and nurtured
from early each weekday morning until the last
second of air time every night. Over at rival
CBS they called it the Fishbowl, at ABC the
Rim, at NBC the Desk. But whichever name
was used, the meaning was the same.

Here, reputedly, were the network's best
brains when it came to making judgments and
decisions about news: executive producer,
anchorman, senior producers, director, editors,
writers, graphics chief and their ranking aides.
There were also, like the instruments of an or-
chestra, a half-dozen computer terminals, wire
news service printers, a phalanx of state-of-the-
art telephones, and TV monitors on which
could be called up instantly anything from
unedited tape, through a prepared news segment ready for broadcast, to competitors' transmissions.

The Horseshoe was on the fourth floor of
the CBA News Building, in a central open area
with offices on one side—those of the National
Evening News senior staff members who, at various times of day, would retreat from the often
frenzied Horseshoe to their more private work
quarters.

Today, as on most days, presiding at the
Horseshoe's head was Chuck Insen, executive
producer. Lean and peppery, he was a veteran

newsman with a print press background in his early years and, even now, a parochial preference for domestic news over international. At age fifty-two Insen was elderly by TV standards, though he showed no sign of diminished energy, even after four years in a job that often burned people out in two. Chuck Insen could be curt and often was; he never suffered fools or small talk. One reason: under the pressures of his job there wasn't time.

At this moment—it was a Wednesday in mid-September—the pressures were at maximum intensity. Through the entire day, since early morning, the lineup of the National Evening News, the selection of subjects and their emphasis, had been reviewed, debated, amended and decided. Correspondents and producers around the world had contributed ideas, received instructions and responded. In the whole process the day's news had been whittled down to eight correspondent reports averaging a minute and a half to two minutes each, plus two voice-overs and four "tell stories." A voice-over was the anchorman speaking over pictures, a "tell story," the anchorman without pictures; for both the average was twenty seconds.

Now, suddenly, because of the breaking story from Dallas and with less than eight minutes remaining before broadcast air time, it had become necessary to reshape the entire news lineup. Though no one knew how much more information would come in or whether pictures would be available, to include the Dallas story at least one intended item had to be dropped, others shortened. Because of balance and timing the sequence of stories would be changed. The broadcast would start while rearrangement was continuing. It often happened that way.

"A fresh lineup, everybody." The crisp order came from Insen. "We'll go with Dallas at the top. Crawf will do a tell story. Do we have wire copy yet?"

"AP just in. I have it." The answer was from Crawford Sloane, the anchorman. He was reading an Associated Press bulletin printout handed to him moments earlier.

Sloane, whose familiar craggy features, gray-flecked hair, jutting jaw and authoritative yet reassuring manner were watched by some seventeen million people almost every week-night, was at the Horseshoe in his usual privileged seat on the executive producer's right. Crawf Sloane, too, was a news veteran and had climbed the promotion ladder steadily, especially after exposure as a CBA correspondent in Vietnam. Now, after a stint of reporting from the White House followed by three years in the nightly anchor slot, he was a national institution, one of the media elite.

In a few minutes Sloane would leave for the

broadcast studio. Meanwhile, for his tell story he would draw on what had already come from Dallas over the speakerphone, plus some additional facts in the AP report. He would compose the story himself. Not every anchor wrote his own material but Sloane, when possible, liked to write most of what he spoke. But he had to do it fast.

Insen's raised voice could be heard again. The executive producer, consulting the original broadcast lineup, told one of his three senior producers, "Kill Saudi Arabia. Take fifteen seconds out of Nicaragua . . ."

Mentally, Sloane winced on hearing the decision to remove the Saudi story. It was important news and a well-crafted two and a half minutes by CBA's Middle East correspondent about the Saudis' future marketing plans for oil. But by tomorrow the story would be dead because they knew that other networks had it and would go with it tonight.

Sloane didn't question the decision to put the Dallas story first, but his own choice for a deletion would have been a Capitol Hill piece about a U.S. senator's malfeasance. The legislator had quietly slipped eight million dollars into a gargantuan appropriations bill, the money to oblige a campaign contributor and personal friend. Only through a reporter's diligent scrutiny had the matter come to light.

While more colorful, the Washington item was less important, a corrupt member of Congress being nothing out of the ordinary. But the decision, the anchorman thought sourly, was typical of Chuck Insen: once more an item of foreign news, whose emphasis Sloane favored, had gone into the discard.

The relationship between the two—executive producer and anchorman—had never been good, and had worsened recently because of disagreements of that kind. Increasingly, it seemed, their basic ideas were growing further apart, not only about the kind of news that should have priority each evening, but also how it should be dealt with. Sloane, for example, favored in-depth treatment of a few major subjects, while Insen wanted as much of that day's news as could be crammed in, even if—as he was apt to express it—"we deal with some of the news in shorthand."

In other circumstances Sloane would have argued against dropping the Saudi piece, perhaps with positive effect because the anchorman was also executive editor and entitled to some input—except right now there wasn't time.

Hurriedly, Sloane braced his heels against the floor, maneuvering his swivel chair backward and sideways with practiced skill so that he confronted a computer keyboard. Concentrating, mentally shutting out the commotion around him, he tapped out what would be the opening sentences of tonight's broadcast.

> *From Dallas–Fort Worth, this word just in on what may be a tragedy in the making. We know that minutes ago there was a midair collision between two passenger planes, one a heavily loaded Airbus of Muskegon Airlines. It happened over the town of Gainesville, Texas, north of Dallas, and Associated Press reports the other plane—a small one, it's believed—went down. There is no word at this moment on its fate or of casualties on the ground. The Airbus is still in the air, but on fire as its pilots attempt to reach Dallas–Fort Worth Airport for a landing. On the ground, fire fighters and ambulance crews are standing by . . .*

While his fingers raced across the keyboard, Sloane reflected in a corner of his mind that few, if any, viewers would switch off until tonight's news was concluded. He added a sentence to the tell story about staying tuned for further developments, then hit a key for printout. Over at Teleprompter they would get a printout too, so that by the time he reached the broadcast studio, one floor below, it would be ready for him to read from the prompter screen.

As Sloane, a sheaf of papers in hand, quickly headed for the stairs to the third floor,

Insen was demanding of a senior producer, "Dammit, what about pictures from DFW?"

"Chuck, it doesn't look good." The producer, a phone cradled in his shoulder, was talking to the national editor in the main newsroom. "The burning airplane is getting near the airport but our camera crew is twenty miles away. They won't make it in time."

Insen swore in frustration. "Shit!"

If medals were awarded for dangerous service in the field of television, Ernie LaSalle, the national editor, would have had a chestful. Although only twenty-nine, he had served with distinction and frequent peril as a CBA field producer in Lebanon, Iran, Angola, the Falklands, Nicaragua and other messy places while ugly situations were erupting. Though the same kind of situations were still happening, nowadays LaSalle viewed the domestic American scene, which could be equally messy at times, from a comfortable upholstered chair in a glass-paneled office overlooking the main newsroom.

LaSalle was compact and small-boned, energetic, neatly bearded and carefully dressed—a yuppie type, some said. As national editor his responsibilities were large and he was one of two senior functionaries in the newsroom. The other was the foreign editor. Both had newsroom desks which they occupied when any particular story became hot and either was closely involved. The Dallas–Fort Worth Airport story was hot—*ergo,* LaSalle had rushed to his newsroom desk.

The newsroom was one floor below the Horseshoe. So was the news broadcast studio, which used the bustling newsroom as its visual backdrop. A control room, where a director put the technical components of each broadcast together, was in the News Building basement.

It was now seven minutes since the Dallas bureau chief had first reported the wounded Airbus approaching DFW. LaSalle slammed down one phone and picked up another, at the same time reading a computer screen alongside him on which a new AP report had just appeared. He was continuing to do everything he could to ensure coverage of the story, at the same time keeping the Horseshoe advised of developments.

It was LaSalle who reported the dispiriting news about CBA's nearest camera crew— though now rushing toward DFW and ignoring speed limits en route, still twenty miles from the scene of action. The reason was that it had been a busy day at the Dallas bureau, with all camera crews, field producers and correspondents out on assignment, and by sheer bad luck all of the assignments were a long way from the airport.

Of course, there would be some pictures

forthcoming shortly, but they would be after the fact and not of the critical Airbus landing, which was certain to be spectacular and perhaps disastrous. It was also unlikely that pictures of any kind would be available for the first feed of the National Evening News, which went via satellite to most of the eastern seaboard and parts of the Midwest.

The only consolation was that the Dallas bureau chief had learned that no other network or local station had a camera crew at the airport either, though like CBA's others were on the way.

From his newsroom desk Ernie LaSalle, still busy with telephones, could see the usual prebroadcast action in the brightly lit news studio as Crawford Sloane came in. Television viewers watching Sloane during a broadcast had the illusion that the anchorman was in, and part of, the newsroom. But in fact there was thick soundproof glass between the two so that no newsroom noises intruded, except when deliberately faded in as an audio effect.

The time was 6:28 P.M., two minutes before first-feed air.

As Sloane slipped into the anchor desk chair, his back to the newsroom and facing the center camera of three, a makeup girl moved in. Ten minutes earlier Sloane had had makeup applied in a small private room adjoining his office, but since then he had been sweating. Now the girl mopped his forehead, dabbed on powder, ran a comb through his hair and applied a touch of hair spray.

With a hint of impatience Sloane murmured, "Thanks, Nina," then glanced over his papers, checking that the opening words of his tell story on top corresponded with those displayed in large letters on the Teleprompter in front of him, from which he would read while appearing to look directly at viewers. The papers which news readers were often seen to shuffle were a precaution, for use only if the Teleprompter failed.

The studio stage manager called out loudly, "One minute!"

In the newsroom, Ernie LaSalle suddenly sat up straight, attentive, startled.

About a minute earlier, the Dallas bureau chief had excused himself from the line on which he had been talking with LaSalle to take another phone call. Waiting, LaSalle could hear the bureau chief's voice but not what was being said. Now the bureau man returned and what he reported caused the national editor to smile broadly.

LaSalle picked up a red reporting telephone on his desk which connected him, through amplified speakers, to every section of the news operation.

"National desk. LaSalle. Good news. We now have immediate coverage at DFW airport. In the terminal building, waiting for flight connections, are Partridge, Abrams, Van Canh. Abrams just reported to Dallas bureau—they are onto the story and running. More: A mobile satellite van has abandoned another assignment and is en route to DFW, expected soonest. Satellite feed time, Dallas to New York, is booked. We expect pictures in time for inclusion in the first-feed news."

Though he tried to sound laconic, LaSalle found it hard to keep the satisfaction from his voice. As if in response, a muffled cheer drifted down the open stairway from the Horseshoe above. Crawford Sloane, in the studio, also swung around and gave LaSalle a cheerful thumbs up.

An aide put a paper in front of the national editor who glanced at it, then continued on the speakerphone, "Also from Abrams, this report: *On board Airbus in distress are 286 passengers, eleven crew. Second plane in collision, a private Piper Cheyenne, crashed in Gainesville, no survivors. There are other casualties on ground, no details, numbers or seriousness. Airbus has one engine ripped off, is attempting landing on remaining engine. Air Traffic Control reports fire is from the location of missing engine.* Report ends."

LaSalle thought: Everything that had come from Dallas in the past few minutes was totally professional. But then, it was not surprising because the team of Abrams, Partridge and Van Canh was one of the crack combinations of CBA News. Rita Abrams, once a correspondent and now a senior field producer, was noted for her quick assessment of situations and a resourcefulness in getting stories back, even under difficult conditions. Harry Partridge was one of the best correspondents in the business. He normally specialized in war stories and, like Crawford Sloane, had reported from Vietnam, but could be relied on to do an exceptional job in any situation. And cameraman Minh Van Canh, once a Vietnamese and now an American citizen, was noted for his fine pictures sometimes shot in dangerous situations with disregard for his own safety. The fact that the three of them were onto the Dallas story guaranteed that it would be well handled.

By now it was a minute past the half hour and the first-feed National Evening News had begun. Reaching for a control beside his desk, LaSalle turned up the audio of an overhead monitor and heard Crawford Sloane doing the top-of-the-news tell story about DFW. On camera, a hand—it was a writer's—slipped a paper in front of him. Clearly it contained the additional report LaSalle had just dictated and, glancing down and ad-libbing, Sloane incorporated it into his prepared text. It was the kind of thing the anchorman did superbly.

Upstairs at the Horseshoe since LaSalle's announcement, the mood had changed. Now, though pressure and urgency remained, there was cheerful optimism with the knowledge that the Dallas situation was well in hand and pictures and a fuller report would be forthcoming. Chuck Insen and others were huddled, watching monitors, arguing, making decisions, squeezing out seconds, doing still more cutting and rearranging to leave the needed space. It looked as if the report about the corrupt senator would fall by the way after all. There was a sense of everyone doing what they did best—coping in a time-confined, exigency situation.

Swift exchanges, jargon-loaded, flowed back and forth.

"This piece is picture-poor."

"Make that copy shorter, pithy."

"Tape room: We're killing '16: Corruption.' But it may come back in if we don't get Dallas."

"The last fifteen seconds of that piece is deadly. We'll be telling people what they already know."

"The old lady in Omaha doesn't know."

"Then she never will. Drop it."

"First segment just finished. Have gone to commercial. We're forty seconds heavy."

"What did the competition have from Dallas?"

"A tell story, same as us."

"I need a bumper and cutline fast for 'Drug Bust.' "

"Take out that sequence. It does nothing."

"What we're trying to do here is put twelve pounds of shit into a ten-pound bag."

An observer unfamiliar with the scene might wonder: *Are these people human? Don't they care? Have they no emotion, no feelings of involvement, not an ounce of grief? Have any of them spared a thought for the nearly three hundred terrified souls on that airplane approaching DFW who may shortly die? Isn't there anyone here to whom that matters?*

And someone knowledgeable about news would answer: *Yes, there are people here to whom it matters, and they* will *care, maybe right after the broadcast. Or, when some have reached home, the horror of it all will touch them, and depending on how it all turns out, a few may weep. At this moment, though, no one has the time. These are news people. Their job is to record the passing parade, the bad with the good, and to do it swiftly, efficiently, plainly so that—*

*in a news phrase from an older time—"he who
runs may read."*

Therefore at 6:40 P.M., ten minutes into the
National Evening News half hour, the key remaining question for those around the Horseshoe and others in the newsroom, studio and
control room was: Will there or won't there be a
story soon, with pictures, from DFW?

2

For the group of five journalists at Dallas–Fort
Worth Airport, the sequence of events had begun a couple of hours earlier and reached a high
point at about 5:10 P.M., central daylight time.

The five were Harry Partridge, Rita
Abrams, Minh Van Canh, Ken O'Hara, the
CBA crew's sound man, and Graham Broderick, a foreign correspondent for the *New York
Times.* That same morning, in predawn darkness, they had left El Salvador and flown to
Mexico City, then, after delay and a flight
change, traveled onward to DFW. Now they
were awaiting other flight connections, some to
differing destinations.

All were weary, not just from today's long journey, but from two months or more of rough and dangerous living while reporting on several nasty wars in unpleasant parts of Latin America.

While waiting for their flights, they were in a bar in Terminal 2E, one of twenty-four busy bars in the airport. The bar's décor was mode-utilitarian. Surrounded by an imitation garden wall containing plants, it sported hanging fabric panels overhead in pale blue plaid, lit by concealed pink lighting. The *Times*man said it reminded him of a whorehouse he had once been in in Mandalay.

From their table near a window they could see the aircraft ramp and Gate 20. It was from that gate Harry Partridge had expected to leave, a few minutes from now, on an American Airlines flight to Toronto. But this evening the flight was late and an hour's delay had just been announced.

Partridge, a tall and lanky figure, had an untidy shock of fair hair that had always made him look boyish and still did, despite his forty-odd years and the fact that the hair was graying. At this moment he was relaxed and not much caring about flight delays or anything else. He had ahead of him three weeks of R&R, and rest and relaxation were what he sorely needed.

Rita Abrams' connecting flight would be to Minneapolis–St. Paul, from where she was headed for a holiday on a friend's farm in Minnesota. She also had a weekend rendezvous planned there with a married senior CBA official, a piece of information she was keeping to herself. Minh Van Canh and Ken O'Hara were going home to New York. So was Graham Broderick.

The trio of Partridge, Rita and Minh was a frequent working combination. On their most recent trip, O'Hara had been with them, as sound recordist, for the first time. He was young, pale, pencil-thin, and spent most of his spare time absorbed in electronics magazines; he had one open now.

Broderick was the odd man out, though he and the TV-ers often covered the same assignments and mostly were on good terms. At this moment, however, the *Times*man—rotund, dignified and slightly pompous—was being antagonistic.

Three of the group had had a little too much to drink. The exceptions were Van Canh, who drank only club soda, and the sound man, who had nursed a beer for a long time and declined more.

"Listen, you affluent son of a bitch," Broderick said to Partridge, who had pulled a billfold from his pocket, "I said I'd pay for this round, and so I will." He put two bills, a twenty and a five, on a waiter's tray on which three double scotches and a club soda had been delivered. "Just because you pull down twice as much as I do for half the work is no reason to hand the print press charity."

"Oh, for chrissakes!" Rita said. "Brod, why don't you throw away that old cracked record."

Rita had spoken loudly, as she sometimes did. Two uniformed officers from the airport's Department of Public Safety force, which policed DFW, had been walking through the bar; they turned their heads curiously. Observing them, Rita smiled and waved a hand. The officers' eyes took in the group and, around them, the assortment of cameras and equipment on which the CBA logo was prominent. Both DPS men returned the smile and moved on.

Harry Partridge, who had been watching, thought: Rita was showing her age today. Even though she exuded a strong sexuality which had drawn many men to her, there were telltale lines on her face; also, the toughness which made her as demanding of herself as of those she worked with came through in imperious little mannerisms, not always attractively. There was recent reason, of course—the strain and heavy work load which she, Harry and the other two had shared through the past two months.

Rita was forty-three, and six years ago was still appearing on camera as a news correspondent, though far less often than when she was younger and more glamorous. Everyone knew it was a rotten, unfair system that allowed men to continue as correspondents, to keep on facing the camera even when their faces revealed them to be growing older, whereas women couldn't and were shunted aside like discarded concubines. A few women had tried to fight and beat the system—Christine Craft, a reporter and anchorwoman, pursued the issue through the courts, but had not succeeded.

But Rita, instead of starting a fight she knew she wouldn't win, had switched to producing and, behind the camera instead of in front of it, had been triumphantly successful. Along the way she had badgered senior producers into giving her some of the tough foreign assignments which almost always went to men. For a while her male bosses had resisted, then they had given in, and soon Rita was sent automatically —along with Harry—to where the fighting was fiercest and the living hardest.

Broderick, who had been pondering Rita's last remark, now said, "It isn't as if your glamour gang is doing anything important. Every night that tiny news hole has only tooth pickings of all that's happened in the world. How long is it—nineteen minutes?"

"If you're shooting at us sitting ducks," Partridge said amiably, "at least the print press should get its facts straight. It's twenty-one and a half."

"Leaving seven minutes for commercials," Rita added, "which, among other things, pay Harry's excessive salary which turns you green with jealousy."

Rita, with her usual bluntness, was on the nose about jealousy, Partridge thought. With print press people, the difference between their own and TV news pay was always a sour point. In contrast with Partridge's earnings, which were $250,000 a year, Broderick, a first-class, highly competent reporter, probably got $85,000.

As if his train of thought had not been interrupted, the *Times*man continued, "What your entire network news department produces in a day would only fill half of one of our paper's pages."

"A dumb comparison," Rita shot back, "because everyone knows a picture is worth a thousand words. We have hundreds of pictures and we take people to where the news is so they can see it for themselves. No newspaper in history ever did that."

Broderick, holding in one hand the fresh double scotch he had been sipping, waved the other hand dismissingly. " 'S not relevant." The last word gave him trouble; he pronounced it "revelant."

It was Minh Van Canh, not usually a great talker, who asked, "Why not?"

"Because you people are dodos. TV network news is dying. All you ever were was a headline service and now the local stations are taking over even that, using technology to bring in outside news themselves, picking off pieces of you like vultures at a carcass."

"Well," Partridge said, still agreeably relaxed, "there are some who've been saying that for years. But look at us. We're still around, and still strong, because people watch network news for quality."

"You're goddamn right," Rita said. "And something else you have wrong, Brod, is the notion that local TV news is getting better. It isn't. It's getting worse. Some of the people who left networks with high hopes to work in local news have gone back to the networks in disgust."

Broderick asked, "Why so?"

"Because local station managements see news as hype, promotion, massive revenue. They use that new technology you talk about to pander to the lowest viewer tastes. And when they send someone from their news department on a big outside story, it's usually a kid, out of his depth, who can't compete with a network reporter's know-how and backup."

Harry Partridge yawned. The thing about this conversation, he realized, was that it was a retread, a game that filled vacant time but required no intellectual effort, and they had indulged in the game many times before.

Then he became aware of some activity nearby.

The two DPS officers were still in the bar through which they had moved casually, but had suddenly become attentive and were listening to their walkie-talkies. An announcement was being transmitted. Partridge caught the words, ". . . condition Alert Two . . . midair collision . . . approaching runway one-seven left . . . all DPS personnel report . . ." Abruptly, hurrying, the officers left the bar.

The others in the group had heard too. "Hey!" Minh Van Canh said. "Maybe . . ."

Rita jumped up. "I'll find out what's happening." She left the bar hurriedly.

Van Canh and O'Hara began to gather together their camera and sound gear. Partridge and Broderick did the same with their belongings.

One of the DPS officers was still in sight. Rita caught up with him near an American Airlines check-in counter, noting that he was youthfully handsome with the physique of a football player.

"I'm from CBA News." She showed her network press card.

His eyes were frankly appraising. "Yes, I know."

In other circumstances, she thought briefly, she might have introduced him to the pleasures of an older woman. Unfortunately there wasn't time. She asked, "What's going on?"

The officer hesitated. "You're supposed to call the Public Information Office—"

Rita said impatiently, "I'll do that later. It's urgent, isn't it? So tell me."

"Muskegon Airlines is in trouble. One of their Airbuses had a midair. It's coming in on fire. We're on Alert Two, which means all the emergency stuff is rolling, heading for runway one-seven left." His voice was serious. "Looks pretty bad."

"I want my camera crew out there. Now and fast. Which way do we go?"

The DPS man shook his head. "If you try it unescorted, you won't get beyond the ramp. You'll be arrested."

Rita remembered something she had once been told, that DFW airport prided itself on cooperating with the press. She pointed to the officer's walkie-talkie. "Can you call Public Information on that?"

"I could."

"Do it. *Please!*"

Her persuasion worked. The officer called and was answered. Taking Rita's press card, he read from it, explaining her request.

A reply came back. "Tell them they must first come to public safety station number one to sign in and get media badges."

Rita groaned. She gestured to the walkie-talkie. "Let me speak."

The DPS officer pressed a transmit button. He held the radio out.

She spoke urgently into the built-in mike: "There isn't time; you must know that. We're network. We have every kind of credential. We'll do any paperwork you want afterward. But please, *please,* get us to the scene now."

"Stand by." A pause, then a new voice with crisp authority. "Okay, get to gate nineteen fast. Ask someone there to direct you to the ramp. Look for a station wagon with flashing lights. I'm on my way to you."

Rita squeezed the officer's arm. "Thanks, pal!"

Then she was hurrying back toward Partridge and the others who were leaving the bar. Broderick was last. As he left, the *New York Times* man cast a regretful glance back at the unconsumed drinks for which he had paid.

Briskly, Rita related what she had learned, telling Partridge, Minh and O'Hara, "This can be big. Go out on the airfield. Don't waste time.

I'll do some phoning, then come to find you."
She glanced at her watch: 5:20 P.M., 6:20 in
New York. "If we're fast we can make the first
feed." But privately she doubted it.

Partridge nodded, accepting Rita's orders.
At any time, the relationship between a correspondent and producer was an imprecise one.
Officially, a field producer such as Rita Abrams
was in charge of an entire crew, including the
correspondent, and if anything went wrong on
an assignment the producer got the blame. If
things went right, of course, the correspondent
whose face and name were featured received the
praise, even though the producer undoubtedly
helped shape the story and contributed to the
script.

However, in the case of a "Big Foot" senior
correspondent like Harry Partridge, the official
pecking order sometimes got turned around,
with the correspondent taking charge and a
producer being overawed and sometimes over-
ruled. But when Partridge and Rita worked together, neither gave a damn about status. They
simply wanted to send back the best reports
that the two of them, in harness, could produce.

While Rita hurried to a pay phone, Partridge, Minh and O'Hara moved quickly toward
gate 19, looking for an exit to the air traffic
ramp below. Graham Broderick, quickly

sobered by what was happening, was close behind.

Near the gate was a doorway marked:

RAMP—RESTRICTED AREA
EMERGENCY EXIT ONLY
ALARM WILL SOUND

No official person was in sight and without
hesitation Partridge pushed his way through,
the others following. As they clattered down a
metal stairway, a loud alarm bell sounded behind them. They ignored it and emerged onto
the ramp.

It was a busy time of day and the ramp was
crowded with aircraft and airline vehicles. Suddenly a station wagon appeared, traveling fast,
with roof lights flashing. Its tires screeched as it
halted at gate 19.

Minh, who was nearest, opened a door and
jumped inside. The others piled in after him.
The driver, a slim young black man in a brown
business suit, pulled away, driving as swiftly as
he had come. Without looking back he said,
"Hiya, guys! I'm Vernon—Public Info."

Partridge introduced himself and the others.

Reaching down to the seat beside him,
Vernon came up with three green media badges.
He passed them back. "These are temp; better
clip them on. I already broke some rules, but

like your girlfriend said, we ain't burdened with time."

They had left the ramp area, crossed two taxiways and were traveling east on a parallel access road. Two runways were ahead and to the right. Alongside the farther runway, emergency vehicles were assembling.

Rita Abrams, in the terminal, was talking on a pay phone with CBA's Dallas bureau. The bureau chief, she had discovered, already knew of the airport emergency and had been trying to get a local CBA crew to the scene. He learned with delight of the presence of Rita and the others.

She told him to advise New York, then asked, "What's our satellite feed situation?"

"Good. There's a mobile satellite van on the way from Arlington."

Arlington, she learned, was only thirteen miles away. The van, which belonged to a CBA affiliate station, KDLS-TV, had been setting up for a sports broadcast from Arlington Stadium, but now that story had been abandoned and the van dispatched to DFW. The driver and technician would be advised by cellular phone to cooperate with Rita, Partridge and the others.

The news excited and elated her. There was, she realized, now a good possibility of getting a

story and pictures to New York in time for the
first-feed National Evening News.

The station wagon carrying the CBA trio
and the *Times*man was nearing runway 17L—
the figures denoted a magnetic heading of 170
degrees, almost due south; the L showed it to be
the left runway of two that were parallel. As at
all airports, the designation was in large white
characters on the runway surface.

Still driving fast, Vernon explained, "A pilot
in distress gets to choose the runway he wants.
Here it's usually one-seven left. That baby is
two hundred feet wide and closest to emergency
help."

The station wagon halted on a taxiway that
intersected 17L and from where the incoming
aircraft's approach and landing would be seen.

"This will be the on-site command post,"
Vernon said.

Emergency vehicles were still arriving, some
converging around them. From the airport's
fire-fighting force were seven yellow trucks—
four mammoth Oshkosh M15 foam vehicles, an
aerial ladder truck and two smaller Rapid Intervention Vehicles. The foam trucks, riding on
giant tires nearly six feet high, with two engines,
front and rear, and high-pressure projection
nozzles, were like self-contained fire stations.
The RIV's, fast and maneuverable, were de-

signed to go in close and quickly to a burning
aircraft.

A half-dozen blue-and-white police cruisers
disgorged officers who opened the cars' trunks,
pulled out silver fire suits and climbed into
them. Airport police were cross-trained in fire
fighting, Vernon explained. On the station wagon's DPS radio a stream of orders could be
heard.

The fire trucks, supervised by a lieutenant in
a yellow sedan, were taking positions on ramps
at intervals down the runway's length. Ambulances summoned from nearby communities
were streaming into the airport and assembling
nearby, but clear of the runway area.

Partridge had been the first to jump from
the station wagon and, standing beside it, was
scribbling notes. Broderick, less hurriedly, was
doing the same. Minh Van Canh had clambered
to the station wagon's roof and now, standing,
his camera ready, was scanning the sky to the
north. Behind him was Ken O'Hara, trailing
wires and a sound recorder.

Almost at once the stricken inbound flight
was visible, about five miles out, with heavy
black smoke behind it. Minh raised his camera,
holding it steady, one eye tight against the viewfinder.

He was a sturdy, stocky figure, not much
more than five feet tall, but with broad shoul-

ders and long, muscular arms. His squarish dark face, pockmarked from a childhood bout with smallpox, held wide brown eyes which looked out impassively, unrevealing of what thoughts might lie behind them. Those who were close to Minh said it took a long time to get to know him.

About some things, though, there was consensus—namely, that Minh was industrious, reliable, honest, and one of the best TV cameramen in the business. His pictures were more than good; they were invariably attention-getting and oftentimes artistic. He had worked for CBA first in Vietnam, as a local recruit who learned his trade from an American cameraman for whom Minh carried equipment amid the jungle fighting. When his mentor was killed after stepping on a land mine, Minh, unaided, carried his body back for burial, then returned with the camera into the jungle where he continued filming. No one at CBA could ever remember hiring him. His employment simply became a *fait accompli.*

In 1975, with the fall of Saigon imminent, Minh, his wife and two children were among the all-too-few lucky ones airlifted from the U.S. Embassy courtyard by CH-53 military helicopter to the safety of the American Seventh Fleet at sea. Even then Minh filmed it all, and

much of his footage was used on the National
Evening News.

Now he was filming another aerial story,
different but dramatic, whose ending had yet to
be determined.

In the viewfinder the shape of the approaching Airbus was becoming clearer. Also clearer
was a halo of bright flame on the right side with
smoke continuing to stream behind. It was possible to see the fire coming from where an engine had been, and where now only a part of the
engine pylon remained. To Minh and others
watching, it seemed amazing that the entire airplane had not yet been engulfed.

Inside the station wagon, Vernon had
switched on an aviation band radio. Air Traffic
Control could be heard speaking with the
Airbus pilots. The calm voice of a controller,
monitoring their approach by radar, cautioned,
"You are slightly below glide path . . . drifting left of center line . . . Now on glide path,
on center line . . ."

But the Airbus pilots were clearly having
trouble holding altitude and an even course.
The plane seemed to be crabbing in, the damaged right wing lower than the left. At moments
the plane's nose veered away; then, as if from
urgent efforts in the cockpit, swung back toward the runway. There was an uneven up-and-
down movement as at one moment too much

height was lost, at the next retrieved, but barely. Those on the ground were asking themselves the tense, unspoken question: Having come this far, would the Airbus make it all the way in? The answer seemed in doubt.

On the radio, the voice of one of the pilots could be heard. "Tower, we have landing-gear problems . . . hydraulic failure." A pause. "We are trying the gear down 'free fall' . . . *now.*"

A fire captain, also listening, had stopped beside them. Partridge asked him, "What does that mean?"

"On big passenger planes there's an emergency system to get the landing wheels down if hydraulic power is out. The pilots release all hydraulic power so the gear, which is heavy, should fall under its own weight, then lock. But once it's down they can't get it up again, even if they want to."

As the fireman spoke, the Airbus landing gear could be seen slowly coming down.

Moments later, once more the calm voice of an air traffic controller: "Muskegon, we see your gear down. Be advised that flames are close to the right front gear."

It was obvious that if the right front tires were consumed by fire, as seemed probable, that side of the landing gear might collapse on impact, skewing the airplane to the right at high speed.

Minh, fondling a zoom lens, had his camera running. He too could see the flames which had now reached the tires. The Airbus was floating over the airport boundary . . . Then it was closer in, barely a quarter mile from the runway . . . It was going to make it to the ground, but the fire was greater, more intense, clearly being fed by fuel, and two of the four right-side tires were burning, the rubber melting . . . There was a flash as one of the tires exploded.

Now the burning Airbus was over the runway, its landing speed 150 mph. As the aircraft passed the waiting emergency vehicles, one by one they swung onto the runway, following at top speed, tires screaming. Two yellow foam trucks were the first to move, the other fire trucks close behind.

On the runway, as the airplane's landing gear made contact with the ground, another right-side tire exploded, then another. Suddenly all right tires disintegrated . . . the wheels were down to their rims. Simultaneously there was a banshee screech of metal, a shower of sparks, and a cloud of dust and cement fragments rose into the air . . . Somehow, miraculously, the pilots managed to hold the Airbus on the runway . . . It seemed to continue a long way and for a long time . . . At last it stopped. As it did, the fire flared up.

Still moving fast, the fire trucks closed in, within seconds pumping foam. Gigantic whorls of it piled up with incredible speed, like a mountain of shave cream.

On the airplane, several passenger doors were opening, escape slides tumbling out. The forward door was open on the right side, but on that side fire was blocking the mid-fuselage exits. On the left side, away from the fire, another forward door and a mid-fuselage door were open. Some passengers were already coming down the slides.

But at the rear, where there were two escape doors on each side, none had so far opened.

Through the three open doors, smoke from inside the airplane was pouring out. Some passengers were already on the ground. The latest ones emerged coughing, many vomiting, all gasping for fresh air.

By now the exterior fire was dying down under a mass of foam on one side of the airplane.

Firemen from the RIV's, wearing silver protective clothing and breathing apparatus, had swiftly moved in and rigged ladders to the unopened rear doors. As the doors were opened manually from outside, more smoke poured out. The firemen hurried inside, intent on extinguishing any interior fire. Other firemen, entering the wrecked Airbus through the forward doors, helped passengers to leave, some of them dazed and weak.

Noticeably, the outward flow of passengers slowed. Harry Partridge made a quick estimate that nearly two hundred people had emerged from the plane's interior, though from the information he had gathered he knew that 297, including crew, were reportedly aboard. Firemen began to carry some who appeared badly burned—among them two women flight attendants. Smoke was still drifting from inside, though less of it than earlier.

Minh Van Canh continued to videotape the action around him, thinking only professionally, excluding other thoughts, though aware that he was the only cameraman on the scene and in his camera he had something special and unique. Probably not since the Hindenburg airship disaster had a major air crash been recorded visually in such detail, while it happened.

Ambulances had been summoned to the on-site command post. A dozen were already there, with more arriving. Paramedics worked on the injured, loading them onto numbered backboards. Within minutes the crash victims would be on their way to area hospitals alerted to receive them. With the arrival of a helicopter bringing doctors and nurses, the command post near the Airbus was becoming an improvised field hospital with a functioning triage system.

The speed with which everything was happening spoke well, Partridge thought, of the airport's emergency planning. He overheard the fire captain report that a hundred and ninety passengers, more or less, were out of the Airbus and alive. At the same time that left nearly a hundred unaccounted for.

A fireman, pulling off his respirator to wipe the sweat from his face, was heard to say, "Oh Christ! The back seats are chock full of dead. It must have been where the smoke was thickest." It also explained why the four rear escape doors had not been opened from inside.

As always with an aircraft accident, the dead would be left where they were until a National Transportation Safety Board field officer, reportedly on the way, gave authority to move them after approving identification procedures.

The flight-deck crew emerged from the Airbus, pointedly declining help. The captain, a grizzled four-striper, looking around him at the injured and already knowing of the many dead, was openly crying. Guessing that despite the casualties the pilots would be acclaimed for bringing the airplane in, Minh held the captain's grief-stricken face in closeup. It proved to be Minh's final shot as a voice called, "Harry! Minh! Ken! Stop now. Hurry! Bring what you've got and come with me. We're feeding to New York by satellite."

The voice belonged to Rita Abrams, who had arrived on a Public Information shuttle bus. Some distance away, the promised mobile satellite van could be seen. The van's satellite dish, which folded like a fan for travel, was being opened and aimed skyward.

Accepting the order, Minh lowered his camera. Two other TV crews had arrived on the same shuttle bus as Rita—one from KDLS, the CBA affiliate—along with print press reporters and photographers. They and others, Minh knew, would carry the story on. But only Minh had the real thing, the crash exclusive pictures, and he knew with inward pride that today and in days to come, his pictures would be seen around the world and would remain a piece of history.

They went with Vernon in the PIO station wagon to the satellite van. On the way Partridge began drafting the words he would shortly speak. Rita told him, "Make your script a minute forty-five. As soon as you're ready, cut a sound track, do a closing standup. Meanwhile, I'll feed quick and dirty to New York."

As Partridge nodded acknowledgment, Rita glanced at her watch: 5:43 P.M., 6:43 in New York. For the first-feed National Evening News, there was barely fifteen minutes left of broad-cast time.

Partridge was continuing to write, mouthing words silently, changing what he had already written. Minh handed two precious tape cassettes to Rita, then put a fresh cassette in the camera, ready for Partridge's audio track and standup close.

Vernon dropped them immediately along-side the satellite van. Broderick, who had come too, was going on to the terminal to phone his own report to New York. His parting words were, "Thanks, guys. Remember, if you want the in-depth dope tomorrow, buy the *Times.*"

O'Hara, the high-technology buff, regarded the equipment-packed satellite van admiringly. "How I love these babies!"

The fifteen-foot-wide dish mounted on the van's platform body was now fully open and elevated with a 20-kilowatt generator running. Inside, in a small control room with editing and transmitting equipment tightly packed in tiers, a technician from the two-man crew was align-ing the van's uplink transmitter with a Ku-band satellite 22,300 miles above them—Spacenet 2. Whatever they transmitted would go to tran-sponder 21 on the satellite, then instantly by downlink to New York to be rerecorded.

Inside the van, working alongside the tech-nician, Rita expertly ran Minh's tape cassettes through an editing machine, viewing them on a TV monitor. Not surprisingly, she thought, the pictures were superb.

On normal assignments, and working with an editor as an extra team member, producer and editor together would select portions of the tapes, then, over a sound track of a correspondent's comments, put all components together as a fully edited piece. But that took forty-five minutes, sometimes longer, and today there wasn't time. So, making fast decisions, Rita chose several of the most dramatic scenes which the technician transmitted as they were—in TV jargon, "quick and dirty."

Outside the satellite van, seated on some metal steps, Partridge completed his script and, after conferring briefly with Minh and the sound man, recorded a sound track.

Having allowed for the anchorman's introduction, which would be written in New York and have the story's up-front facts, Partridge began:

"Pilots in a long-ago war called it comin' in on a wing and a prayer. There was a song with that name . . . It's unlikely anyone will write a song about today.

"The Muskegon Airlines Airbus was sixty miles out from Dallas–Fort Worth . . . with a near-full passenger load . . . having come from

*Chicago . . . when the mid-air collision hap-
pened . . ."*

As always, when an experienced correspondent wrote for TV news, Partridge had written
"slightly off the pictures." It was a specialized
art form, difficult to learn, and some in television never quite succeeded. Even among professional writers the talent did not receive the recognition it deserved, because the words were
written to accompany pictures and seldom read
well alone.

The trick, as Harry Partridge and others
like him knew, was *not* to describe the pictures.
A television viewer would be seeing, visually,
what was happening on the screen and did not
need verbal description. Yet the spoken words
must not be so far removed from the pictures as
to split the viewer's consciousness. It was a lit-
erary balancing act, much of it instinctive.

Something else TV news people recognized:
The best news writing was not in neat sentences
and paragraphs. Fragments of sentences worked
better. Facts must be taut, verbs strong and active; a script should crackle. Finally, by manner
and intonation the correspondent should convey a meaning too. Yes, he or she had to be an
excellent reporter, but an actor also. At all
those things Partridge was expert, though today
he had a handicap: he had not seen the pictures,

as a correspondent normally did. But he knew, more or less, what they would be.

Partridge concluded with a standup—himself, head and shoulders, speaking directly to the camera. Behind him, activity was continuing around the wrecked Airbus.

"There is more of this story to come . . . tragic details, the toll of dead and injured. But what is clear, even now, is that collision dangers are multiplying . . . on the airways, in our crowded skies . . . Harry Partridge, CBA News, Dallas–Fort Worth."

The cassette with the narration and standup was passed to Rita inside the van. Still trusting Partridge, knowing him too well to waste precious time checking, she ordered it sent to New York without review. Moments later, watching and listening as the technician transmitted, she was admiring. Remembering the discussion half an hour earlier in the terminal bar she reflected: with his multitalents, Partridge was demonstrating why his pay was so much higher than that of the reporter for the *New York Times.*

Outside, Partridge was performing still one more of a correspondent's duties—an audio report, spoken from notes and largely ad-libbed, for CBA Radio News. When the TV transmission was finished, that would go to New York by satellite too.

3

The CBA News headquarters building in New York was a plain and unimpressive eight-story brownstone on the east side of upper Manhattan. Formerly a furniture factory, now only the shell of the original structure remained, the interior having been remodeled and refurbished many times by an assortment of contractors. Out of this piecemeal work had come a maze of intersecting corridors in which unescorted visitors got lost.

Despite the drab domicile of CBA News, the place contained a sultan's fortune in electronic wizardry, a considerable portion of it in technicians' country, two floors below street level, sometimes referred to as the catacombs. And here, among a multitude of functions, was a vital department with a prosaic name—the One-inch-tape Room.

All news reports from CBA crews around the world came in, via satellite and occasionally by landline, to the One-inch-tape Room. From there, too, all taped recordings of finished news went out to viewers, via a broadcast control room and again by satellite.

Endemic to the One-inch-tape Room were enormous pressures, taut nerves, tension, instant decision making and urgent commands, especially just before and during broadcasts of the National Evening News.

At such times, someone unaware of what was happening might consider the scene disorganized bedlam, a technological nightmare. The impression would be heightened by surrounding semidarkness, necessary for watching a forest of TV screens.

But in fact the operation functioned smoothly, quickly and with skill. Mistakes here could be disastrous. They rarely happened.

A half-dozen large and sophisticated reel-to-reel tape machines, built into consoles and with TV monitors above, dominated the activity; the machines used one-inch magnetic tape, the highest-quality and most reliable. At each tape machine and console sat a skilled operator receiving, editing and transmitting tapes swiftly, according to instructions. The operators, older than most workers in the building, were a motley group who seemed to take pride in dressing shabbily and behaving boisterously. Because of this, a commentator once described them as the "fighter pilots" of TV broadcasting.

Every weekday, an hour or so before National Evening News broadcast time, a senior news producer moved down five floors from his seat at the Horseshoe to preside over the One-inch-tape Room and its operators. There, acting as a maestro, shouting instructions while semaphoring with his arms, he viewed incoming material for that night's news, ordered further editing if necessary, and kept colleagues at the Horseshoe informed of which expected items were now in-house and how, at first glance, each looked.

Everything, it always seemed, arrived at the One-inch-tape Room in haste and late. It was a tradition that producers, correspondents and editors working in the field polished and repolished their pieces until the last possible moment, so that most came in during the half hour before the broadcast and some after the broadcast had begun. There were even nail-biting occasions when the front half of a report was going out from one tape recorder and being broadcast while the back portion was still feeding into another machine. During those moments nervous, sweating operators pushed themselves to the limit of their skills.

The senior producer most often in charge was Will Kazazis, Brooklyn-born of an excitable Greek family, a trait he had inherited. His excitability, though, seemed to fit the job and despite it he never lost control. Thus it was

Kazazis who received Rita Abrams' satellite transmission from DFW—first Minh Van Canh's pictures sent "quick and dirty," then Harry Partridge's audio track, concluding with his standup.

The time was 6:48 . . . ten minutes of news remaining. A commercial break had just begun.

Kazazis told the operator who had taken the feed in, "Slap it together fast. Use all of Partridge's track. Put the best pictures over it. I trust you. Now move, move, move!"

Through an aide, Kazazis had already let the Horseshoe know that the Dallas tape was coming in. Now, by phone, Chuck Insen, who was in the broadcast control room, demanded, "How is it?"

Kazazis told the executive producer, "Fantastic! Beautiful! Exactly what you'd expect of Harry and Minh."

Knowing there wasn't time to view the piece himself, and trusting Kazazis, Insen ordered, "We'll go with it after this commercial. Stand by."

With less than a minute to go, the tape operator, perspiring in his air-conditioned work space, was continuing to edit, hurriedly combining pictures, commentary and natural sound.

Insen's command was repeated to the anchorman and a writer seated near him. A lead-in was already prepared and the writer passed the single sheet to Crawford Sloane who skimmed it, quickly changed a word or two, and nodded thanks. A moment later on the anchor's Teleprompter, what were to have been the next segment's opening words switched over to the DFW story. In the broadcast studio as the commercial break neared its conclusion, the stage manager called, "Ten seconds . . . five . . . four . . . two . . ."

At a hand signal Sloane began, his expression grave. *"Earlier in this broadcast we reported a midair collision near Dallas between a Muskegon Airlines Airbus and a private plane. The private plane crashed. There are no survivors. The Airbus, on fire, crash-landed at Dallas–Fort Worth Airport a few minutes ago and there are heavy casualties. On the scene is CBA News correspondent Harry Partridge who has just filed this report."*

Only seconds before had the frantic editing in the One-inch-tape Room been completed. Now, on monitors throughout the building and on millions of TV sets in the Eastern and Midwestern United States and across the Canadian border, a dramatic picture of an approaching, burning Airbus filled the screen and Partridge's voice began, *"Pilots in a long-ago war called it comin' in on a wing and a prayer . . ."*

The exclusive report and pictures had, as the final item, made the first-feed National Evening News.

There would be a second feed of the National Evening News immediately after the first. There always was and it would be broadcast— in the East by affiliate stations who did not take the first feed, widely in the Midwest, and most Western stations would record the second feed for broadcast later.

The Partridge report from DFW would, of course, lead the second feed and while competing networks might, by now, have after-the-fact pictures for *their* second feeds, CBA's while-it-happened pictures remained a world exclusive and would be repeated many times in the days to follow.

There were two minutes between the end of the first feed and the beginning of the second and Crawford Sloane used them to telephone Chuck Insen.

"Listen," Sloane said, "I think we ought to put the Saudi piece back in."

Insen said sarcastically, "I know you have a lot of pull. Can you arrange an extra five minutes' air time?"

"Don't play games. That piece is important."

"It's also dull as oil. I say no."

"Does it matter that I say yes?"

"Sure it matters. Which is why we'll talk about it tomorrow. Meanwhile, I'm sitting here with certain responsibilities."

"Which include—or ought to—sound judgments about foreign news."

"We each have our jobs," Insen said, "and the clock is creeping up on yours. Oh, by the way, you handled the Dallas thing—at both ends—nicely."

Without answering, Sloane hung up the telephone at the broadcast desk. As an afterthought he told the writer beside him, "Ask someone to get Harry Partridge on the phone at Dallas. I'll talk with him during the next break. I want to congratulate him and the others."

The stage manager called out, "Fifteen seconds!"

Yes, Sloane decided, there would be a discussion between himself and Insen tomorrow and it would be a showdown. Perhaps Insen had outlived his usefulness and it was time for him to go.

Chuck Insen was tight-lipped and unsmiling when, after the end of the second feed and before going home, he returned to his office to gather up a dozen magazines for later reading.

Reading, reading, reading, to keep informed on a multitude of fronts, was a news executive producer's burden. Wherever he was and no matter what the hour, Insen felt obliged to reach for a newspaper, a magazine, a newsletter, a nonfiction book—sometimes obscure publications in all categories—the way others might reach for a cup of coffee, a handkerchief, a cigarette. Often he awoke in the night and read, or listened to overseas news on short-wave broadcasts. At home, through his personal computer, he had access to the major news wire services and each morning, at 5 A.M., reviewed them all. Driving in to work, he listened to radio news— mainly to CBS whose radio network news he, like many professionals, acknowledged as the finest.

It was, as Insen saw it, this widest possible view of the *ingredients* of news, and of subjects which interested ordinary people that made his own news judgments superior to those of Crawford Sloane, who thought too often in elitist terms.

Insen had a philosophy about those millions out there who watched the National Evening News. What most viewers wanted, he believed, was the answers to three basic questions: Is the world safe? Are my home and family safe? Did anything happen today that was interesting? Above all else, Insen tried to ensure that the news each evening supplied those answers.

He was sick and tired, Insen thought angrily, of the anchorman's I-know-best, holier-than-thou attitude about news selection, which was why tomorrow the two of them would have a slam-bang confrontation during which Insen would say exactly what he was thinking now, and to hell with consequences.

What were those consequences likely to be? Well, in the past, in any kind of contest between a network news anchorman and his executive producer, the anchor had invariably won, with the producer having to look for work elsewhere. But a lot of things were changing in network news. There was a different climate nowadays, and there could always be a first, with an anchor departing and a producer staying on.

With just that possibility in mind, a few days ago Insen had had an exploratory, strictly confidential phone talk with Harry Partridge. Would Partridge, the executive producer wanted to know, be interested in coming in from the cold, settling down in New York, and becoming anchor of the National Evening News? When he chose to, Harry could radiate authority and would fit the part—as he had demonstrated several times by filling in while Sloane was on vacation.

Partridge's response had been a mixture of surprise and uncertainty, but at least he hadn't said no. Crawf Sloane, of course, knew nothing of that conversation.

Either way, concerning himself and Sloane, Insen was convinced they couldn't go on feuding without some kind of a resolution soon.

4

It was 7:40 P.M. when Crawford Sloane, driving a Buick Somerset, left the garage at CBA News headquarters. As usual, he was using a CBA car; one was always available as part of his employment contract and he could have a driver if he wanted, though most of the time he didn't. A few minutes later, as he turned onto Fifty-ninth Street from Third Avenue, heading east toward the FDR Drive, he continued thinking about the broadcast just concluded.

At first his thoughts had gone in the direction of Insen, then he decided to put the executive producer out of his mind until tomorrow. Sloane had not the slightest doubt of his ability to cope with Insen and send him on his way—

perhaps to a network vice presidency which, despite the high-sounding title, would be a demotion after the National Evening News. It did not occur to Sloane for a moment that the reverse of that process could possibly happen. Had it been suggested to him, he would undoubtedly have laughed.

Instead, he turned his thoughts to Harry Partridge.

For Partridge, Sloane recognized, the hasty but excellent reporting job from Dallas had been one more solid performance in an outstanding professional career. Through DFW's airport paging system Sloane had been successful in reaching Partridge by phone and had congratulated him, asking him to pass on the same message to Rita, Minh and O'Hara. From an anchorman that kind of thing was expected—a matter of _noblesse oblige_—even though, where Partridge was concerned, Sloane did it without any great enthusiasm. That underlying feeling was why, on Sloane's part, the conversation had a touch of awkwardness, as conversations with Partridge often did. Partridge had seemed at ease, though he sounded tired.

Within the moving car, in a moment of silent, private honesty, Sloane asked himself: _How do I feel about Harry Partridge?_ The answer, with equal honesty, came back: _He makes me feel insecure._

Both question and answer had their roots in recent history.

The two of them had known each other for more than twenty years, the same length of time they had been with CBA News, having joined the network almost simultaneously. From the beginning they were successful professionally, yet opposites in personality.

Sloane was precise, fastidious, impeccable in dress and speech; he enjoyed having authority and wore it naturally. Juniors were apt to address him as "sir" and let him go through doorways first. He could be cool, slightly distant with people he did not know well, though in any human contact there was almost nothing his sharp mind missed, either spoken or inferred.

Partridge, in contrast, was casual in behavior, his appearance rumpled; he favored old tweed jackets and seldom wore a suit. He had an easygoing manner which made people he met feel comfortable, his equal, and sometimes he gave the impression of not caring much about anything, though that was a contrived deception. Partridge had learned early as a journalist that he could discover more by not seeming to have authority and by concealing his keen, exceptional intelligence.

They had differences in background too.

Crawford Sloane, from a middle-class Cleveland family, had done his early television training in that city. Harry Partridge served his main TV news apprenticeship in Toronto with the CBC—Canadian Broadcasting Corporation —and before that had worked as an announcer-newscaster-weatherman for small radio and TV stations in Western Canada. He had been born in Alberta, not far from Calgary, in a hamlet called De Winton where his father was a farmer.

Sloane had a degree from Columbia University. Partridge hadn't even finished high school, but in the working world of news his de facto education expanded rapidly.

For a long time at CBA their careers were parallel; as a result they came to be looked on as competitors. Sloane himself considered Partridge a competitor, even a threat to his own progress. He was not sure, though, if Partridge ever felt the same way.

The competition between the two had seemed strongest when both were reporting the war in Vietnam. They were sent there by the network in late 1967, supposedly to work as a team, and in a sense they did. Sloane, though, viewed the war as a golden opportunity to advance his own career; even then he had the anchor desk of the National Evening News clearly in his sights.

One essential in his advancement, Sloane knew, was to appear on the evening news as often as possible. Therefore, soon after arriving in Saigon he decided it was important not to stray too far from "Pentagon East"—headquarters of the United States Military Assistance Command for Vietnam (MACV) at Tan Son Nhut air base, five miles outside Saigon—and, when he did travel, not to be away too long.

He remembered, even after all these years, a conversation between himself and Partridge, who had remarked, "Crawf, you'll never get to understand this war by attending the Saigon Follies or hanging around the Caravelle." The first was the name the press corps gave to military briefings; the second, a hotel that was a popular watering hole for the international press, senior military and U.S. Embassy civilians.

"If you're talking about risks," Sloane had answered huffily, "I'm willing to take as many as you are."

"Forget risks. We'll all be taking them. I'm talking about coverage in depth. I want to get deep into this country and understand it. Some of the time I want to be free from the military, not just tagging along on fire fights, reporting bang-bang the way they'd like us to. That's too easy. And when I do military stuff I want it to be in forward areas so I can find out if what the USIS flacks say is happening really is."

"To do all that," Sloane pointed out, "you'll have to be away for days, maybe weeks at a time."

Partridge had seemed amused. "I thought you'd catch onto that quickly. I'm sure you've also figured that the way I plan to work will make it possible for you to get your face on the news almost every night."

Sloane had been uncomfortable at having his mind read so easily, though in the end that was how it worked out.

No one could ever say about his time in Vietnam that Sloane didn't work hard. He did, and he also took risks. On occasion he went along on missions to where the Viet Cong were operating, was sometimes in the midst of firefights, and in dangerous moments wondered, with normal fear, whether he would make it back alive.

As it turned out, he always did and was seldom away more than twenty-four hours. Also, when he came back it was invariably with dramatic combat pictures plus human interest stories about young Americans in battle, the kind of fare that New York wanted.

Following his plan shrewdly, Sloane didn't overdo the dangerous exploits and was usually available in Saigon for military and diplomatic

briefings which, at the time, were newsworthy.
Only much later would it be realized how su-
perficial Sloane's kind of coverage had been and
how—for television—dramatic pictures were a
first priority, with thoughtful analysis and
sometimes truth trailing far behind. But by the
time that became apparent, to Crawford Sloane
it didn't matter.

Sloane's overall ploy worked. He had always
been impressive on camera and was even more
so in Vietnam. He became a favorite with the
New York Horseshoe producers and was frequently on the evening news, sometimes three
or four times a week, which was how a correspondent built up a following, not only among
viewers but with senior decision makers at CBA
headquarters.

Harry Partridge, on the other hand, stayed
with his own game plan and operated differ-
ently. He sought out deeper stories which required longer investigation and which took him,
with a cameraman, to more distant parts of
Vietnam. He made himself knowledgeable
about military tactics, American and Viet
Cong, and why sometimes those of both sides
didn't work. He studied the balance of forces,
stayed in forward areas gathering facts on
ground- and air-attack effectiveness, casualties
and logistics. Some of his reports contradicted
official military statements in Saigon, others

confirmed them, and it was that second kind of reporting—fairness to the U.S. military—that separated Partridge and a handful of others from the majority of correspondents reporting out of Vietnam.

The bulk of reportage on the Vietnam war was, by that time, negative and adversary. A generation of young journalists—some of them sympathetic to anti-war protesters at home— distrusted, at times despised, the U.S. military, and most media coverage reflected that conviction. An example was the enemy's Tet offensive. The media proclaimed Tet as a total, smashing communist victory, a claim which calmer research two decades later showed to be untrue.

Harry Partridge was one who, at the time, reported that U.S. forces at Tet were doing much better than they were being given credit for; also that the enemy was doing less well than generally reported and had failed in some of its objectives. At first senior Horseshoe producers queried those reports and wanted to delay them. But after discussion, Partridge's record of solid accuracy won out and most were aired.

One Partridge report which was *not* aired involved a criticism of negative personal opinion presented in a news context by the venerable Walter Cronkite, then anchorman for CBS.

Cronkite, reporting from Vietnam, declared during a CBS "post-Tet special" that "the bloody experience of Vietnam" would "end in stalemate," and "for every means we have to escalate, the enemy can match us . . ."

He continued, "To say that we are closer to victory today is to believe . . . the optimists who have been wrong in the past." Therefore, Cronkite urged, America should "negotiate, not as victors, but as an honorable people who lived up to their pledge to defend democracy, and did the best they could."

Because of its source, this strong editorializing—intertwined with honest news—had tremendous effect and gave, as a commentator put it, "strength and legitimacy to the anti-war movement." President Lyndon Johnson was reported as saying that if he had lost Walter Cronkite, he had lost the country.

Partridge, through interviews with a series of people on the scene, managed to suggest that not only might Cronkite be wrong but that, well aware of his power and influence, the CBS anchorman had behaved, in one interviewee's words, "like an unelected President and contrary to his own vaunted tenets of impartial journalism."

When Partridge's piece reached New York it was discussed for hours and went to the highest CBA levels before a consensus was reached that to attack the national father figure of "Walter" would be a no-win gambit. However, unofficial copies of the Partridge report were made and circulated privately among TV news insiders.

Partridge's excursions into areas of heavy fighting usually kept him away from Saigon for a week, sometimes longer. Once, when he went underground into Cambodia, he was out of touch for nearly a month.

Every time, though, he returned with a strong story, and after the war some were still remembered for their insights. No one, including Crawford Sloane, ever disputed that Partridge was a superb journalist.

Unfortunately, because his reports were fewer and therefore less frequent than Sloane's, Partridge didn't get noticed nearly as much.

Something else in Vietnam affected the future of Partridge and Sloane. She was Jessica Castillo.

Jessica . . .

Crawford Sloane, driving almost automatically over a route he traveled twice each working day, had by now turned off Fifty-ninth Street onto York Avenue. After a few blocks he swung right to the northbound ramp of the FDR Drive. Moments later, alongside the East River and free from intersections and traffic lights, he allowed his speed to increase. His home in Larchmont, north of the city on Long

Island Sound, was now half an hour's driving time away.

Behind him, a blue Ford Tempo increased its speed also.

Sloane was relaxed, as he usually was at this time of day, and as his thoughts drifted they returned to Jessica . . . who, in Saigon, had been Harry Partridge's girlfriend . . . but in the end had married Crawford Sloane.

In those days, in Vietnam, Jessica had been twenty-six, slim, with long brown hair, a lively mind and, on occasion, a sharp tongue. She took no nonsense from the journalists with whom she dealt as a junior information officer at the United States Information Agency (known as USIS overseas).

The agency had its headquarters on Le Qui Don Street, in the tree-shrouded "Lincoln Library" which used to be the Rex Theater, and the old theater sign remained in place throughout the USIS tenure. Members of the press went to the agency sometimes more than they needed, bringing queries that they hoped might allow them time with Jessica.

Jessica played along with the attention, which amused her. But in her affections when Crawford Sloane first knew her, Harry Partridge was firmly number one.

Even now, Sloane thought, there were areas in that early relationship between Partridge and Jessica of which he had no knowledge, some things he had never asked about and now would never know. But the fact that certain doors had been closed more than twenty years ago, and had remained closed ever since, never had . . . never would . . . stop him wondering about the details and intimacies of those times.

5

Jessica Castillo and Harry Partridge were drawn instinctually to each other the first time they met in Vietnam—even though the meeting was antagonistic. Partridge had gone to USIS seeking information that he knew existed but that had been refused him by the United States military. It concerned the widespread drug addiction of American troops in Vietnam.

Partridge had seen plenty of evidence of addiction during his travels through forward areas. The hard drug being used was heroin and it was plentiful. Through Stateside inquiries made at his request by CBA News, he learned that veter-

ans' hospitals back home were filling up alarmingly with addicts sent back from Vietnam. It was becoming a national problem, rather than just military.

The New York Horseshoe had given a green light to pursue the story, but official sources had clammed up tight and would provide no information.

When he entered Jessica's cubicle office and broached the subject, she reacted in the same way. "I'm sorry. That's something I can't talk about."

Her attitude offended him and he said accusingly, "You mean you won't talk because you've been told to protect somebody. Is it the ambassador, who might be embarrassed by the truth?"

She shook her head. "I can't answer that either."

Partridge, growing angry, bored in hard. "So what you're telling me is that you, in this cozy billet, don't give a goddamn about the GIs out in the jungle who are shit-scared, suffering, and then—for an outlet, because they don't know any better—destroy themselves with drugs, becoming junkies."

She said indignantly, "I said nothing of the kind."

"Oh, but you said exactly that." His voice was contemptuous. "You said you won't talk about something rotten and stinking which needs

a public airing, needs people to know a problem exists so something can be done. So other green kids coming out here can be warned and maybe saved. Who do you think you're protecting, lady? For sure, not the guys doing the fighting, the ones who count. You call yourself an information officer. I call you a concealment officer."

Jessica flushed. Unused to being talked to that way, her eyes blazed with anger. A glass paperweight was on her desk and her fingers clenched around it. For a moment Partridge expected her to throw it and prepared to duck. Then, noticeably, the anger diminished and Jessica asked quietly, "What is it you want to know?"

Partridge moderated his tone to match hers. "Statistics mostly. I know someone has them, that records have been kept, surveys taken."

She tossed back her brown hair in a gesture he would later become used to and love. "Do you know Rex Talbot?"

"Yes." Talbot was a young American vice-consul at the Embassy on Thong Nhut Street, a few blocks away.

"I suggest you ask him to tell you about the MACV Project Nostradamus report."

Despite the seriousness, Partridge smiled, wondering what kind of mind dreamed up that title.

Jessica continued, "There's no need to have

Rex know I sent you. You could let him think you know . . ."

He finished the sentence. ". . . a little more than I really do. It's an old journalist's trick."

"The kind of trick you just used on me."

"Sort of," he acknowledged with a smile.

"I knew it all the time," Jessica said. "I just let you get away with it."

"You're not as soulless as I thought," he told her. "How about exploring that subject some more over dinner tonight?"

To her own surprise, Jessica accepted.

Later, they discovered how much they enjoyed each other's company and it turned out to be the first of many such meetings. For a surprisingly long time, though, their meetings remained no more than that, which was something Jessica, with her blunt, plain speaking, made clear at the beginning.

"I'd like you to understand that whatever else goes on around here, I am no pushover. If I go to bed with someone it has to mean something special and important to me, and also to the other person, so don't say you weren't warned."
Their relationship also endured long separations, due to Partridge's travels to other parts of Vietnam.

But inevitably a moment came when desire overwhelmed them both.

They had dined together at the Caravelle,

where Partridge was staying. Afterward, in the hotel garden, an oasis of quiet amid the discord of Saigon, he had reached for Jessica and she came to him eagerly. As they kissed, she clung tightly, urgently, and through her thin dress he sensed her physical excitement. Years later, Partridge would remember that time as one of those rare and magic moments when all problems and concerns—Vietnam, the war's ugliness, future uncertainties—seemed far away, so all that mattered was the present and themselves.

He asked her softly, "Shall we go to my room?"

Without speaking, Jessica nodded her consent.

Upstairs in the room, with the only lighting from outside and while they continued to hold each other, he undressed her and she helped him where his hands proved awkward.

As he entered her, she told him, "Oh, I love you so!"

Long after, he could never remember if he told her that he truly loved her too, but knew he had and always would.

Partridge was also deeply moved by the discovery that Jessica had been a virgin. Then, as time went by and their lovemaking continued, they found the same delight in each other physically that they had in other ways.

In any other time and place they might have

married quickly. Jessica wanted to be married; she also wanted children. But Partridge, for reasons he afterward regretted, held back. In Canada he had had one failed marriage and knew that marriages of TV newsmen so often were disastrous. TV news correspondents led peripatetic lives, could be away from home two hundred days a year or more, were unused to family responsibilities and encountered sexual temptations on the road which few could permanently resist. As a result, spouses often grew away from each other—intellectually as well as sexually. When reunited after long absences, they met as strangers.

Combined with all that was Vietnam. Partridge knew his life was at risk each time he left Saigon and, though luck had been with him so far, the odds were against that luck enduring. So it wasn't fair, he reasoned, to burden someone else—in this case Jessica—with persistent worry, and the likelihood of heartbreak later on.

He confided some of this to Jessica early one morning after they had spent the night together, and he could not have picked a worse occasion. Jessica was shocked and jolted by what she perceived as a puerile cop-out by a man to whom she had already given her heart and body. She told Partridge coldly that their relationship was at an end.

Only much later did Jessica realize she had

misread what, in reality, was kindness and deep caring. Partridge left Saigon a few hours afterward, and that was the time he went into Cambodia and was away a month.

Crawford Sloane had met Jessica several times while she was in Harry Partridge's company, and saw her occasionally in the USIS offices when he had queries that took him there. On all occasions Sloane was strongly attracted to Jessica and longed to know her better. But recognizing she was Partridge's girl, and being punctilious in such matters, he had never asked her for a date, as others often did.

But when Sloane learned, from Jessica herself, that she and Partridge had "split up," he promptly asked Jessica to dine with him. She agreed to, and they went on seeing each other. Two weeks later, confiding that he had loved her for a long time from a distance and now with closer knowledge adored her, Sloane proposed marriage.

Jessica, taken by surprise, asked for time to think.

Her mind was a tumult of emotions. Jessica's love for Harry had been passionate and all-consuming. No man had ever swept her away as he had done; she doubted if anyone ever would again. Instinct told her that what she and Harry had shared was a once-in-a-lifetime experience. And she still loved him, she was sure of that.

Even now Jessica missed him desperately; if he came back and asked her to marry him she would probably say yes. But, clearly, Harry wasn't going to ask. He had rejected her and Jessica's bitterness and anger lingered. A part of her wanted to . . . just show him! So there!

On the other hand, there was Crawf. Jessica liked Crawford Sloane . . . No—more than that! . . . She felt a strong affection for him. He was kind and gentle, loving, intelligent, interesting to be with. And Crawf was solid. *He possessed—Jessica had to admit—a stability that Harry, while an exciting person, sometimes lacked. But for a lifetime, which was how Jessica saw marriage, which of the two loves on different levels—one with excitement, the other with stability—was more important? She wished she could be positive about the answer.*

Jessica might also have asked herself the question, but did not: Why make a decision at all? Why not wait? She was still young . . .

Unacknowledged, but implicit in her thinking, was the presence of all of them in Vietnam. The fervor of war surrounded them; it was all-pervading like the air they breathed. There was a sense of time being compressed and accelerated, as if clocks and calendars were running at extra speed. Each day of life seemed to spill in a precipitous torrent through the open floodgates of a dam. Who among them knew how many days remained? Which of them would ever resume a normal pace of living?

In every war, throughout all human experience, it had been ever thus.

After weighing everything as best she could, the next day Jessica accepted Crawford Sloane's proposal.

They were married at once, in the U.S. Embassy by an army chaplain. The ambassador attended the ceremony and afterward gave a reception in his private suite.

Sloane was ecstatically happy. Jessica assured herself that she was too; determinedly she matched Crawf's mood.

Partridge did not learn of the marriage until his return to Saigon and only then did it dawn on him, with overpowering sadness, how much he had lost. When he met Jessica and Sloane to congratulate them, he tried to conceal his emotions. With Jessica, who knew him so well, he did not wholly succeed.

But if Jessica shared some of Partridge's feelings, she kept them to herself and also put them behind her. She reasoned that she had made her choice and was determined to be a good wife to Sloane which, across the years, she was. As in any normal marriage there were some midway conflicts and disruptions, but they healed. Now—

incredibly, it seemed to all concerned—Jessica and Crawford's silver wedding anniversary was less than five years distant.

6

At the wheel of the Buick Somerset, Crawford Sloane was midpoint in his journey home. The Triboro Bridge behind him, he was on the Bruckner Expressway and would shortly join Interstate 95, the New England Thruway, exiting at Larchmont.

The same Ford Tempo that had followed him from CBA News headquarters was still behind.

It was not surprising that Sloane had failed to notice the other car, either tonight or on other occasions during the past several weeks when it had followed him. One reason was that the driver—a young, thin-lipped, cold-eyed Colombian currently using the code name Carlos —was expert at stalking any quarry.

Carlos, who had entered the United States two months earlier using a forged passport, had been involved in this stealthy surveillance for almost four weeks, along with six others from Colombia—five men and a woman. Like Carlos, the others were identified only by fictitious first names, which in most cases covered criminal records. Until their present task began, the members of the group were unknown to one another. Even now, only Miguel, the leader, who tonight was several miles away, was aware of real identities.

The Ford Tempo had been repainted twice during the short period of its use. Also, it was just one of several vehicles available, the objective being not to create a detectable pattern.

What had accumulated from the surveillance was a precise and detailed study of Crawford Sloane's movements and those of his family.

In the fast-moving expressway traffic, Carlos allowed three other cars to move up between himself and Sloane, though keeping the trailed Buick still in sight. Beside Carlos, another man noted the time and made an entry in a log. This was Julio—swarthy, argumentative and bad-tempered, with an ugly scar from a knifing down the left side of his face. He was the group's communications specialist. Behind them, in the back seat, was a mobile cellular phone, one of six that linked vehicles and a hidden temporary headquarters.

Both Carlos and Julio were ruthless, trained marksmen and were armed.

After slowing down and negotiating a traffic diversion caused by a multiple rear-end collision in the Thruway's left lane, Sloane resumed his speed and also his thoughts about Vietnam, Jessica, Partridge and himself.

Despite his own great success in Vietnam and since, Crawford Sloane had continued to worry about Partridge, just a little. It was why he was slightly uncomfortable in Partridge's company. And on a personal level he occasionally wondered: Did Jessica ever think about Harry, remembering the privileged, private moments there must have been between them?

Sloane had never asked his wife any truly intimate questions about her long-ago relationship with Harry. He could have done so many times, including at the beginning of their marriage, and Jessica, being Jessica, would probably have answered frankly. But posing that kind of question was simply not Sloane's style. Nor, he supposed, did he really want to know the answers. Yet, paradoxically, after all these years those old thoughts came back to him at times with newer questions: Did Jessica still care about Harry? Did the two of them ever communicate? Did Jessica, even now, have residual regrets?

And professionally . . . Guilt was not a word that preoccupied Sloane in relation to himself, but down in some private corner of his soul he knew that Partridge had been the better journalist in Vietnam, though he himself gained more acclaim and on top of that married Partridge's girl . . . All of it illogical, he knew, an insecurity that need not be . . . but the visceral unease persisted.

The Ford Tempo had now switched places and was several vehicles ahead of Sloane. The Larchmont exit from the Thruway was only a few miles farther on and Carlos and Julio, by this time knowing Sloane's habits, were aware that he would exit there. Getting ahead of a quarry on occasions was an old trick of tailing. Now, the Ford would take the Larchmont exit first, be waiting for Sloane when he turned off, then would fall in behind him once more.

Some ten minutes later, as the CBA anchorman entered the streets of Larchmont, the Ford Tempo followed discreetly at a distance, stopping well short of the Sloane house which was located on Park Avenue, facing Long Island Sound.

The house, befitting someone with Sloane's substantial income, was large and imposing. Painted white under a gray slate roof, it was set in a sculptured garden with a circular driveway. Twin pine trees marked the entrance. A wrought-iron lantern hung over double front doors.

Sloane used a remote control in the car to open the door of a three-car garage, then drove in, the door closing behind him.

The Ford moved forward and, from a discreet distance, the surveillance continued.

7

Sloane could hear voices and laughter as he walked through a short, closed corridor between the garage and the house. They stopped as he opened a door and entered the carpeted hallway onto which most of the downstairs rooms opened. He heard Jessica call out from the living room, "Is that you, Crawf?"

He made a standard response. "If it isn't, you're in trouble."

Her melodious laugh came back, "Welcome, whoever you are! Be with you in a minute."

He heard a clink of glasses, the sound of ice being shaken, and knew that Jessica was mixing martinis, her nightly homecoming ritual to help

him unwind from whatever the day had
brought.

"Hi, Dad!" the Sloanes' eleven-year-old son,
Nicholas, shouted from the stairway. He was
tall for his age and slimly built. His intelligent
eyes lit up as he ran to hug his father.

Sloane returned the embrace, then ran his
fingers through the boy's curly brown hair. It
was the kind of greeting he appreciated, and he
had Jessica to thank for that. Almost from the
time Nicky was born, she had conveyed to him
her belief that feelings about loving should be
expressed in tactile ways.

At the beginning of their marriage, being de-
monstrative did not come easily to Sloane. He
held back in matters of emotion, left certain
things unsaid, to be assumed by the other party.
It was part of his built-in reserve, but Jessica
would have none of it, had worked hard at
smashing the reserve and, for herself, then
Nicky, had succeeded.

Sloane recalled her telling him early on,
"When you're married, darling, barriers come
down. It's why we were 'joined together'—remember those words? So for the rest of our
lives, you and I are going to say to each other
exactly what we feel—and sometimes show it
too."

That final phrase had been about sex, which
for a long time after their marriage held sur-

prises and adventure for Sloane. Jessica had acquired several of the explicit, illustrated sex books which were plentiful in the East and loved to experiment, trying new positions. After being slightly shocked and diffident at first, Sloane came around to enjoying it too, though it was always Jessica who took the lead.

(There were times when he couldn't help wondering: Had she owned those sex books when she and Partridge were going together? Had they made use of what was in them? But Sloane had never summoned the nerve to ask, perhaps because he feared both answers might be yes.)

With other people his reserve lived on. Sloane couldn't remember when he had last hugged his own father, though a few times recently he had considered doing so but held back, uncertain how old Angus—stiff, even rigid in his personal behavior—might react.

"Hello, darling!" Jessica appeared wearing a soft green dress, a color he always liked. They embraced warmly, then went into the living room. Nicky came in for a while, as he usually did; he had eaten dinner earlier and would go to bed soon.

Sloane asked his son, "How's everything in the music world?"

"Great, Dad. I'm practicing Gershwin's Prelude Number Two."

His father said, "I remember that. Didn't Gershwin write it when he was young?"

"Yes, twenty-eight."

"Near the beginning, I think, it goes dum-de-dah-dum-DEE-da-da-de-dum-de-dum-de-dum-de-dum." As he attempted to sing, Nicky and Jessica laughed.

"I know the part you mean, Dad, and maybe why you remember it." Nicky crossed to a grand piano in the room, then sang in a clear young tenor, accompanying himself.

> "In the sky the bright stars glittered
> On the bank the pale moon shone
> And from Aunt Dinah's quilting party
> I was seeing Nellie home."

Sloane's forehead creased with an effort of memory. "I've heard that before. Isn't it an old song from the Civil War days?"

Nicky beamed. "Right on, Dad!"

"I think I understand," his father said. "What you're telling me is, some of those notes are the same as in Gershwin's Prelude Two."

Nicky shook his head. "The other way 'round—the song was first. But no one knows if Gershwin knew the song and used it, or if it was just chance."

"And we'll never know." Amused, and impressed with Nicky's knowledge, Sloane exclaimed, "I'll be damned!"

Neither he nor Jessica could remember exactly how old Nicky had been when he began to exhibit an interest in music, but it was in his very early years and now music was Nicky's dominant concern.

Nicky had gravitated to the piano and took lessons from a former concert pianist, an elderly Austrian living in nearby New Rochelle. A few weeks earlier, speaking with a heavy accent, the tutor had told Jessica, "Your son already has a mastery of music unusual for his age. Later he may follow one of several paths—as a performer or composer, or perhaps a scholar and savant. But more important is that for Nicholas, music speaks with the tongues of angels and of joy. It is part of his soul. It will, I predict, be the mainstream of his life."

Jessica glanced at her watch. "Nicky, it's getting late."

"Ah, Mom, let me stay up! Tomorrow's a school holiday."

"And your day will be as full as any other. The answer is no."

Jessica was the family disciplinarian and, after affectionate good-nights, Nicky left. Soon after, they could hear him playing on a portable electronic keyboard in his bedroom which he

used when the living-room piano was unavailable.

In the softly lighted room, Jessica returned
to the martinis she had been mixing earlier.
Watching her dispense them, Sloane thought,
How lucky can you get? It was a feeling he often
had about Jessica and the way she looked after
more than twenty years of marriage. She no
longer wore her hair long and didn't bother to
conceal streaks of gray. There were also lines
around her eyes. But her figure was slim and
shapely and her legs still brought men's eyes
back for a second glance. Overall, he thought,
she really hadn't changed and he still felt proud
to enter a room, any room, with Jessica beside
him.

As she handed him a glass she commented,
"It sounded like a rough day?"

"It was pretty much that way. You watched
the news?"

"Yes. Those poor passengers on that airplane! What a terrible way to die! They must
have known for the longest time they didn't
have a chance, then just had to sit there, waiting."

With a pang of conscience, Sloane realized
he hadn't thought about that at all. Sometimes
as a professional news person you became so
preoccupied with *gathering* the news, you forgot
the human beings who *made* it. He wondered:

Was it callousness after long exposure to the news or a necessary insulation, the kind acquired by doctors? He hoped it was the second, not the first.

"If you saw the airplane story," he said, "you saw Harry. What did you think?"

"He was good."

Jessica's answer seemed indifferent. Sloane watched her, waiting for more, wondering: In her mind, was the past completely dead?

"Harry was better than good. He did it like that," Sloane said, snapping his fingers. "Without warning. With hardly any time." He went on to describe CBA's luck in having the crew in the DFW terminal. "Harry, Rita and Minh all came through. We beat the pants off the other networks."

"Harry and Rita seem to be working a lot together. Is something going on there?"

"No. They're simply a good working team."

"How do you know?"

"Because Rita's having an affair with Les Chippingham. The two of them think nobody knows. Of course everybody does."

Jessica laughed. "My god! You're an incestuous little group."

Leslie Chippingham was the president of CBA News. It was Chippingham whom Sloane intended to see the next day about the removal of Chuck Insen as executive producer.

"Don't include me in any of that," he told Jessica. "I'm happy with what I have at home."

The martini had relaxed him, as it always did, though neither he nor Jessica was a heavy drinker. One martini plus a glass of wine with dinner was their limit, and during the day Sloane never drank at all.

"You're feeling good tonight," Jessica said, "and you have another reason to." She got up and from a small bureau across the room brought back an envelope, already opened—a normal procedure since Jessica handled most of their private business. "It's a letter from your publisher and a royalty statement."

He took the papers out and studied them, his face lighting with a smile.

Crawford Sloane's book *The Camera and the Truth* had been published several months earlier. Written with a collaborator, it was his third.

In terms of sales, the book got off to a slow start. The New York critics savaged it, leaping at the opportunity to humble someone of Crawford Sloane's stature. But in places like Chicago, Cleveland, San Francisco and Miami, reviewers liked the book. More important, as weeks passed, certain comments in it gained attention in general news columns—the best kind of publicity any book can have.

In a chapter about terrorism and hostages

Sloane had written bluntly of "the shame most Americans felt after the 1986–87 revelations that the U.S. Government bought freedom for a handful of our hostages in the Middle East at the expense of thousands of Iraqi deaths and mutilations, not only on the Iran-Iraq battle-field but among civilians."

The war casualties, he pointed out, resulted from weaponry supplied by the U.S. to Iran in payment for the hostages' release. "A modern dirty thirty pieces of silver" was how Sloane had described the payment, and he quoted Kipling's *Dane-geld:*

We never pay any-one Dane-geld,
No matter how trifling the cost;
For the end of that game is oppression and shame,
And the nation that plays it is lost!

Other applauded Sloane remarks were:
—*No politician anywhere has the guts to say it aloud, but hostages, including American hostages, should be regarded as expendable. Pleas from hostages' families should be heard sympathetically, but should not sway government policy.*

—*The only way to deal with terrorists is by counterterrorism, which means whenever possible seeking out and covertly destroying them—the only language they understand. It includes not striking bargains with terrorists or paying ransom, directly or indirectly, ever!*

—Terrorists who observe no civilized code should not expect, when caught red-handed, to shelter under laws and principles which they despise. The British, in whom respect for law is deeply ingrained, have been forced to bend that law at times in defending themselves from a depraved and ruthless IRA.

—No matter what we do, terrorism will not go away because the governments and organizations backing terrorists don't really want settlements or accommodations. They are fanatics using other fanatics and perverted religions as their weapons.

—We who live in the United States will not remain free from terrorism in our own backyard much longer. But neither mentally nor in other ways are we prepared for this pervasive, ruthless kind of warfare.

When the book came out, some of CBA's brass were nervous about the "hostages should be regarded as expendable" and "covertly destroying" statements, fearing they would create political and public resentment of the network. As it turned out, there was no reason for concern and the executives quickly joined the chorus of approval.

Sloane beamed as he put aside the impressive royalty accounting.

"You deserve what's happened and I'm proud of you," Jessica said. "Especially because it isn't like you to take chances in being controversial." She paused. "Oh, by the way, your father phoned. He's arriving early tomorrow and would like to stay a week."

Sloane grimaced. "That's pretty soon after the last time."

"He's lonely and he's getting old. Maybe if you're that way someday you'll have a favorite daughter-in-law you'll want to be with."

They both laughed, knowing how fond Angus Sloane was of Jessica and vice versa, and that in some ways the two were closer than the father and son.

Angus had been living alone in Florida since the death of Crawford's mother several years earlier.

"I enjoy having him around the house," Jessica said. "So does Nicky."

"Okay then, that's fine. But while Dad's here, try to use your great influence to stop him sounding off so much about honor, patriotism and all the rest."

"I know what you mean. I'll do what I can."

Behind the exchange was the fact that the elder Sloane could never quite let go of his

World War II hero status—as an Army Air
Forces lead bombardier who won a Silver Star
and the Distinguished Flying Cross. After the
war he had been a certified public accountant—
not a spectacular career, though on retirement
it provided him a reasonable pension and independence. But the military years continued to
dominate Angus's thoughts.

While Crawford respected his father's war
record, he knew the old man could be tedious
when launched on one of his favorite themes—
"the disappearance nowadays of integrity and
moral values," as he was apt to put it. Jessica,
though, managed to let her father-in-law's
preachments flow over her.

Talk between Sloane and Jessica continued
over dinner, always a favorite time. Jessica had
a maid come in daily but prepared dinner herself, managing to be organized so that she spent
minimal time in the kitchen after her husband's
arrival for the evening.

Sloane said thoughtfully, "I know what you
meant back there, that it isn't like me to venture
out on limbs. I guess, in my life, I haven't taken
chances as often as I might. But I felt strongly
about some things in the book. Still do."

"The terrorism part?"

He nodded. "Since that was written I've
done some thinking about how terrorism might,
how it *could,* affect you and me. It's why I've

taken some special precautions. Until now I haven't told you, but you ought to know."

While Jessica regarded him curiously, he went on. "Have you ever thought that someone like me could be kidnapped, become a hostage?"

"I have when you've been overseas."

He shook his head. "It could happen here. There's always a first and I, like some others on television, work in a goldfish bowl. If terrorists begin operating in the U.S.—and you know I believe they will, quite soon—people like me will be attractive bait because anything we do, or is done to us, gets noticed in a big way."

"What about families? Could they be targets too?"

"That's highly unlikely. Terrorists would be after a name. Someone everybody knows."

Jessica said uneasily, "You spoke of precautions. What kind?"

"The kind that would be effective *after* I'd been taken hostage—if it happened. I've worked it out with a lawyer I know, Sy Dreeland. He has all the details, and authority to make them public if and when that's needed."

"I don't much like this conversation," Jessica said. "You're making me nervous, and how can precautions be any good after something bad has already happened?"

"Before it happens," he said, "I have to

trust the network to provide some kind of security protection, and they do that now, more or less. But afterward, just as I said in the book, I wouldn't want any kind of ransom to be paid by anyone, including from our own money. So one thing I've done is make a solemn declaration—it's all in legal form—to that effect."

"Are you telling me all our money would be tied up, frozen?"

He shook his head. "No. I couldn't do that, even if I wanted. Almost everything we have—this house, bank accounts, stocks, gold, foreign currencies—you and I own jointly and you could do whatever you wanted with them, just as you can now. But after that solemn declaration was made public and everybody knew the way I felt, I'd like to think you wouldn't go some other route."

Jessica protested, "You'd rob me of the right to make a decision!"

He said gently, "No, dearest. I'd relieve you of a terrible responsibility and a dilemma."

"But supposing the network were willing to pay a ransom?"

"I doubt they would be, but certainly not against my wishes which are on record in the book and repeated in the declaration."

"You said the network is giving you some kind of security protection. It's the first I've heard of it. Just what kind?"

"When there are telephoned threats, or screwball letters which sound a certain way, or a rumor of some kind of possible attack—it happens at all networks and especially to anchor people—then private security men are called in. They hang around the CBA News Building, wherever I'm working, doing whatever security people are supposed to. It's happened with me a few times."

"You've never told me."

"No, I guess I never have," he conceded.

"What else haven't you told me?" There was an edge to Jessica's voice, though clearly she had not made up her mind whether to be angry at the concealment or just anxious.

"Nothing else at the network, but there are some other things I've arranged with Dreeland."

"Would it be too much to let me know about those too?"

"It's important that you know." Sloane ignored the sarcasm which his wife sometimes resorted to when emotional. "When someone is kidnapped, no matter where in the world, nowadays it's a certainty they will make, or be compelled to make, videotape recordings. Then those recordings turn up, sometimes are played on television, but no one knows for sure whether they were voluntary or forced and, if forced, to what extent. But if there's a *prear-*

rangement of signals, someone who is taken hostage has a good chance of getting a message back that is clearly understood. Incidentally, more and more people who might one day be hostages are doing that, leaving instructions with their lawyers and establishing a signal code."

"If this weren't so serious, it would sound like a spy novel," Jessica said. "So what kind of signals have you arranged?"

"Licking my lips with my tongue, which is something anyone might do without its being noticed, would mean, *'I am doing this against my will. Do not believe anything I am saying.'* Scratching or touching my right earlobe would mean, *'My captors are well organized and strongly armed.'* Doing the same thing to my left earlobe would mean, *'Security here is sometimes lax. An attack from outside might succeed.'* There are some others, but we'll leave it for now. I don't want all this to distress you."

"Well, it does distress me," Jessica said. She wondered: *Could* it happen? Could Crawf be kidnapped and spirited away? It seemed unbelievable, but almost every day unbelievable things did happen.

"Apart from fear," she said thoughtfully, "I have to admit some of this fascinates me, because it's a side of you I don't believe I've ever seen before. But I do wonder why you haven't taken that security course we talked about."

It was an anti-terrorism course put on by a British company, Paladin Security, that had been featured on several American news programs. The course lasted a week, and in part was intended to prepare people for just the possibility Sloane had raised—how to behave as a victim in a hostage situation. Also taught was unarmed self defense—something Jessica had urged her husband to learn after a savage attack on the CBS anchorman Dan Rather on a New York street in 1986. The unprovoked attack by two unknown men had sent Rather to a hospital; the assailants were never found.

"Finding time for that course is the problem," Sloane said. "Speaking of that, are you still taking CQB lessons?"

CQB was shorthand for close quarters battle, a specialized version of unarmed combat practiced by the elite British Army SAS. The instruction was given by a retired British brigadier now living in New York, and that was something else Jessica had wanted Crawford to do. But when he simply couldn't find time she took the lessons herself.

"I'm not taking them regularly anymore," she answered. "Though I do an hour every month or two to keep refreshed, and Brigadier Wade sometimes gives lectures which I go to."

Sloane nodded. "Good."

That night, still troubled by what had passed between them, Jessica found it difficult to sleep.

Outside, the occupants of the Ford Tempo watched as one by one the lights in the house went off. Then they made a report by cellular phone and, ending that day's vigil, drove away.

8

Shortly after 6:30 A.M. the surveillance of the Sloanes' Larchmont house resumed. A Chevrolet Celebrity was being used this morning, and slouched down in the car's front seats—a standard observation technique so the occupants would not be noticed by other passing vehicles —were the Colombians, Carlos and Julio. The Chevy was parked beyond the Sloane house on a convenient side street, the observation being carried on through side and rearview mirrors.

Both men in the car were feeling tense, knowing that this would be a day of action, the culmination of long and careful planning.

At 7:30 A.M. an unforeseen event occurred

when a taxi arrived at the Sloane house. From the taxi an elderly man carrying a suitcase emerged. He went into the house and remained there. The newcomer's unexpected presence meant a complication and prompted a call by cellular phone to the watchers' temporary head-quarters some twenty miles away.

Their efficient communications and ample transport typified an operation on which expense had not been spared. The conspirators who had inspired and organized the surveillance and what was to follow were expert, resourceful and had access to plenty of money.

They were associates of Colombia's Medellín cartel, a coalition of vicious, criminal, fabulously wealthy drug lords. Operating with bestial savagery, the cartel had been responsible for countless violent, bloody murders including the 1989 assassination of Colombian presidential candidate Senator Luís Carlos Galán. Since 1981 more than 220 judges and court officials had been murdered, plus police, journalists and others. In 1986, a Medellín alliance with the socialist-guerrilla faction M-19 resulted in a killing orgy of ninety deaths, including half the members of Colombia's Supreme Court.

Despite the Medellín cartel's repulsive record, it enjoyed close ties with the Roman Catholic Church. Several cartel bosses boasted private chapels. A cardinal spoke favorably of

Medellín's people and a bishop blandly admitted taking money from drug traffickers.

Murder was not the only process by which the cartel ruled. Large-scale bribery and corruption financed by the drug lords ran like a massive cancer through Colombia's government, judiciary, police and military, beginning at topmost levels and filtering to the lowest. A cynical description of the drug trade's standard offer to officialdom was *plata o plomo*—silver or lead.

For a while, through 1989 and 1990 during a wave of horror following the Galán assassination, cartel leaders were inconvenienced by law enforcement efforts against them, including some modest intervention by the United States. A retaliatory response, accurately described by the drug conspirators as "total war," involved massive violence, bombings and still more killings, a process which seemed certain to continue. But survival of the cartel and its ubiquitous drug trade—perhaps with fresh leaders and bases—was never in doubt.

In the present instance, while operating undercover in the United States, Medellín was working not for itself but for the Peruvian Maoist-terrorist organization *Sendero Luminoso,* or "Shining Path." Recently in Peru, Sendero Luminoso had grown more powerful while the official government became increasingly inept and weak. Where once Sendero's domain had been limited to the Andes Mountains, Huallaga Valley and centers like Ayacucho and Cuzco, nowadays its bombing teams and assassination squads roamed the capital city, Lima.

Two strong reasons existed for linkages between Sendero Luminoso and the Medellín cartel. First, Sendero customarily employed outside criminals to conduct kidnappings which were frequent in Peru, though not widely reported by the American media. Second, Sendero Luminoso controlled most of Peru's Upper Huallaga Valley where sixty percent of the world's coca crop was grown. The coca, in leaf form, was converted to coca paste—the basis of cocaine—and afterward flown from remote airstrips to the Colombian cartels.

In the whole process drug money contributed heavily to Sendero finances, the group exacting a substantial tribute both from coca growers and traffickers—the Medellín connection among them.

Now, in the surveillance Chevrolet, the two Colombian hoodlums were searching through a collection of Polaroid photos which Carlos, an adept photographer, had taken of all persons seen to have entered the Sloane house during the past four weeks. The elderly man who had just arrived was not among them.

Julio, on the telephone, spoke in code phrases.

"A blue package has arrived. Delivery number two. The package is in storage. We cannot trace the order." Translated: _A man has arrived. Delivered by taxi. He has gone into the house. We do not know who he is; there is no Polaroid of him._

The sharp-edged voice of Miguel, the project's leader, snapped back through the phone, "What is the docket number?"

Julio, not comfortable with codes, swore softly as he leafed through a notebook to decipher the question. It asked him: _What age is this person?_

He looked to Carlos for help. "_Un viejo._ How old?"

Carlos took the book and read the question. "Tell him, _docket seventy-five._"

Julio did, producing another terse question. "Is anything special about the blue package?"

Abandoning code, Julio lapsed into plain language. "He carried a suitcase in. Looks like he plans to stay."

South of Hackensack, New Jersey, in a dilapidated rented house, the man whose code name was Miguel silently cursed Julio's carelessness. _Those_ pendejos _he was forced to work with! In the code book was a phrase that would_ *have answered the question, and he had warned all of them, over and over, that on radio phones* anyone *could be listening.* Scanning devices that could eavesdrop on cellular phone conversations were available in stores. Miguel had heard of a radio station that used a scanner and boasted of foiling several criminal plots.

¡Estúpidos! He simply could not get through to the idiots assigned to him—when the success of their mission, plus all their lives and freedoms were at stake—the importance of being vigilant, cautious, on guard, not just *most* of the time, but *all* of it.

Miguel himself had been obsessively cautious for as long as he could remember. It was why he had never been arrested, even though he was on "most wanted" lists of police forces in North and South America and some in Europe too, including Interpol. In the Western Hemisphere he was becoming as keenly sought after as his brother-in-terrorism Abu Nidal, on the other side of the Atlantic. About that, Miguel permitted himself a certain pride, though never failing to remember that pride could beget overconfidence, and *that* was something else he guarded against.

Despite all the turmoil he had been a part of, he was still a young man—in his late thirties. In appearance he had always been unremarkable, with average good looks but no more; anyone passing him on a street might think he was a bank clerk or, at best, manager of a small store. In part, this was because he worked hard at seeming unimportant. He also made a habit of being polite to strangers, but not to the point of creating a memorable impression; most who met him casually, not knowing who he was, tended to forget having done so.

In the past, this ordinariness had been Miguel's great good fortune, as was the fact that he did not radiate authority. His power of command remained hidden except to those on whom he exercised it, and then it was unmistakable.

An advantage to Miguel in his present enterprise was that, although Colombian, he could appear and sound American. In the late-1960s and early '70s he had attended the University of California at Berkeley as a foreign student, majoring in English and patiently learning to speak the language without an accent.

In those days he was using his real name, Ulises Rodríguez.

His well-to-do parents had provided the Berkeley education. Miguel's father, a Bogotá neurosurgeon, hoped his only son would follow him into medicine, a prospect in which Miguel had no interest, even then. Instead, as the 1970s neared, the son foresaw basic changes ahead for Colombia—conversion from a prosperous democratic country with an honest legal base to a lawless, unbelievably rich mobsters' haven ruled through dictatorship, savagery and fear. The pharaoh's gold of the new Colombia was marijuana; it would later be cocaine.

Such was Miguel's nature that the coming transition did not faze him. What he coveted was part of the action.

Meanwhile he indulged in some action of his own at Berkeley where he discovered himself to be totally devoid of conscience and able to kill other human beings, swiftly and decisively, without compunction or unpleasant aftertaste.

The first time it happened was after a sexual session with a young woman he had met earlier on a Berkeley street while both were getting off a bus. Walking from the bus stop, they got into conversation and discovered they were both freshmen. She seemed to like him and invited him to her apartment, which was at the seedy Oakland end of Telegraph Avenue. It was at a time when such encounters were normal, long before the AIDS-anxiety era.

After some energetic sex he fell asleep, then awakened to find the girl quietly looking through the contents of his wallet. In it were several identification cards in fictitious names; even then he was practicing for his international beyond-the-law future. The girl was too interested in the cards for her own good; perhaps she was some kind of informant, though he never found out.

What he did was spring from the bed, seize and strangle her. He still remembered her look of unbelief as she thrashed around, trying to release herself; then she looked up at him with desperate, silent pleading just before consciousness ebbed. He was interested, in a clinical way, to discover that killing her did not trouble him at all.

Instead, with icy calm he calculated his chances of being caught, which he assessed as nil. While on the bus the two of them had not sat together; in fact they had not known each other. It was unlikely that anyone observed them walking away from the bus stop. On entering the apartment building, and in an elevator going to the fourth floor, they encountered no one.

Taking his time, he used a cloth to wipe the few surfaces where he might have left fingerprints. Then, using a handkerchief to cover his right hand, he turned out all lights and left the apartment, allowing the door to lock behind him.

He avoided the elevator and went down by the emergency stairs, checking that the lobby was empty before passing through it to the street outside.

The next day, and for several days after, he

watched local newspapers for any item about the dead girl. But it was nearly a week before her partially decomposed body was discovered, then after two or three days more, with no developments and apparently no clues, the newspapers lost interest and the story disappeared.

Whatever investigation there was had not connected him with the girl's murder.

During Miguel's remaining years at Berkeley he killed on two other occasions. Those were across the Bay in San Francisco—what he supposed could be called "thrill killings" of total strangers, though he considered both as serving a need to hone his developing mercenary skills. He must have honed them well because in neither case was he a suspect, or even questioned by police.

After Berkeley, and home in Colombia, Miguel flirted with the developing alliance of mad-dog drug lords. He had a pilot's license and made several flights conveying coca paste from Peru to Colombia for processing. Soon a developing friendship with the infamous but influential Ochoa family helped move him on to larger things. Then came M-19 with its orgy of murders and the Medellín cartel's "total war," beginning in late 1989. Miguel participated in all the major killings, many minor ones, and had long since lost count of the corpses in his wake. Inevitably his name became known internationally, but due to his meticulous precautions there was little else on record.

Miguel's—or Ulises Rodríguez's—connections with the Medellín cartel, M-19 and, more recently, Sendero Luminoso, expanded as the years went by. Through it all, though, he maintained his independence, becoming an international outlaw, a gun-for-hire terrorist who was, because of his efficiency, constantly in demand.

Of course, politics was supposedly a part of it all. Miguel was by instinct a socialist, hated capitalism passionately and despised what he thought of as the hypocritical, decadent United States. But he was also skeptical about politics of any kind and simply enjoyed, as one might an aphrodisiac, the danger, risk and action of the life he led.

It was that kind of life which had brought him to the United States a month and a half ago, to work undercover, preparing for what would happen today, which the entire world would shortly learn of.

The route he had originally planned to the U.S. was roundabout but safe—from Bogotá, Colombia, through Rio de Janeiro to Miami. In Rio he would change passports and identities, appearing in Miami as a Brazilian publisher en route to a New York book fair. But an undercover contact in the American State Department had warned Medellín that U.S. Immigration at Miami had urgently requested all available information on Miguel, especially about identities he was known to have used in the past.

Miguel had, in fact, used the Brazilian publisher identity once before and although he believed it was still unexposed, it seemed wiser to avoid Miami altogether. Therefore, even though it meant some delay, he flew from Rio to London where he acquired an entirely new identity and a brand-new, official British passport.

The process was easy.

Ah, the innocent democracies! How stupid and naïve they were! How simple it was to subvert their vaunted freedoms and open systems to advance the purposes of those who, like Miguel, believed in neither!

He had been briefed, before reaching London, on how it was done.

First he went to St. Catherine's House, at the junction of Kingsway and Aldwych, where births, marriages and deaths for England and Wales are recorded. There Miguel applied for three birth certificates.

Whose birth certificates? Those of anyone whose date of birth was the same as, or close to, his own.

Without speaking to anyone or being questioned, he picked up five blank birth certificate applications, then walked to where a series of large volumes were on shelves, identified under various years. Miguel chose 1951. The volumes were divided into quarters of the year. He selected M to R, October–December.

His own birth date was November 14 that year. Leafing through pages, he came across the name "Dudley Martin" who had been born in Keighley, Yorkshire, on November 13. The name seemed suitable; it was neither too distinctive nor as obviously common as Smith. ¡Perfecto! Miguel copied the details onto one of the red-printed application forms.

Now he needed two other names. It was his intention to apply for three passports; the second and third applications would be backups in case anything went wrong with the first. It was always possible that a current passport had already been issued to the same Dudley Martin. In that case a new one would be refused.

He copied the remaining names onto two more forms. Deliberately, he had selected surnames whose initial letters were widely spaced from the "M" of Martin; one began with "B," the other "Y." That was because, at the Passport Office, different clerks handled different letter groups of applications. The spread ensured that the three applications would be dealt with by separate persons, so any similarity would not be noticed.

At all points Miguel was careful not to touch any of the forms on which he wrote. That was why he had picked up five forms; the two outside ones were to protect the others from his fingerprints and he would destroy those later. He had learned since Berkeley that nothing could take away fingerprints totally, not even careful wiping —new high-tech fingerprint tests, the Ninhydrin and ion-argon laser, would reveal them.

Next was a short walk to a cashier's window. There he presented the three applications, still managing not to touch any of those he would leave. A male cashier asked him for a fee of five pounds for each certificate, which he paid in cash. He was told the birth certificates would be ready in two days' time.

During those intervening days he arranged to use three accommodation addresses.

From Kelly's London Business Directory he noted several secretarial agencies to whose unembellished street addresses mail could be sent and then collected. Going to one of the agencies, he paid a fee of fifty pounds, again cash. He had a cover story ready—that he was starting a small business but could not yet afford an office or secretary. As it turned out, no questions were asked. He repeated the process at two other agencies which were equally incurious. He now had three separate addresses for the trio of passport applications, none of them traceable to himself.

Then, making use of automatic photography machines, he obtained three sets of passport photographs, each time varying his appearance. For one picture he applied a neat mustache and beard, in another he was clean-shaven and changed his hair parting, for the third he wore heavy, distinctive glasses.

Next day he collected the three birth certificates from St. Catherine's House. As before, no one was in the least interested as to why he wanted them.

He had already obtained passport applications from a post office, again being careful not to touch them. Now, wearing disposable plastic gloves, he completed the forms. On each, as the applicant's address he used one of the accommodation addresses already arranged.

Two photographs had to accompany each passport application. One photo was required to have on it a statement by a "professionally qualified person," such as a doctor, engineer or lawyer, identifying the applicant; also the same person affirmed that he or she had known the applicant for at least two years. Based on advice he had received, Miguel wrote and signed the statements himself, disguising his handwriting and using names and addresses selected at random from a phone book. He had also bought a rubber stamp set which he used to make the names and addresses more convincing.

Despite a warning on the passport form that checks of support signatories were made, in fact they rarely were, and the chance of a false statement's being discovered was extremely remote. There were simply too many applications and too small a staff.

Finally, Miguel dealt with the three "identified" photos—those that had writing on them and therefore would not appear in any of the passports he was applying for, but were destined for Passport Office files. Using a soft sponge, he applied a weak solution of Domestos, a household bleach similar to the North American product Clorox. This ensured that within two or three months the photographs on file would fade and blur, and thus no picture would exist of Miguel, alias Dudley Martin or the other names.

Now Miguel mailed the three applications, each with a postal order for fifteen pounds, knowing it would take at least four weeks for the passports to be processed and sent back. It was a tedious wait but, for safety's sake, worthwhile.

During this hiatus he mailed several letters to himself at the accommodation addresses. In each instance, after waiting a day or two he telephoned to inquire whether mail was there, and when the answer was "yes" stated that a messenger would make the collection. He then used unknown youths from the street for the pickups, paying them a few pounds and, before revealing *himself afterward, watching carefully to ensure that none was followed. It was Miguel's intention to collect the passports, when delivered, in the same way.*

All three passports arrived within a few days of each other during the fifth week and were collected without a hitch. When the third was in his hands, Miguel smiled to himself. ¡Excelente! He would use the Dudley Martin passport now, retaining the other two for future use.

One final step remained—to buy a round trip ticket to the United States. Miguel did so that same day.

Before 1988, all holders of British passports required a visa to enter the U.S. Now a visa was not needed, provided the intended visit would not exceed ninety days and the traveler possessed a return ticket. Though Miguel had no intention of using his return portion and later would destroy it, its cost was trifling compared with the risk of another sally through bureaucracy. As to the ninety-day rule, it made no difference to him either way. While he did not expect to stay that long in the U.S., when he left it would be either secretly or with another identity, the Dudley Martin passport having been discarded.

America's rule change about visas had delighted Miguel. Once more those convenient open systems were being helpful to his kind!

The next morning he flew to New York and,

at John F. Kennedy Airport, was admitted without hindrance.

After reaching New York, Miguel went immediately to where a sizable Colombian community lived in the borough of Queens and where a safe house had been arranged by a Medellín cartel agent.

"Little Colombia" in Jackson Heights extended from Sixty-ninth to Eighty-ninth streets. A thriving narcotics center, it was one of New York's most dangerous high-crime areas where violence was a hiccup and murder commonplace. Uniformed police officers seldom ventured there alone, and even in pairs did not move around on foot at night.

The district's reputation did not bother Miguel at all; in fact, he thought of it as protection while he began his planning, drew on money made secretly available, and assembled the small force he would lead. That force's seven members, including Miguel, had been selected in Bogotá.

Julio, at this moment on surveillance duty, and Socorro, the only woman in the group, were Colombians who had been "sleeping agents" of Medellín. Several years ago both were sent to the United States, ostensibly as immigrants, their only instructions to establish themselves and wait until such time as their services were needed for drug-related activity or some other criminal purpose. That time had now arrived.

Julio was a communications specialist. Socorro, during her waiting period, had trained and qualified as a nursing aide.

Socorro had an additional affiliation. Through friends in Peru she had become a sympathizer and part-time U.S. agent for the revolutionary Sendero Luminoso. Among Latin Americans such crossovers between politically motivated and profit-motivated crime were common and now, because of her dual connection, Socorro held a watching role also on Sendero's behalf.

Of the remaining four, three others were Colombians, who had been assigned the code names Rafael, Luís and Carlos. Rafael was a mechanic and general handyman. Luís had been chosen for his driving skills; he was expert at eluding pursuit, especially from crime scenes. Carlos was young, quick-witted and had organized the surveillance of the past four weeks. All three spoke English fluently and had been in the U.S. several times before. On this occasion they had come in unknown to each other and using forged passports with false names. Their instructions were to make themselves known to the same Medellín agent who arranged Miguel's safe house, after which they received orders directly from Miguel.

The final member of the group was an American, his name for this operation, Baudelio. Miguel mistrusted Baudelio totally, yet this man's knowledge and skills were essential to the mission's chances of success.

Now, in Hackensack at the Colombian group's temporary operating center, thinking about the renegade American, Baudelio, Miguel felt a surge of frustration. It compounded his anger with Julio for the careless lapse into plain language during the telephoned report from outside the Sloane house in Larchmont. Still holding the telephone, disciplining himself to subdue personal feelings, Miguel considered his reply.

The surveillance report had referred to a man aged about seventy-five, who arrived at the Sloane house a few minutes earlier with a suitcase he had carried inside—in Julio's careless words, "like he plans to stay."

Before leaving Bogotá, Miguel had received extensive intelligence, not all of which he had shared with the others under his command. Included in this dossier was the fact that Crawford Sloane had a father who fitted the description of the new arrival. Miguel reasoned: Well, if the old man had joined his son, expecting to see him for a while, it constituted a nuisance but nothing more. The father would almost certainly have to be killed later that day, but that presented no problem.

Depressing the telephone transmitter, Miguel ordered, "Take no action about the blue package. Report new billing only." "New billing" meant: *if the situation changes.*

"Roger," Julio acknowledged curtly.

Replacing the cellular phone, Miguel glanced at his watch. Almost 7:45 A.M. In two hours all seven members of his group would be in place and ready for action. Everything that would follow had been carefully planned, with problems anticipated, precautions taken. When the action started, some improvisation might be needed, but not much.

And there could be no postponement. Outside the United States, other movements, dovetailing with their own, were already in motion.

9

Angus Sloane gave a contented sigh, put down his coffee cup and patted his mouth and silver-gray mustache with a napkin. "I'll state positively," he declared, "that no better breakfast has been served this morning in all of New York State."

"And not one with higher cholesterol either," his son said from behind an opened *New York Times* across the table. "Don't you know all those fried eggs are bad for your heart? How many was it you had? Three?"

"Who's counting?" Jessica said. "Besides, you can afford the eggs, Crawf. Angus, would you like another?"

"No thank you, my dear." The old man, sprightly and cherubic—he had turned seventy-three a few weeks earlier—smiled benevolently at Jessica.

"Three eggs isn't many," Nicky said. "I saw a late movie once about a Southern prison. Somebody in it ate fifty eggs."

Crawford Sloane lowered the *Times* to say,

"The movie you're speaking of was *Cool Hand Luke.* It starred Paul Newman and came out in 1967. I'm sure, though, that Newman didn't really eat those eggs. He's a fine actor who convinced you that he did."

"There was a salesman here once from the Britannica," Jessica said. "He wanted to sell us an encyclopedia. I told him we already had one, living in."

"Can I help it," her husband responded, "if some of the news I live with sticks to me? It's like fluff, though. You can never tell which bits will stay in memory and what will blow away."

They were all seated in the bright and cheerful breakfast room, which adjoined the kitchen. Angus had arrived a half hour earlier, embracing his daughter-in-law and grandson warmly and shaking hands more formally with Crawford.

The constraint between father and son—sometimes translating to irritation on Crawford's part—had existed for a long time. Mainly it had to do with differing ideas and values. Angus had never come to terms with the easing in national and personal moral standards which had been accepted by most Americans from the 1960s onward. Angus ardently believed in "honor, duty and the flag"; further, that his fellow countrymen should still exhibit the uncompromising patriotism that existed during World War II—the high point of Angus's life, about which he reminisced ad infinitum. At the same time he was critical of many of the rationales that his own son, in his news-gathering activities, nowadays accepted as normal and progressive.

Crawford, on the other hand, was intolerant of his father's thinking which, as Crawford saw it, was rooted in antiquity and failed to take into account the greatly expanded knowledge on all fronts—notably scientific and philosophical—in the four-plus decades since World War II. There was another factor, too—a conceit on Crawford's part (though he would not have used that word) that having attained the top of his professional tree, his own judgments about world affairs and the human condition were superior to most other people's.

Now, in the early hours of this day, it already appeared that the gap between Crawford and his father had not narrowed.

As Angus had explained on countless other occasions, and did so once again, all his life he had liked to arrive wherever he was going early in the morning. It was why he had flown from Florida to La Guardia yesterday, stayed overnight with an American Legion crony who lived near the airport, then, soon after dawn, came to Larchmont by bus and taxi.

While the familiar recital was proceeding,

Crawford had raised his eyes to the ceiling. Jessica, smiling and nodding as if she had never heard the words before, had prepared for Angus his favorite bacon and eggs, and for herself and the other two served a more healthful homemade granola.

"About my heart and eggs," Angus said— he sometimes took a few minutes to absorb a remark that had been made, and then returned to it—"I figure if my ticker's lasted this long, I shouldn't worry about that cholesterol stuff. Also, my heart and I have been in some tight spots and come through them. I could tell you about a few."

Crawford Sloane lowered his newspaper enough to catch Jessica's eye and warn her with a glance: *Change the subject quick, before he gets launched on reminiscences.* Jessica gave the slightest of shrugs, conveying in body language: *If that's what you want, do it yourself.*

Folding the *Times,* Sloane said, "They have the casualty figures here from that crash at Dallas yesterday. It's pretty grim. I imagine we'll be doing follow-up stories through next week."

"I saw that on your news last night," Angus said. "It was done by that fellow Partridge. I like him. When he does those bits from overseas, especially about our military forces, he makes me feel proud to be American too. Not all your people do that, Crawford."

"Unfortunately there's a joker in there, Dad," Sloane said. "Harry Partridge isn't American. He's a Canadian. Also you'll have to do without him for a while. Today he starts a long vacation." Then he asked curiously, "Who, of our people, *doesn't* make you feel proud?"

"Just about all the others. It's the way almost all you TV news folk have of denigrating everything, especially our own government, quarreling with authority, always trying to make the President look small. No one seems to be proud of anything anymore. Doesn't that ever bother you?"

When Sloane didn't answer, Jessica told him, *sotto voce,* "Your father answered your question. Now you should answer his."

"Dad," Sloane said, "you and I have been over this ground before, and I don't think we'll ever have a meeting of the minds. What you call 'denigrating everything' we in the news business think of as legitimate questioning, the public's right to know. It's become a function of news reporting to challenge the politicians and bureaucrats, to question whatever we're told—and a good thing too. The fact is, governments lie and cheat—Democrat, Republican, liberal, socialist, conservative. Once in office they all do it.

"Sure we who seek out the news get tough at times and occasionally—I admit it—go too far. But because of what we do, a lot of crookedness and hypocrisy gets exposed, which in older days those in power got away with. So because of sharper news coverage, which TV pioneered, our society is a little better, slightly cleaner, and the principles of this country nudged nearer what they should be.

"As to presidents, Dad, if some of them look small, and most of them have, they've accomplished that themselves. Oh sure, we news guys help the process now and then, and that's because we're skeptics, sometimes cynics, and often don't believe the soothing syrup that presidents hand out. But skulduggery in high places, *all* high places, gives us plenty of reason to be the way we are."

"I wish the President sort of belonged to everybody, not one party," Nicky said. He added thoughtfully, "Wouldn't it have been better if the Founding Fathers had made Washington the king, and Franklin or Jefferson the President? Then Washington's kids and their children and grandchildren could have been kings and queens, so we'd have a head of state to feel proud of and a President to blame for things, the way the British do with their prime minister."

"America's great loss, Nicky," his father said, "is that you weren't at the Constitutional Convention to push that idea. Despite Washington's kids being adopted, it's more sensible than a lot else that happened then and since."

They all laughed, then becoming serious Angus said, "The reporting in my war—that's World War II to you, Nicky—was different from what it is today. We had the feeling then that those who wrote about it, talked on the radio, were always on our side. It's not that way anymore."

"It was a different war," Crawford said, "and a different time. Just as there are new ways of gathering news, concepts about news change too. A lot of us don't believe any more in 'My country right or wrong.' "

Angus complained, "I never thought I'd hear a son of mine say that."

Sloane shrugged. "Well, you're hearing it now. Those of us who aim at truth in news want to be *sure* our country's right, that we're not being fed hocus-pocus by whoever is in charge. The only way you can find out about that is to ask tough, probing questions."

"Don't you believe there were tough questions asked in my war?"

"Not tough enough," Sloane said. He paused, wondering whether to go farther, then decided he would. "Weren't you one of those who went on the first B-17 bombing raid to Schweinfurt?"

"Yes." Then to Nicholas: "That was deep in

Germany, Nicky. At the time, not a nice place to go."

With a touch of ruthlessness, Crawford persisted. "You told me once that the objective at Schweinfurt was to destroy ball-bearing factories, that those in charge of the bombing believed they could bring Germany's war machine to a halt because it had to have ball bearings."

Angus nodded slowly, knowing what was coming. "That's what they told us."

"Then you also know that after the war it was discovered that it didn't work. Despite that raid and others, which cost so many American lives, Germany never *was* short of ball bearings. The policy, the plans, were wrong. Well, I'm not saying that the press in those days could have stopped that awful waste. But nowadays questions would be asked—not after it was over, but while it was happening, so the questioning and public knowledge would be a restraint and probably lessen the loss of life."

As his son spoke, the old man's face was working, creased by memory and pain. With the others' eyes upon him he seemed to diminish, to sink into himself, suddenly to become older. He said, his voice quavering, "At Schweinfurt we lost fifty B-17s. There were ten people in a crew. That's five hundred fliers lost that single day. And in that same week of October '43, we lost another eighty-eight B-17s—

near enough nine hundred people." His voice dropped to a whisper. "I was on those raids. The worst thing afterward was at night being surrounded by so many empty beds—of people who didn't come back. In the night, waking up, looking around me, I used to wonder, Why me? Why did I get back—in that week and others after—when so many didn't?"

The effect was salutary and moving, causing Sloane to wish he had not spoken, hadn't tried to score a debater's point against his father. He said, "I'm sorry, Dad. I didn't realize how much I was opening an old wound."

As if he had not heard, his father went on, "They were good men. So many good men. So many of my friends."

Sloane shook his head. "Let's leave it. As I said, I'm sorry."

"Gramps," Nicky said. He had been listening intently. "When you were in the war, doing those things, were you frightened very much?"

"Oh god, Nicky! Frightened? I was terrified. When the flak was exploding all around, throwing out razor-sharp hunks of steel that could cut you into slices . . . when the German fighters swarmed in, with guns and cannon firing and you always thought they were aiming just at you . . . when other B-17s went down, sometimes in flames or in tight spirals so you knew the crews could never get out to use their parachutes . . . all of it at 27,000 feet, in air so cold and thin that if the fear made you sweat it froze, and even with oxygen you could hardly breathe . . . Well, my heart was in my mouth and sometimes, it seemed, my guts too."

Angus paused. There was silence in the breakfast room; somehow this was different from his usual reminiscing. Then he went on, speaking only to Nicky who was following every word, so there seemed a communion between the two, the old man and the boy.

"I'll tell you something, Nicky, and it's something I've never told a soul before, not anybody in this world. One time I was so scared, I . . ." He glanced around as if appealing for understanding. ". . . I was so scared, I messed my pants."

Nicky asked, "What did you do then?"

Jessica, concerned for Angus, seemed about to interrupt but Crawford gestured her to silence.

The old man's voice strengthened. Visibly, a little of his pride returned. "What could I do? I didn't like it, but I was there, so I got on with what I'd been sent for. I was the group bombardier. When the group commander—he was our pilot—reached the IP and set us on our target course, he told me over the intercom, 'It's yours, Angus. Take it.' Well, I was stretched out over the Norden bombsight and I steadied myself and took my time. For those few minutes, Nicky, the bombardier flew the airplane. I got the target exactly in the cross hairs, then the bombs were away. It was the signal to the group to release theirs too."

Angus went on, "So let me tell you, Nicky, there's nothing wrong with being scared to death. It can happen to the best. What counts is hanging on, somehow staying in control and doing what you know you should."

"I hear you, Gramps." Nicky's voice was matter-of-fact and Crawford wondered how much he had understood. Probably a good deal. Nicky was smart and sensitive. Crawford also wondered if he himself, in the past, had taken the trouble to understand as much as he should about his own father.

He glanced at his watch. It was time to leave. Usually he arrived at CBA News at 10:30 A.M.; today though, he would be earlier because he wanted to see the division president about firing Chuck Insen as National Evening News executive producer. The memory of last night's clash with Insen still rankled, and Sloane was as determined as ever to ensure changes in the news selection process.

He rose from the breakfast table and, excusing himself, went upstairs to finish dressing.

Selecting a tie—the same one he would wear on camera that evening—and carefully tying it in a Windsor knot, he thought about his father, envisaging the scenes the old man had described, in the air over Schweinfurt and elsewhere. Angus, at that time, would have been in his early twenties—half Crawford's age now, just a raw kid who had hardly lived and was terrified he was about to die, most likely horribly. Certainly not even during his time as a journalist in Vietnam had Crawford endured anything comparable.

Suddenly he had a pang of conscience for what he had failed to understand sooner, in any deep or caring way.

The trouble was, Crawford thought, he was so caught up professionally in each day's current, breaking news that he tended to dismiss the news of earlier eras as history and therefore irrelevant to the brimming, bustling here and now. That mind-set was an occupational hazard; he had seen it in others. But the older news was *not* irrelevant, and never would be, to his father.

Crawford was well informed. He had read about the raid on Schweinfurt in a book, *Black Thursday.* The author, Martin Caidin, compared the attack with the "immortal struggles of Gettysburg, St. Mihiel and the Argonne, of Midway and the Bulge and Pork Chop Hill."

My father, Crawford reminded himself, was a part of that long saga. He had never viewed that fact before in quite the same perspective as today.

He put on the jacket of his suit, inspected himself in the mirror, then, satisfied with his appearance, returned below.

He said goodbye to Jessica and Nicky, then approached his father and told the old man quietly, "Stand up."

Angus seemed puzzled. Crawford repeated himself. "Stand up."

Pushing his chair back, Angus slowly rose. Instinctively, as he so often did, he brought his body to the equivalent of military attention.

Crawford moved close to his father, put his arms around him, held him tight, then kissed him on both cheeks.

The old man seemed surprised and flustered. "Hey, hey! What's all this?"

Looking him directly in the eye, Crawford said, "I love you, you old coot."

At the doorway, on the point of leaving, he glanced back. On Angus's face was a small, seraphic smile. Jessica's eyes, he saw, were moist. Nicky was beaming.

The surveillance duo of Carlos and Julio were surprised to see Crawford Sloane leaving his home by car earlier than usual. They reported the fact immediately by code to the leader, Miguel.

By now, Miguel had left the Hackensack operating center and, accompanied by others in a Nissan passenger van equipped with a cellular phone, was crossing the George Washington Bridge between New Jersey and New York.

Miguel was unperturbed. He issued, also in code, the order that prearranged plans were now in effect, their time of implementation to be advanced if needed. He reasoned confidently: What they were about to do was the totally unexpected; it would turn logic upside down, then soon after raise the frantic question, *Why?*

10

At about the same time Crawford Sloane left his Larchmont home to drive to CBA News headquarters, Harry Partridge awakened in Canada —in Port Credit, near Toronto. He had slept deeply and spent the first few moments of the new day wondering where he was. It was a frequent experience because he was used to waking in so many different places.

As his thoughts arranged themselves he took in familiar landmarks of an apartment

bedroom and knew that if he sat up in bed—
which he didn't feel like doing yet—he would
be able to see, through a window ahead, the
broad expanse of Lake Ontario.

The apartment was one Partridge used as
his base, a retreat, and the nomadic nature of
his work meant that he got to it for only a few
brief periods each year. And even though he
stored his few possessions here—some clothes,
books, framed photographs, and a handful of
mementos from other times and places—the
apartment was not registered in his name. As a
card alongside a bell push in the lobby six floors
below advised, the official tenant was V. Wil-
liams (the V for Vivien), who resided here permanently.

Every month, from wherever in the world
Partridge happened to be, he sent Vivien a
check sufficient to pay the apartment rent and,
in return, she lived here and kept it as his
haven. The arrangement, which had other con-
veniences including casual sex, suited them
both.

Vivien was a nurse who worked in the
Queensway Hospital nearby, and he could hear
her now, moving around in the kitchen. In all
probability she was making tea, which she knew
he liked each morning, and would bring it to
him soon. Meanwhile he let his thoughts drift
back to the events of yesterday and the journey

the night before on his delayed flight from Dallas to Toronto's Pearson International . . .

The experience at DFW Airport had been a professional one which he took in stride. It was Partridge's job to do what he did, a job for which he was well paid by CBA News. Yet thinking about it last night and again this morning, he was conscious of the tragedy behind the surface of the news. From the latest reports he heard, more than seventy aboard the Muskegon Airlines flight lost their lives, with others critically injured, and all six people died aboard the smaller airplane that had collided with the Airbus in midair. Today, he knew, many grief-stricken families and friends were struggling, amid tears, to cope with their abrupt bereavement.

The thought reminded him that there were times when he wished he could cry too, could shed tears along with others because of things he had witnessed in his professional life, including perhaps the tragedy of yesterday. But it hadn't happened—except on one unparalleled occasion which, as it came to mind, he thrust away. What he did remember was the first time he ever wondered about himself and his apparent inability to cry.

Early in his reporting career, Harry Partridge was in Britain when a tragedy occurred in

Wales. It was in Aberfan, a mining village where a vast pile of coal waste—slurry—slid down a hillside and engulfed a junior school. A hundred and sixteen children died.

Partridge was on the scene soon after the disaster, in time to see the dead being pulled out. Each small pathetic body, covered with black, evil-smelling sludge, had to be hosed down before it was carted away for identification.

Around him, watching the same scene, other reporters, photographers, police, spectators, were weeping, choking on their tears. Partridge had wanted to cry too, but couldn't. Sickened but dry-eyed, he had done his reporting job and gone away.

Since then there had been countless other witnessed scenes where there was cause for tears, but he hadn't cried there either.

Was there some deficiency, some inner coldness in himself? He asked that question once of a woman psychiatrist friend, after both of them, following an evening of drinking, had been to bed together.

She told him, "There's nothing wrong with you, or you wouldn't care enough to ask the question. What you have is a defense mechanism which depersonalizes what you feel. You're banking it all, tucking the emotion away inside you somewhere. One day everything will overflow, crack open, and you'll cry. Oh, how you'll cry!"

Well, his knowledgeable bed partner had been right, and there *had* come a day . . . But again he didn't want to think about it, and pushed the image away just as Vivien came into the bedroom, carrying a tray with morning tea.

She was in her mid-forties, with angular, strong features and straight black hair, now streaked with gray. While neither beautiful nor conventionally pretty, she was warm, easygoing and generous. Vivien had been widowed before Partridge knew her and he gathered the marriage had not been good, though she rarely talked about it. She had one child, a daughter in Vancouver. The daughter occasionally stayed here, though never when Partridge was expected.

Partridge was fond of Vivien though not in love with her, and had known her long enough to be aware he never would be. He suspected that Vivien was in love with him and would love him more if he encouraged it. But as it was, she accepted the relationship they had.

While he sipped his tea, Vivien regarded Partridge quizzically, noting that his normally lanky figure was thinner than it should be; also, despite a certain boyishness he still retained, his face showed lines of strain and tiredness. His unruly shock of fair hair, now noticeably grayer, was in need of trimming.

Aware of her appraisal, Partridge asked, "Well, what's the verdict?"

Vivien shook her head in mock despair. "Just look at you! I send you off healthy and fit. Two and a half months later you come back looking tired, pale and underfed."

"I know, Viv." He grimaced. "It's the life I lead. There's too much pressure, lousy hours, junk food and booze." Then, with a smile, "So here I am, a mess as usual. What can you do for me?"

She said, with a mixture of affection and firmness, "First I'll give you a good healthful breakfast. You can stay in bed—I'll bring it to you. For other meals you'll have nutritious things like fish and fowl, green vegetables, fresh fruit. Right after breakfast I'm going to trim your hair. Later, I'm taking you for a sauna and massage—I've already made the appointment."

Partridge lay back and threw up his hands. "I love it!"

Vivien went on, "Tomorrow, I figured you'll want to see your old cronies at the CBC—you usually do. But in the evening I have tickets for an all-Mozart concert in Toronto at Roy Thomson Hall. You can let the music wash over you. I know you like that. Apart from all that, you'll rest or do whatever you wish." She shrugged. "Maybe in between those other things you'll feel like making love. You tried last night but were too tired. You fell asleep."

For a moment Partridge felt more gratitude for Vivien than he had ever felt before. She was rock-solid, a refuge. Late last night, when his flight finally arrived at Toronto Airport, she had been patiently waiting, then had brought him here.

He asked, "Don't you have to work?"

"I had some vacation due. I've arranged to take it, starting today. One of the other nurses will fill in for me."

He told her, "Viv, you're one in a million."

When Vivien had gone and he could hear her preparing breakfast, Partridge's thoughts returned to yesterday.

There had been that congratulatory call—they had paged him for it in the DFW terminal —from Crawford Sloane.

Crawf had sounded awkward, as he often was when they talked. There were times when Partridge wanted to say, "Look, Crawf, if you think I have any grudge against you—about Jessica or your job or *anything,* forget it! I haven't and I never did." But he knew that kind of remark would strain their relationship even more, and probably Crawf would never believe it anyway.

In Vietnam, Partridge had known perfectly

well that Sloane was taking only short air trips
so he could hang around Saigon and get on
CBA network news as often as possible. But
Partridge hadn't cared then, and still didn't. He
had his own priorities. One of them could even
be called an addiction—the addiction to the
sights and sounds of war.

War . . . the bloody bedlam of battle . . .
the thunder and flame of big artillery, the whis-
tle scream and awesome crump of falling bombs
. . . the stentorian chatter of machine guns
when you didn't know who was firing at whom
or from where . . . the near-sensuous thrill of
being under attack, despite fear that set you
trembling . . . all of it fascinated Partridge, set
his adrenaline flowing, his other juices running . . .

He discovered the feeling first in 'Nam, his
initial war experience. It had been with him
ever since. More than once he had told himself,
Face it—you love it; then acknowledged, *Yes, I
do, and a stupid son of a bitch I am.*

Stupid or not, he had never objected to being sent to wars by CBA. Partridge knew that
among his colleagues he was referred to as a
"bang-bang," the slightly contemptuous name
for a TV correspondent addicted to war—a
worse addiction, it was sometimes said, than to
heroin or cocaine and with a final ending almost
as predictable.

But they also knew at CBA News headquarters—which was what mattered most—that for that kind of news coverage, Harry Partridge was the best.

Therefore he had not been overly concerned when Sloane won the National Evening News anchor chair. Like every news correspondent, Partridge had had ideas about getting that top-of-the-pile appointment, but by the time it happened to Sloane, Partridge was enjoying himself so much it didn't matter.

Strangely, though, the question of the anchorman's job had come up recently and unexpectedly. Two weeks ago, during what Chuck Insen warned was "a delicate private conversation," the executive producer confided to Partridge that there might be major changes soon in the National Evening News. "If that happens," Insen had asked, "would you be interested in coming in from the cold and anchoring? You do it damn well."

Partridge had been so surprised that he hadn't known how to respond. Then Insen had said, "You don't have to answer now. I just want you to think about it in case I come back to you later."

Subsequently, through his own inside contacts, Partridge had learned of the ongoing power struggle between Chuck Insen and Crawford Sloane. But even if Insen won, which

seemed unlikely, Partridge doubted if permanent anchoring was something he would want
or could even endure. Especially, he told himself half mockingly, when in so many places of
the world there was still the sound of gunfire to
be heard and followed.

Inevitably, when thinking in a personal way
about Crawford Sloane, there was always the
memory of Jessica, though it was never more
than memory because there was nothing between them now, not even occasional communication, and they seldom met socially—perhaps
only once or twice a year. Nor had Partridge
ever blamed Sloane for his loss of Jessica, having recognized that his own foolish judgment
was the cause. When he could have married
her, Partridge had decided not to, so Sloane
simply stepped in, proving himself the wiser of
the two, with a better sense of values at that
time . . .

Vivien reappeared in the apartment bedroom, bringing breakfast in stages. It was, as
she had promised, a healthful meal: freshly
squeezed orange juice, thick hot porridge with
brown sugar and milk, followed by poached
eggs on whole wheat toast, strong black coffee,
the beans freshly ground, and finally more toast
and Alberta honey.

The thoughtfulness about the honey especially touched Partridge. It reminded him, as it

was intended to, of his native province where he
made his start in journalism on local radio. He
remembered telling Vivien that he had worked
for what was known as a 20/20 radio station; it
meant that rock 'n' roll, the staple programming, was interrupted every twenty minutes by
a few shouted news headlines ripped from the
AP wire. A young Harry Partridge had done
the shouting. He smiled at the recollection; it
seemed a long time ago.

After breakfast, prowling around the apartment in pajamas, he observed, "This place is
getting tacky. It needs repainting and new furniture."

"I know," Vivien acknowledged. "I've been
after the building owners about repainting. But
they say this apartment isn't due to have money
spent on it."

"Screw 'em! Do it without the owners. You
find a painter and order whatever's needed. I'll
leave enough money before I go."

"You're always generous about that," she
said; then added, "do you still have that wonderful arrangement where you don't pay income
tax?"

He grinned. "Sure do."

"To anybody, anywhere?"

"Not to anyone, and it's perfectly legal and
honest. I don't file any income tax return, don't
have to. Saves a lot of time and money."

"I've never understood how you manage it."

"I don't mind telling you," he said, "though normally I don't talk about it. People who pay income tax get jealous; that's because misery likes company."

The critical factor, he explained, was being a Canadian citizen, using a Canadian passport, and working overseas.

"What a lot of people don't realize is that the United States is the only major country in the world that taxes its citizens no matter where they live. Even when Americans reside outside the U.S., they still get taxed by Uncle Sam. Canada doesn't do that. Canadians who move out of the country aren't liable for Canadian taxes, and once the revenue service is satisfied you're gone, they've no further interest in you. The British are the same."

He continued, "The way it works is that CBA News pays my salary each month into a New York account I have at Chase Manhattan. From there I move the money to accounts in other countries—the Bahamas, Singapore, the Channel Islands, where savings earn interest, totally tax-free."

"What about taxes in countries you go to—those you work in?"

"As a TV correspondent I'm never in one place long enough to be liable for tax. That even includes the U.S., provided I'm there no more than 120 days a year, and you can be sure I never stay that long. As for Canada, I don't have a domicile here, not even this one. This is solely your place, Viv, as we both know."

Partridge added, "The important thing is not to cheat—tax evasion's not only illegal, it's stupid and not worth the risk. Tax avoidance is quite different . . ." He stopped. "Hold it! I have something here."

Partridge produced a wallet and from it extracted a folded, well-fingered news clipping. "This is from a 1934 decision by Judge Learned Hand, one of America's great jurists. It's been used by other judges many times."

He read aloud, " *'Any one may so arrange his affairs that his taxes shall be as low as possible; he is not bound to choose that pattern which will best pay the Treasury; there is not even a patriotic duty to increase one's taxes.'* "

"I can understand why people envy you," Vivien said. "Are there others in TV who do the same?"

"You'd be surprised how many. The tax advantages are a reason Canadians like to work overseas for American networks."

Though he didn't mention them, there were other reasons, including U.S. network pay scales, which were substantially higher. But even more important, to work for an American network was to have made the prestigious "big time" and be on the exciting center stage of world affairs.

For their part, the U.S. networks were delighted to have Canadian correspondents, who came to them well trained by CBC and CTV. They had learned also that American viewers liked a Canadian accent; it was a contributing reason for the popularity of many news figures —Peter Jennings, Robert MacNeil, Morley Safer, Allen Pizzey, Barrie Dunsmore, Peter Kent, John Blackstone, Hilary Bowker, Harry Partridge, others . . .

Continuing to prowl through the apartment, Partridge saw on a sideboard the tickets for the Mozart concert the next day. He knew he would enjoy it and was grateful once more to Vivien for remembering his tastes.

He was grateful too for the three weeks of vacation—restful idleness, as he thought of it— that lay ahead.

11

Jessica went household shopping every Thursday morning and she intended to follow her usual routine today. When Angus learned this, he volunteered to accompany her. Nicky, who was home because of a school holiday, asked to go as well so he could be with his grandfather.

Jessica asked doubtfully, "Don't you have some music to practice?"

"Yes, Mom. But I can do it later. I'll have time."

Knowing that Nicky was conscientious about practicing, sometimes for as long as six hours a day, Jessica raised no objection.

The three of them left the Park Avenue house in Jessica's Volvo station wagon shortly before 11 A.M., about an hour and a quarter after Crawford's departure. It was a beautiful morning, the trees rich with fall colors and sunlight glistening off Long Island Sound.

The Sloanes' day maid, Florence, was in the house at the time and, through a window, watched the trio leave. She also saw a car parked on a side street start up and follow in the same direction as the Volvo. At the time she gave no thought to the second vehicle.

Jessica's first stop was, as usual, the Grand Union supermarket on Chatsworth Avenue. She parked the Volvo in the store lot, then, accompanied by Angus and Nicky, went inside.

The Colombians, Julio and Carlos, in the Chevrolet Celebrity which had trailed the station wagon from a discreet distance, observed their movements. Carlos, who had already reported the departure from the house, now made another cellular phone call, announcing that "the three packages are in container number one."

This time Julio was driving, and he did not turn into the store parking lot, instead making observations from the street outside. Following instructions given earlier by Miguel, Carlos now left the Chevy and moved on foot to a position near the store. Unlike other days when he had been casually dressed, today he was wearing a neat brown suit and tie.

When Carlos was in place, Julio drove the Chevrolet away, in case it had been noticed, to the safe seclusion of the Hackensack operating center.

When the first of the two phone messages reached Miguel, he was in the Nissan passenger van, parked near the New Haven Railroad's Larchmont station. The van was inconspicuous, surrounded by other parked vehicles left by New York commuters. With Miguel were Luís, Rafael and Baudelio, though all four occupants were mostly out of sight because of dark, thin plastic sheets covering the side and rear windows. Luís, because of his specialized driving skills, was at the wheel.

When it became known that three people had left the house, Rafael exclaimed, "*¡Ay!* That means the *viejo*'s along. He'll be in our goddamn way."

"Then we'll 'off' the old fart," Luís said. He touched a bulge in his suede jacket. "One bullet will do."

Miguel snapped, "You'll follow the orders you have. Do nothing else without my say-so." He was aware that Rafael and Luís were perpetually aggressive, like smoldering fires likely to burst into angry flame. Rafael, heavily built, had been a professional boxer for a while and bore visible fight scars. Luís had been in the Colombian army—a harsh, rough schooling. There could be a time when the belligerence of both men would be useful, but until then it needed to be curbed.

Miguel was already considering the complication of the third person. Their long-standing plan had involved, at this point, only the Sloane woman and the boy. All along, they—not Crawford Sloane—had been the Sendero Luminoso/Medellín objective. The two were to be seized and held as hostages for as yet unspecified demands.

But now the question was how to handle the old man? Killing him, as Luís suggested, would be easy, but that could create other problems. Most probably Miguel would not make up his mind until the crucial moment, which was coming soon.

One thing was fortunate. The woman and the boy were now together. The several weeks of careful surveillance had shown that the woman always shopped on Thursday mornings. Miguel had also known that the boy had a school holiday today. Carlos, posing on the telephone as a parent, had obtained that information from the Chatsworth Avenue grammar school, which Nicholas attended. What had remained in doubt was how to corral the woman and the boy together. Now, without knowing it, they had solved that problem for him.

When the second message from Carlos came, indicating that all three Sloanes were inside the supermarket, Miguel nodded to Luís. "Okay. Roll!"

Luís put the Nissan van in gear. The next stop, just a half-dozen blocks away, would be the store parking lot.

While they were moving, Miguel turned his head to look at Baudelio, the American in the Medellín group, who continued to be a source of worry.

Baudelio—the name had been chosen for him and, like the others, it was an alias—was in his mid-fifties but looked twenty years older. Gaunt, lantern-jawed, with a sallow skin and a droopy gray mustache he seldom trimmed, he had the appearance of a walking ghost. He had once been a medical doctor, a specialist in anesthesiology practicing in Boston, and a drunk. When left to his own devices he was still a drunk, but no longer a doctor, at least officially. A decade earlier Baudelio's license to practice medicine had been revoked for life, because while in an alcoholic haze he had overanesthetized a patient undergoing surgery. There had been similar lapses before and colleagues had covered for him, but in this instance it cost the patient's life and could not be overlooked.

There had been no future for him in the United States, no family ties, no children. Even his wife had left him several years before. He had visited Colombia several times and, for want of a better place, decided to go there. After a while he found he could use his considerable medical skills for shady, sometimes criminal purposes, without arousing any questions. He was in no position to be particular and took whatever came his way. Amid it all he managed, by reading medical journals, to stay up to date in his specialty. This last was why he had been chosen for this assignment by the Medellín cartel, for whom he had worked before.

All of this background had been made known to Miguel in advance, with a warning that while the assignment lasted Baudelio was to be deprived of any alcohol. Antabuse pills would be used to enforce the prohibition, one pill to be taken by the ex-doctor every day. The effect of Antabuse was that anyone drinking liquor afterward became violently ill, a fact of which Baudelio was well aware.

Since it was common practice among alcoholics to spit out the pill secretly if they wanted to cheat, Miguel was cautioned to be sure the Antabuse was always swallowed. While Miguel carried out the instructions, they did not please him. In the comparatively short time available he had a multitude of responsibilities and acting as a "wet nurse" was one he could have done without.

Also in light of Baudelio's weakness, Miguel decided not to trust him with a firearm. Thus he was the only one in the group not armed.

Now, regarding Baudelio warily, Miguel asked, "Are you ready? Do you understand everything that is to be done?"

The ex-doctor nodded. Briefly a vestige of

professional pride returned to him. Looking Miguel directly in the eye, he said, "I know precisely what is necessary. When the moment comes, you may rely on me, and concentrate on what you have to do yourself."

Not entirely reassured, Miguel turned away. The Grand Union supermarket was now directly ahead.

Carlos saw the Nissan passenger van arrive. The parking lot was not crowded and the Nissan entered a conveniently vacant slot alongside Jessica's Volvo station wagon. When Carlos had observed this, he turned into the store.

Jessica gestured to her partly filled shopping cart and told Angus, "If there's something you especially like, just drop it in."

Nicky said, "Gramps likes caviar."

"I should have remembered that," Jessica said. "Let's get some."

They moved to the gourmet section to discover it was featuring a special caviar assortment. Angus, inspecting prices said, "It's awfully expensive."

Jessica said softly, "Have you any idea how much that son of yours earns?"

The old man smiled; he kept his voice low too. "Well, I did read somewhere it was close to three million dollars a year."

"Close is right." Jessica laughed; being with

Angus always made her feel good. "Let's blow some of it." She pointed to a seven-ounce can of beluga caviar in a locked display case, priced at $199.95. "We'll have some of this with drinks before dinner tonight."

It was at that moment that Jessica noticed a young man, slightly built and well dressed, approaching another woman shopper nearby. He appeared to ask a question. The woman shook her head. The young man approached a second shopper. Again an apparent question and a negative reply. Mildly curious, Jessica watched the young man as he approached her.

"Excuse me, ma'am," Carlos said. "I'm trying to locate someone." He had been aware of Jessica all the time but deliberately had not gone to her first, instead positioning himself so that she could see him speaking with the other people.

Jessica noticed a Spanish accent, though that was not unusual in New York. She also thought the speaker had cold, hard eyes, but that was none of her business. All she said was, "Oh?"

"It's a Mrs. Crawford Sloane."

Jessica was startled. "I'm Mrs. Sloane."

"Oh ma'am, I have some bad news for you." The facial expression of Carlos was serious; he was playing his part well. "Your husband has been in an accident. He's badly injured. The

ambulance took him to Doctors Hospital. I was
sent to find you and take you there. The maid at
your house told me you would be here."

Jessica gasped and turned deathly pale. Instinctively her hand went to her throat. Nicky,
who had returned in time to hear the last few
words, looked stunned.

Angus, though equally shocked, was the
first to recover and take charge. He gestured to
the shopping cart. "Jessie, leave all this. Just
let's go."

"It's Dad, isn't it?" Nicky said.

Carlos answered gravely, "I'm afraid so."

Jessica put her arm around Nicky. "Yes,
dear. We're going to him now."

"Please come with me, Mrs. Sloane," Carlos
said. Jessica and Nicky, still dazed by the sudden shattering news, went quickly with the
brown-suited young man toward the store's
main door. Angus followed. Something was
bothering him, though he wasn't quite sure
what.

Outside in the parking lot, Carlos preceded
the others. He moved toward the Nissan van.
Both doors on the side next to the Volvo were
open. Carlos could see that the Nissan's engine
was running and Luís was in the driver's seat. A
shadowy form in the back had to be Baudelio.
Rafael and Miguel were out of sight.

Alongside the Nissan, Carlos said, "We'll go in this vehicle, ma'am. It will be . . ."

"No, no!" Jessica, tense and anxious, was groping in her purse for car keys. "I'll take my car. I know where Doctors Hospital—"

Carlos interposed himself between the Volvo and Jessica. Grasping her arm, he said, "Ma'am, we'd rather you—"

Jessica attempted to withdraw her arm; as she did, Carlos held her more firmly and pushed her forward. She said indignantly, "Stop that! What is this?" For the first time Jessica began to think beyond the impact of the awful news she had been given.

A few feet behind, Angus now realized what had been troubling him. Inside the store the strange young man had said, "He's badly injured. The ambulance took him to Doctors Hospital."

But Doctors Hospital didn't take emergencies. Angus happened to know because over several months the year before he had visited an old Army Air Forces comrade who was a patient there and got to know the hospital well. Doctors Hospital was big and famous; it was close to Gracie Mansion, the mayor's residence, and alongside the route Crawford used on the way to work. *But emergencies were sent to New York Hospital, a few blocks south . . .* Every ambulance driver knew it.

So the young man was lying! The setup in the store had been a fake! What was happening out here wasn't right either. Two men—Angus didn't like their looks at all—had just appeared from around the back of the passenger van. One of them, a huge bruiser, had joined the first man; they were forcing Jessica inside! Nicholas, a little way behind, was not yet involved.

Angus shouted, "Jessica, don't go! Nicky, run! Get—"

The sentence was never finished. A pistol butt crashed down on Angus's head. There was a fierce, searing pain, everything around him spun, then he fell to the ground unconscious. It was Luís who had jumped out of the driver's seat, rushed around, and attacked him from behind. In almost the same motion, Luís grabbed Nicholas.

Jessica began screaming and crying out. *"Help! Someone—anyone—please help!"*

The burly Rafael, who had joined Carlos in seizing Jessica, now clamped a massive hand across her mouth, set another in her back and flung her inside the van. Then, jumping in himself, he continued to hold her while she screamed and struggled. Jessica's eyes were wild. Rafael snarled at Baudelio, *"¡Apúrate!"*

The ex-doctor, with a medical bag open on the seat beside him, produced a gauze pad which moments earlier he had soaked in ethyl chloride. He slapped the pad over Jessica's nose and mouth and held it there. Instantly Jessica's eyes closed, her body sagged and she became unconscious. Baudelio gave a grunt of satisfaction, though he knew the effect of ethyl chloride would last only five minutes.

By now, Nicholas, struggling too, had been hauled inside. Carlos held him while he received the same treatment.

Baudelio, still working quickly, used scissors to cut the sleeve of Jessica's dress, then injected the contents of a hypodermic syringe intramuscularly into her upper arm. The drug was midazolam, a strong sedative that would ensure continued unconsciousness for at least an hour. He gave the boy a similar injection.

Miguel, meanwhile, had dragged the unconscious Angus over to the van. Rafael, now freed of Jessica, jumped down and pulled out a pistol, a Browning automatic. Clicking the safety off, he urged Miguel, "Let me finish him!"

"No, not here!" The entire operation of seizing the woman and boy had gone with incredible speed, occupying barely a minute. To Miguel's amazement, no one else appeared to have witnessed what had happened. One reason: They had been shielded by the two vehicles; also, fortuitously, there had been no passersby. Miguel, Carlos, Rafael and Luís had all come armed and there was a Beretta sub-

machine gun in the van for use if they had to
fight their way out of the parking lot. Now a
fighting exit wasn't necessary and they would
have a head start on any pursuit. But if they left
the old man behind—his head was bleeding pro-
fusely, with blood dripping to the ground—an
immediate alarm would be raised. Making a decision, Miguel ordered, "Help me get him in."

It was accomplished in seconds. Then, as he
entered the van himself and closed the side
door, Miguel saw he had been wrong about no
witnesses. An elderly woman, white-haired and
leaning on a cane, was watching from between
two cars some twenty yards away. She appeared
uncertain and puzzled.

As Luís moved the Nissan van forward, Rafael caught sight of the old woman too. In a
single swift movement he grabbed the Beretta,
raised it, and through a rear window was taking
aim. Miguel shouted to him, "No!" He didn't
care about the woman, but the chances looked
good that they could still get away without raising an alarm. Pushing Rafael aside and making
his voice cheerful, Miguel called out, "Don't be
alarmed. It's just part of a film we're making."

He saw relief and the beginning of a smile
on the woman's face. Then they left the parking
lot and, soon after, Larchmont. Luís was driv-

ing skillfully, wasting no time. Within five minutes they were on Interstate 95, the New England Thruway, heading south and moving fast.

12

There had been a time when Priscilla Rhea possessed one of the sharpest minds in Larchmont. She had been a schoolteacher who pounded into several generations of area youngsters the fundamentals of square roots, quadratic equations, and how to discover—she always made it sound like the search for a holy grail—the algebraic values of x or y. Priscilla also urged them to have a sense of civic responsibility and never to shirk their obvious duty.

But all of that was prior to Priscilla's retirement fifteen years earlier, and before the toll of age and illness slowed her body, then her mind. Nowadays, white-haired and frail, she walked slowly, using a cane, and had recently described her thought processes, disgustedly, as "having the speed of a three-legged donkey going uphill."

Nevertheless Priscilla was exercising her

thought processes now, moving them along as best she could.

She had watched two people—a woman and a boy—being taken into what looked like a small bus, apparently against their will. They were certainly struggling and Priscilla thought she'd heard the woman cry out, though about that she wasn't sure, her hearing having deteriorated along with everything else. Then another person, a man who seemed unconscious and hurt, was lifted into the same small bus before it drove away.

Her natural anxiety at seeing this was immediately relieved by the shouted information that it was all part of a film show. That made sense. Film and television crews seemed to be everywhere nowadays, photographing their stories against real backgrounds and even interviewing people for TV news, right on the street.

But then, the moment the little bus had gone Priscilla looked around for the cameras and film crew which should have been recording the action she had watched, and for the life of her she couldn't find any. She reasoned that if there *had* been a film crew, it couldn't possibly have disappeared that fast.

The whole thing was a worry Priscilla wished she didn't have, in part because she knew that perhaps she was all mixed up in her mind, the way she had been some other times.

The sensible thing to do, she told herself, was go into the Grand Union store, do her bit of shopping and mind her own business. Just the same, there was her lifelong credo of not shirking responsibility, and perhaps she shouldn't, even now. She only wished there were someone handy whom she could ask for advice, and just at that moment she saw Erica McLean, one of her old pupils, also on her way into the supermarket.

Erica, now a mother with children of her own, was in a hurry but stopped to ask courteously, "How are you, Miss Rhea?" (No one who had ever been a pupil of Miss Rhea *ever* presumed to address her by her first name.)

"Slightly bewildered, my dear," Priscilla said.

"Why, Miss Rhea?"

"Something I just saw . . . But I'm not sure what I saw. I'd like to know what you think." Priscilla then described the scene, which was still remarkably clear in her mind.

"And you're sure there was no film crew?"

"I couldn't see one. Did you, as you came in?"

"No." Within herself, silently, Erica McLean sighed. She had not the least doubt that dear old Priscilla had been subject to some kind of hallucination and it was Erica's bad luck to have come along just then and be roped in. Well, she couldn't walk away from the old duck, for whom she had a genuine fondness, so she had better forget being in a hurry and do what she could to help.

"Just where did all this happen?" Erica asked.

"Over there." Priscilla pointed to the still-empty parking slot next to Jessica's Volvo station wagon. They walked to it together. "Here!" Priscilla said. "It happened right here."

Erica looked around her. She had not expected to see anything significant, and didn't. Then, about to turn away, her attention was caught by a series of small pools of liquid on the ground. Against the blacktop surface of the parking lot the liquid seemed dark brown. It was probably oil. Or was it? Curiously, Erica leaned down to touch it. Seconds later she looked with horror at her fingers. They were covered in what was unmistakably blood, still warm.

It had been a quiet morning in the Larchmont police department, a small but efficient local force. In a glass cubicle a uniformed desk officer was sipping coffee and glancing through the local *Sound View News* when the call came in—from a pay phone on the corner of Boston Post Road, a half block from the supermarket.

Erica McLean spoke first. After identifying

herself she said, "I have a lady here, Miss Priscilla Rhea . . ."

"I know Miss Rhea," the desk officer said.

"Well, she thinks she may have seen something criminal, perhaps some kind of abduction. I'd like you to speak to her."

"I'll do better than that," the desk officer said. "I'll send an officer in a patrol car and you can tell it to him. Where are you ladies?"

"We'll be outside the Grand Union."

"Stay there, please. Someone will be with you in a few minutes."

The desk officer spoke into a radio microphone. "Headquarters to car 423. Respond to Grand Union store. Interview Mrs. McLean and Miss Rhea waiting outside. Code one."

The answer came back, "Four twenty-three to headquarters. Ten four."

Eleven minutes had now passed since the passenger van carrying Jessica, Nicholas and Angus had left the supermarket parking lot.

The young police officer, named Jensen, had listened carefully to Priscilla Rhea who was more confident in reporting for the second time what she had seen. She even remembered two additional details—the color of what she continued to call the "little bus"—a light tan—and the fact that it had dark windows. But no, she had not noticed a license number, or even if the license plates were New York's or out-of-state.

The officer's first reaction, though he kept it to himself, was of skepticism. Police forces were used to citizens who became alarmed about matters that turned out to be harmless; such incidents happened every day, even in a small community like Larchmont. But the officer was conscientious and listened attentively to all that was said, making careful notes.

His interest began to mount when Erica McLean, who seemed a responsible, rational woman, told him about some splotches on the parking lot that looked like blood. The two of them walked over to inspect. By this time most of the liquid had dried, though there was enough that was moist to reveal it as red to the touch. There was no proof it was human blood, of course. But, Officer Jensen reasoned, it gave more credence to the story, more urgency too.

Hurrying back to where they had left Priscilla, they found her talking with several other people who were curious about what was going on.

One man volunteered, "Officer, I was inside and saw four people leave in a hurry—two men, a woman and a boy. They were in such a hurry that the woman left her shopping cart. It was full, but she just left it."

"I saw them too," a woman said. "That was

Mrs. Sloane, the TV anchorman's wife. She often shops here. When she left she looked up-set—like something bad happened."

Another woman said. "That's funny. A man came to me and asked if I was Mrs. Sloane. He asked others, too."

Now several people were talking at once. The police officer raised his voice. "Did anyone see what this lady"—he motioned to Priscilla—"calls a 'small bus,' color light tan?"

"Yes, I saw that," the first man said. "It pulled into the lot as I was walking to the store. It was a Nissan passenger van."

"Did you notice the license plate?"

"It was a New Jersey plate, but that's all I saw. Oh, one other thing, it had dark windows —the kind of glass where you can see out, but can't see in."

"Hold it!" the officer said. He addressed the growing crowd. "Any of you who have more information, and those who've given me some already, please stay. I'll be right back."

He jumped into the white police cruiser he had parked alongside the supermarket and grabbed the radio mike.

"Car 423 to headquarters. Possible kidnap at Grand Union parking lot. Request help. De-scription of suspect vehicle: Nissan passenger van, color light tan. New Jersey plates, license unknown. Dark windows, believed one-way glass. Three persons may have been seized by unknown occupants of Nissan van."

The officer's transmission would be heard by all Larchmont police cars as well as those in neighboring Mamaroneck Town and Mamaroneck Village. The headquarters desk officer, through a "hot line" phone, would automatically alert all other police forces in surrounding Westchester County and the New York State Police. The New Jersey State Police would not, at this point, be informed.

Already, at the supermarket, two sirens could be heard from other approaching police cruisers responding to the request for help.

Nearly twenty minutes had elapsed since the Nissan passenger van's departure.

Some eight miles away, the Nissan van was about to leave the I-95 Thruway and enter a maze of streets in the Bronx.

From Larchmont, Luís had made good progress heading south. He had been driving at five miles above the legal speed limit, which most motorists did—a good speed but not fast enough to attract attention from any cruising State Police. Now, Thruway exit 13, an intermediate objective, was ahead. Luís eased into a right-hand lane to take the turn. Both Luís and Miguel had been looking behind for signs of any pursuit. There was none.

Just the same, as they left the I-95 Miguel urged Luís, "Move it! Move it!" Since the departure from Larchmont, Miguel had been wondering if he had made a mistake in not letting Rafael kill the old woman on the parking lot. She might not have believed the phony story about what she had seen being part of a film. By now she could have spread the alarm. Descriptions could be circulating.

Luís was pushing his speed, going as fast as he could on the roughly paved Bronx streets.

Baudelio, since leaving Larchmont, had several times checked vital signs of their two sedated captives, and all appeared to be well. He estimated that the drug midazolam which he had administered would keep the woman and boy unconscious for another hour. If it didn't he would give them more, though he preferred not, since it might delay the much more complex medical task needed at the end of this journey.

He had also stanched the bleeding of the older man and applied a dressing to his head. The old man was now stirring, slight moans escaping him as he neared a return to consciousness. Anticipating possible trouble, Baudelio prepared another hypodermic of midazolam and injected it. The stirring and moans subsided. Baudelio had no idea what would happen to the old man. Most likely Miguel would shoot him and dispose of the body in a safe place; during his association with the Medellín cartel, Baudelio had seen it happen often. Not that he cared one way or the other. Caring about other human beings was an emotion he had long since discarded.

Rafael had produced some brown blankets and he and Carlos, with Baudelio watching, wrapped the woman, boy and old man in one each, so that only their heads protruded. In each case sufficient blanket was left folded at the top so it could be turned back to cover the face when the three were removed from the Nissan van. Carlos tied each rolled bundle with a length of cord around the middle so that in transit it would resemble nothing more than a piece of conventional cargo.

Conner Street in the Bronx, which they had reached, was desolate, gray and depressing. Luís knew where he was going; in rehearsals for today they had traveled the route twice before. At a corner with a Texaco station they turned right into a semideserted industrial area. Trucks were parked at intervals, some looking as if they had been there a long time. Few people were in sight.

Luís brought the van to a halt against a long, unbroken wall of an unoccupied warehouse. As he did, a truck that had been waiting on the opposite side of the street pulled across and stopped slightly ahead of the Nissan. The truck was a white GMC with a painted sign, "Superbread," on either side.

Inquiry would have shown there was no such product as Superbread. The truck was one of a total of six vehicles obtained by Miguel soon after his arrival, employing a fake rental agency as a front. The GMC truck had been used occasionally for the Sloane surveillance duty and otherwise for general use. As with other vehicles in the small fleet, the truck had been repainted several times, the legend on its sides changed too—all of it the handiwork of Rafael. Today the truck was being driven by the remaining member of the group, the woman, Socorro, who jumped down from the driver's seat and went around to open the double rear doors.

At the same time the door of the Nissan van was opened and the rolled bundles, with all three faces covered, were quickly transferred by Rafael and Carlos to the GMC truck. Baudelio, having gathered up his medical equipment, followed.

Miguel and Luís were busy in the Nissan van. Miguel peeled off the dark, thin plastic sheets from the windows; they had been useful for concealment but were now an identifying feature to be disposed of. From beneath the driver's seat Luís took a pair of New York State license plates he had put there earlier.

Going outside, and after looking around to make sure he was not observed, Luís removed the Nissan van's New Jersey plates, replacing them with the New York plates. The process took only a few seconds because all of the group's vehicles had special license plate holders, with one side hinged. The hinged portion could be lifted upward while the original plate was slid out and a fresh one put in. The side of the holder was then snapped back and held in place by a spring fastener.

Miguel, soon after his arrival in New York, had arranged through an underworld contact to buy a series of New York and New Jersey plates from vehicles no longer in use but on which license fees had been kept up to date.

The licensing systems of New York, New Jersey and most other states made it possible to get license plates for any vehicle long after it was totally dismantled and all of its parts discarded. All that a state registration agency cared about was receiving a license fee along with evidence—equally easy to obtain—that the nonexistent vehicle was insured. Neither the state agency nor the insurance company, which would renew an old insurance policy by mail as long as the required premium was tendered, ever required the vehicle to be produced.

Consequently in criminal circles a brisk business existed in such plates which, while illegal, were not on any police "hot list" and were for that reason worth many times their actual cost.

Miguel emerged from the Nissan van with the plastic sheets, which he dumped in an overflowing trash container nearby. Luís hurriedly brought the discarded New Jersey plates and stuffed those in too.

Luís then took over the wheel of the GMC truck which now contained the unconscious Jessica, Nicholas and Angus, as well as Miguel, Rafael, Baudelio and Socorro. After a swift U-turn they headed back to the Thruway and, within less than ten minutes after leaving it, were back on the I-95 in the new vehicle, continuing south.

Carlos, now driving the empty Nissan passenger van, also made a U-turn. He too went to I-95, but headed north. With the van's appearance changed by removal of the dark windows and the substitution of New York for New Jersey license plates, it was now like thousands of others in normal use and *unlike* the description circulated by the Larchmont police.

Carlos's assignment was to dispose of the Nissan passenger van and that, too, had been carefully planned. After three miles he left the

Thruway, then continued north for twelve miles on secondary roads as far as White Plains. There he drove to a public parking garage, a four-story structure adjoining an indoor shopping complex—Center City Mall.

Parking on the third level, Carlos moved with apparent casualness through his next activities. Among shoppers parking nearby and getting in or out of cars, no one seemed remotely interested in him or the Nissan van.

First, Carlos wiped all obvious surfaces to make fingerprint detection difficult. That was in case the van was recovered by law authorities in its present condition. The next step was to ensure it wasn't.

From a locker in the van's interior Carlos withdrew a Styrofoam container. Opened, it contained a formidable quantity of plastic explosive, a small detonator unit with a release pin, two lengths of pliant wire and a roll of adhesive tape. With the tape he fastened the explosive and detonator behind the front seats, low down and out of sight. He ran wires from the detonator release pin to the inside handles of each front door. After fastening a wire to each handle with the door almost closed, he shut each door carefully, then locked it. Now, opening either door would pull the release pin from the detonator.

Peering into the van, Carlos satisfied himself

that neither the plastic explosive nor the wires were visible from outside.

Miguel had reasoned that several days would pass before the van was noticed, by which time the kidnappers and their victims would be far away. But when the van was found, a typical terrorist surprise would emphasize that those who had been involved with the kidnap were to be taken very seriously.

Carlos left the parking garage through the shopping mall, then used public transport to head for Hackensack where he would rejoin the others.

The GMC truck continued south for five miles, as far as the Cross Bronx Expressway where it turned west. About twelve minutes later it crossed the Harlem River and, soon after, the George Washington Bridge spanning the Hudson River.

Halfway across the bridge the truck and its occupants left New York State and entered New Jersey. Now, for Miguel and the others in the Medellín gang, the haven of their Hackensack headquarters was reassuringly close.

13

Bert Fisher lived and worked in a tiny apartment in Larchmont. He was sixty-eight and had been a widower for a decade. His business cards described him as a news reporter, though in the parlance of journalism he was more realistically a stringer.

Like other stringers, Bert was the local representative of several news organizations based in larger centers, some of which paid him a small retainer. He submitted information or written copy and got paid for what was used, if anything. Since small-town local news rarely had national or even area-wide significance, getting something published in a major newspaper or reported on radio or television was difficult, which was why no one ever made a fortune as a stringer and most—like Bert Fisher—barely scraped by.

Still, Bert enjoyed what he was doing. During World War II, as an American G.I. in Europe he had worked for the armed forces newspaper, *Stars and Stripes*. It had put journalism in his bloodstream and ever since he had happily been a modest part of it. Even now, though age had slowed him a little, he still made telephone calls each day to local sources and kept several scanner radios switched on, thus hearing communications of local police, fire departments, ambulances and other public services. He always hoped that something might be worth following up and reporting to a major chronicler of news.

That was how Bert heard the Larchmont police transmission ordering an officer in car 423 to go to the Grand Union supermarket. It seemed like a routine call until, soon after, the officer alerted police headquarters to a possible kidnap. At the word "kidnap," Bert sat up straight, locked the radio on the Larchmont police frequency, and reached for copy paper to make notes.

By the time the transmission finished, Bert knew he must hurry to the scene of action. First, however, he needed to call New York City television station WCBA.

At WCBA-TV an assistant news director took Bert Fisher's call.

WCBA, a wholly owned affiliate of the CBA network, was a prestigious local station serving the New York area. It operated out of three floors of a Manhattan office building a mile or so from its network parent. Although a local station, it had an enormous audience; also, because of the amount of news which New York generated, WCBA's news organization was in many ways a microcosm of the network's.

In a bustling, noise-filled newsroom where thirty people worked at closely clustered desks, the assistant news director checked Bert Fisher's name against a list in a loose-leaf binder. "Okay," he said, "what do you have?"

He listened while the stringer described the police radio message and his intention to go to the Larchmont scene.

"Just a 'possible' kidnap, eh?"

"Yes, sir."

Although Bert Fisher was almost three times as old as the young man he was addressing, he still observed a deference to rank, carried forward from another age.

"All right, Fisher, get going! Call back immediately if there's anything real."

"Right, sir. Will do."

Hanging up, the assistant news director realized the call might be just a false alarm. On the other hand, big-breaking news sometimes tiptoed in through unlikely doorways. For a moment he considered dispatching a camera crew to Larchmont, then decided not. At this point the stringer's report was nebulous. Besides, the available crews were already on assignment, so it would mean pulling one away from an active story. Nor, without more information, was there anything which could be broadcast.

The assistant did, however, walk over to the elevated newsroom desk where the station's woman news director presided, and tell her about the call.

After hearing him out, she confirmed his decision. But afterward a thought occurred to her and she picked up a telephone that connected her directly to CBA network news. She asked for Ernie LaSalle, the national editor with whom she sometimes exchanged information.

"Look," she said, "this may turn out to be nothing." Repeating what she had just heard, she added, "But it *is* Larchmont and I know Crawford Sloane lives there. It's a small place, it might involve someone he knows, so I thought you'd want to tell him."

"Thanks," LaSalle said. "Let me know if there's anything more."

When he hung up the phone, Ernie LaSalle momentarily weighed the potential importance of the information. The likelihood was, it would amount to zero. Just the same . . .

On instinct and impulse he picked up the red reporting phone.

"National desk. LaSalle. We are advised

that at Larchmont, repeat Larchmont, New York, the local police radio reports a possible kidnapping. No other details. Our friends at WCBA are following up and will inform us."

As always, the national editor's words were carried throughout the CBA News headquarters. Some who heard wondered why LaSalle had put something so insubstantial on the speaker system. Others, unconcerned, returned their attention to whatever else they had been doing. One floor above the newsroom, senior producers at the Horseshoe paused to listen. One of them, pointing to Crawford Sloane who could be seen through the closed glassed doorway to his private office, observed, "If there's a kidnapping let's be thankful it's someone else in Larchmont and not Crawf. Unless that's his double in there." The others laughed.

Crawford Sloane heard LaSalle's announcement through a speaker on his desk. He had closed the door for a private meeting with the president of CBA News, Leslie Chippingham. While Sloane, in asking for the meeting, had suggested he go to Chippingham's office, the other man had chosen to come here.

Both paused until the national editor's words concluded and Sloane's interest was quickened by the mention of Larchmont. At any other time he would have gone to the newsroom to seek more information. But as it was, he did not want to stop what had suddenly become a no-holds-barred confrontation which, to the anchorman's surprise, was not going at all the way he had expected.

14

"My instinct tells me, Crawf, you have a problem," the CBA News president said, opening their conversation.

"Your instinct is wrong," Crawford Sloane responded. "It's you who have the problem. It's readily solvable, but you need to make some structural changes. Quickly."

Leslie Chippingham sighed. He was a thirty-year veteran of TV news who had begun his career at age nineteen as a messenger at NBC's Huntley-Brinkley Report, the premier news show of its day. Even then he had learned that an anchorman must be handled as delicately as a Ming vase and receive the deference accorded heads of state. It was Chippingham's success in doing both which, along with other talents, had raised him to executive producer, then kept him a senior management survivor while other high climbers—including a bevy of network news presidents—were exiled to TV's backwaters or the oblivion of early retirement.

Chippingham had a facility for being at ease with everyone and making others feel the same way. It was once said of him that if he fired you, he made you feel good about it.

"So tell me," he asked Sloane. "What changes?"

"I can't continue to work with Chuck Insen. He has to go. And when we choose a new exec producer I want the casting vote."

"Well, well. You're right about there being a problem." Chippingham chose his words cautiously and added, "Though it's perhaps a different one, Crawf, from what you think."

Crawford Sloane regarded his nominal superior. What he saw was a towering figure, even seated—Chippingham was six-foot-four and weighed a trim 205 pounds. The face was more rugged than handsome, the eyes bright blue and the hair a forest of tight curls, now mostly gray. Across the years a succession of women had taken pleasure in running their fingers through Chippingham's curls, that particular pleasure invariably preceding others. Women, in fact, had been Les Chippingham's lifelong weakness, their conquest an irresistible hobby. At this moment, because of those indulgences, he was facing marital and financial disaster—a fact unknown to Sloane, though he, like others, was aware of Chippingham's womanizing.

Chippingham, however, knew he must put his own concerns aside to cope with Crawford Sloane. It would be like walking a high wire, as any colloquy with an anchorman always was.

"Let's quit futzing around," Sloane said, "and come to the point."

Chippingham agreed, "I was about to. As we both know, many things in network news are changing . . ."

"Oh for chrissakes, Les, of course they are!" Sloane cut in impatiently. "That's why I have problems with Insen. We need to change the shape of our news—with fewer quick headlines and more important stories developed thoroughly."

"I'm aware of your feelings. We've been over this before. I also know what Chuck believes and, by the way, he came to see me earlier this morning, complaining about you."

Sloane's eyes widened. He had not expected the executive producer to take the initiative in their dispute; it was not the way things usually happened. "What does he think you can do?" he asked.

Chippingham hesitated. "Hell, I suppose there's no point in not telling you. He believes the two of you are so far apart that your differences aren't reconcilable. Chuck wants you out."

The anchorman threw back his head and laughed. "And him stay? That's ridiculous."

The news president met his gaze directly. "Is it?"

"Of course. And you know it."

"I knew it once; I'm not sure I do now." Ahead of them both was untrodden ground. Chippingham eased onto it guardedly.

"What I'm trying to get through to you, Crawf, is that nothing anymore is the way it used to be. Since the networks were bought out, everything's in flux. You know as well as I do there's a good deal of feeling among our new masters—at this network and the others—about the power of the evening anchormen. Those goliaths running the parent companies want to diminish that power; also they're unhappy about some of the big salaries for which they think they're not getting value. Recently there's been talk about private, quiet agreements."

Sloane said sharply, "What kind of agreements?"

"The way I hear, the kind big entrepreneurs reach in their exclusive clubs and private homes. For example: *'We'll tell our network not to try to hire away your network news people, provided you agree not to go after ours. That way*

*we won't push salaries up all around, and can
work on reducing some of the big ones.'"*

"That's collusion, restraint of trade. It's
goddamned illegal!"

"Only if you can prove it happened," Chippingham pointed out. "How can you, though, if
the agreement's made over drinks at the Links
Club or the Metropolitan, and no record is
kept, nothing ever written down?"

Sloane was silent and Chippingham pressed
the message home. "What it amounts to, Crawf,
is that this is not the best of times to push too
hard."

Sloane said abruptly, "You said Insen envisaged someone else in my place. Who?"

"He mentioned Harry Partridge."

Partridge! Once more, Sloane thought, he
was looming as a competitor. He wondered if
Partridge had planted the idea. As if divining
the thought, Chippingham said, "Apparently
Chuck mentioned the idea to Harry, who was
surprised but didn't think he'd be interested."

Chippingham added, "Oh, another thing
Chuck Insen told me: If it comes to a choice
between him and you, he isn't going without a
fight. He's threatened to take it personally to
the top."

"Meaning what?"

"Meaning he'll talk to Margot Lloyd-Mason."

Crawford Sloane exploded. "Go to that bitch! He wouldn't dare!"

"I believe he would. And she may be a bitch, but Margot has the power."

As Leslie Chippingham well knew.

CBA had been the last of the major broadcast networks to fall victim to what those in the business privately labeled "the invasion of the Philistines." That was the description given to the takeover of the networks by industrial conglomerates whose insistence on constantly enlarging profits outweighed their sense of privilege and public duty. This, in contrast to the past when leaders like CBS's Paley, NBC's Sarnoff and ABC's Goldenson, while dedicated capitalists, were consistent demonstrators of their public obligations too.

Nine months before, after failed attempts to keep CBA independent, the network had been swallowed by Globanic Industries Inc., a corporate giant with worldwide holdings. Like General Electric, which had earlier acquired NBC, Globanic was a major defense contractor. Also like GE, Globanic's record included corporate criminality. On one occasion, following grand jury investigations, the company was fined and top-rank executives sentenced to prison terms for rigging bids and price-fixing. On another the company pleaded guilty to defrauding the U.S.

Government by falsifying defense contract ac-
counting records; a million-dollar fine was levied
—the maximum under law, though a small
amount compared with a single contract's total
value. As a commentator wrote at the time of
Globanic's takeover, "Globanic has just too
many special interests for CBA not to have lost
some editorial independence. Can you envisage
CBA ever again digging deeply into a sensitive
area where its parent is involved?"

Since the takeover of CBA, there had been
public assurances from the network's new owners
that the traditional independence of CBA News
would be respected. The view from inside,
though, was that such promises were proving hol-
low.

The transformation of CBA began with the
arrival of Margot Lloyd-Mason as the network's
new president and chief executive officer. Known
to be efficient, ruthless and exceedingly ambi-
tious, she was already a vice president of
Globanic Industries. It was rumored that her
move to CBA was a trial run to see whether she
would demonstrate sufficient toughness to qual-
ify as eventual chairman of the parent company.

Leslie Chippingham first encountered his
new chieftain when she sent for him a few days
after her arrival. Instead of the usual personal
phone call—a courtesy extended by Mrs. Lloyd-
Mason's predecessor to divisional presidents—he

received a peremptory message through a secre-
tary to appear immediately at "Stonehenge," the
colloquial network name for CBA's Third Ave-
nue headquarters. He went there in a chauffeur-
driven limousine.

Margot Lloyd-Mason was tall, with upswept
blond hair, a high-cheekboned, lightly tanned
face and shrewdly appraising eyes. She wore an
elegant taupe Chanel suit with a paler-toned silk
blouse. Later, Chippingham would describe her
as "attractive but formidable."

The chief executive's manner was both
friendly and cool. "You may use my first name,"
she told the news president, while making it
sound like an order. Then, without wasting time,
she got down to business.

"There will be an announcement sometime
today about a problem Theo Elliott is having."

Theodore Elliott was chairman of Globanic
Industries.

"The announcement's already been made,"
Chippingham said. "By the IRS in Washington,
this morning. They claim our king-of-kings has
underpaid his personal taxes by some four mil-
lion dollars."

By chance, Chippingham had seen the story
on the AP wire. The circumstances were that El-
liott had made investments in what was now ex-
posed as an illegal tax shelter. The creator of the
tax shelter was being criminally prosecuted. El-

liott was not, but would be required to pay back taxes plus large amounts in penalties.

"Theo has telephoned," Margot said, "assuring me he had no idea the arrangement was illegal."

"I suppose there are some who'll believe that," Chippingham said, aware of the army of lawyers, accountants and tax advisers which someone like the Globanic chairman would have at his disposal.

Margot said icily, "Don't be flippant about this. I sent for you because I want nothing about Theo and taxes to appear on our news, and I'd like you to ask the other networks not to report it either."

Chippingham, shocked and scarcely believing what he had just heard, struggled to keep his voice calm. "Margot, if I were to call the other networks with that request, not only would they turn it down, but they would report on the air that CBA News had attempted to arrange a cover-up. And frankly, if something similar happened in reverse, at CBA we'd do the same."

Even while speaking, he realized that the new network head had demonstrated in a single brief exchange not only her lack of knowledge of the broadcast business, but a total insensitivity to news-gathering ethics. But then, he reminded himself, it was public knowledge that neither of those things had brought her here, but instead, _her financial acumen and an ability to create profits._

"All right," she said grudgingly, "I suppose I have to accept what you say about the other networks. But I want nothing on our own news."

Chippingham sighed inwardly, knowing that from now on his job as news president was going to be monumentally more difficult. "Please believe me, Margot, when I tell you as a certainty that tonight the other networks will use that piece of news about Mr. Elliott and his taxes. And if we don't use it also, it will create more attention by far than if we do. That's because everyone will be watching to see how fair and impartial we are, especially after the statements by Globanic that the freedom of our News Division will not be interfered with."

The network president's strong face was set grimly, her lips compressed, but her silence showed she understood the point Chippingham had made. At length she said, "You'll keep it short?"

"That will happen automatically. It's not something that's worth a long report."

"And I don't want some smart-ass reporter implying that Theo knew about the illegality when he says he didn't."

"The one thing I'll promise you," Chippingham said, "is that whatever we do will be fair. I'll see to it myself."

Margot made no comment and instead picked up a slip of paper on her desk. "You came here in a chauffeured limo."

Chippingham was startled. "Yes, I did." The car and driver were one of the perks of his job, but the experience of being spied on—which had obviously happened—was new and unsettling.

"In future, use a taxi. I do. So can you. And something else." She fixed him with a steely glance. "The News Division's budget is to be cut by twenty percent immediately. You'll receive a memo from me tomorrow and 'immediately' means just that. I shall expect a report within a week on how economies have been made."

Chippingham was too dazed for more than a polite, formal leave-taking.

The item about Theodore Elliott and income taxes appeared on the CBA National Evening News and the Globanic chairman's statement about his innocence was left unchallenged. As a Horseshoe producer observed a week later, "If it had been a politician, we'd have poured skepticism on him, then peeled away his skin like an onion. As it is, we haven't even done a follow-up."

In fact, a follow-up was considered; there was sufficient new material. But during a discussion at the Horseshoe in which the news president participated, it was decided that other news that day was more important, so the follow-up didn't run.

The decision was subtle; few, even to themselves, conceded it to be a cop-out.

The matter of budget cutting was something else. It was an area where all networks were vulnerable to their conquerors and everyone knew it, including Leslie Chippingham. The News Divisions in particular had become fat, overstaffed and ripe for pruning.

When it happened at CBA News—the result of the demanded cost economies—the process was painful, mainly because more than two hundred lost their jobs.

The firings produced cries of outrage from those left jobless, and their friends. The print press had a bonanza, with newspapers running human interest stories slanted sympathetically toward the economy wave's victims—even though, quite frequently, print publishers exercised the same kind of economies themselves.

A group within CBA News, all of whose members were on long-term contracts, sent a letter of protest to the New York Times. *The signatories included Crawford Sloane, four senior correspondents and several producers. Their letter lamented that among those abruptly unemployed were veteran correspondents who had served CBA News for most of their working lives. It also pointed out that CBA overall was in no financial difficulty and that the network's profits compared favorably with those of major industrial companies. The published letter was discussed and quoted nationwide.*

The letter and the attention accorded it infuriated Margot Lloyd-Mason. Once more she sent for Leslie Chippingham.

With the Times *open in front of her she railed, "Those overpaid, conceited bastards are part of management. They should be supporting management decisions, not undermining us by public bellyaching."*

The news president ventured, "I doubt if they consider themselves management. They're news people first and are unhappy about their colleagues. And I may as well tell you, Margot, so am I."

The network head impaled him with a glare. "I've enough problems without any from you, so forget that brand of garbage. See to it that you ream out the people who signed that letter and let them know I expect no more disloyalty. You may also inform them that their kind of double-dealing will be remembered at contract renewal time. Which reminds me—some of the amounts we're paying news people are insanely exorbitant, especially for that arrogant son of a bitch Crawford Sloane."

Subsequently, Leslie Chippingham relayed a softer version of Margot's comments, reasoning that he was the one who had to hold the News

Division together, something that was becoming increasingly difficult.

The difficulty was compounded a few weeks later when a new proposal by Mrs. Lloyd-Mason was announced through a CBA internal memo. The intention was to create a political action fund to pay for lobbying in Washington on behalf of CBA network. Money for the fund would be contributed "voluntarily" by network executives and deducted from their salaries. Senior personnel in the News Division would be included. The announcement pointed out that the arrangement conformed to a similar one within the parent company, Globanic Industries.

The same day the announcement arrived, Chippingham was near the Horseshoe when a producer asked him, "Les, you're going to fight that political action shit for all of us, aren't you?"

From several feet away, Crawford Sloane interjected, "Of course he is. Les would never agree to anything which had the News Division asking for political favors instead of reporting them. We can all rely on him for that."

The news president found it hard to tell whether or not there was irony in the anchorman's voice. Either way, Chippingham recognized he had another serious problem, originating through Margot's ignorance—or was it plain uncaring?—about news integrity. Should

*he go to her and argue against the political ac-
tion fund? He doubted, though, that it would
make any difference since Margot's main objective was clearly to please her Globanic masters
and advance her own career.*

*In the end he solved his problem by leaking
the story, along with a copy of the internal CBA
memo, to the* Washington Post. *He had a contact there whom he had used before and who
could be trusted not to reveal a source. The resulting* Post *report, which was picked up by other
papers, ridiculed the idea of involving a news organization in political lobbying. Within days the
plan was officially abandoned—according to rumors, on the personal orders of Globanic's chairman, Theodore Elliott.*

*Once more the CBA network president sent
for Chippingham.*

*Coldly, without greeting or preliminaries, she
asked, "Who in the News Division gave my
memo to the* Post?*"*

"I have no idea," he lied.

*"Bullshit! If you don't know for sure, you
have a damn good notion."*

*Chippingham decided to keep quiet, though
noting with relief that it had not occurred to
Margot he himself might be responsible for the
leak.*

*She broke the silence between them. "You
have been uncooperative ever since I came here."*

"I'm sorry you feel that way because I don't believe it's true. In fact, I've tried to be honest with you."

Ignoring the disclaimer, Margot continued, *"Because of your persistent attitude I've had inquiries made about you and have learned several things. One is that your job is important to you at this moment, because financially you can't afford to lose it."*

"My job has always been important to me. As to financially important, isn't that true of most people? Perhaps even of you." Chippingham wondered uneasily what was coming.

With a thin, superior smile the network chief said, *"I'm not in the middle of a messy divorce action. You are. Your wife wants a large financial settlement, including most of your joint property and, if she doesn't get it, will produce evidence in court of a half-dozen adulterous relationships which you were careless about concealing. You also have debts, including a big personal bank loan, so you desperately need a continuing income; otherwise you'll be a personal bankrupt and the next thing to a pauper."*

Raising his voice, he objected, *"That's insulting! It's an intrusion on my personal privacy."*

Margot said calmly, *"It may be, but it's true."*

Despite the protest, he was jolted by the extent of her knowledge. He was in a near-desper-

ate financial bind, in part because he had never been able to manage his personal money and across the years had not only spent his substantial salary as it came in, but had borrowed heavily. He had also never been able to resist the temptations of other women, a weakness that Stasia, his wife of twenty years, had appeared to accept—until three months ago. Then, without warning, Stasia's pent-up rage and stored-up evidence exploded into a ferocious divorce action. Even with that to contend with, he had foolishly started another affair, this time with Rita Abrams, a CBA News producer. He hadn't intended it to happen but it had. Now he found it exciting and wanted to go on. But the thought of losing his job frightened him.

"Now listen to me carefully," Margot said. "It isn't hard to replace a News Division president and if I need to, I will. Before you even know what's happening, you'll be out on your ass and someone else in. There are plenty of candidates for your job, here and at the other networks. Is that clear?"

Chippingham said resignedly, "Yes, it's clear."

"However, if you play ball with me, you'll stay on. But News Division policy will be the way I want it. Remember that. And one more thing: When I want something done which you don't like, don't waste my time with crap about news

ethics and purity. You stopped being pure—if you ever were—when you didn't use those follow-up pieces about Theo Elliott's taxes." Margot gave her thin smile again. "Oh yes, I know about that. So you've been corrupted already and a few more times won't make any difference. That's all. You can go."

That conversation had taken place two days before Chuck Insen, and then Crawford Sloane, had come to the news president with their personal problems about the National Evening News. Chippingham knew that their differences must be settled promptly within the News Division. For as long as possible he wanted no more visits to Margot, no more confrontations.

"I'm telling you, Crawf, just as I told Chuck," Chippingham said, "right now you'll do the greatest harm to all of us in news if the two of you go public with your infighting. Over at Stonehenge, the News Division is out of favor. As for Chuck's idea of involving Margot Lloyd-Mason, she won't take his side or yours. What she'll probably do is more cost cutting on the grounds that if we have time for internal feuding we're not busy enough, and are therefore overstaffed."

"I can fight that," Sloane said.

"And I guarantee you'll be ignored." Unusually, Chippingham was becoming angry. At

times it was a news president's function to protect his reporting staff, including an anchorman,
from the network's top management. But there
were limits; for once he decided to be rough.
"Something you may as well know is that our
new boss doesn't have a lot of time for you.
Because of that damnfool letter you and the
others wrote to the *Times,* she described you as
arrogant and overpaid."

Sloane protested, "That letter was on target.
I'm entitled to a free opinion and I expressed
it."

"Balls! You had no business putting your
name there. In that I agree with Margot. For
god's sake, Crawf, grow up! You can't take the
kind of money you do from the network and
continue being 'one of the boys,' shooting off at
the mouth when you feel like it."

There was no reason, Chippingham
thought, why he should take all the flak from
the network's new owners. Let other senior
staffers, including Sloane and Insen, carry their
share! The news president also had a private
reason for irritation. Today was Thursday. Tonight he planned to leave for a long, love-filled
weekend with Rita Abrams in Minnesota. Rita
was already there, having arrived the night before. What he didn't want was to have this stupid brawl fomenting in his absence.

"I still come back to what we started with,"

Sloane said. "There need to be changes in our news format."

"There can be," Chippingham told him. "I have some ideas myself. We'll work them out here."

"How?"

"Starting next week I'll hold meetings with you and Chuck Insen—as many as it takes to get agreement. Even if I have to slam your heads together, we'll find an acceptable compromise."

"We can try it," Sloane said doubtfully, "but it's not totally satisfactory."

Chippingham shrugged. "Tell me something that is."

When the news president had gone, Sloane sat silently in his office brooding over their discussion. Then he remembered the speakerphone announcement about Larchmont. Curious to know if there was any more information, he left his office and headed for the newsroom.

15

Bert Fisher, the Larchmont stringer, was continuing to pursue a potential news story stemming from the police radio message about a "possible kidnap." After telephoning WCBA-TV, Bert hurried out of his apartment, hoping that his battered twenty-year-old Volkswagen bug would start. Following an anxious minute of abortive whines and grunts, it did. He kept a scanner radio in the car and set it to the Larchmont police frequency. Then he headed for downtown—the Grand Union supermarket.

Partway there some more police radio exchanges caused him to change direction.

"Car 423 to headquarters. Proceeding to house of possible victims of reported incident. Address, 66 Park Avenue. Request a detective meet me there."

"Headquarters to 423. Ten four."

A brief pause, then, *"Headquarters to car 426. Proceed urgently to 66 Park Avenue. Meet post officer, car 423. Investigate officer's report."*

In local police usage, Bert realized, "proceed urgently" meant: *with flashing lights and siren.* Clearly, the action was heating up and Bert increased his own speed as much as the ancient Volkswagen would allow. Now, heading for Park Avenue, he felt excited about that address number—66. He wasn't sure, but if the house belonged to the person he thought it did, this was really a big story.

Officer Jensen, who had responded to the original call from the Grand Union supermarket and interviewed the old lady, Priscilla Rhea, now had a feeling he was involved in something serious. In his mind, he went over the situation so far.

During his questioning of others at the supermarket, several witnesses confirmed seeing a fellow shopper—identified by two of them as Mrs. Crawford Sloane—leave the store suddenly, apparently in distress. She was accompanied by her young son and two other men, one about thirty, the other elderly. The thirty-year-old appeared to have come to the store on his own. At first he had asked other shoppers whether they were Mrs. Sloane. Then, when he encountered the real Mrs. Sloane, the hasty exodus ensued.

From that point, the only person claiming to have seen any of those described was Miss Rhea. Her story about an attack, with the victims being carried away in a "little bus," was increasingly believable. Contributing to the credibility was that Mrs. Sloane's Volvo station wagon—pointed out to Officer Jensen by someone who knew her—was still parked in the supermarket lot, with no sign of Mrs. Sloane or the others with her. There were also those splotches on the ground which possibly were blood. Jensen had asked one of the other officers now on the scene to protect them as evidence, for examination later.

Another onlooker, who lived near the Sloanes, had given Jensen the family's home address. This, coupled with the fact that there was nothing more for him to do at the supermarket, had prompted Jensen's radio message asking for a detective to meet him at 66 Park Avenue. In other circumstances, and because Larchmont police radio conversations were casual compared with those of larger forces, he would have included the Sloane name with the address. But knowing that Larchmont's most famous resident was involved, and being aware that outsiders might be listening, he withheld the name for the time being.

Jensen was on his way to Park Avenue now —a journey of only a few minutes.

He had just entered the driveway of number 66 when a second police car—unmarked, though with a portable flashing roof light and screaming siren—pulled in behind. Detective Ed York, an old-timer on the force whom Jensen knew well, stepped out. York and Jensen conferred briefly, then walked to the house together. The policemen identified themselves to Florence, the Sloanes' day maid, who had come to the front door at the sound of the siren. She let them in, her face showing a mixture of surprise and alarm.

"There's a possibility, *only* a possibility," Detective York informed her, "that something may have happened to Mrs. Sloane." He began asking questions which Florence answered, her concern mounting as she did.

Yes, she had been in the house when Mrs. Sloane, Nicky, and Mr. Sloane's father left to go shopping. That was about eleven o'clock. Mr. Sloane had left for work just as Florence arrived, which was 9:30. No, she had not heard from anyone in the family since Mrs. Sloane left, though she hadn't expected to. In fact there had been no phone calls at all. No, there had been nothing unusual when Mrs. Sloane and the others drove away. Except . . . well . . .

Florence stopped, then asked anxiously, "What's this all about? What's happened to Mrs. Sloane?"

"Right now there isn't time to explain," the detective said. "What did *you* mean by 'except . . . well'?"

"Well, when Mrs. Sloane, her father-in-law and Nicky were leaving, I was in there." Florence motioned toward a sun-room at the front of the house. "I saw them drive away."

"And?"

"There was a car parked on the side street; you can see it from there. When Mrs. Sloane left, all of a sudden the car started and went the same way she did. I didn't think anything about it at the time."

"No reason why you should," Jensen said. "Can you describe the car?"

"It was dark brown, I think. Sort of medium size."

"Did you see a license plate?"

"No."

"Did you recognize the make?"

Florence shook her head. "They all look the same to me."

"Leave that for now," Detective York told Jensen. Then to Florence, "Think about that car. Try to remember anything else, and we'll come back to you."

The detective and Jensen returned outside. As they did, two more police cruisers arrived. One brought a uniformed sergeant, another the Larchmont chief of police. The chief, in uniform, was tall and rangy, with a deceptively low-key manner. The four began a hasty conference in the driveway.

Near the end of it the chief asked Detective York, "Do you think this is for real—a kidnap?"

"At this moment," York said, "everything points that way."

"Jensen?"

"Yes, sir. It's for real."

"You said the Nissan van that was seen leaving had New Jersey plates?"

"According to a witness, yes, sir."

The chief mused. "If it *is* a kidnap and they cross a state line, it becomes the FBI's jurisdiction. That's the Lindbergh law." He added, "Not that that kind of detail worries the FBI."

The last words came out sourly, reflecting the conviction of many local lawmen that the FBI moved in on any high-profile case they wanted and found reasons to decline the ones they didn't. Then the chief said decisively, "I'm calling in the FBI now."

He returned to his car and picked up the radio mike.

A minute or two later, rejoining the others, the chief ordered Detective York to go back to the house and stay inside. "The first thing you do, have that maid put you in touch with Mr. Sloane and speak to him yourself. Tell him as much as you know, and that we're doing all we can. After that, answer any incoming phone calls. Keep a note of everything. You'll be getting help soon."

The sergeant and Jensen were instructed to remain on protective duty outside. "Soon, there'll be more people here than flies around a shithouse. Let no one past the front gate except the FBI. When the press get here with their questions, direct them to headquarters."

At that moment they heard the sound of a noisy approaching car. Their heads turned. It was a battered white Volkswagen bug and the chief said glumly, "Here's the first."

Bert Fisher had no need to check which house on Park Avenue was number 66. The assembled police cars were direction enough.

As he stopped his VW at the curb and climbed out, the police chief had entered his own car and was about to leave. Bert hurried forward. "Chief, can you make a statement?"

"Oh, it's you!" The chief ran down his window on the driver's side; he had encountered the old news stringer many times before. "A statement about what?"

"Oh, come on, Chief! I've heard all the radio buzz, including your instruction just now to call in the FBI." Bert looked around him, realizing that his hunch was right. "This is Crawford Sloane's home, isn't it?"

"Yes, it is."

"And is it Mrs. Sloane who's been kidnapped?"

As the chief hesitated, Bert pleaded, "Look, I'm the first here. Why not give a local boy a break?"

The chief, who was a reasonable man, thought, *Well, why not?* He was even a little fond of Fisher, a nuisance at times like a persistent mosquito, though never vicious the way some press people could be.

"If you heard all the messages," the chief said, "you'll know we aren't certain of anything yet. But yes, we do think Mrs. Sloane may have been abducted, along with the Sloanes' son Nicholas and Mr. Sloane's father."

Bert, scribbling as the chief spoke, knew this was the most important story of his life and he wanted to be careful. "So what you're telling me is that the Larchmont police are acting on the assumption there have been three kidnappings."

The chief nodded. "That's an okay quote."

"Do you have any idea who might have done this?"

"No. Oh, just one thing. Mr. Sloane has not been informed and we're trying to get in touch with him. So before you start sounding off, for god's sake give us time to do that."

With that, the chief pulled away and Bert dived for his VW. Despite the chief's caveat, he had no intention of waiting for anything. The only question in his mind was: Where was the nearest pay phone?

Moments later, as Bert turned out of Park Avenue, he saw another car turning in and recognized the occupant—the local stringer for WNBC-TV. So the competition was onto the story. Now, if Bert was to stay ahead he had to move fast.

Not far away, on Boston Post Road, he found a pay phone. As he punched out the numbers of WCBA-TV, his hand was trembling.

16

At 11:20 A.M. in the pressure-driven newsroom of WCBA-TV, tension was rising as it always did during the hour preceding the local New York station's News at Noon. Today especially, there was a heavy budget of news with several developing stories competing for the lead position.

A famous evangelist, in New York to receive a religious prize, had been found dead in his Waldorf suite, apparently from a cocaine overdose, and a prostitute who had spent the night with him was being questioned by police. In midtown Manhattan an office building was on fire; people trapped on high floors were being rescued by helicopter. A Wall Street billionaire, terminally ill with cancer, was being wheeled around the Bronx in an invalid chair as he handed out fistfuls of one-hundred-dollar bills. Every few minutes, from a trailing armored car, his supply was replenished.

Amid a scene of near-bedlam, Bert Fisher's phone call was routed to the same assistant news director as before who, on hearing who was calling, snapped, "We're swamped here. Make it short and quick!"

Bert did, at which the young newsman said incredulously, "You're sure? Absolutely sure? Do you have confirmation?"

"From the chief of police." Bert added proudly, "He gave me an exclusive statement and, to be safe, I had him repeat it."

The assistant news director was already on his feet, signaling to the news director, shouting urgently, "Line four! Line four!" He told an assignment editor at a desk beside him, "We need a camera crew in Larchmont fast. Don't ask me how to find one, just pull them off something else, anything else, and get them there."

The woman news director was already listening to Bert Fisher. When she had made notes of the essentials, she asked him, "Who else has the story?"

"I was the first. Still am. But WNBC's man was arriving as I left."

"Did he have a camera crew?"

"No."

The assistant news director crossed the newsroom to report, "I've a crew on the way. We pulled them from the Bronx."

The news director spoke into the phone, instructing Bert Fisher, "Stay on the line." Then to a writer at a desk nearby: "Take line four. It's Fisher, Larchmont. Get everything he has, then write it as our noon lead."

At the same time the news director picked up a telephone connecting her directly to the network. Ernie LaSalle, CBA's national editor, answered and she told him, "The kidnap in Larchmont is confirmed. Half an hour ago unknown persons violently seized Crawford Sloane's wife, his son, and Crawford's father."

"Good Christ!" LaSalle's shock and incredulity came down the line. "Has Crawf been told?"

"I don't think so."

"Are the police involved?"

"Very much so, and they've called in the FBI. Our man Fisher has a statement from the Larchmont chief." Checking her notes, the news director read aloud the chief's statement,

Bert Fisher's query, and the chief's words, "That's an okay quote."

"Run that past me again." LaSalle was frantically typing as he spoke.

The WCBA news director did so, adding, "We've heard that WNBC is onto the story, though a tad behind us. Look, we'll go with this at noon anyway, and I'm considering breaking into programming now. But I thought, since this is family . . ."

Before she could finish, LaSalle snapped, "Don't do a damn thing over there. The brass will be in on this. And if anybody breaks it, we will."

Taking seconds only, Ernie LaSalle debated his options.

He had several.

One was to take whatever time was necessary to first contact Crawford Sloane, who might or might not be in the building, then personally and gently as possible convey to Crawf the frightening information. A second was to pick up the red reporting phone in front of him and announce to the entire News Division the kidnapping of the Sloane family, after which urgent action to make an on-air report would undoubtedly begin. The third was to issue an order to network master control that CBA News would "take air" in approximately three minutes, interrupting network programming with a special bulletin. LaSalle was one of a half-dozen people who had the power to authorize such intrusion and, in his judgment, the news just received was not only preeminent, but of immense public interest.

He made his decision, opting for the second choice. Influencing his judgment was the knowledge that another New York station, WNBC-TV—owned by NBC network—was on the Larchmont scene. Undoubtedly NBC News would receive a report swiftly from their affiliate, just as CBA had. Therefore there wasn't time for humane niceties. As for going on the air at once, there were plenty of other people around, including the News Division president, Les Chippingham, to make that decision.

I'm sorry as hell to do this to you, Crawf, LaSalle thought, then picked up the red reporting phone.

"National desk. LaSalle. The earlier reported kidnapping at Larchmont, New York, has been confirmed by the local chief of police who has called in the FBI. According to police, the reported victims are Mrs. Crawford Sloane, young Nicholas Sloane and . . ." Despite his resolve and professionalism, LaSalle found his voice breaking. Steeling himself he continued. ". . . and Crawford's father, who were violently seized and driven away by unknown persons. WCBA has reliable on-scene coverage, details available here. NBC is believed to be working on this story, though we have a slight lead. National desk recommends taking network air immediately."

Horror and consternation swept through the News Division like a tidal wave. Everyone stopped working. Many looked at each other, asking silently, *Did I really hear that?* When confirmation was forthcoming, unanswerable questions sprang to lips: *How could it happen? Who would do such a thing? Is it a kidnap for ransom? What do the kidnappers want? What are the chances the police will catch them quickly? Oh god, how must Crawford feel?*

One floor above the newsroom, senior staffers at the Horseshoe were equally appalled, though their shock lasted only moments. After it, out of habit and discipline, they were galvanized to action.

Chuck Insen, as senior producer in the building, left his office on the run. All his newsman's instincts told him that the national desk advice to take network air immediately would be followed. When that happened, Insen's appointed place was in the broadcast control room four floors below. Reaching a bank of elevators, he jabbed a down button with his thumb.

Impatiently awaiting for an elevator, Insen's

mind overflowed with sympathy for Sloane, their differences for the moment totally erased. He wondered: Where was Crawf? Earlier, Insen had seen him briefly in the distance and knew that he and Les Chippingham had had their heads together in Sloane's office for reasons Insen already knew. Presumably Crawf was somewhere in the building and must have heard the hot-line call. Which raised a crucial question.

When urgent breaking news was deemed significant enough to interrupt the network with a special report, it was the evening news anchorman—in CBA's case, Crawford Sloane —who faced the cameras. If the anchorman wasn't on the scene, he would be sent for, with any available correspondent filling in until the anchor arrived. But, Insen realized, there was absolutely no way Sloane could be expected to handle this sudden, harrowing news about his own family.

At that moment a "down" elevator arrived and the business correspondent of CBA News, Don Kettering, prepared to step out. Kettering, middle-aged with a thin mustache and looking like a well-to-do businessman himself, opened his mouth to say something but never got started. This was because Insen shoved him back inside the elevator and hit the B1 button for first basement. The elevator doors closed.

Kettering spluttered, "What the—"

"Hold it," Insen said. "You heard the speakerphone just now?"

"Yes, I'm damn sorry. I was going to tell Crawf—"

"Where you're going," Insen said, "is on the air. Get to the flash studio and take the hot seat. Crawf can't do this. You're available. I'll talk to you from the control room."

Kettering, a quick thinker and an experienced general reporter before he became a business specialist, nodded. He even seemed a little pleased at the prospect. "Do I get some briefing?"

"We'll give you all we have so far. You'll get maybe a minute to do a quick study, then ad-lib. More will be fed to you as it comes in."

"Right."

As Insen left the elevator, Kettering pressed a button which would take him upward to the broadcast floor.

Elsewhere, other activity was in high gear, some proceeding automatically.

In the newsroom, the Northeast assignment editor was rounding up two network camera crews and correspondents. Their instructions were to proceed posthaste to Larchmont and obtain pictures of the kidnap scene as well as interview police and any witnesses. A mobile transmitting van would follow right behind.

In a small research department adjoining

the Horseshoe, an offshoot of a larger research library in another building, a half-dozen people were hastily assembling a computer biography of Crawford Sloane and the few known facts about his family—few because Jessica Sloane had always insisted on privacy for herself and Nicholas.

From somewhere, though, main research had acquired a photograph of Jessica which was coming through on a fax machine; a graphics editor hovered over the machine, waiting to remove the picture and convert it to a slide. Printing out from another computer was the war record of Crawford's father, Angus Sloane. There would be a photo of him too. No picture of Nicky had been located so far.

A research assistant grabbed all the material available and ran down a flight of stairs to the flash facility studio where Don Kettering had just arrived. Right behind research, a messenger from the national desk brought a printout of Bert Fisher's Larchmont report, received from WCBA-TV. Kettering sat down at the studio's central desk and, blocking out all else, immersed himself in reading. Around him technicians were arriving, lights coming on. Someone clipped a microphone onto Kettering's jacket. A cameraman framed Kettering in his lens.

The flash facility was the smallest studio in the building, no bigger than a modest living room. It had a single camera and was kept for occasions such as this when it could be activated and ready in moments.

Meanwhile, in the darkened control room where Chuck Insen had now established himself, a woman director slid into her central seat facing a bank of TV monitors, some illumined, others black. On her right, an assistant with an open notebook joined her. Operators and technicians were taking their places, a stream of orders flowing.

"Standby camera one. Mike check."

"Bill, this will be a live announce. 'We interrupt this programming' open and a 'resume programming' close. Okay?"

"Okay. Got it."

"Do we have a script yet?"

"Negative. Don may go ad-lib."

"Bring the video up ten units."

"Camera one, let's see Kettering."

More monitors were coming alight, among them one from the flash facility. The face of Don Kettering filled the screen.

The director's assistant was talking with network master control. "This is news. We're expecting to break into the network with a bulletin. Please stand by."

The director inquired, "Is the special slide ready?"

A voice responded, "Here it is."

On another monitor, bright red letters filled the screen:

CBA NEWS
SPECIAL
BULLETIN

"Hold it there." The director turned in her chair to speak to Insen. "Chuck, we're ready as we'll ever be. Do we go or not?"

The executive producer, a telephone cradled in his shoulder, told her, "I'm finding out now."

He was talking to the News Division president who was in the main newsroom where Crawford Sloane was pleading for delay.

The time was 11:52 A.M.

When the shattering national desk announcement began, Crawford Sloane was at the head of a stairway on the fourth floor, about to descend to the newsroom. His intention had been to find out more, if he could, about the earlier report from Larchmont.

As the speakerphones went live, he stopped to listen, then, scarcely believing what he had heard, stood briefly, dazed and in a state of shock. His momentary trance was interrupted by one of the Horseshoe secretaries who had seen him leave and now came running after him, calling out breathlessly, "Oh, Mr. Sloane!

The Larchmont police are on your line. They
want to talk to you urgently."

He followed the girl back and took the call
in his office.

"Mr. Sloane, this is Detective York. I'm at
your home and have some unfortunate—"

"I just heard. Tell me what you know."

"Actually, sir, it's very little. We know that
your wife, son and father left for the Grand
Union supermarket about fifty minutes ago. Inside the store, according to witnesses, they were
approached . . ."

The detective continued his recital of known
facts, including the trio's apparently forced departure in a Nissan van. He added, "We've just
heard that FBI special agents are on the way
here, and someone from FBI is coming over to
you. I've been asked to tell you there's concern
about your own safety. You'll receive protection, but for the time being you should not leave
the building you are in."

Sloane's mind was whirling. Consumed with
anxiety, he asked, "Is there any idea who might
have done this?"

"No, sir. It all happened suddenly. We're
absolutely in the dark."

"Do many people know about this—what's
happened?"

"As far as I know, not many." The detective

added, "The longer we can keep it that way, the better."

"Why?"

"With a kidnapping, Mr. Sloane, publicity can be harmful. We may be hearing from the kidnappers—they'll probably try to contact you first. Then we, or more likely the FBI, will want a dialog with them, a start to negotiating. We won't want the whole world in on that. Nor will they because . . ."

Sloane interrupted. "Detective, I'll talk to you later. Right now there are things I have to do."

Aware of activity around the Horseshoe and knowing what it meant, Sloane wanted to curb precipitate action. Hurrying from his office he called out, "Where's Les Chippingham?"

"In the newsroom," a senior producer said. Then, more gently, "Crawf, we're all damn sorry, but it looks as if we're going on the air."

Sloane scarcely heard. He raced for the stairs and descended them swiftly. Ahead he could see the news president in hasty conference with several others around the national desk. Chippingham was asking, "How sure are we of that Larchmont stringer?"

Ernie LaSalle answered, "WCBA say he's a little old guy they've had for years—foursquare, reliable."

"Then I guess we should go with what we have."

Sloane broke into the circle. "No, no, no! Les, *don't* go with it. We need more time. The police just told me they may hear from the kidnappers. Publicity could harm my family."

LaSalle said, "Crawf, we know what you're going through. But this is a big story and others have it. They won't hold off. WNBC—"

Sloane shook his head. "I still say no!" He faced the news president directly. "Les, I beg of you—delay!"

There was an embarrassed silence. Everyone knew that in other circumstances, Sloane would be the first to urge going ahead. But no one had the heart to say, *Crawf, you're not thinking coherently.*

Chippingham glanced at the newsroom clock: 11:54.

LaSalle had taken over the phone call from Insen. Now he reported, "Chuck says everyone's set to go. He wants to know: Are we breaking into the network or not?"

Chippingham said, "Tell him I'm still deciding." He was debating: Should they wait until noon? On monitors overhead he could see the national feeds of all networks. On CBA a popular soap opera was still in progress; when it concluded, commercials would follow. Cutting in now would be a costly disruption. Would less

than another six minutes make much difference?

At that moment, simultaneously, several
newsroom computers emitted a "beep." On
screens a bright "B" appeared—the signal for
an urgent press wire bulletin. Someone reading
a screen called out, "AP has the Sloane kidnap
story."

On the national desk another phone rang.
LaSalle answered, listened, then said quietly,
"Thank you for telling us." Hanging up, he in-
formed the news president, "That was NBC.
They called us as a courtesy to say they have
the story. They're going with it on the hour."

The time was fifteen seconds short of 11:55.

Making a decision, Chippingham said, "We
go now!" Then to LaSalle, "Tell Chuck to break
the network."

17

In the CBA News headquarters building, two
floors below street level in a small, plain room,
two male operators sat facing complex switching systems with a galaxy of colored lights and

dials, computer terminals and television monitors. Two sides of the room had glass surrounds looking out onto drab corridors. Passersby, if so inclined, could look in. This was network master control, technical command post for the entire CBA national network.

Through here all network programming flowed—entertainment, news, sports, documentaries, presidents' addresses, Capitol Hill follies, assorted live coverage and prerecordings, and national commercials. Surprisingly, for all its importance as an electronic pulse center, master control's location and appearance were uninspiring.

At master control, each day usually advanced routinely according to a meticulous plan which codified each twenty-four hours of broadcasting in terms of minutes, sometimes seconds. Principally, execution of the plan was by computer, with the two operators overseeing—and occasionally interceding when unexpected events required regular programming to be interrupted.

An interruption was occurring now.

Moments earlier on a direct line from the News Division control room, Chuck Insen had instructed, "We have a news special. It's for the full network. We're taking air—*now!*"

As Insen spoke, the slide "CBA News Special Bulletin," fed from the news control room, came up on a master control monitor.

The experienced master control operator who received the call knew the command "now" meant exactly that. In the absence of that word, if a program in progress were within a minute and a half of finishing, he would wait until its conclusion before breaking into the network feed. Similarly, if a commercial were airing, he would allow it to finish.

But "now" meant no delay, no holding. A one-minute commercial was being broadcast and had thirty seconds to go. But moving a switch, the operator cut it, thereby costing CBA in lost revenue some $25,000. With another switch he put the "Special Bulletin" slide on the network video feed. Instantly the bright red words appeared on the screens of more than twelve million television sets.

For five seconds, as he watched a digital clock in front of him, the master control operator kept the audio feed silent. This was to allow control rooms of affiliate stations which had not been broadcasting the network program to interrupt their local programming and take the special bulletin. Most did.

At the end of five seconds the audio feed was opened and an announcer's voice heard.

"We interrupt our regular programming to bring you a special report from CBA News.

Now, from New York, here is correspondent Don Kettering."

In the news control room, the director ordered, "Cue Don!"

Across the nation, the face of CBA's business correspondent filled television screens.

His voice and expression serious, Kettering began, "Police in Larchmont, New York, have reported the apparent kidnapping of the wife, young son and father of CBA News anchorman Crawford Sloane."

A slide of Sloane's familiar face appeared as Kettering continued, "The kidnapping, by unidentified persons, occurred about forty minutes ago. According to police and a witness at the scene, it was preceded by a violent assault . . ."

The time was 11:56 A.M.

Beating out its competitors, CBA News had broken the story first.

PART
TWO

1

The aftereffects of CBA's special bulletin announcing the Sloane family kidnap were instantaneous and widespread.

NBC News, whose decent, courteous gesture of informing CBA had robbed it of a possible lead, followed with its own bulletin barely a minute later—ahead of its original plan to break the story at noon.

CBS, ABC and CNN, alerted by wire reports from AP and Reuters, were all on the air with the news within minutes. So were TV stations across the country not connected to a network, but with their own news services.

Canadian television also made the Sloane kidnapping the lead item on noon news broadcasts.

Radio stations, with their lightning immediacy, were even faster than television in spreading the story.

From coast to coast, afternoon newspapers at once began replating front pages with banner headlines. Major out-of-state papers instructed their New York correspondents to work on individual by-line stories.

News photo agencies began a frantic search for pictures of Jessica, Nicholas and Angus Sloane. There was no shortage of Crawford Sloane photos.

The main switchboard of CBA was flooded with calls for Crawford Sloane. When the callers were told politely that Mr. Sloane was not available, most left sympathetic messages.

The press and other media reporters, knowing better than to call a switchboard, used direct lines into CBA News. As a result, some telephones were constantly blocked, making outside communication difficult. Journalists who got through, wanting to interview Sloane, were advised that he was too distressed to talk with anyone and that, in any case, there was no more information than had already been broadcast.

One caller who did reach Sloane was the President of the United States.

"Crawf, I've just been told this awful news," the President said. "I know you have too much on your mind to talk right now, but I wanted you to know that Barbara and I are thinking about you and your family, and hoping for good news very soon. Like you, we want this ordeal to be over."

"Thank you, Mr. President," Sloane said. "That means a lot."

"I've given orders to the Justice Department," the President said, "that the FBI's search for your family is to have priority, and any other resources of government that are needed will be used."

Sloane repeated his thanks.

The substance of the President's call was immediately made public by a White House spokesman, adding to the growing flow of information which clearly would dominate the evening news broadcasts of all networks.

TV camera crews from New York stations and the networks reached Larchmont shortly after the initial bulletins, and interviewed—as an observer put it—"almost every breathing body in sight," including some with only a tenuous connection to the case. The ex-schoolteacher, Priscilla Rhea, blossoming under all the attention, proved to be the favorite interviewee, with the Larchmont police chief a close second.

A startling new development emerged when several people living near the Sloanes came forward with information that the Sloane house had apparently been under observation for several weeks, perhaps a month. A succession of different cars, and several times a truck, had been seen to arrive. They remained parked near the house for long periods, with whoever came in the vehicles remaining inconspicuously inside. Some makes of cars were mentioned, though detailed information was sketchy. There was agreement among the observers that sometimes the cars had New York license plates, at other times New Jersey's. No one, though, remembered numbers.

One of the cars described by a neighbor matched the description of that seen by the Sloanes' maid, Florence—the same car that followed Jessica Sloane's Volvo when Jessica, Nicky and Angus left to do the household shopping.

Press and TV interviewers asked the obvious question: Why had no one reported the apparent surveillance to the police?

In each case the answer was the same. It was assumed that some kind of security protection was being provided for the famous Mr. Crawford Sloane, and why would neighbors interfere with that?

Now, belatedly, information about the various vehicles was being sought by police.

Overseas media, too, were showing keen interest in the kidnap story. While the face and voice of Crawford Sloane were not as familiar to foreigners as to North Americans, the involvement of a major TV personality seemed of international consequence in itself.

This overwhelming reaction was proof that the modern network anchorman—species *Homo promulgare ancora,* as the next day's *Wall Street Journal* would dub it—had become a special breed, ranking in public idolization with kings and queens, movie and rock stars, popes, presidents and princes.

Crawford Sloane's mind was a turmoil of emotions.

He moved through the next several hours partly in a daze, half-expecting to learn at any moment that the entire episode was a misunderstanding, a readily explained mistake. But as time went by, with Jessica's Volvo still standing unclaimed in the Larchmont supermarket parking lot, this seemed increasingly less likely.

What troubled Sloane greatly was the memory of his conversation the preceding evening with Jessica. It was he who had brought up the possibility of kidnap, and it was not the coincidence which exercised him—he knew from long experience that real life and real news were full of coincidences, sometimes incredible ones. But, as he saw it at this moment, his own selfishness and self-importance made him assume that only he could be a kidnap victim. Jessica had even asked, *"What about families? Could they be targets too?"* But he had dismissed the idea, not believing it could happen or that Jessica and Nicky should be protected. Now, blaming himself for indifference and neglect, his sense of guilt was overwhelming.

He was greatly concerned, of course, about his father, though clearly Angus's inclusion in today's events was accidental. He had arrived unexpectedly and, unhappily, had been caught in the kidnappers' net.

At other moments during the day Sloane fretted impatiently, wanting to take some action, any action, yet knowing there was little he could do. He considered going to Larchmont, then realized he would gain nothing and would be out of touch if any fresh news broke. Another reason for staying put was the arrival of three FBI field agents who began a flurry of activity centering around Sloane.

Special Agent Otis Havelock, who was senior in the trio, at once demonstrated himself to be, in the words of an observing Horseshoe producer, "a take-charge guy." He insisted on being conducted directly to Crawford Sloane's office and there, after introducing himself to Sloane, demanded from his escort the presence of the head of the network's security force. Next, the FBI agent used a telephone to summon help from the New York City Police Department.

Havelock—small, dapper and balding—had deep-set green eyes and a direct gaze which seldom shifted from the person with whom he was conversing. His permanently suspicious expression appeared to say, *I've seen and heard it all before.* Later, Sloane and others would learn that the unspoken assertion was the truth. A twenty-year FBI veteran, Otis Havelock had spent the greater part of his life dealing with the worst of human infamies.

CBA's security chief, a grizzled retired New York police detective, arrived speedily. Havelock told him, "I want this entire floor secured immediately. The people who've taken Mr. Sloane's family may make an attempt on Mr. Sloane himself. Station two of your security guards at the elevators and post other guards at any stairways. They're to check, *carefully* check, the identity of all persons entering or leaving the floor. As soon as that's done, begin a thorough check of everyone who is on this floor already. Is that clear?"

The older man protested, "Sure it's clear, and we're all concerned for Mr. Sloane. But I don't have unlimited people and what you're asking is excessive. I have other security responsibilities I can't neglect."

"You've neglected them already," Havelock snapped. He produced a plastic identity card. "Look at this! I used it to get in this building.

Just showed it to the guard downstairs and he waved me past."

The security head peered at the card on which was a photo of a man in uniform. "Whose picture is that?"

"Ask Mr. Sloane." Havelock handed Crawford Sloane the card.

As Sloane glanced at it, despite his anxieties he burst out laughing. "It's Colonel Qaddafi."

"I had it specially made," the FBI man said. "I use it sometimes to prove to companies like this how lousy their security is." He told the crestfallen security chief, "Now get on with what I said. Secure this floor and tell your people to look at ID cards carefully, *including pictures.*"

When the other man had gone, Havelock told Sloane, "The reason security's bad in most big companies is because security's not a revenue-producing department; therefore budget people cut it to the bone. If you'd had proper security here, it would have included protection for you and your family at home."

Sloane said ruefully, "I wish you'd been around to suggest it."

A few minutes earlier, when Havelock phoned the New York Police Department, he had spoken with the chief of detectives, explaining that a kidnapping had taken place and asking for police protection of Crawford Sloane.

Now, from outside, the sound of several rapidly approaching sirens grew louder, then stopped. Minutes later a uniformed police lieutenant and a sergeant marched in.

"What I'd like you to do," Havelock told the lieutenant after introductions, "is keep a couple of radio cars outside to advertise police presence, also post an officer at every outside entrance, with one inside the main lobby. Tell your men to stop and question anyone suspicious."

The police lieutenant said, "Will do." To Crawford Sloane, he added almost reverently, "We'll take good care of you, sir. Whenever I'm home, my wife and I always watch you on the news. We like the way you do it."

Sloane nodded. "Thank you."

The policemen, looking around them, seemed inclined to linger, but Havelock had other ideas. "You can do a perimeter check by sending someone up to the roof. Take a look at the building from above. Make sure all exits are covered."

With assurances that everything possible would be done, the lieutenant and the sergeant left.

"You'll be seeing a lot of me, I'm afraid, Mr. Sloane," the special agent said when they were alone. "I've been ordered to stay close to you.

You heard me say that we think you could be a kidnap target too."

"I've sometimes thought I might be," Sloane said. Then, expressing the guilt that had been building in him, "It never occurred to me that my family could be in danger."

"That's because you were thinking rationally. But clever criminals are unpredictable."

Sloane asked nervously, "You think that's the kind of people we may be dealing with?"

The FBI man's expression did not change; he seldom wasted time with words of comfort. "We don't know yet what kind they are. But I've found it useful never to underestimate the enemy. Then if it turns out later that I overrated him, that's to my advantage."

Havelock continued, "Some more of our people will be moving in soon, here and at your home, with electronic gadgetry. We'll want to monitor your incoming phone calls, so while in this building you should take all calls on your regular line." He motioned to Sloane's desk. "If there's a call from the kidnappers, do the obvious thing—keep talking as long as possible, though nowadays calls can be traced much faster than they used to be, and criminals know that too."

"You realize our phones at home have unlisted numbers?"

"Yes, but I'm assuming the kidnappers have

those numbers. Quite a few people are bound to know them." Havelock produced a notebook. "Now, Mr. Sloane, I need answers to some questions."

"Go ahead."

"Have you, or members of your family, received any threats that you remember? Think carefully, please."

"I'm not aware of any."

"Is there anything you might have reported on the news which could have caused special antagonism on the part of someone, or some group?"

Sloane threw up his hands. "Once a day, at least."

The FBI man nodded. "I guessed that, so two of my colleagues will view tapes of your broadcasts, working backward through the past two years, to see if ideas suggest themselves. How about antagonistic mail? You must get some."

"I never see it. People in network news are shielded from the mail. It's a management decision."

Havelock's eyebrows went up as Sloane continued, "Everything we broadcast generates a phenomenal amount of mail. Reading all those letters would take too much time. Then we'd probably want to respond, which would take more time still. Something else management believes is that we're better able to keep our sense of perspective and fairness if protected from individual reactions to the news." Sloane shrugged. "Some may disagree, but that's the way it is."

"So what happens to the mail?"

"It's handled by a department called Audience Services. All letters are answered and anything judged important is sent to the News Division president."

"I presume all incoming mail is kept."

"I believe so."

Havelock made a note. "We'll assign people to go through that too."

During a pause, Chuck Insen knocked on the office door and came in.

"If I can interrupt . . ." As the other two nodded, the executive producer said, "Crawf, you know we all want to do the best we can—for you, for Jessica, Nicky . . ."

Sloane acknowledged, "Yes, I know."

"We feel you shouldn't do the news tonight. For one thing, it will be heavily *about* you. For another, even if you anchored the remainder, it would look too much like business as usual, almost as if the network wasn't caring, which of course isn't true."

Sloane considered, then said thoughtfully, "I suppose you're right."

"What we're wondering is if you'd feel up to being interviewed—live."

"Do you think I should?"

"Now that the story's out," Insen said, "I think the wider attention it gets, the better. There's always a chance that someone watching might come through with information."

"Then I'll do it."

Insen nodded, then continued, "You know the other networks and the press want to interview you. How do you feel about a press conference this afternoon?"

Sloane made a gesture of helplessness, then conceded, "All right, yes."

Insen asked, "When you're through here, Crawf, can you join Les and me in my office? We'd like your views about some other plans."

Havelock interjected, "As much as possible, I'd like Mr. Sloane to stay in his office and be close to this telephone."

"I'll be close to it anyway," Sloane assured him.

Leslie Chippingham had already telephoned Rita Abrams in Minnesota with the unhappy news that their planned lovers' weekend would have to be abandoned. There was no way, he explained, that in the midst of this breaking story he could leave New York.

Rita, while disappointed, was understanding. People in TV news were used to unexpected events disrupting their lives, even their illicit affairs.

She had asked, "Do you need me on the story?"

He told her, "If we do, you'll hear soon enough."

It appeared that Special Agent Havelock, having attached himself to Crawford Sloane, intended to follow the anchorman into the meeting in Insen's office. But Insen blocked his way.

"We're going to discuss some private network business. You can have Mr. Sloane again as soon as we've finished. In the meantime, if there's anything urgent, feel free to barge in."

"If it's all the same to you," Havelock said, "I'll barge in now and see where Mr. Sloane will be." He eased determinedly past Insen and surveyed the room inside.

Behind Insen's desk were two doors. Havelock opened both. One was to a supplies closet; after looking inside, he closed it. Another opened onto a toilet and washroom. The FBI man stepped inside, looked around, then came out.

"Just wanted to be sure," he told Insen, "that there was no other way in or out of here."

"I could have told you there wasn't," Insen said.

Havelock smiled thinly. "Some things I prefer to check myself." He left the office and found himself a chair outside.

Leslie Chippingham was already seated in the office when the FBI agent made his inspection. Now, as Sloane and Insen joined him, he said, "Chuck, you spell it out for Crawf."

"The fact is," Insen said, looking at Sloane directly, "we do not have confidence in government agencies and their ability to handle this situation. Now, Les and I don't want to depress you, but we all remember how long it took the FBI to find Patricia Hearst—more than a year and a half. And there's something else."

Insen reached among the papers on his desk and produced what Sloane recognized as a copy of his own book, *The Camera and the Truth.* Insen opened it at a page with a bookmark.

"You wrote, yourself, Crawf: 'We who live in the United States will not remain free from terrorism in our own backyard much longer. But neither mentally nor in other ways are we prepared for this pervasive, ruthless kind of warfare.' " Insen closed the book. "Les and I agree with that. Totally."

A silence followed. The reminder of his own words startled and shocked Sloane. In the privacy of his mind he had begun to wonder if some terrorist motive, perhaps relating to himself, could be behind the seizure of Jessica,

Nicky and his father. Or was the idea too pre-posterous even to consider? Seemingly not, as the thinking of the other experienced newsmen was obviously moving in that direction.

At length he said, "Do you seriously think that terrorists . . ."

Insen responded, "It's a possibility, isn't it?"

"Yes." Sloane nodded slowly in agreement. "I've begun wondering too."

"Remember," Chippingham put in, "that at this point we've no idea who the people are who have taken your family, or what they want. It could turn out to be a conventional kidnapping with demands for ransom money and, god knows, that's bad enough. But we're also con-sidering—because of who and what you are—other long-shot options."

Insen picked up the thread of what had been said earlier. "We mentioned the FBI. Again, we don't want to worry you, but if Jessica and the others are spirited out of this country in some way, which is a possibility, I'm afraid, then what government has to fall back on is the CIA. Well, in all the years that U.S. nationals have been prisoners in Lebanon, the CIA, with all its power and resources, spy satellites, intelligence and infiltration, has never been able to discover where a semiliterate, ragtag band of terrorists was holding them. And that in a tiny country only slightly larger than the state of Delaware.

So who can say if the same old CIA would do any better in other parts of the world?"

It was the news president who offered a conclusion.

"So that's what we mean, Crawf," Chippingham said, "by saying we don't have confidence in the government agencies. But what we do believe is that we ourselves—an experienced news organization accustomed to investigative reporting—have a better than average chance to discover where your family has been taken."

For the first time that day, Sloane's spirits rose.

Chippingham continued, "So what we've decided is to set up our own CBA News investigative task force. Our effort will be nationwide at first, then, if necessary, worldwide. We'll use all our resources plus investigative techniques that have worked in the past. As for people, we'll throw in the best talent we have, starting now."

Sloane felt a surge of gratitude and relief. He started to say, "Les . . . Chuck . . ."

Chippingham stopped him with a gesture. "Don't say it. There's no need. Of course, some of this is because of you, but also it's our business."

Insen leaned forward. "There's one thing we want to ask you at this point, Crawf. The task force needs to be headed by an experienced correspondent or producer, someone who can take charge, who's good at investigative reporting and in whom you have confidence. Is there anyone you'd like to name?"

Crawford Sloane hesitated for the briefest moment, weighing his personal feelings against what was at stake. Then he said firmly, "I want Harry Partridge."

2

The kidnappers, like foxes returning to a hidden burrow, had gone to ground in their temporary headquarters, the rented property south of Hackensack, New Jersey.

It was a collection of old, decaying structures—a main house and three outbuildings—which had been unused for several years until Miguel, after studying alternative locations and real estate advertisements, signed a one-year lease with full payment in advance. A year was the shortest rental period suggested by the agents. Miguel, not wishing to reveal that the place would be used for little more than a month, agreed to the terms without question.

The type of property and its location—a thinly occupied, run-down neighborhood—were ideal in numerous ways. The house was large, could accommodate all seven members of the Colombian gang, and its state of disrepair didn't matter. The outbuildings made it possible to keep six vehicles under cover and out of sight. No other occupied properties were close by, and privacy was aided by surrounding trees and other foliage. A further advantage was the nearness of Teterboro Airport, not much more than a mile away. Teterboro, used mainly by private aircraft, figured largely in the kidnappers' plans.

From the beginning of the conspiracy, Miguel foresaw that immediately after the victims' seizure a hue and cry would follow, with police roadblocks and intensive searches. He therefore decided that any immediate attempt to travel a long distance would be unsafe. On the other hand, there must be a temporary hideaway, well clear of the Larchmont area.

The Hackensack property was roughly twenty-five road miles from where the kidnapping had occurred. The ease with which they had returned here and the absence of pursuit proved that Miguel's planning had been effective—so far.

The three prisoners—Jessica, Nicholas and Angus Sloane—were now in the main house.

Still drugged and unconscious, they had been carried to a large room on the second floor. Unlike other rooms in the dilapidated, mildewed house, this one had been thoroughly cleaned and repainted in white. Additional electric outlets and overhead fluorescent lights had been installed. There was new pale-green linoleum on the floor. The ex-doctor, Baudelio, had specified and overseen the changes which were carried out by the group's handyman-mechanic, Rafael.

Two hospital cots with side restraining rails now stood in the center of the room. Jessica was on one, the boy, Nicholas, on the other. Their arms and legs were secured by straps—a precaution against their regaining consciousness, though for the time being that was not intended.

While anesthesiology was seldom an exact science, Baudelio was confident that his "patients"—as he now thought of them—would remain sedated for another half hour, perhaps longer.

Alongside the two cots was a narrow metal bed and mattress which had been hastily brought in and set up to accommodate Angus, whose presence had not been expected. As part of the improvisation, his limbs were secured with lengths of rope instead of straps. Even now, Miguel, watching from across the room, was unsure about what to do with the old man.

Should he be killed and his body buried outside after dark? Or should he somehow be included in the original plan? A decision had to be made soon.

Baudelio was working around the three recumbent forms, setting up intravenous stands, putting fluid bags in place. On a table covered with a green cotton cloth he had laid out instruments, drug packages and trays. Although intravenous catheters for entering veins through the skin were all that was likely to be needed, Baudelio had a long-established habit of having other equipment available for use in difficulty or emergencies. Assisting him was Socorro, the woman with ties to both the Medellín cartel and Sendero Luminoso; during her several undercover years in the United States she had qualified as a nursing aide.

With raven-dark hair twisted into a bun behind her head, Socorro had a slim, lithe body, olive skin, and features that might have been beautiful had she not worn a permanently sour expression. Although she did whatever was required of her and expected no favors because of her sex, Socorro seldom spoke and never revealed what went on within her mind. She had also rejected, with blunt profanity, sexual overtures from some of the men.

For these reasons Miguel had labeled Socorro mentally "the inscrutable one." While he was aware of her dual affiliation and that Sendero Luminoso had, in fact, insisted on Socorro's inclusion in the kidnap group, he had no reason to mistrust her. He occasionally wondered, though, if Socorro's long exposure to the American scene had diluted her Colombian and Peruvian loyalties.

The question was one Socorro herself would have had trouble answering.

On the one hand, she had always been a revolutionary, initially finding an outlet for her fervor with the Colombian M-19 guerrillas, then more recently—and profitably—with the Medellín cartel and Sendero Luminoso. Her conviction about the Colombian and Peruvian governments was that she wanted the villainous ruling class killed and would happily join the slaughter. At the same time she had been indoctrinated to consider the U.S. power structure as equally evil. Yet after three years of living in the United States and receiving friendly fairness where hostility and oppression would have been easier to handle, she found it difficult to continue despising and regarding as enemies America and its people.

Right now she was doing her best to hate these three captives—*rico bourgeois scum,* she assured herself—but not wholly succeeding . . . *damnably* not succeeding . . . because *pity,* in a revolutionary, was a *contemptible emotion!*

But once out of this perplexing country, as all of them would be very soon, Socorro was sure she could do better and be stronger, more consistent in her hatreds.

From a tilted-back chair on the far side of the room, Miguel said to Baudelio, "Tell me what it is you are doing." His tone made clear it was an order.

"I am working quickly because the midazolam I administered will very soon wear off. When it does, I shall begin injections of propofol, an intravenous anesthetic, a longer-acting drug than the earlier one and more suitable for what is ahead."

As he moved and spoke, Baudelio seemed transformed from his normal gaunt and ghostlike self to the teacher and practicing anesthesiologist he had once been. The same effect, a stirring of long-discarded dignity, had occurred shortly before the kidnap. But he showed no concern, then or now, that his skills were being criminally debased or that the circumstances he was sharing were despicable.

He continued, "Propofol is a tricky drug to use. The optimum dose for each individual varies, and if too much accumulates in the bloodstream death can result. So initially there must be experimental doses, closely monitored."

Miguel asked, "Are you sure you can handle it?"

"If you have doubts," Baudelio said sarcastically, "you are free to get someone else."

When Miguel failed to answer, the ex-doctor went on, "Because these people will be unconscious when we transport them, we must be certain there is no vomiting and aspiration into the lungs. Therefore while we are waiting there will be a period of enforced starvation. However, they must not become dehydrated, so I shall give them fluids intravenously. Then at the end of two days, which you tell me is the time I have, we shall be ready to put them into those." With his head, Baudelio gestured to the wall behind him.

Propped upright against the wall were two open funeral caskets, solidly constructed and silk-lined. One was smaller than the other. The ornamented hinged lids for both had been removed and stood alongside.

The caskets reminded Baudelio of a question. Pointing to Angus Sloane, he asked, "Do you want him prepared, or not?"

"If we take him, do you have the medical supplies to handle it?"

"Yes. There's a reserve of everything in case something goes wrong. But we'd need another . . ." His eyes returned to the caskets by the wall.

Miguel said irritably, "I do not need to be told that."

Still, he wondered. The original orders from Medellín and Sendero Luminoso specified abduction of the woman and the boy and then, as soon as possible afterward, their transfer to Peru. The caskets were to be a covert means of transportation; a phony cover story had been devised to forestall an exit search by U.S. Customs. Once in Peru the prisoners would become prize hostages—high-stakes bargaining chips against the fulfilment of unique demands by Sendero Luminoso, their nature yet to be disclosed. But would the unexpected addition of Crawford Sloane's father be regarded as an added prize or, at this point, a needless risk and burden?

If there had been some way to do so, Miguel would have sought an answer from his superiors. But the only secure communication channel was not open to him at that moment, and to telephone on one of the cellular phones would leave the record of a call. Miguel had been emphatic with everyone in the Hackensack operating group that the phones were solely for vehicle-to-vehicle or vehicle-to-headquarters use. Positively no calls were to be made to other numbers. The few outside calls that were necessary had been made from public pay phones.

Therefore the decision was his alone. He

must also consider that obtaining an extra casket meant taking additional risks. Was it worth
it?

Miguel reasoned that it was. From experience, he knew it was almost a certainty that
after Sendero Luminoso's ransom demands
were made known, one of the captives would
have to be killed and the body dumped where it
would be found—all to make the point that the
kidnappers were serious. Possession of Angus
Sloane would mean an extra body for that purpose, leaving either the woman or the boy to be
executed later if it became necessary to make
the same point twice. So in that sense the extra
captive was a bonus.

Miguel told Baudelio, "Yes, the old man
goes."

Baudelio nodded. Despite his outward assurance, he was nervous around Miguel today
because, the night before, Baudelio had committed what he now recognized as a serious mistake, a possible breach of everyone's security.
While he was alone, in a moment of profound
loneliness and dejection, he had used one of the
cellular phones to call Peru. It was a woman he
had spoken to, his slatternly live-in companion
and only friend, whose frequently drunken
companionship he sorely missed.

It was because of Baudelio's continuing anxiety about that call that he was slow to react

when suddenly, unexpectedly, a crisis confronted him.

Jessica, during the struggle outside the Larchmont supermarket, had had only a minute or two, first of shock, then horror, to grasp the enormity of what was happening. Even after her screams had been silenced by the gag slapped over her mouth, she continued to struggle fiercely and desperately, aware that Nicky, too, had been seized by the unknown brutes around them and that Angus had been savagely struck down. But moments later, as the strong injected sedative circulated through her bloodstream, blackness supervened and she fell into deep unconsciousness.

But now, without knowing how long it had lasted, she was reviving, her memory returning. She became aware, dimly at first and then more clearly, of sounds around her. She tried to move, to speak, but found she could do neither. When she transferred the effort to her eyes, they would not open.

It was as if she were at the bottom of a well of darkness, attempting to do *something, anything,* but able to do nothing.

Then, as more moments passed, the voices became clearer, the awful memory of events at Larchmont sharpened.

At last Jessica's eyes opened.

Baudelio, Socorro and Miguel were all looking elsewhere and failed to see it happen.

Jessica was aware of feeling coming back into her body but could not understand why her arms and legs wouldn't move, except for the smallest distance. Then she saw that her nearer arm, the left, was constricted by a strap and realized she was on what looked like a hospital bed, and that her other arm and both legs were restricted in the same way.

She turned her head slightly and froze in horror at what she saw.

Nicky was on another bed, imprisoned like herself. Beyond him Angus, too, was tied down with ropes. And then—*Oh, no! Oh, god!*—she glimpsed the two open funeral caskets, one smaller than the other, clearly intended for herself and Nicky.

In a single instant she began to scream and struggle wildly. Somehow, in her demented terror, she managed to get her left arm free.

Hearing the scream, the three conspirators swung toward her. For a moment Baudelio, who should have taken instant action, was too startled to move. By then Jessica had seen them all.

Still struggling wildly, she reached out with her left hand, trying desperately to find something to use as a weapon to protect herself and Nicky. The table of instruments was beside her.

As her fingers groped frantically, she seized what felt like a kitchen paring knife. It was a scalpel.

Now Baudelio, having collected his wits, raced toward her. Seeing Jessica's free arm, he tried to refasten it with Socorro's help.

But Jessica was faster. In her desperation she reached out with the metal object, slashing wildly, managing to gash Baudelio's face, then Socorro's hand. At first, thin red lines appeared on both. A moment later blood gushed out.

Baudelio ignored the pain and tried to secure that flailing arm. Miguel, hurrying forward, hit Jessica savagely with his fist, then helped Baudelio. With Baudelio's wound dripping blood onto Jessica and the cot, they managed to re-strap Jessica's arm.

Miguel retrieved the scalpel. Though Jessica still struggled, it was to no avail. Defeated and helpless, she broke down in tears.

Then, another complication. Nicky's sedation was also wearing off. Becoming aware of the shouting, and of his mother nearby, he returned to consciousness more quickly. He too began screaming, but despite his struggles couldn't free himself from the restraining straps.

Angus, who had been sedated later than the other two, did not stir.

By now the noise and confusion were over-

whelming, but Baudelio and Socorro both knew
their own wounds had to be treated ahead of
anything else. Socorro, with the lesser injury,
put a temporary adhesive dressing on her own
cut hand, then turned to aid Baudelio. She
taped gauze pads over his face, though they
were quickly soaked with blood.

Recovering from initial shock, he nodded an
acknowledgment, then pointed to the assembled
equipment and murmured, "Help me."

Socorro tightened the strap above Jessica's
left elbow. Then Baudelio inserted a hypodermic needle into a vein and injected the propofol
he had prepared earlier. Jessica, watching and
screaming, fought against the drug's effect until
her eyes closed and once more she was unconscious.

Baudelio and Socorro moved on to Nicky
and repeated the process. He, too, stopped his
painful cries and slumped back, his brief period
of awareness ended.

Then, rather than take a chance on the old
man regaining consciousness and causing trouble, Angus was also given propofol.

Miguel, while not interfering in the latter
stages, had been glowering. Now he accused
Baudelio, "You incompetent asshole!" Eyes
blazing, he stormed on, "*¡Pinche cabrón!* You
could ruin everything! Do you *know* what you
are doing?"

"Yes, I know," Baudelio said. Despite the gauze pads, blood was streaming down his face. "I made an error of judgment. I promise it will not happen again."

Without replying, his face flushed with anger, Miguel stalked out.

When he had gone, Baudelio used a portable mirror to inspect his bloody wound. Immediately he knew two things. First, he would carry a scar, running the full length of his face, for the remainder of his life. Second, and more important, the gaping, open cut needed to be closed and sutured at once. In present circumstances he could not go to a hospital or another doctor. Baudelio knew there was no other choice than to do it himself, however difficult and painful that might be. As best she could, Socorro would have to help.

During his early medical training, Baudelio, like any student, had learned to suture minor wounds. Later, as an anesthesiologist, he watched hundreds of incisions being stitched. Then, while working for the Medellín cartel, he had done some wound repairs himself and knew the procedures needed now.

Feeling weak, he sat himself in front of the mirror and told Socorro to bring his regular medical bag. From it he selected surgical needles, silk thread and a local anesthetic, lidocaine.

He explained to Socorro what, between them, they would do. As usual, she said little except an occasional *"¡Sí!"* or *"¡está bien!"* Then, without further discussion, Baudelio began to inject lidocaine along the margins of his wound.

The whole procedure took almost two hours and, despite the local anesthetic, the pain was excruciating. Several times Baudelio came close to fainting. His hand shook frequently, which made the sutures uneven. Adding to his difficulties was the awkward, reverse effect of working with a mirror. Socorro passed him what he asked for and, once or twice when he was near collapse, supported him. In the end he managed to hold on and, though some clumsy sutures meant the residual scar would be worse than he had at first supposed, the gap in his cheek was closed and he knew the wound would heal.

Finally, knowing the most difficult part of his Medellín/Sendero assignment was still ahead and that he needed rest, Baudelio took two hundred milligrams of Seconal and slept.

3

At about 11:50 A.M., in the apartment at Port Credit, Harry Partridge had switched the living room TV to a Buffalo, New York, station—a CBA affiliate. All Buffalo TV stations, whose signals had only to travel an unobstructed sixty miles across Lake Ontario, were received clearly in the Toronto area.

Vivien had gone out and would not be back until midafternoon.

Partridge hoped to learn, from the noon news, the latest developments following yesterday's Muskegon Airlines disaster at Dallas–Fort Worth. Consequently at 11:55, when programming was interrupted by the CBA News Special Bulletin, Partridge was watching.

He was as shocked and horrified as everyone else. Could it really be true, he wondered, or just some incredible snafu? But experience told him that CBA News would not have put out a bulletin without satisfying itself of the story's authenticity.

As he watched Don Kettering's face on the

screen and heard the continuing report, he felt, more than anything, a personal concern for Jessica. And mixed with his emotions was a surge of camaraderie and pity for Crawford Sloane.

Partridge also knew, without even thinking about it, that his vacation, which had scarcely begun, was already over.

It was no surprise, then, to receive a phone call some forty-five minutes later, asking him to come to CBA News headquarters in New York. What did surprise him was that it was a personal appeal from Crawford Sloane.

Sloane's voice, Partridge discerned, was barely under control. After the preliminaries, Sloane said, "I desperately need you, Harry. Les and Chuck are setting up a special unit; it will work on two levels—daily reports on air and deep investigation. They asked me who I wanted in charge. I told them there's only one choice—you."

In all the years that he and Sloane had known each other, Partridge realized they had never been closer than at this moment. He responded, "Hang in there, Crawf. I'll be on the next flight."

"Thank you, Harry. Is there anyone you especially want to work with?

"Yes. Find Rita Abrams, wherever she is— in Minnesota somewhere—and bring her in. The same for Minh Van Canh."

"If they're not waiting when you get here, they'll be with you soon after. Anyone else?"

Thinking quickly, Partridge said, "I want Teddy Cooper from London."

"Cooper?" Sloane sounded puzzled, then remembered. "He's our bureau researcher, isn't he?"

"Right."

Teddy Cooper was an Englishman, a twenty-five-year-old product of what the British snobbishly called a red-brick university, and a cheerful Cockney who might have auditioned successfully for *Me and My Girl.* He was also, in Partridge's opinion, a near-genius at turning ordinary research into detective work and following it up with shrewd deductions.

While working in Europe, Partridge had discovered Cooper, who at the time held a minor librarian's job at the British Broadcasting Corporation. Partridge had been impressed with some inventive research work that Cooper had done for him. Later he was instrumental in having Cooper employed, with more money and better prospects, by CBA's London bureau.

"You've got him," Sloane replied. "He'll be on the next *Concorde* out of England."

"If you feel up to it," Partridge said, "I'd like to ask some questions, so I have something to think about on the way down."

"Of course. Go ahead."

What followed was a near-replay of queries already put by FBI agent Havelock. Had there been threats? . . . Any special antagonism? . . . Unusual experiences? . . . Was there any notion, even the wildest, as to who . . . ? Was there anything known that had not been broadcast?

The asking was necessary, but the answers were all negative.

"Is there anything at all you can think of," Partridge persisted, "some little incident, perhaps, which you may have dismissed at the time or even hardly noticed, but which might relate to what has happened?"

"The answer's no at the moment," Sloane said. "But I'll think about it."

After they hung up, Partridge resumed his own preparations. Even before Sloane's call he had begun packing a suitcase that only an hour earlier he had unpacked.

He telephoned Air Canada, making a reservation on a flight leaving Toronto's Pearson International at 2:45 P.M. It was due into New York's La Guardia Airport at 4 P.M. Next, he called for a taxi to collect him in twenty minutes.

After his packing was finished, Partridge scribbled a goodbye note to Vivien. He knew she would be disappointed at his abrupt departure, as he was himself. Along with the note he left a generous check to cover the apartment refurbishing they had discussed.

As he looked around for a place to leave the note and check, a buzzer sounded in the apartment. It was the intercom from the lobby below. The taxi he ordered had arrived.

The last thing he saw before leaving was, on a sideboard, the tickets for the next day's Mozart concert. He reflected sadly that those—as well as other unused tickets and invitations in the past—represented, more than anything else, the uncertain pattern of a TV newsman's life.

The Air Canada flight was non-stop, a 727 with all-economy seating. A light passenger load enabled Partridge to have a three-seat section to himself. He had assured Sloane that he would apply his mind to the kidnapping while en route to New York and had intended to begin planning the direction he and the CBA News investigative group should take. But the information he had was sketchy, and obviously he needed more. So after a while he gave up and, sipping a vodka-tonic, allowed his thoughts to drift.

He considered, on a personal level, Jessica and himself.

Over the years since Vietnam he had grown accustomed to regarding Jessica as belonging only in the past, as someone he had once loved but who was no longer relevant to him and in any case far beyond his reach. To an extent, Partridge realized, his thinking had been an act of self-discipline, a safeguard against feeling sorry for himself, self-pity being something he abhorred.

But now, because Jessica was in danger, he admitted to himself that he cared as much about her as ever, and always had. *Face it, you're still in love with her. Yes I am.* And not with some shadowy memory, but with a person who was living, vital, real.

So whatever his role was to be in searching for Jessica—and Crawf himself had asked that it be a major one—Harry Partridge knew that his love for Jessica would drive and sustain him, even though he would hold that love secret, burning out of sight within himself.

Then, with what he recognized as a characteristic touch of quirky humor, he asked himself, *Am I being disloyal?*

Disloyal to whom? Of course, to Gemma who was dead.

Ah, dearest Gemma! Earlier today, when he had remembered the one exception to his apparent inability to cry, he had almost let memories about her crowd in. But he had pushed them away as being more than he could handle. But now thoughts of Gemma were flooding back. *She will always come back,* he thought.

A few years after his duty tour in Vietnam and some other hard-living assignments, CBA News sent Partridge to be resident correspondent in Rome. He remained there almost five years.

Among all television networks, an assignment to a Rome bureau was considered a plum. The standard of living was high, living costs modest by comparison with big cities elsewhere, and though pressures and tensions were inevitably transmitted from New York, the local pace of life was leisurely and easy.

As well as reporting on area stories and sometimes roving far afield, Partridge covered the Vatican. Also, several times he traveled on papal airplanes, accompanying Pope John Paul II on the pontiff's international peregrinations.

It was on one of those papal journeys he met Gemma.

Partridge was often amused at the assumption by outsiders that a papal air journey was an exercise in decorum and restraint. In fact, it wasn't. In particular, in the press section at the rear of the airplane the reverse was true. Invariably there was much partying and drinking—the liquor unlimited and free—and during long overnight flights, sexual dalliance was not unknown.

Partridge once heard the papal airplane described by a fellow correspondent as having different levels, ranging—as in Dante's Inferno—*all the way from hell to heaven. (While there was never any permanent aircraft earmarked for the Pope's flights, the special interior configuration for each journey was usually the same.)*

At the front of the airplane on every trip was a spacious cabin outfitted for the Pope. It contained a bed and two large comfortable seats, sometimes three.

The next section back was for senior members of the Pope's entourage—his Secretary of State, some cardinals, the Pope's doctor, secretary and valet. Then, behind another divider was a cabin for bishops and lower-ranking priests.

In between one of the forward cabins, and depending on the type of airplane was an open space where all the gifts the Pope received on his journey were stored. It was inevitably a large, rich pile.

Finally there was the last cabin in the plane —for journalists. The seat configuration here was tourist, but with first-class service, many flight attendants, and superb food and wine. There were generous gifts for journalists too, usually from the airline involved which, more often than not, was Alitalia. Airlines, astute in public relations, recognized a chance for good publicity when they saw one.

As to the journalists themselves, they were an average group from their profession, an international mixture of newspaper, television and radio reporters, the television people accompanied by technical crews—all with normal interests, normal skepticism, and a penchant at times for irreverent behavior.

While no TV network would ever admit it openly, they privately preferred that correspondents reporting on religious subjects, such as a papal journey, not be committed deeply to any faith. A religious adherent, they feared, would send in cloying reports. A healthy skepticism was preferred.

In that regard, Harry Partridge filled the bill.

Some seven years after his own experiences on papal flights, Partridge greatly admired a 1987 TV news report by ABC's Judd Rose who was covering a visit by Pope John Paul II to Los Angeles. Rose successfully trod a hairline between hard news and pyrrhonism with his commentary.

For the media capital that is Hollywood, it's a media event that's heaven-sent. All the pomp of a royal wedding, all the hype of a Super Bowl— all this with a cast of thousands and a star straight from central casting . . . Space age technology and dramatic imagery—it's the sort of thing John Paul favors and the camera loves.

[The Pope is] carefully crafted and controlled. He speaks out often but is seldom spoken to. The only time reporters can ask questions is in brief sessions on his plane when he travels . . . Media coverage has been exhaustive. The papal trip has become an electronic extravaganza like Live Aid or Liberty Weekend, and some Catholics wonder if anyone will know the difference.

Theology and technology—it's a powerful union and John Paul's using it to preach his message as no Pope before him ever could. The world is watching, but the real test of the great communicator is whether we're listening too.

Rose was absolutely right, Partridge reminisced, about that brief opportunity to ask the Pope questions aboard the papal airplane. In fact, if it had not been for one short question-and-answer exchange, what developed between himself and Gemma might never have . . .

It was one of Pope John Paul's longer journeys—to nearly a dozen countries in Central America and the Caribbean, and was on an Alitalia DC-10. There had been an overnight flight and early the next morning, about two hours before a scheduled landing, the Pope appeared unannounced in the rear press section. He was in everyday attire—a white cassock, a zucchetto on his head, and on his feet, brown loafers—which was normal, except when specially dressed for a papal mass.

He stopped near Harry Partridge, appearing pensive. Within the press cabin, TV camera lights were coming on; several reporters had tape recorders running.

Partridge stood and, hoping to ease into a reportable conversation, inquired politely, "Your Holiness, did you sleep well?"

The Pope smiled and answered, "Very few."

Puzzled, Partridge asked, "Very few, your Holiness. Very few hours?"

There was no answer, only a slight shake of the head. While John Paul was an accomplished linguist in several languages, sometimes his English was solecistic. Partridge could have conversed adequately in Italian, but wanted the Pope's words in the language of CBA viewers.

He decided to try a more newsworthy question. For several weeks there had been discussion and controversy about a possible papal visit to the Soviet Union. "Your Holiness," Partridge asked, "do you want to go to Russia?"

This time there was a clear, "Yes." Then the Pope added, "The Poles, the Russians, they are all slaves. But they are all my people."

Before anything else could be said, the Pope

turned and walked away, returning to his private quarters in the airplane.

Among the reporters there was an instant hum, in several languages, of questioning and speculation. The Alitalia flight attendants, who had been preparing breakfast, had stopped work and were listening intently. Someone in the press group asked, "Did you hear what he said— slaves!"

Partridge glanced at his own cameraman and sound man. Both nodded. The sound man said, "We got it."

Somebody else was playing back a tape recording. The word "slaves" was heard distinctly.

A reporter from a British news syndicate said doubtfully, "He meant 'Slavs.' He's a Slav himself. It figures."

" 'Slaves' makes a helluva better story," another voice rejoined.

And so it did. Partridge knew it too. A literal reporting of the "slaves" description would arouse worldwide interest and discussion, perhaps create an international incident, with accusations and exchanges between the Kremlin, Warsaw and the Vatican. There could be embarrassment for the Pope, marring his triumphal journey.

Partridge was one of the older, more experienced hands aboard and was respected by his colleagues. Some of the others looked to him for a lead.

He considered briefly. It was a lively story, something seldom encountered on a papal trip. There might not be another. His inclination, as a skeptic, was to use it. And yet . . . skepticism did not override ordinary decency; and for some in the business, journalistic ethics did exist.

Making up his mind, Partridge said clearly, so that everyone could hear. "He meant 'Slavs.' It's obvious that he did. I'm not going to use it."

There was no discussion, no spoken consensus or agreement, but afterward it became clear that no one else used the incident either.

As the reporters and technical crews returned to their seats, the Alitalia flight attendants resumed work.

When Partridge's breakfast tray came, it contained something extra, not served to the others—a small glass vase containing a single rose.

He looked up at the young stewardess who, smiling, in her smartly tailored green and black uniform, had brought the tray. He had noticed her several times before and heard other flight attendants call her Gemma. But now he was unexpectedly breathless at her closeness and, for an instant, tongue-tied.

Forever after, especially at times of terrible loneliness, he remembered Gemma as she was at that magic moment—age twenty-three, beauti-

ful, with long, dark, lustrous hair, brown and sparkling eyes, and joyous with life like a fragrant morning flower in fresh spring air on a green and sunlit hillside.

With unaccustomed awkwardness, he pointed to the rose. Later he would learn that she had gone forward and purloined it from the Pope's own cabin. Now he asked, "Why this for me?"

She smiled down at him and, with a soft Italian accent, said, "I brought it because you are a good, sweet man. I like you."

Even to himself his answer seemed inadequate and banal. "I like you, too."

But banal or not, in those few moments his great and lasting love for Gemma had begun.

Partridge drew his thoughts back to the present shortly before the Air Canada flight landed in New York. He was first off the airplane and strode quickly through La Guardia terminal. With only hand baggage, he was able to leave the airport without delay, taking a taxi to CBA News headquarters.

He headed for Chuck Insen's office, but found it unoccupied. A senior producer at the Horseshoe called across, "Hi, Harry! Chuck's at a press conference that's been arranged for Crawf. The whole thing's being taped. You'll be able to see it."

Then, as Partridge walked toward the Horseshoe, the producer added, "Oh, in case no one's told you, Crawf's on the sidelines tonight. You'll be anchoring the news."

4

That evening, in the Medellín gang's hideaway at Hackensack, Miguel kept a radio tuned to an all-news station. With several of the others, he also watched a portable television, switching between news programs, all featuring reports on the Sloane family kidnap.

Despite the intense interest and speculation, it was evident that nothing had been learned so far about the kidnappers' identities or motivations. Nor did law enforcement authorities know the escape route taken or of any specific areas where the kidnappers and their victims might have gone to ground. Some reports suggested that by now they could be many miles from New York. Others revealed that suspicious vehicles had been stopped and detained at roadblocks as far away as Ohio, Virginia and the Canadian border. Several criminal arrests had resulted from the police activity, but none was connected to the Sloanes.

Descriptions of a Nissan passenger van believed to have been used by the kidnappers were still circulating. It meant that the van abandoned by Carlos at White Plains had not been found. Carlos had returned safely to the Hackensack house hours ago.

Among Miguel and the others there was a sense of relief, though everyone knew that police forces all over North America were looking for them and their safety was only temporary. Because of the dangers still ahead, Miguel had established a guard roster. Even now Luís and Julio were patrolling outside with Beretta submachine guns, trying to stay in the shadows of the house and outbuildings.

Miguel knew that if their hideaway was discovered and the police moved in in force, there was little chance of any of them getting away. In that event, his original orders were clear: Neither of the kidnap victims was to be taken back alive. Now, the only thing that had changed was that the order applied to three instead of two.

Of the various TV news broadcasts Miguel watched, the one that interested him most was the National Evening News from CBA. It amused him that Crawford Sloane was not in his usual anchor position; the substitute was someone named Partridge whom Miguel remembered vaguely seeing before. Sloane, however, was interviewed on air and shown at a previously recorded press conference.

The press conference had been well attended by print, television and radio reporters, along with camera and sound crews. It was held in another CBA building, a block away from news headquarters. On a sound stage, folding chairs had been hastily set up; all were occupied, with many participants standing.

There were no formal introductions and Crawford Sloane began with a brief statement. He expressed his shock and anxiety, then appealed to the news media and the public for any information which might help disclose where his wife, son and father had been taken, and by whom. He announced that a CBA phone center with a WATS line number had been set up to receive information. The center was already staffed by operators and a supervisor.

A voice injected, "You'll be swamped with crank calls."

Sloane responded, "We'll take our chances. All we need is one solid piece of knowledge. Someone, somewhere, has it."

Twice during his statement Sloane had to pause to control emotion in his voice. Each time there was a sympathetic silence. A *Los Angeles*

Times report next day described him as "dignified and impressive in agonizing circumstances."

Sloane announced that he would answer
questions.

At first the questioning was also sympathetic. But then, inevitably, some in the press
corps weighed in with tougher queries.

An Associated Press woman reporter asked,
"Do you think it's possible, as some are already
speculating, that your family may have been
seized by foreign terrorists?"

Sloane shook his head. "It's too early even
to think about that."

AP objected, "You're ducking the question.
I asked if you thought it *possible.*"

Sloane conceded, "I suppose it's possible."

Someone from a local TV station asked the
perennial question, "How do you feel about
that?"

Someone else groaned and Sloane wanted to
answer, *How the hell would you feel?* Instead he
replied, "Obviously, I hope it isn't true."

A gray-haired former CBA correspondent,
now with CNN, held up a copy of Sloane's
book. "Do you continue to believe, as you wrote
here, that 'hostages should be expendable,' and
are you still opposed to paying ransom—as you
put it, 'directly or indirectly, ever'?"

Sloane had anticipated the question and answered, "I don't believe that anyone as emotionally involved as I am at this moment can be objective about that."

"Oh, come on, Crawf," the CNN man persisted. "If you were standing here instead of me, you wouldn't let anyone get away with that. I'll put the question another way: Do you regret having written those words?"

"At this moment," Sloane said, "I find myself wishing they weren't being quoted against me."

Another voice called out, "They're not being used against you and that's still no answer."

A woman reporter from an ABC magazine program raised her penetrating voice. "I'm sure you're aware that your statement about American hostages being expendable caused a great deal of distress to families who have relatives still imprisoned in the Middle East. Do you have more sympathy for those families now?"

"I've always had sympathy," Sloane said, "but right now I probably have a better understanding of those people's anguish."

"Are you telling us that what you wrote was wrong?"

"No," he said quietly, "I'm not saying that."

"So if a ransom is demanded, you'll say adamantly no?"

He raised his hands helplessly. "You're asking me to speculate on something that hasn't occurred. I won't do that."

While not enjoying what was happening, Sloane acknowledged mentally that at plenty of press conferences in the past he had played hardball as an interrogator himself.

An offbeat query came from *Newsday*. "Not much is known about your son Nicholas, Mr. Sloane."

"That's because we keep our family life private. In fact, my wife insists on it."

"It isn't private anymore," the reporter pointed out. "One thing I've been told is that Nicholas is a talented musician and might become a concert pianist one day. Is that true?"

Sloane knew that in other circumstances Jessica would object to the question as an intrusion. At this moment, though, he didn't see how he could avoid answering it.

"Our son does love music, always has, and his teachers say he's advanced for his age. As to his being a concert pianist or anything else, only time will tell."

At length, when the questions seemed to be winding down, Leslie Chippingham stepped forward and declared the session at an end.

Sloane was immediately surrounded by some who wanted to shake his hand and wish him well. Then, as quickly as he could, he slipped away.

Miguel, having seen all the news he wanted, switched the television off and considered carefully what he had learned.

First, neither the Medellín cartel nor Sendero Luminoso was suspected of involvement in the kidnappings. At this point, that was helpful. Second, and equally helpful, was the fact that no descriptions existed of himself or the other six conspirators. If the authorities had somehow obtained descriptions, almost certainly they would have been made public by now.

All of which, Miguel reasoned, made slightly less dangerous what he proposed to do next.

He needed more money and, to get it, he must telephone tonight and arrange a meeting at, or near, the United Nations tomorrow.

From the beginning, getting sufficient money into the United States had been a problem. Sendero Luminoso, which was financing this operation, had plenty of money in Peru. The difficulty was in circumventing Peru's exchange control laws and transferring hard currency in U.S. dollars to New York, at the same time keeping the movement of money—its source, routing and destination—secret.

It had been done ingeniously, with help from a revolutionary sympathizer, a Sendero ally highly placed inside the Lima, Peru, banking system. His accomplice in New York was a Peruvian diplomat, a senior aide to Peru's ambassador to the United Nations.

The amount of operating funds allocated during planning by Sendero and Medellín was $850,000. This included payments to personnel, their transportation and living expenses, leasing a secret headquarters, the purchase of six vehicles, medical supplies, the funeral caskets, payments in the Little Colombia district of Queens for covert aid and firearms, commissions in Peru and New York on money transfers, plus bribes to an American woman banker. There would also be the cost of flying the captives by private aircraft from the U.S. to Peru.

Almost all the money spent in New York had been drawn in cash by Miguel, through the United Nations source.

The way it worked was that the Lima banker surreptitiously converted the funds entrusted to him by Sendero Luminoso into U.S. dollars, $50,000 at a time. He then made transfers to a New York bank at Dag Hammarskjöld Plaza near United Nations headquarters, where the money was placed in a special sub-account of the Peruvian UN delegation. The account's existence was known only to José Antonio Salaverry, the UN Ambassador's trusted aide, who had authority to sign checks, and to the bank's assistant manager, Helga Efferen. The woman banker personally took care of the special account.

José Antonio Salaverry was another secret supporter of Sendero, though not above taking a commission on the transferred funds. Helga was sleeping regularly with the duplicitous Salaverry and both were living a lavish New York lifestyle beyond their means, partying and keeping up with the free-spending United Nations diplomatic crowd. For that reason the extra money they made by secretly channeling the incoming funds was warmly welcomed.

Whenever Miguel had needed money he telephoned Salaverry and stated the amount. A meeting was then arranged for a day or two later, usually at UN headquarters, occasionally elsewhere. In the meantime Salaverry would obtain a briefcase full of cash. Miguel would walk away with it.

Only one thing bothered Miguel. On one occasion, Salaverry let slip that while not knowing the money's specific purpose or where Miguel and the others from Medellín were hiding out, he had a pretty good idea of their objective. This, Miguel realized, could only mean there had been a security leak in Peru. At this point there was nothing he could do, but it made him wary of contacts with José Antonio Salaverry.

Miguel glanced at the cellular phone beside

him. For a moment he was tempted to use it, but knew he shouldn't and must go out. In a café eight blocks away was a pay phone he had used before. He checked his watch: 7:10 P.M. With luck, Salaverry would be in his mid-Manhattan apartment.

Miguel put on a topcoat and walked quickly, keeping a lookout for any sign of unusual activity in the area. There was none.

During the walk he thought again about the televised press conference with Crawford Sloane. Miguel had been interested in the reference to a book by Sloane which apparently included statements about never paying ransom and that "hostages should be expendable." Miguel hadn't known about the book nor, he was sure, had others in the Medellín cartel or Sendero Luminoso. He doubted, though, if the knowledge would have affected the decision to abduct Sloane's family; what someone wrote for publication and what they felt and did in private were often different. But either way, it made no difference now.

Something else of interest coming out of the press conference was the description of the *mocoso* Sloane brat as a possible concert pianist. Without any clear notion of how he might use it, Miguel tucked the nugget of information away.

When he reached the café Miguel could see

that only a few people were inside. Entering, he headed for the phone, which was at the rear, and dialed a number he had memorized. After three rings Salaverry answered. "'Allo," he said with a strong Spanish accent.

Miguel tapped three times on the phone mouthpiece with a fingernail, a signal that identified him. Then he said, keeping his voice low, "Tomorrow morning. Fifty cases." A "case" was a thousand dollars.

He heard a quick gasp at the other end. The voice which came back sounded frightened. "*¿Estás loco?,* phoning here tonight? Where are you? Can this call be traced?"

Miguel said contemptuously, "Do you think I am a *pendejo?*" At the same time he realized that Salaverry had connected him with today's events; therefore meeting him would be dangerous. Still, there was no alternative. He needed cash to purchase—among other things—the additional casket for Angus Sloane. Also, Miguel knew there was plenty left in the New York account and wanted some extra money for himself before leaving the country. He was certain that more than just commissions had stuck to José Antonio Salaverry's grubby fingers.

"We cannot meet tomorrow," Salaverry said. "It is too soon, and too short notice for the money. You must not . . ."

"*¡Cállate!* Do not waste my time." Miguel

gripped the phone tightly, controlling his anger, still speaking softly so others in the café would not hear. "I am giving you an order. Get the fifty cases early. I will come to you in the usual way, shortly before noon. If you fail, you know how furious our mutual friends will be, and their arm has a long reach."

"No, no! There is no need for their concern." There was a hasty, conciliatory change in Salaverry's voice. A threat of vengeance by the infamous Medellín cartel was not to be taken lightly. "I will do my best."

Miguel said curtly, "Do better than that. I will see you tomorrow." He hung up the phone and left the café.

Inside the Hackensack hideaway the three captives remained sedated under Socorro's watchful guard. Throughout the night she administered additional dosages of propofol as Baudelio had instructed; she monitored vital signs and kept a record. Shortly before daylight Baudelio awakened from his own sedated sleep. After studying Socorro's medical log he nodded approval, then relieved her.

In the early morning Miguel, who had slept only fitfully, watched TV news again. The Sloane kidnapping was still the top item, though there were no reports of new leads.

Soon after, Miguel informed Luís that at

eleven o'clock the two of them would be driving into Manhattan in the hearse.

The hearse was the group's sixth vehicle, a Cadillac in good condition, bought secondhand. So far they had only used it twice. The remainder of the time the hearse had stayed out of sight at the Hackensack house, where it was referred to by the others as *el angel negro,* the black angel. The vehicle's inside floor, where a casket normally rested, was of handsome rosewood; built-in rubber rollers ensured that a casket's passage would be smooth. Interior sides and roof were lined with dark blue velvet.

Miguel had originally planned to use the hearse only as a final means of transportation before the air journey to Peru, but now, clearly, it was their safest vehicle. The cars and the GMC truck had had too much exposure, especially during the Larchmont surveillance, and it was possible that descriptions of them had by this time been given to police and circulated.

The weather had changed to pouring rain, with fiercely blowing gusts, the sky a sullen gray.

With Luís driving, they took a circuitous route from Hackensack, several times changing direction and twice stopping to be sure they were not followed. Luís handled the hearse with extra care because of slick roads and poor forward visibility beyond the monotonously slapping windshield wipers. Having gone south on the New Jersey side of the Hudson River as far as Weehawken, they entered the Lincoln Tunnel and emerged in Manhattan at 11:45 A.M.

Both Miguel and Luís were wearing dark suits and ties, appropriate to their presence in a hearse.

After leaving the tunnel they headed east on Fortieth Street. The heavy rain made for bumper-to-bumper crosstown traffic and painfully slow progress. Miguel watched pedestrians moving slowly and uncomfortably on crowded sidewalks.

The paradox of riding through New York City in a hearse amused him. On one hand the vehicle was far too conspicuous for their purpose; on the other it commanded respect. At a previous intersection, a uniformed traffic agent —a "brownie," as New Yorkers called them— had even stopped other vehicles and waved them by.

Miguel also noticed that many people who glanced at the hearse immediately looked away. He had observed the same thing before and wondered: Was it the reminder of death, the great oblivion, that disturbed them? He had never feared his own death, though he had no intention of making it easy for others to hasten its arrival.

But whatever the reason, it didn't matter. What did was that no one in the crowds around them was likely to consider that this particular hearse, so close that they could touch it, contained two of the most sought-after criminals in the country, perpetrators of a crime that was the nation's hottest news story. The thought intrigued Miguel. It was also reassuring.

They turned north onto Third Avenue, and a little short of Forty-fourth Street Luís pulled over to the curb and let Miguel out. Turning his collar up against the driving rain, Miguel walked the last two blocks east to United Nations headquarters. Despite his earlier thoughts about the hearse, arriving in it would court attention he didn't need. In the meantime Luís had instructions to keep moving and come back to the drop-off point in an hour. If Miguel did not appear, Luís would return every subsequent half hour.

On the corner of Forty-fourth, Miguel bought an umbrella from a street vendor but found it hard to handle in the wind. A few minutes later he crossed First Avenue to the white-fronted UN General Assembly Building. Because of the rain, the many flagpoles stood forlornly bare, bereft of flags. Passing an iron-grille fence and the delegates' entrance, he ascended steps to a wide platform where visitors were admitted. Miguel, empty-handed, was quickly cleared through a checkpoint inside where others were having their handbags and packages opened for inspection.

In the large hall beyond, benches were filled with waiting visitors, their faces and clothes as diverse as the UN itself. A Bolivian woman in a bowler hat sat stoically. Beside her a small black child played with a stuffed white lamb. Nearby sat an old, weathered man wearing Afghan-type headgear. Two bearded Israelis argued over papers spread between them. And interspersed throughout the crowd were white-skinned Americans and British tourists.

Ignoring those waiting, Miguel walked toward a prominent "Guided Tours" sign at the far end of the hall. Beside it, holding an attaché case, José Antonio Salaverry was waiting.

Just like a weasel, Miguel thought, as he took in Salaverry's narrow, pinched face, receding hair and thin mustache. The Peruvian diplomat, usually exuding self importance, today appeared ill at ease.

They exchanged the slightest of nods, then Salaverry led the way to an information desk where, with a delegate's authority, he signed Miguel in, using a bogus name. Miguel received a visitor's pass.

As the two walked down an avenue flanked by pillars, a garden was visible through glass panels, and beyond it the East River. An escala-

tor took them upward to the next floor where
they entered the Indonesian Lounge, available
only to diplomats and guests.

The large, impressive room, where heads of
state were entertained, contained magnificent
art including the curtain of the Holy Kaabe entry to Mecca, a black tapestry inlaid with gold
and silver and presented by the Saudis. A deep
green carpet complemented white leather sofas
and chairs, the furnishings ingeniously arranged
so that several meetings could take place at
once, with none intruding on another. Miguel
and Salaverry seated themselves in a small private section.

As they faced each other, José Antonio
Salaverry's thin lips twisted with displeasure. "I
warned you it was dangerous to come here!
There is already enough risk without creating
more."

Miguel asked calmly, "Why is coming here
a risk?" He needed to find out how much this
weakling knew.

"You fool! You know why. The television,
the newspapers, are full of what you have done,
those people you have seized. The FBI, the police, are throwing everything into the search for
you." Salaverry swallowed, then asked anxiously, "When are you going—all of you getting
out of the country?"

"Assuming what you say is true, why do

you want to know? What difference does it make to you?"

"Because Helga is frantic with anxiety. So am I."

So the loose-tongued idiot had shared what he knew with his whoring woman banker. It meant that the original breach of security had widened and was now an imminent danger which had to be erased. Though Salaverry had no means of knowing, his foolish admission had sealed the fate of his woman and himself.

"Before I answer," Miguel said, "give me the money."

Salaverry manipulated a combination lock on his attaché case. From the case he removed a bulging pressboard wallet tied with tape, and passed it over.

Miguel opened the wallet, surveyed the money inside, then retied the tape.

Salaverry asked petulantly, "Don't you want to count it?"

Miguel shrugged. "You would not dare cheat me." He considered, then said with apparent casualness, "So you want to know when I and certain others will leave."

"Yes, I do."

"Where will you and the woman be tonight?"

"In my apartment. We are too upset to go out."

Miguel had been to the apartment and remembered the address. He told Salaverry, "Stay
there. I cannot telephone because of reasons
which will become clear. Therefore a messenger
will come to you tonight with the information
you want. He will use the name Plato. When
you hear that name, it is safe to let him in."

Salaverry nodded eagerly. He seemed relieved.

Miguel added, "I am doing you this service
in return for your obtaining the money
promptly." He touched the pressboard wallet.

"Thank you. You understand I have no wish
to be unreasonable . . ."

"I understand. But stay home tonight."

"Oh, I will."

From the UN building, Miguel crossed First
Avenue to the United Nations Plaza Hotel. On
the main floor he went to a pay phone near the
newsstand.

He tapped out the memorized digits for a
call to Queens. When a voice answered, he
knew he was connected with a fortress-like private house in the Little Colombia distict of
Jackson Heights. Miguel spoke briefly, avoiding
use of names, gave the number of the pay phone
from which he was calling and then hung up.

He waited patiently by the phone; on two
occasions when other people approached, he

pretended to be using it. After seven minutes it rang. A voice confirmed that it was speaking from another pay phone. The call would not be traced or overheard.

Speaking softly, Miguel stated his requirements. He was assured they could be met. A contract was arranged, a price of six thousand dollars agreed. Miguel gave Salaverry's apartment address and explained that the name "Plato" would ensure admittance. He emphasized, "It is to be done tonight and must appear to be a murder-suicide."

His instructions, he was promised, would be carried out precisely.

Miguel arrived at the Third Avenue rendezvous point a little less than an hour from the time he had left. Moments later Luís brought the hearse to the curb.

Getting in, out of the rain, Miguel told Luís, "We go now to the funeral place—the same one as before. You remember?"

Luís nodded and, soon after, turned east toward the Queensboro Bridge.

5

At times, when news was quiet, a network news organization was like a slumbering giant.

It operated at considerably less than a hundred percent utilization and a substantial number of its talented people had what was referred to in the trade as "down time"—meaning they were not actively at work.

Which was why, when a major news event occurred, there were experienced hands who could be—as another trade phrase went— "grabbed and fired up."

On Friday morning, one day after the Sloane family kidnapping, the firing-up process had begun as the special task force headed by Harry Partridge, with Rita Abrams as senior producer, began assembling within CBA News headquarters.

Rita, who had reached New York from Minnesota late the night before, came in to the newly assigned task force offices at 8A.M. Harry Partridge, having spent the night in a luxury suite provided by the network at the Inter-Continental Hotel, joined her soon after.

Wasting no time, he asked, "Any new developments?"

"Zilch on the kidnap," Rita answered. "But there's a mob scene outside Crawf's house."

"What kind of mob?"

The two were in what would be the group conference room and Rita leaned back in a swivel chair. Despite the brevity of her vacation, she seemed refreshed, her usual vitality and drive restored. Nor had she lost the quirky cynicism which those who worked with her enjoyed.

"These days, everyone wants to touch the hem of an anchorman. Now that they've learned his address, Crawf's fans are pouring into Larchmont. Hundreds of them, maybe thousands. The police are having trouble coping and they're setting up road barriers."

"We have a camera crew on site?"

"Sure have. They camped out all night. I've told them to stay in place until Crawf leaves for work. By then, I'll have another crew out to replace them."

Partridge nodded his approval.

"It makes sense to assume the kidnappers, and therefore the action, have moved on from Larchmont," Rita said, "but I think we should protect ourselves by being around for a couple of days in case anything fresh breaks. That is, unless you have other ideas."

"Not yet," he said; then added, "you know we've been given pretty much a blank check where talent is concerned?"

"I was told last night. So I've asked for three producers to begin—Norman Jaeger, Iris Everly and Karl Owens. They'll be here soon."

"Great choices." Partridge knew all three well. Their abilities were among the best in CBA News.

"Oh, I've allocated offices. Do you want to see yours?"

Rita led the way around five adjoining offices which would constitute the task force operating base. Network news departments were perpetually in a state of flux, with temporary projects being created and disbanded, so when need arose, required accommodation could usually be found.

Partridge would have an office to himself, as would Rita. Two other offices, already jammed with desks, would be shared by the additional producers, camera crews and support staff, some of whom were already moving in. Partridge and Rita exchanged greetings with them before returning to the fifth and largest office, the conference room, to continue planning.

"What I'd like," Partridge said, "is to have a meeting as soon as possible with everyone

who'll be working with us. We can allocate responsibilities, then begin work on a spot for tonight's news."

Rita glanced at her watch: 8:45 A.M.

"I'll set it up for ten o'clock," she said.
"Right now I want to find out more about
what's happening at Larchmont."

"In all the years I've lived here," the Larchmont police sergeant said, "I've never seen anything like it."

He was speaking with FBI Special Agent
Havelock who had emerged from the Sloane
house a few minutes earlier to survey a throng
of spectators outside. The crowd had been
growing in size since dawn and now packed the
sidewalks in front of the house. In some places
they spilled onto the road where police officers
were trying, not too successfully, to control the
crowd and keep passing cars moving. Otis
Havelock, having stayed in the house overnight,
was concerned that Sloane, who was inside getting ready for work, might be mobbed on his
way out.

Clustered by the front gate were television
crews and other reporters. As Havelock appeared, TV cameras swung toward him amid
shouted questions:

"Have you heard from the kidnappers?"

"How's Sloane holding up?"

"Can we talk to Crawford?"

"Who are you?"

In response Havelock shook his head and waved his hands dismissingly.

Beyond the press group, the crowd appeared orderly, though Havelock's appearance had increased the buzz of conversation.

The FBI man complained to the police sergeant, "Can't you people keep this street clear?"

"We're trying. The Chief has ordered barriers. We'll stop traffic and pedestrians, except for those who live on the street, then we'll try to clear these others out. It'll take at least an hour. The Chief doesn't want anyone hassled, not with all those cameras around."

"Any idea where these people are from?"

"I asked a few," the sergeant said. "They mostly drove in from outside Larchmont. I guess it's seeing all that excitement on TV, and wanting a glimpse of Mr. Sloane. The streets around are full of their cars."

Rain had begun to fall, but it didn't seem to discourage the watchers. Instead they put up umbrellas or huddled in their coats.

Havelock returned to the house. Inside he told Crawford Sloane, who looked tired and gaunt, "When we leave, it will be in two unmarked FBI cars. I want you in the second. Crouch down in the back and we'll drive away fast."

"No way," Sloane said. "There are media people out there. I'm one of them and I can't sail by as if I were the President."

"There may also be someone out there from the people who seized your wife and family." Havelock's voice sharpened. "Who knows what they might try, including shooting you? So don't be a damn fool, Mr. Sloane. And remember I'm responsible for your safety."

In the end they agreed to invite the camera crews and reporters into the hallway of the house for an impromptu press conference which Sloane would handle. As the journalists trooped in they looked around the luxurious home with curiosity, some with unconcealed envy. The questions and answers that followed were mostly repetitive of those the preceding day, the only new information being that there had been no communication from the kidnappers during the night.

"I can't tell you any more," Sloane said finally. "There simply isn't anything. I wish there were."

Havelock, while present and watchful, declined to participate in the exchanges and eventually the reporters, some of whom seemed resentful at the lack of news, left as they had come.

"Now, Mr. Sloane," Havelock said, "I want us to leave here in the way I described—with you in the back of the car, down low and out of sight." Reluctantly, Sloane agreed.

But in the execution of the plan, an unforeseen misfortune happened.

Crawford Sloane entered the FBI car so quickly that it was observed by only a few people in the crowd outside. However, those few promptly passed the word to others so that the message spread like fire—"Sloane's in the second car." Within the same car Havelock and another FBI agent were in the backseat, with Sloane uncomfortably on his hands and knees between them. A third FBI agent was at the wheel.

Two more FBI men were in the first car and both cars began moving immediately.

With the crowd now apprised of Sloane's departure, some at the rear pushed forward, impelling those at the front off the sidewalk and onto the road. At that point several things occurred in swift succession.

The lead car emerged from the Sloanes' driveway, waved out by a policeman. It was traveling fast, with the second car close behind. Then suddenly, as spectators opposite the driveway were pushed even farther onto the road, the first car's previously clear path was blocked. Its driver, shocked to see a line of people facing him, jammed on his brakes.

In other circumstances the lead car might

have stopped in time. As it was, on a wet road surface slick from recent rain, it skidded sideways. To the sound of screeching tires followed by a series of horrifying thuds and human screams, the car plowed a path through the front ranks of spectators.

The occupants of the second car—excepting Sloane, who could not see—gasped in horror and braced for a similar collision. But as people scrambled hastily to the opposite side of the road, the crowd parted and Havelock, his face set grimly, ordered the driver, "Don't stop! Keep going!" Afterward, Havelock would defend his apparently callous action by explaining, "It all happened so fast, I wasn't sure of anything and figured it could be an ambush."

Crawford Sloane, aware only that something unexpected was in progress, raised his head to peer out. At that precise moment, a TV camera already focused on the car caught Sloane's face in closeup, then stayed with the car as it sped from the accident scene. Viewers who later saw the videotape on air had no means of knowing that Sloane was pleading to go back, but Havelock insisted, "There are police right there. They'll do whatever's needed."

The Larchmont police did control the situation and several ambulances were rushed to the scene. When the toll was reckoned, eight people had been injured—six with minor lacerations and bruises, two seriously. Of the seriously hurt, one man sustained a broken arm and crushed ribs while a young woman had a leg so badly mangled that it required amputation.

The accident, though tragic, in other circumstances would not have gained wide attention. Because of the association with the Sloane family kidnap, it received national coverage and some of the blame appeared, by implication, to attach to Crawford Sloane.

The researcher from CBA's London bureau, Teddy Cooper, had been flown in, as promised, on that morning's *Concorde*. He came directly to the task force offices, arriving shortly before 10A.M., and reported first to Harry Partridge, then to Rita. The three went to the conference room where the group meeting was assembling.

On the way in, Cooper met Crawford Sloane who also had arrived a few minutes earlier, still shaken from his experience at Larchmont.

Cooper, a wiry slip of a man, radiated energy and confidence. His brown lank hair, worn longer than was now fashionable, framed a pale face that bore signs of adolescent acne. The effect was to make him seem even younger than his twenty-five years. Though a born-and-bred Londoner, he had been in the U.S. several times before and was familiar with New York.

To Crawford Sloane, he declared, "Sorry to

hear about your missus and family, Mister S, but cheer up! I'm here now! I'll have those buggers before you know it. It's what I'm good at!"

Sloane, glancing at Partridge, raised his eyebrows inquiringly, as if to ask, *Are you sure we want this bird?*

Partridge said dryly, "Modesty has never been Teddy's problem. We'll give him some rope and see what happens." The exchange seemed not to bother Cooper in the least.

To Partridge, Cooper said, "First thing, Harry, is to check out the reports. Then I'll suss out the scene of the crime. I want a word with the geezers who saw it happen—and I mean everyone. There's no point pissin' about. If I'm going to do this, I'm going to do it right."

"You do it your way." Partridge remembered previous occasions when he had witnessed Cooper at work. "You'll be in charge of research here, with two assistants."

The assistant researchers, a young man and woman who had been borrowed from another CBA project, were already in the conference room. While waiting for the meeting to begin, Partridge introduced them.

Cooper shook hands and said, "Working with me will be a great experience for you, kids. Don't be nervous, though—I'm very informal. Just call me 'your excellency,' and you need only salute first thing each morning."

The researchers seemed amused by Cooper and the trio began discussing a "Sequence of Events" board, already in place in the conference room and occupying an entire wall. A standard procedure in task force reporting, it would record every known detail about the Sloane kidnapping, in proper sequence. On another wall was a second large board, headed "Miscellaneous." This would contain incidental intelligence, some of it speculation or rumor, whose sequence was irrelevant or not known. From time to time, as "miscellaneous" items developed, they would be transferred to the other board—all of it a research responsibility.

The boards' purpose was twofold: first, to apprise everyone in the task force inner circle of all available information and new developments; second, to provide a focus for progress reviews and brainstorming sessions which could, and often did, provoke new ideas.

Punctually at ten o'clock, Rita Abrams raised her voice, cutting across the general buzz of conversation. "All right, everyone! Let's get to work."

She was seated at the head of a long table, Harry Partridge beside her. Leslie Chippingham arrived and took his place at the table too. As he caught Rita's eye, they exchanged discreet smiles.

Crawford Sloane seated himself at the far end. He did not expect to contribute to the discussion at this point and had confided to Partridge, "I feel helpless right now, like a loose nut."

Also at the table were the three producers Rita had recruited. Norman Jaeger, oldest of the three, was a CBA veteran who had worked in every phase of news. Soft-spoken, imaginative and scholarly, he was a producer for the network's highly acclaimed magazine program, "Behind the Headlines." His abrupt temporary reassignment today pointed up the exceptional resources of the task force.

Next to Jaeger was Iris Everly, in her mid-twenties and a brightly shining star on the news production scene. Petite, pretty, a Columbia Journalism School graduate, she had a shrewd mind which functioned at lightning speed. When working to pursue an elusive news story, her reputation for toughness and cunning matched Rasputin's.

Karl Owens, the third producer, was a workhorse who had gained his reputation through persistent, tireless plodding; sometimes his joint investigative work with correspondents succeeded after competitors had given up. Midway in age between Jaeger and Iris Everly and not as imaginative as either, Owens could be

counted on for solidity and a thorough knowledge of his craft.

In other seats at the table and immediately
behind were Teddy Cooper and the two assistant researchers, a staff writer borrowed from
the National Evening News, Minh Van Canh,
who would be senior cameraman, and a woman
secretary, appointed unit manager.

"Okay, we all know why we're here," Rita
said, opening the meeting with a businesslike
tone. "What we'll discuss now is how to go
about our work. First, I'll talk about organization. After that, Harry will direct us on the way
we should march editorially."

Rita paused and looked the length of the
table at Crawford Sloane. "Crawf, we won't
make speeches here. I don't think any of us
could without becoming emotional, and you
have enough distress to carry without our adding to that burden. But I want to tell you, very
simply and from all of us—for your sake, your
family's, and our own because we care—we're
going to do our *damnedest!*"

From the other task force members there
was an approving, sympathetic murmur.

Sloane nodded twice, then managed to utter,
"Thank you," his voice choked.

"From here in," Rita said, "we shall operate
on two levels—the long-term project and the
daily breaking story. Norm," she continued, ad-

dressing the older producer, "you're to be in charge of long term."

"Right."

"Iris, you'll do the day-by-day, starting with a spot for the news tonight, which we'll discuss shortly."

Iris Everly said crisply, "Got it, and the first thing I'll want is the video of that melee this morning outside Crawf's house."

Sloane winced at the mention of the incident and glanced half pleadingly at Iris, though she took no notice.

"You'll get it," Rita told her. "The tape's on the way in."

To the third producer, Owens, Rita said, "Karl, you'll move between the two project sides as needed." She added, "And I'll be working closely with all three of you."

Her attention turned to Cooper. "Teddy, I understand you want to go to Larchmont."

Cooper looked up with a grin. "Yes, ma'am. To dig around and make like the famed Sherlock H." Turning his head, he added for the others, "At which I'm exceptionally good."

"Teddy," Partridge said, speaking for the first time, "everyone in this room is exceptionally good. It's why they're here."

Unabashed, Cooper beamed. "Then I oughta feel right at home."

"After we finish this meeting," Rita advised

him, "Minh will go to Larchmont, heading two fresh camera crews. You'll go with him, Teddy, and meet Bert Fisher who's a stringer for our local affiliate station. I've arranged it. Fisher was first to break the story yesterday. He'll drive you around and introduce you to whoever you want to see."

"Wizard! I'll make a note o' that: Go fishing with Fisher."

Norm Jaeger said softly to Karl Owens, "Before this assignment's over I may strangle that Limey."

"Minh," Iris Everly said to the cameraman, "let's you and me talk, please, before you leave for Larchmont."

Minh Van Canh, his square dark face impassive as usual, nodded.

"For the time being that takes care of the nuts and bolts," Rita said. "Now, more important, there's editorial direction. Harry—over to you."

"Our first objective, as I see it," Partridge began, "is to find out more about the kidnappers. Who are they? Where are they from? What are they aiming for? Of course, very soon they may tell us that themselves; however, we won't wait for it to happen. At this point I can't tell you how we'll learn the answers to those questions, except that together we will focus our brains on everything that's occurred so far, plus each new piece of information that comes in. Today I want everyone here to study all the data that we have, memorizing details. The boards will help." He motioned to the "Sequence of Events" and "Miscellaneous" boards, adding, "Both will be up to date later this morning.

"After everyone has caught up I want us, separately and collectively, to keep picking over the pieces, worrying at them. If we do that, based on past experience something will come out."

Around the table the group listened attentively as Partridge continued.

"One thing I'll tell you for sure. Somewhere, those people—the kidnappers—have left traces. Everybody leaves traces, no matter how carefully they try to hide them. The trick is to locate some." He nodded to Jaeger. "Concentrating on that will be your job, Norman."

"Got it," Jaeger said.

"Now the short term. Iris, about our spot for tonight's evening news. I know you've been thinking. How do you see the bones? Do you have a framework?"

She answered crisply. "If there's no fresh dramatic news like communication from the kidnappers, after saying there isn't, we may go to the snafu this morning outside Crawf's house. Then, since this will be the first full day since the event, a recap of yesterday. I've watched the tape of last night; it was a mish-mash. Tonight we can do better, be more orderly. Also I'd like re-interviews with witnesses at Larchmont"—Iris consulted notes—"especially the old lady, Priscilla Rhea, who's video-rich. She and the others may have remembered something new."

"What about reactions?" Jaeger asked. "As in Washington."

Partridge answered. "A short bite only, from the President, I think. Maybe some citizen interviews if we have time."

"But nothing from Capitol Hill?"

"Maybe tomorrow," Partridge said. "Maybe never. Everyone on the Hill will want to get in the act." He motioned for Iris to continue.

"To wrap up," she said, "we should do some analysis at the end—an interview with an authority on kidnapping."

Partridge asked, "Anyone in mind?"

"Not yet."

Karl Owens volunteered, "I know of a guy. Name's Ralph Salerno, an ex-New York cop, lives at Naples, Florida. He lectures about crime to police forces all over and has written books. Knows a lot about kidnap. I've seen him on air. He's good."

"Let's get him," Iris said, glancing at Partridge who nodded his approval.

Les Chippingham interjected, "Karl, we have an affiliate in the Naples area. Work through them if you can; otherwise fly Salerno to Miami."

"And either way," Iris added, "book satellite time for Harry to do the interview."

"I'll get onto it," Owens said, and made a note.

After another fifteen minutes of discussion, Rita tapped the table. "That'll do," she announced. "The rap is over. Real work begins."

Amid the serious business, a marginal tempest.

For research purposes, Harry Partridge had decided to interview Crawford Sloane. Partridge believed that Sloane, like many people who became involved in a complex episode, knew more than he realized and that skilled, persistent questioning might bring out new facts. Sloane had already agreed to the session.

In the conference room after the meeting, as Partridge reminded Sloane of the arrangement, a voice behind them broke in, "If you don't mind, I'd like to sit in and listen. I may learn something too."

Surprised, they turned. Confronting them

was Special Agent Otis Havelock who had walked in as the meeting broke up.

"Well," Partridge said, "since you ask, I do mind."

Rita Abrams queried Havelock, "Aren't you Mr. FBI?"

He answered amiably, "You mean like 'Miss America?' My colleagues might not think so."

"What I really mean," Rita said, "is you shouldn't be in here at all. This area is off limits to anyone except those working here."

Havelock seemed surprised. "Part of my job is to protect Mr. Sloane. Besides, you're investigating the kidnapping. Right?"

"Yes."

"Then we have the same objective, to locate Mr. Sloane's family. So anything you people discover, such as what goes up there"—he gestured to the "Sequence of Events" board—"the FBI needs to know as well."

Several others in the room, among them Leslie Chippingham, had fallen silent.

"In that case," Rita said, "it should be a two-way deal. Can I send a correspondent, right now, over to the FBI's New York office to examine all your reports that have come in?"

Havelock shook his head. "I'm afraid that isn't possible. Some are confidential."

"Exactly!"

"Look, folks." Havelock, aware of the grow-

ing attention around the room, was clearly trying to be restrained. "I'm not sure you fully
understand that we're dealing with a crime.
Anyone with knowledge has a legal obligation
to pass it on, in this instance to the FBI. Failing
to do so could be a criminal offense."

Rita, seldom long on patience, objected,
"For chrissakes, we're not children! We do investigations all the time and know the score."

Partridge added, "I should tell you, Mr.
Havelock, that I've worked close to the FBI on
several stories and your people are notorious for
taking all the information they can get and giving back nothing."

Havelock snapped, "The FBI isn't obliged
to give anything back." His earlier restraint was
gone. "We're a government agency with the
power of the President and Congress behind us.
What you people seem to be doing here is setting yourself up as competitors. Well, let me advise you that if anyone impedes the official investigation by withholding information, they're
likely to face serious charges."

Chippingham decided it was time to intervene.

"Mr. Havelock," the news president said, "I
assure you we are not people who break the
law. However, we *are* free to do all the investigating we want and sometimes we're more suc-

cessful at it than what you call the 'official investigation.'

"What's really involved here," Chippingham continued, "is something called 'reporter privilege.' While I admit there are some gray areas, what's important is that reporters can investigate, then protect their sources unless a court rules otherwise. So you see, it would be an infringement on our freedom if we allowed you to have instant, total access to whatever comes in. Therefore I must tell you that while we're glad to have you here, there's a limit to your clearance and a line you may not cross—right there." He pointed to the conference-room doorway.

"Well, sir," Havelock said, "I'm not sure I buy all that, and you won't mind if I discuss the whole matter with the Bureau."

"Not in the least. I'm sure they'll tell you we're acting within our rights."

What Chippingham did not say was that CBA, like any news organization, would make its own decisions about what to reveal and when, even if it meant ruffling some FBI feathers. He knew that most others in the News Division felt the same way. As to possible consequences, the network would have to deal with those as and if they happened.

After Havelock had left to make a phone call, Chippingham told Rita, "Call the building superintendent. Ask for some keys to these offices and keep them locked."

In the privacy of Partridge's office, he and Sloane began their interview with a tape recorder running. Partridge covered the now familiar ground, repeating earlier questions in more detailed ways, but nothing new emerged. At length, Partridge asked, "Is there anything in your mind, Crawf, even down in your subconscious that you might have to search for, something that could vaguely relate to what has happened? Is there the smallest incident you might have wondered about, then dismissed?"

"You asked me that yesterday," Sloane answered thoughtfully. His attitude to Partridge had changed noticeably over the past twenty-four hours. In one sense it was friendlier. In another, Sloane was less wary of Partridge, even relying on him mentally in a way he never had before. Strangely, Sloane was almost deferential, as if seeing in Harry Partridge his greatest hope of getting Jessica, Nicky and his father back.

"I know I did," Partridge said, "and you promised to think about it."

"Well, I thought last night and maybe there is something, though I can't be sure, and it's only the vaguest feeling." Sloane spoke awkwardly. He was never comfortable with hazy, unformed ideas.

Partridge urged, "Keep talking."

"I think, before this happened, I might have had a feeling of being followed. Of course, it could be I'm thinking this way after discovering there was a watch on the house . . ."

"Forget that. So you think you were followed. Where and when?"

"That's the trouble. It's so hazy I could have made it up, maybe feeling I *had* to find something."

"Do you think you made it up?"

Sloane hesitated. "No, I don't."

"Give me more details."

"I've a feeling I might have been followed sometimes while driving home. Also I have an instinct, and it's damned elusive, that someone may have been observing me here, inside CBA News—someone who should not have been here."

"All this over how long a period?"

"Maybe a month?" Sloane threw up his hands. "I simply can't be sure I'm not inventing. In any case, what difference does it make?"

"I don't know," Partridge said. "But I'll talk it over with the others."

Afterward, Partridge typed out a summary of the Sloane interview and pinned it on the conference room "Miscellaneous" board. Then, back in his office, he began the procedure known to all journalists as "working the phones."

Open in front of him was his private "blue book"—a catalog of people he knew worldwide who had been useful before and might be again. It also included others he had helped by supplying information when they, in turn, needed it. The news business was full of debits and credits; at times like this, credits were called in. Also helpful was that most people were flattered to be sought after by TV news.

The night before, referring to the blue book, Partridge had made a list of those he would call today. The names beside him now included contacts in the Justice Department, White House, State Department, CIA, Immigration, Congress, several foreign embassies, New York's Police Department, the Royal Canadian Mounted Police in Ottawa, Mexico's Judicial Police, an author of real-life crime books, and a lawyer with organized crime clients.

The ensuing phone conversations were mostly low-key and began, "Hi, this is Harry Partridge. We haven't been in touch for a while. Just called to see how life is treating you." The personal mode continued with inquiries about wives or husbands, lovers, children—Partridge kept notes of those names too—then eased into the current scene. "I'm working on the Sloane kidnapping. I wonder if you've heard any rumbles, or have ideas of your own."

Sometimes the questions were more specific. *Have you heard speculation on who might be responsible? Do you think terrorist involvement is a possibility; if so, from where? Are any rumors floating, even wild ones? Will you ask around and call me back if you hear anything?*

It was standard practice, at times tedious and always requiring patience. Sometimes it produced results, occasionally delayed ones, often none. From today's telephoning nothing specific emerged, though the most interesting conversation, Partridge decided afterward, was with the organized crime lawyer.

A year ago Partridge had done him a favor —or so the lawyer thought. The man's daughter, on a college trip to Venezuela, had been part of a messy drug orgy that made U.S. national news. Eight students were involved; two had died. Through a Caracas agency, CBA News had obtained exclusive on-the-spot pictures, with close-ups of participants—the lawyer's daughter among them—being arrested by police. Partridge, who was in Argentina, flew north to cover the story.

In New York, the girl's father somehow learned about the coverage, also the pictures, and tracked Partridge down by phone. He pleaded with Partridge not to use his daughter's name or image, arguing she was the youngest of the group, had never been in trouble before, and national exposure would ruin her life.

Partridge had by that time seen the pictures; he knew about the girl and had decided not to use her in his story. Even so, keeping his options open, he merely promised to do the best he could.

Later, when it became clear that CBA had made no direct reference to the girl, the lawyer sent Partridge a check for a thousand dollars. Partridge returned the check with a polite note, and since then the two had not communicated.

Today, after listening to Partridge's casual opener, the lawyer responded bluntly, "I owe you. Now you want something. Tell me what it is."

Partridge explained.

"I haven't heard anything, except on TV," the lawyer said, "and I'm sure as I can be that none of my clients are involved. It isn't the kind of thing they'd touch. Sometimes, though, they get to hear about things that others don't. Over the next few days I'll do some discreet asking around. If I find out anything I'll call you."

Partridge had a feeling that he would.

At the end of an hour, when he had covered half the names on his list, Partridge took a break and went to the conference room to pour himself coffee. Returning, he did what almost everyone in TV news did daily—went through the *New York Times* and *Washington Post.* It always surprised visitors to TV news centers to see how many copies of those newspapers were around. The fact was, despite TV's own news achievements, a subtle, ingrained attitude persisted that nothing was really news until printed in the *Times* or *Post.*

The strong voice of Chuck Insen broke into Partridge's reading.

"I bring tonight's lineup, Harry," the executive producer said, entering the office. "The word is, we'll do a split-anchor news. You're to be half the horse."

"Rear end or front?"

Insen smiled faintly. "Which of us ever knows? Anyway, from tonight on, you'll anchor anything to do with the Sloane family kidnap which—unless the President gets shot before air time—will be our lead again. Crawf will anchor the rest of the news as usual, the point being that all of us feel we're damned if a bunch of thugs, whoever they are, are going to dictate how life goes on at CBA."

"Fine with me," Partridge said. "I presume it is with Crawf."

"Frankly, it was Crawf's idea. Like any king he feels insecure if off his throne too long. Besides which, his staying invisible would achieve nothing. Oh, another thing—right at the end of the news, Crawf will say a few spontaneous words thanking those who've sent messages about his family, or otherwise care."

"Spontaneous?"

"Of course. We have three writers toiling over them now."

Amused, despite the circumstances, Partridge said, "You two are managing to agree for the time being."

Insen nodded. "We've declared an unspoken armistice until all this is over."

"And afterward?"

"Let's wait and see."

6

Almost a month earlier, soon after Miguel had entered the United States illegally, he had attempted to buy funeral caskets to be used for transporting his two intended kidnap victims to Peru. The plan had been developed well before his arrival on the scene and Miguel assumed their purchase could be accomplished quickly and quietly—a simple matter. He discovered it was not.

He had gone to a funeral home in Brooklyn, wanting to spread out his activities rather than confine them to the Little Colombia area of Queens, his operating center at the time. The establishment he chose was near Prospect Park —an elegant white building labeled "Field's," with a spacious parking lot.

Miguel entered through heavy oak doors which opened onto a lobby with golden-beige carpeting, tall potted plants and paintings of peaceful landscapes. Inside he was greeted by a decorous middle-aged man wearing a black jacket with a white carnation, black-and-gray-striped trousers, white shirt and a dark tie.

"Good morning, sir," the sartorial paragon said. "I am Mr. Field. How can I be of service?"

Miguel had rehearsed what he would say. "I have two elderly parents who wish certain planning to be done about their eventual . . . er, passing."

With an inclination of his head, Field conveyed approval and sympathy. "I understand, sir. Many older people, at the sunset of their years, wish to be comfortable and assured about their future."

"Exactly. Now, what my parents would like . . ."

"Excuse me, sir. It might be more suitable if we stepped into my office."

"Very well."

Field led the way. Perhaps intentionally, they passed several salon-type rooms with settees and armchairs, one with rows of chairs prepared for a service. In each room was a corpse, gilded with cosmetics and propped on a frilly pillow in its open casket. Miguel noticed a few visitors, but some rooms were empty.

The office was at the end of a corridor, discreetly hidden. On the walls were framed diplomas, much as in a doctor's office, except that one was for "beautification" of dead bodies (it was adorned with purple ribbons), and another for embalming. At Field's gesture, Miguel took a chair.

"May I ask your name, sir."

"Novack," Miguel lied.

"Well, Mr. Novack, to begin we should discuss the overall arrangements. Do you or your parents have a cemetery plot chosen and obtained?"

"Well, no."

"Then that must be our first consideration. We ought to get that for you right away because it's becoming difficult to obtain a plot, especially a choice one. Unless, of course, you are considering cremation."

Miguel, curbing his impatience, shook his

head. "No. But what I really want to talk about . . ."

"Then there's the question of your parents' religion. What service will be required? And there are other decisions to be made. Perhaps you would care to study this."

Field passed over what resembled an elaborate restaurant menu. It included a long list of separate items and costs such as, "Bathing, disinfecting, handling and cosmetizing of deceased —$250," "Special care for autopsied cases— $125" and "Clerical assistance in the completion of various forms—$100." A "full traditional service" at $5,900 included, among other things, a $30 crucifix placed in the deceased's hands. A casket was extra, ranging up to $20,600.

"It's the caskets I came to discuss," Miguel said.

"Certainly." Field stood up. "Please come with me."

This time he led the way down a stairway to a basement. They entered a display room where the carpeting was red and Field went first to the $20,600 casket. "This is our very best. It's of 18-gauge steel, has three covers—glass, brass and quilted brass—and will last and last and last." Elaborate ornaments adorned the casket's exterior. The inside was lined with lavender velvet.

"Maybe something a little simpler," Miguel told him.

They settled on two caskets, one smaller than the other, priced at $2,300 and $1,900. "My mother is a tiny lady," Miguel explained. *About the size of an eleven-year-old boy,* he thought.

Miguel's curiosity had been piqued by several plain, simple boxes. When asked about them, Field explained, "They are for religious Jews who require simplicity. The boxes have two holes in the bottom, the theory being 'earth to earth.' You are not Jewish?" When Miguel shook his head, Field confided, "Frankly, that is not the kind of repository I would choose for my own loved ones."

They went back to the office where Field said, "Now I suggest we go over the other matters. The burial plot first."

"That's not necessary," Miguel said. "What I would like to do is pay for the caskets and take them."

Field looked shocked. "That isn't possible."

"Why not?"

"It simply isn't done that way."

"Perhaps I should have explained." Miguel was beginning to see that this might not be as simple as expected. "What my parents would like is to have their caskets now, in their present home, placing them where they can be seen each day. That way they can get used, so to speak, to their future accommodation."

Field appeared devastated. "We couldn't possibly do that. What we arrange here is—if I may use that word—a 'package.' It would be possible for your parents to come to view the caskets they will eventually rest in. But after that we would insist on keeping them until the need arose."

"Couldn't you . . ."

"No, sir, absolutely not."

Miguel had sensed the other man losing interest, even possibly becoming suspicious.

"Very well. I'll think about it and perhaps come back."

Field escorted Miguel out. Miguel had not the slightest intention of coming back. As it was, he knew he'd already left too strong an impression.

The next day he tried two more funeral homes farther afield, making his inquiries shorter. But the response was the same. No one would sell him caskets separate from "the package."

At that point Miguel decided the attempt to move away from his operating center had been a mistake and he returned to Queens and his Little Colombia contacts. After a few days' delay they sent him to a small, drab funeral home in Astoria, not far from Jackson Heights. There he met Alberto Godoy.

In terms of funeral establishments, Godoy's was to Field's what K mart was to Tiffany— geared to a down-scale clientele. Not only that, but shabbiness prevailed, extending to the proprietor himself.

Godoy was obese, bald, with nicotine-stained fingers and the bloated features of a heavy drinker. Food stains were conspicuous on his undertaker's uniform of black coat and gray-striped pants. His voice was raspy and punctuated by a smoker's cough. During the meeting with Miguel, which began in Godoy's tiny, cluttered office, he smoked three cigarettes, lighting one from another.

"My name is Novack, and I've come for information," Miguel had said.

Godoy nodded, "Yes, I know."

"I have two elderly parents . . ."

"Oh, is that the line?"

Miguel persisted, repeating his earlier story while Godoy listened with a mixture of boredom and disbelief. At the end his only question was, "How will you pay?"

"Cash."

Godoy became a shade more friendly. "This way."

Once more a basement provided the setting for sample caskets, though here the carpeting was dull brown and worn, with the choices fewer than at Field's. Expeditiously Miguel found two suitable caskets, one of average size, the other smaller.

Godoy announced, "For the regular size, three thousand dollars. For the child's, twenty-five hundred."

Though the "child" reference ran counter to his story and was dangerously near the truth, Miguel ignored it. Also, while convinced the $5,500 total was at least twice the normal price, he agreed to it without discussion. He had brought cash and paid in hundred-dollar bills. Godoy asked for another $454 for New York City sales tax which Miguel added, though he doubted that the city's coffers would ever see the money.

Miguel backed his recently acquired GMC truck to a loading dock where, under Godoy's watchful supervision, the caskets were wheeled aboard. Miguel then took them to the safe house where they were stored until their later transfer to Hackensack.

Now, almost a month later, he had returned to Alberto Godoy's establishment in search of one more casket.

Miguel was uneasy about going back because of the risks involved. He remembered Godoy's offhand reference to the second casket being for a child. So was there a chance, Miguel wondered, that Godoy had connected yesterday's kidnapping of a woman and boy with the earlier purchase of the caskets? It wasn't likely, but one reason Miguel had survived so long as a terrorist was by weighing every possibility. However, having decided to transport the third captive to Peru, at this point there was no alternative to Godoy. The risk had to be taken.

Slightly more than an hour after leaving the United Nations, Miguel instructed Luís to park their hearse a block from the Godoy Funeral Home. Again Miguel used his umbrella in the pouring rain.

Inside the funeral home a woman receptionist spoke to Godoy via an intercom, then directed Miguel to the proprietor's office.

From behind a cloud of cigarette smoke the fat man regarded Miguel warily. "So it's you again. Your friends didn't tell me you were coming."

"No one knew."

"What do you want?" Whatever Godoy's motivations in doing business with Miguel in the first place, it was clear he now had reservations.

"I've been asked to do a favor for an elderly friend. He's seen the caskets I bought for my parents, likes the idea, and asked if I would . . ."

"Aw, cut it out!" An old-fashioned cuspidor was beside Godoy's desk. Removing his cigarette, he spat into it. "Listen, mister, don't waste time with what both of us know is a potful of crap. I said what is it you want?"

"One casket. To be paid for as before."

Godoy peered forward through shifty eyes. "I run a business here. Sure, sometimes I oblige your friends; they do the same for me. But what I want to know from you is: Am I setting myself up to land in some shit?"

"There'll be no shit. Not if you cooperate." Miguel let his own voice take on menace and it had an effect.

"All right, you got it," Godoy said, his tone more moderate. "But since last time the price has gone up. For that same adult model, four thousand."

Without speaking, Miguel opened the pressboard wallet José Antonio Salaverry had given him and began counting hundred-dollar bills. He handed forty to Godoy who said, "Plus two hundred 'n' fifty New York tax."

Re-tying the tape of the the pressboard wallet, Miguel told Godoy, "You and New York go fuck yourselves." Then: "I have transport outside. Get the casket to your loading dock."

On the dock, Godoy was mildly surprised to see a hearse appear. The two previous caskets, he remembered, had been taken away in a truck. Still suspicious of his visitor, Godoy memorized the numbers and letters on the hearse's New York license plate and, when back in his office, wrote them down, though not really knowing why. He pushed the piece of scratch paper into a drawer and promptly forgot it.

Despite a belief that he had been involved in something it would be safer not to know more about, Godoy smiled as he put away the four thousand dollars in an office safe. Some of the previous cash his recent visitor had paid a month ago was also in the safe, and not only did Godoy have no intention of paying New York sales tax on either transaction, he did not intend to declare it on his tax returns either. Juggling his business inventory to make the three caskets disappear from his books would be easy. The thought so cheered him that he decided to do what he often did—go to a nearby bar for a drink.

Several of Godoy's cronies at the bar welcomed him. A short time later, mellowed by three Jack Daniel's whiskeys, he related to the group how some punk had bought two caskets and put them—so he said—in his parents' home, ready for the old folks to croak, and then come back for another casket, all of it like he was buying chairs or saucepans.

As the others roared with laughter, Godoy further confided that he'd outsmarted the dumb punk by charging three times the caskets' regular price. At that, one of his friends added a cheer to the laughter, prompting Godoy—all his worry now dissipated—to order another round.

Among those at the bar was a former Colombian, now a U.S. resident, who wrote a column for an obscure Spanish-language weekly published in Queens. On the back of an envelope, using a stub of pencil, the man wrote the gist of Godoy's story, translating it to Spanish as he did. It would make a good little item, he thought, for next week's column.

7

At CBA News it had been a frantic day, especially for the Sloane kidnap task force.

Producing a comprehensive report on the kidnapping for the National Evening News continued to be the focus of activity, though other events, some major, were happening elsewhere in the world.

The kidnap story had been allotted five and a half minutes—an extraordinary duration in a business where fifteen-second segments were fiercely fought over. As a result, almost the entire effort of the task force was devoted to that day's production, leaving virtually no time for longer-term planning or reflection.

With Harry Partridge anchoring the opening portion of the news, the evening broadcast began:

> *"After thirty-six hours of agonized waiting there is no fresh news about the family of CBA anchorman Crawford Sloane, whose wife, young son and father were kidnapped yesterday morning in Larchmont, New York. The whereabouts of Mrs. Jessica Sloane, eleven-year-old Nicholas, and Mr. Angus Sloane remain unknown."*

As each name was mentioned, a still photo appeared over Partridge's shoulder.

> *"Also unknown are the identities, objectives, or affiliations of the kidnappers."*

A fast cut to Crawford Sloane's troubled face filling the screen. Sloane's distraught voice pleaded, *"Whoever you are, wherever you are, for god's sake make yourself known! Let us hear from you!"*

Partridge's voice returned over an exterior

shot of FBI headquarters, the J. Edgar Hoover Building in Washington. *"While the FBI, now in charge of the investigation, is withholding comment . . ."*

Briefly the scene changed to the FBI press office and a spokesman saying, *"At this moment it would not be helpful to make any statement."*

Partridge again: *". . . privately, FBI officials admit no progress has been made.*

"Since yesterday an outpouring of concern and anger have come from highest levels . . ."

A dissolve to the White House press room, the President speaking: *"Such evil has no place in America. The criminals will be hounded down and punished."*

Partridge: *". . . and in humbler places . . ."*

From Pittsburgh, a hard-hatted black steel-worker, his face shining in the light from a fiery furnace: *"I'm ashamed something like this could happen in my country."*

In a bright Topeka kitchen, a white house-wife: *"I cannot understand why no one foresaw what's happened and took precautions. My heart goes out to Crawford."* Gesturing to a TV set: *"In this house he's like family."*

Seated at her classroom desk in California, a young, soft-voiced Eurasian girl: *"I'm worried about Nicholas Sloane. It isn't fair they took him."*

During the day, camera crews of CBA and affiliated stations across the country had sought public reactions. The network had viewed fifty and selected those three.

The scene shifted to the Sloane house at Larchmont that morning in the rain—a long shot of the waiting crowd in the street, then, moving in close, a pan across their faces. Over the image, Partridge's voice: *"In part because of intense public interest, today new tragedy intruded."*

The voice-over continued, alternating with natural sound, more pictures: emergence of the two unmarked FBI cars from the driveway . . . the surge of onlookers into the first car's path . . . the first car braking, then out of control and sliding . . . a shriek of tires followed by screams from the injured . . . others frantically scrambling clear of the second car, which then continued on . . . a close-up of Crawford Sloane's bewildered face . . . the second car speeding away.

During editing, some objections had been raised about including the shots of Sloane's face and the disappearing car. Sloane himself claimed, "It gives a wrong impression."

But Iris Everly, who put most of the spot together, working through the day with one of

CBA's best tape editors, Bob Watson, argued for its inclusion and won. "Whether Crawf likes it or not," she pointed out, "it's news and we should stay objective. Also, we're looking at the only piece of action since yesterday." Rita and Partridge had supported Iris.

The tempo changed to a skillful recap of the previous day. It began with Priscilla Rhea, the frail and elderly ex-schoolteacher, again describing the brutal seizure of Jessica, Nicky and Angus Sloane outside the Larchmont supermarket.

Minh Van Canh had used his camera creatively, going in for an extreme close-up of Miss Rhea's face. It showed the deep lines of age with every wrinkle in sharp relief, but also brought out her intelligence and sturdy character. Minh had coaxed her with gentle questions, an occasionally used procedure. When no correspondent was present, experienced camera people sometimes asked questions of those they were photographing. The questions were erased later from the audio recording, but the answers remained for use as statements.

After describing the struggle on the parking lot and the Nissan van's departure, Miss Rhea said of the kidnappers, her voice rising, *"They were brutal men, beasts, savages!"*

Next, the Larchmont police chief confirmed that there had been no breakthrough in the case and the kidnappers had not been heard from.

Following the recap was an interview with the criminologist, Ralph Salerno.

With Salerno in a Miami studio and Harry Partridge in New York, the interview had been recorded via satellite late that afternoon. The recommendation by Karl Owens proved a good one and Salerno, an authoritative figure, was eloquent and well informed. He so impressed Rita Abrams that she arranged for him to be available exclusively to CBA for the duration of the crisis. He would be paid $1,000 for each broadcast appearance, with a minimum guarantee of four.

Although TV networks claimed not to pay for news interviews—a statement not always true—a consultant fee was different and acceptable.

"The progress of investigation after any efficiently executed kidnap," Ralph Salerno declared, *"depends on hearing from the kidnappers. Unless and until that happens, there is usually a stalemate."*

Answering a question by Partridge, he continued: *"The FBI has a high success ratio in kidnappings; they solve ninety-two percent of cases. But if you look carefully at who was caught and how, you'll find most solutions depended on first hearing from the kidnappers, then trapping them during negotiations or payment of a ransom."*

Partridge prompted, *"So the likelihood is that not much will happen until these kidnappers are heard from."*

"Exactly."

A final statement in the special news segment was made by CBA's corporate president, Margot Lloyd-Mason.

It had been Leslie Chippingham's idea to include Margot. Soon after breaking into the network with the kidnap bulletin yesterday, he reported to her by telephone and did so again this morning. Her reaction had, on the whole, been sympathetic and after their first conversation she telephoned Crawford Sloane, expressing hope that his family would be recovered quickly. While speaking with the news president, though, she added two caveats.

"Part of the reason something like this happens is that networks have misguidedly let anchor people become larger than life, so the public thinks of them as something extra-special, almost gods." She did not elaborate on how a network could control public concepts, even if it wished, and for his part, Chippingham saw no point in arguing the obvious.

The other proviso concerned the kidnap task force.

"I don't want anyone—and that principally means you," Margot Lloyd-Mason asserted, "going wild about spending money. You should be able to do whatever is necessary within the existing news budget."

Chippingham said doubtfully, "I'm not so sure of that."

"Then I'll give you a firm ruling. No activity exceeding budget is to be embarked on without my advance approval. Is that clear?"

Chippingham wondered whether the woman had blood in her veins or ice?

Aloud, he answered, "Yes, Margot, it's clear, though I'll remind you that our ratings for the National Evening News shot up last night and I expect that to continue while this crisis lasts."

"Which merely goes to show," she answered coolly, "that unfortunate events can be turned to profit."

While involving the corporate president in this evening's broadcast seemed appropriate, Chippingham also hoped it might soften her attitude toward some special expenditures which, in his view, would be needed.

On air, Margot spoke with authority, using words scripted for her but with revisions of her own.

> *"I am speaking for all the people of this network and our parent company, Globanic Industries,"* Margot said, *"when I declare that our total resources are available in the search for the missing members of the Sloane family. For all of us, in fact, it is a family affair.*
>
> *"We deplore what has happened. We urge law enforcement agencies to continue their strongest efforts to bring the criminals to justice. We hope to see our friend and colleague, Crawford Sloane, united with his wife, son and father in the shortest possible time."*

In the original draft there had been no reference to Globanic Industries. When Margot proposed it while reviewing her script in the privacy of Chippingham's office, he advised, "I wouldn't do that. The public has an image of CBA as an entity, a piece of Americana. Bringing in Globanic's name makes that image cloudy, to no one's advantage."

"What you'd like to pretend," Margot retorted, "is that CBA is some kind of crown jewel, and independent. Well, it's neither. Over at Globanic they're more apt to think of CBA as a pimple on their ass. The reference stays in. What you can take out, *à propos* Sloane, are those words, 'our friend and colleague.' Kidnap or not, I might choke on them."

Chippingham suggested dryly, "How about a trade-off? I'll promise to love Globanic if, for one broadcast, you'll be Crawford's friend."

For once, Margot laughed aloud. "Shit, yes."

The lack of progress after a frantic first day for the task force did not surprise Harry Partridge. He had been involved in similar projects in the past and knew it took members of any new team at least a day to orient themselves. Just the same, it was imperative there be no more delay in formulating plans.

"Let's have a working dinner," he told Rita during the afternoon.

She then arranged for the six principals in the task force—Partridge, Rita, Jaeger, Iris, Owens, Cooper—to meet for Chinese food immediately after the National Evening News. Rita chose Shun Lee West on West Sixty-fifth, near Lincoln Center, a favorite with TV news folk. In making the reservation she told the maître d', Andy Yeung, "Don't bother us with menus. You order a good meal and give us a table out of the mainstream, where we can talk."

During a commercial that followed the five-minute kidnap report at the top of the National Evening News, Partridge eased out of the anchor desk chair and Crawford Sloane moved in. As he did, Sloane gripped Partridge's arm and murmured, "Thank you, Harry—for everything."

"Some of us will be working tonight," Partridge assured him, "trying to come up with ideas."

"I know. I'm grateful." Routinely, Sloane skimmed through the scripts an assistant placed in front of him and, watching, Partridge was shocked by the other man's appearance. Not even makeup could conceal ravages the past day and a half had wrought. Sloane's cheeks appeared hollow, there were bags beneath his eyes, which were red-rimmed; perhaps, Partridge thought, he had been crying in private.

"Are you okay?" he whispered. "Sure you want to do this?"

Sloane nodded. "Those bastards won't put me out of action."

The studio floor manager called out, "Fifteen seconds."

Partridge moved from camera range, then quietly left the news studio. Outside he watched a monitor until satisfied that Sloane would make it through to the end of the news. Then he left by taxi for Shun Lee West.

Their table was at the rear of the restaurant in a relatively quiet corner.

Near the end of the first course—a steaming, delicately flavored winter melon soup—Partridge addressed Cooper. The young Englishman had spent most of the day in Larchmont, talking with everyone who had knowledge of the kidnapping, including the local police. He had returned to task force headquarters in the late afternoon.

"Teddy, let's hear your impressions so far, and any ideas on where we go from here?"

Cooper pushed his empty soup dish away and wiped his lips. He opened a well-worn exercise book and answered, "Okay, impressions first."

The pages in front of him were crowded with scribbled notes.

"First off, it was a pro job all the way. The blokes who put this together didn't muck about. They planned it like a railway timetable and made sure they left no evidence behind. Secondly, these were pros who had lotsa money."

Norman Jaeger asked, "How do you know?"

"Hopin' you'd ask." Cooper grinned as he looked around the table. "For one thing, everything suggests that whoever did the snatch kept a close eye on the house for a long time before they made their move. You've heard about the neighbors who now say they saw the motors outside the Sloane house, and once or twice vans, and thought the people in 'em were *protecting* Mr. S, not spying on him? Well, five people've reported that since yesterday; today I talked to four. They all said they saw those motors on and off for three weeks, maybe a month. Then we've got to consider Mr. S, who now believes he was followed."

Cooper glanced at Partridge. "Harry, I read your notes on the info board and I believe Mr. S was right; he *was* trailed. I've a theory about that."

While they were talking, fresh dishes had appeared—sautéed shrimp with peppers, fried prawns, snow peas, fried rice. There was a pause to enjoy the hot food, then Rita urged, "How about that theory, Teddy?"

"Okay. Mr. S is a big TV star; he's used to being a public figure, watched wherever he goes, and that becomes a way of life. So as a sort of counterbalance he builds up a *subconscious* feeling of invisibility. He's not going to let stares from strangers, the turning heads or pointing fingers bother him. That's why he may have screened out the notion of being followed—which I reckon he was, because it fits in with full-blown reconnaissance of the whole Sloane family."

"Even if that's true," Karl Owens asked, "where does it get us?"

Partridge said, "It helps us build a picture of the kidnappers. Keep going, Teddy."

"Okay, so it cost the snatchers to take all that time and do all that spying. The same thing goes for all those motors they used; also a van, maybe two, and the Nissan van yesterday—a regular fleet. And there's something special about those motors."

Cooper turned a notebook page. "The Larchmont cops let me see those motor reports. Some interesting things come out.

"Now, when somebody sees a car, they may not remember much about it, but one thing most of us do remember is the color. Well, those people who reported seeing the motors described *eight different colors.* So I asked myself: Did the gang really have eight different cars?"

"They could have," Iris Everly said, "if they were rental cars."

Cooper shook his head. "Not our lads; they'd be too cagey. They'd know that renting motors means identification—drivers' licenses, credit cards. Also, rental cars have license plates which can be traced."

"So you've another theory," Iris prompted. "Right?"

"Right. What I think happened is the snatchers most probably had three motors and resprayed them, say once a week, hoping to lessen the chances of being noticed. Okay, it worked. Only thing was, in the respraying these blokes made a stupid mistake."

More food had arrived—two heaped platters of Peking duck. The others reached out with chopsticks and ate hungrily while Cooper continued.

"Let's go back a mo. One of those Larchmont neighbors noticed more than the others about these motors. That's because he's in the motor insurance business, knows makes and models."

Jaeger interrupted. "All this is interesting, my British friend, but if you want any of this delicious duck you'd best dive in before us greedy Yanks finish it."

"International duck!" Cooper joined with relish in the eating, then resumed.

"Anyway, this insurance geezer noticed the makes and models of the motors and he says he saw three, no more—a Ford Tempo, a Chevy Celebrity and a Plymouth Reliant, all this year's models, and he remembers some of the colors."

Partridge asked, "So how do you figure the repainting?"

"This afternoon," Cooper said, "your mate, Bert Fisher, phoned some car dealers for me. What came out was that some of the colors people say they saw aren't available for those models. For instance, the insurance geezer, he said he saw a yellow Ford Tempo, but there's no such color made. Same goes for a blue Plymouth Reliant. Someone else described a green motor, yet not one of those three makes comes in green."

Owens said thoughtfully, "You may be on to something. It's possible, of course, that one car could have been in an accident and repainted, but not likely three."

"Something else about that," Jaeger put in, "is that when auto body shops repaint cars, they mostly do it in manufacturer's colors. Unless somebody asks for an offbeat shade."

"Which wouldn't be likely," Iris contributed, "remembering what Teddy said just now about the people we're looking for being savvy. They'd want to be inconspicuous, not the other way."

"All of which I agree with, folks," Cooper said, "and it leads to the thought that the mob we're looking for did the spray jobs themselves, not giving much thought to current colors, perhaps not even knowing about them."

Partridge said doubtfully, "That's moving pretty far into supposition country."

It was Rita who asked, "But is it? Let me remind you of what Teddy pointed out earlier. That the people we're talking about practically ran a fleet of vehicles—at least three cars, one

truck and maybe two, a Nissan passenger van
for the kidnap . . . Anyway, five we know of.
Now, it makes sense that they'd want to keep
them together in one place, which would have
to be sizable. So isn't it likely it would be somewhere big enough to include a paint shop?"

"An operating headquarters is what you
mean," Jaeger said. He turned to Teddy; an increasing respect had replaced the older man's
skepticism of the morning. "Isn't that what
you're talking about? Where you're leading
us?"

"Yep." Cooper beamed. "Sure am."

Their meal—eventually to include eight
courses—had continued. Now before the group
was sautéed lobster with ginger and scallions.
They reached for portions thoughtfully, concentrating on what had just been said.

"An operating center," Rita mused.
"Maybe for the people involved, whoever they
are, as well as vehicles. We know from the old
lady's description there were either four or five
men at the kidnap scene. There could be others
offstage. Wouldn't it make sense for everything
to be together?"

"Including the hostages," Jaeger added.

"If we assume all that," Partridge said, "and
okay, let's do it for the moment, obviously the
next question is where?"

"We don't know, of course," Cooper said,

"but some hard thinking might suggest the *kind* of place it could be; also, maybe, how far it was —or is—from Larchmont."

With amusement, Iris queried, "Hard thinking you've already done?"

"Well," Cooper said, "since you ask . . ."

"Quit showing off, Teddy," Partridge said sharply. "Get to the point."

Cooper responded, unperturbed, "I tried to think the way a snatcher would plan. So I asked the question: After the snatch, when I'd grabbed what I wanted, what would I want next?"

"How's this for an answer?" Rita said. "To be safe from pursuit; therefore go like hell and get under cover quickly."

Cooper smacked his palms together. "Bleedin' right! And where better to be under cover than at that HQ hangout?"

Owens asked, "Am I reading you right? You're suggesting the HQ wasn't far away?"

"Here's how I see it," Cooper said. "First off, it needs to be well clear of Larchmont; staying anywhere in the area would be too risky. But, second, it shouldn't be too far. The snatchers would know that in the shortest time, maybe minutes, there'd be an alarm and police crawling all over the place. Therefore they'd have calculated how much time they'd got."

Rita asked, "If you're still inside their minds, how much time?"

"Guessing, I'd say half an hour. Even that long would be a bit iffy, but they'd have to chance it to get far enough away."

Owens said slowly, "Translating that to miles . . . remembering the area . . . I'd say twenty-five."

"Just what I figured." Cooper produced a folded New York area map and opened it. On the map, taking Larchmont as the center, he had drawn a crayon circle. He prodded within the circle with a finger. "Twenty-five-mile radius. I reckon the headquarters is somewhere inside here."

8

At 8:40 P.M. on Friday evening, while the CBA News group was still dining at Shun Lee West, a buzzer sounded in the mid-Manhattan apartment of the Peruvian diplomat, José Antonio Salaverry. It signaled a visitor.

The apartment, on Forty-eighth Street near Park Avenue, was part of a twenty-floor complex. Although a doorman was stationed on the main floor, visitors used an outside intercom system to announce their arrival, then were admitted directly by the building's tenants.

Salaverry had been edgy since his meeting with Miguel that morning at United Nations headquarters and was anxious to hear that the Medellín/Sendero Luminoso group was safely out of the country. Their departure, he thought, would end his own association with the frightening matter that had filled his mind since yesterday.

He and his banker friend, Helga Efferen, had been drinking vodka-tonics in front of a fireplace for more than an hour, neither of them feeling inclined to go to the kitchen to prepare food or to telephone and order it sent in. While the liquor had relaxed them physically, it had removed none of their anxiety.

They were an oddly matched pair—Salaverry, small and weasely; Helga, whom the single word "ample" best described. She was big-boned, abundantly fleshed, with cornucopian breasts, and a natural blonde. Nature, however, had stopped short of making her beautiful; there was a harshness to her face and an acidic manner that repelled some men, though not Salaverry. From their first meeting in the bank he had been drawn to Helga, perhaps seeing in her a reflection of himself and sensing, too, her hidden but strong sexuality.

If so, he had been right on both counts. They shared the same points of view, which were based mainly on pragmatism, selfishness and avarice. As to sex, during their frequent fornicating an aroused Helga became a frenzied whale to José Antonio's Jonah, surrounding and almost swallowing him. He loved it. Helga was also given to crying out loudly, sometimes screaming, at her climax, which made him feel macho and—in every way—bigger than he was.

A rare exception to this erogenous enjoyment had occurred earlier that evening. They had begun copulating, hoping to erase, even temporarily, their great worry. But it didn't happen and after a while they both realized that they didn't have their hearts in the enterprise and gave up.

The mental empathy, though, remained intact and was typified by their attitude to the Sloane family kidnapping.

Both were aware that they possessed important knowledge about a sensational crime which dominated the news and whose victims and perpetrators were being sought by almost every law enforcement agency in the country. Worse, they had aided and abetted the financing of the kidnap gang.

However, it was not the safety of the kidnap

victims that troubled José Antonio and Helga. It was their own. Salaverry knew that if his involvement were exposed, not even his diplomatic immunity would save him from exceedingly unpleasant consequences, including expulsion from the UN and the United States, the extinction of his career and, more than probably, the vengeance of Sendero Luminoso back in Peru. Helga, with no diplomatic protection, could be sent to prison for criminally withholding information and also, perhaps, for accepting bribes to channel funds secretly in the bank she worked for.

Those thoughts were running through her mind when the buzzer sounded and her paramour jumped up, hurrying to the wall-mounted intercom connected with the main floor entrance. Pressing a button, he queried, "Yes?"

A voice, made metallic by the system, announced, "This is Plato."

With relief, Salaverry informed Helga, "It's him." Then into the intercom, "Come up, please." He pressed a button which would release an entrance lock downstairs.

Seventeen floors below, the man who had been speaking with Salaverry entered the apartment building through a heavy plate-glass door. He was of average build, thin-faced and swarthy, with deep-set, brooding eyes and glossy dark hair. His age could have been anywhere from thirty-eight to fifty-five. He wore a trench coat, unbuttoned at the front, over an unremarkable brown suit. He had come in wearing lightweight gloves and despite the building's warmth did not remove them.

A uniformed doorman who had seen the man arrive and use the intercom waved him to an elevator. Three other people already waiting in the lobby entered the elevator too. The man in the trench coat ignored them. After pressing a button for the eighteenth floor, he stood expressionless, looking straight ahead. By the time the elevator reached his floor, the other occupants had left.

He followed an arrow to the apartment he sought, carefully noting there were three other apartments on the floor and an emergency stairway to the right. He did not expect to use the information, but memorizing escape routes was a habit. At the apartment doorway he pressed a button and heard a soft chime inside. Almost at once the door opened.

The man asked, "Mr. Salaverry?" His voice was soft, with a Latin accent.

"Yes, yes. Come in. Let me take your coat?"

"No. I will not be staying." The visitor looked swiftly around. Seeing Helga, he inquired, "This woman is the banker?"

It seemed an ungracious way of putting it, but Salaverry answered, "Yes, Miss Efferen. And your name?"

"Plato will do." Nodding to the area in front of the fire, "Can we go there?"

"Of course." Salaverry noticed that the man kept his gloves on. Maybe, he thought, it was a personal fetish or perhaps the fellow had a deformity.

They were now in front of the fireplace. After the slightest of nods to Helga, the man asked, "Is anyone else here?"

Salaverry shook his head. "We are alone. You may speak freely."

"I have a message," the man said, reaching into his trench coat. When his hand emerged, it was holding a nine-millimeter Browning pistol with a silencer on the muzzle.

The liquor he had drunk slowed Salaverry's reactions, though even had they been normal it was unlikely he could have done anything to change what happened next. While the Peruvian froze in amazement, and before he could move, the man put the gun against Salaverry's forehead and squeezed the trigger. In his last brief moment of life the victim's mouth hung open in surprise and disbelief.

The wound was small where the bullet entered—a neat red circle surrounded by a powder burn. But the exit wound at the rear of the head was large and messy as bone fragments, brain tissue and blood splattered out. In an instant before the body fell, the man in the raincoat had time to notice the powder burn, an effect he had intended. Then he turned to the woman.

Helga, too, had been riveted by shock. By now, however, surprise had turned to terror. She began to scream, and at the same time attempted to run.

In both efforts she was too late. The man, an accurate marksman, put one bullet through her heart. She fell and died, her blood pouring onto the rug where she had fallen.

The hit man, who was Miguel's paid assassin dispatched from Little Colombia, paused to listen carefully. The silencer on the Browning had effectively muffled the sound of both shots, but he took no chances, waiting for possible intervention from outside. If there had been any noise from neighbors or other signs of curiosity, he would have left immediately. As it was, the silence continued and he proceeded, swiftly and efficiently, with the remaining things he had been instructed to do.

First, he removed the silencer from the pistol and pocketed it. He put the pistol down temporarily near Salaverry's body. Then, from another pocket of his coat, he produced a small can of spray paint. Crossing to a wall of the apartment, he sprayed across it in large black letters the word *CORNUDO.*

Returning to Salaverry, he allowed some of the black paint to drip onto the dead man's right hand, then wrapped the limp fingers around the can and pressed them, so Salaverry's fingerprints were on the can. The hit man stood the can on a nearby table, then picked up the gun and placed it in the dead man's hand, again squeezing the fingers so that Salaverry's prints were on the gun. He arranged the gun and the hand so it would appear Salaverry had shot himself, then fallen to the floor.

The hit man did nothing to the woman's body, leaving it where it had fallen.

Next, the intruder took a folded sheet of stationery from his pocket on which were typed words. They read:

So you would not believe me when I told you she is a nymphomaniac whore, unworthy of you. You think she loves you when all she feels for you is contempt. You trusted her, gave her a key to your apartment. What she did with it was take other men there for vile sexual acts. Here are photographs to prove it. She brought the man and allowed his photographer friend to take pictures. Her nymphomania extends to collecting such pictures for herself. Surely, her use of your home so monstrously is the ultimate insult to a machismo man such as you.

—Your Former (and True) Friend

Moving from the living room, the hit man entered what obviously had been Salaverry's bedroom. He crumpled the typed sheet into a ball and threw it into a wastebasket. When the apartment was searched by police, as it would be, the paper was certain to be found. The probability was strong that it would be regarded as a semianonymous letter, the authorship known only to Salaverry when he was alive.

A final touch was an envelope, also produced by the hit man, containing some fragments of black-and-white glossy photos, each fragment burned at the edges. Entering a bathroom that adjoined the bedroom, he emptied the envelope's contents into the toilet bowl, leaving the pieces floating.

The pieces were too small to be identified. However, a reasonable assumption would be that Salaverry, after receiving the accusatory letter, had burned the accompanying photos and flushed the ashes down the toilet, though a few unburned portions still remained. Then, having learned of his apparent betrayal by his beloved Helga, in a jealous rage he shot and killed her.

Salaverry would then have sprayed the single word on the wall, a pathetic message describing what he felt himself to be. (If the investigating police officers did not speak Spanish, someone would quickly enlighten them that the English version of the word was "cuckold.")

There was even a touch of artistry in that crudely printed parting cry. While not, perhaps, the kind of thing an Anglo-Saxon or native American might do, it bespoke the volatile frenzy of a Latin lover.

A final assumption: In despair, unwilling to face the consequences of his act, Salaverry killed himself, the powder burn on his forehead being typical of a self-inflicted head wound.

As the experienced planners of the scene well knew, in New York City where unsolved homicides were commonplace and the police detective force severely overburdened, little time and effort would be spent investigating a crime where the circumstances and solution were so plainly in view.

The hit man surveyed the apartment living room, making a final check, then quietly left. When he walked out of the building unhindered, he had been inside less than fifteen minutes. A few blocks away, he peeled off his gloves and threw them into a sidewalk trash can.

9

Norman Jaeger asked, "Do you think Teddy Cooper will come up with something?"

"It wouldn't surprise me," Partridge said. "He has before."

It was after 10:30 and they were walking south on Broadway, near Central Park. The dinner meeting at Shun Lee West had broken up a quarter of an hour earlier, shortly after Cooper's declared opinion that the kidnap gang's headquarters was within a twenty-five-mile radius of Larchmont. He had followed the first opinion with a second.

The kidnappers and their victims, he believed, were at that operating center now, the gang members lying low until the initial searching eased up and police roadblocks were decreased or abandoned—both of which would inevitably happen soon. Then the gang and prisoners would move to some more distant location, perhaps in the United States, possibly elsewhere.

Cooper's reasoning had been considered seriously by the others. As Rita Abrams put it, "It makes as much sense as anything so far."

But Karl Owens pointed out, "That's an enormous area you're talking about, densely populated, and there's no way of searching it effectively, even with an army." He added, needling Cooper, "That is, unless you have another brilliant idea breezing up behind."

"Not right now," Cooper had answered. "I need a good night's kip. Then maybe I'll come up with—as you so kindly put it—something 'brilliant' in the morning."

They ended the discussion there, and though the next day was Saturday, Partridge had summoned another task force meeting for 10 A.M. For tonight, most of the group went their separate ways by taxi, though Partridge and Jaeger, enjoying the night air, decided to walk to their hotels.

"Where did you latch on to this guy Cooper?" Jaeger asked.

Partridge told him about discovering Teddy at the BBC, being impressed with his work and, soon after, finding him a better job with CBA.

"One of the first things he did for us in London," Partridge continued, "was in 1984, at the time the Red Sea was being mined. A lot of ships were getting blown up and sunk all over the place, but no one knew who the hell was laying the mines. Remember?"

"Sure I remember," Jaeger said. "Iran and Libya were prime suspects, but nothing more. Obviously a ship was doing the filthy work, but no one knew what ship, or whose it was."

Partridge nodded. "Well, Teddy started researching and spent days and days at Lloyds of London, patiently going through their records of ship movements. He began by believing that whatever ship had done the minelaying had passed through the Suez Canal. So he made lists of all the ships that had gone through Suez since just before the mine sinkings started—and that was a helluva lot of ships.

"Then he went through more records and traced the subsequent movements of *each ship he'd listed* as it went from port to port, comparing those movements with the dates of mine sinkings in particular areas. Finally—and I mean after a *long, long search*—he came up with the name of one ship, the *Ghat*. It had been *everywhere* where other ships had struck mines, and in each case just a day or two before. Talk about a 'smoking gun.' Teddy found it."

Partridge went on, "As we know now, the ship was Libyan and once the name was in the open, it didn't take long to put proof together that Qaddafi was behind it all."

"I knew we were ahead of others on the story," Jaeger said. "But I didn't know the rest of the yarn behind it."

"Isn't that usually the way?" Partridge grinned. "We correspondents get credit for work that guys like you and Teddy do."

"I'm not complaining," Jaeger said. "And I'll tell you one thing, Harry—I wouldn't change places with you, especially at my age." He ruminated, then went on. "Cooper's just a kid. They're all kids. This has become a kids' business. They have the energy and the smarts. Do you have days like me when you get to feeling old?"

Partridge grimaced. "Just lately, all too often."

They had reached Columbus Circle. To their left was the formidable darkness of Central Park where few New Yorkers ventured at night. Immediately ahead lay West Fifty-ninth Street, beyond it the brighter lights of mid-Manhattan. Partridge and Jaeger carefully crossed the confluence of thoroughfares as traffic swirled about them.

"You and I have seen a lot of changes in this business," Jaeger said. "I guess, with luck, we'll be around for more."

Partridge asked, "What do you think's ahead?"

Jaeger considered before answering. "I'll tell you first what I *don't* see happening, and that's network news disappearing or even changing much, despite some dire predictions. Maybe

CNN will move into top rank—it has the distri-
bution; all that's needed is network quality. But
the important thing is, there's an enormous appetite out there for news, more than ever before
in history, and in every country."

"Television did it."

"Damn right! TV's the twentieth-century
equivalent of Gutenberg and Caxton. What's
more, for all of television's failings, its news has
made people hungry to know more. It's why
newspapers are stronger and will stay that
way."

"I doubt they'll give us credit," Partridge
said

"They may not give credit, but they give attention. Don Hewitt at CBS has pointed out
that the *New York Times* has four times as
many people assigned full-time to television as
they have reporters covering the United Nations. And a lot of that writing is about *us*—TV
news, its people, what we do.

"Turn it around, though," Jaeger continued.
"When was there anything important enough
about the *Times* to be featured on TV? All of
that applies to the rest of the print press, and so
you ask yourself, which is being acknowledged
as the more important medium?"

Partridge chuckled. "Color me important."

"Color!" Jaeger seized the word. "That's
something else TV has changed. Newspapers

are looking more like television screens—something *USA Today* began. You and I, Harry, will live to see four colors on the *New York Times* front page. The public will demand it and the old gray *Times* will heed the writing on the tube."

"You're full of homespun tonight," Partridge said. "What else do you foresee?"

"I see the weekly newsmagazines disappearing. They're dinosaurs. When *Time* and *Newsweek* get to subscribers, much of what's inside is a week to ten days old, and nowadays who wants to read stale news? Incidentally, the way I hear it, advertisers are asking the same question."

Jaeger went on, "So despite their dishonest cover dates and classy writing, eventually the weekly newsies will go the way of *Collier's, Look* and the *Saturday Evening Post.* Incidentally, most kids working in news nowadays have never heard of those."

They had come to the Parker-Meridien on West Fifty-seventh, where Jaeger was staying. Partridge had preferred what he thought of as the more cozy Inter-Continental on East Forty-eighth.

"We're a couple of old war-horses, Harry," Jaeger said. "See you in the morning." They shook hands and said good night.

———

A half hour later, in bed and surrounded by several newspapers he had bought on the way to his hotel, Partridge began reading. But before long the newsprint blurred and he pushed the papers aside. He would go through them in the morning along with fresh editions which would arrive with breakfast.

Still, sleep did not come easily. Too much had happened in the preceding thirty-six hours. His mind was full—a kaleidoscope of events, ideas, responsibilities, all of them intertwined with thoughts of Jessica, the past, the present . . . memories revived . . .

Where was Jessica now? Was Teddy right about a twenty-five-mile radius? Was there a chance that somehow he, Harry the Seasoned Warrior, like some medieval knight in shining armor, could successfully lead a crusade to find and free his former love?

Cut the whimsy! Save thoughts about Jessica and the others for tomorrow. He tried to clear his mind to rest, or at least to think of something else.

Inevitably, that something else became Gemma . . . the *other* great love of his life.

Yesterday, during the journey from Toronto, he had relived that memorable papal flight: The Alitalia DC-10 . . . the press section and an encounter with the Pope . . . Partridge's decision not to use the pontiff's "slaves" remark,

rewarded by a rose from Gemma . . . the beginning of their mutual passion and commitment . . .

No longer avoiding thoughts of Gemma, as
he had for so long, he resumed in memory
where he had ended the day before.

*That papal tour, through Central America
and the Caribbean, was long and arduous. It was
one of the most ambitious undertaken by the
Pope. The itinerary included eight countries and
long flights, with some at night.*

*From the moment of their initial encounter,
Partridge decided he wanted to know Gemma
better, but his CBA reporting duties allowed him
little time to see her during stops. Yet they became increasingly aware of each other and sometimes in the air, when Gemma wasn't busy, she
came to sit beside him. Soon they began holding
hands and once, before leaving, she leaned over
and they kissed.*

*When it happened, his already strong desire
for her increased.*

*They talked as often as they could and he
began to learn about her background.*

*Gemma was born in Tuscany, the youngest of
three sisters, in a small mountain resort town,
Vallombrosa, not far from Florence. "It is not a
fashionable place where the rich go, Harry caro,
but very beautiful."*

Vallombrosa, she told him, was a haven of the Italian middle class, who stayed there during summers. A mile away was Il Paradisino where John Milton once lived and, legend claimed, found the inspiration for Paradise Lost.

Gemma's father was a talented artist who made a good living restoring paintings and frescoes; he often worked in Florence. Her mother was a music teacher. Art and music were an integral part of the family's life and continued to be part of Gemma's.

She had joined Alitalia three years earlier. "I wanted to see the world. There was no other way I could afford it."

Partridge asked, "This way, have you seen very much?"

"Some pieces. Not as many as I would like, and I am growing tired of being a cameriera del cielo.*"*

He laughed. "You're much more than a waitress in the sky. But you must have met many people." With a jealous twinge, he added, "A lot of men?"

Gemma shrugged. "Most I would not want to meet again outside an airplane."

"But there were others?"

She smiled, that flashing sweet smile, so much a part of her. "There has been no one I have liked as much as you."

It was said simply and Partridge, the profes-

*sional skeptic, wondered if he was being naïve
and foolish in believing her. Then he thought,
Why shouldn't I believe when I feel exactly the
same way, when no other woman since Jessica
has had the same effect on me as Gemma?*

*Both of them, he sensed, felt the journey was
going too quickly. So little time remained. At the
end of it they would probably walk away, never
seeing each other again.*

*Perhaps because of that sense of time run-
ning out, one memorable night when the cabin
lights were turned low and most others were
asleep, Gemma curled up beside him and, under
a blanket, they made love. In the confines of a
tourist three-seat section, they should have been
uncomfortable but somehow weren't, and he remembered it always as among the more beautiful experiences of his life.*

*It was immediately after their lovemaking—
on impulse, and reminded that he had lost Jessica through indecision—he whispered,
"Gemma, will you marry me?"*

*She had whispered back, "Oh, amor mio, of
course I will."*

*The next stop would be Panama. In a low
voice, Partridge asked questions and made plans
while Gemma, laughing softly, mischievously in
the semidarkness, agreed to everything.*

*In daylight they landed at Panama's
Tocumen Airport. The Alitalia DC-10 taxied in.*

*The Pope disembarked and, like the trained ac-
tor he had once been, smoothly kissed the ground
as a multitude of cameras zoomed in. After that,
the standard formalities began.*

*Before the landing, Partridge had talked
with his field producer and camera crew, asking
them to cover the Pope's activities during the
next few hours without him. He would join them
later in narrating and helping edit the regular
National Evening News report. Panama, which
did not have daylight saving time, was only an
hour behind New York, so there would be sufficient time.*

*While clearly curious, the other CBA staffers
asked no questions, though Partridge knew it was
unlikely that his and Gemma's growing attach-
ment had passed unnoticed.*

He also approached the New York Times *reporter on the flight, who happened to be Graham
Broderick, asking if he would share his notes for
that day with Partridge. Broderick, while raising
his eyebrows quizzically, agreed. Working journalists often made such trades, never knowing
when they might need help themselves.*

*When the others disembarked, Partridge
held back. He had no idea what explanation
Gemma gave to her chief, the senior purser, but
she joined him and they left the DC-10 together.
Gemma, still in Alitalia uniform, began explaining she had no means of changing into other*

clothes. But he stopped her and said, "I love you as you are."

She turned to face him, her expression serious. "Do you truly, Harry?"

He nodded slowly. "Truly."

They looked into each other's eyes and each seemed satisfied with what they saw.

Inside the airport terminal, Partridge left Gemma briefly. Going to a tourist booth, he asked several questions of a pimply youth behind a counter. The young man, smirking, told him he must go with the señora to Las Bóvedas, part of the Old City wall in the Plaza de Francia. There he would find the Juzgado Municipal.

Partridge and Gemma took a taxi to the Old City. They got out near a towering obelisk topped by a chanticleer, the crowing rooster commemorating French canal builders, among them the famed Ferdinand de Lesseps.

Some twenty minutes later, inside the old wall and standing before a juez in an ornate office that had once been a prison cell, Harry Partridge and Gemma Baccelli became husband and wife. During a five-minute ceremony the judge, casually dressed in a cotton guayabera, signed an Acta Matrimonial which cost twenty-five dollars and Partridge paid twenty dollars each to two stenographers who served as witnesses.

The bride and groom were informed that the

*additional formality of registering their marriage
was optional and, in fact, unnecessary until they
came back for a divorce.*

*"We will register," Partridge said, "and we
will not be back."*

At the end, without great conviction, the juez
*wished them, "¡Que vivan los novios!" They had
the feeling he had said it many times before.*

*Both then and later, Partridge wondered how
Gemma, who unhesitatingly agreed to a civil ceremony, reconciled it with her religion. She had
been born Catholic and her early education, she
had told him, was at a Sacré Coeur school. But
each time he asked, she merely shrugged and
said, "God will understand." It was, he supposed, typical of a casualness many Italians had
about religion. He had once heard someone say
that Italians always assumed God to be Italian
too.*

*Inevitably, aboard the papal airplane the
news of the marriage spread—as the London*
Times *correspondent put it, quoting* Revelation,
*faster than "the four winds of the earth." In the
press section, after takeoff from Panama, a cele-
bratory party was held with great quantities of
champagne, liquor and caviar. As much as their
duties allowed, the pursers and cabin crew joined
in and told Gemma there would be no work for
her through the remainder of that day. Even the*

Alitalia captain left the flight deck briefly to come back with congratulations.

Amid the revelry and good wishes, Partridge sensed strong doubts by some that the marriage would last, but also among the men, a feeling of envy.

Notably, but not surprisingly, there was no representation at the party from the ecclesiastics, and for the remainder of the trip Partridge was aware of their coolness and disapproval. Whether or not the Pope was ever informed of what had happened was something none of the journalists learned, despite inquiries. However, on that journey the Pope did not visit the press section again.

In the limited time they were able to spend together, Partridge and Gemma began planning for their future.

In a New York hotel room . . . slowly, sadly . . . the image of Gemma faded. The present replaced the past. At last, exhausted, Harry Partridge slept.

10

In the kidnappers' Hackensack base Miguel received a message by telephone at 7:30 Saturday morning. He took the call in a small room on the first floor of the main building, which he had kept for himself as an office and for sleeping.

Of the six portable cellular phones the group had used, one was earmarked to receive special calls, the number known only to those with authority to make them. Miguel always kept that phone close to him.

The caller, following orders, was using a public pay phone so the call could not be traced, in or out.

Miguel, alert and waiting, had been expecting the call for the past hour. He picked up the handset on the first ring and answered, *"¿Sí?"*

The caller then challenged him with a prearranged code word, *"¿Tiempo?"* to which Miguel responded, *"Relámpago."*

There was an alternative reply. If Miguel's answer to the query "weather?" had been "thunder" instead of "lightning," it would have meant that, for whatever reason, his group required a twenty-four hours' delay. As it was, *"relámpago"* conveyed: "We are ready to go. Name place and time."

The crucial message followed: *"Sombrero profundo sur* twenty hundred."

Sombrero was Teterboro Airport, slightly more than a mile away, *profundo sur* the airport's southern end gate. The words "twenty hundred" indicated the time—2000 hours or 8 P.M.—when the kidnap victims and those to accompany them would board a Colombia-registered Learjet 55LR which would be there, waiting. The 55, as Miguel already knew, was a larger model with a more spacious interior than the familiar 20 and 30 series Lears. The LR signified Long Range.

Miguel acknowledged curtly, *"Lo comprendo,"* and the conversation ended.

The caller had been another diplomat, this time attached to the Colombian Consulate General in New York; he had been a conduit for messages since Miguel's arrival in the United States a month earlier. Both the Peruvian and Colombian diplomatic corps were riddled with defectors, either Sendero Luminoso sympathizers or on the Medellín cartel payroll, sometimes both, and performing their double-crosses for the large amounts of money which Latin America drug lords paid.

After receiving the call, Miguel walked through the house and buildings and informed the others, though preparations for departure were already in hand and each group member knew what was required. Those to travel on the Learjet, accompanying the kidnap victims in their caskets, were Miguel, Baudelio, Socorro and Rafael. Julio would remain behind in the United States, resuming his previous identity and becoming, once more, a Medellín cartel sleeping agent. Carlos and Luís would quietly leave the country within the next few days, flying separately to Colombia.

Julio, Carlos and Luís, though, had a concluding duty after the Learjet had gone: to disperse the remaining vehicles and abandon them.

Miguel had given considerable thought about what to do with the Hackensack hideaway. He had considered, as a final act, burning the whole place down, vehicles with it. The collection of buildings was old and would go up like a furnace, especially with the help of gasoline.

But a fire would draw attention and, if investigated, the ashes might yield clues. While in some ways it wouldn't matter since everyone would be gone, it went against reason to make things easier for the American law agencies. So the idea of a fire was out.

If they simply vacated the building, leaving it as it was, their use of the place as a kidnap way station might not be discovered for weeks or months, perhaps never. But that required the disposition of the vehicles—driving them all in different directions for a good distance and then abandoning them. True, there were risks involved, specifically for those who would drive the three cars, the GMC truck and the hearse, but Miguel believed they weren't great. In any case it was what he had decided on.

He encountered Rafael first and told him, "We leave here this evening at 7:40."

The burly handyman-mechanic, who was in the outbuilding they used as a paint shop, grunted and nodded, seeming more interested in the GMC truck, which he had repainted the day before. The former white truck with the legend "Superbread" had been transformed to an almost totally black one with the name "Serene Funeral Homes" in discreet gold lettering on both sides.

Miguel had ordered the change himself. Satisfied, he told Rafael, *"¡Bien hecho!* A pity it will only be used once."

The big man swung around, clearly pleased, a slight smile on his scarred and brutish face. It was strange, Miguel thought, that Rafael who could be so savage in action, taking demoniac delight in inflicting suffering or killing, at other moments behaved like a child in need of approval.

Miguel pointed to the truck's New Jersey license plates. "These are fresh ones?"

Again Rafael nodded. "From the last set. Ain't been used yet, an' I switched the others."

It meant that all five remaining vehicles now had license plates which could not have been seen during the Larchmont surveillance, so that driving and abandoning them would be that much safer.

Miguel went outside to where, within a cluster of trees, Julio and Luís were digging a deep hole. The ground was wet from yesterday's rain and the work heavy going. Julio was using his spade to sever a rugged tree root and, seeing Miguel, he stopped, wiped his swarthy, sweating face with a sleeve, and cursed.

"*¡Pinche árbol!* This is shit work—for oxen, not men."

On the point of snapping back an obscenity, Miguel checked himself. The ugly knifing scar on Julio's face was turning crimson, a signal of the man's foul temper and that he was spoiling for a fight.

"Take a rest," Miguel said curtly. "There's time. We all leave at 7:40."

Brawling in these last few hours would be a

stupid waste. Besides, Miguel needed the men to finish digging the hole in which they would bury all the cellular phones and some medical equipment Baudelio would leave behind.

Burying the phones, in particular, was not an ideal arrangement and Miguel would have preferred to dump them somewhere in deep water. But while there was plenty of water in the New Jersey–New York area, the chances of doing something like that without being observed were not good—at least in the short time available.

Later that day, when the hole was refilled, Julio and Luís should be able to rake leaves over the surface, leaving no trace of what was beneath.

Carlos, to whom Miguel went next, was in another of the outbuildings, burning papers in an iron stove. Carlos, young and well educated, had organized the month-long surveillance records and photos of visitors to the Sloane house, all of which was now feeding the fire.

When Miguel told him about the evening departure, Carlos seemed relieved. His thin lips twitched and he said, *"¡Que bueno!"* Then his eyes resumed their normal hardness.

Miguel had been aware of the strain of the past forty-eight hours on everyone, Carlos especially, perhaps because of his youth. But commendably the younger man had kept himself under control and Miguel foresaw a command terrorism role for Carlos before too long.

A small pile of what appeared to be Rafael's clothing was beside the stove. Miguel, Rafael and Baudelio would all wear dark suits during the departure process by air when, to anticipate a possible U.S. Government inspection, they would pose as mourners, using a carefully designed cover story. Everything else would be left behind.

Miguel pointed to the clothes, "Don't burn those—too much smoke. Go through the pockets, take everything out and remove any labels. Then bury the rest." He gestured in the direction of the digging outside. "Tell the others."

"Okay." When he had attended to the fire again, Carlos said, "We should have flowers."

"Flowers?"

"Some on the casket that goes in the hearse, maybe on the others. It's what a family would do."

Miguel hesitated. He knew Carlos was right and it was something he hadn't thought of himself in planning their exit from the U.S., first via Teterboro, then aboard the Learjet to Opa Locka Airport, Florida, from where they would fly directly to Peru.

Originally, when Miguel had expected only two unconscious captives, he had planned to make two journeys with the hearse between the

Hackensack house and Teterboro Airport, conveying one casket at a time, which was all the hearse would hold. But three journeys with three caskets were too many and would entail too great a risk; therefore Miguel had devised a new plan.

One casket—Baudelio would decide which —would be transported to Teterboro in the hearse. The repainted GMC truck of "Serene Funeral Homes" would carry the other two.

The Lear 55LR, Miguel knew, was configured with a cargo door that allowed plenty of room for loading two caskets. Getting a third in might be difficult, but he was sure it could be done.

Still weighing Carlos's suggestion, he thought: The addition of flowers *would* make their cover story more convincing. At Teterboro they would have to pass through airport security. Probably, too, there would be supplemental police because of the kidnap alert, and questions were almost certain to be asked about the caskets and their contents. Some tense moments were likely and Teterboro, as Miguel saw it, was the key to their safe departure. At Opa Locka, from where they would actually leave the U.S., he anticipated no problems.

Miguel decided to take a small risk now to help offset the large one later. He nodded. "Yes, flowers."

"I'll take one of the cars," Carlos said. "I know where to go in Hackensack. I'll be careful."

"Use the Plymouth." It had been repainted dark blue and had license plates not previously used, as Rafael had pointed out.

After leaving Carlos, Miguel sought out Baudelio. He found him, with Socorro, in the large room on the second floor of the main house which by this time resembled a hospital ward. Baudelio, appearing like a patient himself, had dressings over the right side of his face, covering the stitches he had put in following Jessica's wild slashing during her brief consciousness.

Normally Baudelio appeared gaunt, pallid and older than he was, but today the effect was intensified. His face was sickly white and his movements clearly required an effort. But he was continuing with preparations for departure and after Carlos informed him of the 7:40 P.M. time, Baudelio acknowledged, "We will be ready."

Under prompting from Miguel, the ex-doctor confirmed that his day and a half of experimenting with the drug propofol had shown him how much should be administered to each of the three captives to achieve deep unconsciousness for specific periods. This knowledge was necessary for the times when each "patient" would be left unattended and unmonitored in one of the sealed caskets.

Also, the enforced starvation period for all three—which would be fifty-six hours by departure time—was satisfactory. There should be no vomiting or aspiration into the lungs, though as extra precautions against choking and suffocation, Baudelio added, an airway tube would be placed in each throat and the bodies turned on their sides before the caskets were closed. Meanwhile, the intravenous injection of fluids had prevented dehydration. From transparent bags of glucose, on stands beside each of the unconscious trio, drip tubes led to catheters in their arms.

Miguel paused, looking down at the three bodies. They appeared peaceful, their faces untroubled. The woman had a certain beauty, he thought; later, if opportunity arose, he might make use of her sexually. The man looked dignified, like an old soldier at rest which, according to news reports, he was. The boy seemed frail, his face thin; perhaps the enforced starvation had left him weak, which didn't matter as long as he was alive on arrival in Peru, as had been promised to Sendero Luminoso. All three were pale with only a little color in their cheeks, but were breathing evenly. Satisfied, Miguel turned away.

The funeral caskets into which Angus, Jes-

sica and Nicky would be moved shortly before
the general exodus to Teterboro Airport were
horizontal on trestles. Miguel was aware, because he had watched Rafael do it under guid-
ance from Baudelio, that a series of tiny vent
holes had been drilled into each. Almost invisible, they would admit fresh air.

"What is that?" Miguel pointed to a jar of
crystals next to the caskets.

"Soda lime granules," Baudelio answered.
"They're spread around inside to counter car-
bon dioxide from exhaled breath. There'll also
be an oxygen cylinder, controllable from outside."

Mindful that during the difficult hours
ahead Baudelio's medical skills would be vital
to them all, Miguel queried, "What else?"

The ex-doctor motioned to Socorro. "Tell
him. You'll be doing it with me."

Socorro had been watching and listening,
her face inscrutable as always. Miguel still had
questions in his mind about the woman's total
commitment, but today was distracted by her
provocative body, its sensuous movements, her
blatant sexuality. As if she read his thoughts,
there was a hint of taunting in her voice.

"If any of them needs to piss, even unconscious, they might move and make noise. So before closing those"—Socorro pointed to the cas-

kets—"we'll insert catheters. That's tubes in the men's cocks and the bitch's cunt. *¿Entiendes?*"

Miguel said testily, "I know about catheterization." On the point of telling her his father was a doctor, he checked himself. A moment's weakness, the influence of a woman, had almost led him to reveal a detail of his background, something he never did.

Instead he asked Socorro, "When we need it, can you cry?"

As part of the planned tableau, she also would be a grieving mourner.

"*Sí.*"

Baudelio added, with the professional pride which occasionally surfaced, "I will place a grain of pepper beneath each of her lower eyelids. The same for mine. The tears are then copious and will not stop until the pepper is out." He regarded Miguel. "I will do the same for you if you wish."

"We'll see."

Baudelio completed his strategy catalog. "Finally, in all three caskets will be tiny EKG monitors to record breathing and depth of sedation. I'll have a connection to read them from outside. The propofol infusion can be adjusted from outside too."

Reviewing their exchange, and despite earlier misgivings, Miguel felt satisfied that Baudelio knew what he was doing. Socorro too.

Now it was simply a question of waiting through the day. The hours ahead seemed interminable.

11

At CBA News headquarters on Saturday morning, the special task force meeting called for 10 A.M. had scarcely begun when it was abruptly interrupted.

Harry Partridge, seated at the head of the conference table, had opened a discussion when a speakerphone broke in—an announcement from the main newsroom. Partridge paused as he and the six others at the table listened.

"Assignment desk. Richardson. This bulletin just in from UPI . . .

"White Plains, New York—A passenger van, believed to be the vehicle used in Thursday's kidnap of the Crawford Sloane family, exploded violently a few minutes ago. At least three persons are dead, others injured. Police were on their way to inspect the van when the explosion occurred in a parking building adjoining Center City shopping mall. It happened as many weekend shoppers were

arriving in their cars. The building is extensively damaged. Fire fighters, rescue crews and ambulances are on the scene which a witness describes as 'like a nightmare from Beirut.' "

Even as the bulletin was continuing, chairs in the conference room were being pushed back, the task force members scrambling to their feet. As the speakerphone fell silent, Partridge was first out, on the run, hurrying to the newsroom one floor below, with Rita Abrams close behind.

Saturday morning in any network news department was a relatively informal time. Most of the Monday-to-Friday staff stayed home. The few on weekend duty, while sometimes under pressure, were aware of the absence of the high command. For this reason dress was casual, jeans predominating, and men showed up without ties.

The main CBA newsroom was eerily quiet, with barely a third of the desks occupied and that day's assignment manager, Orv Richardson, covering for the national desk as well. Young, fresh-faced and eager, Richardson had recently come to the network from a regional bureau. While not unhappy to be in charge, the important breaking story from White Plains made him slightly nervous. He wanted to be sure of doing the right thing.

It was with some relief, therefore, that he saw a Big Foot correspondent, Harry Partridge, and a senior producer, Abrams, burst into the newsroom and hurry his way.

While Partridge skimmed a printout of the United Press bulletin and read a follow-up story feeding in on a computer monitor, Rita told Richardson, "We should go on air immediately. Who has authority?"

"I have a number." With a phone tucked into his shoulder and consulting a note, the assignment manager tapped out digits for a CBA News vice president available at home. When the man answered, Richardson explained the situation and asked for authorization to take air with a special bulletin. The vice president shot back, "You have it. Go!"

What followed was a near-replay of Thursday's intrusion into the network when the kidnap news broke shortly before noon. The differences were the nature of today's report and the cast involved. Partridge was in the flash facility studio, occupying the correspondent's hot seat, Rita was acting executive producer, and in the control room a different director appeared, having come hastily from another section of the building after hearing a "special bulletin" call.

CBA was on air within four minutes after

receiving the UPI bulletin. The other networks
—observed from control room monitors—
broke into their own programming at almost
the same time.

Harry Partridge was, as always, collected
and articulate, the ultimate professional. There
was no time to write a script or use a Teleprompter. Partridge simply memorized the contents of the wire reports and ad-libbed.

The special broadcast was over in two minutes. There were the bare facts only, few details,
and no on-scene pictures—merely hastily gathered stills, projected over Partridge's shoulder,
of the Sloane family, their Larchmont home
and the Grand Union store where the Thursday
kidnap had taken place. A fuller report with
pictures from White Plains, Partridge promised
viewers, would be aired later on CBA's Saturday National Evening News.

As soon as the red camera lights went out in
the flash studio, Partridge phoned Rita in the
control room. "I'm going to White Plains," he
told her. "Will you set it up?"

"I have already. Iris, Minh and I are going
as well. Iris will produce a piece for tonight.
You can do a standup there and cut a sound
track later. There's a car and driver waiting."

The city of White Plains had a long history
going back to 1661 when it was an encampment

of the Siwanoy Indians who called it Quarropas
—which means white plains, or white balsam—
after the trees that grew there. In the eighteenth
century it was an important iron-mining center
and a transportation crossroads. In 1776, during the American Revolution, a battle on
nearby Chatterton Hill forced Washington's retreat, but in the same year a Provincial Congress in White Plains approved the Declaration
of Independence and the creation of New York
State. There were other milestones, good and
bad, though none exceeded in infamy the explosion engineered by the Medellín cartel and
Sendero Luminoso in the Center City Mall
parking building.

There was, it became clear later, a certain
inevitability to the cycle of events.

During the preceding night a patrolling security guard had recorded the license numbers
and makers' names of vehicles left there overnight—a normal procedure and a precaution
against cheating by drivers who might claim to
have lost their parking stub and to have parked
for one day only.

The presence of a Nissan passenger van with
New York plates had also been noted the night
before which, again, was not unusual. Sometimes, for a variety of reasons, vehicles were left
parked for a week or more. But during the second night a different and more alert security

guard wondered if the Nissan van could be the one he had heard about as being sought in connection with the Sloane family kidnapping.

He wrote a query to that effect on his report and the maintenance supervisor, on reading it next morning, promptly called the White Plains Police who ordered a patrol car to investigate. The time, according to police records, was 9:50 A.M.

The maintenance supervisor, however, did not wait for the police arrival. Instead he went to the Nissan van, taking along a large bunch of car keys he had accumulated over the years. It was a source of pride with him that there were few locked vehicles which, aided by his key collection, he could not open.

All of this was at a time when Saturday shoppers, in their cars, were beginning to stream into the parking building.

Quite quickly the supervisor found a key that fitted the Nissan van and opened the driver's door. It was his final act in the few remaining seconds of his life.

With a roar which someone later described as "like fifty thunderstorms," the Nissan van disintegrated in an intense, engulfing ball of flame. So did a substantial part of the building and several cars nearby, fortunately unoccupied, though what was left of them burned fiercely. The explosion punched wide holes in the parking building above and below where the Nissan van had been and caused flaming cars to cascade through the holes to the lower floors.

Nor was the effect confined to the parking building. The Center City Mall itself sustained structural damage and, in the mall and beyond, windows and glass doors were shattered. Other debris, initially blown upward, descended on adjoining streets, traffic and people.

The shock effect was total. When the initial roar subsided, apart from the quieter sound of fires and falling objects, there was a measurable silence. Then the screams began, followed by incoherent shouts and curses, hysterical pleas for help, unintelligible orders and, soon after, sirens approaching from all directions.

In the end it seemed extraordinary that the human toll, when added up, was no greater than it was. In addition to the maintenance supervisor's instant death, two others died soon after from their injuries and four more victims were critically hurt and hovering between life and death. Twenty-two more, including a half-dozen children, were injured and hospitalized.

Overall, the reference to Beirut in the UPI bulletin did not seem inappropriate.

Afterward there would be debate, focusing on the question: Would the explosion have happened if the maintenance supervisor had awaited the arrival of police? The police said no, claiming they would have called the FBI whose forensic experts would have examined the van, discovered the explosive material, and then disarmed it. But others were skeptical, believing the police would have opened the van anyway, either themselves or using the maintenance man's keys. Eventually, though, the discussion was seen as pointless and petered out.

One thing became self-evident. The destroyed Nissan van had indeed been used by the kidnappers of the Sloane family members two days earlier. The proximity to Larchmont, the van's recorded appearance in the Center City parking building Thursday and the fact that it was booby-trapped all pointed to that conclusion. So did the license number which, when checked against motor vehicle records, was shown as belonging to a 1983 Oldsmobile sedan. However, the owner name, address and insurance data in official files were quickly discovered to be phony; also the registration and insurance fees had been paid in cash, the payer leaving no true identity behind.

What it all meant was that the Oldsmobile had disappeared, probably junked, but its registration was kept alive for illicit use. Thus the license plates on the Nissan were illegal, though not on any police "hot list."

A question was raised because a witness at Larchmont had described the Nissan van as having New Jersey plates, whereas those seen in the White Plains parking building were New York's. But, as investigators later pointed out, it was normal for criminals to switch license plates immediately after a crime was committed.

One other conclusion was expressed by the White Plains police chief at the explosion scene. He told reporters grimly, "This was clearly the work of hardened terrorists."

When asked if, extending that reasoning, it was foreign terrorists who had abducted the Sloane family trio, the chief answered, "That didn't happen on my turf, but I would think so."

"Let's make that foreign terrorist theory our main focus for this evening's news," Harry Partridge told Rita and Iris Everly when he heard about the police chief's comment.

The CBA contingent had arrived a few minutes ago in two vehicles—the camera crew aboard a Jeep Wagoneer, Partridge, Rita, Iris and Teddy Cooper in a Chevrolet sedan driven by a network courier—both having covered the twenty-five miles from mid-Manhattan in a sizzling thirty minutes. As well as an assemblage of news people at the scene, a growing crowd of spectators was being herded behind police barriers. Minh Van Canh and the sound man, Ken

O'Hara, were already getting videotape and natural sound of the wrecked building, the injured who continued to be removed, and of piles of twisted, tortured vehicles, some still burning. They had also joined an impromptu press conference in time to tape the police chief's statement.

After making a general assessment of the situation, Partridge summoned Minh and O'Hara and began conducting on-camera interviews with some of those involved in rescue efforts as well as several spectators who had witnessed the explosion. It was work that could have been performed by the camera crew alone or with a producer. But it gave Partridge a sense of involvement, being in action, of *touching* the story directly for the first time.

Touching an ongoing news story was psychologically essential to a correspondent, no matter how well informed he or she might be about that story's background. Partridge had been working on the Sloane family kidnap for some forty-two hours, but until now without direct contact with any of its elements. At moments he had felt caged, with only a desk, a telephone and a computer monitor connecting him with the reality outside. Going to White Plains, tragic as the circumstances were, fulfilled a need. He knew the same applied to Rita.

The thought of her caused him to seek Rita out and ask, "Has anyone talked with Crawf?"

"I just phoned him at home," she said. "He was about to come here, but I pleaded with him not to. For one thing, he'd be mobbed. For another, seeing what those bastards are capable of would upset him terribly."

"Still, he'll see the pictures."

"He wants to. He'll meet us at the network, so will Les, and I have what's been shot already." Rita was holding several tape cassettes. She added, "I think you and I should go. Iris and Minh can stay a while longer."

Partridge nodded. "Okay, but give me a minute."

They were on the third floor of the parking garage. Leaving Rita, he walked to an unoccupied, undamaged corner. It provided a view of White Plains and the city going about its regular business. In the distance was the highway to New England and, beyond, the green hills of Westchester—all scenes of normalcy in contrast to the devastation close at hand.

He had walked away from that chaos, wanting a quiet moment to think, to ask and answer a tormenting question: Having accepted a commitment to somehow find and perhaps free Jessica, her son and Crawford's father, was there any hope . . . the slightest hope . . . of his succeeding? At this moment Partridge feared the answer would be no.

What had happened here today, observing what his adversaries were capable of, had been a chastening encounter. It raised still more questions: Could such merciless savagery be matched? Now that a terrorist connection was virtually confirmed, were any civilized resources capable of tracking and outwitting so evil an enemy? And even if the answer happened to be yes, and despite initial optimism at CBA News headquarters, wasn't it an empty conceit to believe that an unarmed news reporting cadre could succeed where police, governments, intelligence and military so often failed?

As to himself, Partridge thought, this was no open battle, the kind of warfare which, perversely or not, excited him and set his juices flowing. This was furtive and filthy, the enemy unknown, the victims innocent, the contest sickening . . .

But personal feelings aside, should he advise for pragmatic reasons the abandonment of active engagement by CBA, advocate their return to a standard role of news observing or, failing that, at least pass on responsibility to someone else?

He was conscious of movement behind him. Turning, he saw that it was Rita. She asked, "Can I help?"

He told her, "We've never had one quite like this before, with so much depending not just on what we report, but what we do."

"I know," she said. "Were you thinking of turning it in, handing the burden back?"

Rita had surprised him before with her perceptiveness. He nodded. "Yes, I was."

"Don't do it, Harry," she urged. "Don't give up! Because if you do, there isn't anyone else that's half as good as you."

12

Partridge, Rita and Teddy Cooper rode back to Manhattan together—at a pace considerably less frantic than their drive out. Partridge was in the front seat with the network driver, Teddy and Rita in the rear.

Cooper, whose decision to go to White Plains had been made at the last moment, had stayed in the background there, observing; then and now he appeared preoccupied, as if concentrating on a problem. Partridge and Rita, too, at first seemed disinclined to talk. For both, this morning's experience had been portentous.

While they had witnessed, many times, the effects of terrorism overseas, to observe its invasion of American suburbia was traumatic. It was as if barbarian madness had at last arrived, poisoning an environment which, if not calm, had until now possessed a base of reason. The erosion of that base begun today, they suspected, would be extensive and perhaps irreversible.

After a while Partridge turned in his seat, facing the other two, and said, "The British were convinced that imported terrorism couldn't happen in their country, but it did. A good many believed the same thing here."

"They were wrong from the beginning," Rita said. "It was always inevitable, never *if* but *when?*"

Both assumed with some certainty—acknowledged by the White Plains police chief— that the Sloane kidnapping had been a foreign terrorist act.

"So who the hell are they?" Partridge pounded a fist into his palm. "That's what we must concentrate on. *Who?*"

It was clear to Rita that Harry had put behind him the notion of abdicating the leadership of CBA's task force. She answered, "It's natural to think first of the Mideast—Iran, Lebanon, Libya . . . the religious lineup: Hezbollah,

Amal, Shiites, Islamic Jihad, FARL, PLO, you name it."

Partridge acknowledged, "I've been thinking that way too. Then I ask myself, *Why would they?* Why would they bother extending their reach so far, taking the risks of operating here, with so many easier targets close to home?"

"To make an impression, perhaps. To convince the 'great Satan' there's no safety anywhere."

Partridge nodded slowly. "You might be right." He looked at Cooper. "Teddy, should we consider the IRA as possibles?"

The researcher snapped out of his reverie. "I don't think so. The IRA are scum who'll do anything, though not in America because there are still idiot Irish-Americans who feed them money. If they went active here, they'd cut that payola off."

"Any other thoughts?"

"I agree with what you say, Harry, about the Mideast mob. Maybe you should be looking south."

"Latin America," Rita said. "It makes sense. Nicaragua's the most likely, Honduras or Mexico possibilities, even Colombia."

They continued to theorize but had reached no conclusion when Partridge said to Teddy, "I know something's at work in that convoluted mind of yours. Are you ready to share it with us?"

"I guess so." Cooper considered, then began, "I reckon they've left this country."

"The kidnappers?"

The researcher nodded. "And taken Mr. S's family. What happened back there this morning"—he inclined his head toward White Plains—"was like a signature. To let us know the kind of people they are, how rough they play. It's a reminder for later on, for anyone who has to deal with them."

"Let's be sure I read you," Partridge said. "You believe they estimated how long it would take for the van to be discovered and blow up, and planned to have it happen *after* they had gone?"

"That's the size of it."

Partridge objected, "You're simply guessing. You could be wrong."

Cooper shook his head. "Better than guessing—say an intelligent assessment. Which is probably dead right."

Rita asked, "Supposing you *are* right, where does that leave us?"

"It leaves us," Cooper said, "having to decide if we want to make a big expensive effort to find their hideaway, even though it's empty when we get there."

"Why would we care about that if, as you assume, the birds have flown?"

"Because of what Harry said yesterday: Everybody leaves traces. No matter how careful they've been, these blokes will have too."

Their network car was nearing Manhattan. They were on the Major Deegan Expressway, the Third Avenue Bridge ahead, and the driver slowed in increased traffic. Partridge looked out, confirmed his bearings, then returned his attention to the other two.

"Last night," he reminded Cooper, "you told us you'd try for an idea to locate the gang's headquarters. Is that 'big expensive effort' part of it?"

"It would be. It would also be a long shot."

Rita said, "Let's hear about that."

Cooper consulted a notebook and began, "What I figured on first was the kind of a place this mob would need to do all those things we discussed last night—park at least five vehicles, most likely out of sight, set up a workshop big enough to spray those motors, then have enough living, sleeping and eating quarters for four people and probably a couple more for good measure. They'd want space for storage, then somewhere safe to lock up the three Sloanes after they'd snatched 'em, and—for that size of operation—an office of some kind. So it wouldn't be anything small, especially not some ordinary house with nosey parker neighbors around."

"Okay," Partridge agreed, "I'll buy that for starters."

"So what kind of place would it be?" Cooper continued. "Well, the way I see it, it would most likely be one of three things—either a small disused factory, or an empty warehouse, or a big house with outbuildings. But whichever, it would need to be somewhere with not much going on around—isolated, lonely—and as we've already agreed, it shouldn't be more than twenty-five miles from Larchmont."

"You've already agreed," Rita pointed out. "The rest of us have gone along because we couldn't think of anything better."

"The trouble is," Partridge objected, "even in that twenty-five-mile radius there could be twenty thousand places answering that description."

Cooper shook his head. "Not that many. After our dinner last night, I talked with some of the others and what we reckoned, when you include the lonely part, was maybe one to three thousand."

"Even then, how in hell would we find the one we want?"

"I already said it would be a long shot, but there might just be a way."

As Partridge and Rita listened, Cooper described his plan.

"Start out by mulling this over: When those snatchers got here, wherever they came from, they had to set up base close to Larchmont, but not too close—just the way we said. So how would they most likely find one? First, pick a general area. After that, do what anyone else would, 'specially when they're short of time— look through the newspaper property ads, and the kind of place they'd need to lease or rent would be in the classifieds. Of course we can't be certain, but there's a good chance that's how they got the setup they used."

"Sure it's a possibility," Partridge said. "It's also a possibility they had local advance help, with the base set up before they got here."

Cooper sighed. "Too bloody true! But when all you have to work with is possibles, you go for those you can put your hands on."

"So I'm being a devil's advocate, Teddy. Keep going."

"Okay, moving on . . . What we should do now is study the estate agents' ads in every paper, regional and local, published over the last three months inside that twenty-five-mile radius, with Larchmont as the center. Going through those papers, we'd look for ads of certain types—for the kinds of buildings we just talked about—especially any ad that ran for a while, then suddenly stopped."

Rita gasped. "Have you *any idea* how many papers, dailies and weeklies, and how many people—"

Partridge told her, "I'm thinking the same way, but let him finish."

Cooper shrugged. "Do I know the number of papers? No, not exactly, except it's a bleedin' lot. But what we'd do is hire people—bright young kids—to go around and look through them all. I'm told there's a book . . ." Cooper paused to check his notes. *"Editor and Publisher International Year Book,* which lists every paper, big and small. We'd start with that. From there we'd go to libraries which have files of newspapers, some on microfilm. For the others we'd go direct to the papers and ask to look through their back numbers. It'll take a lot of bodies, and it has to be done fast, before the trail gets cold."

Partridge said, "And you figure three months of advertising would cover . . ."

"Look, we know these people were snooping on the Sloanes for about a month and, when it started, you can bet they had their pad set up. So three months is a sane spread."

"What happens when we find some advertising that fits the kind of place we're searching for?"

"There should be a big number of 'possibles,'" Cooper said. "We'd sort them into priorities, then have some of the same people we hired to check the newspapers do the follow-up too. First, by contacting the advertisers and asking the odd question. After that, according to the answers, we'd decide which places we should take a look at." Cooper shrugged. "Most of the look-sees would be goose eggs, but some might not. I'd expect to do some of the follow-up myself."

There was a silence as Partridge and Rita weighed what they had heard.

Partridge announced his judgment first. "I salute you for an original idea, Teddy, but you said it was a long shot and it sure as hell is. A *long,* long shot. Right at this moment, I just can't see it working."

"Frankly," Rita said, "I think what you'd be trying to do is impossible. First, because of the number of papers involved—there's a multitude! Second, the amount of help you'd need would cost a fortune."

"Wouldn't it be worth it," Cooper asked her, "to get Mr. S's family back?"

"Of course it would. But what you're suggesting *wouldn't* get them back. At best it might produce some information and even that's unlikely."

"Either way," Partridge ruled, "we're not

making a decision here. Because of the money, Les Chippingham will do that. When we meet with him later today, Teddy, you can spell out your idea again."

The two-and-a-half-minute spot produced by Iris Everly for the Saturday National Evening News was dramatic, shocking and—as the jargon went—video-rich. At White Plains, Minh Van Canh had, as always, employed his camera creatively. Iris, back at CBA News headquarters and working again with the tape editor, Bob Watson, had fashioned a small masterpiece of news theater.

The process began with Iris and Partridge joining Watson in a tiny editing room—one of a half dozen side by side and in constant use as air time neared. There the three viewed all available videotapes while Iris made rough logs of the contents of each cassette. A late tape certain to be used showed the arrival of FBI agents at the White Plains explosion scene. Asked if there had been any communication from the kidnappers, the senior FBI man gestured around him and said, grim-faced, "Just this."

Other tapes included scenes of devastation and Partridge's on-scene interviews.

When they had finished viewing, Iris said, "I think we should begin with that pile of burning cars, show where those floors of the building were torn apart, then cut to the dead and injured being carried out." Partridge agreed and, with more discussion, they crafted a general plan.

Next, still in the editing booth, Partridge recorded an audio track, the correspondent's commentary over which pictures would be superimposed. Reading from a hastily typed script, he began, *"Today, any remaining doubt that the kidnappers of the Crawford Sloane family are full-fledged terrorists was savagely dispelled . . ."*

That evening, Partridge's participation in the broadcast would differ from the two preceding days when, on Thursday, he had anchored the news, then the following evening been co-anchor with Crawford Sloane. Tonight he would be in his normal role as a correspondent, since CBA's Saturday news had its own regular anchor person, Teresa Toy, a charming and popular Chinese-American. Teresa had initially discussed with Partridge and Iris the general line their report would take. From then on, aware that she was dealing with two of the network's top professionals, she wisely left them alone.

When Partridge finished the audio track, he left to do other things. After that it took Iris and Watson another three hours to complete the painstaking editing process, a facet of TV news seldom understood by viewers who watched the polished end result.

Externally, Bob Watson seemed an unlikely candidate for the meticulous, patient work his editing job required. He was chunky and simian, with stubby fingers. Though he shaved each morning, by midafternoon he looked as if he had a three-day growth of beard. And he chain-smoked fat, pungent cigars which those obliged to work with him in his tiny cubicle repeatedly complained about. However, he told them, "If I cain't smoke, I don't think so good, then you get a piss-poor piece." Producers like Iris Everly suffered the smoke because of Watson's skill.

The video and sound editing of TV news reports was done in network headquarters, distant bureaus around the world, or could even be on the spot near some breaking news scene. The news served up daily by the networks consisted of all three.

The standard tools of a TV editor, which Watson faced with the petite, strong-willed Iris seated beside him, were two machines, each an elaborate video recorder with precise controls and meters. Linked to the recorders and displayed above them was an array of TV monitors and speakers. Alongside and behind the editor, racks contained dozens of tape cassettes received from network cameramen, the network's tape library or affiliate stations.

The objective was to transfer to a master tape, inserted in the left recorder, snippets of scenes and sounds from a multitude of other tapes which were reviewed and rereviewed in the recorder on the right. Transferring a scene, seldom more than three seconds long, from a right-hand tape to the master required artistic and news judgment, infinite patience and a watchmaker's delicacy of touch. In the end, the contents of the master tape would be broadcast on air.

Watson began putting together the opening sequence already agreed on—the burning cars and shattered building. With the speed of a mail sorter, he plucked cassettes from racks, inserted one into the right-hand video machine and, using fast forward, found the required scene. Dissatisfied, he fiddled with rewind, went back and forth, stopped at another shot, returned to the first. "No," he said, "somewhere there's a wide shot from the opposite angle that's better." He switched cassettes, viewed and discarded a second, then chose a third and found what he sought. "We should start with this, then go to the first for a closeup."

Iris agreed and Watson transferred images and sound to the master tape. Dissatisfied with his first and second tries, he wiped them out, then was happy with the third.

Sometime later, Iris said, "Let's see that stock shot of a Nissan." They viewed it for a second time; it showed a new and spotless Nissan passenger van moving in sunshine down a leafy country lane. "Idyllic," she commented. "What do you think of using it, then cutting to what's left of the kidnap van after the explosion?"

"It'll work." After several experiments, Watson combined the two with maximum shock value.

"Beautiful!" Iris murmured.

"You ain't so dumb yourself, kid." The tape editor picked up his cigar and emitted a cloud of smoke.

Ideas and exchanges continued flowing back and forth. The working alliance of a line producer and tape editor had been described as a duet. It often was.

Within the process, though, the possibilities for prejudice and distortion were infinite. Individuals could be shown doing things out of sequence. A political candidate, for example, might be seen laughing at the sight of homeless people when in reality he had wept, the laughter having occurred earlier and been directed at something else. Using a technique known as "slipping audio," sound or speech could be transposed from one scene to another, with only an editor and producer knowing of the change. When such things were about to be done, a correspondent who happened to be in an editing room was asked to leave. The correspondent might guess what was intended but prefer not to know.

Officially such practices were frowned on, though they happened at all networks.

Iris had once asked Bob Watson if he ever let his political prejudices—known to be strongly socialist—influence his editing. He answered, "Sure, at election times if I think I can get away with it. It ain't hard to make someone look good, bad or downright ridiculous, providing the producer goes along."

"Don't ever try it with me," Iris had said, "or you'll be in trouble."

Watson had touched his forehead in mock salute.

Now, continuing with the White Plains report, Iris suggested, "Try that shot with the doughnut effect."

"It's better—Oh, goddamn that inconsiderate schmuck!" The head of a still photographer had popped up, ruining the video shot, a reminder of a perpetual war between press photographers and TV camera crews.

At one point, pictures on the master tape

didn't fit the sound track. Watson said, "We need Harry to change some words."

"He will. Let's finish our stuff first."

Watson chafed over limiting to three seconds the length of several shots. "In British TV news they let their shots run five; you can build a mood that way, use sound to help. Did you know the Brits have a longer attention span than we do?"

"I've heard people say so."

"Over here, if you use five-second shots more than occasionally, twenty million assholes'll get bored and change channels."

When they took a few minutes' break for coffee and Watson had a fresh cigar going, Iris asked him, "How did you get into this?"

He chuckled. "If I told you, you wouldn't believe."

"Try me."

"I lived in Miami, was the night janitor for a local TV station. One of the young news guys who was on at nights saw I was interested and showed me how the edit machines worked; that was back when they were using film, not tape. After that, I'd work like hell to get the cleaning work done fast. Come three or four in the morning, I'd be in an edit room splicing yesterday's outtakes they'd thrown away, putting stories together. After a while I guess I got good."

"So what happened."

"One time in Miami, while I was still a janitor, there was a race riot. It was at night. Everything was going wild, a lot of the black area, Liberty City, burning up. The TV station I worked for had called in all its people, but some had trouble getting through. They didn't have a film editor, needed one real bad."

Iris said, "So you volunteered."

"At first, nobody'd believe I could do it. Then they got desperate and let me try. Right away, my stuff was going on air. They sent some to the network. The network used it all next day. I stayed on the job ten hours. Then the station manager came in and fired me."

"Fired you!"

"As a janitor. Said I was goofing off, didn't have my mind on my work." Watson laughed. "Then he hired me as an editor. Haven't looked back since."

"That's a lovely story," Iris said. "When I write my book someday, I'll use it."

Soon after, at Watson and Iris's suggestion, Partridge changed some words of commentary to match the editing and Watson slipped the rerecording in. Partridge also recorded a final standup for the piece, facing a camera on the street outside the CBA News building.

Since returning from White Plains, Partridge had thought deeply, at moments ago-

nized, about what he would say. If this had
been a normal news story a summation would
have been easy. What made this story different
was Crawford Sloane's involvement. Some of
the words he had considered using would, Partridge knew, bring anguish to Crawf. So should
he soften them, waffle just a little, or be the
hard-nosed newsman with a single standard—
objectivity?

In the end, the decision simply happened.
Outside the CBA News building, with a camera
crew waiting and curious pedestrians watching,
Partridge scribbled the sense of what he would
say, then, memorizing the notes, ad-libbed.

*"The events in White Plains today—a mon-
strous tragedy for that city's innocent victims—is
also the worst of news for my friend and colleague, Crawford Sloane. It means, without
doubt, that his wife, young son and father are in
the hands of savage, merciless outlaws, their identities and origins unknown. The only thing clear is
that whatever their motives, they will stop at nothing to achieve them.*

*"The nature and timing of the crime at White
Plains also raise a question which many are now
asking: Have the kidnap victims by this time been
removed from the United States and conveyed to
some distant place, wherever that may be?*

"Harry Partridge, CBA News, New York."

13

Teddy Cooper was wrong. The kidnappers and their victims had not left the United States. However, according to present plans, a few more hours would see them gone.

For the Medellín group still holed up at Hackensack on Saturday afternoon, tension was at a peak, nerves stretched to their limit. The immediate cause for concern was radio and TV reports about that morning's events at White Plains.

Miguel, restless and anxious, snapped back answers to questions from the others, several times swearing at those who asked them. When Carlos, usually the mildest of the five Colombian men, suggested angrily that booby-trapping the Nissan van with explosives had been *una idea imbécil,* Miguel snatched up a knife. Then, gaining control of himself, he put it down.

In truth, Miguel knew that booby-trapping the passenger van at White Plains had been a bad mistake. The intention was to provide a

harsh warning about the kidnappers' seriousness, after they had gone.

After was the operative word.

Miguel had been confident that because of
changes in the van's appearance made following
the kidnap—eliminating the dark windows and
switching from New Jersey to New York license
plates—it would remain unnoticed in the White
Plains parking garage for five or six days, perhaps much longer.

Clearly, his judgment had been wrong.
Worse, that morning's explosion and aftermath
had refocused national attention on the Sloane
family's kidnappers and raised police and public
alertness to a peak, just when they were ready
to steal quietly out of the country.

Neither Miguel nor the others cared in the
least about the deaths and general mayhem at
White Plains. In other circumstances they
would have been amused. They cared only to
the extent that they themselves were now in
greater peril *and it need not have occurred.*

The conspirators at Hackensack batted
questions back and forth: Would police roadblocks, which according to news reports had
eased since Thursday, be reinstated? If so,
would there be one or more between the hideaway and Teterboro Airport? And what about
the airport? Would security be tighter because
of the new alert? And even if the four who were

going, plus captives, managed to leave Teterboro safely in the private Learjet, what of the stop at Florida's Opa Locka Airport? How great was the danger there?

No one, including Miguel, had any answers. All they knew for sure was that they were committed to going; the machinery of their transfer was in motion and they must take their chances.

Another reason for tension, perhaps inevitable, was the increasing disenchantment of the conspirators with one another. Having been in close confinement for more than a month with only the most limited outside contacts, some personal irritations became magnified into something close to hatred.

Particularly obnoxious to the others was Rafael's habit of coughing up mucus, then spitting it out wherever he found himself, including at the meal table. At one mealtime Carlos was so offended that he called Rafael *¡un bruto odioso!,* prompting Rafael to grab Carlos by the shoulders, throw him against a wall, then pummel him with hamlike fists. Only Miguel's intervention saved Carlos from injury. Since then, Rafael had not changed his habit though Carlos seethed.

Luís and Julio had also become antagonists. The week before, Julio had accused Luís of cheating at cards. A fistfight ensued which neither won, but next day they had swollen faces and the two had scarcely spoken since.

Now, Socorro was another source of friction. Despite her earlier rejection of sexual overtures, last night she had bedded with Carlos. The animal noises had aroused envy in the other men and intense jealousy in Rafael, who had wanted Socorro for himself and reminded her this morning. But, she told him in front of the others during breakfast, "You will have to change your filthy manners before you stick your *verga* in me."

That situation was complicated by Miguel's own strong desire for Socorro. But as the group's leader he continually reminded himself that he could not afford to join in the competition over her.

His leadership role, he realized, had had other effects as well. Looking in his shaving mirror recently, he realized he was shedding his unremarkable "everyman" appearance. Less and less did he resemble an innocuous clerk or minor manager, which had once been his natural camouflage. Age and responsibility were giving him the look of what he was—a seasoned, strong commander.

Well, he thought today, all commanders made mistakes and White Plains clearly had been one of his.

Thus, for everyone's varying reasons, it was

a big relief as 7:40 P.M. neared and final pullout procedures got underway.

Julio would drive the hearse, Luís the "Serene Funeral Homes" truck. Both vehicles were loaded and ready.

The hearse contained a single casket in which Jessica lay, under deep sedation. Angus and Nicholas, also unconscious and in closed caskets, were in the truck. On top of each casket Carlos had placed a garland of white chrysanthemums and pink carnations, the flowers he had obtained that morning.

Strangely, the sight of the caskets and flowers subdued the conspirators, as if the roles they had rehearsed in their minds and were about to act out had somehow become easier to assume.

Only Baudelio, fussing around the three caskets, taking last-minute readings with his external equipment, remained solely attuned to immediate concerns, this being one of several times during the next few hours when the success of the enterprise would depend totally on his prior judgments. If one of the captives should regain consciousness and struggle or cry out while the group was en route, especially while being questioned, all could be lost.

Even a suspicion that the caskets were in any way unusual could result in their being opened and the entire plan foiled—as happened

at Britain's Stansted Airport in 1984. On that
occasion a Nigerian, Dr. Umaru Dikko, having
been kidnapped and drugged, was about to be
flown to Lagos in a sealed crate. Airport workers reported a strong "medicine-type smell" and
British Customs officers insisted that the crate
be opened. The victim was discovered, unconscious but alive.

Miguel and Baudelio both knew of that
1984 incident and wanted no repetition.

As the moment to leave for Teterboro approached, Socorro had appeared, strikingly se-
ductive in a black linen dress with matching
jacket trimmed with braid. Her hair was tucked
under a black cloche and she wore gold earrings
and a thin gold necklace. She was crying copi-
ously, the result of Baudelio's prescription of a
grain of pepper beneath each lower eyelid. She
now gave the same treatment to Rafael; at first
he had objected, but Miguel insisted and the big
man gave in. Soon after Rafael adjusted to the
mild discomfort, his tears rolled out too.

Rafael, Miguel and Baudelio, each wearing
their dark suits and ties, looked suitably cast as
mourners. If questions were asked, Rafael and
Socorro would pose as brother and sister of a
dead Colombian woman, killed in a fiery auto
accident while visiting the U.S., whose remains
were being flown home for burial. And since the
woman's young son—so the cover story went—

was one of two others killed in the same accident, Rafael and Socorro would be Nicky's sorrowful uncle and aunt. The third "dead" person, Angus, would be described as an older distant relative who had been traveling with the other two.

Baudelio would be a supportive member of the bereaved family, Miguel a close family friend.

Elaborate documentation corroborated the cover story—fake death certificates from Pennsylvania where the fatal accident supposedly occurred, graphic photos of a turnpike traffic disaster scene, and even press clippings purportedly from the *Philadelphia Inquirer,* but in fact printed on a private press. The documents had included new passports for Miguel, Rafael, Socorro and Baudelio and two spare death certificates, one of which had since been used for Angus. The document "package" had been obtained through another of Miguel's Little Colombia contacts and cost more than twenty thousand dollars.

Included in the cover story and false news reports was a critical feature: All three bodies were so badly mangled and burned that they were unrecognizable. Miguel counted on that to deter any opening of the caskets during their removal from the United States.

The hearse and truck now had their engines

running and behind them was the Plymouth Reliant, with Carlos in the driver's seat. He would follow the other vehicles at a distance, though ready to intervene in case of trouble. With the exception of Baudelio, they were all armed.

The immediate plan was to proceed directly to the airport, which should take about ten minutes, fifteen at the most.

In the courtyard of the Hackensack house, Miguel checked his watch. 7:35 P.M. He instructed the others, "Everyone aboard."

Alone he made a final inspection of the house and outbuildings, satisfying himself that no significant traces of their occupancy remained. Only one thing troubled him. The ground where the hole had been dug to bury the cellular phones and other equipment was uneven compared with the area surrounding it. Julio and Luís had done their best to level the earth and spread leaves, but signs of disturbance remained. Miguel supposed it didn't matter greatly and at this point nothing could be done.

Returning to the hearse, he climbed into the front seat and told Julio tersely, "Go!"

Dusk had settled in, with the last traces of sunset on their right as they headed for Teterboro.

———

Luís was first to see the flashing police lights ahead. He swore softly as he braked. From the passenger side of the hearse, Miguel saw the lights too, then craned to survey their own position in relation to other traffic. Socorro was in the middle, seated between the two men.

They were on State Highway 17 headed south, with the elevated Passaic Expressway a mile behind. Traffic both ways on 17 was heavy. Between themselves and the flashing lights there was no turnoff to the right, and central dividers made a U-turn out of the question. Miguel, beginning to sweat, tightened his hold on himself and instructed Luís, "Keep going." He checked to make sure the "Serene Funeral Homes" truck was immediately behind.

Carlos in the Plymouth would be farther back, though it was impossible to see him.

Now they could see that the traffic ahead was being funneled into two right-hand lanes by several state troopers. Between the lanes was some kind of portable structure like a tollbooth and additional troopers appeared to be speaking with drivers as they stopped. Off to the right were more state police vehicles and flashing lights.

Miguel told the other two, "Stay cool. Leave any talking to me."

They inched forward for another ten minutes before gaining a better view of the head of the line. Even then it was not clear exactly what was happening; by now it was dark, the many lights confusing. It appeared, though, that after exchanges between the police and each vehicle's occupants, some cars and trucks were being directed to the side for closer examination, others waved on.

Miguel checked his watch. Almost 8 P.M. There was no way they could make the Learjet rendezvous on time.

Despite warning the others to stay cool, Miguel's own tension was mounting. After their remarkable success so far, was this to be the end of the line, resulting in capture or death in a shoot-out with police? Of the two, Miguel knew he would prefer death. The chances of bluffing their way out of this present jeopardy seemed slight. He wondered: Was it best to make a run for it now, at least put up a fight, or should they continue sitting here, letting the minutes tick away, with their only hope the unlikely gamble of getting through?

Luís muttered, "The fuckers are looking for us!" Reaching under his coat, he produced a Walther P38 pistol and laid it on the seat beside him.

Miguel snarled, "Keep that out of sight!"

Luís covered the gun with a newspaper.

Beside him, Miguel felt Socorro tremble. He put a hand on her arm and the movement stopped. He saw her looking steadily ahead, her eyes on an approaching state trooper.

The uniformed figure appeared to be alone, unattached to the group at the head of the line. He was glancing into stopped cars as he passed, pausing occasionally, apparently responding to questions. When the officer was a few yards away Miguel decided to take the initiative. He depressed the switch which lowered the electric window beside him.

"Officer," Miguel called out, "can you please tell me what this is about?"

The state trooper, who seemed little more than a youth, came closer. A name tag identified him as "Quiles."

"It's just a driver sobriety check, sir, in the interest of public safety," he said with a smile that seemed forced.

Miguel didn't believe him.

Then, as the trooper took in the hearse and its contents, he added, "I hope you haven't all come from a wake where there was a big booze-up."

It was a feeble lunge at humor which came out clumsily, but Miguel saw his chance and grabbed it. Riveting Trooper Quiles with a glare, he said sternly, "If that was meant as a joke, officer, it was in extremely poor taste."

The young trooper's expression changed instantly. He said, chagrined, "I'm sorry . . ."

As if he hadn't heard, Miguel pressed on, "The lady beside me has been visiting this country with her sister. That is her beloved sister in the casket behind us—tragically killed in a traffic accident, along with two others in the funeral van behind. Their bodies are being flown from here to be buried in their own land. We have an airplane waiting at Teterboro and we appreciate neither your humor nor the delay."

Taking her cue, Socorro turned her head so the trooper could see tears streaming down her face.

Quiles said penitently, "I said I was sorry, sir and madam. It just slipped out. I do apologize."

"We accept your apology, officer," Miguel said with dignity. "Now, I wonder if you could help us proceed on our way."

"Hold on, please." The trooper walked quickly forward to the head of the line where he consulted a sergeant. The sergeant listened, looked their way, then nodded. The young officer returned.

He told Miguel, "I'm afraid we're all a bit on edge, sir." Then lowering his voice in confidence, "The truth is, what's happening here is a cover and we're really looking for those kidnappers. Did you hear what they did in White Plains today?"

"Yes, I did," Miguel answered gravely. "It was terrible."

The car immediately ahead had moved forward, leaving a gap.

"Both of your drivers can pass around to the left, sir. Just follow me to the barrier, then join the onward traffic. Again, I'm sorry for what I said."

The trooper motioned the hearse and GMC truck out of line, at the same time signaling a car behind to continue forward. Glancing back, Miguel could still see no sign of the Plymouth Reliant. Well, he reasoned, Carlos would have to take care of himself.

The trooper preceded them on foot until they were level with the portable booth they had seen from a distance, then waved them by. The road ahead was clear.

As the hearse passed him, Trooper Quiles snapped a smart salute, holding it until both vehicles were gone.

Put to its first test, Miguel thought, their cover story had worked. With the challenge of Teterboro still to come, he wondered: Would it work again?

During the weeks they had been at Hackensack, Miguel had visited Teterboro Airport twice to study the layout.

It was a busy airport used exclusively by pri-

vate planes. During an average twenty-four
hours some four hundred flights might land and
take off, many of them at night. About a hundred aircraft made Teterboro their base and
were parked along the northeast perimeter.
Along the northwest perimeter were the headquarters buildings of six companies which provided operating services for visiting and resident
aircraft. Each company had a private entrance
to the airport and handled its own security.

Of Teterboro's six service companies, the
largest was Brunswick Aviation, the one which,
at Miguel's suggestion, the incoming Learjet
55LR from Colombia would use.

During one of his visits Miguel masquer-
aded as the owner of a private plane and met
with Brunswick's general manager as well as
the managers of two other companies. From
those meetings it became evident that, for the
purpose of loading an aircraft, certain areas of
the airport were more secluded and private than
others. The least private and most popular arrival and parking area was known as the Table,
centrally located near the operators' buildings.

The least-used parking area, regarded as in-
convenient, was at the south end. Requests for
space there were granted gladly since it relieved
pressure at the Table. Also nearby was a locked
gate, opened on request by any of the Teterboro
operating companies.

Armed with this knowledge, Miguel had sent a message to Bogotá through his contact at New York's Colombian consulate, advising that the incoming Learjet should request space at the south end near the gate. Then today, making one final use of a cellular phone, he had called Brunswick Aviation requesting that the south gate be opened from 7:45 to 8:15 P.M.

Miguel knew from his earlier conversations at Teterboro that such a request was not unusual. Owners of private aircraft often had business they preferred others not to know about and the airport's operators had a reputation for discretion. One of the airport managers had even described to Miguel an incident concerning an incoming load of marijuana.

After observing suspicious-looking bales being moved from an airplane to a truck, the manager had telephoned police, prompting the drug traffickers' arrest. But afterward the aircraft owner, a regular Teterboro user, complained bitterly about invasion of his privacy when, as he put it, "This is supposed to be a discreet, dependable airport."

Now, as the hearse and truck neared Teterboro, Miguel directed Luís toward the south gate. Though he did not expect to avoid security attention entirely, he was gambling on its being more informal there than at a main entrance.

There had been a stressful silence in the hearse since the encounter with the State Police. But with tensions easing, Socorro told Miguel, "Back there you were *¡magnifico!*"

"Yeah," Luís added.

Miguel shrugged. "Don't relax. There may be more to come."

As they neared the airport fence, he checked his watch: 8:25. They were already a half hour late, also ten minutes after the time he had asked for the south gate to stay open.

When the headlights of the hearse lit up the gate, it was closed and locked. Beyond was darkness—no one in sight. Frustrated, Miguel slammed a fist onto the dashboard, exclaiming, "*¡Mierda!*"

Luís got out of the hearse to inspect the lock. From the truck behind, Rafael joined him, then walked back to the hearse. "I can blow that mother open with one bullet," he told Miguel.

Miguel shook his head, wondering why one of the Learjet pilots had not met them here. In the darkness he could make out several parked aircraft inside the fence, but no lights or activity. Could the flight have been delayed? Whatever the answer, he knew they must use the Brunswick Aviation main entrance.

He told Luís and Rafael, "Get back in."

As they turned away from the south gate,

the Plymouth Reliant fell in behind. Obviously, Carlos had come safely through the police road-block. His instructions were to follow as far as the airport entrance, then wait outside until the hearse and truck returned.

Approaching the brightly lit Brunswick building, they saw that another gate blocked their way. Beside it, at the doorway to a guard post, stood a uniformed security man. Next to him a tall, balding man in civilian clothes was peering intently at the oncoming hearse. A police detective? Once more Miguel felt a tighten-ing of his gut.

The second man stepped forward. Probably in his early fifties, he moved with authority. Luís lowered his window and the man asked, "Do you have an uncommon shipment for Se-ñor Pizarro?"

A wave of relief swept over Miguel. It was a coded question, prearranged. He used an an-swering code he had memorized, "The consign-ment is ready for transfer and all papers are in order."

The newcomer nodded. "I'm your pilot. Name's Underhill." His accent was American. "Goddamn, you're late!"

"We had problems."

"Don't bother me with them. I've filed a flight plan. Let's get going." As he went around to the passenger side, Underhill motioned to the guard and the gate swung open.

Clearly, there was to be no security check, no police inspection. Their cover story, so painstakingly prepared, was not needed. Miguel found he didn't mind at all.

It was a squeeze with four on the hearse front seat, but they managed to close the door. The pilot directed Luís as the hearse moved onto a taxi strip between blue lights and headed for the airport's south side. The GMC truck was behind.

Several aircraft loomed ahead. The pilot pointed to the largest, a Learjet 55LR. From its shadows a figure emerged.

Underhill said tersely, "Faulkner. Copilot."

On the Learjet's left side a clamshell door was open; the lower half included steps from the fuselage to the ground. The copilot had gone inside and lights were coming on.

Luís maneuvered the back of the hearse close to the Lear's steps for unloading. The truck stopped a short distance away and from it, Julio, Rafael and Baudelio jumped down.

With everyone assembled around the Learjet doorway, Underhill asked, "How many live ones are flying?"

"Four," Miguel answered.

"I need those names for the manifest," the pilot said, "also the names of the dead. Apart from that, Faulkner and I don't want to know anything about you or your business. We're providing a contract charter flight. Nothing else."

Miguel nodded. He had no doubt both pilots would earn golden pay for this journey tonight. The Latin America–U.S. air routes were loaded with air crews, Americans and others, who flirted with the law, taking high risks for big money. As for these two, Miguel didn't care one way or the other about their wish to distance themselves from what was happening. He doubted, though, that it would make any difference if they fell into real trouble. The pilots would share it too.

With the copilot supervising and Rafael, Julio, Luís and Miguel lifting, the first casket containing Jessica was transferred from the hearse to the jet. Making the turn through the fuselage doorway was difficult, with barely an inch to spare. Inside, the right-side seats had been removed. Straps to hold cargo in place—in this instance the caskets—were attached to tracks on the floor and other fittings overhead.

By the time the first casket was loaded, the hearse had been moved away and the truck backed in. The other two caskets followed speedily, after which Miguel, Baudelio, Socorro and Rafael boarded and the clamshell door was closed. No one bothered with goodbyes. As Miguel seated himself and looked through a window, the lights of the two vehicles were already receding.

With the copilot still fastening straps around the caskets, the pilot flipped switches in the cockpit and the whine of engines began. The copilot went forward and the radio crackled as tower clearance was asked for and received. Moments later they were taxiing.

Reaching over from his seat, Baudelio began connecting external monitoring equipment to the caskets. He continued to work at it as the Learjet took off, climbed swiftly through the darkness and headed south for Florida.

On the ground, some unfinished business remained.

As the hearse and GMC truck emerged from the airport, Carlos, waiting outside, put the Plymouth in gear and followed the hearse to Paterson, some ten miles west. There Luís drove the hearse to a modest funeral home which had been randomly selected in advance and parked on the establishment's lot. He left the keys inside, walked quickly to the Plymouth and drove away with Carlos.

Perhaps, in the morning, the funeral home owner would wrestle with his conscience about calling police or waiting to see what happened, if anything, about an apparent gift of a valuable hearse. Whatever the outcome, Carlos, Luís and the others would be far away.

From Paterson, Carlos and Luís traveled six miles north to Ridgewood where Julio had, by this time, driven the GMC truck. He left it outside the premises of a used-truck dealership which had closed for the night. It seemed possible that an unclaimed, almost-new truck might eventually be absorbed, its presence never reported.

The other two picked up Julio at a prearranged point nearby, then the trio returned to the Hackensack hideaway for the last time. There, Julio and Luís switched to the Chevrolet Celebrity and Ford Tempo. Without further delay, they and Carlos dispersed.

They would leave the cars at widely divergent points, with the doors unlocked and ignition keys in place—the last in the hope that someone would steal the cars, thus making any connection with the Sloane family kidnapping highly improbable.

14

It was not until after the first-feed Saturday National Evening News that the special task force meeting, interrupted by that morning's harrowing events at White Plains, resumed at CBA News headquarters. By then it was 7:10 P.M. and the task force members had resignedly canceled any weekend plans. It was often said of TV news people that their irregular working hours, long absences from home and the impossibility of leading any predictable social life produced one of the highest occupational divorce rates.

Seated once more at the head of the conference-room table, Harry Partridge surveyed the others—Rita, Norman Jaeger, Iris Everly, Karl Owens, Teddy Cooper. Most looked tired; Iris, for once, was less than immaculate, her hair awry and white blouse ink-stained. Jaeger, in shirtsleeves, had his chair tilted back, feet up on the table.

The room itself was messy, with waste containers overflowing, ash trays full, dirty coffee cups abounding and discarded newspapers littering the floor. A price paid for keeping the task force offices locked was that cleaners had been unable to get in. Rita reminded herself to arrange for the place to be spruced up before Monday morning.

The "Sequence of Events" and "Miscellaneous" boards had been added to considerably. The most recent contribution was a summary of that morning's White Plains havoc, typed by Partridge. Frustratingly, though, there was still nothing conclusive on the boards about the kidnappers' identities or their victims' whereabouts.

"Reports, anyone?" Partridge asked.

Jaeger, who had lowered his feet and propelled his chair to the table, raised a hand.

"Go ahead, Norm."

The veteran producer spoke in his quiet, scholarly fashion. "For most of today I've been telephoning Europe and the Middle East—our bureau chiefs, correspondents, stringers, fixers —asking questions: What have they heard that is fresh or unusual about terrorist activity? Are there signs of peculiar movements of terrorism people? Have any terrorists, especially groups, disappeared from sight recently? If they have, is it possible they could be in the United States? And so on."

Jaeger paused, shuffling notes, then continued, "There are some semipositive answers. A whole group of Hezbollah disappeared from Beirut a month ago and haven't surfaced. But rumor puts them in Turkey, planning a new attack on Jews, and there's confirmation from Ankara that the Turkish police are searching for them. No proof, though. They could be anywhere.

"The FARL—Lebanese Armed Revolutionary Factions—are said to have people on the move, but three separate reports, including one from Paris, say that they're in France. Again no proof. Abu Nidal has disappeared from Syria and is believed to be in Italy where there are rumbles that he, the Islamic Jihad and Red Brigades are plotting something vicious." Jaeger threw up his hands. "All these hoodlums are like slippery shadows, though the sources I've used have been reliable in the past."

Leslie Chippingham entered the conference room, followed a moment later by Crawford Sloane. They joined the others at the table. As the meeting fell silent, the news president urged, "Carry on, please."

As Jaeger continued, Partridge observed Sloane and thought the anchorman looked ghastly, even more pale and gaunt than yesterday, though it was not surprising with the growing strain.

Jaeger said, "The intelligence grapevine re-

ports some more individual terrorist movements. I won't bother you with details except to
say they're apparently confined to Europe and
the Middle East. More important, the people I
talked to don't believe there's been any terrorist
exodus, certainly not in sizable numbers, to the
U.S. or Canada. If there were, they say it's unlikely there'd be no word at all. But I've told
everybody to keep looking, listening and reporting."

"Thanks, Norm." Partridge turned to Karl
Owens. "I know you've been inquiring south-
ward, Karl. Any results?"

"Nothing really positive." The younger producer had no need to shuffle notes from his day
of telephoning. Typical of his precise methodol-
ogy, he had each phone call summarized on a
four-by-six card, the handwriting neat, the
cards sorted into order.

"I've talked with the same kind of contacts
as Norm, asking similar questions—mine in
Managua, San Salvador, Havana, La Paz, Bue-
nos Aires, Tegucigalpa, Lima, Santiago, Bogotá,
Brasilia, Mexico City. As always, there's terrorist activity in most of those places, also reports
about terrorists changing countries, crossing
borders like commuters switching trains. But
nothing in the intelligence mill fits a group
movement of the kind we're looking for. I did

stumble on one thing. I'm still working on it . . ."

"Tell us," Partridge said. "We'll take it raw."

"Well, it's something from Colombia. About a guy called Ulises Rodríguez."

"A particularly nasty terrorist," Rita said. "I've heard him referred to as the Abu Nidal of Latin America."

"He's all of that," Owens agreed, "and he's also believed to have been involved in several Colombian kidnappings. They don't get reported much here, but they happen all the time. Well, three months ago Rodríguez was reported as being in Bogotá, then he simply disappeared. Those who should know are convinced he's active somewhere. There was a rumor he might have gone to London, but wherever he is, he's stayed successfully out of sight since June."

Owens paused, referring to a card. "Now something else: On a hunch I called a Washington contact in U.S. Immigration and floated Rodríguez's name. Later, my source called me back and said that three months ago, which is about the time Rodríguez dropped out of sight, Immigration was warned by the CIA that he might attempt a U.S. entry through Miami. There's a federal arrest warrant out for him and Miami Immigration and Customs went on red alert. But he didn't show."

"Or managed to get through undetected," Iris Everly added.

"That's possible. Or he could have come in through a different doorway—from London, perhaps, if the rumor I mentioned was right. That's something else about him. Rodríguez studied English at Berkeley and speaks it without an accent—or, rather, with an American accent. What I'm saying is, he can blend in."

"This gets interesting," Rita said. "Is there anything more?"

Owens nodded. "A little."

The others around the table were listening intently and Partridge reflected that only those in the news business understood just how much information could be assembled through contacts and persistent telephoning.

"The little that's on record about Rodríguez," Owens said, "includes what I've just told you and that he graduated from Berkeley with the class of '72."

Partridge asked, "Are there pictures of him?"

Owens shook his head. "I asked Immigration and came up nil. They say no one has a photo, which includes the CIA. Rodríguez has been careful. However, on that score we may have got lucky."

"For chrissakes, Karl!" Rita complained.

"If you must act like a novelist, get on with the story!"

Owens smiled. Patient plodding was his personal style. It worked and he had no intention of changing it for Abrams or anyone else.

"After learning about Rodríguez I called our San Francisco bureau and asked to have someone sent over to Berkeley to do some checking." He glanced at Chippingham. "I invoked your name, Les. Said you'd authorized zip priority."

The news president nodded as Owens continued.

"They sent Fiona Gowan who happens to be a Berkeley graduate, knows her way around. Fiona got lucky, especially on Saturday and—if you'll believe it—located an English Department faculty member who actually remembers Rodríguez from the Class of '72."

Rita sighed. "We believe it." Her tone said: *Get on!*

"Rodríguez, it seems, was a loner, had no close friends. Something else the faculty guy recalled was that Rodríguez was camera-shy, would never let anyone take his picture. The *Daily Cal,* the student newspaper, wanted to feature him in a group of foreign students; he turned them down. Eventually it got to be a joke, so a classmate who was a pretty good artist did a charcoal sketch of Rodríguez without his knowing. When the artist showed it around, Rodríguez flew into a rage. Then he offered to buy the picture and did, paying more than it was worth. The Catch-22 was that the artist had already made a dozen copies which he doled out to his friends. Rodríguez never knew that."

"Those copies . . ." Partridge began.

"We're on to it, Harry." Owens smiled, still refusing to be hurried. "Fiona's back in San Francisco, been working the phones all afternoon. It was a big job because the Berkeley English class of '72 had three hundred and eighty-eight members. Anyway she managed to scrape up names and some alumni home numbers, one leading to another. Just before this meeting she called me to say she's located one of the copy sketches and will have it by tomorrow. Soon as it's in, San Fran bureau will transmit it to us."

There was an approving murmur around the table. "Nice staff work," Chippingham said. "Thank Fiona for me."

"We should keep a sense of proportion, though," Owens pointed out. "At the moment we've nothing more than coincidence and it's only a guess that Rodríguez might be involved with our kidnap. Also, that charcoal drawing is twenty years old."

"People don't change all that much, even in twenty years," Partridge said. "What we can do is show the picture around Larchmont and ask if anyone remembers seeing him. Anything else?"

"Washington bureau checked in," Rita said. "They say the FBI has nothing new. Their forensic people are working on what was left of the Nissan van at White Plains, but they're not hopeful. Just as Salerno said on Friday's broadcast, the FBI in kidnap cases depend on the kidnappers making contact."

Partridge looked down the table toward Sloane. "I'm sorry, Crawf, but that seems to be all we have."

Rita reminded him, "Except for Teddy's idea."

Sloane said sharply, "What idea? I haven't heard it."

"Best let Teddy explain," Partridge said. He nodded to the young Englishman, also seated at the table, and Cooper brightened as attention focused on him.

"It's a possible way to find out where the snatchers had their hideout, Mr. S. Even though by now I'm sure they've scarpered."

Chippingham asked, "If they've gone, what good would that do us?"

Sloane gestured impatiently. "Never mind that. I want to hear the idea."

Despite the intervention, Cooper answered Chippingham first. "Traces, Mr. C. There's always a chance people leave traces, showing who they are, where they came from, maybe even where they've gone."

Including the others in his remarks, Cooper repeated the proposal made to Partridge and Rita earlier that day . . . described the kind of property and location he visualized as the kidnappers' headquarters . . . his belief the kidnappers could have obtained their base by responding to newspaper advertising . . . the plan to examine classified ads appearing over the past three months in newspapers within twenty-five miles of Larchmont . . . Objective of the search: to match the theoretical HQ description . . . The detail work, in libraries and newspaper offices, to be done by bright young people hired especially . . . Later, the same group, under supervision, would investigate possible locations the search produced . . .

Cooper ended, "It's a long shot, I admit."

"I wouldn't even put it that high," Chippingham said. He had been frowning during the recital, his frown deepening as the hiring suggestion emerged. "How many people are we talking?"

Rita said, "I've done some checking. In the area we're speaking of, there are approximately a hundred and sixty newspapers, including dailies and weeklies. Libraries don't carry back numbers of more than a few of those, so mostly it would mean going to publication offices and searching through files. Doing that, reading back through three months of ads and making notes, would be a monumental job. But if it's to be of value, it will need to be done fast . . ."

Chippingham cut in. "Will someone please answer my question. How many people?"

"I estimate sixty," Rita told him. "On top of that, some supervision."

Chippingham turned to Partridge. "Harry, are you seriously recommending this?" His tone conveyed, *You couldn't be that crazy!*

Partridge hesitated. He shared Chippingham's doubts. This morning, during the drive back from White Plains, he had mentally labeled Teddy's notion a harebrained scheme; nothing since then had changed his mind. Then he reasoned: Sometimes taking a stand was a good idea, even with a long shot.

"Yes, Les," he said, "I'm recommending it. It's my opinion that we ought to try everything. Right now, we aren't overburdened with leads or fresh ideas."

Chippingham was unhappy with the answer. He felt apprehensive at the thought of employing sixty extra people, plus their travel and other expenses, for what could turn out to be several weeks—to say nothing of the supervisory help Rita had mentioned. That kind of hiring always added up to horrendous sums. Of course, in the old free-spending days of TV news he wouldn't have thought twice about it. No one did. But now, Margot Lloyd-Mason's edict about the kidnap task force echoed in his mind: *"I don't want anyone . . . going wild about spending money . . . No activity exceeding budget is to be embarked on without my advance approval."*

Well, Chippingham thought, as much as anyone else he wanted to find out where Jessica, the Sloane kid and the old man had been taken and, if he had to, he'd go to bat with Margot on the money crunch. But it would have to be on behalf of something he believed in and not this piece of idiot shit from the arrogant Limey.

"Harry, I'm going to veto that one, at least for the time being," Chippingham said. "I simply don't think it has enough possibility to justify the effort." Even now, he supposed, if the others knew the part of his thinking that included Margot, they would call him craven. Well, never mind, he had problems—including hanging on to his own job—they didn't know about.

Jaeger began, "I would have thought, Les . . ."

Before he could finish, Crawford Sloane said, "Norm, let me." As Jaeger subsided, the anchorman's voice sharpened. "When you talk about not justifying the effort, Les, aren't you really saying you won't spend the money?"

"That's a factor; you know it always is. But mostly it's a judgment call. What's been suggested isn't a good idea."

"Perhaps you have a better one."

"Not at this moment."

Sloane said icily, "Then I have a question and I'd like an honest answer. Has Margot Lloyd-Mason put a spending freeze on?"

Chippingham said uneasily, "We've discussed budget, that's all." He added, "Can you and I talk privately?"

"No!" Sloane roared, jumping to his feet, glaring at Chippingham. "No goddamn privacy for that cold-hearted bitch! You answered my question. There *is* a money freeze."

"It's not significant. For anything worthwhile, I'll simply call Stonehenge . . ."

Sloane stormed, "And what *I'll* call is a press conference—right here, tonight! To tell the world that while my family is suffering in some hellhole, god knows where, this wealthy network is huddling with accountants, reviewing budgets, haggling over pennies . . ."

Chippingham protested, "No one's haggling! Crawf, this isn't necessary. I'm sorry."

"And what the hell good does that do?"

The others around the table could scarcely believe what they were hearing: In the first

place, that a spending freeze had been applied
secretly to their own project, and second, in the
present desperate situation, not to try all possibilities was inconceivable.

Something else was equally incredible: That
CBA should so offend its most illustrious citizen, the senior anchorman. Margot Lloyd-Mason had been mentioned; therefore it could only
be concluded she represented the ax-wielding
hand of Globanic Industries.

Norman Jaeger stood up too, the simplest
form of protest. He said quietly, "Harry thinks
we should give Teddy's idea a chance. So do I."

Karl Owens joined him. "Me too."

"Add me to the list." Iris Everly.

Rita, a touch reluctantly, caring about
Chippingham, said, "I guess you'd better count
me in."

"Okay, okay, let's cut the histrionics,"
Chippingham said. He realized he had been
guilty of misjudgment, knew that either way he
was the loser, and silently cursed Margot. "I
reverse myself. Maybe I was wrong. Crawf,
we'll go ahead."

But he wouldn't, Chippingham decided, go
to Margot and ask for approval; he knew too
well, had known from the beginning, what her
response would be. He would authorize the expense and take his chances.

Rita, practical as always and seeking to

defuse the scene, said, "If we're moving on this, we can't afford to lose time. We should have researchers working by Monday. So where do we begin?"

"We'll call in Uncle Arthur," Chippingham said. "I'll speak to him at home tonight and have him here tomorrow to begin recruiting."

Crawford Sloane brightened. "A good idea."

Teddy Cooper, seated beside Jaeger, whispered, "Who the hell is Uncle Arthur?"

Jaeger chuckled. "You haven't met Uncle Arthur? Tomorrow, my young friend, you are in for a unique experience."

"The drinks are on me," Chippingham said. Mentally he added, *I brought you all here to bind up any minor wounds.*

He and the others had adjourned to Sfuzzi, a restaurant and bar near Lincoln Center with a nouveau-Ancient Roman décor. It was a regular rendezvous for TV news people. Though Sfuzzi's was crowded on a Saturday night, they managed to squeeze around a table supplemented by extra chairs.

Chippingham had invited everyone who had been at the task force meeting, including Sloane, but the anchorman declined, deciding to go home to Larchmont with his FBI escort, Otis Havelock. There they would wait through another night for the hoped-for telephone message from the kidnappers.

When everyone had their drinks and with tensions eased, Partridge said, "Les, there's something I think needs saying. At the best of times, I wouldn't want your job. But especially right now, I'm certain that none of us here could juggle the priorities and people that you're having to—at least, not any better."

Chippingham looked at Partridge gratefully and nodded. It was a testament of understanding from someone Chippingham respected and was a reminder from Partridge to the others that not all issues were straightforward or decisions easy.

"Harry," the news president said, "I know the way you work, and that you get a 'feel' for situations quickly. Has that happened with this story?"

"I think so, yes." Partridge glanced toward Teddy Cooper. "Teddy believes our birds have flown the country; I've come to that conclusion too. But something else I have an instinct about is that we're close to a breakthrough—either through our doing or it will happen. Then we'll know about the kidnappers: who and where."

"And when we do?"

"When it happens," Partridge said. "I'll be on my way. Wherever the break leads, I want to be there fast and first."

"You shall be," Chippingham said. "And I promise you'll get all the support you need."

Partridge laughed and looked around the table. "Remember that, everybody. You all heard."

"We sure did," Jaeger said. "Les, if we have to, we'll remind you of those words."

Chippingham shook his head. "That won't be needed."

The talk continued. While it did, Rita appeared to be searching in her bag, though what she was doing was scribbling on a piece of paper. Discreetly, under the table, she put it into Chippingham's hands.

He waited until attention was directed away from him, then looked down. The note read: *Les, feel like getting laid? Let's get out of here.*

15

They went to Rita's. Her apartment was on West Seventy-second, only a short taxi ride from Sfuzzi's. Chippingham was living farther uptown in the Eighties while his and Stasia's divorce was being fought over, but the apartment was small, cheap for New York, and he wasn't proud of it. He missed the plush Sutton Place co-op he and Stasia had shared for a decade before their breakup. The co-op was forbidden territory to him now, a lost utopia. Stasia's lawyers had seen to that.

Anyway, right now he and Rita wanted the nearest private place. Their hands were busy in the taxi until he told her, "If you keep doing that, I'll explode like Vesuvius and it may be months before the volcano's in business again."

She laughed and said, "Not you!" but desisted just the same.

On the way, Chippingham had the cab driver stop at a newsstand. He left the taxi and returned burdened with the early Sunday editions of the *New York Times, Daily News,* and *Post.*

"At least I know where I rate in your priorities," Rita observed. "I only hope you're not planning to read those before . . ."

"Later," he assured her. "Much, *much* later."

Even as he spoke, Chippingham wondered if he would ever grow up where women were concerned. Probably not, or at least not until his libido burned lower. Some men, he knew, would envy his virility which, with his fiftieth birthday only a few months away, was almost as good as when he was half that age. On the other hand, a permanent horniness had its penalties.

While Rita excited him now, as she had on earlier occasions, and he knew there was pleasure ahead for them both, he knew also that in an hour or two he would ask himself: *Was it worth all the trouble?* Along the same lines, he often wondered: Had his sexual dalliances been worth losing a wife he genuinely cared about and, at the same time, putting his entire career in jeopardy—the last a reality made clear by Margot Lloyd-Mason during their recent meeting at Stonehenge?

Why did he do it? In part, because he could never resist a carnal romp when opportunity arose and, in the news business, such openings were legion. Then there was the thrill of the chase, which never lessened, and finally the invasion and physical fulfillment—getting and giving, both equally important.

Les Chippingham kept a notebook, carefully hidden, recording his sexual conquests—a list of names in a special code that only he could decipher. All the names were women he had liked and some who, for a while, he truly loved.

Rita's name, recently added to his book, was the one hundred and twenty-seventh entry. Chippingham tried not to think of the list as a scorecard, though in a way it was.

Some people who led quieter or more inno-

cent lives might find that figure excessive, perhaps difficult to believe. But those employed in
television or working in any other creative field
—artists, actors, writers—would have no trouble believing it at all.

He doubted if Stasia had any idea of the
number of his side excursions—which brought
to mind another recurring question: Was there
any way to repair their marriage, a chance of
returning to the closeness he and Stasia had enjoyed even while she knew of his philandering?
He wished the answer could be yes, but knew it
was too late. Stasia's bitterness and hurt were
overwhelming now. A few weeks ago he had
tried writing her a letter with a tentative approach. Stasia's lawyer had replied, warning
Chippingham not to communicate directly with
his client again.

Well, he reflected, even if that particular ball
game was lost, nothing would hinder the pleasure of the next hour or two with Rita.

Rita, too, had been considering relationships, though on a simpler level. She had never
married, never having met an available man to
whom she wanted to tie herself permanently. As
to her current affair with Les, she knew there
was no long-term future. Having known and
watched him for a long time, she believed Les
incapable of fidelity. He moved from one
woman to the next with the casualness that

other men changed underwear. What he did
have, though, was that big, long body with ac-
cessories to match, so that a sexual escapade
with him was a euphoric, joyous, heavenly
dream. As they arrived at her apartment building and Les paid off the taxi, she was dreaming
of it now.

Rita shut and bolted her apartment door
and a moment later they were kissing. Then,
wasting no more time, she led the way to her
bedroom as Les followed, dropping his jacket,
tossing his tie aside, unbuttoning his shirt.

The bedroom was typical Rita—organized,
yet in a casual, comfortable way with pastel-
colored chintzes, and cushions everywhere.
Deftly, she pulled back and roughly folded the
bedspread, throwing it onto a nearby armchair.
She undressed quickly, flinging her clothes in all
directions, an instinctive lover's gesture of shedding inhibitions too. As each garment flew she
smiled across at Les. He in turn appraised her
as he slipped out of his undershorts, sending
them sailing after Rita's panties and brassiere.

As he had before, he liked what he saw.

Rita, a natural brunette, began dying her
hair in her early thirties when a few gray
strands appeared. But after changing her job
and image from correspondent to producer, she
let nature have its way and now her hair was an

attractive mixture of dark brown and silver.
Her figure, too, had matured and she carried an
extra ten pounds over an earlier sleek hundred
and twenty. "You could say," she told Les on
the first occasion he had viewed her nude, "that
I went from Aphrodite to a comfortable Venus."

"I'll take your Venus," he had said.

Either way, Rita's five-foot-six body was in
excellent shape, the hips well rounded, breasts
high and firm.

As her eyes dropped, she knew Les needed
no further arousal. Yet he came to her slowly,
bending down to kiss her forehead, her eyelids
and her mouth. Then, gently cupping his hands
around her breasts, he drew the nipples, each in
turn, into his mouth. A quiver of bliss ran
through her as she felt them harden.

Breathing deeply, each movement of her
body a growing delight, Rita's hands reached
down to Les's groin, moving her fingers gently,
slowly, her touch feather-light, experienced. She
felt his whole body stiffen, heard the sharp intake of his breath and a soft low sigh of pleasure.

Gently, Chippingham pushed her down on
the bed, his hands and tongue continuing to explore the sweet, warm wetness of her body.
When neither could wait any longer, he slid in-

side her. Rita cried out, then moments later soared to a final, glorious peak.

Rita floated for a while, savoring the lazy moments until her ever-active mind posed questions. Each time, their lovemaking was so smooth, so perfect, so experienced, that she wondered: Was it always like this for the women who had sex with Les? She supposed it must be. He had a way of handling a woman's body that had given Rita—and probably all the others—an undiluted ecstasy. And Rita's own excitement undoubtedly enhanced his own. Only after her exquisite climax—and how wonderful not to have to fake or strain toward it!—did he, too, explode within her.

Later, bodies damp, sweat mingling in its own sweet union, they lay side by side breathing deeply, evenly.

"Leslie Chippingham," Rita said, "has anyone told you you're the world's most perfect lover?"

He laughed, then kissed her. "Loving is poetry. Poetry feeds on inspiration. At this moment, you are mine."

"You're good with words, too," she told him. "Maybe you should be in the news business."

After a while they slept, then, awakening, made love again.

———

Eventually, inevitably, Chippingham and Rita turned from sex to the pile of Sunday papers which Les had stopped to buy. They spread them on the bed and he started with the *Times,* Rita the *Post.*

Both devoured the latest developments from the Sloane family kidnap, emphasis being on Saturday morning's explosion at White Plains in the vehicle the kidnappers had used, and the resulting devastation. From a professional viewpoint, Rita was pleased to see that CBA News had missed nothing major in its Saturday evening coverage. While the print press had longer stories with more reactions, the essentials were the same.

From the kidnap, Rita and Les moved on to major national and international stories to which they had paid less than usual attention in the past few days. Neither spent any time reading, and scarcely noticed, a single-column report appearing only in the *Post* and buried on an inside page.

UN DIPLOMAT
SLAYS LOVER, SELF
IN JEALOUS RAGE

A United Nations diplomat, José Antonio Salaverry, and his woman friend, Helga Efferen, were found shot dead Saturday in

Salaverry's 48th St. apartment. Police describe the shootings as "a jealous lover's murder-suicide."

Salaverry was a member of the Peruvian delegation to the UN. Efferen, an American citizen, formerly a Lebanese immigrant, was employed by the American-Amazonas Bank at its Dag Hammarskjöld Plaza branch.

The bodies of the dead couple were discovered early Saturday by a janitor. A medical examiner fixed the time of death between 8 and 11 P.M. the previous day. Substantial evidence, police say, points to the discovery by Salaverry that Efferen was using his apartment as a base for her sexual affairs with other men. Enraged, he shot her, then himself.

16

With the grace of a gull the Learjet 55LR descended through the night, its powerful engines momentarily curbed. It settled toward two parallel strands of lights ahead, marking runway one-eight of Opa Locka Airport. Beyond the airport were the myriad lights of Greater Miami, their reflection a vast halo in the sky.

From his seat in the passenger cabin Miguel peered through a window, hoping that America's lights and all they represented would be behind him soon.

He checked his watch. 11:18 P.M. The flight from Teterboro had taken slightly more than two and a quarter hours.

Rafael, in the seat ahead, was watching the approaching lights. Socorro, beside him, appeared to be dozing.

Miguel turned his head toward Baudelio who, a few feet away, was continuing to monitor the three caskets, using the external equipment he had fastened to them. Baudelio nodded, indicating all was well, and Miguel turned his mind to another potential problem which had just arisen.

A few minutes earlier he had gone forward to the flight deck and asked, "At Opa Locka, how quickly can you do what's needed and get us on our way?"

"Shouldn't take more than half an hour," the pilot, Underhill, had said. "All we have to do is refuel and file a flight plan." He hesitated, then added, "Though if Customs decide to take a look at us, it could be longer."

Miguel said sharply, "We don't have to clear Customs here."

The pilot nodded. "Normally true; they don't bother with outgoing flights. Lately, though, I've heard they've been making occasional checks, sometimes at night." Though attempting to sound casual, his voice betrayed concern.

Miguel was jolted by the information. His own and the Medellín cartel's intelligence about the rules and habits of U.S. Customs was the reason Opa Locka had been chosen as the airport of departure.

Like Teterboro, Florida's Opa Locka was used by private aircraft only. Because of incoming flights from overseas, it had a U.S. Customs office—a small, makeshift affair housed in a trailer, with a correspondingly small staff. Compared with Customs departments at important international airports like Miami, New York, Los Angeles or San Francisco, Opa Locka was a poor relation, obliged to use less exacting procedures than elsewhere. Usually no more than two Customs officers were on duty, and even then only from 11 A.M. to 7 P.M. on weekdays and 10 A.M. to 6 P.M. Sundays. The present Learjet journey had been scheduled on the assumption that by this late hour Customs would be closed, the staff long gone.

Underhill added, "If anyone's in Customs

and their airport radio is on, they'll hear us talking with the tower. After that, they may be interested in us, maybe not."

Miguel realized there was nothing he could do except go back to his seat and wait. When he was there he mentally ran over possibilities.

If they did encounter U.S. Customs tonight, unlikely as it seemed, the cover story was in place and they could use it. Socorro, Rafael and Baudelio would play their parts, Miguel his. Baudelio could quickly disconnect his controls connected to the caskets. No, the problem was not with the cover story and all that supported it, but with the rules a Customs inspector was supposed to follow when a dead body left the country.

Miguel had studied the official regulations and knew them by heart. Specific papers were required for each body—a death certificate, a permit of disposition from a county health department, an entry permit from the country of destination. The dead person's passport was not needed, but—most critically—a casket must be opened, its contents inspected by a Customs officer, then the casket sealed.

With careful foresight Miguel had obtained all the needed documents; they were forgeries, but good ones. Supplementary were the gory traffic accident photographs, unidentified but fitting the general story, also the bogus press clippings, the latter stating that the bodies were so badly burned and mangled as to be un-recognizable.

So if a Customs man was on duty at Opa Locka and came their way, all papers were in order, but would he insist on looking into the caskets? Equally to the point, having read the descriptions, would he *want* to?

Once more Miguel felt himself tense as the Learjet landed smoothly and taxied in to Hangar One.

Customs Inspector Wally Amsler figured that some game-plan-happy bureaucrat in Washington must have dreamed up Operation Egress. Whoever it was, he (or maybe she) was probably in bed and asleep by now, which was where Wally would prefer to be instead of wandering around this godforsaken Opa Locka Airport, which was off the beaten track in daytime and lonely as hell at night. It was half an hour before midnight and there were two more hours after that before he and the other two Customs guys on special duty here could put Egress behind them and go home.

The grouchiness was unusual for Amsler who was basically cheerful and friendly, except to those who broke the laws he upheld. Then he could be cool and tough, his sense of duty inflexible. Mostly he liked his work, though he had never cared for night duty and avoided it whenever possible. But a week ago he had had a bout with flu and still didn't feel good; earlier tonight he had considered calling in sick, though he decided not to. And something else had been distressing him lately—his status in the Customs Service.

Despite doing his job conscientiously for more than twenty years, he hadn't advanced to where he believed he should have been by his present age, a few months short of fifty. His status was Inspector, GS-9, which was really a journeyman grade, no more. There were plenty of others younger than himself and with far less experience who were already Senior Inspectors, GS-11. Amsler took orders from them.

He had always assumed that someday he would move up to Senior Inspector but now, being realistic, he knew his chances were remote. Was that fair? He wasn't sure. His record was good and he had always put duty to the Service above other considerations, including some personal ones. At the same time, he had never pushed hard to become a leader and nothing he had done in line of duty was spectacular; perhaps that had been the problem. Of course, even as a GS-9, the pay wasn't bad. With overtime, working a six-day week, he earned about $50,000 a year and there would be a good pension in another fifteen years.

But pay and pension weren't, by themselves, enough. He needed to activate his life, to do something by which, even in a modest way, he would be remembered. He wished it would happen and he felt he deserved it. But at Opa Locka, late at night and working Operation Egress, it wasn't likely to.

Egress was a program involving the random inspection of aircraft about to depart the United States for other countries. There was no way all of them could be checked; Customs didn't have the staff. So a blitz-type operation was used in which a team of inspectors descended on an airport unannounced and for the next several hours boarded foreign-destined flights—mostly private planes. The program was often in effect at night.

Officially the objective was to search for high-tech equipment being exported illegally. Unofficially, Customs was also looking for currency in excess of authorized amounts, particularly large sums of drug money. The latter motive had to be unofficial because legally, under the Fourth Amendment, there could be no search for money without "probable cause." However, if a lot of money was discovered during another type of search, Customs had the right to deal with it.

Sometimes Egress produced results—occasionally sensational. But nothing of that kind had happened when Amsler was around, a reason he wasn't enthusiastic about the program. Just the same, Egress was why he and two other inspectors were at Opa Locka tonight, though outbound foreign flights had been fewer than usual and it seemed unlikely there would be many more.

One of the few was preparing to leave shortly—a Learjet that had arrived from Teterboro and, a few minutes ago, filed a flight plan for Bogotá, Colombia. Amsler was now on his way to Hangar One to take a look at it.

In contrast to most of southern Florida, the small town of Opa Locka was an unattractive place. Its name derived from a Seminole Indian word, *opatishawockalocka,* meaning "high, dry hummock." The description fitted, as did a more recent one by author T. D. Allman who described Opa Locka as an impoverished "ghetto" appearing like "a long-abandoned and vandalized amusement park." The adjoining airport, though busy, had few buildings, and the area's overall dry flatness—on top of that natural hummock—conveyed the impression of a desert.

Amid that desert, Hangar One was an oasis.

It was a modern, attractive white building, only part of which was a hangar, the whole comprising a luxury terminal catering to private aircraft, their passengers and pilots.

Seventy people worked at Hangar One, their duties ranging from vacuuming incoming planes' interiors and disposing of their trash, through restocking galleys with meals and beverages, to mechanical maintenance—minor repairs or a major overhaul. Other staffers tended to VIP lounges, showers, and a conference room equipped with audiovisual, fax, telex and copying aids.

Across an almost but not quite invisible dividing line, similar facilities existed for pilots, plus a comprehensive flight planning area. It was in that area that Customs Inspector Wally Amsler approached the Learjet pilot, Underhill, who was studying a printout of weather data.

"Good evening, Captain. I believe you're scheduled out for Bogotá."

Underhill looked up, not entirely surprised at the sight of the uniform. "That's right."

In fact, both his answer and the flight plan were lies. The Learjet's destination was a dirt landing strip in the Andes near Sion in Peru and the flight there would be nonstop. But the exacting instructions Underhill had been given, and for which the pay would be munificent, specified that his departure data should show Bogotá. In any case, it didn't matter. As soon as he had shed U.S. Air Traffic Control, shortly after takeoff, he could fly anywhere he chose and no one would check or care.

"If you don't mind," Amsler said politely, "I'd like to inspect your ship and your people aboard."

Underhill did mind, but knew it would do no good to say so. He only hoped that his oddball quartet of passengers could satisfy this Customs guy sufficiently to have him clear the airplane and let the flight get on its way. He was uneasy, all the same, not for the passengers but about his own potential involvement with whatever was going on.

There was something unusual, possibly illegal, about those caskets, Denis Underhill suspected. His best guess was that either they contained items other than bodies, being smuggled out of the country, or, if bodies, they were victims of some kind of Colombian-Peruvian gang war and were being removed before U.S. authorities realized it. Not for a moment did he believe the story told to him at the time the charter was arranged in Bogotá, about accident victims and a grieving family. If that was true, why all the cloak-and-dagger secrecy? Added to that, Underhill was sure at least two of those people aboard the Lear were armed. Why, also, the obvious attempt to avoid what had now happened—an encounter with U.S. Customs?

Though Underhill didn't own the Learjet—

it belonged to a wealthy Colombian investor and was registered in that country—he managed it, and along with salary and expenses received a generous share of profits. He was certain his employer knew that corners were sometimes cut with charters that were either downright illegal or on the borderline, but the man trusted Underhill to handle such situations and keep his investment and his airplane out of jeopardy.

Remembering that trust and his own vested interest, Underhill decided to use the accident victims yarn now, thereby putting himself on the record and, he hoped, the Learjet in the clear whatever else might happen.

"It's a sad situation," he told the Customs man and went on to describe the tale he had been told in Bogotá, which—though Underhill didn't know it—tallied with the documents in Miguel's possession.

Amsler listened noncommittally, then said, "Let's go, Captain."

He had encountered Underhill's type before and was not impressed. Amsler assessed the pilot as a soldier of fortune who for the right kind of money would fly anywhere with any cargo, then later, if trouble erupted, depict himself as an innocent victim deceived by his hirers. All too often, in Amsler's opinion, such people were flagrant lawbreakers who got away with it.

They walked together from the Hangar One main building to the Learjet 55LR, parked under an overhead canopy. The Lear's clamshell door was open and Underhill preceded Inspector Amsler up the steps into the passenger cabin. He announced, "Lady and gentlemen, we have a friendly visit from United States Customs."

During the preceding fifteen minutes, since landing and taxiing in, the four Medellín group members had remained aboard the Learjet on Miguel's orders. Then, after the engines were shut down and both pilots left—Underhill to file a flight plan, Faulkner to supervise refueling —Miguel talked seriously to the other three.

He warned them of the possibility of a Customs inspection and that they must be prepared to play their rehearsed roles. There was a sense of tension, clearly some anxiety, but all indicated they were ready. Socorro, using the mirror in a makeup compact, slipped a grain or two of pepper beneath each lower eyelid. Almost at once her eyes filled with tears. Rafael this time said no to the pepper and tears; Miguel didn't argue. Baudelio had already disconnected his exterior equipment from the three caskets, after making sure their occupants were still deeply sedated and would not stir for an hour or more if left unattended.

Miguel made clear he would be principal spokesman. The others would respond to his prompting.

Consequently it was not a total shock when Underhill made his announcement and a Customs officer appeared.

"Good evening, folks." Amsler used the same polite tone he had with Underhill. At the same time he looked around, taking in the caskets secured on one side of the cabin and the passengers on the other—three of them seated, Miguel standing.

Miguel answered, "Good evening, officer." He was holding a sheaf of documents and four passports. He proffered the passports first.

Amsler accepted them but didn't look down. Instead he asked, "Where are you all going and what is the purpose of this flight?"

Having seen the flight plan, Amsler already knew the declared destination and Underhill had described to him the journey's motive. But a Customs and Immigration technique was to start people talking; sometimes their manner, plus any sign of nervousness, revealed more than actual answers.

"This is a tragic journey, officer, and a once happy family is now overwhelmed with grief."

"And you, sir. What is your name?"

"I am Pedro Palacios, not a member of the bereaved family but a close friend who has

come to this country to give help in time of
need." Miguel was using a new alias for which
he had a matching Colombian passport. The
passport was real and the picture inside was of
himself, but the name and other details, including a U.S. entry visa dated a few days earlier,
were skillful fakes. He added, "My friends have
asked me to speak for them because they are not
proficient in English."

Amsler looked at the passports in his hand,
located Miguel's and, glancing up, compared
the photo with the face in front of him. "You
speak English very well, Señor Palacios."

Miguel thought quickly, then answered with
assurance, "Part of my education was at Berkeley. I love this country dearly. If it were for
some reason other than the present one, I would
be happy to be here."

Opening the remaining passports, Amsler
compared the photos in them with the other
three people, then addressed Socorro. "Madam,
have you understood what we have been saying?"

Socorro raised her tear-streaked face. Her
heart was beating fast. Haltingly, forsaking her
normal fluent English, she answered, "Yes . . .
a little."

Nodding, Amsler returned to Miguel. "Tell
me about those." He gestured to the caskets.

"I have all the required documents . . ."

"I'll look at them later. Tell me first."

Miguel let his voice become choked. "There was a terrible accident. This lady's sister, her sister's young son, an older gentleman also of the family, were on vacation in America. They had reached Philadelphia and were driving . . . A truck, out of control, crossed the turnpike at great speed . . . It struck the family's car head-on, killing everyone. Traffic was heavy . . . eight more vehicles crashed into the wreckage, with other deaths . . . a fierce fire burned and the bodies—*Oh, my god, the bodies!*"

At the mention of bodies, Socorro wailed and sobbed. Rafael had his head down in his hands, his shoulders shaking; Miguel conceded mentally that it was more convincing than the tears. Baudelio simply looked wan and sad.

While speaking, Miguel had watched the Customs inspector carefully. But the man revealed nothing and simply stood waiting, listening, his expression inscrutable. Now Miguel thrust the remaining documents forward. "It is all here. Please, officer, I ask you—read for yourself."

This time Amsler took the papers and leafed through them. The death certificates appeared to be in order; so did the body disposition permits and the entry permissions for Colombia. He went on to read the press clippings, and at

the words "bodies burned . . . mutilated beyond recognition," his stomach turned. The
photographs were next. One glance was enough
and he covered them quickly. He was reminded
that earlier tonight he had considered calling in
sick. Why in hell hadn't he? At this moment he
felt physically nauseated, and sicker still at the
thought of what he had to do next.

Miguel, facing the Customs inspector, had
no idea that the other man was worrying as
well, but for a different reason.

Wally Amsler believed what had been told
to him. The documentation was okay, the other
material supportive and nobody, he decided,
could fake the kind of grief he had witnessed in
the past few minutes. A decent family man himself, Amsler's sympathy went out to these people and he wished he could send them on their
way right now. But he couldn't. By law the caskets had to be opened for inspection and that
was the cause of his own distress.

For Wally had a quirk. He could not bear to
see dead bodies and was filled with horror at the
thought of seeing the mutilated remains described, first by Palacios, then in the news clippings he had read.

The problem had started when Wally, at age
eight, had been forced to kiss his dead grand-
mother lying in a coffin. The memory of waxen,
lifeless flesh against his lips while he struggled

and screamed in protest still caused him to shudder, so that for the rest of his life Wally never wanted to see a dead person again. As an adult he learned that psychiatry had a name for what he felt—necrophobia. Wally didn't care about that. All he asked was that the dead be kept away from him.

Only once before in his many years as a Customs inspector had he viewed a dead body in line of duty. That was when the corpse of an American arrived late at night from overseas when Amsler was at work alone. An accompanying passport showed the deceased's weight as a hundred and fifty pounds, yet the shipment weight was three hundred pounds. Even allowing for a coffin and container, the difference seemed suspicious and Amsler reluctantly ordered the coffin opened. The result was horrible.

The dead man inside was gross, having put on tremendous weight since issuance of the passport. Even worse, death and a botched embalming job had horribly bloated the body, causing it to putrefy and produce an unbelievably offensive stench. As Amsler breathed the disgusting air, he frantically motioned for the coffin to be closed. Then he ran outside and was violently sick. The sense of sickness and that awful smell remained with him for days afterward and the memory, never eclipsed, came back to him now.

Yet stronger than memory, stronger than his fears, was that inflexible sense of duty. He told Miguel, "I'm truly sorry, but regulations require that the caskets be opened for inspection."

It was what Miguel had most feared. He made one last attempt to win by reason. "Oh, please, officer. I beg of you! There has been so much anguish, so much pain. We are friends of America. Surely, for compassion's sake, an exception can be made."

He spoke in Spanish to Socorro, *"El hombre quiere abrir los ataúdes."*

She screamed in horror, *"¡Ay, no! ¡Madre de Dios, no!"*

Rafael joined in. *"Le suplicamos, señor. ¡En el nombre de decencia, por favor, no!"*

Baudelio, his face ashen, whispered, *"¡Por favor, no lo haga, señor! ¡No lo haga!"*

Without knowing all the words, Amsler grasped the essentials of what was being said. He told Miguel, "Please inform your friends that I did not write the regulations. Sometimes I have no pleasure in enforcing them, but it is my job, my duty."

Miguel didn't bother. There was no point in prolonging this charade. A moment of decision had arrived.

The Customs idiot was prattling on. "I suggest the caskets be taken from the airplane to somewhere private. Your pilot can arrange it. He will get help from Hangar One."

Miguel knew he could not allow it. The caskets must not leave the plane. Therefore only one recourse remained—armed force. They had not come this far to be defeated by a single Customs *cabrón,* and he would either kill the man here in the airplane or take him prisoner and execute him later in Peru. The next few seconds would decide. The pilots, too, must be held at gunpoint; otherwise, fearful of later consequences, they would refuse to take off. Miguel's hand slipped under his coat. He felt the Makarov nine-millimeter pistol he was carrying and slid off the safety. Glancing at Rafael, he saw the big man nod. Socorro had reached into her handbag.

"No," Miguel said, "the caskets will not be moved." He shifted position slightly, placing himself between the Customs man, both pilots and the clamshell door. His fingers tightened on the gun. This was the moment. *Now!*

In that same instant, a new voice spoke. "Echo one-seven-two. Sector."

It startled everyone except Wally Amsler, who was used to hearing the walkie-talkie he carried on his belt. Unaware that anything had changed, he lifted the radio to his lips. "Sector, this is Echo one-seven-two."

"Echo one-seven-two," the male voice

rasped back, "Alpha two-six-eight requests you terminate present assignment and contact him immediately by landline at four-six-seven twenty-four twenty-four. Do not, repeat do not, use radio."

"Sector. Ten-four. This is Echo one-seven-two out." Transmitting the acknowledgment, Amsler found it hard to keep elation from his voice. At this very last moment before removing the caskets he had received an honorable reprieve—a clear order he could not disobey. Alpha two-six-eight was the code number of his sector boss for the Miami area and "immediately," in his superior's parlance, meant "move your ass!" Amsler also recognized the phone number given; it was in the cargo section at Miami International.

What the message most likely meant was that an intelligence tip had been received about an incoming flight carrying contraband—most big Customs breaks came that way—and Amsler was needed to assist. A need to protect the intelligence would be the reason for using landline instead of radio. He must get to a phone fast.

"I have been summoned away, Señor Palacios," he said. "Therefore I will clear your flight now and you may leave."

Scribbling to complete the needed paper work, Amsler was unaware of the suddenly lowered tension and relief, not only of the passengers but of the pilots. Underhill and Miguel exchanged glances. The pilot, who had sensed that guns were about to be produced, wondered if he should demand that they be turned over to him before takeoff. Then, assessing Miguel and those glacial eyes, he decided to leave well enough alone. There had already been delay and complication. They would take their clearance and go.

Moments later, as Amsler hurried toward the interior of Hangar One and a phone, he heard the Learjet's clamshell door close and the engines turning over. He was glad to have that minor episode behind him and wondered what was ahead at Miami International. Would it be the big, important opportunity he had waited for so long?

The Learjet 55LR, clear of United States air space and on course for Sion, Peru, climbed . . . upward, upward . . . through the night.

PART
THREE

1

Within CBA News, Arthur Nalesworth—urbane, dignified and nowadays known to everyone as Uncle Arthur—had, in his younger years, been a very big wheel. During three decades at the network he worked his way to a series of top appointments, among them vice president of world news coverage, executive producer of the National Evening News, and executive vice president of the entire News Division. Then his luck changed and, like many before and since, he was shunted to the sidelines at age fifty-six, informed that his days of big responsibility were over and given the choice of early retirement or a minor, make-work post.

Most people faced with those alternatives chose retirement out of pride. Arthur Nalesworth, not consumed by self-importance but with a great deal of eclectic philosophy, chose to keep a job—any job. The network, not having expected that decision, then had to find him something to do. First they made it known he would have the title of vice president.

As Uncle Arthur himself was apt to tell it later, "Around here we have three kinds of vice presidents—working veeps who do honest, productive jobs and earn their keep; headquarters-bureaucrat vice presidents who are nonproducing but positioned to take the blame for those above them if anything goes wrong; and 'has-been' vice presidents, now in charge of paper clips, and I am one of those."

Then, if encouraged, he would confide still further, "One thing those of us who achieve some success in this business should all prepare for, but most don't, is the day we cease to be important. Near the top of the greasy pole we ought to remind ourselves that sooner than we think we'll be discarded, quickly forgotten, replaced by someone younger and probably better. Of course" . . . and here Uncle Arthur liked to quote Tennyson's *Ulysses* . . . *"Death closes all: but something ere the end, Some work of noble note, may yet be done . . ."*

Unexpectedly, after his high-flying days ended, and surprising both the network and himself, Uncle Arthur found his own "work of noble note."

It involved young people, candidates for jobs.

TV executives found it a nuisance and sometimes a dilemma when asked an almost identical question by a succession of people—friends, relatives, business contacts, politicos, doctors, dentists, optometrists, stockbrokers, guests at parties, a list ad infinitum. The question was: "Will you help my son/daughter/nephew/niece/godchild/pupil/protégé get a job in television news?"

There were days, especially at college graduation time, when it seemed to those already in the business that an entire generation of young people was attempting to batter down the gates and enter.

As to their would-be sponsors, some could be brushed off easily by the TV executives so approached, but by no means all. Among the non-brushables were important advertisers or their agencies, members of CBA's board of directors, Washingtonians having clout at the White House or on Capitol Hill, other politicians whom it would be foolish to offend, important news sources, and many more.

In BUA days—the initials signifying "Before Uncle Arthur"—CBA executives would spend more time than they should making phone calls to one another about vacancies, then attempting to placate those whose sons/daughters, *et al.*, simply could not be accommodated.

But not anymore. Arthur Nalesworth's assignment, created partly out of desperation by CBA News management, saved his colleagues all of that trouble.

Now, when confronted by a job applicant's sponsor, a CBA big shot could say, "Certainly I'll help. We have a special vice president to deal with bright young people. Tell your candidate to call this number, mention my name, and he (or she) will be given an appointment for an interview."

The interview was always given, because Arthur Nalesworth, in the tiny, windowless office he had been assigned, interviewed *everybody*. There had never been so many job applicant interviews before and all were lengthy, lasting an hour, sometimes more. During the interview wide-ranging questions were asked and answered, confidences exchanged. At the end, the interviewee left feeling good about CBA even if no job resulted—as was mostly the case—and Nalesworth was left with a perceptive insight into the personality and potential of the young person he had faced across his desk.

At first the number of interviews and the time they took became a news department joke, with sardonic references to "time filling" and "empire building." Also, because of Nalesworth's sympathetic encouragement of every applicant, promising or not, the description "Uncle Arthur" was coined and stuck.

But gradually a grudging respect replaced the skepticism. It evolved still further when Uncle Arthur strongly urged employing certain young people who, when hired, moved quickly and successfully into the news department's mainstream. In time it became a source of pride, like possessing a diploma, to have been an Uncle Arthur choice.

Now, with Uncle Arthur in his sixty-fifth year and normal retirement only five months away, there was talk among the News Division brass of pleading with him not to go. Suddenly, to everyone's surprise, Arthur Nalesworth was important once again.

Thus, on a Sunday morning in the third week of September, Uncle Arthur arrived at CBA News headquarters to play his part in the search for Jessica, Nicholas and Angus Sloane. As instructed by Les Chippingham on the telephone the night before, he came to the special task force conference room where Partridge, Rita and Teddy Cooper were on hand to greet him.

The man they met was broad-shouldered and stocky, of medium height, with a cherubic face and a full head of carefully brushed and parted silver hair. He had an assured, easy manner. Acknowledging that it was not a regular working day, instead of his usual dark suit Uncle Arthur wore a brown Harris tweed jacket, light gray slacks with a knife-edge crease, a bolo tie and highly polished brogues.

When Uncle Arthur spoke it was with a sonorous, almost-Churchillian delivery. A former colleague once remarked that any opinion Arthur Nalesworth expressed was as if engraved on tablets of stone.

After shaking hands with Partridge and Rita and being introduced to Cooper, Uncle Arthur said, "I understand you need sixty of my brightest and best—*if* I can assemble that many at short notice. First, though, I suggest you tell me what's in the wind."

"Teddy will do that," Partridge said. He motioned to Cooper to begin.

Uncle Arthur listened while the British researcher described the attempts to identify the kidnappers and the apparent dead end now reached. Cooper then outlined his idea of searching through newspaper real estate advertising in an attempt to locate the headquarters the kidnappers might have used, based on his theory of their renting space within a twenty-five-mile radius of the crime scene.

Partridge added, "We know it's a long shot, Arthur, but at the moment it's the best we have."

"My own experience," Uncle Arthur replied, "is that when you have nothing whatever to proceed on, long shots are the way to go."

"I'm glad you think so, sir," Cooper said.

Uncle Arthur nodded. "A thing about long shots is that while you seldom find exactly what you're looking for, you're likely to stumble over something else that will help you in a different way." He added, speaking to Cooper directly, "You'll also find, young man, that among the young people I'm about to call, some are dynamos, very much like yourself."

Cooper accompanied Uncle Arthur to his small office where the older man spread files and index cards around until they covered the surface of his desk. He then began telephoning —a steady procession of calls having a common pattern, though each sounding personal and as if a familiar friend were on the line.

". . . Well, Ian, you said you wanted an opportunity to get into this business, no matter how modest, and one has just come up." . . . "No, Bernard, I cannot guarantee that two weeks' work will lead to something permanent, but why not take a chance?" . . . "Quite so, Pamela, I agree this temporary job isn't much for a journalism major. Remember, though, that some of broadcasting's biggest names began as gofers." . . . "Yes, Howard, you're right in saying five dollars fifty cents an hour is not a bountiful wage. But if money's your main concern, forget a news career and head for Wall Street." . . . "Felix, I do understand the timing may not be convenient; it seldom is. If you wish to be a TV news person you'll have to walk out, if necessary, on your wife's birthday party." . . . "Don't lose sight of the fact, Erskine, that you'll be able to put on your résumé you did a special job for CBA."

At the end of an hour Uncle Arthur had made twelve calls resulting in seven "sures" who would report for work the following day, plus one probable. He continued to work patiently through his lists.

One call made outside his lists by Uncle Arthur was to his longtime friend Professor Kenneth K. Goldstein, associate dean of the Columbia School of Journalism. When the CBA network problem was explained, the educator was instantly sympathetic and helpful.

While both men knew that heavy scholastic pressures made the involvement of undergraduate students impossible, some graduate students working on master's degrees in journalism would likely be interested and available. So might other recent graduates who had not yet found employment.

"What we'll do here," the associate dean said, "is rate this an emergency. I'll do my best to come up with a dozen or so names and will be back to you later."

"Columbia forever!" Uncle Arthur affirmed, then continued with other phoning.

Teddy Cooper, meanwhile, returned to the conference room to prepare a task plan for the temporary workers who would arrive the next day. His two assistant researchers had come in to help and together they pored over *Editor and Publisher International Year Book,* local maps and phone directories, selecting libraries and newspaper offices to be visited and routes and schedules to be followed.

At the same time Cooper drew up specifications to guide the young recruits who would sift through three months of classified advertising in some one hundred and sixty newspapers. What would they look for?

As well as the proviso of being within twenty-five miles of Larchmont, Cooper envisaged:

- A relatively lonely location with little other activity around. The people being sought would want privacy, also the ability to come and go without arousing curiosity. Any house or premises in a busy or densely populated location should be discounted.
- The premises would probably be a small abandoned factory or warehouse, or a large house. If a house, most likely old, run-down and therefore not much sought after. The house probably with outbuildings having space to garage several vehicles and contain a vehicle paint shop. An untenanted farm a strong

possibility. Other types of accommodation matching the general concept to be looked for and imagination utilized.

- Living accommodation for at least four or five people and possibly other housing space. However, the
occupants would be capable of "roughing it," so
living quarters might not be evident in any advertised description. (In "other housing" Cooper mentally included imprisonment of the kidnap victims,
but would not mention that specifically.)

- The location and premises might be undesirable to
someone seeking normal business space or somewhere to live. Therefore special attention should be
paid to any advertisement appearing for an extended time, then abruptly stopping. That sequence
might indicate no takers, followed by a sudden renting or sale for an unusual purpose.

- The cost of renting, leasing or even ownership
should not be a factor in the advertising search. The
people being pursued almost certainly had ample
funds.

That was sufficient, Cooper decided. While
he wanted to convey a broad general idea, he
didn't wish to be too limiting or discourage initiative. He also intended to talk to Uncle Arthur's recruits when they arrived early the next
day and had asked Rita to arrange a suitable
place.

Shortly after noon, Cooper joined Uncle Arthur for lunch in the CBA News cafeteria. Uncle Arthur chose a tuna sandwich and milk,

Cooper a rectangle of meat covered by glutinous gravy, a canary-yellow pie and—with a look of resignation—a cup of warm water and a tea bag.

"Unfortunately," Uncle Arthur said apologetically, " '21' is closed today. Perhaps some other time."

Because it was Sunday, with fewer people than usual in the building, they had a table to themselves. Soon after settling down Cooper began, "I'd like to ask you, sir . . ."

Uncle Arthur stopped him with a gesture. "Your British respect is refreshing. But you are now in the land of great leveling where commoners address kings as 'Joe' or 'Hey you!' and a decreasing number of people use 'Mr.' on an envelope. Here I'm known to all and sundry by my first name."

"Well, Arthur," Cooper said, a shade awkwardly, "I was only wondering how you feel about TV news right now compared with when . . ."

"Compared with the olden days when I counted for something? Well, my answer may surprise you. It's much better all around. The people who do reporting and producing are an improvement over those in my time, including myself. But that's because coverage of the news is always getting better. It always has."

Cooper raised his eyebrows. "Lotsa people feel the other way."

"That's because, my dear Teddy, there are those who suffer from nostalgia constipation. What those people need is a mental enema. One way to get it is to visit the Museum of Broadcasting here in New York and watch—as I did recently—some of the old news broadcasts, from the sixties for example. Measured by the standards of today, most seem weak, even amateurish, and I speak not just of technical quality but the depth of journalistic probing."

"Some who don't like us say nowadays we probe too much."

"A criticism coming usually from those with something to hide."

As Cooper chuckled, Uncle Arthur continued expansively, "One measure of our improving journalism is that fewer things which ought to be exposed stay hidden. Abuses of the public trust are dragged into the open. Of course, even the good people in public life pay penalties for that. Their loss of privacy is one. But in the end society is better served."

"So you don't think the old-time reporters were better than those today?"

"Not only were they not better, but most didn't have the ruthlessness, the indifference to authority, the willingness to go for the jugular that a first-rate newsperson requires today. Of course, the old reporters were good by the standards of their times and a few were exceptional. But even those, if around today, would be embarrassed by the sainthood now conferred on them."

Cooper wrinkled his eyes in curiosity. "Sainthood?"

"Oh, yes. Didn't you know we dedicated news people regard our calling as a religion? We use buzz words like news being a 'sacred trust.' We pontificate about a 'golden age of television' —in the past, naturally—and then we canonize our journalistic stars. Over at CBS they've created Saint Ed Murrow—who was outstanding, no doubt about it. But Ed had his worldly weaknesses, though legend prefers to overlook them. Eventually CBS will create Saint Cronkite, though Walter, I'm afraid, will have to die first. A living person can't sustain such eminence. And that's just CBS, the senior news establishment. The other, younger networks will create their saints in time—ABC inevitably will have Saint Arledge. After all, Roone, more than any other single person, shaped network news into its modern form."

Uncle Arthur rose. "Listening to your views, my dear Teddy, has been most enlightening. But I must now return to that ubiquitous master of our lives, the telephone."

By the end of the day Uncle Arthur made

known that fifty-eight of his "brightest and best" would be reporting for duty Monday morning.

2

Early on Sunday the Learjet 55LR entered airspace over San Martín Province in the sparsely populated Selva, or jungle, region of Peru. Aboard the jet Jessica, Nicholas and Angus Sloane were still in caskets and sedated.

After a five-and-a-quarter-hour flight from Opa Locka, Florida, the Lear was nearing its destination—Sion airstrip in the Andes foothills. The local time was 4:15 A.M.

On the dimly lighted flight deck both pilots craned forward, their eyes searching the darkness ahead. The airplane's altitude was 3,500 feet above sea level, though only 1,000 feet above the jungle floor below. Not far ahead were high mountain ranges.

Eighteen minutes earlier they had left a regular airway with its dependable radio beacons and, to locate the airstrip, had switched to a GNS-500 VLF navigation system, a device so precise that pilots sometimes described it as "able to find a pimple on a fly's ass." However, when they were near or over the airstrip, there should be a visual signal from the ground.

They had reduced airspeed substantially, but were still cruising at more than 300 knots.

The copilot, Faulkner, was first to see the white light of the ground beacon. It flashed three times, then went out, but not before Faulkner, who was at the controls, had put the aircraft into a turn and settled on a compass heading to where the light had been.

Captain Underhill, who had seen the light a moment after Faulkner, was now busy with a radio, using a special frequency and a message in code. *"Atención, amigos de Huallaga. Éste es el avión 'La Dorada.' Les traemos el embarque Pizarro."*

The prearranged call sign had been given to Underhill when the charter was negotiated. It worked, and a reply shot back, *"Somos sus amigos de la tierra. Les estamos esperando. 'La Dorada,' se puede aterrizar. No hay viento."*

The permission to land was welcome, but the news of no ground wind to help slow the heavy 55LR was not. However, as Underhill transmitted an acknowledgment, the same beacon light came on again and continued flashing intermittently. Moments later, beyond it, three flares sprang into view along the hard-dirt strip.

Underhill, who had been here twice before, was sure the radio that had just been used was hand-held field equipment and probably carried on the same truck as a portable searchlight. The sophisticated gear did not surprise him. Drug traffickers frequently landed here, and when it came to equipment the drug cartels spent freely.

"I'll take us in," Underhill said, and the co-pilot surrendered the controls.

Staying a thousand feet above the ground, the pilot made a pass over the area, sizing up what little could be seen of the airstrip and gauging his approach. He knew they would need every foot of ground available, knew too there were trees and heavy foliage on both sides of the landing strip, so for all reasons, touch-down would have to be perfectly placed. Satis-fied, he began an approach pattern, swinging onto a downwind leg, flying parallel with the strip and losing height.

Beside him, Faulkner was performing a pre-landing check. At "gear down," the rumble of descending wheels began. As they turned left onto a base leg, the landing gear's three green lights winked on.

On final approach their two bright landing lights sliced the darkness ahead and Underhill let the speed fall back to 120 knots. He found himself wishing this landing could have been in daylight, but they had too little fuel to stooge around until sunrise at six o'clock. As the strip became nearer, Underhill realized they were too high. He reduced power. Now the threshold was barely fifty feet distant. Throttles right back, power off, trimmed at nearly full nose-up. This was it! They touched the rough, uneven ground with a bump. Hard rudder to stay straight, those trees a blur of shadows in the landing lights. Reverse thrust . . . brakes! Now they had passed the middle flare and were slowing. Was it slow enough? The end of the strip was disconcertingly close, but speed was almost off. They were going to make it and they did—with nothing to spare.

"Nice," Faulkner said. He didn't like Underhill much; his superior was selfish, inconsiderate and usually aloof. Just the same he was a superb pilot.

As Underhill swung the Lear around and taxied back toward the approach end of the airstrip, they caught glimpses of a truck and several moving figures. Beyond the truck and off to one side was a small, roughly constructed hut, beside it a dozen or so metal drums.

"There's our fuel," Underhill said, pointing. "Those guys will help you pump it in, and do it fast because I want us the hell out of here at first light." Bogotá, Colombia, was their next destination and the culmination of this charter.

Once airborne, it would be a short and easy flight.

Something else Underhill knew was that this area of jungle was a no-man's-land, regularly fought over by Sendero Luminoso, the Peruvian Army, and sometimes the government's anti-terrorism police. With all three groups noted for extreme brutality, it was not a place to linger. But the Learjet's passengers would be disembarking here, so Underhill motioned to Faulkner who reached behind him and opened the door between the flight deck and the main cabin.

Miguel, Socorro, Rafael and Baudelio were relieved to be on the ground after the descent through darkness. But with relief came an awareness that a new part of their enterprise was beginning. In particular, Baudelio, who had been monitoring the caskets with external instruments, began to diminish the sedation, knowing that very soon the caskets would be opened and his patients—as he continued to think of them—removed.

Moments later the Learjet stopped, the engines fell silent and Faulkner left his seat to open the clamshell door. In sudden contrast to the controlled temperature inside, the outside air was suffocatingly hot and humid.

As the airplane's occupants filed out it was

evident that the attention and respect of those waiting on the ground were focused on Miguel and Socorro. Obviously, Miguel's reception was due to his role as leader and Socorro's because of her affiliation with Sendero Luminoso.

The waiting force comprised eight men. Even in the darkness, reflected light made it possible to see their light brown, weathered faces and that all were sturdy peasant types, stockily built. The youngest-looking of the eight stepped forward and quickly identified himself as Gustavo. To Miguel he said, *"Tenemos ordenes de ayudarle cuando lo necesite, señor."*

Having acknowledged his willingness to accept orders, Gustavo turned to Socorro with a bow, *"Señora, la destinacíon de sus prisioneros será Nueva Esperanza. El viaje será noventa kilometros, la mayor parte por el río. El barco está listo."*

Underhill emerged in time to hear the last exchange. He asked sharply, "What prisoners are to be taken ninety kilometers by boat?"

Miguel had not wanted Underhill to hear the name of their final destination, Nueva Esperanza. But in any case he had had more than enough of this imperious pilot, remembering the greeting at Teterboro, *"Goddamn, you're late!"* and other times during the journey when the pilot's hostility had been thinly veiled. Now that Miguel was on ground where the other

man had no authority, he said contemptuously,
"This is not your business."

Underhill snapped back, "Everything that
happens in this airplane is my business." He
glanced toward the caskets. Originally he had
insisted that the less he knew about them, the
better. Now, more from instinct than reason, he
decided for his own protection later he had better know. "What *is* in those?"

Ignoring the pilot, Miguel told Gustavo,
*"Dígale a los hombres que descarguen los
ataudes cuidadosamente sin moverlos dema-
siado, y que los lleven adentro de la choza."*

"No!" It was Underhill. He blocked the
clamshell doorway. "You will not unload those
caskets until you have answered me!" Already,
responding to the heat, sweat was streaming
down his face and balding head.

Miguel caught Gustavo's eye and nodded.
Instantly there was a flurry of movement, a series of sharp metallic clicks and Underhill
found himself looking into the barrels of six Kalashnikov rifles, all held steady by the ground-
force men, safeties off, their fingers curled
around the triggers.

With sudden nervousness the pilot called
out, "For chrissakes, all right!" His eyes swung
from the weapons to Miguel. "You've made
your point. Just let us take on fuel and get out
of here."

Ignoring the request, Miguel snarled, "Move your ass away from that door!" When Underhill had done so, Miguel nodded again, the rifles were lowered and four of the ground men entered the airplane, going to the caskets. The copilot accompanied them, releasing the cargo straps, then one by one the caskets were unloaded and carried into the small hut. Baudelio and Socorro followed.

An hour and a half had passed since the Learjet's landing and now, a few minutes before sunrise, the landing strip and its surroundings were becoming clearer. During the intervening time the Learjet had been refueled for the flight to Bogotá, the fuel taken from the drums and transferred through a portable pump. Underhill was now looking for Miguel to inform him of their imminent departure.

Miguel and the others were in the makeshift hut, Gustavo indicated. Underhill walked toward it.

The hut door was partially closed and, hearing voices inside, the pilot pushed it open. The next instant he stopped—shocked and horrified at what he saw.

Seated on the dirt floor of the hut were three figures, their backs to the wall, heads lolling, mouths open, comatose but certainly alive. Two of the caskets taken from the Learjet—now open and empty—had been placed on either side of the trio to help prop them up. A single oil lantern illuminated the scene.

Underhill knew immediately who the three were. It was impossible not to know. He listened daily to U.S. radio news and read American newspapers, available at foreign airports and hotels. Colombian news media, too, had carried reports about the kidnapped family of a famous U.S. anchorman.

Fear, icy fear, crept over Denis Underhill. He had skirted the borderlines of crime before —anyone flying Latin American charters inevitably did. But he had never, ever before, been involved in anything as utterly felonious as this. He knew, without having to think about it, that if his role in conveying these people became known in the U.S., he could go to jail for life.

He knew others in the hut were watching him—the three men and the woman who had been his passengers from Teterboro through Opa Locka to Sion. They too appeared to have been startled by his entry.

It was at that moment that the semiconscious woman on the ground stirred. She raised her head weakly. Looking directly at Underhill, her eyes came into focus and she moved her lips though no sound emerged. Then she managed to gasp, "Help . . . please help . . . tell someone . . ." Abruptly her eyes lost their focus, her head slumped forward.

From the far side of the hut a figure moved quickly toward Underhill. It was Miguel. With a Makarov nine-millimeter pistol in his hand, he motioned. "Out!"

Underhill moved ahead of Miguel and his gun to the jungle outside. There, Miguel said matter-of-factly, "I can kill you now. No one will care."

A sense of numbness overwhelmed Underhill. He shrugged. "You've done me in anyway, you bastard. You've made me part of kidnapping those people, so whatever comes next won't make a helluva lot of difference." His eyes dropped to the Makarov; the safety catch was off. Well, it figured, he thought. He had been in tight situations before and this looked like one he wouldn't get out of. He had known others like this thug Palacios—or whatever his real name was. A human life meant nothing to them, snuffing one out no more than spitting in the dust. He just hoped the guy would shoot straight. That way it should be quick and painless . . . *Why hadn't he done it yet?* . . . Suddenly, despite his reasoning, desperate fear seized Underhill. Though sweat still poured from him, he was shivering. He opened his mouth to plead, but saliva filled it and words failed him.

For some reason, he perceived, the man facing him with the gun was hesitating.

In fact, Miguel was calculating. If he killed one pilot, he would have to kill both, which meant the Learjet could not be flown out for the time being—a complication he could do without. He knew also that the airplane's Colombian owner had friends in the Medellín cartel. The owner could make trouble . . .

Miguel thumbed the safety on. He said menacingly, "Maybe you just thought you saw something. Maybe you didn't after all. Maybe, this whole journey, you saw nothing."

Underhill's mind flashed a message: *For a reason he didn't understand, he was being given a chance.* He responded hastily, breathlessly, "That's right. Didn't see a goddamn thing."

"Get the fucking airplane out of here," Miguel snarled, "and afterward keep your mouth shut. If you don't, I promise wherever you are you'll be found and killed. Is that clear?"

Trembling with relief, knowing he had been closer to death than ever before in his life, and also that the closing threat was real, Underhill nodded. "It's clear." Then he turned and walked back to the airstrip.

Morning mist and broken cloud hung over the jungle. The Learjet passed through it as they climbed. The ascending sun was blurry amid haze, the sign of a scorching, steamy day ahead for those left on the ground.

But Underhill, going through piloting motions automatically, was thinking only of what lay ahead.

He reasoned that Faulkner, seated beside him, hadn't seen the Sloane family captives and knew nothing of Underhill's involvement or what had happened just a few minutes ago. *And they would keep it that way.* Not only was there no need for Faulkner to be told now that there had been live, kidnapped people in those caskets they had carried, but if he weren't told, the co-pilot could swear later on that Underhill didn't know either.

That was the essential thing for Underhill to insist on whenever inquiry was made, as he was certain it would be: *He didn't know.* From beginning to end, he didn't know about the Sloanes.

Would he be believed? Perhaps not, *but it didn't matter,* he thought with growing confidence. *It made no difference as long as there was no one who could prove the contrary.*

He was reminded of the woman who had spoken to him. Her name was Jessica, he recalled from the reports. Would she remember seeing him? Could she identify him later? Considering her state, it was highly unlikely. It was also unlikely, the more he thought about it, that she would ever leave Peru alive.

He signaled for Faulkner to take over the flying. Leaning back in his seat, the hint of a smile crossed the senior pilot's face.

At no point did Underhill give any thought to a possible rescue of the Sloane family captives. Nor did he consider reporting to authorities who was holding them and where.

3

After less than three full days of investigation an important success had been achieved by the CBA News special task force.

In Larchmont, New York, an infamous Colombian terrorist, Ulises Rodríguez, had been positively identified as one of the kidnappers of the Sloane family trio and, perhaps, the leader of the kidnap gang.

On Sunday morning—as had been promised the preceding day—a copy of a charcoal sketch of Rodríguez, drawn twenty years earlier by a fellow student at the University of California at Berkeley, arrived at CBA News headquarters.

Producer Karl Owens, who had uncovered Rodríguez's name through contacts in Bogotá and U.S. Immigration, personally received the sketch and later took it to Larchmont. A camera crew and a hastily summoned New York correspondent accompanied him.

As the camera rolled, Owens had the correspondent show six photos to Priscilla Rhea, the retired schoolteacher who had witnessed the kidnap on the Grand Union parking lot. One photo was of the Rodríguez sketch, the other five had been taken from files and were of men of similar appearance. Miss Rhea pointed instantly to the Rodríguez picture.

"That's him. That's the one who shouted that they were making a movie. He's younger in the picture, but it's the same man. I'd know him anywhere." She added, "When I saw him, it seemed he was in charge."

At this point CBA News had the information exclusively.

(It was not, of course, known that Ulises Rodríguez was using the code name Miguel or that during the Learjet flight to Peru he employed the alias Pedro Palacios. But since a terrorist habitually used many names, this was not important.)

The discovery was discussed late Sunday at an informal session by four task force members —Harry Partridge, Rita Abrams, Karl Owens and Iris Everly. Owens, justly pleased by his breakthrough, urged that the new development be included in Monday's edition of the National Evening News.

When Partridge hesitated, Owens argued forcefully.

"Look, Harry, no one else has this yet. We're ahead of the whole pack. If we go on air tomorrow, everyone else will pick it up and have to give us credit which includes—even though we know they hate doing it—the *New York Times* and *Washington Post.* But if we hold off and wait too long, word about Rodríguez may get out and we'll lose our exclusive. You know as well as I do, people talk. There's the Rhea woman in Larchmont; she may tell someone and they'll pass it on. Even our own people blab, and there's a chance of someone at another network hearing."

"I second all that," Iris Everly said. "You're expecting me to do a follow-up tomorrow, Harry. Without Rodríguez, I have nothing new."

"I know," Partridge said. "I'm thinking about going with it, but there are also some reasons to wait. I won't make a decision until tomorrow."

With that, the others had to be content.

One decision Partridge made privately was that Crawford Sloane must be informed of the fresh discovery. Crawf, he reasoned, was suffering such mental agony that any forward step, even though an inconclusive one, would come as a relief. Late as it was—nearing 10 P.M.—Partridge decided to visit Sloane himself. Obviously he could not telephone. All phone calls to Sloane's Larchmont house were being monitored by the FBI and Partridge was not ready yet to give the FBI the new information.

Using a phone in his temporary private office, he ordered a CBA car and driver to meet him at the news building's main entrance.

"I'm grateful you came out, Harry," Crawford Sloane said after Partridge made his report. "Will you go on air with this tomorrow?"

"I'm not sure." Partridge described his reasoning both ways, adding, "I want to sleep on it."

They were having drinks in the living room where, only four evenings earlier, Sloane thought sadly, he had sat talking with Jessica and Nicholas after his own return from work.

On Partridge's way in, an FBI agent had regarded him inquiringly. The agent was substituting that night for Otis Havelock who was at home with his family. But Sloane had firmly closed the door connecting with the outside hallway and the two newsmen talked in low voices.

"Whatever you decide," Sloane said, "I'll back your judgment. Either way, do you have enough reason to take off for Colombia?"

Partridge shook his head. "Not yet, because Rodríguez is a gun-for-hire. He's operated all over Latin America, Europe too. So I need to know more—specifically, where this operation is based. Tomorrow I'll work the phones again. The others will do the same."

One call in particular Partridge intended to make was to the lawyer for organized crime figures he had spoken to on Friday, but who hadn't yet called back. Instinct told him that anyone operating in the U.S. as Rodríguez appeared to have done would need an organized crime connection.

As Partridge was leaving, Sloane put his hand on the other's shoulder. "Harry, my friend," he said, his voice emotional, "I've come to believe that the only chance I have of getting Jessica, Nicky and my Dad back is through you." He hesitated, then went on. "I guess there have been times when you and I weren't the closest companions, or even allies, and whatever's been my fault in that, I'm sorry. But apart from that, I just want you to know that most of what I have and care about in this world is riding on you."

Partridge tried to find words to reply, but couldn't. Instead he nodded several times, touched Sloane on the shoulder too, and said, "Good night."

"Where to, Mr. Partridge?" the CBA driver inquired.

It was close to midnight and Partridge answered tiredly, "The Inter-Continental Hotel, please."

Leaning back in the car and remembering Sloane's parting words, Partridge thought that, yes, he did know what it meant to have lost, or face the chance of losing, someone you loved. In his own case, long ago, there had first been Jessica, though the circumstances then were in no way comparable to Crawf's desperate situation now. Then later there was Gemma . . .

He stopped. *No!* He would not let himself think of Gemma tonight. The remembrance of her had come back to him so much lately . . . it seemed to happen with tiredness . . . and always, along with memory, there was pain.

Instead, he forced his mind back to Crawf who, in circumstances equally dire as those affecting Jessica, was also suffering the loss of a child, his son. Partridge himself had never known what it was to have a child. Still, he knew that the loss of one must be unbearable, perhaps the most unbearable burden of all. He and Gemma had wanted children . . .

He sighed . . . *Oh, dearest Gemma . . .*

He gave in . . . relaxed as the smoothly moving car closed the distance to Manhattan . . . allowed his mind to drift.

For always, after that simple marriage ceremony in Panama City when he and Gemma stood before the municipal juez in his cotton guayabera and took their unpretentious vows, Partridge nursed a conviction that simple ceremonies produced the better marriages and flamboyant, ritzier circuses were more likely to be followed by divorce.

He admitted it was a prejudice, based heavily on his own experience. His first marriage, in Canada, had begun with a "white wedding" complete with bridesmaids, several hundred guests and incantations in a church—the bride's mother insisting on it all—and preceded by theatrical rehearsals which seemed to rob the ceremony itself of meaning. Afterward the marriage simply didn't work, something Partridge conceded to be at least fifty percent his fault, and the rhetorical pledge of "until death us do part" was—by mutual agreement, this time in court before a judge—shortened to a year.

The marriage to Gemma, however, from its unlikely beginning aboard the Pope's airplane, had strengthened as their love had grown. At no point in his life had Partridge ever been happier.

He continued to be the network's correspon-

dent in Rome where foreign journalists were able, as a colleague working for CBS expressed it, "to live like kings." Almost at once after returning from the papal flight Partridge and Gemma found an apartment in a sixteenth-century palazzo. Located midway between the Spanish Steps and the Trevi Fountain, it had eight rooms and three balconies. In those days, when networks consumed money as if there were no tomorrow, correspondents found their own accommodation and were reimbursed. More recently, with leaner budgets and accountants in catbird seats, the network supplied living quarters—of lesser quality and cheaper.

As it was, on looking over what would be their first home, Gemma declared, "Harry, mio amore, *it is heaven now. I will make it seven heavens for you." And she did.*

Gemma had a gift for imparting laughter and joy and love of living. As well, she ran the home proficiently and was a superb cook. What she could not do, as Partridge quickly learned, was manage money or balance a checkbook. When Gemma wrote a check she often forgot to fill in a counterfoil, so the balance in their account was invariably less than she believed. Coupled with that, even when she remembered the counterfoil her arithmetic was unreliable—she would sometimes add instead of subtract—so that Gemma and the bank were constantly at odds. *"Harry, tesoro,"* she complained after one stern lecture from the manager, *"bankers have no tenderness. They are . . . what is that English word?"*

He said, amused, *"How about pragmatic?"*

"Oh, Harry, you have such a clever mind! Yes," Gemma said decisively, *"bankers are too pragmatic."*

Partridge found the solution easy. He simply took over their household finances, which seemed a small contribution in return for the many agreeable condiments now added to his life.

Another problem with Gemma required more delicate handling. She adored cars, owned a dilapidated Alfa Romeo and, like many other Italians, drove like a crazed fiend. There were times when Partridge, seated beside her either in the Alfa or his own BMW, which she enjoyed driving too, closed his eyes, convinced that disaster was about to happen. Each time it didn't, he equated himself with a cat having lost one more of its nine lives.

He was down to four when he summoned the courage to ask Gemma if she would consider not driving anymore. *"It's because I love you so much,"* he assured her. *"When I'm away I have nightmares, dreading something may happen with the car and you may be hurt when I get back."*

"But Harry," Gemma protested, not understanding at all, "I am a safe, prudente *driver.*"

For the moment Partridge left it there, though managing to bring the subject up again from time to time, his revised strategy being that Gemma was indeed a safe driver but he himself was neurotically nervous. The best he could get, though, was a conditional promise.

"Mio amore, *as soon as I am pregnant I will not drive a car. That I swear to you.*"

It was a reminder of how much they both wanted children. "At least three," Gemma announced soon after their marriage and Partridge saw no reason to disagree.

Meanwhile he traveled away from Rome periodically on CBA News assignments and, at the beginning, Gemma continued with her stewardess job. Very quickly, though, it became evident they would see little of each other that way because sometimes when Partridge returned from a trip Gemma would be flying; at others the reverse was true. It was Gemma who decided she would make the adjustment for them both by ceasing to fly.

Fortunately, when she let it be known at Alitalia that she was prepared to quit, the airline assigned her to ground duties that kept her permanently in Rome. Both Gemma and Partridge were delighted because now they had much more time together.

They used their spare hours to explore and enjoy Rome, dipping into its millennium of history about which, Partridge discovered, Gemma's mind held a treasure trove of bric-a-brac.

"The Emperor Augustus, Harry—he was Julius Caesar's stepson—started a fire brigade of slaves. But there was a big fire they didn't put out, so he got rid of the slaves and had freemen as firemen, vigiles, *who were better. That's because people who are free* want *to put out fires."*

Partridge said doubtfully, "Is all that true?" *Gemma only smiled, though later research showed him she was right and that the switch to freemen happened in* A.D. *6. Subsequently, when the United Nations held a Freedom Symposium in Rome, which Partridge covered, he adroitly slipped the ancient fire brigade story into his CBA News script.*

On another occasion: "The Sistine Chapel, Harry, where new popes are chosen, was named after Pope Sixtus IV. He licensed brothels in Rome and had sons, one by his own sister. He made three of his sons cardinals."

And: "Our famous Spanish Steps, Scala di Spagna, *have a wrongful name. They ought to be* Scala di Francia. *The French suggested the steps, a Frenchman left the money for them in his will. The Spanish Embassy—poof!—just happened to be there. Spain had nothing,* nothing, *Harry, to do with those steps at all."*

When work and time permitted, Partridge and Gemma journeyed farther afield to Florence, Venice and Pisa. It was while returning from Florence by train that Gemma appeared pale and excused herself several times to enter the toilet. When Partridge expressed concern, she dismissed it as unimportant. "I probably ate something I should not. Do not worry."

In Rome, away from the train, Gemma seemed her normal self and next day Partridge went as usual to the CBA bureau. In the evening, however, when he returned home he was surprised to find an extra small plate at his dinner place and, on it, the keys of Gemma's Alfa Romeo. When he asked about them, Gemma, a small smile on her face, answered, "A promise is for keeping."

For a moment he was puzzled, then with a surge of love and a shout of joy, he remembered her statement, "As soon as I am pregnant I will not drive a car."

Gemma had tears of happiness in her eyes as they kissed and held each other tightly.

One week later Partridge received word from CBA News that he would no longer be Rome correspondent and was being given a more important assignment—as senior correspondent in London.

His immediate reaction was to wonder how

Gemma would feel about the change. He need not have been concerned.

"It is wondrous news, Harry caro," *she told him. "I adore London. I flew there with Alitalia. We will make a good life there together."*

"We're here, Mr. Partridge."

Partridge, who had closed his eyes in the CBA car—momentarily, as he thought—opened them to discover they had reached Manhattan and were on Forty-eighth Street outside the Inter-Continental Hotel. He thanked the driver, said good night, then went inside.

In the elevator on the way to his room he realized it was now Monday—the beginning of what was likely to be a crucial week.

4

Jessica was trying desperately to hold on to awareness, to keep her mind functioning and to understand what was going on around her, but mostly she was not succeeding. She would have moments of clarity in which she could see other

people and feel her own body—its pain and discomfort, nausea, an acute thirst. Yet even while
this was happening, panic possessed her with
one dominating thought: *Nicky! Where was he?
What had happened?* Then abruptly everything
would ebb away, becoming a swirling, misty
montage in which she could grasp nothing mentally, not even who she was. During such lapses
she seemed engulfed by some sluggish, opaque
liquid.

Somehow, even while teetering in and out of
consciousness, she managed to hold on to memories of what she had briefly perceived. She
knew that something which had been connected
to her arm was now removed and in its place
was a throbbing ache. She was aware of being
helped from some resting place, then partly
walked and partly carried to wherever she was
now seated, which seemed—again in moments
of awareness—to be a flat surface. There was
something solid—she wasn't sure what—behind
her back.

In between such thoughts, as fright and
panic returned, she tried to tell herself what she
knew to be important: *Keep control!*

One thing she was clear about was the sudden sight, and now the memory, of a man. The
image of him was sharp and strong. He was tall
and partly bald, held himself straight, and
looked as if he had authority. It was that im-

pression of authority which made her attempt to speak to him, to plead for help. She knew he had been startled by her voice; that response was also precisely etched, though the reality of the man had disappeared. But did her plea get through? Would he return to help? . . . *Oh god! Who knew?*

Now . . . once more awareness had swirled in. There was another man, this time leaning over her . . . *Wait!* She had seen this one before, recognized his cadaverous face . . . *Yes!* Just minutes ago, while she was desperately fighting with some kind of knife, she had slashed his face, seen blood spurt out . . . *But why wasn't he bleeding now? How was it that his face was bandaged?*

In Jessica's mind her long interval of unconsciousness did not exist . . .

She reasoned: *This man was an enemy.* Now she remembered: *He had done something to Nicky. Oh, how she hated him! . . .* Wild anger sent adrenaline pumping, brought back movement to her limbs. She reached up, seized the adhesive bandage and pulled it off. Then, following through, her nails raked flesh and scab.

With a startled cry, Baudelio leaped back. Putting a hand to his cheek, it came away red with blood . . . *That goddamn woman!* She had messed up his face again. Instinctively he had been thinking like a doctor, and of her as a

patient, but not now! Enraged, he clenched a
fist, leaned forward and hit her hard.

An instant later, for clinical reasons, he regretted having done it. He had wanted to see
how far all three captives were advanced in consciousness—up to this point they had come out
of sedation satisfactorily and their pulses and
breathing were okay. The woman had seemed a
little ahead of the others. He thought ruefully:
She had just proved it.

They would all suffer aftereffects, of course
—from his anesthesiology experience he knew
them well. There would be a sense of confusion
probably followed by depression, some numbness, a severe headache, almost certainly nausea. The general effect would be much like a
drunkard's hangover. They should all be given
water soon; he would attend to that. No food,
though—at least not until they had reached
their next destination. Hell camp, Baudelio
thought.

Socorro appeared beside him and he told
her about the need for water. She nodded and
went out to see what she could find. Paradoxically, as Baudelio knew, in this sparsely inhab-
ited, damp jungle, drinking water was a problem. Rivers and streams, though plentiful, were
fouled by chemicals—sulfuric acid, kerosene
and other by-products used by drug dealers in
transforming coca leaves into coca paste, the

substance of cocaine. As well, there were dangers of malaria and typhoid, so that even impoverished peasants drank soft drinks, beer and, when possible, boiled water.

Miguel had entered the hut in time to see the incident involving Jessica and Baudelio and hear the latter's instruction to Socorro. He called after her, "And get something to tie these scumbags' hands, then do it—behind their backs."

Turning to Baudelio, Miguel ordered, "Get the prisoners ready to move. First we go by truck. After that, everyone will walk."

Jessica, now only feigning unconsciousness, heard it all.

In hitting her, Baudelio had actually done a favor. The blow's jolting effect had brought her borderline awareness suddenly into focus. She now knew who she was and memory was returning. But instinct cautioned her to keep that knowledge, for the moment, to herself.

She knew she had been frightened and panicked a few minutes ago, but now must try to keep her thinking orderly. First: Where was she? How had she got here?

Answers accumulated . . . *Everything was coming back:* The Grand Union supermarket and the report conveyed to her about Crawford and an accident—obviously a lie. Then in the parking lot, the brutal seizure of herself, Nicky and . . .

Nicky! Had he been harmed? Where was he now?

Still striving to maintain control, she remembered glimpsing Nicky briefly on some kind of bed, tied down . . . and so was Angus. *Oh, poor Angus!* She'd seen them while she struggled with the man and cut his face . . . Was she still in that same place? She didn't think so. More important, was Nicky with her? Barely opening her eyes, keeping her head low, she shifted to look. *Oh, thank god! Nicky was right alongside!* His eyes were opening and closing; he was yawning.

And Angus? *Yes!* Angus was beyond Nicky, eyes closed, but she could see that he was breathing.

Which raised the question: *Why had the three of them been taken?* She decided the answer to that would have to be postponed.

More immediately: *Where were they?* Jessica's quick glimpses of this place had shown her a small semidarkened room, windowless and lit by an oil lantern. *Why no electricity?* She and the other two were seated on what felt like a dirt floor and she thought she could feel insects, though she tried not to think about them. It was incredibly hot and sticky here, which puzzled her since September this year had been unusually cool and no change was forecast.

So . . . because this was a different place from where Nicky and Angus had been tied down, how had they got here? Had she been drugged? The thought caused her to recall something else: the pad over her nose and mouth after she had been pulled into the van on the Grand Union parking lot.

She remembered nothing more that happened in the van; therefore she *had* been drugged, probably the other two as well. For how long? Half an hour, she estimated—an hour at the most. The memory of the skirmish on the parking lot was too close for it to be more.

So the likelihood was, they were still not far from Larchmont, which meant somewhere in New York State, New Jersey or Connecticut. Jessica considered Massachusetts and Pennsylvania, then dismissed them. Both were too far away . . . Voices interrupted . . .

"The bitch is faking," Miguel said.

"I know," Baudelio replied. "She's fully conscious and thinks she's cunning. She's been listening to what we're saying."

Miguel extended his right shoe and shoved it hard into Jessica's ribs. "On your feet, bitch! We have places to go."

The shoe made her wince and because there

seemed no advantage in pretending, Jessica lifted her head and opened her eyes. She recognized both men looking down at her—the one whose face she had cut, the other whom she had caught sight of briefly in the van. Her mouth was dry and her voice raspy, but she managed to say, "You'll be sorry for this. You'll be caught. Punished."

"Silence!" Miguel used his foot again, this time to kick her stomach. "From now on, you will speak only when questioned."

From beside her, she heard Nicky stir and say, "What's happened? Where are we?" She sensed in his voice the same panic she had experienced herself.

It was Angus who answered softly, "It looks to me, old son, as if we've been kidnapped by some pretty nasty people. But keep your cool! Be strong! Your Dad'll find us."

Jessica, still fighting pain from the savage kick, felt a hand placed on her arm and heard Nicky's voice say gently, "Mom, are you okay?"

Tears sprang to her eyes at the thought that Nicky's concern should be for her. Turning her head, she tried to nod reassuringly, only to see Nicky being kicked viciously too. In a moment of horror she thought: What was all this doing to him?

Miguel shouted, "That silence rule means you too, idiot boy! Remember it!"

"Oh, he'll remember." It was Angus, his voice dry and cracked, but he managed to impart contempt. "Who could forget a piece of human offal, so brave he'll kick a helpless woman and a boy?" The old man was struggling to rise.

Jessica breathed, "Angus, don't!" She knew that nothing at this moment could improve their situation; hard words would make it worse.

Angus had trouble balancing and rising to his feet. In the meantime Miguel looked around him and seized part of a tree branch lying on the floor. He crossed to Angus and belabored him savagely about the head and shoulders. The old man fell back, one eye closed where the wood had struck him, grunting with the pain.

"All of you will use that as a lesson!" Miguel barked. "Keep silent!" He turned to Baudelio. "Get them ready to go."

Socorro had returned carrying a water jug in a wicker cover and a length of coarse rope.

"They should have water first," Baudelio said. He added with a hint of petulance, "That is, if you want them kept alive."

"First tie their hands," Miguel ordered. "I want no more trouble."

Scowling, he left the hut. Outside, as the sun ascended, the humid heat was overpowering.

Jessica was growing increasingly puzzled about their location.

A few minutes ago she, Nicky and Angus had been moved from what Jessica now realized was a crudely constructed hut and were in the grimy back portion of an open truck, along with a miscellaneous cargo of crates, boxes and sacks. After being marched out of the hut with their hands tied behind them, the three were partially lifted, partially shoved roughly over the truck's tailgate by several pairs of hands. Then a half-dozen motley-dressed men, who could have been farmhands except they carried guns, had boarded also, followed by the man Jessica labeled mentally "Cutface," and another man whom she remembered vaguely having seen before. After that the tailgate was raised and fastened.

While it was all happening she had concentrated on their surroundings, trying to see as much as she could, but it hadn't helped. There were no other buildings in view, nothing but dense woodland all around, and the dirt track to the hut could scarcely be called a road. She attempted to see the truck's license plate, but if there was one the lowered tailgate covered it.

Physically, Jessica felt better for having re-

ceived water. Before leaving the hut, Nicky and
Angus had been given water too, by a sour-
faced woman whom Jessica also remembered
seeing briefly before—she believed during her
initial struggle with Cutface.

Trying to appeal as one woman to another,
Jessica whispered softly between mouthfuls fed
to her from a battered tin cup. "Thank you for
the water. Please!—will you tell me where we
are and why?"

The response was harsh and unexpected.
Putting down the cup, the woman administered
two hard slaps, forehand and backhand, to Jessica's face, each time sending her reeling sideways. The woman hissed, "You heard the order.
¡Silencio! Speak again and you will go without
water for a day."

After that, Jessica stayed silent. So did
Nicky and Angus.

The same woman was now in the front seat
of the truck, next to the driver who had just
started the engine. Also in front was the man
who had kicked Jessica and Nicky and beaten
Angus. Jessica had heard one of the others call
him Miguel and he appeared to be in charge.
The truck began to move, bouncing unevenly
over rugged ground.

The heat was even more intense than in the
hut. Perspiration streamed from everyone. *So
where were they?* Jessica's notion about being in

the general area of New York State seemed less plausible every minute. Nowhere she could think of would be as hot at this time of year. Unless . . .

Was it possible, Jessica wondered, that she and the others had been unconscious, drugged, much longer than she first believed? And if so, could they have been taken to someplace much farther away, farther south, like Georgia or Arkansas? The more she thought about the type of country they were in, the more it resembled the remoter parts of those states, and it would be hot there too. The prospect dismayed her because, if true, the hope of imminent rescue had just receded.

Still seeking clues, she began listening to snatches of speech between the men with the guns. She recognized the language as Spanish and while Jessica didn't speak it, she knew a smattering of words.

. . . *"¡Maldito camión! Me hace daño en la espalda."* . . . *"¿Por qué no te acuestas encima de la mujer? Ella es una buena almohada."* . . . Some raucous laughter . . . *"No, esperaré hasta que termine el viaje. !Entonces, ella debe tener cuidado!"* . . . *"Los Sinchis, esos cabrónes, torturaron a mi hermano antes de matarlo."* . . . *"El río no puede llegar tan pronto como yo desearía que llegara. La Selva ve y oye todo."* . . .

Hearing them, she supposed they were recent immigrants; so many Hispanics nowadays
were flooding into the United States. Abruptly
she remembered the man who first accosted her
in the Larchmont supermarket. He spoke English with a Spanish accent. Was there a connection? She couldn't think of one.

The thought of Larchmont, though, reminded her of Crawf. What torment he must be
going through! There was something that
Angus had said to Nicky in the hut. *"Your
Dad'll find us."* For sure, by now, Crawf would
be moving heaven and earth in the search for
them, and he had plenty of influence, lots of
friends in high places who would help. *But
would they have any idea of where to look?*
Somehow she must discover where they were
and devise a way to get word back to Crawf.

Something else Angus had said to Nicky
was that they had been kidnapped. Jessica
hadn't thought that through before—there
hadn't been time—but she supposed Angus was
right. But why kidnapped? For money? Wasn't
that the usual reason? Well, sure the Sloanes
had money, but not in huge amounts, not the
kind Crawf sometimes talked about as "industrial or Wall Street money."

And how incredible, Jessica thought, that
only last evening—if it *was* last evening; she was

losing track of time—Crawf had spoken of the possibility of being kidnapped himself . . .

Her thoughts were distracted by the sight of Nicky. Since the truck began moving, Nicky had had trouble keeping his body upright and now, because of his tied hands, had slid down horizontally so that with every bump his head was hitting the floor.

Jessica, frantic and unable to help, was about to break silence and appeal to Cutface when she saw one of the gun-toting men take notice of Nicky's plight and move toward him. Partially lifting Nicky, the man moved the boy so his back was against a sack and his feet touching a box, ensuring that he wouldn't slip again. Jessica tried to thank the man with her eyes and a half smile. In return he gave the slightest of nods. It was small reassurance, she thought, but at least there was someone among these brutal people who had feelings.

The man continued to sit near Nicky. He mumbled some words which Nicky, having recently begun Spanish lessons at school, seemed to understand. As the journey continued, there were two more exchanges between the man and the boy.

After about twenty minutes, at a point where the track they had been driving on disappeared and there were only trees, the truck stopped. Jessica, Nicky and Angus were again partially shoved and lifted off the truck. When they were standing, Miguel came around from the front and announced curtly, "From here we walk."

Gustavo and two other armed men led the way through thick foliage over an uneven, barely discernible trail. Leaves and branches pressed in on either side and though the trees overhead provided shade, the incredible heat persisted amid a constant buzz of insects.

At moments, the three captives were close together. At one point Nicky said in a low voice, "This leads to a river, Mom. Then we're going in a boat."

Jessica whispered back, "Did that man tell you?"

"Yes."

Soon after, Jessica heard Angus murmur, "I'm proud of you, Nicky. You're being brave."

It was the first time Jessica had heard Angus's voice since leaving the hut. She was relieved the old man was at least coping, though she dreaded the effect of this awful experience on him and, for that matter, on Nicky too. Jessica still kept wondering about rescue. What were their chances? When and how would help arrive?

Nicky awaited an opportunity, then answered Angus softly, "It's the way you told me, Gramps. When you're really scared, hang on."

With sudden emotion Jessica remembered the conversation at breakfast—the four of them, including Crawf, talking about that bombing raid on Germany . . . Schweinfurt? . . . What Nicky had said just now was almost exactly Angus's words then. And how long ago was that breakfast? . . . Today; yesterday; the day before? . . . Again she realized she had lost all reckoning of time.

A little later, Nicky asked, "Gramps, how about you?"

"There's life in this old dog." Another pause, then, "Jessie—how is it with you?"

At the next opportunity she said, "I've been trying to guess where we are. Georgia? Arkansas? Where?"

It was Nicky who supplied the answer. "They took us out of America, Mom. The man told me. We're in Peru."

5

"Earlier this morning," Teddy Cooper told the rows of attentive young faces in front of him, "I was planning to stand here and spin you a cock-

'n'-bull story about why you've been hired and what you'll be doing. Like a real smart-ass, I had what I thought was a convincing cover story all worked out. But a few minutes ago, after talking to some of you, I realized you're all too smart to be taken in. Also, I believe that when you know the real facts, you'll leave here keen, tight-lipped and caring. So sit up straight, lads and lassies. You're about to be trusted with the truth."

The approach was rewarded by some smiles and continued attention.

It was 9:30 A.M. Monday. Within the past half hour exactly sixty young men and women, the sexes almost equally divided, had reported for temporary work at CBA News, Uncle Arthur having persisted with his telephoning through Sunday evening to make up the full complement required. All were now assembled in the CBA auxiliary building a block away from news headquarters, which the preceding Thursday had been used for the press conference conducted by Crawford Sloane. On the same sound stage, folding chairs had again been set up, facing a lectern.

Most of the recruits were about twenty-two years old and recent university graduates with good scholastic records. They were also articulate, competitive and anxious to break into the TV news milieu.

About a third of the group was black and among these was one Uncle Arthur had drawn to Cooper's attention—Jonathan Mony. "You may want to use Jonathan as a supervisor," the older man advised. "He's a Columbia Journalism graduate who's been working as a waiter because he needs the money. But if you're as impressed as I am, when this is over maybe the two of us can somehow bring him into CBA."

Mony, who had been one of the earliest to report this morning, had the build and agility of a professional basketball player. His features were finely cut, with compelling, confident eyes. Mony's voice was a clear baritone and he spoke without jargon in concise sentences. His first question to Cooper after introducing himself was, "May I help you set this up?"

Cooper, who liked Mony instantly, responded, "Sure," and handed over the batch of forms which the network required all of today's newcomers to complete. Within minutes, Mony was showing fresh arrivals to seats and explaining the forms he had glanced over only moments before.

Soon after, Cooper asked Mony to make two phone calls and pass along messages. Without asking any questions, Mony simply nodded and disappeared. A few minutes later he was back, reporting, "Okay, Mr. Cooper. Both answers were yes."

That was ten minutes ago. Now Teddy Cooper was continuing his introductory remarks, having paused for effect after telling his audience they would be "trusted with the truth."

"So what this is really all about is the kidnapping—which of course you've heard of—of Mrs. Crawford Sloane, Master Nicholas Sloane and Mr. Angus Sloane. The work you'll be doing is aimed at helping those kidnap victims and is triple-X important. When you leave here you'll be detailed off to local newspaper offices and certain libraries where you will read every issue published over the past three months. Not just reading, though, but Sherlock Holmesing for clues on which I'll brief you, clues which could lead us to the body snatchers."

Interest on the faces before him was now even greater than before, accompanied by a hum of conversation which quickly quieted as Cooper continued. "As soon as I'm through sounding off up here, you'll be divided into groups and given the gen about where to go and what to do. Some of the newspaper offices have already been phoned by us this morning; they're cooperative and expecting you. At others you'll have to introduce yourselves, saying you represent CBA. Before leaving here everyone gets a CBA identification card. Save it—a souvenir for your grandchildren.

"About transport, we have some motors waiting which will take several groups each day, dropping off one person at a time at their starting point. After that, you'll make your own way. You all have initiative; you'll get the chance to use it. Some of you will get where you're going by bus and train. Either way, travel expenses are on CBA.

"You needn't come back here at the end of each day, but you *must* report by telephone— we'll give you numbers—and also call immediately if you find anything important."

The arrangements Teddy Cooper was describing had been worked on through Sunday and early this morning by himself, his two assistant researchers and a secretary borrowed from the news staff. Some backup work, including phoning local papers, was continuing.

"Now," Cooper declared, "that was for starters. Next let's get to the big picture. Somewhere about now you should be getting several sheets of paper . . . Yes, here they are."

The ebullient Jonathan Mony had been consulting with Cooper's assistants, busy at a desk across the room. Mony now returned, burdened by a pile of papers—copies of the task plan and guidelines developed yesterday by Cooper and printed overnight. Mony began handing copies to his fellow temporaries.

"When you get to those local newspaper offices," Cooper said, "you'll ask first to see issues published three months back from last Thursday—that is, starting June 14. When you have them in front of you, go to classified ads for estate agents and look for any ad offering to rent a small factory, or a warehouse, or a large old house—but not just *any* old place like that . . . and to get specific, let's turn to page one of those notes you just received."

As he explained his reasoning and planning, Teddy Cooper was relieved about his decision to disclose the truth. How much or how little he should tell these helpers had been left to his discretion, and now *not* using a bogus story made everything simpler. There were risks involved, of course. One was the chance that what CBA News was attempting would become known to a competitor, another network perhaps, who would either publicize the fact or run a parallel project of its own. Cooper intended to caution these young people not to reveal any details of CBA's behind-scenes purpose. He hoped his trust would be justified. Surveying his audience, still attentive and with a majority scribbling notes, he believed it would.

Cooper was also keeping his eye on an outer doorway. The phone calls he had asked Jonathan Mony to make were messages to Harry Partridge and Crawford Sloane requesting they make a brief appearance here. He had been pleased when the response from both was positive.

They arrived together. Cooper, in the midst of describing his imagined picture of the kidnappers' operating base, stopped and pointed to the door. All heads turned and despite the group's sophistication, there was an audible gasp as Sloane came forward, followed by Partridge.

With suitable deference, Cooper stepped down from the lectern. He would not presume to introduce the National Evening News anchorman, but simply made way.

"Hello, Teddy," Sloane said. "What would you like me to do?"

"Mostly, sir, I think everyone would like to meet you."

Sloane kept his voice low. "Tell me, how much have you let these people know?"

Partridge had joined them near the lectern and was listening.

"Pretty much the lot. I decided they'll be more keen that way and we should trust them."

"I go along with that," Partridge said.

Sloane nodded. "Okay by me." He moved toward the rows of chairs, ignoring the lectern. His face was serious; no one would expect him to be smiling and happy today, and when he spoke his voice matched the sober mood.

"Ladies and gentlemen, it may be that in

days to come, what any one or some of you are about to do will contribute directly to the safe return of my wife, my son and my father. If by great good fortune that should happen, you may be sure I will seek you out to thank you personally. For the time being I would like to express my appreciation of your being here, and wish you well. Good luck to us all!"

Sloane remained in place as many of the young people rose to their feet and some came forward, reaching out to shake his hand and offer genuine good wishes; among them Teddy Cooper saw a few eyes glistening with tears. At the end, Sloane signaled goodbye and left as unobtrusively as he had come. Partridge, who also shook hands and spoke with some of the temporary workers, went with him.

Cooper continued his briefing, describing what these investigative neophytes should look for. When he invited questions several hands shot up.

A youth in an NYU sweat shirt was first. "Okay, so one of us has found an ad that fits the specs you've given, and it might be the place you're looking for. So we phone it in. What next?"

"For starters," Cooper replied, "we find out who placed the ad. Usually a name will be there and you'll tell us. If there's no name, just a box number, try to get the info from the paper where you are, and if they're sticky about that, let us handle it."

"And after that?"

"If we can, we'll contact the advertiser by phone and ask some questions. If we can't, we'll go to visit them. Then, if the lead still looks promising, we'll take a look—very cautiously— at the place that was advertised."

"You've been saying 'we.'" The new questioner was an attractive young woman in a fashionable beige suit. "Does that mean just you and other big shots, or will some of us here get to share the interesting part, where the action is?"

There were some cheers, and laughter in which Teddy Cooper joined.

"Let's get something straight," he responded, "I'm a little shot, and be careful how you spell it." (More laughter.) "But this I promise you: As far as we can, we'll bring you in on any developments, especially those you have a hand in launching. One reason is, we'll need you. We don't have many bodies for this job and if there's a target, chances are you'll be headed for it."

"When you get to that stage," a petite redhead asked, "will there be camera crews?"

"You mean might *you* be on camera?"

She smiled. "Something like that."

"That won't be my decision, but I'd say it's likely."

When the questions ended, Cooper concluded with some thoughts he had discussed with no one else, but had considered carefully the night before.

"As well as looking for the kind of advertised buildings I've described, I want you to use the chance, with those three months of newspapers in front of you, to look at every page and be alert for anything unusual.

"Don't ask me what that might be because I have no clue myself.

"But remember this: Those kidnappers we're trying to track down have been lurking in this area we reckon for at least a month, probably two. In that time, no matter how careful they've tried to be, possibly they've done some small thing which left a trace behind. The other possibility is that that small thing may somehow have found its way into print."

"Sounds pretty chancy," someone said.

Teddy Cooper nodded agreement. "You could say it's a chance in ten thousand that something happened which got reported, and another long-shot chance that one of you will find it if it did. So okay, the odds are against us. But don't forget that someone always wins the lottery when the odds are a million to one.

"All I can tell you is *think, think, think!*

Look hard, and look intelligently. Use your imagination. You were hired because we think you're smart, so prove us right. Yep, search for our first target—the ads for premises—but watch out for that other long shot as you go."

At the end of his remarks, to Cooper's considerable surprise, the young people facing him rose to their feet and applauded.

Earlier that morning, as soon as businesses were open, Harry Partridge had telephoned his contact, the lawyer with organized crime clients. The response was less than cordial. "Oh, it's you. Well, I told you Friday I'd do some discreet checking and I've already done that twice with no result. What I don't need is you climbing on my back."

"I'm sorry if I . . ." Partridge began, but the other wasn't listening.

"What you newshounds never realize is that in something like this, it's my goddamn head that's on the block. The people I deal with, my clients, trust me and I intend to keep it that way. I also know that one thing they don't give a shit about is other people's problems, including yours and Crawford Sloane's, however bad you think they are."

"I understand that," Partridge protested. "But this is a kidnapping and . . ."

"Shut up and listen! I told you when we

talked, I was sure none of the people I represent
did the kidnapping or were even involved. I'm
still sure. I also conceded that I owe you and
would try to find out what I could. But I have
to walk like I'm in a minefield and, second, convince anyone I talk to that it's to their advantage to help if they know anything or have
heard rumors."

"Look, I said I'm sorry if . . ."

The lawyer pressed on. "So it isn't something to be done with a bulldozer or an express
train. Understand?"

Inwardly sighing, Partridge said, "I understand."

The lawyer's voice moderated. "Give me a
few more days. And don't call me; I'll call
you."

Hanging up, Partridge reflected that while
contacts could be useful, you didn't necessarily
have to like them.

Before his arrival at CBA News that morning Partridge had reached a decision on
whether or not to reveal on the National Evening News that a known Colombian terrorist,
Ulises Rodríguez, had been linked conclusively
to the Sloane family kidnap.

His decision was to withhold the information for the time being.

Following the session with Cooper's recruits, Partridge sought out special task force members to inform them. In the group conference room he found Karl Owens and Iris Everly and explained his reasoning.

"Look at it this way: Right now Rodríguez represents the only lead we have and he doesn't know we have it. But if we broadcast what we know, chances are strong that Rodríguez himself will hear of it and we'll have tipped our hand."

Owens asked doubtfully, "Does that matter?"

"I think it does. Everything points to Rodríguez having been under cover, and the effect would be to drive him further under. I don't have to tell you how much that would lessen our chances of discovering where he is—and, of course, the Sloanes."

"I can see all that," Iris acknowledged, "but do you really think, Harry, that a red-hot piece of news like this, already known to at least a dozen people, is going to stay conveniently under wraps until we're ready? Don't forget every network, every newspaper, every wire service has their best people working on this story. I give it twenty-four hours at most before everybody knows."

Rita Abrams and Norman Jaeger had joined them and were listening.

"You may be proved right," Partridge told

Iris, "but I think it's a risk we have to take." He
added, "I hate to sound corny but I think we
should remember once in a while that this news
thing we do is not some holy grail. When reporting endangers life and liberty, news has to
take second place."

"I don't want to seem stuffy either," Jaeger
put in. "But in that, I'm with Harry."

"There's one other thing," Owens said,
"and that's the FBI. By witholding this from
them, we could be in trouble."

"I've thought about that," Partridge acknowledged, "and decided to take our chances.
If that bothers any of you, I'll remind you I'm
the one responsible. The thing is, if we tell the
FBI, we know from experience they're as likely
as not to discuss it with other news people, then
we'll have blown our exclusive that way."

"Coming back to the main issue," Rita said,
"there are precedents for what we'd be doing. I
remember one at ABC."

Iris prompted, "So tell us."

"You recall the TWA hijack—Beirut,
1985?"

The others nodded, reminded that during
the mid-1980s Rita had worked for ABC News;
also that the hijacking was a terrorist outrage,
holding world attention for two weeks during
which a U.S. Navy diver, a passenger aboard
TWA Flight 847, was savagely murdered.

"Almost from the beginning of that hijack," Rita said, "we knew at ABC that there were three American servicemen aboard that plane, in civilian clothes, and we believed we had the information exclusively. The question was: Should we use it on the air? Well, we never did, believing that if we did, the hijackers would learn of it and those servicemen would be as good as dead. In the end the terrorists found out themselves but we always hoped, because of doing the decent thing, we helped two of those three survive."

"Okay," Iris said, "I suppose I go along. Though if no one's used the story by tomorrow, I suggest we take another look."

"I'll buy that," Owens agreed, and the discussion ended.

However, because of its importance Partridge decided to share his decision with Les Chippingham and Chuck Insen.

The news president, who received Partridge in his paneled office, merely shrugged when told, and commented, "You're the one making task force decisions, Harry; if we didn't trust your judgment you wouldn't be there. Thanks for telling me, though."

The National Evening News executive producer was in his presiding seat at the Horseshoe. As he listened, Insen's eyes brightened. At the end he nodded. "Interesting, Harry; nice piece of research. When you give it to us, we'll run it top of the show. But not until you say so."

Which left Partridge free to resume telephoning and he settled down in his temporary private office.

Once more he had his blue book of names and phone numbers, but unlike last week when his calls were directed mainly at U.S. sources, today Partridge tried to reach contacts in Colombia and the countries immediately adjoining —Venezuela, Brazil, Ecuador, Panama and Peru—plus Nicaragua. In all those places, from where he had frequently reported for CBA News, there were people he knew who had helped him, and for some of whom he had done return favors.

Something else different today was having the positive Rodríguez lead, which translated into a double-barreled question: *Do you know of a terrorist named Ulises Rodríguez; if so, have you any idea where he is or what he's reputed to be doing?*

Although Karl Owens had talked on Friday with Latin American contacts, as far as Partridge could tell there was no overlapping—a fact not surprising since producers as well as correspondents cultivated their own sources and, once they had them, kept them to themselves.

Today, responses to the first part of the question posed were almost entirely "yes" and to the second portion, "no." Confirming Owens's earlier report, Rodríguez seemed to have disappeared from sight three months ago and had not been seen since. An interesting point, though, emerged from a conversation with a longtime Colombian friend, a radio news reporter in Bogotá.

"Wherever he is," the broadcaster said, "I'd almost guarantee it isn't this country. He's a Colombian after all, and even though he stays out of reach of the law, he's too well known to be in his home territory for long without word getting around. So my bet is, he's somewhere else." The conclusion made sense.

One country Partridge had suspicions about was Nicaragua, where the Sandinista regime was notorious for duplicity and tyranny and was antagonistic to the United States. Could the regime be involved in some way with the kidnapping, hoping to gain from it an advantage yet to be disclosed? The question didn't entirely make sense, but neither did much else. However, a half-dozen calls to the capital, Managua, produced a consensus that Ulises Rodríguez was not in Nicaragua, nor had he been there.

Then there was Peru. Partridge made several calls to that country and one conversation in particular left him wondering.

He had spoken with another old acquaintance, Manuel León Seminario, owner-editor of the weekly magazine *Escena,* published in Lima.

After Partridge announced his name, Seminario had come on the line at once. His greeting was in impeccable English and Partridge could picture him—slight and dapper, fashionably and fastidiously dressed. "Well, well, my dear Harry. How excellent to hear from you! And where are you? In Lima, I hope."

When informed that the call was from New York, the owner-editor expressed disappointment. "For a moment I hoped we might have lunch tomorrow at La Pizzeria. The food, I assure you, is as good as ever. So why not hop on a plane and come?"

"I'd love to, Manuel. Unfortunately I'm up to my eyebrows in important work." Partridge explained his role in the Sloane kidnap task force.

"My god! I should have realized you'd be involved. That's a terrible thing. We've followed the situation closely and we'll have a full-page piece in this week's issue. Is there anything new we should include?"

"There *is* something new," Partridge said, "and it's the reason I'm calling. But for now we're keeping it under wraps, so I'd appreciate this talk being off the record."

"Well . . ." The response was cautious. "As long as it's not information we possess already."

"We can trust each other, Manuel. On the basis you just said—okay?"

"With that understanding, okay."

"We have reason to believe that Ulises Rodríguez is involved."

There was a silence before the magazine man said softly, "You are speaking of bad company, Harry. Around here that name is a nasty, feared word."

"Why feared?"

"The man is suspected of masterminding kidnappings, skulking in and out of Peru from Colombia for employment by others here. It is a way our criminal-revolutionary elements work. As you know, in Peru nowadays kidnapping is almost a way of life. Well-to-do businessmen or their families are favorite targets. Many of us employ guards and drive protected cars, hoping to forestall it."

"I did know that," Partridge said. "But until this moment I'd forgotten."

Seminario sighed audibly. "You are not alone, my friend. The Western press attention to Peru is spotty, to put it kindly. As to your TV news, we might as well not exist."

Partridge knew the statement held some truth. He was never sure why, but Americans seldom took the same continuing interest in Peru that they did in other countries. Aloud he said, "Have you heard any talk of Rodríguez being in Peru, perhaps right now, or recently working for anyone there?"

"Well . . . no."

"Did I sense some hesitation?"

"Not about Rodríguez. I have not heard anything, Harry. I would tell you if I had."

"What then?"

"Everything here, on what I call the criminal-revolutionary front, has been strangely quiet for several weeks. Scarcely anything happening. Nothing of significance."

"So?"

"I have seen the signs before and I believe they are unique to Peru. When things are quietest it often means something big is about to happen. Usually unpleasant and of a nature unexpected."

Seminario's voice changed tempo, becoming businesslike. "My dear Harry, it has been a pleasure talking to you and I am glad you called. But *Escena* will not edit itself and I must go. Do come to see me soon in Lima, and remember: Lunch at La Pizzeria—a standing invitation."

Through the remainder of the day the words

kept coming back to Partridge: *"When things are quietest it often means something big is about to happen."*

6

Coincidentally, on the same day Harry Partridge talked with the owner-editor of *Escena,* Peru was discussed at an ultra-private, top-echelon meeting of CBA network's corporate owners, Globanic Industries Inc. The meeting was a twice-yearly, three-day "policy workshop" chaired by the conglomerate's chairman and chief executive officer, Theodore Elliott. Attendance was confined to other CEO's—those of Globanic's nine subsidiaries, all major companies themselves, most with their own ancillaries.

At such meetings corporate confidences were exchanged and secret plans revealed, some capable of making or breaking competitors, investors and markets around the world. However, no written agenda or minutes of the biannual parleys ever existed. Security was strict and each day, before proceedings began, the meeting room was electronically swept for bugs.

Outside the meeting, but never in it, were support staffs of aides—a half dozen or so for each subsidiary company—poised to provide data or briefings that their various chiefs might need.

The locale of the meetings seldom varied. On this occasion, as on most others, it was at the Fordly Cay Club near Nassau in the Bahamas.

Fordly Cay, one of the world's most exclusive private clubs, with a resort facility including a yacht harbor, golf course, tennis courts and white-sand beaches, occasionally allowed special VIP groups the expensive use of its facilities. Larger conventions were *verboten;* sales meetings, as far as Fordly Cay was concerned, did not exist.

Ordinary membership in the club was hard to come by; a waiting list caused many aspirants to linger for long periods, some in vain. Theodore Elliott was a recent member, though approval of his application had taken two years.

The day before, when everyone arrived, Elliott had been proprietorial, especially welcoming Globanic spouses who would appear only at social, tennis, golfing and sailing breaks. Today the first morning meeting was in a small, comfortable library with deep rattan chairs upholstered in beige leather, and wall-to-wall patterned carpeting. Between book-lined walls, softly lit cases held silver sporting trophies. Above a fireplace—seldom used—a portrait of the club's founder beamed down on the select small group.

Elliott was appropriately dressed in white slacks and a light-blue polo shirt, the latter bearing the club crest—a quartered shield with palm tree rampant, engrailed crossed tennis racquets, golf clubs and a yacht, all on waves of the sea. With or without such accoutrements, Theo Elliott was classically handsome—tall, lean, broad-shouldered, with a strong jaw and a full head of hair, now totally white. The hair was a reminder that in two years' time the chairman-in-chief would reach retirement age and be succeeded, almost certainly, by one of the others present.

Allowing for the fact that some heads of companies were too old to be eligible, there were three strong candidates. Margot Lloyd-Mason was one.

Margot was conscious of this as she reported early in the proceedings on the state of CBA.

Speaking precisely, she disclosed that since Globanic Industries' acquisition of CBA television and radio network and affiliated stations, strict financial controls had been introduced, budgets pared and redundant personnel dismissed. As a result, third-quarter profits would be up twenty-two percent compared with the pre-Globanic year before.

"That's a fair beginning," Theodore Elliott commented, "though we'll expect even better in future." There were confirming nods from others in the room.

Margot had dressed carefully today, not wanting to appear too feminine, yet at the same time not wishing to lose the advantage of her sex. At first she considered wearing a tailored suit, as she often did in her office at Stonehenge, but decided it was inappropriate in the semi-tropics. In the end she chose beige linen slacks and a cotton sweater in a soft peach shade. The outfit emphasized her well-proportioned body, a judgment confirmed by lingering glances from some of the men.

Continuing her report, Margot mentioned the recent kidnapping of the Crawford Sloane family.

The chairman of International Forest Products, a hard-driving Oregonian named DeWitt, injected, "That's too bad and we all hope they catch those people. Just the same, your network's getting a lot of attention from it."

"So much attention," Margot informed him, "that our National Evening News ratings have soared from 9.2 to 12.1 within the past five days, which means an additional six million viewers and puts us strongly in front as number one. It's also raised the rating of our daily game show, carried by our five owned and operated stations immediately after the news. And the same is true of our prime-time shows, especially the Ben Largo Show on Friday which went from 22.5 to 25.9. The sponsors all around are delighted; as a result we're pushing hard with next season's advertising."

Someone asked, "Does that spread of good ratings mean most people don't change channels?" The question reminded Margot that even among this exalted group there was an inherent fascination with the minutiae of broadcasting.

"Networks know from experience that if viewers tune in to the evening news the odds are they will stay with that network for the next ninety minutes, sometimes more. At the same time, others join the audience."

"So it's an ill wind . . . as the old saying goes," the forest products chief said, smiling.

Margot smiled back. "Since we're here in private I'll agree, though please don't quote me."

"No one quotes anybody," Theo Elliott said. "Privacy and truth are why we hold these sessions."

"Speaking of your advertisers, Margot." The voice belonged to Leon Ironwood of West World Aviation, a tanned, athletic Californian and another of the three contenders to be Elliott's successor. The company Ironwood headed was a successful defense contractor making fighter airplanes. "What's the latest on that ongoing problem of video recording machines? How many households have them anyway?"

"About fifty percent," Margot acknowledged, "and you're right about the problem. Most of those who record network programs later zip through commercials without watching, thereby diminishing our advertising effectiveness."

Ironwood nodded. "Especially since VCR owners represent an affluent population group. It's how I watch TV."

Someone else added, "And don't forget mute buttons. I use mine whenever there's a commercial."

"The truth is," Margot said, "the whole VCR and mute problems are like permanent storm clouds over us, which is why networks have dragged their feet in researching their effects. There could have been a measuring technique long ago, except we don't *want* to know the bad news, and in that we have an ally— advertising agencies who fear that knowledge would turn off big advertisers, depriving the agencies of enormous business."

"I'm sure," Elliott prompted, "that your fiscal planning has taken that into account."

"It has, Theo. Looking ahead and accepting that network advertising money will diminish, we're seeking additional revenue sources, and it's why CBA and others have quietly bought up TV cable operators and will acquire more. The networks have the capital and one day soon cable TV may wake up to find itself almost entirely owned by broadcast networks. At the same time, we're exploring joint-venture agreements with the phone companies."

"Joint venture?" Ironwood asked

"I'll explain. First, accept the fact that terrestrial broadcasting—over-the-air television—is near the end of its useful life. Within ten to fifteen years about the only place you'll find an old-fashioned TV antenna is the Smithsonian; also by then, TV stations will have abandoned their conventional transmitters as uneconomic."

"With cable and satellite dishes taking over?"

"Partly, but not entirely." Margot smiled. She was dealing with a familiar subject as well as demonstrating, she hoped, her own farsightedness.

"The next thing to realize," she continued, "is that there is no important future in this business for cable operators alone. To survive, they must pool resources—and so shall we—with the telephone people *whose lines already go into every home.*"

Several nodded approvingly as Margot declared, "The technology for a combination phone and TV line, using fiber-optic cable, is available now. It's simply a matter of getting the system working, which includes a network like ours developing specialized cable programming. The potential revenues are enormous."

"Aren't there government restrictions," Ironwood asked, "on phone companies entering the broadcast business?"

"Restrictions which the Congress will change. We're working on that; in fact legislation has been drafted."

"And you're convinced Congress will go along?"

Theo Elliott laughed. "If she is, it's with good reason. I assume most of us here have read the book *The Best Congress Money Can Buy*. If not, it's must reading for people like ourselves . . . What's the author's name?"

"Philip Stern," Margot said.

"Right. Well, just the way Stern described, Globanic Industries contributes handsomely to every Political Action Committee affecting our concerns, which means congressional votes are bought and ready when we need them. When Margot wants those regulations changed, she can let me know. I'll pass the word."

"There's talk of abolishing the PAC system," DeWitt said.

"And that's all it is—talk," Elliott responded. "Besides, even if the name is changed, you can be sure those in Congress will find some other way to do exactly what they're doing now."

The forthright, off-the-record talk continued. However, the subject of the Sloane family kidnapping was not brought up again.

Late in the morning it was the turn of K. Phocis ("Fossie") Xenos, chairman of Globanic Financial Services, to address his fellow CEO's.

Three years earlier Tri-Trade Financial Services, as it was then, was a consumer credit enterprise making loans to middle-class Americans from a chain of storefront offices; it also sold life and casualty insurance. Globanic then bought out Tri-Trade, Theo Elliott seeing it as a ready-made base—much simpler than starting a new company—for attracting international investors seeking entrepreneurial risk and glamour. He put Fossie Xenos in charge—a young second-generation Greek-American with an MBA degree from Wharton, who had come to Elliott's attention through some artful investment-bank maneuvers.

Almost the first thing Xenos did was dispose of the consumer credit business, which produced only modest profits, and close the storefront offices; soon after, he terminated the insurance activity, describing it as "small-time humdrum for mental midgets." He was more interested in something fresh and exciting on the monetary scene—leveraged buyouts, known as LBO's, financed by junk bonds.

Since then, working with whatever happened to be "hot" financially, Fossie Xenos had created sparkling profits for Global Financial, plus a dynamic reputation for himself. The last was why Margot Lloyd-Mason viewed Fossie, who was the third possible candidate for the conglomerate chairmanship, as her most formidable rival.

Despite his manipulative skills and conquests, Fossie retained a boyish manner, appearing at least eight years younger than the forty-one he was. His clothes were mostly casual, his hair untidy, the result of running his hands through it as he talked in a rapid-fire staccato. He was persuasive and convincing; that and a dazzling smile he flashed at everyone were his personality strengths.

Today Fossie Xenos reported on a complex, delicate and largely secret project, now in its early stages but expected to produce a multibillion-dollar bonanza for Global. It involved so-called debt-to-equity swaps and a gigantic real estate investment fund, both relating to Peru, with Globanic working hand-in-glove with that country's government.

As described by Fossie to his fellow CEO's, the steps and conditions were:

- Currently, Peru had more than $16 billion of foreign debt on which it had defaulted, thereby cutting itself off from the international financial community which would lend it no more money. Peru, however, suffering a desperate economic crisis, was anxious to get back into reputable status and begin borrowing once more.

- Globanic Financial Services had quietly bought up $4.5 billion of Peru's outstanding debt—better than one quarter—paying an average five cents on the dollar, an outlay of $225 million. The original lenders of the money, mainly U.S. banks, were glad to sell even at that low price since they long ago figured they would get nothing back at all. Globanic had now "securitized" the Peruvian debt—that is, converted it into negotiable paper.

- The government of Peru, through three of its ministers controlling finance, tourism and public works, had been informed they now had a matchless opportunity to wipe out that $4.5 billion of debt by buying the securitized debt from Globanic for ten cents on the dollar, *but with all bookkeeping payments in Peru's own weak currency, the inti.* This was Fossie's cleverly baited hook because in that way the country's small and precious store of other countries' hard currency—mainly dollars—would remain untouched.

- Three critical conditions were attached to Globanic's acknowledgment of Peruvian currency. Globanic didn't want cash but instead the debt-to-equity swap, giving it total ownership of two spectacular resort locations now owned by the Peruvian Government. Globanic Financial would develop and eventually operate these, believing both to have gigantic potential as premium holiday destinations. One resort city with a coastal location was foreseen as the "Punta del Este of the Pacific." The other, a mountain-locked site in the Andes, would be a sensational staging point for excursions to Machu Picchu and Cuzco, among the world's most popular tourist attractions.

- Along with those vast amounts of land would go government guarantees that Globanic could do the developing freely, in its own way. At the same time Globanic would bring in hard currency to pay for development while also creating massive local employment, both helpful to Peru.

- The final condition, to be secret between the Peruvian Government and Globanic, was that the price paid for the two resort sites should be twenty-five percent less than their real value.

- Globanic would benefit in several ways: Initially by selling the securitized debt for twice what it paid—an instant bonus of $225 million. Next, by obtaining two magnificent locations for only three quarters of their worth. After that, attracting worldwide investment for the resorts' development and eventually reaping gargantuan profits from their operation.

Fossie's report ended with the information that following long and delicate negotiations, agreement between the Peruvian Government and Globanic Financial had been reached a few days earlier, with all of Globanic's demands accepted.

As K. Phocis Xenos concluded and sat down, there was spontaneous applause from the small, high-powered audience.

Theo Elliott, beaming, inquired, "Questions, anyone?"

"About those government ministers you spoke of," a CEO named Warren Graydon began; he headed Empire Chemical Corporation. "Is there any kind of assurance that they'll keep their word?"

"Let me handle that one," Elliott said. "The answer is yes, we have taken precautions. But I don't believe we need lay out details, even here."

There were subtle smiles, the answer indicating that bribery was involved. In fact, when the Peru-Globanic agreement was signed and sealed, the three ministers would receive Swiss bank accounts, opened in their names, with a million and a half dollars deposited in each. They would also have the free use, whenever required, of luxury condominiums in London, Paris and Geneva, with accompanying fringe benefits. International companies like Globanic

Industries frequently made such arrangements for their political friends.

Margot spoke up. "Tell us about Peru's stability, Fossie. Lately there's been an increase in revolutionary activity, not just in the usual Andes areas, but in Lima and elsewhere. Under those circumstances will resorts be practical? Will vacationers want to go there?"

She was walking a tightrope, Margot knew. On one hand, because of their competitive relationship, she could not afford to let Fossie Xenos get away with his presentation entirely unchallenged; also if something went wrong with the resort scheme later, she wanted it remembered that she had doubts in the beginning. On the other hand, if Margot became Globanic Industries' new chairman, she would need Fossie's friendship and his impressive contributions to conglomerate revenues. Keeping that in mind, she tried to make her questions rational and down the middle.

If Fossie sensed the maneuvering, he showed no sign of it and answered cheerfully. "All my information is that the revolutionary outlook is short-term and over the long haul Peru will survive with a solid, law-abiding democracy favorable to expanded tourism. Supporting that, there's a long tradition in the country based on democratic values."

Margot made no further contribution but

noted that Fossie had just exhibited a weakness which someday she might exploit. She had observed the same thing before with others, especially in real estate deals where glamorous objectives could outweigh normally cautious judgments. Psychologists called it the suspension of reality and, as Margot viewed it, anyone who believed an end was in sight to armed insurrection in Peru had done exactly that.

Of course, she reasoned, the resorts could still go ahead and be protected; after all, there were an increasing number of places in the world where holiday-making and danger existed side by side. But in Peru's case, only time and large expenditures would make the outcome clear.

Theo Elliott clearly did not share Margot's doubts. "If that's all the questioning," he pronounced, "let me just say this: For some time I've known what Fossie has just told you, but have brought you into it today for two good reasons. First, I know all of us can keep secrets and it's to our advantage to keep this one. Second, I don't want anything to damage our still delicate relationship with the government of Peru and thereby spoil what can evolve into the deal of the century." The chairman rose. "Now that's understood, let's have lunch."

7

It took several minutes for Jessica to accept the possibility that what Nicky had told her—that they were actually in Peru—might conceivably be true.

It couldn't have happened! Surely there had not been time!

But gradually, discarding earlier assumptions and with specific memories returning, the likelihood grew stronger. Wasn't it possible, she reasoned, that she, Nicky and Angus had been unconscious far longer than she had considered possible, even when she thought they might be in a southern U.S. state? Obviously, yes.

Yet if this was Peru, how had they been brought here? It could not have been easy to smuggle three unconscious people . . .

A sudden flash of memory! An image sharp and clear, yet totally forgotten until now.

During that brief interval when she struggled and managed to wound Cutface . . . in those desperate moments she had seen *two empty funeral caskets, one smaller than the other.* That terrifying sight had convinced her she and Nicky were about to be killed.

But now, with a shudder, Jessica realized they must have been brought here in those caskets—*like dead people!* The thought was so horrific that she wouldn't, *couldn't* think of it. Instead, she forced her mind back to the present, grim and painful as it was.

Jessica, Nicky and Angus, with their hands tied behind them, were still walking, stumbling over the narrow trail hemmed in by densely growing trees and undergrowth. Some armed men were ahead, others behind. At any sign of slowing, those behind shouted, *"¡Andale! ¡Apúrense!,"* prodding with their rifles to urge the captives on.

And it was hot. Incredibly hot. Sweat poured from them all.

Jessica worried desperately about the other two. She herself was suffering an intense headache, nausea, and a myriad of buzzing insects she was unable to brush away. *How long could this go on?* Nicky had said they were going to a river. *Surely they must get there soon!*

Yes, Jessica decided, Nicky's informant must have been right. This *was* Peru and, realizing how far from home they had come and how remote were the chances of their being rescued here, she felt like weeping.

The ground beneath her feet had become

soggy, making it increasingly difficult to walk. Suddenly, behind her, Jessica heard a sharp cry, a commotion and a thud. Turning, she saw that Angus had fallen. His face was in mud.

Gamely, the old man struggled to get up, but failed because of his tied hands. Behind him the men with guns laughed. One of them lunged forward with his rifle, ready to thrust the barrel in Angus's back.

Jessica screamed at the man, "No, no, no!"

The words briefly startled him and before he could recover, Jessica ran to Angus and dropped to her knees beside him. She managed to keep her body upright, even with her hands tied, though was helpless to assist Angus to his feet. The man with the gun moved angrily toward her, but stopped at the sound of Miguel's sharp voice. From the front of the column, Miguel now appeared, with Socorro and Baudelio behind him.

Before anyone else could speak, Jessica raised her voice, strong with emotion. "Yes, we are your prisoners. We don't know why, but we know we can't escape, and so do you. Why, then, tie our hands? All we want is to help ourselves, to keep from falling. Look what happens when we can't! Please, please, show some mercy! I beg you, free our hands!"

For the first time, Miguel hesitated, especially as Socorro told him softly, "If one of them breaks a leg or arm, or even has a cut, it could be infected. In Nueva Esperanza we'll have no means of dealing with infection."

Beside her, Baudelio said, "She's right."

Miguel, with an impatient gesture, snapped an order in Spanish. One of the men with guns stepped forward—the same man who had helped Nicky in the truck. From a sheath fastened to his belt he produced a knife and reached behind Jessica. She felt the rope binding her wrists loosen, then fall away. Nicky was next. Angus was propped up while his bonds were severed too, then Jessica and Nicky helped him stand.

Amid shouted commands, they again moved forward.

In the past few minutes, despite her emotion, Jessica had learned several things. First, their destination was Nueva Esperanza, though the name meant nothing to her. Second, the man who had befriended Nicky was Vicente— she'd heard his name used when he cut the bonds. Third, the woman who interceded with Miguel, the same one who struck Jessica in the hut, possessed some medical knowledge. So did Cutface. Possibly one or the other was a doctor, perhaps both.

She squirreled the nuggets of information away, instinct telling her that whatever she could learn might prove useful later.

Moments later, as the column rounded a bend in the trail, a wide river appeared ahead.

Miguel remembered reading in his early nihilist days that a successful terrorist must divest himself of conventional human emotions and achieve his ends by instilling terror in those who opposed his wishes and his will. Even the emotion of hatred, while useful in providing terrorists with psychic passion, could be a liability in excess, obscuring judgment.

In his terrorist career, Miguel had followed those dicta faithfully, adding one more: Action and danger were a terrorist's stimulants. For himself, he needed them the way an addict needed drugs.

Which was the reason for his disenchantment with what lay immediately ahead.

For four months, commencing with his flight to London and his acquisition of the illegal passport he used to enter the United States, he had been driven by the zest of ever-present danger, the life-and-death necessity for careful planning, more recently the heady flavor of success and, overall, a constant vigilance to assure survival.

But now, in these jungle backwaters of Peru, the dangers were less great. While there was always a possibility of government forces appearing suddenly, spraying automatic weapons fire and asking questions after, most other pressures were reduced or absent. Yet Miguel had contracted to remain here—or at least in Nueva Esperanza, the small village they would reach today—for an unspecified length of time because when this deal was made with the Medellín cartel, Sendero Luminoso had wanted it that way. For what reason? Miguel didn't know.

Nor did he know precisely why the prisoners had been taken and what would happen now they had been brought here. He did know they were to be strictly guarded, which was probably the reason for his staying on since he had a reputation for reliability. As to anything more, that was presumably in the hands of Abimael Guzmán, the raving lunatic—as Miguel thought of him nowadays—who had founded Sendero Luminoso and considered himself the immaculate Maoist-Jesus. Of course, that was assuming Guzmán was still alive. Rumors that he was or wasn't came with the persistence—and unreliability—of jungle rain.

Miguel hated the jungle—or Selva, as Peruvians called it. Hated the all-pervading dampness, decay and mold . . . the sense of confinement, as if the swiftly growing, impenetrable undergrowth was forever closing in . . . the never-ceasing dissonance of insects until you longed for a few minutes of silence and relief . . . the loathsome legion of soundless, slithering snakes. And the jungle was huge: almost twice the size of California and representing three fifths of Peru, though only five percent of the country's inhabitants lived there.

Peruvians were fond of declaring there were three Perus: the bustling coastal region with a thousand miles of cities, commerce, beaches; the South Andean mountains, their magnificent peaks rivaling the Himalayas and the area perpetuating Inca history and tradition; and finally this jungle, the Amazonian Selva—Indian, wild and tribal. Well, Miguel could take and even enjoy the first and second. Nothing, though, would change his aversion to the third. The jungle was *asquerosa*.

His thoughts returned to Sendero Luminoso —the "Shining Path" to revolution, the name taken from the writings of Peru's late Marxist philosopher, José Carlos Mariátegui. In 1980, Abimael Guzmán followed that lead, soon afterward anointing himself "the fourth sword of world revolution," his predecessors, as he saw it, being Marx, Lenin and Mao Tse-tung. All other revolutionaries were spurned by Guzmán as pallid charlatans, the rejects including Lenin's Soviet successors and Cuba's Castro.

The guerrillas of Sendero Luminoso believed they would overthrow the existing government and rule all of Peru. But not quickly. The movement claimed to count time in decades, not in years. Yet Sendero was large and strong already, its corps of leaders and its power growing, and Miguel expected to see the overthrow happen in his lifetime. Not, however, from this *odiosa* jungle.

For the moment, though, Miguel was awaiting instructions about the prisoners, instructions which would probably originate in Ayacucho, a historic town in the Andes foothills where Sendero exercised almost total control. Not that Miguel cared who gave the orders as long as some, involving action, reached him soon.

But now, the Huallaga River was directly ahead—a sudden opening in the constricting jungle scene. He paused to survey it.

Wide and a muddy orange-brown from Andean lateritic silt, the Huallaga flowed steadily toward its confluence with the Marañón River three hundred miles away and, soon after, its merging with the mighty Amazon. Centuries ago, Portuguese explorers named this whole Amazon complex *O Rio Mar,* The River Sea.

As they drew nearer, Miguel could see two wooden workboats, each about thirty-five feet long and with twin outboard motors, moored close to the riverbank. Gustavo, leader of the small force that had met them at the airstrip, was giving orders about loading stores the arriving group had brought. He also indicated how those traveling in the boats would be divided; the prisoners were to be in the first. Miguel noted approvingly that Gustavo's instructions included posting two armed guards while loading was taking place, a precaution against a sudden appearance by government forces.

Satisfied with what was being done, Miguel saw no reason to interfere. He would resume full command at Nueva Esperanza.

For Jessica, the river magnified the sense of isolation she felt. It seemed to her a desolate opening to an unknown world, unconnected to the one behind them. Prodded by guns, she, Nicky and Angus waded knee-deep through water to board one of the boats and, after climbing in, were ordered to sit on the damp boat bottom, a flat surface formed by boards running fore and aft above the keel. It was possible to lean back, if they chose, against the edge of a single board athwart the top of the boat, but this merely provided a choice between two discomforting positions, neither one endurable for long.

Jessica noticed then that Nicky had gone pale and was suddenly racked by vomiting. Though nothing came from his mouth except a little mucus, his chest heaved. Jessica moved closer and held him, at the same time looking desperately for help.

She immediately saw Cutface who had waded out from shore and was beside the boat. Before Jessica could speak, the woman she had observed several times before appeared and Cutface ordered, "Give them all more water— the boy first."

Socorro filled a tin cup with water and passed it to Nicholas who drank greedily; as he did, the shaking of his body subsided. Then he said in a weak voice, "I'm hungry."

"There is no food here," Baudelio told him. "You will have to wait."

Jessica protested, "There must be *something* he can have."

Cutface did not answer, but the order he had given about water had made his status clear and Jessica said accusingly, "You're a doctor!"

"That is no concern of yours."

"And he's American," Angus added. "Listen to his voice." The water seemed to have revived Angus who turned toward Baudelio. "That's right isn't it, you disgusting bastard? Don't you ever feel ashamed?"

Baudelio merely turned away and climbed into the other boat.

"Please, I'm hungry," Nicky repeated. He turned to Jessica. "Mom, I'm scared."

Jessica, holding him again, admitted, "Darling, so am I."

Socorro, who heard all the exchanges, appeared to hesitate. Then reaching into her shoulder bag, she produced a large bar of Cadbury's chocolate. Without speaking, she tore open the package, broke off a half-dozen squares and offered two to each prisoner. Angus was last and shook his head. "Give mine to the boy."

Socorro clucked her annoyance, then impulsively tossed the entire chocolate bar into the boat. It fell at Jessica's feet. At the same time Socorro moved away, boarding the second boat.

Some of the armed men who had been in the truck and on the wooded trail now climbed into the same boat as the prisoners and both boats started to move. Jessica noticed that other men who had been in charge of the boats were also armed. Even the two helmsmen, each seated forward of the twin outboard motors, had rifles across their knees and looked ready to use them. The chances of getting away, even if there were somewhere to go, seemed nonexistent.

As both boats headed upriver against the current, Socorro fumed at herself for what she had done. She hoped no one else had seen, because giving the prisoners that good chocolate, unobtainable in Peru, was a sign of weakness, of foolish pity—a contemptible sentiment in a revolutionary.

The problem was, she had moments of vacillation within herself, a psychic tug-of-war.

Less than a week ago, Socorro had reminded herself of the need to guard against banal emotions. That was the evening following the kidnap while the Sloane woman, the boy and the old man were unconscious in the second floor medical room of the Hackensack house. At that time Socorro was doing her best to hate the captives—*rico bourgeois scum,* she had labeled them mentally, and still did. But the hatred had to be forced on that other occasion and even now, she thought to her discredit, the same seemed true.

Earlier today, in the airstrip hut when the Sloane woman asked a question after Miguel ordered silence, Socorro deliberately hit her hard, sending the woman reeling. At the time, believing Miguel was watching, Socorro had simply tried to be supportive. Yet moments later she felt ashamed at what she had done. *Ashamed!* She *should not* feel that way.

Socorro told herself: She must be resolute in putting behind her, once and for all, memories of those things she had liked—*correction:* deluded herself into liking—during her three years in the United States. She had to *hate, hate, hate* America. And these prisoners too.

Soon afterward, while the river and its dense green uninhabited shores slipped by, she dozed.

Then, some three hours after departure, both boats slowed, their bows turning from the main river into a smaller stream, the banks on either side closing in and rising steeply as the boats progressed. They were nearing Nueva Esperanza, Socorro presumed, and there, she assured herself, she would strengthen and revive her radical fervor.

Baudelio, watching the boat ahead lead the way along a side valley from the Huallaga River, knew this journey was almost ended and he was glad. His time spent with this project was close to ending too, and very soon he hoped to be in Lima. That had been promised him as soon as the captives were delivered here in a healthy state.

Well, they *were* healthy, even in this ghastly, humid heat.

As if the thought of humidity had prompted more of the same, the sky overhead suddenly darkened to a somber gray and a torrent of rain arrived in sheets, soaking everything in sight. While a protruding jetty could be seen ahead, with other boats moored or beached, there were still several minutes to go before landing and, for captives and captors both, there was nothing to do but sit and get wet.

Baudelio was indifferent to the rain as he was indifferent nowadays to most else that came

his way—for example, the abuse directed at him
by the old man prisoner and the Sloane woman.
He was long past caring about that, and any
humane feelings he once had concerning those
he worked on medically had been extinguished
years ago.

What he really longed for at this moment
was a drink—several drinks; in fact, Baudelio
wanted to get drunk as soon as possible. While
he had continued taking the Antabuse tablets
which made it impossible to drink liquor without becoming violently ill—Miguel still insisted
on the alcoholic ex-doctor swallowing one tab-
let in his presence daily—Baudelio intended to
stop the Antabuse the instant he and Miguel
parted company. As far as Baudelio was concerned, that could not be too soon.

Something else Baudelio wanted was his
woman in Lima. He knew she was a slut, had
been a prostitute, and was a drunkard like himself, but in the messy detritus of his shattered
life, she was all he had and he missed her. His
own empty loneliness had been the reason for
his illicit use, a week ago, of one of the cellular
phones to call his woman from the Hackensack
house. Since making that call, against Miguel's
orders, Baudelio had worried a lot, dreading
that Miguel would find out. But the call had

apparently gone undiscovered, for which he was relieved.

Oh, how he needed that drink!

The chocolate, while not a lasting substitute for food, had helped.

Jessica did not waste mental effort wondering why the sour-faced woman had so impetuously left a chocolate bar, apart from noting that she was a person of unpredictable moods. Instead Jessica concealed the chocolate in a pocket of her dress, keeping it out of sight of the armed men aboard.

While traveling upriver, Jessica gave most of the chocolate to Nicky, but ate some herself and insisted that Angus have some too. It was important, she pointed out, keeping her voice low, that they all preserve their strength—which was clearly ebbing after the time in the open truck, then the exhausting march through the jungle and now their several hours in the boat.

As to the length of time the three of them had been unconscious, Jessica realized there was a clue in Angus's growth of beard. She hadn't noticed before, but the unshaved gray hairs on his face were surprisingly long. When she pointed this out, Angus felt his face and estimated it was four or five days since his last shave.

Perhaps that wasn't important now, but Jessica was still absorbing all the information she could, a reason she tried to stay alert during the river journey.

There wasn't much to see, except thickly growing trees and foliage on both banks, and the river itself winding sinuously, hardly ever in a straight line. Several times small canoes were visible in the distance, but none came close.

Throughout the journey Jessica was plagued by constant itching. Earlier, in the hut where she first returned to consciousness seated on the dirt floor, she had been aware of insects crawling on her. Now she realized they were fleas, which had stayed with her and were biting persistently. But short of stripping, there was no way she could remove them. She hoped that wherever she and the others were being taken, there would be ample water so she could wash the fleas away.

Like everyone else, Jessica, Nicky and Angus were soaked in the deluge of rain shortly before landing at Nueva Esperanza. But as their boat made fast against a crude wooden jetty, the rain stopped as suddenly as it had begun, and at that same moment the spirits of all three sank as they saw the awful, forbidding place ahead.

Beyond a rough and muddy path from the riverbank was a series of dilapidated houses, about two dozen in all, some merely shacks

built partly from old packing cases and rusted
corrugated iron and supplemented by bamboo
stems. Most of the houses were windowless,
though two had what appeared to be small
storefronts. Thatched roofs showed disrepair,
and some had gaping holes. Discarded cans and
other garbage littered the surrounding area. A
few scrawny chickens ran loose. Off to one side,
a dead dog was being pecked by buzzards.

Could there possibly be something better
farther on? The dismal answer appeared when a
rough, now muddy road leading out of the hamlet came into sight. The road climbed a hill and
on either side, beyond the few houses already in
view, was nothing but two barricading walls of
jungle. At the top of the hill the road disappeared.

Later, Jessica and the others would learn
that Nueva Esperanza was basically a fishing
village, though Sendero Luminoso used it from
time to time for purposes the organization
wanted hidden.

"*¡Váyanse a tierra! ¡Muévanse! ¡Apúrense!*"
Gustavo shouted at the prisoners, at the same
time signaling them to move. Dejected, dreading whatever was to come, Jessica and the other
two obeyed.

What happened minutes later was even
worse than they had feared.

After being escorted by Gustavo and four

more armed men up the muddy path, they were herded into a shack which stood farthest from the river. Inside, it took a few moments for their eyes to adjust to the semidarkness. When they did, Jessica screamed in anguish.

"Oh, my god, no! You can't shut us in those! Not in cages, like animals! *Please! Please no!*"

What she had seen set against the far wall were three partitioned cells about eight feet square. Thin but strong bamboo stalks, securely fastened, were a substitute for bars. Additionally, between each cell, wire screening had been nailed so there could be no physical contact between adjoining occupants or anything passed from one enclosure to another. At the front of each cell was a door fitted with a sliding steel bar and, outside, a heavy padlock.

Inside each cell was a low wooden bed and a thin, soiled mattress, alongside the bed a galvanized pail, presumably intended as a toilet. The whole place stank.

While Jessica pleaded and protested, Gustavo seized her. Though she continued struggling, his hands were like steel. Impelling her forward, he ordered, *"¡Vete para adentro!"* Then in halting English, "You go in there."

"In there" was the enclosure farthest from the shack's outer door and, with a forceful shove, Gustavo pushed Jessica to the inside wall. As she fell against it, the cell door closed

and she heard the padlock's metallic click. Outside, at the opposite end of the shack, she could
hear Angus fighting and arguing too, but he was
subdued, thrown in, and the padlock fastened.
In the cell next to her own, Jessica heard Nicky
sobbing.

Tears of rage, frustration and despair
coursed down her cheeks.

8

A week and a half had passed since the sixty
temporary recruits had been turned loose by
CBA News to make a study of the region's local
newspapers, searching for a headquarters that
the Sloane family's kidnappers might have used.
However, no progress had been made, nor had
there been developments in other areas.

The FBI, while not saying specifically it had
reached a dead end, had nothing new to report.
The CIA, now rumored to be involved, would
make no statement.

What everyone was waiting for, it seemed,
was some word from the kidnappers, presum-

ably accompanied by demands. So far it hadn't happened.

The kidnap story was still very much in the news, though on TV newscasts it had ceased to be the lead item, and in newspapers was usually on an inside page.

Despite the apparent waning of the public interest, there was no shortage of speculation. Among the news media there appeared a growing belief that the kidnap victims had somehow been spirited from the country and were overseas. As to precisely where, most hypotheses centered on the Middle East.

Only at CBA News were there contrary indications. Because of the special task force identification of a Colombian terrorist, Ulises Rodríguez, as a kidnap gang participant and perhaps the gang's leader, Latin America had become the focus of attention. Unfortunately, no particular country had been determined as the kidnappers' base.

To the surprise of everyone involved, knowledge of the Rodríguez connection remained exclusively with CBA News. It had been expected that the discovery would quickly be duplicated by other networks and newspapers and thus become public information, but while that could still occur at any time, it hadn't yet. There was even some unease at CBA about the News Division's continuing to withhold its knowledge concerning Rodríguez from the FBI.

Meanwhile CBA, more than other networks, kept the kidnap story aggressively alive, using a technique borrowed from rival CBS. During the 1979–81 Iran hostage crisis, Walter Cronkite, then CBS Evening News anchorman, concluded each broadcast with the words, "And that's the way it is [the date], the ____th day of captivity for the American hostages in Iran." (The number of days eventually totaled 444).

As Barbara Matusow, broadcasting's historian and conscience, recorded in her book *The Evening Stars,* Cronkite made "a decision that the hostages . . . were so important that the spotlight of national attention should not stray from them, even for a single night."

Similarly, Harry Partridge, still acting as second anchor for any item concerning the Sloane kidnap, now began, "On this the [numbered] day since the brutal kidnapping of the wife, son and father of CBA News anchorman Crawford Sloane . . ." The item itself then followed.

As a matter of policy, approved by Les Chippingham and agreed to by executive producer Chuck Insen, there was always a Sloane kidnap reference in every National Evening

News, even if only to record the absence of any new development.

But on a Wednesday morning, ten days after the search of local newspapers began, an event occurred which put everything at CBA News in high gear once more. It also ended the inactivity that had frustrated all members of the special task force.

At the time Harry Partridge was in his private office. He looked up to see Teddy Cooper in the doorway and, behind him, Jonathan Mony, the young black man who had made so strong an impression earlier when the temporary researchers were assembling.

"We may have something, Harry," Cooper said.

Partridge waved the two in.

"Jonathan will tell you." Cooper motioned to Mony. "Go ahead."

"Yesterday I went to a local newspaper in Astoria, Mr. Partridge," Mony began confidently. "That's in Queens, near Jackson Heights. Did all the things you said, found nothing. Then, coming out, I saw the office of a Spanish-language weekly called *Semana*. It wasn't on the list, but I went in."

"You speak Spanish?"

Mony nodded. "Pretty well. Anyway, I asked to check their issues for those dates we've been watching and they let me. Nothing there either, but as I was leaving they gave me their latest issue. I took it home, looked through it last night."

"And brought it to me this morning," Cooper said. He produced a tabloid-style newspaper which he spread on Partridge's desk. "Here's a column we think will interest you, and a translation Jonathan has written."

Partridge glanced at the paper, then read the translation, typed on a single sheet.

Hello, you wouldn't think, would you, that some people buy funeral caskets the way you and me pick up cheese at the grocery. Happens, though; ask Alberto Godoy of Godoy's Funeral Home.

Seems this guy came in from the street and bought two caskets just like that off the shelf—one regular, one small. Said he wanted to take them to his old Mom and Dad, the tiny one for Mom. Hey, how's that for a hint to the old folks? "Time to beat it, Mom and Dad, the party's over!"

Don't go away, there's more. Last week, that's six weeks later, this same guy comes back, he wants another casket like before, regular size. He took it away, paid cash, same as he did for the other two. Didn't say who this one was for. Wonder if his wife's been cheating.

Tell you who doesn't care, that's Albert Godoy. Says he's ready and eager for more business of the same kind.

"There's something else, Harry," Cooper said. "A few minutes ago we phoned the *Semana* office. Jonathan talked and we got lucky. The bloke who wrote the column was there."

"What he told me," Mony said, "was that the day he wrote the piece you read was a week ago last Friday. He'd just seen Godoy in a bar and Godoy had sold the third casket that same day."

"Which also," Cooper added, "happened to be right after the snatch, the very next day."

"Wait," Partridge said. "Don't talk. Let me think."

While the others were silent, he considered.

Stay calm, he told himself. *Don't get carried away!* But the possibilities were unmistakable: The first two caskets, purchased six weeks before the kidnap, only slightly ahead of the estimated one-month surveillance of the Sloane family, and within the three-months' maximum operation time also estimated by the task force. Then the size of the two caskets: one regular, one small, the second said to be for an old woman, *but it could also be for an eleven-year-old boy.*

Next, the third casket—according to the newspaper, a regular size. Established fact: Crawf's father, the old man, Angus, had arrived at the Sloane house virtually unexpected, having phoned only the day before. So if the family hadn't expected him, neither had the kidnappers. Yet they captured him and took him with Jessica and the boy. Three captives instead of two.

Questions: Did the kidnappers already have two caskets? Did the old man cause them to acquire a third? Was it for him the extra one was bought from Godoy's Funeral Home *the next day after the kidnap?*

Or was the whole thing merely an incredible coincidence? It might be. Or might not.

Partridge raised his eyes to the other two who were regarding him intently.

Cooper said, "Raises a few questions, don't it?"

"Do you think . . ."

"What I think is, we may have found how Mrs. Sloane and the others could have been taken out of the country."

"In caskets? Do you believe they were dead?"

Cooper shook his head. "Doped. It's been done before."

The statement confirmed what Partridge was already thinking.

"What happens next, Mr. Partridge?" The question was from Mony.

"As soon as we can, we'll interview that funeral man . . ." Partridge glanced at the typed translation to which had been added the funeral home's address. "Godoy. I'll do it myself."

"I'd like to come with you."

"I think he earned it, Harry," Cooper urged.

"So do I." Partridge smiled at Mony. "Nice going, Jonathan."

The young researcher beamed.

They would leave immediately and take a cameraman, Partridge decided. He instructed Cooper, "Minh Van Canh is in the conference room, I think. Tell him to grab his gear and join us."

As Cooper left, Partridge picked up a telephone and ordered a network car.

On the way out, passing through the main newsroom, he and Mony encountered Don Kettering, CBA's business correspondent. When news of the Sloane kidnap broke, it had been Kettering who was assigned to the flash studio "hot seat" and became first to go on the air with a special bulletin.

Now he asked, "Anything new, Harry?" Impeccably dressed in a brown tailored suit, his thin mustache neatly trimmed, Kettering, as always, looked like a prosperous businessman himself.

About to make a perfunctory answer and hurry by, Partridge hesitated. He respected Kettering not only as a specialist, but as a first class reporter. With his background, Kettering might be more at home than Partridge with the subject they were about to tackle.

"Something *has* come up, Don. What are you doing now?"

"Not much. Wall Street's quiet today. Need some help?"

"Could be. Come with us. I'll explain as we go."

"Let me tell the Horseshoe." Kettering picked up a phone on the nearest desk. "Be right behind you."

A network Jeep Wagoneer reached the main entrance of CBA News headquarters less than a minute after Partridge, Mony and Minh Van Canh emerged onto the street. The cameraman climbed into the rear seat with his equipment, Mony helping. Partridge took the front seat beside the driver. As the front door slammed, Don Kettering arrived and squeezed into the rear.

"We're going to Queens," Partridge told the driver. He had brought the *Semana* newspaper and Mony's translation with him and read out the Godoy's Funeral Home address.

Making a fast U-turn and facing east, the driver headed for the Queensboro Bridge.

"Don," Partridge said, swiveling around in his seat. "Here's what we know and what we're wondering . . ."

Twenty minutes later, in Alberto Godoy's cluttered, smoky office, Harry Partridge, Don Kettering and Jonathan Mony faced the obese, bald funeral home proprietor across his desk. The trio had simply walked in after resisting questions from a woman receptionist.

On Partridge's instructions, Minh Van Canh remained outside in the Jeep Wagoneer. If any pictures were needed, he would be called in later. Meanwhile, from the vehicle, Van Canh was discreetly videotaping the Godoy building.

From behind his usual lighted cigarette, the undertaker regarded the visitors suspiciously. For their part, they had already taken in the shabby establishment, Godoy's bloated features which suggested heavy drinking, and the food stains on his black coat and gray-striped pants. This was not a quality establishment and probably not a scrupulously run one either.

"Mr. Godoy," Partridge said, "as I told your lady outside, we're all from CBA News."

Godoy's expression changed to interest. "Ain't I seen you on the tube? Comin' from the White House?"

"That's John Cochran; people sometimes mix us up. He works for NBC. I'm Harry Partridge."

Godoy slapped a hand against his knee. "You been doin' all them kidnap bits."

"Yes, I have, and that's partly why we're here. May we sit down?"

Godoy motioned to chairs. Partridge and the others sat facing him.

Producing his copy of *Semana,* Partridge asked. "May I ask if you've seen this?"

Godoy's features soured. "That lousy, snooping son of a bitch! He had no right to print something he overheard, that wasn't said to him."

"Then you *have* seen the paper and know what's in it."

"Sure I know. So what?"

"We'd appreciate your answering some questions, Mr. Godoy. First, what was the name of the man who bought the caskets? What did he look like? Can you describe him to us?"

The undertaker shook his head. "All that's my private business."

"It *is* important." Deliberately, Partridge kept his voice low-keyed and friendly. "It's even possible there's a connection to something you just mentioned—the Sloane family kidnapping."

"Don't see how there could be." Then Godoy added stubbornly, "Anyway, it's private, so nothin' doing. And if you all don't mind, I've got work to do."

Don Kettering spoke for the first time.

"How about the price you charged for those caskets, Godoy? Want to tell us what it was?"

The undertaker's face flushed. "How many times I gotta tell you people? I'm minding my business. You mind yours."

"Oh, we'll do that," Kettering said. "In fact we'll make it our business to go directly from here to the New York City sales tax office. Even though it says in this report"—he touched the copy of *Semana*—"that you were paid all cash for those three caskets, I'm sure you collected, reported and paid New York sales tax, which will be a matter of public record, including the purchaser's name." Kettering turned to Partridge. "Harry, why don't we leave this uncooperative person and go to the sales tax people now?"

Godoy who a moment earlier had paled, now spluttered, "Hey, hold it! Just a minute!"

Kettering turned, his expression innocent. "Yes?"

"Maybe I . . ."

"Maybe you didn't pay any sales tax, didn't report it either, though I'll bet you charged it." Kettering's voice became harsh; abandoning any pretense of friendliness, he leaned forward over the undertaker's desk. Partridge, who had not seen the business correspondent in action in this way before, was delighted he had brought him.

"Listen to me carefully, Godoy," Kettering continued. "A network like ours has a lot of clout and if we have to, we'll use it, especially because right now we're fighting for one of our own—against a filthy crime, the seizure of his family. We need answers to questions fast, and if you help us we'll try to help you by not revealing what isn't important as far as we're concerned, like the sales tax or income tax—you've probably cheated the IRS, too. But if we don't get honest answers, we'll bring in—here, today —the FBI, the New York police, the sales tax force and the IRS. So take your choice. You can deal with us or them."

Godoy was licking his lips. "I'll answer your questions, fellas." His voice sounded strained.

Kettering nodded. "Your turn, Harry."

"Mr. Godoy," Partridge said, "who was it bought those caskets?"

"He said his name was Novack. I didn't believe him."

"You were probably right. Know anything else about him?"

"No."

Partridge reached into a pocket. "I'm going to show you a picture. Simply tell me your reaction." He held out a photocopy of the twenty-year-old charcoal sketch of Ulises Rodríguez.

Without hesitation Godoy said, "That's

him. That's Novack. He's older than the picture . . ."

"Yes, we know. You're absolutely sure?"

"Dead sure. Seen him twice. He sat where
you are."

For the first time since today's procession of
events began, Partridge felt a surge of satisfaction. Once more the special task force had
scored an investigative breakthrough. A positive connection between the caskets and the kidnap was established. Glancing at Kettering and
Mony, he knew they realized it too.

"Let's go over this Novack's conversation
with you," he told Alberto Godoy. "From the
beginning."

During the questions and answers following,
Partridge extracted as much from the undertaker as he could. In the end, however, it was
not a lot and it became clear that Ulises Rodríguez had been careful not to leave a trail behind
him.

Partridge asked Kettering, "Any other
thoughts, Don?"

"One or two."

Kettering addressed Godoy. "About that
cash Novack paid you. I believe you said, adding both lots, it was nearly $10,000, mainly in
hundred-dollar bills. Right?"

"Right."

"Anything special about them?"

Godoy shook his head. "What's special about money, except it's money?"

"Were they new bills?"

The undertaker considered. "A few may have been, but mostly no."

"What has happened to all that cash?"

"It's gone. I used it, spent it, paid some bills." Godoy shrugged. "Nowadays money goes fast."

Jonathan Mony had been watching the undertaker intently throughout the questioning. Earlier, when the talk turned to the cash, he was sure he detected nervousness on Godoy's part. He had the same feeling now. On a notepad he scribbled a message and passed it to Kettering. It read: *He's lying. He has some of the cash left. He's scared to tell us because he's still worrying about taxes—sales and income.*

The business correspondent read the note, gave the slightest of nods and passed it back. Speaking mildly, at the same time rising as if ready to leave, he asked Godoy, "Is there anything else you remember, or that you might have, which could be helpful to us?" As he concluded, Kettering turned away.

Godoy, now relaxed and confident, obviously wanting this to end, answered, "Not a damn thing."

Kettering spun on his heels. His face contorted, red with anger, he strode to the desk, leaned over and gripped the undertaker by the shoulders. Pulling the other forward until their faces were close, Kettering spat out the words, "You're a goddamn liar, Godoy. You still have some of that cash. And since you won't show it to us, we'll see if the IRS can get to see it. I told you we wouldn't call them if you helped us. Well, that's all over now."

Kettering pushed Godoy back into his chair, reached into a pocket for a slim address book and pulled a desk telephone toward him.

Godoy shouted, "No!" He wrenched the telephone away. Breathing heavily, he growled, "You bastard! All right, I'll show you."

"Understand," Kettering said, "this is the last time we fool around. After this . . . ."

Godoy, standing, was already removing a framed embalmer's certificate from the wall behind his desk. It revealed a safe. The undertaker spun the combination lock.

A few minutes later, while the others watched, Kettering carefully examined the cash Godoy had extracted from the safe—nearly $4,000. During his inspection the business correspondent looked closely at both sides of every bill, at the same time separating them into three piles—two fairly small, the third larger. At the end he pushed the larger pile toward Godoy and motioned to the two remaining.

"We need to borrow these. We'll give you a

proper receipt on behalf of CBA News. You can add the serial numbers if you like, and Mr. Partridge and I will both sign the receipt. I personally guarantee you will have all the money back within forty-eight hours with no more questions."

Godoy said grudgingly, "I guess that's okay."

Kettering motioned Partridge and Mony closer to the two small piles of bills. All were of one-hundred dollar denomination.

"Lots of business people," Kettering said, "are wary of hundred-dollar bills for fear they might be counterfeit. So what they often do is write on a bill, showing where it came from. For instance, if you take out a rental car and pay with hundred-dollar bills when turning it in, Hertz or whoever will write the rental contract number on each bill, which means they can trace you later if a bill is bad. For the same reason some tellers in banks note the depositor's name or account number on hundred-dollar bills paid in."

"I've seen that on hundreds sometimes," Partridge said, "and wondered why."

"Not me," Mony interjected. "That kind of paper doesn't come my way."

Kettering smiled. "Stick with TV, kid. It will in time."

The business correspondent continued, "All

those marks on money are illegal, of course. Defacing the currency can be a criminal offense, though it's seldom, if ever, enforced. Anyway, what we have in this first stack of bills is written numbers, and in the second, names. If you like, Harry, I'll show the number groups to banking friends who may recognize who uses them, then will float them through computers. As to the names, I'll go through the phone book and try to locate whoever had those hundred-dollar bills and used them."

"I think I see where we're headed," Partridge said. "But just spell out, Don, exactly what we're looking for."

"We're looking for banks. Whatever information we get should lead us to banks which at some point received those bills; maybe someone in a bank wrote on them the names or numbers that you see. Then, if we're exceptionally lucky, we may identify the bank that actually handled all of this money and paid it out."

"I get it," Mony said. "Paid it out to the kidnappers who used it to buy those caskets from Mr. Godoy."

Kettering nodded. "Exactly. Of course, it's all a long shot, but if it works *we shall know the bank the kidnappers used* and where they probably had an account." The business correspondent shrugged. "Once we have that, Harry, your investigation can move on from there."

"That's great, Don," Partridge said. "And we've done well on long shots so far."

Catching sight of the copy of *Semana* that had brought them here, he remembered Uncle Arthur's words when the search of local newspapers was begun: *"A thing about long shots is that while you seldom find exactly what you're looking for, you're likely to stumble over something else that will help you in a different way."*

9

In Alberto Godoy's office, tensions were easing.

Now that the demands of his high-pressure visitors from TV news were satisfied and the overhanging threat to himself removed, the funeral director relaxed. After all, Godoy reminded himself, he had done nothing illegal in selling the three caskets to Novack, or whatever his real name was. How was he supposed to know the goddamn caskets would be used for something criminal? Oh sure, he had suspicions about Novack both times he came in, and hadn't believed a word of his phony story about why he wanted caskets. But let anyone try to prove that. No way! They couldn't!

The two things he had been worried about when today's shindig started were the city sales tax, which he collected for the first two caskets but hadn't reported, and the fact that he'd cooked his books so that the ten grand cash he took from Novack didn't appear anywhere as income. If the IRS found out, they'd create seventeen kinds of shit from that. Well, these TV dudes had promised not to squeal about either of those finagles and he reckoned they'd keep their word. The way he'd heard it, making those kinds of deals was how TV news people gathered a lot of their information. And he had to admit, now that it was over, he'd got a charge out of watching them at work. But he sure as hell wouldn't talk about anything that happened today if that snooping asshole from the *Semana* rag was anywhere around.

"If you'll give me a sheet of paper," Don Kettering said, pointing to the two small piles of bills still remaining on the desk, "I'll write out a receipt for this money we'll be taking."

Godoy opened a drawer behind his desk in which he kept odds and ends and removed a pad of lined paper. As he was closing the drawer, he caught sight of a single sheet torn from a scratch pad, bearing his own handwriting. He had stuffed the paper in more than a week ago and forgotten it until now.

"Hey, here's something! That second time Novack showed . . ."

"What is it?" Partridge asked sharply.

"I told you he had a Caddy hearse, with another guy driving. They took the casket away in it."

"Yes, you did."

Godoy held out the scratch-pad sheet. "This was the hearse license number. I wrote it down, put it in here, forgot."

Kettering asked, "Why did you do that?"

"Maybe a hunch." Godoy shrugged. "Does it matter?"

"No," Partridge said, "it doesn't. Anyway, thanks; we'll check this out." He folded the paper and put it in a pocket, though was not hopeful about the outcome. He remembered that the license number of the Nissan van in the White Plains explosion had been phony and led nowhere. Still, any lead had to be pursued, nothing taken for granted.

Partridge's thoughts moved on to more specific reporting. He reasoned that some or most of what they had uncovered, including the involvement of Ulises Rodríguez, would have to go on air soon, almost certainly within the next few days. There was a limit to how much information could remain dammed up at CBA;

though luck had been with them so far, it could change at any moment. Also they *were* in the news business. Partridge felt his excitement rise at the prospect of reporting progress and decided that *right now* he had to think in terms of presentation.

"Mr. Godoy," Partridge said, "we may have got off on the wrong foot to begin, but you've been pretty helpful to us. How would you feel about making a video recording, repeating most of what you've told us here?"

The idea of being on TV, and a network no less, appealed to Godoy. Then he realized the publicity would expose him to all kinds of questions, including those about taxes which had worried him earlier. He shook his head. "No thanks."

As if reading his mind, Partridge said, "We needn't say who you are or show your face. We can do what's called a silhouette interview, using backlighting so viewers will only see a shadow. We can even disguise your voice."

"It'll sound like it's coming through a coffee grinder," Kettering added. "Your own wife won't recognize it. Come on, Godoy, what have you got to lose? We've a cameraman sitting outside who's a real expert, and you'll be helping us get those kidnapped people back."

"Well . . ." The undertaker hesitated.

"Would you guys promise to keep it confidential, not to tell anybody else?"

"I promise that," Partridge said.

"Me too," Kettering agreed.

Mony added, "Count me in."

Kettering and Partridge glanced at each other, aware that the promise they had made and would keep—the way honest journalists did, no matter what the consequences—could cause them problems later. The FBI and others might object to the secrecy, demanding to know who the silhouette subject was. Well, the network's lawyers would have to handle that; there had been brouhahas of the same kind before.

Partridge remembered when NBC in 1986 had secured a much-sought-after but controversial interview with the Palestinian terrorist Mohammed Abul Abbas. Afterward, a bevy of critics denounced NBC, not only for holding the interview but for a prior agreement—which the network honored—not to disclose its location. Even a few media people joined in, though clearly some professional jealousy was involved. While argument thrived, a U.S. State Department spokesman huffed and puffed and the Justice Department threatened subpoenas and interrogation of an on-the-scene TV crew, but eventually nothing happened. (The then Secretary of State, George Shultz, only said when questioned, "I believe in freedom of the press.")

The fact was, and everyone knew it, broadcast networks were in many ways a law unto themselves. For one thing, few government departments or politicians wanted to tangle with them legally. Also, free-world journalism, on the whole, stood for disclosure, freedom and integrity. Sure, it wasn't totally that way; standards fell short more often than they should because journalism's practitioners were human too. But if you became an inexorable opponent of what journalism stood for, the chances were you belonged on the side of "dirty" instead of "clean."

While Harry Partridge considered those fundamentals of his craft, Minh Van Canh was setting up for the videotape interview of Alberto Godoy which Don Kettering would conduct.

Partridge had suggested that Kettering do the interview, in part because the business correspondent clearly wanted to continue his involvement with the Sloane kidnapping—it was, after all, a subject close to the hearts and minds of the entire News Division. Also, there were other aspects of the subject that Partridge intended to handle himself.

He had already decided that he would leave for Bogotá, Colombia, as soon as he could get away. Despite sharing the opinion of his Colombian radio reporter friend that Ulises Rodríguez was not in that country, Partridge believed the time had come to begin his own search of Latin America, and Colombia was the obvious place to start.

Minh Van Canh announced he was ready to begin.

A few minutes earlier, on being called in from outside and looking around the funeral establishment, Minh had decided to set up the interview in the basement where caskets were exhibited. Because of the special backlighting, not much of the display room would be seen; only the wall behind where Godoy was seated was floodlit, with the interviewee in gloom. However, alongside the silhouette of Godoy was now another of a casket, an ingeniously macabre effect. The disguising of the undertaker's voice would be done later at CBA News headquarters.

Today there was no sound man present and Minh was using one-man equipment, a Betacam with half-inch tape incorporating picture and sound. He had also brought along a small viewing monitor and placed it so that Godoy, now seated, could observe exactly what the camera was seeing—a technique calculated to make the subject, in such special circumstances, more relaxed.

Godoy was not only relaxed, but amused. "Hey," he told Kettering, seated nearby, off camera, "you cats are smart."

Kettering, who had his own ideas about the way this interview should go, gave only a thin smile as he looked up from notes scribbled a few minutes earlier. At a nod from Minh, he began, having allowed for an introduction to be written later, which would precede the on-air showing.

"The first time you saw the man whom you now know to have been the terrorist Ulises Rodríguez, what was your impression?"

"Nothing special. Seemed ordinary to me." Even under this concealment, Godoy decided, he wasn't going to admit being suspicious of Novack-alias-Rodríguez.

"So it didn't trouble you at all when you sold him two caskets initially, then one more later on?"

The silhouette shrugged. "Why should it? That's the business I'm in."

" 'Why should it?' you say." Repeating Godoy's words, Kettering managed to convey skepticism. "But isn't that kind of sale exceedingly unusual?"

"Maybe . . . sort of."

"And as a funeral director, don't you normally arrange, or sell, what's called a package —a complete funeral?"

"Most of the time, sure."

"In fact, isn't it true that before you made those two sales to the terrorist Rodríguez, you had never, *ever,* sold caskets in that way before?" Kettering was guessing, but reasoned Godoy wouldn't know he was, and in a recorded exchange would not lie.

"I guess so," Godoy muttered. The interview was already not going the way he had expected. In the partial gloom he glared at Kettering, but the newsman persisted.

"In other words, the answer is no, you hadn't sold caskets that way before."

The undertaker's voice rose. "I figured it was none of my business what he wanted them for."

"Did you give any thought at all to communicating with authorities—the police, for example—and saying something like, 'Look, I've been asked to do something strange, something I've never been asked before, and I wonder if you'd like to check this person out.' Did you consider that?"

"No, I didn't. There was no reason to."

"Because you weren't suspicious?"

"Right."

Kettering bored in. "Then if you were not suspicious, why is it that on the second occasion Rodríguez visited you, you covertly wrote down the license number of the hearse he was using to take away the casket and kept that information hidden until today?"

Godoy roared angrily, "Now, look! Because

I told you something confidential, it don't mean . . ."

"Correction, Mr. Funeral Director! You did not say *anything* about that being confidential."

"Well, I meant to."

"There's quite a difference. And incidentally, neither did you say it was confidential when you revealed before this interview that the price you charged for those three take-out caskets was almost ten thousand dollars. For the kind of caskets you described, wasn't that a high price?"

"The guy who bought them didn't complain. Why should you?"

"Perhaps he didn't complain for his own good reasons." Kettering's voice became icy and accusatory. "Didn't you ask that excessively high price because you knew the man would pay it, knew all the time there was something suspicious, and you could take advantage of the situation, get yourself some extra money . . ."

"Hey, I don't have to sit here and take that garbage! Forget all this! I'm getting out." Angrily, Godoy rose from his chair and walked away, the line from a microphone separating as he did. The route brought him closer to the Betacam, and Minh, swinging it as a reflex action, caught him full-face and in light so, in effect, Godoy violated his own confidentiality.

There would be discussion later as to whether that closing sequence should be used or not.

"You bastard!" Godoy stormed at Kettering.

The business correspondent told him, "I don't like you either."

"Listen," Godoy said to Partridge, "I cancel the arrangement." He pointed to the Betacam. "You're not to use that. Understand?"

"I understand what you're saying," Partridge said. "But I can't guarantee we won't use it. That will be up to the network."

"Get the hell out of here!" Alberto Godoy glowered as the recording equipment was dismantled and the CBA News quartet departed from his premises.

During the ride back from Queens, Don Kettering announced, "I'd like to drop off as soon as we're in Manhattan. I want to start tracing that marked money and there's an office on Lex where I can do some phoning."

"Is it possible," Jonathan Mony said, "that I could come with you?" He glanced at Partridge. "I'd very much like to see how the other half of what we did today works out."

"Okay with me," Kettering assured him. "If Harry says yes, I'll show you some nuts-and-bolts reporting."

Partridge agreed and they separated after

crossing the Queensboro Bridge. While the Jeep Wagoneer continued on to CBA News, Kettering and Mony took a taxi to a brokerage office off Lexington Avenue near the Summit Hotel.

On entering, they were in a spacious room where about two dozen people—some seated, others standing—faced an overhead screen displaying swiftly moving stock market quotations. A dark green carpet contrasted with light green walls; comfortable chairs, fixed to the floor in rows, were upholstered in green and orange tweed. Some of those intently watching the market figures held notebooks with pencils poised; others were less concerned. A young oriental man was studying sheets of music; a few more were reading newspapers; several dozed.

Off to one side was a row of computers and some extension phones, a sign above them reading, LIFT RECEIVER FOR TRADING. Several phones were in use; despite lowered voices, snatches of conversation could be heard. "You bought two thousand? Sell." . . . "Can you get five hundred at eighteen? Do it." . . . "Okay, get out at fifteen and a quarter."

On the room's far side a receptionist saw the two newsmen come in and with a smile of recognition at Kettering, picked up a telephone. Behind her were several doors, some open, leading to interior offices.

"Take a look around you," Kettering told Mony. "This kind of stock shop will be history soon; this is one of the last. Most others have disappeared the way speakeasies did after prohibition ended."

"Stock trading hasn't ended, though."

"True. But brokers looked at their costs and found places like this don't pay. Too many people coming in to rest or just out of curiosity. Then the homeless began joining them—in winter, what better place to spend a warm, relaxing day? Unfortunately, the homeless don't generate a lot of brokerage commissions."

"Maybe you should do a piece for the news," Mony said. "Nostalgic, the way you just said, before the last of these goes."

Kettering looked at him sharply. "That's a helluva good idea, young fella. Why didn't I think of it? I'll talk to the Horseshoe next week."

Behind the receptionist, a closed door opened and a beetle-browed, burly man came forward, greeting Kettering warmly. "Don, it's good to see you. You haven't been around lately, though we're your faithful followers on the news. Is there something we can do?"

"Thanks, Kevin." Kettering pointed to Mony. "My young colleague, Jonathan, would like the name of a stock he can buy today which will quadruple in value by tomorrow. Apart from that, is there a desk and a phone I can use for half an hour?"

"The desk and phone, no problem. Come through to the back and use mine; you'll be more private. About the other thing—sorry, Jonathan, our crystal ball's out being serviced. If it comes back while you're here, I'll let you know."

They were shown into a small comfortable office with a mahogany desk, two leather chairs, the inevitable computer and a phone. A name on the door read: Kevin Fane.

"Make yourself at home," Fane said, "and I'll send in coffee and sandwiches."

When they were alone, Kettering told Mony, "When Kevin and I were at college, during summers we worked as runners on the floor of the New York Stock Exchange and we've kept in touch since. Want some professional advice?"

Mony nodded. "Sure do."

"As a correspondent, which it looks as if you may be, always keep lots of contacts, not just at high levels but lower ones too, and drop in to keep them green, the way we're doing now. It's a means of picking up information, sometimes when you least expect. Also remember that people like to help TV reporters; even just letting you use their phone makes them feel closer to you and, in a strange way, grateful."

While speaking, Kettering had withdrawn from an inside pocket the several hundred-dollar bills borrowed from Alberto Godoy, and spread them on the desk. He opened a drawer and found a sheet of paper to make notes.

"First we'll try our luck with the bills that have names written on them. Later, if needed, we'll work on those with account numbers only." Picking up a bill, he read out, "James W. Mortell" and added, "this hundred smackeroos passed through his hands at some time. See if you can find him in the Manhattan phone book, Jonathan."

Within moments Mony announced, "He's here." He read the number aloud while Kettering tapped out digits on the phone. After two rings a pleasant woman's voice answered, "Mortell Plumbing."

"Good morning. Is Mr. Mortell in, please?"

"He's out on a job. This is his wife. Can I help?" Not only pleasant, but young and charming, Kettering thought.

"Thank you, Mrs. Mortell. My name is Don Kettering. I'm the business correspondent of CBA News."

A pause, then a hesitant response. "Is this a joke?"

"No joke, ma'am." Kettering was relaxed and affable. "At CBA we're making some inqui-

ries and think Mr. Mortell may be able to help
us. In his absence, perhaps you can."

"You *are* Don Kettering. I recognize the
voice. How could we help *you?*" A soft laugh.
"Unless you have a water leak over there."

"Not that I know of, though if I hear about
one I'll remember you. Actually, it's concerning
a hundred-dollar bill which has your husband's
name written on it."

"We've done nothing wrong, I hope."

"Absolutely not, Mrs. Mortell. It simply
looks as if the bill passed through your husband's hands and I'm trying to discover where
it went."

The woman on the phone said thoughtfully,
"Well, we have customers who pay cash, including hundred-dollar bills. But we never ask questions."

"No reason why you should."

"Later on at the bank, when we pay those
big bills in, sometimes a teller will write our
name on them. I think they're not supposed to,
but some do." A pause, then, "I once asked
why. The teller said there are so many counterfeit hundreds, it's a precaution to protect themselves."

"Aha! Precisely what I thought, and probably how the bill I'm looking at got marked."
While speaking, Kettering gave Mony a
thumbs-up sign. "Do you have any objection,

Mrs. Mortell, to telling me the name of your bank?"

"I don't see why not. It's Citibank." She named an uptown branch.

"Thank you! That's all the information I need."

"Just a moment, Mr. Kettering. May I ask a question?"

"Of course."

"Is something about this going to be on the news? And if so, how can I be sure not to miss it?"

"Easy! Mrs. Mortell, you've been so helpful that I promise, the day it goes on, I'll call you personally and let you know."

As Kettering hung up the phone, Jonathan Mony said, "I thought I might learn something. I just did."

"What was that?"

"How to make a friend."

Kettering smiled. He had already decided that the Mortell woman sounded so charming, and with a hint of invitation in her voice, that instead of phoning he would drop in to see her. He made a note of the address; it was uptown, not far away. He might be disappointed, of course. Voices were deceptive and she could be older than she sounded and look like the back of a bus, though instinct told him otherwise. Something else Jonathan would undoubtedly learn in time was that a fringe benefit of being on television was frequent romantic opportunities, leading—if one were so inclined—to pleasant sexual dalliance.

He selected another hundred-dollar bill. "Let's try this one," he told Mony and motioned to the phone book. "The name is Nicolini Brothers."

It turned out to be a bakery and pastry store on Third. A man who answered was suspicious at first and after a question or two seemed inclined to hang up. But Kettering, politely persistent, persuaded him otherwise. Eventually the name of a bank was obtained where receipts from the store—including large bills—were regularly paid in. It was the American-Amazonas Bank at Dag Hammarskjöld Plaza.

The names on the next two bills which Kettering chose did not appear in the Manhattan phone book.

The bill after that produced results in the way of a cooperative manager of a men's clothing store. The store, he disclosed, had an account at Bank Leumi, the branch at Third and Sixty-seventh.

Another name on a bill was untraceable. The next led to a distrustful and abusive woman with whom Kettering could make no headway and he gave up.

The fifth phone call resulted in communication with an eighty-six-year-old man living in an East End Avenue apartment. He was too weak to speak on the phone and a nursing attendant did it for him, though clearly there was nothing wrong with the old man's mind. He could be heard whispering cheerfully that his son, who owned several night clubs, often dropped in and gave his father hundred-dollar bills, which were subsequently paid into a bank account that, the eighty-six-year-old declared with a faint chuckle, he was setting aside for his old age. And, oh yes, the account was at American-Amazonas Bank, Dag Hammarskjöld Plaza.

The next call, to a seafood restaurant near Grand Central, resulted in Kettering speaking at length with several people, none of whom would take the responsibility of telling him anything important. Eventually the restaurant owner was located and said impatiently, "What the hell! Sure you can know the name of our bank; in return, I hope you'll give us a mention on the news. Anyway, the bank's on that damn square I never can spell—Dag Hammarskjöld —and is American-Amazonas."

When he hung up, Kettering scooped up the hundred-dollar bills and told Mony, "We hit the jackpot. No more calls needed. We have the answer."

In response to a questioning glance he

added, "Look at it this way: Three out of five people naming the same bank is too much to be coincidence. So those other names, on the bills which went through Citibank and Leumi, had to have been put on earlier and the bills recirculated, probably through American-Amazonas too.

"So that's where the money came from which Novack-Rodríguez paid Godoy for the caskets."

"Exactly!" Kettering's voice hardened. "I'll also wager that same bank is where those fucking kidnappers drew their cash and had—maybe still have—an account."

Mony prompted, "So next step—Dag Hammarskjöld Plaza."

Kettering pushed his chair back from the desk and rose. "Where the hell else? Let's go."

10

Don Kettering was recognized immediately on entering the American-Amazonas Bank and had an instinct early on that his presence was not a total surprise.

When he asked to see the manager, a ma-
tronly secretary informed him, "He has someone with him now, Mr. Kettering, but I'll interrupt and tell him you're here." She glanced at
Jonathan Mony. "I'm sure he won't keep you
gentlemen long."

While waiting, Kettering surveyed the bank.
It was located on the main floor of an elderly
brick building near the Plaza's north extremity
and, viewed from outside, the bank's slate gray
entrance was unimposing. The interior, however, while small for a New York bank, was attractive and colorful. Instead of a conventional
tiled floor, a patterned carpet in muted cherry,
red and orange shades ran the entire length and
width of the business area; a small, gold-lettered
panel noted it was woven in Amazonas, Brazil.

While furnishings were conventional—a line
of tellers' counters on one side, three officers'
desks on the other—the woodwork everywhere
was of highest quality. Occupying most of one
wall, where customers would view it, was a
striking mural—a revolutionary scene of pant-
ing horses with tousled manes carrying uniformed soldiers.

Kettering was studying the mural when the
secretary advised, "Mr. Armando is free now.
Will you come in, please."

As they entered a partially glass-walled office which provided a view of the operations

area outside, the manager came forward with his hand extended. A desk plaque identified him as Emiliano W. Armando, Jr.

"Mr. Kettering, a pleasure to meet you. I see you often and admire much of what you say. But I suppose you hear that all the time."

"Even so, I still appreciate it." The business correspondent introduced Mony. At a gesture from Armando, the three sat down, the visitors facing a hanging tapestry in bright blues and yellows which continued the bank's thematic décor.

Kettering watched the manager, a small figure with a wrinkled face showing signs of tiredness, thinning white hair and bushy eyebrows. Armando moved with a nervous quickness, his expression worried, the general effect reminding Kettering of an aging terrier, uneasy with the changing world around him. Instinctively, though, he found himself liking the man—in contrast to his recent encounter with Alberto Godoy.

Leaning back in a swivel chair, the banker sighed. "I rather guessed that you or someone like you would be around soon. It's been an unhappy, perplexing time for us here, as I'm sure you understand."

Kettering leaned forward. The manager assumed he knew something that he didn't. He acknowledged cautiously, "Yes, that's all too often true."

"As a matter of interest, how did you get to hear?"

The business correspondent resisted saying, *"Hear what?"* and smiled. "In TV news we have sources of information, even though at times we can't reveal them." He noticed Mony following the conversation with interest while keeping his face impassive. Well, that ambitious young man was getting a journalism lesson in spades today.

"I wondered if it was the *Post* report," Armando said. "It left many unanswered questions."

Kettering wrinkled his forehead. "I may have read that. Do you happen to have a copy?"

"Of course." Armando opened a desk drawer and produced a news clipping encased in plastic. The heading read:

UN DIPLOMAT
SLAYS LOVER, SELF
IN JEALOUS RAGE

Kettering skimmed the report, noting it was from a ten-day-old paper, dated the Sunday before last. As he observed references to the two who had died—Helga Efferen of American-Amazonas Bank and José Antonio Salaverry, a member of the United Nations Peruvian delegation—the cause of the manager's distress became clear. What was not clear was whether or not the incident had any connection to the matter that had brought CBA News here.

Kettering passed the report to Mony and returned his attention to Armando, prompting, "Unanswered questions, I believe you said."

The manager nodded. "What the newspaper described is how the police say it happened. Personally, I don't believe it."

Still groping for a possible linkage, Kettering asked, "Would you mind telling me why?"

"The whole business is too complex for that simple explanation."

"Obviously, you knew the woman who was employed here. Did you know the man, Salaverry?"

"Unfortunately—as it's since turned out—yes."

"Will you explain that?"

Armando hesitated before answering. "My inclination is to be frank with you, Mr. Kettering, mostly because I think that what we've learned at this bank during the past ten days will come out anyway, and I know you to be fair in your reporting. However, I have an obligation to the bank. We are a substantial and respected establishment in Latin America, as well as having this and other toeholds in the United States. Is it possible you could wait a

day or two, giving me time to consult with senior management outside this country?"

There *was* a connection! Kettering's instincts again, and he shook his head decisively.
"It isn't possible to wait. There's a critical situation involving safety and lives." It was time, he
decided, to do some revealing of his own.

"Mr. Armando, at CBA we have reason to
believe your bank was involved in some way
with the kidnapping two weeks ago of Mrs.
Crawford Sloane and two other members of the
Sloane family. I'm certain you've heard about
it. So the question arises: Is this other episode—
the deaths of Efferen and Salaverry—related to
the kidnap?"

If Armando had been troubled before, Kettering's pronouncement had the effect of an in-
cremental bolt of lightning. Apparently overwhelmed, he put his elbows on his desk and his
head in his hands. After several seconds he
raised his eyes.

"Yes, it's possible," he said in a whisper.
"Now I see it. It's not only possible, it's likely."
He went on wearily, "A selfish notion, I know,
but I'm due to retire in just a few months and
my thought right now is: Why couldn't all this
have waited until I had gone?"

"I understand your feelings." Kettering
tried to curb his impatience. "But the fact is,
you and I are here and we *are* involved. Obvi-

ously we each have different information and, equally obviously, we'll both be ahead if we exchange it."

"I agree," Armando conceded. "Where should we begin?"

"Let me. A large sum of money, at least ten thousand dollars in cash and probably a good deal more, is known to have passed through your bank and aided the kidnappers."

The manager nodded gravely. "Putting together your knowledge and mine, it is definitely a great deal more money." He stopped. "If I help fill in some details, is it essential that you quote me directly?"

Kettering considered. "Probably not. There's an arrangement called 'background, not for attribution.' If you wish, we'll talk on that basis."

"I'd prefer it." Armando paused, collecting his thoughts. "Within this bank we have a number of accounts for several delegations to the United Nations. I won't go into those, except to say our bank has strong ties with certain countries; it's why this office is conveniently close to the UN. Various people in UN delegations have authority over those accounts and one in particular was controlled by Mr. Salaverry."

"An account belonging to the Peruvian delegation?"

"Connected with the Peruvian delegation—

yes. Though I'm not sure how many people knew about that account, other than Salaverry who had authority to sign and use it. You should understand that any UN delegation may have a number of accounts, some for special purposes."

"Okay, but let's concentrate on the important one."

"Well, for the past several months, substantial sums have been coming into that account and going out—all legitimately, with nothing irregular being done by the bank, except for one unusual thing."

"Which was?"

"Miss Efferen, who had considerable responsibilities here as an assistant manager, went out of her way to handle the account herself, at the same time shielding me and others from direct knowledge of the account's existence or what was going on."

"In other words, the source of the money coming in and who it was paid out to was kept secret."

Armando nodded. "That's the way it was."

"And to whom was it paid out?"

"In every instance to José Antonio Salaverry, on his signature. There are no other signatures in the account and every payment was in cash."

"Let's go back a bit," Kettering said.

"You've told us you reject the police conclusion about the way Efferen and Salaverry died. Why?"

"When I began to discover things last week and this, I thought that whoever was passing money through that account—assuming Salaverry to be an intermediary, which I think he was—probably did the killings, arranging them to look like murder-suicide. But now you tell me that the kidnappers of the Sloane family were involved, it seems likely they could have been the ones."

Though the wizened little manager had been under strain and was near retirement, his reasoning powers were still good, Kettering thought. He observed that Mony was fidgeting and advised, "If you have questions, Jonathan, ask away."

Mony put aside some notes he had been making and sat forward in his chair. "Mr. Armando, if what you say is true, can you make a guess why those two people were killed?"

The manager shrugged. "In my opinion they probably knew too much."

"For instance—the names of the kidnappers?"

"Again, from what Mr. Kettering has told me, that would seem a probability."

"And what about the source of the money

that the man, Salaverry, controlled. Do you know where that money came from?"

For the first time the manager hesitated. "Since Monday, I've had discussions with members of the Peruvian delegation at the UN— they are conducting an investigation of their own. What they've discovered so far and we've conferred about has been confidential . . ."

Kettering cut in, "We're not quoting you directly; we already agreed on that. So come on— let's have it! Who did the money come from?"

Armando sighed. "Let me ask you a question, Mr. Kettering. Have you ever heard of an organization called Sendero Luminoso or—"

Mony completed the sentence. "The Shining Path?"

Kettering's face tightened as he answered grimly, "Yes, I have."

"We're not certain," the manager said, "but they could be the ones who shoveled money into that account."

After leaving Kettering and Mony on the Manhattan side of the Queensboro Bridge, Harry Partridge and Minh Van Canh took time out for an early lunch at Wolf's Delicatessen at West Fifth-seventh and Sixth. Over their mutual choice of gigantic hot pastrami sandwiches, Partridge regarded Minh who had seemed thoughtful today, unusually preoccupied, though it had not affected his efficient work at Godoy's Funeral Home. From across the restaurant table, Minh's squarish pockmarked face above his stocky figure looked back impassively between mouthfuls of mustard-laden pastrami.

"Something on your mind, old friend?" Partridge asked.

"A few things." The answer was typical Van Canh and Partridge knew better than to press his question. Minh would respond with more detail in his own way, in his own good time.

Meanwhile Partridge confided to Minh his intention to fly to Colombia, perhaps the following day. He added that he wasn't sure whether anyone else should travel with him; he would talk with Rita about that. But when there was need for a camera crew, either tomorrow or later, he wanted Minh.

Van Canh considered, weighing a decision. Then he nodded. "Okay, I do it for you, Harry, and for Crawf. But it will be the last time, the last adventure."

Partridge was startled. "You mean you're quitting?"

"I promised my family; we talked last night. My wife wants me at home more. Our children need me, my business too. So after we come back, I go."

"But this is so damn sudden!"

Van Canh gave one of his rare faint smiles.

"Sudden like an order at three in the morning to go to Sri Lanka or Gdansk?"

"I know what you mean, though I'll miss you like hell; things won't be the same without you." Partridge shook his head sadly, though the decision did not surprise him. As a Vietnamese working for CBA News, Minh had survived extraordinary perils in the Vietnam war, near the end managing to get his wife and two children airlifted from the country before the fall of Saigon and all the while taking superb pictures of history on the run.

In the years following, the Van Canh family adapted to their new American life—the children, like so many Vietnamese immigrants, studying hard and earning high grades at school and now college. Partridge knew them well and admired, sometimes envied, the family's solidarity. As part of it, they lived frugally while Minh saved and invested most of his substantial CBA pay, his economies so obvious that among colleagues a rumor now existed that Minh was a millionaire.

The last was possible, Partridge knew, because over the past five years Minh had purchased several small camera stores in New York suburbs, linking them and significantly enlarging their business with the aid of his wife, Thanh.

It was reasonable, too, that at this point in

his life Minh should decide he had had enough of travel and prolonged absences, and had taken sufficient risks, including joining Harry Partridge on dangerous assignments.

"Speaking of your business, how is it going?" Partridge asked.

"Very well." Again Minh smiled, adding, "But it has become more than Thanh can manage while I am away."

"I'm pleased for you," Partridge said, "because no one deserves it more. And I hope we'll still see each other once in a while."

"You can count on it, Harry. In our home your name will stay first on our list of honored guests."

On the way back from lunch, after leaving Van Canh, Partridge stopped at a sporting goods store to buy some heavy socks, a pair of hiking boots and a sturdy flashlight. He suspected he might need all three quite soon. By the time he returned to CBA, it was midafternoon.

In the task force conference room, Rita Abrams waved him over. "A man's been trying to reach you. He's called three times since this morning. Wouldn't leave his name, but said it's essential he speak to you today. I told him sooner or later you'd be back."

"Thanks. There's something I want to tell you. I've decided I should go to Bogotá . . ."

Partridge stopped as he and Rita looked up at the sound of hurried footsteps approaching the conference room. A moment later Don Kettering entered with Jonathan Mony close behind.

"Harry! Rita!" Kettering said, his voice breathless from hurrying, "I think we have the can of worms—wide open!"

Rita glanced around her, aware of others in the room. "Let's go in a private office," she said, and led the way to her own.

It took twenty minutes for Kettering, aided occasionally by Mony, to describe all that they had learned. Kettering produced the *New York Post* report of the Salaverry-Efferen alleged murder-suicide, a copy made by the American-Amazonas Bank manager before they left. The two correspondents and Rita knew that when this meeting was over, CBA News research would routinely obtain all other material on the same subject.

After Rita read the clipping, she asked Kettering, "Do you think we should start investigative work on those two deaths?"

"Maybe some, though it's incidental now. The real story is the Peru connection."

"I agree," Partridge said, "and Peru has come up before." He remembered his conversation two days ago with Manuel León Seminario, owner-editor of the Lima-based *Escena.* While nothing specific had emerged, Seminario had said, "In Peru nowadays kidnapping is almost a way of life."

"Even though we have a Peru involvement," Rita pointed out, "let's not forget that we don't know for sure whether the kidnap victims have been taken out of this country."

"I'm not forgetting," Partridge said. "Don, do you have anything more?"

Kettering nodded. "Yes. Before I left the bank I had the manager agree to an interview on camera, maybe later today. He knows he may be sticking his neck out with the bank's owners, but he's a good old guy with a sense of responsibility and says he'll take his chances. If you like, Harry, I'll do that one too."

"I do like. Anyway, it's your story." Partridge turned to Rita. "Cancel what I said about going to Bogotá. Now it's Lima. I want to be there early tomorrow."

"And how much do we broadcast, when?"

"Everything we know, and soon. Exactly when, we'll discuss with Les and Chuck, but if possible I'd like a clear twenty-four hours in Peru before an army of other correspondents gets there, which will happen as soon as we go with what we have."

He continued, "So starting right now, we'll work all night putting everything together. Call everyone on the task force in for a meeting"—

Partridge glanced at his watch: 3:15 P.M.—"at five o'clock."

"Yessir!" Rita, enjoying action, smiled.

At the same moment, the phone on her desk rang. After answering, she covered the mouthpiece and told Partridge, "It's the same man—the one who's been trying to get you all day."

He took the phone. "This is Harry Partridge."

"Don't use my name at any point in this conversation. Is that clear?" The caller's words sounded muffled, perhaps deliberately, but Partridge recognized the voice of his contact, the organized crime lawyer.

"Yes, it's clear."

"You know who I am?"

"I do."

"I'm calling from a pay phone, so the call's not traceable. And something else: If you ever name me as the source of what I'm about to tell you, I shall swear you're a liar and deny it. That clear too?"

"It is."

"I've taken big risks to get what I have, and if certain people knew of this conversation it could cost me my life. So when this call ends, my debt to you is paid in full. Understood?"

"Fully understood."

The other three in the small office were silent, their eyes fixed on Partridge as the muffled voice, audible only to him, continued.

"Some clients I do business with have Latin American connections." *Connections with the cocaine trade,* Partridge thought, but didn't say it.

"Just as I already told you, they wouldn't touch the kind of thing you've been inquiring about, but there are other things they get to hear."

"I understand that," Partridge said.

"All right, here it is, and the information is solid, I guarantee it. The people you are looking for were flown out of the United States last Saturday and are now imprisoned in Peru. Got that?"

"I have it," Partridge said. "May I ask one question?"

"No."

"I need a name," Partridge pleaded. "Who's responsible? Who is holding them?"

"Goodbye."

"Wait, please wait! All right, I won't ask you to give a name, only do this: I'll speak a name and if I'm wrong, give me some kind of signal saying no. If I'm right, don't say anything. Will you do that?"

A pause, then, "Make it fast."

Partridge took a breath before mouthing, "Sendero Luminoso."

At the other end, silence. Then a click as the caller hung up.

11

Almost from the beginning, when Jessica regained consciousness in the darkened hut at Sion and discovered soon after that she, Nicky and Angus were prisoners in Peru, Jessica had accepted that she alone must provide their beleaguered trio with leadership and inspiration. Both qualities, she realized, were essential to their survival while they waited and hoped for eventual rescue. The alternative was profound despair, leading to an emotional surrender which could perhaps destroy them all.

Angus was courageous, but too old and weak to be more than supportive, and ultimately even he might need to draw from Jessica's strength. Nicky, as always, must be Jessica's first concern.

Assuming they came through this nightmare safely—and Jessica refused to consider any other outcome—it was possible for it to leave forever a mental scar on Nicky. Jessica's intention, no matter what ordeals and privations lay ahead, was to see that it did not. She would teach Nicky, and Angus if necessary, that above all they must retain their self-respect and dignity.

And she knew how. She had taken a training course which some of her friends had thought of as a whim. It happened because Crawford, who really ought to have taken the course himself, had lacked the time. Jessica, feeling someone in the family should, had gone instead.

Oh, thank you and bless you, Brigadier Wade! I never dreamed, when I attended those drills and listened to your lectures, that I would need and make use of what you taught me.

Brigadier Cedric Wade, MC, DCM, had been a British Army sergeant in the Korean War and later an officer in the elite British SAS. Now retired and living in New York, he conducted small-scale anti-terrorism courses. His reputation was such that the U.S. Army sometimes sent him pupils.

In Korea, in 1951, Sergeant Wade was captured by the North Korean forces and for nine and a half months held in solitary confinement in an earthen pit below ground level, approximately ten feet square. Above his head were securely fastened bars, open to the sun and rain. At no point while imprisoned was he ever released from that lonely cell. During his time there he had minimal communication with his guards, had nothing to read, and could see only the sky above.

As he quietly described his experience in a lecture, which even now Jessica remembered almost word for word, *"I knew at the start they intended to break my spirit. I was determined they never would and that however bad it got, even if I died in that hole, I would not lose my self-respect."*

He kept it, Brigadier Wade told members of his classes, by hanging on to whatever threads of normalcy and order he could. To begin, he assigned each corner of his tiny cell a separate function. An unpleasant one came first. He had no choice but to urinate and defecate on the cell floor. One corner was kept for that purpose only; he saw to it that no other portion of the cell was similarly debased. *"At first, the odor was terrible and sickening. After a while I got used to it because I knew I had to."*

The opposite corner, as far away from the first as possible, was used for eating the meager food passed down to him. A third corner was for sleeping, the fourth for sitting to meditate. The center of the cell was used for exercises three times daily, including running in place. *"I reasoned that staying fit was another way to keep myself a person, and preserve my dignity."*

He received a ration of drinking water daily, but none for ablutions. From the drinking water, he always saved a small portion with which he washed. *"It wasn't easy and I was sometimes tempted to drink it all, but I didn't and instead was always clean—something truly important in the way you feel about yourself."*

At the end of nine months, taking advantage of a guard's carelessness, Sergeant Wade escaped. Three days later he was recaptured and returned to the cell, but within two weeks American forces overran the North Koreans' position and released him. He made friendships then which, long afterward, resulted in his residence in the United States.

Something else Brigadier Wade taught Jessica and others was CQB—close quarters battle, a form of unarmed combat in which even a small, lightweight person with the proper skills could disarm an attacker and either blind that person or break an arm, a leg or the neck. Jessica had proved an agile and fast-learning pupil.

Since arriving in Peru as a captive, there had been opportunities to make use of her CQB training, but each time Jessica had restrained herself, knowing such action would be self-defeating. Instead she kept her ability concealed, in reserve for some moment—if one should arise—when it could become decisive.

No such moment had arisen yet at Nueva Esperanza. Nor did the chance of one seem probable.

During those terrible first minutes when Jessica, Nicky and Angus were thrust into their separate cages, and Jessica wept on hearing Nicky sobbing, there was a period of mental dislocation and misery which even the best intentions could not bridge. Jessica, like the others, had succumbed to it.

But not for long.

Before ten minutes had passed, Jessica called out softly, "Nicky, can you hear me?"

After a pause, a subdued answer came back, "Yes, Mom." The reply was followed by movement as Nicky approached the screen between their cells. Their eyes had adjusted to the semidarkness and the two could see each other, though not touch.

Jessica asked, "Are you okay?"

"I think so." Then in a voice which quivered, "I don't like it here."

"Oh, darling, neither do I. But until we can do something, we have to hold on. Keep reminding yourself that your father and a lot of others are searching for us." Jessica hoped her voice sounded reassuring.

"I hear you, Jessie. You too, Nicky." It was

Angus, speaking from the cell on the far side of Nicky's, though his voice seemed weak. "Keep believing that we'll all get out of here. And we will."

"Try to get some rest, Angus." Jessica was remembering the beating her father-in-law had taken from Miguel in the hut where they all returned to consciousness, the grueling trek through the jungle and Angus's fall, the long journey by boat, and then his struggle here.

As she spoke, a shuffling of feet could be heard and from the shadows beyond the cells a figure moved into view. It was one of the gunmen who had accompanied them on the journey, a heavyset mustachioed man they would later identify as Ramón. He carried a Kalashnikov rifle and, aiming it at Jessica, ordered, *"¡Silencio!"*

About to protest, Jessica heard Angus advise softly, "Jessie, don't!" She curbed her impulse and they all fell silent. After a pause, the gun was lowered and Ramón returned to a chair in which he had been seated.

The experience proved to be their first with a succession of armed guards, one of whom was always on duty in the hut, the individual changing every four hours.

As they quickly discovered, the strictness of the guards varied. The most easygoing was Vicente, the man who had helped Nicky in the truck and, on Miguel's orders, had cut the ropes binding their wrists. Apart from motioning them to keep their voices lowered, Vicente allowed them to talk as much as they wished. Ramón was the strictest, permitting no talking at all, with the other guards somewhere in between.

During the times they talked, Jessica shared with Nicky and Angus recollections of her antiterrorism course, especially the ordeal and precepts of Brigadier Wade. Nicky seemed fascinated with the Wade story—probably as a relief from the confinement and monotony. It was a cruel restriction for an active, highly intelligent eleven-year-old, and several times a day Nicky would ask, "What do you think Dad's doing right now, Mom, to get us out of here?"

Jessica always tried answering imaginatively, at one point saying, "Your father knows so many people that there isn't anyone he can't call on for help. I'm sure he must have spoken with the President, who can get lots of people working, looking for us."

Even if true, it was a piece of vanity which in normal times Jessica would not have uttered. But if it bolstered Nicky's hopes, that was all that mattered.

Jessica urged the other two to follow as much of Brigadier Wade's example as they could. In the matter of using the makeshift toi-

let facilities, they respected each other's privacy
by turning away when asked and not comment-
ing about the inevitable odors. On the second
day they all began exercising, Jessica again taking the lead.

As the first few days passed, a pattern of
living—mainly miserable—took shape. Three
times daily, a diet of unappetizing, greasy food
—principally cassava, rice and noodles—was
brought to them. The first day, Nicky choked
on the grease which tasted sour and Jessica
came close to vomiting; hunger eventually outweighed distaste and they forced it down. Every
forty-eight hours, more or less, the stinking san-
itary pails were removed and emptied by an Indian woman. If they were washed at all, it was
superficially; when returned they smelled almost as bad. Drinking water was handed in to
each cell in used soft-drink bottles; occasionally
there were bowls and other water with which to
wash. The guards warned the prisoners by hand
signals that they should not drink the washing
water which was a muddy brown.

Nicky's morale, which was the most important to Jessica, while not high at least remained
stable; he also proved himself to be resilient
once the initial shock of being there had passed.
Jessica, who in New York did part-time social
work among underprivileged families, had observed that in tragic situations, children often

coped better than adults. Possibly, she thought, it was because children's thinking was less complicated and more honest; or perhaps children became mentally adult when the need was thrust upon them. In Nicky's case, for whatever reason, he was visibly coping.

He began attempting conversations with the guards. Nicky's Spanish was rudimentary, but depending on the patience and good nature of the other party, he managed to achieve exchanges and gain information. Vicente was the most cooperative.

From Vicente they learned of the impending departure of "the doctor"—obviously the one whom Jessica thought of as Cutface—and who, Vicente believed, was "going home to Lima." However, "the nurse" would stay on, and this was clearly the sour-faced woman whose name they discovered was Socorro.

They speculated among themselves on why Vicente was different from the other guards and apparently kinder. It was Jessica who cautioned Nicky and Angus, "It's not so much that he's different. Vicente's still one of those who brought us here and are keeping us prisoners— don't let's forget that. But he's not as mean or thoughtless as the others, so by comparison he seems kind."

There were other facets of the subject that Jessica wanted to talk about, but she decided to save them for later. There would be need of fresh themes for thought and discussion during what she foresaw as lonely days ahead. Meanwhile, she added, "Because he's the way he is, let's make all the use of Vicente that we can."

At Jessica's suggestion, Nicky asked Vicente if the prisoners were to be allowed out of the cells at all, to go outside. To this question, Vicente shook his head, though it was not clear whether the answer was negative or he didn't understand. Jessica, persisting, asked to have a message passed to Socorro that the prisoners would like to see her. Nicky did his best, but once more a headshake was the only response, making it seem doubtful the request would be delivered.

Nicky's relative success with the language surprised Jessica since his Spanish lessons at school had begun only a few months earlier. When she mentioned this, Nicky told her that two of his friends at school were Cuban immigrants who chattered in Spanish in the playground. "Some of us listened, we picked up things . . ." Nicky paused, chuckling. "You won't like this, Mom, but they know all the dirty words. They taught us those."

Angus, who had been listening, asked, "Did you learn any dirty insults, too?"

"Sure did, Gramps."

"Could you teach me a few? So I can use them on the people here, if I have to."

"I'm not sure Mom would like . . ."

"Go ahead," Jessica said. "I won't mind." Nicky's laughter had been wonderful to hear.

"All right, Gramps. If you really want to badmouth somebody, you could say . . ." Nicky crossed his cell and whispered to his grandfather through their separating screen.

They had, Jessica reflected, stumbled on one more way to pass the time.

And later that day Socorro came, responding to the message.

She stood in the outer doorway, her slim, lithe body a distinctive silhouette, surveying the three cells, her nose wrinkling at the all-pervading smell.

Without waiting, Jessica spoke. "We know you're a nurse, Socorro. It's why you cared enough to speak up and have our hands untied, and why you gave us chocolate."

Socorro said crossly, "Not a nurse, a nursing aide." She came closer to the cells, her lips set tightly.

"It makes no difference, not here anyway," Jessica said. "Now that the doctor's going, you'll be the one who knows about medicine."

"You're trying to be smart; it won't help you. You wanted to see me. Why?"

"Because you've already shown you want to

keep us alive and well. But unless we get out of here, into some fresh air for a while, we'll all be desperately ill."

"You have to stay inside. They don't want you to be seen."

"Why not? And who are 'they'?"

"That is not your concern, and you have no right to ask questions."

Jessica slammed back, "I have a mother's right to care about my son; also about my father-in-law who is old and has been treated brutally."

"He deserved it. He talks too much. So do you."

Instinct told Jessica that some of Socorro's antagonism was contrived. She attempted a compliment. "Your English is excellent. You must have lived in America a long time."

"That is none of your . . ." Socorro stopped and shrugged. "Three years. I hated it. It is a filthy, corrupt country."

Jessica said softly, "I don't think you really believe that. I think you were treated well, and now you are having trouble hating us."

"Think what you want," Socorro snapped as she walked away, then in the doorway turned. "I will try to have more air let in here." Her lips twitched in the nearest thing to a smile. "It will be healthier for the guards."

Next day two men arrived with tools. They

cut open several spaces, creating unblocked windows in the walls facing the cells. Immediately, the daytime semidarkness was replaced by light so the three captives could see each other clearly, and also the guard. As well, there was a flow of air through the building, occasionally a breeze, and while foul odors were not eliminated, they were greatly reduced.

It was a victory for Jessica and also, she thought, an indication that beneath the surface Socorro was not as hostile as she tried to appear —a vulnerability perhaps to be exploited later in some larger way.

But the light-and-air victory was minor and, as it proved, there were major agonies still to be endured. One, unknown to Jessica, was already taking shape.

12

Six days after the captives and their escorts arrived at Nueva Esperanza, Miguel received a series of written orders from Sendero Luminoso, orders originating in Ayacucho. They were delivered by a messenger traveling in a truck that took two days to cover the five hundred tortuous road miles, a journey extending over perilous mountain passes and soggy jungle trails. Several items of specialized equipment were also delivered.

The most important instruction involved making a videotape recording of the woman prisoner. A script was supplied and no deviation from its wording would be permitted. The project was to be personally supervised by Miguel.

Another instruction confirmed that Baudelio's duties were at an end. He would accompany the messenger in the truck back to Ayacucho, from where he would fly to Lima. The truck would return to Nueva Esperanza in a few days' time to bring more supplies and collect the completed videotape.

The news that Baudelio was going home to Lima, even though expected, displeased Miguel. For one thing, the ex-doctor knew too much. For another, he was certain to resume his alcoholic ways, and liquor and a loose tongue inevitably went together. Therefore Baudelio at large was a threat not only to the security of their small garrison but also—more importantly, as Miguel saw it—to his own safety.

In other circumstances he would have forced Baudelio to take a walk in the jungle from which only Miguel would return. But

Sendero Luminoso, while ruthless in many ways, could become belligerent about an outsider killing one of its own people, for whatever reason.

What Miguel did was send confidentially with the messenger a strongly worded note pointing out the dangers of having Baudelio remain in circulation. Sendero would quickly make its own decision. Miguel had little doubt what that would be.

One thing pleased him. Among the general instructions he received was one to "keep the three hostages in good health until otherwise ordered." The reference to "three hostages," which Sendero's high command would have learned of through news reports, conveyed approval of Miguel's decision to include the old man in the kidnap, something originally not planned.

He turned his attention to the special equipment brought from Ayacucho for the video and sound recording session. It comprised a Sony Camcorder with cassettes, a tripod, photoflood kit and a portable 110-volt generator, gasoline-powered. None of it presented a problem to Miguel, who had handled recording sessions with kidnap victims before.

He realized, though, that he would need support and certain stern measures to ensure obedience from the woman, who he suspected would be difficult. To help him he chose Gustavo and Ramón, both of whom he had observed being tough with the prisoners and who were unlikely to be squeamish, whatever punishment they were asked to inflict.

The recording session, Miguel decided, would take place the following morning.

As soon as there was sufficient daylight, Jessica was busy at work.

Soon after she, Angus and Nicky had recovered consciousness in Peru, all three discovered that at some point almost the entire contents of their pockets had been removed, including any money they had had. A handbag Jessica had been carrying at Larchmont, not surprisingly, had disappeared. Among the few things left were some paper clips, a comb of Jessica's, and a small notebook in Angus's back pants pocket, which apparently was overlooked. Also, in the lining of Nicky's jacket was a ballpoint pen which had fallen through a hole in a pocket and had not been found.

At Jessica's urging, the notebook and pen were carefully hidden and used only if the guard on duty was one of those known to be more easygoing than the martinets like Ramón.

Yesterday Jessica had borrowed the notebook from Angus, and Nicky's ballpoint pen. Although the screens between the prisoners' cages prevented them from passing anything to each other, Vicente, while on guard duty, obligingly collected the objects and handed them to her.

What Jessica intended was to make drawings of the people she had encountered while strong memories of them still remained. While not an accomplished artist, she was a competent amateur and was sure the faces in her drawings would be recognizable if eventually she was able to use them for identifying those involved in the kidnap and this aftermath.

The first drawing, which she had begun the preceding day and was still working on, was of the tall, balding, authoritative man whom Jessica had become aware of as consciousness returned to her in the first darkened hut. Although not totally alert at the time, she did remember her desperately mouthed plea, *"Help! . . . please help . . . tell someone . . ."* A subsequent impression, sharp and clear, was of the man in question reacting, looking startled, but afterward doing nothing, as was now apparent.

Who was he? Why was he there? Since he was present, he had to be involved. Jessica believed that the man was American. Whether he was or wasn't, she hoped that one day her drawing would help track him down.

When she had finished, Jessica had sketched

a recognizable likeness of the Learjet pilot, Captain Denis Underhill.

The sound of footsteps outside caused her to fold the drawing hastily and conceal it in her brassiere, the first place she thought of. The notebook and pen she thrust beneath the thin mattress of her bed.

Almost at once, Miguel, Gustavo and Ramón appeared. All three were carrying equipment which Jessica recognized instantly. "Oh, no!" she called out to Miguel. "Don't waste your time setting that up. We will not help you by making any recording."

Miguel ignored her. Taking his time, he installed the Camcorder on its tripod and arranged the photoflood lights which he plugged into an extension cable. The cable ran out of doors where the sound of a generator starting up could be heard. Moments later the area in front of the three cells was brightly lit, the lights focused on an empty chair which the Camcorder faced.

Still unhurriedly, Miguel walked forward to Jessica's cage. His voice was cold and hard. "You will do precisely what I tell you, when I tell you, bitch." He held out three handwritten pages. "This is what you will say—exactly that and no more, with not one word changed."

Jessica took the pages, read them quickly, then tore them into pieces which she threw outward through the bamboo bars. "I told you I wouldn't do it, and I won't."

Miguel did not react but looked toward Gustavo who was waiting nearby. Miguel nodded. "Get the boy."

Despite her determination a moment earlier, a shiver of apprehension ran through Jessica.

While she watched, Gustavo opened the padlock securing Nicky's cage. Going inside, he seized Nicky by a shoulder and one arm; then, twisting the arm, propelled him outside until both were in front of Jessica's cell. Nicky, though plainly frightened, said nothing.

Becoming frantic, and now sweating, Jessica demanded of the men, "What are you going to do?"

No one answered.

Instead, Ramón brought from the other side of the building the chair usually occupied by the armed guard. Gustavo pushed Nicky into the chair where the two men tied him with rope. Before securing his arms, Gustavo loosened Nicky's shirt, exposing his small chest. Ramón, meanwhile, was lighting a cigarette.

Jessica, with a sense of what was coming, cried out to Miguel, "Wait! Perhaps I was hasty. Please wait! We can talk!"

Miguel did not answer. Stooping to the floor, he picked up several pieces of the paper which Jessica had thrown. "Those were three pages," he said. "Fortunately I thought you might do something foolish so I gave you a copy. But three is the figure you have set us, just the same."

He signaled to Ramon, holding up three fingers. *"Quémelo bien . . . tres veces."*

Ramón inhaled, bringing the tip of the cigarette in his mouth to a glowing red. Then deliberately, with a single swift movement, he removed the cigarette and pressed the burning end against Nicky's chest. For the briefest moment the boy was so surprised that no sound escaped him. Then as he felt the burning, searing agony, he screamed.

Jessica was screaming too—wildly, incoherently, tearfully pleading for the torture to cease, assuring Miguel she would do whatever he wanted. "Anything! Anything! I don't care! Just tell me what it is! But stop! Oh, stop!"

From the third cell, Angus was banging his hands against the screen of his cage and shouting too. His words intermingled with the other din, though a few could be heard. "You filthy bastards! Cowards! You're animals, not men!"

Ramón watched and listened, a slight smile around his lips. Then he returned the cigarette to his mouth, drawing his breath in hard several times to reignite the glow. When it was again strong and red, he quashed the cigarette once more against another part of Nicky's chest.

Nicky's screams intensified while, for the third time, Ramón drew on the cigarette and repeated the process. By this time, a smell of burning flesh accompanied the boy's screams and desperate sobbing.

Miguel remained coolly impassive, outwardly indifferent to it all.

After the third burn he waited until some of the noise had subsided, then informed Jessica, "You will sit in front of the camera and speak when I signal you. I have written on cards what you are to say. It is the same as you read and the cards will be held up. You will follow them exactly. Is that understood?"

"Yes," Jessica said dully, "it's understood."

Hearing her voice, choked and dry, Miguel told Gustavo, "Give her some water."

Jessica protested, "I don't . . . It's Nicky who needs attention—something for those burns. Socorro will know . . ."

"Shut up!" Miguel snarled. "If you give any more trouble, the boy will suffer again. He will stay as he is. You will obey!" He glared at Nicky, who was whimpering. "You shut up too!" Miguel turned his head. "Ramón, keep the hot poker ready!"

Ramón nodded. *"Sí, jefe."* He inhaled until his cigarette was again a glowing red.

Jessica closed her eyes. Her own obstinacy, she thought, had brought them to this. Maybe one day Nicky would forgive her. To protect him now, she would concentrate on what had to be done, completing it without a mistake. But even then, a sudden thought occurred.

At home in Larchmont, the night before the kidnap when Jessica and Crawf were talking, Crawf had described signals which a hostage making a video recording could transmit surreptitiously. The point was that someone back home would know of the signals and be able to recognize them. Crawf had had the notion that someday he might be kidnapped and make such a recording. But now it was Jessica instead—something neither of them had dreamed of—and she struggled to remember the signals, knowing Crawf would see this tape . . . *What were they?*

The conversation at Larchmont was coming back . . . her memory had always been good . . . Crawf had said, *"Licking my lips with my tongue would mean, 'I am doing this against my will. Do not believe anything I am saying.'* . . . *Scratching or touching my right earlobe—'My captors are well organized and strongly armed.'* . . . *Left earlobe—'Security here is sometimes lax. An attack from outside might succeed.'"* . . . There were other signals, Crawf had said, though he hadn't described them. So the three —or rather two, since she could only use one of the earlobe messages—would have to do.

Jessica's cell was opened by Gustavo who motioned her to move outside.

Her impulse when she emerged was to run to Nicky, but Miguel's face was glowering and Ramón, also watching, had lighted a new cigarette. Jessica stopped, her eyes meeting Nicky's, and she knew he understood. Guided by Gustavo, she sat in the chair facing the photofloods and Camcorder. Obediently, she sipped water that he gave her.

The message she would speak was written in large letters on two cards which Gustavo now held up. Miguel had moved to the Camcorder and was squinting into an eyepiece. He ordered, "When I drop my hand, begin."

The signal came and Jessica spoke, trying to keep her voice even.

"We have all been treated well and fairly. Now that the reason we were taken has been explained to us, we understand why it was necessary. We also have been told how easy it will be for our American friends to ensure our safe return home. To have us released . . ."

"Stop!"

Miguel's face was red, his features working angrily.

"Bitch! You are reading like you would a laundry list—without expression, trying to be clever, making it sound unbelieving, as if being forced . . ."

"I *am* being forced!" It was a flash of spirit which, an instant later, Jessica regretted.

Miguel signaled to Ramón who applied his hot cigarette to Nicky's chest, prompting another scream.

Jessica, almost out of her mind, was on her feet, pleading. "No! No more! I'll do it better! . . . The way you want! . . . I promise!"

To her relief this time, there was no second burn. Miguel put a fresh cassette into the Camcorder and waved Jessica back into the chair. Once more Gustavo gave her water. Moments later she began again.

Steeling herself, she did her best to make the opening phrases sound convincing, then continued, "To have us released, you must simply follow—quickly and exactly—the instructions which accompany this recording . . ."

Immediately after the word "recording," Jessica moistened her lips with her tongue. She knew she was taking a risk, for herself and Nicky too, but believed the action would seem natural and pass unnoticed. The absence of objection proved her right and she had now confirmed to Crawf and others that the words she was speaking were not her own. Despite all else that had happened, she felt a thrill of satisfaction as she continued reading from the cards Gustavo held.

" . . . but be sure of this: If you do not

obey those instructions, you will not see any of us, ever again. We beg of you, do not let that happen . . ."

What were the instructions—the price of their release which the kidnappers were asking? Jessica could only wonder, by now knowing better than to ask. Meanwhile, only a little time remained, and how about her other message? A choice must be made . . . left earlobe or right . . . Which?

It was true the people here were armed and perhaps well organized, but security was lax at times, and often at night their guards fell asleep; sometimes one or the other could be heard snoring . . . Making her decision, Jessica reached up and casually scratched her left earlobe. It was done! No one had noticed! She continued with the closing words.

"We will be waiting, counting on you, desperately hoping you will make the right decision and . . ."

Seconds later, it was over. As Jessica closed her eyes in relief, Miguel switched off the floodlights and stepped back, a small smile of satisfaction on his face.

It was an hour before Socorro came, an hour of pain for Nicky and of anguish for Jessica and Angus, who could hear Nicky moaning softly on his bed but could not go to him. Jessica had begged the guard on duty—using words and gestures—to let her leave her cell and join Nicky in his, and it was clear the man, while not speaking English, understood what she was asking. But he had shaken his head and insisted, *"No se permite."*

An overpowering sense of guilt seized Jessica. She told Nicky through the screen, "Oh, darling, I'm so desperately sorry. If I'd known what they would do, I'd have made the recording right away. I never even thought . . ."

"Don't worry, Mom." Despite his pain, Nicky had tried to reassure her. "It wasn't your fault."

"No one could have believed what those savages did, Jessie," Angus had called out from his cell on the far side. "Does it still hurt a lot, old chap?"

"It's pretty bad." Nicky's voice quavered.

Jessica appealed to the guard again. "Get Socorro! The nurse! You understand? Socorro!"

This time the man took no notice. He was seated, reading what appeared to be a comic book, and did not look up.

Eventually Socorro came, apparently of her own volition.

"Please help Nicky," Jessica asked. "Your friends burned him."

"He probably deserved it." Socorro signaled to the guard to open Nicky's cell and went in.

As she saw the four burns, she made a clucking sound with her mouth, then turned away and left the cell, the guard locking it behind her.

Jessica called, "You *are* coming back?"

For a moment Socorro looked as if she would make another sharp answer. Then she nodded curtly and left. A few minutes later she returned, carrying a bowl, a jug of water and a package of what proved to be folded cloths and gauze.

Watching through the screen, Jessica observed Socorro gently bathe the burns with water, Nicky wincing as she did, though he did not cry out. Socorro blotted the burns dry with a cloth, then placed a gauze pad over each, securing the dressings with adhesive tape.

Jessica spoke warily. "Thank you. You are good at that. May I ask . . ."

"They are second-degree burns and will heal. I will take the dressings off in several days."

"Can you do something for the pain?"

"This is not a hospital. He must endure it." Socorro turned to Nicky, her voice edgy, her face unsmiling. "Lie still today, boy. It will hurt less tomorrow."

Jessica decided on one more appeal. "Please, may I be with him? He's eleven years old and I'm his mother. Can't we be together, even if only for the next few hours?"

"I asked Miguel. He said no." Moments later, Socorro was gone.

There was a silence, then Angus said softly, "I wish there were something I could do for you, Nicky. Life isn't fair. You don't deserve any of this."

A pause. Then, "Gramps."

"Yes, old son?"

"There *is* something."

"That I can do? Tell me."

"Talk about those old songs. And maybe sing one."

Angus's eyes moistened. It was a request that did not need explaining.

Anything about songs and music fascinated Nicky, and sometimes on summer evenings at the Sloanes' lakeside cottage near Johnstown in upstate New York, the grandfather and grandson would talk and listen to songs of World War II which, two generations earlier in other arduous times, had sustained Angus and many like him. Nicky never seemed to tire of those exchanges and Angus struggled now to remember words and phrases he had used before.

"Those of us who were flyboys in the Army Air Forces, Nicky, cherished our collections of seventy-eight r.p.m. records . . . Those seventy-eights disappeared long ago . . . bet you've never seen any . . ."

"I did once. The father of one of my friends had some."

Angus smiled. As Nicky knew too, an identical dialog had taken place a few months earlier.

"Anyway, we carried those records personally from air base to air base and because they were so breakable, no one would trust anyone else with transporting them. And every BOQ—that's Bachelor Officers Quarters—was alive with music of the big bands: Benny Goodman, Tommy Dorsey, Glenn Miller. And the singers were young Frank Sinatra, Ray Eberle, Dick Haymes. We'd hear their songs and sing them ourselves in the shower."

"Sing one now, Gramps."

"My goodness, I'm not sure. My voice is getting old."

"Try, Angus!" Jessica urged. "If I can, I'll join you."

He groped in memory. When they had done this before was there a special song Nicky liked? He remembered—yes, there was. Steadying his breathing he began, though glancing first toward the guard, wondering if he would enforce the oppressive silence rule. But the man seemed not to mind them talking and was turning pages of his comic book.

Angus had had a good singing voice once; now, like the rest of him, it was worn and quavery. But the words were clear in his mind, their recollection sharp . . .

> *I'll be seeing you*
> *In all the old familiar places*
> *That this heart of mine embraces all day thru . . .*

Jessica joined in, her memory finding the lyric from somewhere. A moment later, Nicky's young tenor was added.

> *In that small café,*
> *The park across the way,*
> *The children's carousel,*
> *The chestnut trees, the wishing well.*
> *I'll be seeing you*
> *In ev'ry lovely summer's day,*
> *In ev'rything that's light and gay,*
> *I'll always think of you that way,*
> *I'll find you in the morning sun;*
> *And when the night is new,*
> *I'll be looking at the moon*
> *But I'll be seeing you!*

For Angus, the years fell away. Jessica's spirits lifted. For Nicky, briefly, the anguish from his burns was eased.

13

From the moment on Wednesday afternoon when Harry Partridge announced his decision to leave for Peru early the following day, the CBA News special task force moved feverishly into high gear.

Partridge's accompanying decision—to open the floodgates of information some thirty-six hours after his departure—resulted in meetings and consultations during which a priority program covering the next three days was structured and approved.

Immediately ahead, to be written and partially recorded overnight, was a report anchored by Partridge which would dominate the National Evening News on Friday. This would contain all that was known concerning the Sloane family kidnapping, including the latest information about Peru and Sendero Luminoso; identification of the terrorist, Ulises Rodríguez alias Miguel; the caskets and the undertaker, Alberto Godoy; Amazonas-American Bank and the alleged murder-suicide, now suspected to have been a double murder, of José Antonio Salaverry and Helga Efferen.

However, before any preparations began, Harry Partridge visited Crawford Sloane in the anchorman's office on the fourth floor. Partridge still felt that Sloane should be among the first to be informed of any new development or plan.

Since the kidnapping thirteen days earlier, Crawford Sloane had continued to work, though at times it seemed he was merely filling each day and his heart and mind were not immersed in work at all. Today he appeared more gaunt than ever, his eyes more tired, the lines on his face even deeper than a few days earlier. He was conferring with a woman writer and a male producer and looked up as Partridge appeared. "You need to see me, Harry?"

When Partridge nodded, Sloane asked the other two, "Do you mind leaving? We'll finish later."

Sloane waved Partridge to a chair. "You look serious. Is it bad news?"

"I'm afraid it is. We've established that your family is out of the country. They're prisoners in Peru."

Sloane slumped forward, elbows on his desk; he rubbed a hand across his face before responding. "I've been expecting something like this—or rather, dreading it. Do you know who has them?"

"We believe Sendero Luminoso."

"Oh god! Not those fanatics!"

"I'm leaving for Lima in the morning, Crawf."

"I'll go with you!"

Partridge shook his head. "We both know you can't, that it wouldn't work. Besides, the network would never allow it."

Sloane sighed, but didn't argue. He asked, "Do we have any idea what those Sendero jackals want?"

"Not yet. I'm sure we'll hear." A silence followed, then Partridge said, "I've called a task force meeting for five o'clock. I thought you'd like to be there. After that, most of us will work all night." He went on to describe developments during the day and the plan to broadcast all information that they had on Friday.

"I'll be at the meeting," Sloane acknowledged, "and thanks." Then as Partridge rose to leave, "Do you have to go right now?"

Partridge hesitated. He had a great deal to do and time was short, but he sensed a desire on the other's part to talk. He shrugged. "I guess a few minutes won't make any difference."

There was a pause before Sloane said awkwardly, "I'm not sure I know how to say this, or even if I should. But at a time like this you get to thinking about all kinds of things." Partridge waited, curious, as Sloane continued. "Anyway, Harry, I've been wondering what your feelings are about Jessica. After all, years ago you two were pretty close."

So that was it: A secret thought voiced after all this time. Partridge chose his words carefully, knowing this moment was important. "Yes, I do care about Jessica, in part because we were close—as you put it—years ago. But mostly I care because she's your wife and you're my friend. As for anything that once existed between Jessica and me, it finished the day she married you."

"I suppose I'm saying this now because of all that's happened, but there were times when I used to wonder about that."

"I know you did, Crawf, and there were times *I* wanted to tell *you* what I just did; also that I never had any resentment, either about your marrying Jessica or making it big at the anchor desk. No reason why I should. But I always had the feeling that if I did say it, you wouldn't have believed."

"You're probably right." Sloane paused, considering. "But if it's of any interest, Harry, I believe it now."

Partridge nodded. Enough had been said, and he needed to go. At the doorway he turned.

"I'll do my damnedest when I get to Lima, Crawf. I truly will."

On reaching Sloane's office, Partridge had noticed the absence of FBI Agent Otis Havelock, whose presence had been so prominent for a week after the kidnapping. While pausing outside at the Horseshoe, where he informed Chuck Insen of the task force meeting, Partridge asked about the FBI man.

"He's still around a lot," the evening news executive producer said, "though I think he's following other leads."

"Do you know if he's coming back today?"

"I've no idea."

Partridge found himself hoping the FBI man would continue whatever he was doing for the remainder of the day. If he did, it would be easier to keep the knowledge of tonight's activity and Partridge's departure tomorrow restricted to a few people at CBA only. On Friday, of course, assuming word was released in advance that CBA would have new revelations on its evening news, the FBI would probably demand to know what was going on and would have to be stalled until broadcast time. But Partridge would be in Peru by then, and someone else would have that responsibility.

Just the same, he decided coping with the

FBI was one more item to be factored into plans for the next two days.

The five o'clock meeting in the task force conference room was well attended. Les Chippingham and Crawford Sloane were there. Chuck Insen stayed for fifteen minutes, then left because the National Evening News first feed was looming close, and another Horseshoe producer took his place. Partridge was at the head of the long conference table, with Rita Abrams beside him. Iris Everly, who had produced a kidnap segment for the evening news—though it contained none of that day's new material—arrived several minutes late. Teddy Cooper was present, having spent the day with the temporary researchers who were still visiting local newspaper offices to review classified advertising—so far with no positive result. Minh Van Canh came in, as did producers Norman Jaeger and Karl Owens. A new face at the table was Don Kettering's. Jonathan Mony had stayed on and was introduced around. Various support staff members were in attendance.

Partridge began with a summation of what had happened during the day, his intention to leave for Peru early the next morning, and the decision to broadcast everything they knew on Friday evening's news.

Les Chippingham cut in. "I agree with everything you've said, Harry, but I think we should go one step further and do a one-hour News Special, also on Friday night, covering the whole kidnap sequence at length, including the new material."

Around the table there were murmurs of approval as the news president continued. "I remind you we have a prime-time news show already scheduled for the nine o'clock slot which we can yank. You guys sound as if you have plenty to fill an hour."

"Plenty and more," Rita Abrams assured him. A short time earlier she had screened the silhouette interrogation of Alberto Godoy and viewed Don Kettering's interview with the American-Amazonas bank manager, Emiliano Armando, which had just come in. She was enthusiastic about both.

After the screening there had been a discussion between Rita, Partridge and Kettering as to whether the funeral director's identity should be protected after all, since during his antagonistic termination of the interview, Godoy voluntarily brought his face into light and camera range. There was a temptation to reveal his face on television since protecting Godoy's identity could clearly cause the network trouble. Yet because of the original agreement with him, some complex ethics were involved.

In the end, it was decided that since Godoy

had not known, technically, what he was doing,
the original pact must be honored. To make
sure the decision was safeguarded, Partridge
erased on an editing machine the portion of
tape showing Godoy's face, so it could not be
retrieved with outtakes later. At this point the
erasure was not a legal offense, though it would
be if done after official inquiries were begun.

Everyone at the conference room table realized the decision to have a one-hour special was
relatively easy since the prime-time hour in
question belonged to the News Division anyway; therefore the network's programming
brass need not be consulted. The show originally scheduled for nine o'clock Friday was
"Behind the Headlines," a newsmagazine on
which Norman Jaeger was normally a producer
and to which he would undoubtedly return
when this present work was over. Chippingham
decided privately that he need not report immediately to Margot Lloyd-Mason on the change,
though sometime during Friday he would advise her of what was coming up that evening.

From there, other decisions flowed.

Partridge announced that Minh Van Canh
and Ken O'Hara, the sound man who had been
present at the Dallas–Fort Worth air crash two
weeks ago, would accompany him to Peru.

Rita, glancing down the table at Chippingham, added, "Les, the assignment desk has

chartered a Learjet for Harry and the others, out of Teterboro at six A.M. tomorrow. I need your okay."

"Are you sure . . ." Chippingham, conscious of mounting expenses, had been about to continue, ". . . *there isn't a commercial flight available,*" when he caught sight of Crawford Sloane's steely eyes fixed on him. Changing his mind, the news president said tersely, "I approve."

Rita, it was decided, would remain in New York for overall supervision of the Friday evening news report and one-hour special, with Iris doing general production on the first, Norm Jaeger and Karl Owens on the second. Then, during Friday night, Rita would follow Partridge and the others to Lima, with Jaeger taking over in New York as senior producer.

Partridge, who had discussed the subject earlier with Chippingham, disclosed that after his own departure, Don Kettering would head the kidnap task force in New York. Temporarily, Kettering's business correspondent duties would be handled by an assistant.

However, Partridge pointed out, neither the National Evening News report of Friday nor the one-hour special later—on both of which he would be featured—should convey any hint that he had already left for Peru. In fact, if it could be made to appear at some point that he was broadcasting live—though without actually being deceptive—so much the better.

While other networks and the print press were unlikely to be deceived by such tactics, anything that might lessen their own urgency in dispatching reporting teams to Peru would be an advantage. From a practical point of view, apart from competitiveness, Partridge stood a better chance of making investigative headway alone, instead of amid a swarm of other reporters.

Which led to the question of security.

Everything that would happen through that night and the next two days, Les Chippingham declared, must not be discussed, even with others in the News Division who were uninvolved, and certainly not with outsiders, including families. The criterion for discussion was: *Need to know.* "And that's not a request; it's an order."

The news president continued, looking in turn at everyone around the table. "Let us not do or say *anything* that could release our news prematurely and deprive Harry of the twenty-four hours' lead time he so clearly needs. Above all, remember lives are at stake"—he glanced toward Crawford Sloane—"very special lives, close and important to us all."

Other security measures were arranged.

Tomorrow and the next day, while a studio and control room were being used to produce the one-hour News Special, security guards would be posted outside, admitting only those persons on a list to be compiled by Rita. Also, the normal studio output line would be disconnected so that no one beyond the studio and control room could view on a monitor what was happening inside.

It was agreed, however, that on Friday morning security would be relaxed slightly, to the extent of doing broadcast promotional advertising during the day. This would advise viewers that important new information about the Sloane kidnapping would be revealed on that evening's National Evening News and the one-hour special. Also during the day as a professional courtesy, other networks, news wire services and the print press would be advised of the same thing, though no details would be disclosed.

At length, Partridge asked, "Is there anything else, or can we get to work?"

"One more detail." It was Rita, a touch of mischief in her voice. "Les, I need your approval for another Learjet, this one for Friday night when it's my turn for Peru. I'm taking an editor—Bob Watson—and an editpak. Also, I'll have the bankroll."

There was a chuckle among insiders at the table and even a smile from Crawford Sloane. Rita was enhancing her chances of traveling by private plane, first by taking an editor and editpak, the latter consisting of bulky editing equipment, hard to transport otherwise. Second, it was considered unwise to travel commercially with large amounts of U.S. cash; though Rita hadn't mentioned the amount, it would be fifty thousand dollars. Yet hard currency was essential in a country such as Peru where local money was close to worthless and dollars would buy almost anything, including special privileges which were certain to be needed.

Chippingham sighed inwardly. Inconsiderately, he thought, and despite their affair which continued to flourish, Rita had put him on the spot.

"Go ahead," he told her. "Book it."

Only minutes after the meeting ended, Partridge was at a computer terminal working on his co-anchor introduction for Friday's National Evening News.

Several startling new developments, he wrote, *have come to light concerning the kidnapping, fifteen days ago, of the wife, son and father of CBA News anchorman Crawford Sloane. Investigative reporting by CBA has led us to believe that the three kidnap victims have been transported to Peru where they are being held by the Maoist rev-*

olutionary guerrillas Sendero Luminoso, or Shining Path, who have terrorized large portions of Peru for many years.

A motive for the kidnapping is not yet known.

What is known is that a United Nations diplomat, using a New York bank account, supplied money to the kidnappers, which made the abduction, as well as other acts of terrorism, possible.

Our extensive coverage begins, as so many other crimes begin, with money. CBA's business correspondent Don Kettering explains.

It would be, Partridge reflected as he began to revise what he had written, the first of many similar introductions he must compose and record before leaving Manhattan for Teterboro Airport at 5 A.M.

PART
FOUR

1

It was still dark, and raining, a few minutes before 6 A.M. Eastern daylight time when a Learjet 36A took off from New Jersey's Teterboro Airport for Bogotá, Colombia. Aboard were Harry Partridge, Minh Van Canh and Ken O'Hara.

The 36A did not have the range for a nonstop flight to Lima, but they would be in Bogotá only long enough to refuel and hoped to reach the Peruvian capital by 1:30 P.M. Eastern standard time, which Peru stayed on all year round.

Partridge and the other two had come directly from CBA News headquarters to Teterboro in a network car. During the busy night, Partridge managed to slip away for a half hour to the Inter-Continental Hotel and pack a bag. He hadn't wasted time checking out; someone from the network would do that in the morning.

He had also asked the CBA News assignment desk to arrange some sleeping facility in
the Lear and was delighted to find it ready. On
the right side of the passenger cabin, two facing
seats had been lowered to become a bed, with a
mattress, sheets and blankets invitingly in place.
It was possible for another bed to be made up
on the opposite side, but Minh and O'Hara
would have to work that out between them. In
any case, he didn't think their night had been as
arduous as his own.

By the time they were in the air and on
course, Partridge was asleep. He slept soundly
for three hours, then awakened to find the cabin
in semidarkness, someone having thoughtfully
lowered all the window shades, though bright
sunshine—enough to see by—was visible
around their edges. Across the cabin, Minh was
curled up and asleep in a seat. O'Hara, also
sleeping, was in another seat behind.

Partridge checked his watch: 9 A.M. New
York time—still only 8 A.M. in Lima. Reaching
for a flight plan the co-pilot had brought before
takeoff, he calculated it would be another two
hours before the refueling stop in Bogotá. The
hum of jet engines was steady but quiet and
there was no hint of turbulence. A phrase came
to Partridge: *a silky journey.* Enjoying the luxury, he lay down again and closed his eyes.

This time sleep did not come. Perhaps the

three hours had been enough. Perhaps too much had happened in too short a time for him to rest for very long. On other occasions in the past he had found he needed little sleep during periods of stress and action, and this was such a time, or would be very soon. Yes, he was going into action—quite probably and literally into battle—and he felt his senses stir agreeably.

That feeling, he supposed, had always been dormant inside him, though Vietnam had awakened it and, afterward, other wars in other places satisfied his need. It was what made him, in TV news jargon, a "bang-bang" correspondent, a label that used to bother him but didn't anymore.

Why not? Because there were times when a "bang-bang" like himself was needed, just as Balaklava had had soldiery who performed their jobs while

> *Cannon to right of them,*
> *Cannon to left of them,*
> *Cannon in front of them*
> *Volleyed and thundered.*

He smiled, amused by Tennyson's romanticizing, and his own.

It hadn't always been that way with him. For a while, when he and Gemma were together, he consciously avoided wars and danger because life was sweet, too gloriously happy to risk a sudden termination. Around that time, within the network, he knew word had gone out to the effect: *Give Harry some safe assignments; he's earned them. Let the newer reporters follow the sound of gunfire for a while.*

Later, all of that changed, of course. When Gemma was no longer on the scene, Partridge had ceased to be protected and was sent again to wars, in part because he was so good at them, in part because he made it known he didn't care what chances he took. That last was one reason, he supposed, why he was on this journey here and now.

How strange that since this project began he had mentally relived his time with Gemma. It was during the air journey from Toronto immediately after the kidnap that the memory came back to him of the Pope's Alitalia DC-10 and meeting Gemma . . . his own conversation with the Pope and the "Slavs-slaves" mix-up which he resolved . . . then Gemma delivering his breakfast tray and bringing him a rose.

One day later on this assignment—or was it two?—more memories at night in his hotel . . . of falling in love with Gemma and, while still continuing on the papal tour, proposing marriage . . . During a brief stopover, their taxi ride to the old city in Panama, and Gemma standing beside him while the *juez* in his ornate office pronounced them man and wife.

Then barely a week ago, while being driven in darkness from Larchmont to Manhattan after visiting Crawford Sloane, there had been the remembrance of Partridge's and Gemma's idyllic, halcyon days in Rome where their love had grown; Gemma's shining gift of laughter and joy; the checkbook she could never balance; the car she drove like a fiend, arousing his fears . . . until she surrendered the keys on learning she was pregnant. And after that, the news of their move from Rome to London . . .

Now, here he was, on another air journey and with more quiet moments, back again with thoughts of Gemma. This time, unlike the others, he did not resist the memories but let them flow.

Their life in London was unbelievably good.

They took over a pleasant furnished flat in St. John's Wood which Partridge's predecessor had vacated, Gemma quickly adding touches of her own style and color. The rooms were always filled with flowers. She hung paintings they had brought from Rome, shopped for china and table linens in Kensington and added a striking bronze sculpture by a new young artist exhibiting in Cork Street.

At the CBA News London bureau, Par-

tridge's work went well. Some stories he covered were in Britain, others on the continent—in France, the Netherlands, Denmark and Sweden —though he was seldom away from home for long. When he wasn't working, he and Gemma explored London together, delighting in their joint discovery of history, splendor, curiosity and oddity, often in intriguing, narrow streets, some still as Dickens had described them, or around corkscrew, convoluted corners.

The multitude of mazelike streets perplexed Gemma and she often got lost. When Partridge suggested that parts of Rome could be equally difficult, she shook her head in disagreement. "They do not say idly 'the Eternal City,' Harry caro. *In Rome you move onward; it is something you can feel. London plays with you like cat and mouse; it turns you sideways and backward and you never know. But I adore it; it is like a game."*

The traffic bewildered Gemma too. Standing with Partridge on the steps of the National Gallery, watching the speeding circle of massed taxis, cars and double-deck buses rounding Trafalgar Square, she told him, "It is so dangerous, darling. They are all going the wrong way." Fortunately, because she could not adjust mentally to driving on the left, Gemma had no desire at all to use their car and, when Partridge was not available, she either walked a great deal or traveled by Underground or taxi.

The National was one of many galleries they visited and they savored other sights too, both conventional and offbeat, from the changing of the guard at Buckingham Palace to viewing bricked-up windows on old buildings—a holdover from the early 1800s when windows were taxed to finance the Napoleonic wars.

A guide they hired for a day showed them a statue of Queen Anne who, the guide noted, had nineteen pregnancies and was buried in a coffin four feet eight inches square. And at New Zealand House, formerly the Carlton Hotel, he told them Ho Chi Minh once worked there as a kitchen porter—all of it the kind of information Gemma loved, and she squirreled it away in an ever-growing notebook.

A favorite Sunday pastime was visiting Speakers' Corner near Marble Arch where, as Partridge explained, "prophets, loudmouths and lunatics get equal time."

"What is so different about that, Harry?" Gemma once asked after listening. "Some speeches you report seriously on TV are no better. You should do a piece about Speakers' Corner for your news."

Soon after, Partridge passed the suggestion to New York and the Horseshoe shot back approval.

A report was done and became a much-praised, humorous "end piece" on a Friday night.

Another highlight was visiting Brown's Hotel, founded by Lord Byron's butler, and having afternoon tea—the ultimate English experience with impeccable service, dainty sandwiches, scones, strawberry jam and clotted Devonshire cream. "It is a sacred ritual, mio amore," Gemma declared. "Like communion, but tastier."

In short, whatever they did together became a time of joy. And, all the while, Gemma's pregnancy progressed, promising supplemental happiness ahead.

It was during her seventh month of pregnancy that Partridge was sent on a one-day assignment to Paris. CBA News's Paris bureau, short-staffed, needed someone to cover accusations about an American film which portrayed critically—and inaccurately, it was claimed— the French Resistance in World War II. Partridge did the piece, which was sent by satellite to New York via London, though he doubted if it was important enough to make the National Evening News, and in the end it didn't.

Then, in the Paris bureau and about to leave to catch his homebound flight, he was handed a phone and told, "London wants you. Zeke is on the line."

Zeke was Ezekiel Thomson, the London bu-

reau chief—huge, tough, dour and black; also, to those who worked with him, he seemed emotionless. The first thing Partridge became aware of as he listened on the phone was that Zeke's voice was choked and breaking.

"Harry, I've never had to do anything like this . . . I don't know how . . . but I have to tell you . . ." he managed to get out.

Somehow Zeke conveyed the rest.

Gemma was dead. She had begun to cross the street at a busy intersection in Knightsbridge and witnesses said she had been looking to the left instead of to the right . . . Oh, Gemma! Dearest, wonderful, scatterbrained Gemma, who believed that everyone in Britain was driving on the wrong side, who had not yet mastered which way to look when a pedestrian amid traffic . . . A truck, coming from the right, had struck and run over her. Those who saw it happen said the truck driver should not be blamed, he didn't have a chance . . .

Their baby—a boy, Partridge discovered later—had also died.

Partridge returned to London and when what had to be done was done, alone in the flat they had shared, he wept. He stayed alone for days, refusing to see anyone while his tears poured out —not only for Gemma, but all the tears which across the years he had never shed.

He wept at last for the dead Welsh children at Aberfan whose pathetic bodies he had watched brought from that ghastly sea of mud. He cried for the starving in Africa where some had died as cameras turned and Partridge, dry-eyed, made entries in his notebook. He cried for all others in those many tragic places he had visited, where he had stood among the bereaved, hearing their wailing, chronicling their grief, yet was a newsman doing his job and nothing more.

Somewhere amid it all he remembered the words of the woman psychiatrist who once told him, "You're banking it all, tucking the emotion away inside you somewhere. One day everything will overflow, crack open, and you'll cry. Oh, how you'll cry!"

Afterward, as best he could, he had put his life together. CBA News had helped by keeping him busy, not giving him time for introspection, and as fast as one tough assignment ended, another took its place. Soon, wherever there was conflict or danger in the world, Harry Partridge was on the scene. He took risks and got away with them until it seemed, to himself and others, that his life was charmed. And while it happened, the months, then years slipped by.

Nowadays there were stretches of time when he was able, if not to forget Gemma, at least not to think of her for longish periods. Then there were other times—like the two weeks since the

Sloane kidnap—when she was foremost in his mind.

Either way, since those desperate days after Gemma's death, he had not cried again.

Now, aboard the Learjet and still an hour out of Bogotá, sleep was returning after all and in Harry Partridge's mind the past and present were merging . . . Gemma and Jessica were becoming one . . . Gemma-Jessica . . . Jessica-Gemma . . . No matter what the odds against him, he would find her and bring her back . . . Somehow he would save her.

Sleep came.

When he awoke again the Lear was on final approach to Bogotá.

2

The contrasts of Lima, Harry Partridge thought, were as stark and grimly apparent as the crises and conflicts, political and economic, that bitterly, often savagely, divided all Peru.

The immense, dry, sprawling capital city was split into several segments, each displaying opulent wealth or squalid poverty, with hatreds like poisoned arrows speeding between the two extremes. Unlike most other cities he knew, there was seldom any middle ground. Grandiose homes surrounded by manicured gardens, all built on Lima's best land, adjoined hideous *barriadas*—slums jam-packed together—on the worst.

The multitude of "have-not" slum dwellers, many crowded into filthy cardboard shacks, was so visibly wretched, the anger looking out from sullen eyes so fierce, that during past visits to Peru, Partridge had had a sense of revolution in ferment. Now, from what he had already learned during his first day here, some form of insurrection seemed ready to explode.

Partridge, Minh Van Canh and Ken O'Hara had landed at Lima's Jorge Chávez Airport at 1:40 P.M. On disembarking they were met by Fernández Pabur, CBA's regular stringer in Peru and—when required, as now—the network's fixer.

He had whisked them through Immigration and Customs ahead of others waiting—it seemed likely that at some point money had changed hands—and then escorted them to a Ford station wagon, with waiting driver.

Fernández was heavyset, dark, swarthy and energetic, probably about thirty-five, with a protruding mouth and prominent white teeth which he flashed every few seconds in what he clearly hoped was a dazzling smile. In fact, being patently false, it wasn't—but Partridge didn't care. What he liked about Fernández, whom he had used on other occasions, was that the fixer knew instinctively what was needed and got results.

The first result was a suite for Partridge in the elegant five-star Cesar's Hotel in Miraflores, and good rooms for the other two.

At the hotel, while Partridge washed and put on a clean shirt, Fernández phoned ahead at Partridge's request to set up the first appointment. It was with an old acquaintance, Sergio Hurtado, news editor and broadcaster for Radio Andes network.

An hour later, the radio man and Partridge were together in a small broadcast studio which doubled as an office.

"Harry my friend, I have only depressing tidings to convey," Sergio was saying, responding to a question. "In our country the rule of law has disappeared. Democracy is not even a façade; it is nonexistent. We are bankrupt in every sense. Massacres are commonplace, politically inspired. There are private death squads of the President's party; people simply disappear. I tell you we are nearer to a total bloodbath than ever before in the history of Peru. I wish none of this were true. Alas, it is!"

Although coming from a grotesquely obese body, the deep mellifluous voice was compelling and persuasive as ever, Partridge noted. Small wonder that Sergio commanded the country's largest audience, since radio was still the paramount news medium, more important and influential than television. TV viewers were a well-to-do concentration in larger cities only.

Sergio's chair creaked complainingly as he shifted his mountain of flesh. His jowls were like outsize sausages. His eyes, which across the years had receded as his face grew larger, were now porcine. Nothing was wrong with his brain, however, nor his distinguished American education which had included Harvard. Sergio appreciated U.S. reporters visiting him, as many did, seeking his well-informed opinions.

After an agreement that their conversation would be off the record until the following evening, Partridge described the chronology of the Sloane kidnap, then asked, "Do you have any advice for me, Sergio? Is there anything you have heard which might be helpful?"

The broadcaster shook his head. "I have heard nothing, which is not surprising. Sendero is good at secrecy, mainly because they kill any of their people who talk indiscreetly; staying alive is an incentive not to gossip. But I will help you, if I can, by putting out feelers. I have information sources in many places."

"Thank you."

"As to your news tomorrow night, I will obtain a satellite tape and adapt it for myself. Meanwhile we are not short of disaster subjects of our own. This country, politically, financially, every other way, is going down the tubes."

"We hear mixed reports about Sendero Luminoso. Are they really getting stronger?"

"The answer is yes—and not only stronger every day, but controlling more and more of the country, which is why the task you have set yourself is difficult, some might say impossible. Assuming your kidnapped people are here, there are a thousand out-of-the-way places where they may be hidden. But I am glad you came to me first because I will give you some advice."

"Which is?"

"Do not seek official help—that is, from the Peru armed forces or the police. In fact, avoid them as allies because they have ceased to be trustworthy, if they ever were. When it comes to murder and mayhem, they are no better than Sendero and certainly as ruthless."

"Are there recent examples?"

"Plenty. I'll point you toward some if you wish."

Partridge had already begun thinking about reports he would send back for the National

Evening News. He had previously arranged that after the arrival Saturday of Rita Abrams and the editor, Bob Watson, they would put together a piece for Monday's broadcast. In it, Partridge hoped to have sound bites from Sergio Hurtado and others.

Now he asked, "You said democracy is nonexistent. Was that rhetoric or really true?"

"Not only true, but to huge numbers of people here the presence or absence of democracy makes no difference in their lives."

"Pretty strong stuff, Sergio."

"Only because of your finite viewpoint, Harry. Americans see democracy as a remedy for all ills—to be taken three times daily like prescription medicine. It works for them. *Ergo!* —it should work for the world. What America naïvely forgets is that for democracy to function, most of a populace must have something personally that is worth preserving. Generally speaking, most Latin Americans don't. Of course, the next question is—why?"

"So I'll buy it. Why?"

"The areas of the world in deepest trouble, including ours, have two main groups of people —the reasonably educated and affluent on the one hand; on the other, the ignorant and hopeless poor who are largely unemployable. The first group breeds only moderately, the second breeds like flies, inexorably growing larger—a

human time bomb ready to destroy the first."
Sergio gestured airily behind him. "Go outside
and see it happening."

"And you have a solution?"

"America could have. Not by distributing
arms or money, but by flooding the world with
birth-control teaching teams, sent out the way
Kennedy dispatched the Peace Corps. Oh, it
would take several generations, but curbing
population growth could save the world."

Partridge queried, "Aren't you forgetting
something?"

"If you mean the Catholic church, I remind
you I am a Catholic myself. I also have many
Catholic friends—of stature, educated and with
money. Strangely, almost all have small families. I have asked myself: Have they curbed
their sexual passions? Knowing both the men
and women, I am sure that they have not. Indeed, some speak out frankly, disavowing
church dogma on birth control—which is man-
made dogma, incidentally." He added, "With
American leadership, voices in opposition to
that dogma could grow and grow."

"Speaking of speaking out," Partridge said.
"Would you be willing to repeat most of what
we've talked about on camera?"

Sergio threw up his hands. "Well, my dear
Harry, why not? Perhaps the greatest thing
America instilled in me was a passion for free

speech. I have been speaking freely here on radio, though at times I wonder how long they
will let me go on. Neither the government nor
Sendero like what I say and both have guns and
bullets. But one cannot live forever, so yes,
Harry, I will do it for you."

Beneath the gross fat, Partridge acknowledged mentally, was a person of principle and
courage.

Before reaching Peru, Partridge had already
decided there was only one way to go about
locating the kidnap victims. That was to act as a
TV news correspondent would in normal circumstances—meeting known contacts, seeking
out new ones, searching for news, traveling
where he could, questioning, questioning, and
all the while hoping some fragment of information would emerge, providing a clue, a lead to
where the captives might be held.

After that, of course, would come the
greater problem of how to rescue them. But that
would have to be faced when the time arrived.

Unless some lucky, sudden breakthrough
happened, Partridge expected the process to be
demanding, slow and tedious.

Continuing the TV correspondent routine,
he next visited Entel Peru—the national tele-
communications company with headquarters in
downtown Lima. Entel would be CBA's base

for communication with New York, including satellite transmissions. When crews from other U.S. networks arrived, as seemed likely in a day or two, they would use the same facilities.

Victor Velasco was the busy, harried international manager of Entel whom Fernández Pabur had already contacted. In his forties, with graying hair and a permanently worried expression, Velasco was clearly preoccupied with other problems as he told Partridge, "It has been difficult to find space, but we have a booth for your editor, his equipment, and we've run in two phone lines. Your people will need security passes . . ."

Partridge was aware that in places like Peru, where politicians and military leaders strutted and got rich, it was low-profile managers like Velasco—conscientious, overworked and underpaid—who really kept the country running. Back in his hotel suite, Partridge had put a thousand dollars in an envelope which he produced and discreetly handed over.

"A small thank-you for your trouble, Señor Velasco. We'll be seeing you again before we leave."

For a moment Velasco looked embarrassed and Partridge wondered if he might refuse. Then, glancing in the envelope and seeing U.S. currency, Velasco nodded and put it in a pocket.

"Thank you. And if there's anything else . . ."

"There will be," Partridge said. "That's the only thing I'm sure of."

"What took you so long, Harry?" Manuel León Seminario inquired when Partridge phoned from the hotel shortly after 5 P.M., having just returned from Entel Peru. "I've been expecting you since our little talk."

"I had a couple of things to do in New York." Partridge was reminded of his phone conversation ten days earlier with the *Escena* magazine owner-editor; it had been at a time when Peru involvement in the Sloane family kidnapping was a possibility, though not a certainty as now. He asked, "I was wondering, Manuel, if you've a dinner engagement tonight."

"I have indeed. I shall be dining at La Pizzeria at eight o'clock and my guest will be one Harry Partridge."

It was now 8:15 and they were sipping Pisco sours, the popular Peruvian cocktail, piquant and delicious. La Pizzeria was a combination of bistro and traditional restaurant where the movers and shakers of Lima were often to be seen.

The magazine chief, slightly built and dapper, with a neatly trimmed Vandyke beard, was wearing high-fashion Cartier spectacles and a Brioni suit. He had brought with him to the table a slim burgundy leather briefcase.

Partridge had already reported why he was in Peru. He added, "I've been hearing that things around here are pretty bad."

Seminario sighed. "It is true, they are. But then, our life has always been a mixture. We . . . how did Milton put it? . . . *'Can make a heav'n of hell, a hell of heav'n.'* Yet we *limeños* are survivors, something I try to reflect with *Escena*'s covers." He reached for the briefcase and opened it. "Consider these two—our current edition and the artwork for next week. Together, I believe they say something."

Partridge looked at the printed magazine first. Its cover was a color photograph of a tall downtown building's flat roof. The roof contained a mess of debris, obviously from an explosion. Central in the picture was a dead woman, on her back. She appeared to have been young; her face, not badly damaged, might have been beautiful. But her stomach had been blown away, with bloody entrails strewn around the body. Despite his familiarity with scenes of war, Partridge shuddered.

"I'll save you reading the story inside, Harry. A business convention was in session across the street. Sendero Luminoso, in which the woman was an activist, decided to mortar the convention center. Fortunately for the convention, but not the woman, the mortar was homemade and exploded before she could fire it."

Partridge glanced at the picture, then away. "Sendero is increasingly active in Lima, I believe."

"Exceedingly so. Their people move around freely and this bombing, which went wrong, was an exception. Most are successful. Nevertheless, consider next week's cover." The editor passed across the artwork.

It was sex and cheesecake, only a hairbreadth away from pornography. A slim young girl, perhaps nineteen and scantily clad in the briefest of swimsuits, was leaning against a silken pillow, her head thrown back, blond hair tumbled, lips parted, eyes closed, legs partially spread.

"Life goes on and there are always two sides, even in Peru," the magazine man said. "Speaking of which, let us order dinner, then I will make suggestions, Harry, to ensure that your life goes on too."

The food was Italian and excellent, the service faultless. Near the end of the meal, Seminario leaned back.

"One thing you must realize is that Sendero Luminoso may already know of your presence here; their spies are everywhere. But even if not, they will learn of it shortly, probably after your CBA broadcast tomorrow, which will be repeated widely. So beginning at once, you must have a bodyguard accompany you, particularly if you go out at night."

Partridge smiled. "That seems to have happened already." Fernández Pabur had insisted on collecting Partridge from the hotel and bringing him here. Accompanying them in the Ford station wagon had been a silent, burly man who looked like a heavyweight boxer. Judging by a bulge under his jacket, he was armed. At their destination, the new man alighted first, Fernández and Partridge remaining inside the vehicle until signaled to come out. Partridge had not asked questions, but Fernández told him, "We will wait while you have dinner." Presumably the retinue was still outside.

"Good," Seminario acknowledged. "Your man knows what he is doing. Are you carrying a gun yourself?"

Partridge shook his head.

"You must. Many of us do. And to quote American Express, 'Don't leave home without it.' Another thing: Do not go to Ayacucho, a Sendero stronghold. Sendero would learn of your being there and you would be committing suicide."

"At some point I may have to go."

"You mean if I, or others trying to help you,

learn where your friends are being held. In that case you will have to ensure surprise by going in fast and getting out the same way. There will be no other way and you will have to use a charter airplane. Some pilots here will do that if you pay them enough risk money."

When they had finished talking, most other diners were gone and the restaurant was preparing to close.

Outside, Fernández and the bodyguard were waiting.

In the station wagon returning to Cesar's Hotel, Partridge asked Fernández, "Can you get me a gun?"

"Of course. Do you have a preference?"

Partridge considered. The nature of his work had made him knowledgeable about guns and he had learned to use them. "I'd like a nine-millimeter Browning; also a silencer."

"You will have it tomorrow. And about to-morrow—are there plans that I should know of?"

"Just like today, I'll be seeing more people." Partridge added mentally: *And in days beyond that, still more—until the breakthrough comes.*

3

Friday was a day of action at CBA, New York. Some of the activity had been anticipated; a good deal more was unforeseen.

As usual, the network's broadcasting day began with the 6 A.M. "Sunrise Journal." During that program a CBA News promo aired along with commercials, as it would throughout the day. The promo was a recorded message spoken on camera by Harry Partridge.

> *"Tonight . . . on CBA National Evening News . . . an exclusive report of startling new developments in the kidnapping of the Crawford Sloane family.*
>
> *"And at nine P.M. Eastern time, seven central, a one-hour News Special—'Network in Peril: The Sloane Kidnap.'*
>
> *"Be sure not to miss tonight's National Evening News and one-hour News Special."*

The choice of Partridge was appropriate since he had regularly anchored all the evening kidnap news. It was also opportune since his appearance conveyed an unspoken implication that he was in the United States, though at 6 A.M. he had already been in Peru for eighteen hours.

Les Chippingham saw the promo while having a self-serve, on-the-run breakfast in his Eighty-second Street apartment. The news president was in a hurry, knowing there would be a good deal happening during the day, and through the kitchen window he could see his CBA limo and driver already waiting outside. The limousine reminded him of Margot Lloyd-Mason's instruction at their first meeting that he should use taxis instead, an order he had ignored. He must not ignore keeping Margot informed, however, and as soon as he reached the office would call her since she was likely to have seen the promo too.

The decision was unnecessary. When he entered the car, the driver handed him a phone and Margot's voice barked instantly.

"What is all this about new developments and why haven't I been told?"

"It happened suddenly. I intended to call you as soon as I got in."

"John Q. Public has been told. Why should I have to wait?"

"Margot, the public has not been told; they will be this evening. You, on the other hand, are going to be told as soon as I reach my desk, but not on this phone because we've no idea who's listening."

There was a pause during which he could hear heavy breathing. "Do it immediately you get in."

"I will."

Some fifteen minutes later, connected again with the network president and CEO, Chippingham began, "There's quite a lot to tell."

"Get on with it!"

"First, from your point of view the outlook is excellent. Some of our best people have achieved several exclusive breakthroughs which tonight may give CBA the largest news audience in our history, with matching ratings. Unfortunately, the news about the Sloane family is less than good for Crawf."

"Where are they?"

"In Peru. Held by Sendero Luminoso."

"Peru! Are you absolutely sure?"

"As I said, we've had some of our most experienced people working on this, especially Harry Partridge, and what they've discovered is convincing. I've no doubts, and am sure you won't have either." Just the same, Margot's startled reaction at the mention of Peru surprised Chippingham, making him wonder what was behind it.

She said sharply, "I'd like to talk to Partridge."

"I'm afraid that isn't possible. He's already in Peru, and has been since yesterday. We expect to have an update from him for Monday's news."

"Why are you moving so quickly?"

"This is the news business, Margot. We always work that way." The question amazed him. So did a hint of uncertainty, even nervousness, in Margot's voice. It prompted him to say, "You seem concerned about Peru. Do you mind telling me why?"

There was silence and obvious hesitation before an answer. "At the moment Globanic Industries has a substantial business arrangement there. A great deal is at stake and it's essential our alliance with the Peruvian Government remains good."

"May I point out that CBA News doesn't have an alliance with the Peruvian Government —good or bad—or with any other government either."

Margot said impatiently, "CBA *is* Globanic. Globanic has an alliance with Peru; therefore so does CBA. When will you grasp that simple fact?"

Chippingham wanted to answer, *Never!* But he knew he couldn't and said instead, "We're a news organization first and have to report the news the way it is. Also I'll point out, we didn't involve Peru; it's Sendero Luminoso which appears to have kidnapped our anchorman's family. In any case, as soon as our story breaks tonight, everyone else—networks, print press, you name it—will jump on the Peru story too."

In a corner of his mind Chippingham was asking: *Can this conversation really be taking place? And should I laugh or weep?*

"Keep me informed," Margot said. "If there's any change, especially about Peru, I want to know immediately, not next day."

Chippingham heard a click as the connection was severed.

In her elegant office at Stonehenge, Margot Lloyd-Mason pondered. Uncharacteristically, she was uncertain about what to do next. Should she call Globanic Chairman Theo Elliott, or not? She recalled his cautioning words about Peru at the Fordly Cay Club meeting: *"I don't want anything to damage our still-delicate relationship . . . and thereby spoil what can evolve into the deal of the century."* In the end, she decided that she must inform him. Better he should hear the news from her than on some newscast.

When she talked with Elliott, his reaction to her information was surprisingly calm. "Well, if that Shining Path rabble did the kidnapping, I suppose there's no way it can *not* be reported. But let's not forget that the Peruvian Government is in no way involved because they and the Shining Path are deadly enemies. Be sure your news people make that clear."

"I'll see that they do," Margot said.

"They can go even further," Theo Elliott continued. "What's happening presents an opportunity to make the government there look good, and CBA should use it."

The comment puzzled her. "Use in what way?"

"Well, clearly the Peruvian Government will do everything possible to find the kidnapped Americans and free them—using Peru's military and police. So while they're doing that, let's ensure they get proper credit, with upbeat pictures on our TV news. Then I can call President Castañeda, whom I know personally, and say, 'Hey, we're making you and your government look great!'—which should help us when Globanic Financial and Peru put together the final pieces of our debt-to-equity deal."

Even Margot hesitated. "I'm not sure about going quite that far, Theo."

"Then *be* sure! I know what you're thinking —that we're manipulating the news. Well, in something as important to us as this, so be it!" The Globanic chairman's voice rose. "Jesus Christ! We own the goddamn network, don't we? So once in a while let's put that ownership to our advantage. At the same time, remind your news people that this is a competitive, profit-oriented business which pays their fancy salaries and they are a part of it, like it or not. If they don't like it, they've a clear choice—get out!"

"I hear you, Theo," Margot said. While listening and making notes, she had decided on a *modus vivendi* which would have three stages.

First, she would call Chippingham to insist that CBA News indicate clearly the Peruvian Government's innocence of involvement in the kidnappings, precisely as Theo urged. Second, she herself, as president of CBA, would contact the U.S. State Department, asking for immediate pressure on Peru to do everything possible —including use of their military and police—to rescue the three Sloane family members. Third, the cooperation of Peru's government would be reported by CBA headquarters for general release. At the same time, CBA News would report positively the actual efforts made.

Almost certainly there would be difficulties and argument, but one thing Margot was sure of: Her relationship with Theo Elliott and loyalty to Globanic were paramount, overriding everything else.

Les Chippingham was growing used to Margot's unpredictabilities; therefore receiving another call from her so soon after their earlier

conversation did not surprise him. The subject
matter, though, made him uneasy because this
was direct corporate meddling in news content,
which happened occasionally at all networks
but almost never with a major story. Fortunately, in this instance it was possible to be reassuring.

"All of us know the Peruvian Government
was not involved in the kidnapping," the news
president said. "I'm sure that in our news tonight that will be implied and evident."

"I want more than implication. I want a
positive statement."

Chippingham hesitated, knowing he should
take a strong stand about news department independence, but aware of his precarious personal dependency on Margot. "I'll have to look
at scripts," he told her. "Let me call you back
in fifteen minutes."

"Don't make it any longer."

Ten minutes later, Chippingham called. "I
think this will please you. It's something Harry
Partridge wrote before he left for Peru and is in
our news for tonight: *'The government of Peru
and Sendero Luminoso have been fierce enemies
for many years, dedicated to each other's destruction. Peru's President Castanēda has declared, "Sendero's existence imperils Peru.
Those criminals are a knife thrust in my side."'*

That last statement will be a library shot and sound bite by Castañeda."

Chippingham's voice reflected relief as well as humor. "I guess Harry read your mind, Margot. I hope it satisfies."

"It will do. Read it again. I want to write it down."

After the phone call ended, Margot summoned her secretary and dictated a memo to Theo Elliott.

> Theo:
>
> Resulting from our talk, the following will be in the National Evening News tonight:
>
> *"The government of Peru and Sendero Luminoso have been fierce enemies for many years, dedicated to each other's destruction. Peru's President Castañeda has declared, 'Sendero's existence imperils Peru. Those criminals are a knife thrust in my side.' "*
>
> Castañeda will be seen and heard making the last statement.
>
> Thanks for your suggestion and help.
>
> Margot Lloyd-Mason

The memo was to be hand-delivered by special messenger to Globanic Industries headquarters.

Margot's next call was to Washington—the Secretary of State.

———

Throughout Friday at CBA, until the National Evening News first feed at 6:30 P.M., security was strained while outsiders nibbled at its edges, attempting to gain access to the exclusive information about which CBA News had been titillating viewers and competitors all day. News staff at other TV networks, radio stations, news wire services and the print press telephoned friends and contacts at CBA, attempting—sometimes directly, but mostly by inventive ruses—to learn the gist of what was coming. But within CBA, by carefully limiting the number of people with knowledge, and temporary isolation of an inner core of computers, the line was held and secrecy preserved.

Consequently, when the news broke it was immediately copied and repeated throughout the world, with CBA News acknowledged as the source. At other TV networks, testy inquests would soon be held, asking: *How did we miss out on this? What could we have done, but didn't? Why didn't* you *check* this, *or* you *follow through on* that? *Didn't* anyone *think of calling* there? *How do we guard against this happening again?*

Meanwhile, TV networks hastily revised their second newscast feeds, using swiftly supplied videotape displaying "Courtesy CBA," while newspapers reshaped the next day's front pages. At the same time, all major media alerted their regular Peru contacts while rushing to get their own reporters, correspondents and video and sound crews on airplanes to Peru.

Amid it all, a major new development occurred.

Don Kettering, now heading the CBA kidnap task force, heard about it shortly before 10 P.M., as the one-hour News Special was nearing its conclusion. Kettering was still at the anchor desk, where he had presided—apparently, so far as viewers were concerned—jointly with Harry Partridge, though the Partridge contribution was on tape.

Norman Jaeger conveyed the news through an anchor desk telephone during a commercial break. Jaeger was now senior producer since Rita Abrams had left for Teterboro Airport and her Peru flight an hour ago.

"Don, there's to be a task force session immediately after we've finished."

"Has something happened, Norm? Something hot?"

"Hot as hell! I've just had word from Les. Over at Stonehenge they've received the kidnappers' demands along with a videotape of Jessica Sloane."

4

They ran the videotape of Jessica first.

It was 10:30 P.M. on Friday. In a private viewing room at CBA News, used normally by senior executives, ten people were assembled: Les Chippingham and Crawford Sloane; from the task force, Don Kettering, Norm Jaeger, Karl Owens and Iris Everly; from CBA corporate headquarters at Stonehenge, Margot Lloyd-Mason, an executive vice president, Tom Nortandra, and Irwin Bracebridge, president of CBA Broadcast Group; and from the FBI, Special Agent Otis Havelock.

Chance had played a part in the group's assembly. Earlier in the evening, about 7:30 P.M., a small plain package was delivered by messenger to the main lobby of Stonehenge, addressed: *President, CBA Network.* After a routine security check it was sent to Margot Lloyd-Mason's floor where it would normally have waited, unopened, until Monday morning. However, Nortandra, whose office suite adjoined Margot's, happened to be working late, as were his two secretaries. One of the secretaries received the package and opened it. Realizing its importance, she informed Nortandra who telephoned Margot at the Waldorf where she was attending a reception and dinner honoring the President of France.

Margot abandoned the reception and hurried to Stonehenge where she, Nortandra and Bracebridge, who had also been called in, screened the videotape and read an accompanying document. Immediately they realized that the News Division must be informed and arranged a meeting at CBA News headquarters.

A few minutes before the meeting, Bracebridge, a former news president himself, took Crawford Sloane aside. "I know this is hard on you, Crawf, and I have to warn you there are some sounds on the tape I didn't like hearing. So if you'd prefer to watch the video alone first, while the rest of us wait outside, we'll do that and understand."

Crawford Sloane had driven in from Larchmont, along with FBI Agent Havelock who had been in the Sloane house when a call about the videotape of Jessica was received. Now Sloane shook his head. "Thanks, Irwin. I'll see it with the rest of you."

It was Don Kettering, taking charge, who called to an operator behind the small audience, "Okay, let's go!"

Lights in the viewing room dimmed. Almost at once a large, elevated TV screen went to black with scattered pinpoints of light, as was usual when running a blank tape without pictures. But sound was on the tape and was transmitted suddenly—a series of piercing screams. The group was transfixed. Crawford Sloane sat up straight, exclaiming in a broken voice, "Oh, Christ! That's Nicky!"

Then abruptly, as unexpectedly as it had begun, the screaming was cut off. A moment later a picture appeared—of Jessica's head and shoulders against a plain brown background, obviously a wall. Jessica's face was set and serious, and to those in the group who knew her, as most did, she appeared wan and under strain. But her voice, when she began, was firm and controlled, though an impression persisted that Jessica had willed herself to speak normally.

She began, "We have all been treated well and fairly. Now that the reason we were taken has been explained to us, we understand why it was necessary. We also have been told how easy it will be for our American friends to ensure our safe return home. To have us released, you must simply follow—quickly and exactly—the instructions which accompany this recording, but be sure of this . . ."

At the words "be sure of this," there was a

sharp intake of breath by Crawford Sloane and a muted exclamation. The tape continued.

". . . If you do not obey these instructions, you will not see any of us, ever again. We beg of you, do not let that happen . . ."

Again a sudden sound from Crawford Sloane—a whispered exclamation, *"There!"*

"We will be waiting, counting on you, desperately hoping you will make the right decision and bring us safely home."

For a second there was a silence in which Jessica's face remained on screen, her features expressionless, her eyes apparently unfocused, looking straight ahead. Then both sound and picture ended. In the viewing room the lights came on.

"We ran all of the tape earlier," Irwin Bracebridge said. "There's nothing else on it. And about the screams at the beginning, we think that was patched in from another tape. When you watch closely with the tape slowed right down, there's a slight visual break where two tapes were edited together."

Someone asked, "Why would they do that?

Bracebridge shrugged. "Maybe to wake us up, scare us. If so, it worked, didn't it?"

There was a murmur of agreement.

Les Chippingham asked gently, "Are you certain that first sound was Nicky, Crawf?"

Sloane said bleakly, "Positive." Then he added, "Jessica passed two signals."

"What kind of signals?" Chippingham sounded puzzled.

"The first was licking her lips, which means 'I am doing this against my will. Don't believe anything I'm saying.' "

"Clever!" Bracebridge said. "Good for Jessica!"

"Spunky!" someone else added. Others nodded approval.

Sloane went on, "We talked about signals the night before all this happened. I thought that one day I might need them myself . . . Life's full of coincidences. I guess Jessica remembered."

"What else was she able to tell you?" Chippingham asked.

"No, sir!" The voice of the FBI man, Havelock, cut across the conversation. "Whatever else you learned, Mr. Sloane, keep it to yourself for the time being. The fewer people who know, the better. We'll talk in a little while, please."

"I'd like to be in on that," Norm Jaeger said. "The task force has done pretty well in keeping secrets until now." He added pointedly, "Discovering them too."

The FBI agent glared. "It's my understanding you'll be hearing from our director about that—why we weren't kept informed."

Iris Everly said impatiently, "This is wasting time. Mrs. Sloane said something on the tape about instructions. Do we have them?" Though she was the youngest person present, Iris was typically unimpressed by the influx of network heavy brass. She had worked hard all day on the one-hour News Special and was tired, but her fast mind was functioning as usual.

Margot, still wearing a lavender chiffon Oscar de la Renta gown in which she had met the French President, answered, "We have it here." She nodded to Nortandra. "I think you'd better read it aloud."

The executive vice president accepted a half-dozen clipped sheets from Margot, perched a pair of half-moon reading glasses on his nose, and moved under a light; it heightened his thatch of white hair and a brooding face. Nortandra had been a corporate lawyer before becoming a CBA executive; his voice had an assured authority, developed from years of addressing courtrooms.

"The title of this document—or perhaps I should say this extraordinary diatribe—is: 'The Shining Time Has Come.' I shall now read to you, without comment or interjection, exactly what is here.

"In the histories of enlightened revolutions, there have been times when the persons leading and inspiring them have chosen to remain silent, to endure and suffer, sometimes to die miserably, but always to hope and plan. And then there have been other times—moments of glory and victory in the uprising of a downtrodden and exploited majority, the overthrow of imperialism and tyranny, and the deserved destruction of an encrusted capitalist-bourgeois class.

"For Sendero Luminoso the time of silence, patience and suffering has ended. The shining time, along the Shining Path, has come. We are ready to advance.

"In the world at large the self-proclaimed superpowers, while jockeying with each other and pretending to seek peace, are in reality preparing for a catastrophic confrontation between imperialistic and socialist-imperialistic forces, both seeking world hegemony. In all of it, the already enslaved and abused majority will suffer. If left alone to further exploit the world, a few power-mad money masters will, for their own advantages, control mankind.

"But like a volcano ready to explode, revolution is simmering everywhere. The Party— Sendero Luminoso—will lead that revolution. It has the knowledge and experience. Its growing influence is extended throughout the world.

"The time has come to make ourselves better known and understood.

"For many years the lying capitalist-imperialist media, which prints and broadcasts only what

its money-grubbing masters tell it, has ignored or misrepresented the heroic struggle of Sendero Luminoso's people.

"That will now be changed. It is why capitalist captives have been taken and are held as hostages.

"The American CBA television network is hereby ordered to do the following:

"One: Commencing with the second Monday after receipt of this demand, the program CBA National Evening News *(both network feeds) will be canceled for five weekdays—one full week.*

"Two: In place of the canceled program, another program, to be supplied in five tape cassettes delivered to CBA, *will be broadcast. The program's title is, 'World Revolution: Sendero Luminoso Shows the Way.'*

"Three: During the Sendero Luminoso broadcasts no commercial advertising will be allowed.

"Four: Neither CBA *nor any other agency will attempt to trace the source of the cassettes received, the first of which will reach* CBA *by Thursday of next week. Others will follow day by day. A single attempt to find the origin of the cassettes will result in immediate execution of one of the three prisoners held in Peru. Any further foolish attempts will bring a similar result.*

"Five: These orders are not negotiable and will be obeyed exactly.

"If there is full obedience by CBA *network and others with the orders in this document, the three prisoners will be released four days after the fifth Sendero Luminoso broadcast. But if the or-*

ders are not obeyed, the prisoners will not be seen
again and their bodies will never be recovered.

"Then there's something else," Nortandra
said. "It's on a separate sheet of paper.

"Copies of 'The Shining Time Has Come' and
the tape cassette of the woman prisoner have been
sent to other television networks and the press.

"That's all of it," Nortandra concluded.
"Neither paper is signed, but the fact they accompanied the tape makes them, I suppose, au-
thentic."

A silence followed the reading. No one, it
seemed, wanted to be first to speak. Several people glanced at Crawford Sloane who was
slumped in his chair, his face grimly set. The
others shared his sense of hopelessness.

It was Les Chippingham who said finally,
"Well, now we know. All along we've wondered
what these people wanted. We thought it might
be money. It's turned out to be much more."

"Much, much more," Bracebridge added.
"In money terms of course it's incalculable, but
obviously that isn't the issue here."

"As I indicated at the beginning," Nortandra observed, "the whole thing—especially all
that jargon—doesn't make a lot of sense."

Norm Jaeger spoke up. "Revolutionaries

seldom do make sense, except maybe to themselves. But that's no reason not to take them seriously. We learned that from Iran." Jaeger glanced at a clock above their heads, which showed 10:55. He addressed Chippingham. "Les, do we want to break into the network with this? If we're fast, we can do it on the hour and use some of Mrs. Sloane on tape. If what we heard about other networks getting the tape is true, they may go with the story any time."

"Then let them," the news president said firmly. "This is a new element in which we are players and will not rush. We'll put out a bulletin at midnight, which gives us an hour to consider how to handle the news and, more important, what our response—if any—will be."

"There can't be any question about a response," Margot Lloyd-Mason declared. "It's perfectly obvious there is no way that we can accept those ridiculous terms. We will certainly not put our network evening news out of business for one whole week."

"However, we don't have to say that, at least, not in the beginning," Nortandra pointed out. "We can say something like, the demands are being carefully considered and we'll make an announcement later."

"If you'll pardon my saying so," Jaeger told him, "I doubt if that would deceive anyone, least of all Sendero Luminoso. I've spent a lot of research hours on those people and whatever else they may be, they aren't fools; they're sharp. Also, they've clearly learned about our business—for example, that the National Evening News goes out with two feeds and our news audience falls off on Saturdays and Sundays, which they've indicated they don't want."

"So what are you suggesting?"

"That you let the news department handle everything in the way of a response. This calls for finesse, not a blunderbuss approach like speaking of 'ridiculous terms.' In CBA News we're better equipped, more finely tuned, our knowledge of the scene is greater . . ." At a signal from Chippingham, Jaeger stopped.

"Basically, I'm agreeing with Norman," the news president said, "but since it's my responsibility I think I should say that, yes, the News Division ought to handle any response because we *are* better informed, we know the ground, have established contacts, and one of our best correspondents, Harry Partridge, is in Peru already and must be consulted."

"Consult and finesse all you want," Margot snapped; she had flushed at Jaeger's reference to her "ridiculous terms" statement. "But what's involved here is a corporate matter requiring executive decision."

"No! Goddamn, no!" The words were shouted. Heads turned. The speaker was Craw-

ford Sloane, no longer seated and dejected, but standing, eyes fiery, face flushed. When he spoke, his voice was emotional, at moments choked.

"Keep corporate out of this! Norman is right about a blunderbuss approach; we all just witnessed one, and it's because corporate people don't have knowledge or experience to make news judgments. Besides, a corporate decision is already made; we heard that too: *Can't accept those terms. Won't put our news out of business for a week.* Did we really need you to tell us? Didn't we, in news, already know that—yes, all of us, including me? You want it on the record, Mrs. Lloyd-Mason. Well, here it is: I *know* we can't close down CBA News and hand it over to Sendero for one week. God help me!—I accept that. You have witnesses."

Sloane paused, swallowed, and continued. "What we *can* do, here at news, is use our skills, our know-how, play for time. At this moment, time is what we need the most. That, and use Harry Partridge who's the one best hope we have—*my* best hope to get my family home."

Sloane remained standing, but fell silent.

Before anyone could react, Bracebridge, the long-ago newsman, now a corporate wheel, tried a conciliatory tone. "A time like this is hard on everyone. It's emotional, tension is high, tempers short. Some of what's been said tonight could have been put more courteously and probably should have been." He turned toward the network president. "Just the same, Margot, I believe that what's been presented is a viewpoint worth considering, remembering—as Crawf made clear—that your end decision is understood and accepted. There seems no question about that."

Margot, having been offered a face-saving device, hesitated, then approved it. "Very well." She informed Chippingham, "On that basis, you may decide a temporary, stratagem response."

"Thank you," the news president acknowledged. "May we clarify one thing?"

"What is it?"

"That the ultimate decision we've agreed on will, for the time being, remain confidential."

"I suppose so. But you'd better get the same assurance from the others here. In any case, keep me informed."

Everyone else had been listening intently. Chippingham faced them and asked, "May I have that assurance, please?"

One by one they acknowledged their agreement. While they did, Margot walked out.

When Chippingham returned to his office it was 11:25 P.M. At 11:30 he received a printout of a Reuters dispatch originating in Lima, Peru, with information about the Sendero Luminoso demands on CBA. Moments later, AP in Washington came through with a more detailed report which had "The Shining Time Has Come" document in full.

Within the next fifteen minutes, ABC, NBC and CBS all carried bulletins including short segments of the Jessica tape. Fuller details were promised on the networks' news programs next day, with more bulletins if needed. CNN, with a news broadcast in progress, simply inserted the story and was ahead of everyone else. Chippingham stayed with his original decision not to interrupt present programming, but to release at midnight a carefully constructed bulletin, now being prepared.

At 11:45 he left his office for the Horseshoe, which had been activated for the occasion. Norm Jaeger was occupying the executive producer's chair. Iris Everly, in an editing room, was working with the tape of Jessica as well as others to be used for background. Don Kettering, who would anchor the special midnight news, was in makeup, at the same time reading over and amending a draft script.

"We'll just be telling it straight," Jaeger told Chippingham, "with no CBA reaction at all. We figure there's plenty of time for that later— whatever you want it to be. Incidentally, everyone else including the *Times* and *Post* has been phoning, asking for reactions. We've told them all we don't have any and the subject is simply being considered."

Chippingham nodded approval. "Good."

Jaeger gestured to Karl Owens, seated across the Horseshoe. "He has an idea, though, about what a reaction might be."

"I'd like to hear."

Owens, the workhorse, plodding, junior producer who had already come up with a series of ideas and whose painstaking probing had identified the terrorist as Ulises Rodríguez, consulted notes on a four-by-six card, his standard data bank.

"We were told in the Sendero Luminoso document that five tape cassettes, intended to replace our National Evening News, will be delivered to CBA—the first on Thursday of next week, the others following day by day. Unlike the tape of Mrs. Sloane which we watched tonight, those tapes will apparently be delivered to CBA only."

"I know all that," Chippingham said.

Jaeger smiled as Owens continued at his own pace, unperturbed. "What I'm suggesting is that we continue to hold off disclosing any CBA reaction until Tuesday. Except that on Monday, to keep interest alive, you could say there'll be an announcement the following day. Then on Tuesday that announcement would be:

No further comment until we receive the tape promised for Thursday, and after that we'll make our decision known."

"Where does all that get us?"

"It gets us to Thursday, six days from now. Then let's assume the Sendero tape comes in."

"Okay, so it's in. What then?"

"We put it in a safe where no one can get to it, and right away go on the air—breaking into programming, generally making a big fuss— saying we've received the tape, but it's defective. It must have got damaged on the way; most of the content got wiped out. We tried to play it, then fix it, but we can't. As well as putting all that on TV, we'll feed it to the press and wire services, making sure the message is repeated to Peru, so it gets back to Sendero Luminoso."

"I think I follow your reasoning," Chippingham said. "But tell me anyway."

"The Sendero gang won't know whether we're lying or not. What they *will* know—just as we do—is that that kind of thing can happen. So maybe they'll give us the benefit of doubt and send another tape, which could take several days . . ."

Chippingham finished the sentence for him. ". . . and would mean we couldn't possibly start their broadcasts on the day they specified."

"Exactly."

Jaeger added, "I guess Karl would get to

this eventually, Les. But what he's saying is we'll have gained several extra days' reprieve— *if* it works, and it just might. What do you think?"

Chippingham said, "I think it's brilliant. It makes me glad we got the nitty-gritty shifted back to news."

Throughout the weekend the news about Sendero Luminoso's demands and the videotape of Jessica stayed prominently in the news, with growing interest around the world. Calls flooded in to CBA requesting some comment from the network, preferably in the form of an official statement. By arrangement, all such calls were routed to CBA News. Other CBA executives and managers were advised not to respond to questions on the subject, even off the record.

At CBA News three secretaries, summoned for special weekend work, handled the calls. In every case their response to questions was the same: CBA had no comment and, no, it was not possible to say when a comment would be made.

The absence of a CBA reaction, however, did not stop others from expressing opinions. A majority view seemed to be, *Hold the line! Don't give in!*

A surprising number, though, saw no harm

in the kidnappers' demands being met as a price of the prisoners' release, prompting Norm Jaeger to comment in disgust, "Can't those birdbrains grasp the principles involved? Don't they see that by creating a precedent we'd invite every lunatic group in the world to kidnap television people?"

On the Sunday TV talk shows "Face the Nation," "Meet the Press" and "This Week with David Brinkley," the subject was debated and extracts from Crawford Sloane's book *The Camera and the Truth,* read aloud, particularly:

- *Hostages . . . should be regarded as expendable.*
- *The only way to deal with terrorists is . . . not striking bargains or paying ransom, directly or indirectly, ever!*

Within CBA, those who had promised Les Chippingham to keep secret the ultimate decision not to accept Sendero Luminoso's terms appeared to have kept their word. In fact, the only one to break it was Margot Lloyd-Mason who, on Sunday, advised Theodore Elliott by telephone of everything that had transpired the night before.

No doubt Margot would have argued she was acting correctly in keeping the Globanic chairman informed. Unfortunately, right or wrong, her action paved the way for a devastating leak.

5

Globanic Industries World Headquarters occupied a mansion-style office complex set in its own private park at Pleasantville, New York, some thirty miles outside Manhattan. The intent in choosing that locale had been to remove high-level thinking and policy making from the daily pressure-cooker atmosphere of Globanic subsidiaries in industrial or financial areas. Globanic Financial, for example, which was managing the Peru debt-to-equity deal, occupied three floors of One World Trade Center in the Wall Street area.

In reality, however, many ancillary matters affecting Globanic outposts spilled into the Pleasantville headquarters. This was why, at 10 A.M. on Monday morning, Glen Dawson, a preppy young reporter for the *Baltimore Star,* was waiting to interview Globanic's chief comptroller on the subject of palladium. Currently the precious metal was in the news and a Globanic company owned mines producing palladium and platinum in Minas Gerais, Brazil, where labor riots were threatening supplies.

Dawson waited outside the comptroller's office in an elegant circular lounge which gave access to the suites of two other high Globanic officers, one of them the conglomerate's chairman and CEO.

The reporter, seated in an inconspicuous corner, was still waiting when one of the other office doors opened and two figures emerged. One was Theodore Elliott whom Dawson recognized instantly from photographs he had seen. The face of the other man was familiar, though Dawson couldn't place it. The two were continuing a conversation begun inside, the second man speaking.

". . . been hearing about your CBA. Those threats from the Peru rebels put you in a difficult spot."

The Globanic chairman nodded. "In one way, yes . . . carry on, I'll walk you to the elevator . . . We've made a decision, though it hasn't been announced. What we're *not* going to do is let a bunch of crazy Commies push us around."

"So CBA won't cancel their evening news?"

"Absolutely not! As for running those Shining Path tapes, not a hope in hell . . ."

The voices faded.

Using a magazine he had been glancing through as cover for a notepad, Glen Dawson quickly scribbled the exact words he had heard. His pulse was racing. He knew he had exclusive information which countless other journalists had been seeking unsuccessfully since Saturday night.

"Mr. Dawson," a receptionist called over, "Mr. Licata will see you now."

On his way past her desk, he stopped and smiled. "That other gentleman with Mr. Elliott —I'm sure I've met him, but couldn't place his face."

The receptionist hesitated; he sensed her disapproval and renewed the smile. It worked.

"It was Mr. Alden Rhodes, the Under Secretary of State."

"Of course! How could I forget?"

Dawson had seen the Under Secretary of State for Economic Affairs once before—on television, appearing before a House committee. But all that mattered at this moment was that he had the name.

The interview with Globanic's comptroller seemed endless to Dawson, though he tried to conclude it as quickly as he could. The subject of palladium had not interested him much, anyway; he was an ambitious young man who wanted to write on subjects of wide interest, and what he had stumbled on seemed a timely ticket to a more exciting future. The comptroller, however, was unhurried in describing the history and future of palladium. He dismissed the labor unrest in Brazil as temporary and unlikely to affect supplies, which was what Dawson had principally come to find out. At length, pleading a deadline, the reporter made his escape.

Checking his watch, he decided he had time to drive to the *Baltimore Star*'s Manhattan bureau, write both stories there, and still make the paper's main afternoon edition. Driving fast, mentally stringing words and sentences together as the miles flew by, he headed south on Saw Mill River Parkway, then Interstate 87.

Seated at a computer terminal in the bureau's modest office at Rockefeller Plaza, Glen Dawson quickly wrote the palladium story first. It was what he had been sent to do and an original obligation was now decently fulfilled.

He then began the more exciting second story. His first report had gone to the financial desk and, since he was assigned there, so would the second. He was certain, though, it would not remain at financial for very long.

His fingers danced over the keyboard, composing a lead.

As he did, Dawson wondered about an ethical question which he knew would have to be asked and answered soon: Would publication of the information he was now writing place the kidnap victims in Peru in greater peril than they were already?

More specifically: Would the Sloane family hostages be harmed by revelation of the CBA network decision to reject the demands of Sendero Luminoso, a decision which obviously, at this point, was not intended to be disclosed?

Or, on the other hand, was the public entitled to know whatever an enterprising reporter like himself was able to find out, no matter how the information was obtained?

Though such questions existed, the plain fact was, Dawson knew, they were none of his business or concern. The rules in the matter were precise and known to all parties involved.

A reporter's responsibility was to write any worthwhile story he found. If he discovered news, his job was not to suppress or modify it in any way, but to write a full and accurate report, then deliver it to the organization that employed him.

At that point what had been written would go to an editor. It was the editor, or editors, who must consider ethics.

In Baltimore, Dawson thought, where his story would be printing out at another computer terminal, that was probably happening right now.

As he concluded, he pressed a key to get a local printout for himself. However, another hand reached out and got the printout first.

It was the bureau chief, Sandy Sefton, who had just come in. A veteran general reporter, Sefton was a few years from retirement and he and Dawson were good friends. As he read the printout, the bureau chief whistled softly, then looked up.

"You got a hot one all right. Those words of Elliott's—did you write them down right when he said them?"

"Within seconds." Dawson showed the older man his notes.

"Good! Have you talked to this other guy, Alden Rhodes?"

Dawson shook his head.

"Baltimore will probably want you to." A telephone rang. "Want to bet that's Baltimore now?"

It was. Sefton took the call, listened briefly, then said, "My boy's gonna lead the paper tonight, right?" He grinned as he passed the phone to Dawson. "It's Frazer."

J. Allardyce Frazer was executive editor. He wasted no time, his voice authoritative. "You haven't spoken to Theodore Elliott directly yet. Correct?"

"Correct, Mr. Frazer."

"Do it. Tell him what you have and ask if he

has a comment. If he denies saying it, report that too. If he does deny, try for a confirmation from Alden Rhodes. You know the kind of question to ask?"

"I think so."

"Let me talk to Sandy."

The bureau chief took the phone. He winked at Dawson while he listened, then said, "I've seen Glen's notes. He wrote Elliott's words on the spot. They're clear. No chance of a misunderstanding."

Replacing the phone, Sefton told Dawson. "You're not home free yet; they're debating ethics. You carry on with Elliott. I'll try to locate Rhodes; he can't have got back to Washington." Sefton crossed the room to use another phone.

Dawson tapped out Globanic's number. After going through a switchboard, a woman's voice answered. The reporter identified himself and asked for "Mr. Theodore Elliott."

"Mr. Elliott is not available now," the voice said pleasantly. "I'm Mrs. Kessler. Is there something I can do?"

"Perhaps." Dawson carefully explained why he had called.

The voice became cool. "Wait, please."

Several minutes passed. Dawson was about to hang up and call again when the connection came alive. This time the voice was frigid. "Mr.

Elliott advises that whatever you think you heard was confidential and may not be used."

"I'm a reporter," Dawson said. "If I hear or learn something and it wasn't told to *me* confidentially, I'm entitled to use it."

"Mr. Dawson, I see no point in prolonging this conversation."

"Just a moment, please. Does Mr. Elliott deny having used the words I read to you?"

"Mr. Elliott has no further comment."

Dawson wrote down the question and answer, as he had the previous exchange.

"Mrs. Kessler, do you mind telling me your first name?"

"There is no reason to . . . well, Diana."

Dawson smiled, guessing Kessler had reasoned that if her name was to appear in print, it might as well be in full. About to say thank you, he realized the connection had been severed.

As he replaced the phone, the bureau chief handed him a slip of paper. "Rhodes is on his way to La Guardia in a State Department car. Here's the number of the car phone."

Dawson lifted his phone again.

This time, after a ringing tone, a male voice answered. When Dawson asked for "Mr. Alden Rhodes," the response was, "This is he."

Again the reporter identified himself, aware that Sandy Sefton was listening on an extension.

"Mr. Rhodes, my paper would like to know

if you have any comment on Mr. Theodore Elliott's statement that CBA network will reject
the recent Sendero Luminoso demands and, in
Mr. Elliott's words, 'we're not going to let a
bunch of crazy Commies push us around.' "

"Theo Elliott told you *that!*"

"I heard him say it personally, Mr.
Rhodes."

"I thought he wanted it kept confidential."
A pause. "Now wait a minute! Were you sitting
in that hall when we walked through?"

"Yes, I was."

"Dawson, you've tricked me and I insist this
entire conversation be off the record."

"Mr. Rhodes, before we began talking I
identified myself and you did not say anything
about being off the record."

"Fuck you, Dawson!"

"That last was off the record, sir. By then
you'd told me."

The bureau chief, grinning, gave a thumbs-
up signal.

The ethical debate in Baltimore did not last
long.

In any news organization there always existed a predilection toward disclosure. However, with some news stories—and this was one
—certain questions needed to be asked and answered. The executive editor and national edi-

tor, who would oversee the story, posed them to each other.

QUESTION: Would publication of CBA's decision imperil the hostages? ANSWER: The hostages were in peril already; it was hard to see how publication of anything could make much difference. QUESTION: Would anyone be killed because of publication? ANSWER: Unlikely because a dead hostage would cease to be of value. QUESTION: Since CBA would have to make its decision known in a day or two, what difference would it make to be a little early? ANSWER: Not much, if any. QUESTION: Since Globanic's Theo Elliott revealed the CBA decision casually and others must know of it, was it likely to stay secret much longer? ANSWER: Almost certainly no.

At the end, the executive editor expressed the conclusion of both: "There isn't an ethical problem. We go!"

The story led the *Baltimore Star*'s main afternoon edition with a banner headline:

CBA SAYS NO
TO SLOANE KIDNAPPERS

Glen Dawson's by-line story began:

CBA will say an emphatic "No" to demands
by the Sloane family's kidnappers that it cancel its

*televised National Evening News for a week, re-
placing it with propaganda videotapes supplied by
the Peru Maoist rebel group Sendero Luminoso.*

*Sendero Luminoso, or Shining Path, has ad-
mitted holding the kidnap victims at a secret location in Peru.*

*Theodore Elliott, chairman and chief execu-
tive officer of Globanic Industries, the parent company of CBA, declared today, "What we're not
going to do is let a bunch of crazy Commies push
us around."*

*Speaking at Globanic's headquarters at Pleas-
antville, New York, he added, "As for running
those Shining Path tapes, not a hope in hell."*

A Star *reporter was present during the Elliott
statement.*

*Alden Rhodes, Under Secretary of State for
Economic Affairs, who was with Mr. Elliott when
the statement was made, declined to comment
when questioned by the* Star, *though he did say, "I
thought he wanted it kept confidential."*

*An attempt late this morning to reach Mr. El-
liott for additional information was unsuccessful.*

"Mr. Elliott is not available," the Star *was informed by Mrs. Diana Kessler, an assistant to the
Globanic chairman. In response to questions, Mrs.
Kessler insisted, "Mr. Elliott has no further comment."*

There was more—principally background
and the history of the kidnap.

Even before the *Baltimore Star* hit the
streets, the wire services had the story, giving

credit to the *Star*. Later that evening the *Star* was quoted on all network news broadcasts, including CBA's where the premature news was received with near-despair.

Next morning in Peru, where the kidnap story was already prominent in the news, newspapers, as well as radio and TV, featured the disclosure with special emphasis on Theodore Elliott's "bunch of crazy Commies"—*"grupo de Comunistas locos"*—description of Sendero Luminoso.

6

"I like Vicente," Nicky said. "He's our friend."

"I think he is too," Angus called over from his cell. He was lying on the thin, soiled mattress of his makeshift bed and filling empty time by watching two large beetles on the wall.

"Then *un*-think, both of you!" Jessica snapped. "Liking *anyone* here is stupid and naïve."

She stopped, wanting to bite her tongue and call the words back. There was no need to have spoken sharply.

"I'm sorry," she said. "I didn't mean that to come out the way it did."

The trouble was that after fifteen days of close confinement in their tiny cages, the strain was telling on them all, wearing their spirits down. Jessica had done her best to keep morale, if not high, at least at a level above despair. She also made sure they all performed daily exercises, which she led. But clearly, despite best intentions, the close physical restriction, monotony and loneliness were having an inevitable effect.

Additionally, the greasy, unpalatable food was one more burden that sapped their physical resources.

Compounding those miseries, and despite their efforts to stay washed, they were usually dirty, odorous, and frequently sweating, with their soiled clothes sticking to them.

It was all very well, Jessica thought, to remind herself that her anti-terrorism course mentor, Brigadier Wade, had suffered a good deal more and for a longer period in his below-ground hellhole in Korea. But Cedric Wade was an exceptional, committed person serving his country in time of war. There was no war here to stiffen the mind or sinews. They were merely civilians caught in a petty skirmish . . . for what purpose? Jessica still didn't know.

Just the same, the thought of Brigadier

Wade and Nicky's remark about liking Vicente, plus Angus's endorsement, reminded her of something she had learned from Wade. Now seemed a good time to bring it up.

Speaking softly while glancing warily at the guard on duty, she asked, "Angus and Nicky, have either of you heard of the Stockholm syndrome?"

"I think so," Angus said. "Not sure, though."

"Nicky?"

"No, Mom. What is it?"

The guard was the one who sometimes brought a comic book; he seemed engrossed in one now and indifferent to their talking. Jessica also knew he spoke no English.

"I'll tell you," Jessica said.

In memory she could hear Brigadier Wade's voice informing the small study group of which she had been part, "One thing that happens in almost every terrorist hijack or kidnap situation is that after a while at least some of the hostages come to *like* the terrorists. Sometimes hostages go so far as to think of the terrorists as their friends and the police or troops outside, who are trying to rescue the hostages, as the enemy. That's the Stockholm syndrome."

All of which was true, Jessica confirmed subsequently through additional reading. She had also been curious enough to go back and learn how the process got its label.

Now, dipping into memory and using her own words, she described the strange story while Nicky and Angus listened.

It happened in Stockholm, Sweden, on August 23, 1973.

That morning, at Norrmalmstorg, a central city square, an escaped convict, Jan-Erik Olsson, age thirty-two, entered Sveriges Kreditbanken, one of Stockholm's larger banks. From beneath a folded jacket Olsson produced a submachine gun which he fired into the ceiling, creating panic amid a shower of concrete and glass.

The ordeal that followed lasted six days.

In course of it no one participating had any notion that for years and probably centuries to come, an outcropping of the experience they were sharing would become famous as the Stockholm syndrome—a medical and scientific phrase destined to be as familiar worldwide to students and practitioners as Cesarean section, anorexia, penis envy or Alzheimer's disease.

Three women and a man, all bank employees, were taken hostage by Olsson and an accomplice, Clark Olofsson, age twenty-six. The hostages were Birgitta Lundblad, thirty-one, a pretty blond; Kristin Ehnmark, twenty-three, spirited and black-haired; Elisabeth Oldgren, twenty-

one, small, fair and gentle; and Sven Säfström, twenty-five, a tall, slender bachelor. For most of the next six days this sextet was confined to a safe-deposit vault from where the criminals presented their demands by telephone—for three million kronor in cash ($710,000), two pistols and a getaway car.

During the siege, the hostages suffered. They were forced to stand with ropes around their necks so that falling would strangle them. From time to time, as a machine gun was thrust into their ribs, they expected death. For fifty hours they were without food. Plastic wastebaskets became their only toilets. Within the vault, claustrophobia and fear were all-pervading.

Yet all the while a strange closeness between hostages and captors grew. There was a moment when Birgitta could have walked away but didn't. Kristin managed to give information to the police, then acknowledged, "I felt like a traitor." The male hostage, Sven, described his captors as "kind." Elisabeth agreed.

Stockholm's police, waging a war of attrition to free the prisoners, encountered hostility from them. Kristin said by telephone that she trusted the robbers, adding "I want you to let us go away with them . . . They have been very nice." Of Olsson, she declared, "He is protecting us from the police." When told, "The police will not harm you," Kristin replied, "I do not believe it."

It was revealed later that Kristin held hands with the younger criminal, Olofsson. She told an investigator, "Clark gave me tenderness." And after the hostages' release, while being taken by stretcher to an ambulance, Kristin called to Olofsson, "Clark, I'll see you again."

Lab technicians searching the vault found traces of semen. Following a week of questioning, one of the women, while denying having had sex, said that during one night while others were asleep she helped Olsson to masturbate. Investigators, while skeptical about the no-sex statement, dropped the matter.

During questioning by doctors the freed hostages referred to police as "the enemy" and believed it was the criminals to whom they owed their lives. Elisabeth accused a doctor of attempting to "brainwash away" her regard for Olsson and Olofsson.

In 1974, nearly a year after the bank drama, Birgitta visited Olofsson in jail, conversing with him for half an hour.

Investigating doctors eventually declared the hostages' reaction typical of anyone caught in "survival situations." They quoted Anna Freud who described such reactions as "identification with the aggressor." But it took the Swedish bank drama to create a permanent, memorable name: the Stockholm syndrome.

"Hey, that's neat, Mom," Nicky called out.

"I never knew all that, Jessie," Angus added.

Nicky asked, "Got any more good stuff?"

Jessica was pleased. "A little."

Once more she drew on her memories of the Britisher, Brigadier Wade. "I have two pieces of advice for you," he once told his anti-terrorist class. "First, if you're a captive and a hostage: *Beware the Stockholm syndrome!* Second, when dealing with terrorists keep in mind that 'Love your enemies' is vapid nonsense. At the other extreme, don't squander time and effort hating terrorists, because hate is a wasteful, draining emotion. Just never for a moment trust them, or like them, and never stop thinking of them as the enemy."

Jessica repeated the Wade advice for Nicky and Angus. She went on to describe airplane hijackings where people who had been seized and abused developed friendly feelings for their attackers. This proved true with the infamous TWA flight 847 in 1985 when some passengers expressed sympathy for the Shiite hijackers and expounded their captors' propagandist views.

More recently, Jessica explained, a released hostage from the Middle East—a pathetic figure, clearly another victim of the Stockholm syndrome—even delivered a message from his jailers to the Pope and the U.S. President, gaining much publicity while he did. The nature of the message was not disclosed, though unofficially it was called banal and pointless.

Of even greater concern to those who understood the Stockholm syndrome was the case of kidnap victim Patricia Hearst. Unfortunately for Hearst, who was arrested in 1975 and tried the following year for alleged crimes while dominated by her brutish captors, the events in Stockholm were not sufficiently known to allow either sympathy or justice. Speaking at one of the Wade anti-terrorist sessions, an American lawyer declared, "In legal and intellectual values the Patty Hearst trial must be equated with the Salem witchcraft trials of 1692." He added, "Knowing what we do now, and remembering that the wrong done was recognized by President Carter who commuted her prison sentence, it will be a dark day of shame for our country if Patricia Hearst is allowed to die unpardoned."

"So what you're saying, Jessie," Angus said, "is not to be taken in by Vicente's seeming easy. He's still an enemy."

"If he weren't," Jessica pointed out, "we could just walk out of here while he's guarding us."

"Which we know we can't." Angus directed his voice to the middle cell. "Have you got that, Nicky? Your mom's right and you and I were wrong."

Nicky nodded glumly, without speaking. One of the sadnesses of this incarceration, Jessica thought, was that Nicky was being faced— earlier than would have happened normally— with some harsh realities of human infamy.

As always in Peru, the developing news concerning the Sloane family kidnapping traveled over the longest distances and to the country's remotest places by radio.

The first news of the linkage of Peru and Sendero Luminoso to the kidnapping was reported on Saturday, the day following the CBA National Evening News broadcast in which the exclusive material assembled by the network's special task force was revealed. While the kidnapping had been reported earlier by Peru's media in a minor way, the local involvement made it instant major news. Here, too, radio was the means of widest dissemination.

Similarly, on the Tuesday morning following Monday's news breakthrough by the *Baltimore Star,* radio delivered to the Andes mountain city of Ayacucho and the Selva hamlet Nueva Esperanza the first report of Theodore Elliott's rejection of the kidnappers' demands and his low opinion of Sendero Luminoso.

In Ayacucho the radio report was heard by Sendero leaders and in Nueva Esperanza by the terrorist Ulises Rodríguez, alias Miguel.

Soon after, a telephone conversation took place between Miguel and a Sendero leader in Ayacucho, though neither disclosed his name while talking. Both were aware that the telephone connection was poor by modern standards and that the line passed through other locations where anyone could be listening, including the army or police. Thus they talked in generalities and veiled references, at which many in Peru were practiced, though to both men the meaning was understood.

This was: Something must be done immediately to prove to the American TV network, CBA, that they were dealing with neither fools nor weaklings. Killing one of the hostages and leaving the body to be found in Lima was a possibility. Miguel, while agreeing that would be effective, suggested for the moment keeping all three hostages alive, preserving them like capital. Instead of killing, he advised another course of action which—remembering something he had learned while at Hackensack—he believed would be devastating psychologically to those at the other end of the equation in New York.

This was promptly agreed to and, since physical transportation would be needed, a car or truck, whichever proved available, would leave Ayacucho immediately for Nueva Esperanza.

In Nueva Esperanza, Miguel began his preparations by sending for Socorro.

Jessica, Nicky and Angus looked up as a small procession filed into the area immediately outside their cells. It consisted of Miguel, Socorro, Gustavo, Ramón and one of the other men who served as guards. From their sense of purpose it was evident something was about to happen and Jessica and the others waited apprehensively to discover what.

One thing Jessica was sure of: Whatever was expected of her, she would cooperate. It was now six days since she had made the videotape recording in course of which, because of her initial defiance, Nicky had been tortured by agonizing burns. Since then, Socorro had come in daily to inspect the burns, which were sufficiently healed so that Nicky was no longer in pain. Jessica, who still felt guilty about Nicky's suffering, was determined he would not be hurt again.

Consequently, when Nicky's cell was opened and the terrorists crowded in with Nicky, ignoring Jessica and Angus, Jessica cried out anxiously, "What are you doing? I beg of you don't hurt him. He's suffered enough. Do what you have to do to me!"

It was Socorro who swung to face Jessica and shouted through the screen between them,

"Shut up! There's no way you can stop what's going to happen."

Jessica screamed frantically, "What *is* happening?" Miguel, she saw, had brought a small wooden table into Nicky's cell while Gustavo and the fourth man had seized Nicky and were holding him so he was unable to move. Jessica cried again, "Oh, this isn't fair! For god's sake let him go!"

Ignoring Jessica, Socorro said to Nicky, "You're going to have two of your fingers cut off."

At the word "fingers," Nicky, already frantic, screamed and struggled, but to no avail.

Socorro continued, "These men will do it, and there's nothing you can do to change that. But it will hurt more if you struggle, so keep still!"

Ignoring the warning, mouthing incoherent words, his eyes moving wildly, Nicky fought even more desperately to free himself, to somehow pull back his hands, but did not succeed.

Jessica emitted a piercing wail. "Oh, no! Not fingers! Don't you understand? He plays the piano! It's his life . . ."

"I know." This time it was Miguel who turned, a small smile on his face. "I heard your husband say so on television; he was answering a question. When he receives those fingers he'll wish he hadn't."

On the other side of Nicky's cell, Angus was banging his screen and shouting too. He held up his hands. "Take mine! What difference will it make? Why spoil the rest of the boy's life?"

Miguel, this time his face working angrily, flared back. "What do two fingers of a bourgeois brat matter when every year sixty thousand Peru children die before the age of five?"

"We're Americans!" Angus hurled at him. "We're not to blame for that!"

"You are! The capitalist system, *your* system which exploits the people, is depraved, destructive. It *is* to blame . . ."

Miguel's statistics about the deaths of children were a quote from Abimael Guzmán, Sendero Luminoso's founder. As Miguel knew, Guzmán's figure might be exaggerated, but without question Peru's child malnutrition death toll was one of the highest in the world.

While the epithets flowed back and forth, it happened quickly.

The small table Gustavo had brought was moved in front of Nicky. While the boy continued to squirm and wriggle, begging and crying, pleading pitifully, Gustavo forced the boy's right index finger on top of the table so it was there alone, the other fingers curled back against the table's edge. Ramón had produced a sheath knife. Now, grinning, he tested the bright blade's razor sharpness with a thumb.

Satisfied, Ramón moved forward, placed the blade against the second joint of Nicky's exposed finger and, with a single swift movement, brought the heel of his beefy left hand down sharply against the back of the knife. With a *thunk* sound, a spurt of blood, and a piercing scream from Nicky, the finger was almost severed, but not quite. Ramón lifted the knife, then cut away the remaining tissue and flesh to complete the finger's severance. Nicky's despairing cries, now from pain, were shrill and harrowing.

Blood flooded the tabletop and was on the hands of the men holding Nicky. They ignored it and moved the boy's little finger, also of the right hand, from the table's edge to the top. This time the action and result were faster. With a single chop of Ramón's knife, the finger was separated from the hand, falling clear while more blood spurted.

Socorro, who had collected the first severed finger and put it in a plastic bag, now added the second and passed the bag to Miguel. Socorro was pale, her lips compressed. She glanced briefly toward Jessica whose face was covered with her hands, her body racked by sobbing.

By now, Nicky—barely conscious, his features ashen white—had fallen back on the narrow bed, his screaming turned to agonized moans. As Miguel, Ramón and the fourth man moved out from the cell, taking the bloody table with them, Socorro told Gustavo whom she had signaled to wait, *"Agarra el chico. ¡Sientalo!"*

Responding, Gustavo raised Nicky to a seated position and held him while Socorro moved outside, returning with a bowl of warm soapy water she had brought when the group arrived. Taking Nicky's right hand and holding it upright, Socorro carefully washed the raw stumps of the two severed fingers to forestall infection. The water turned bright red as she did. Then, after covering both wounds with several gauze pads, she securely bandaged the entire hand. Even through pads and bandage, bloodstains showed, though it appeared the flow of blood was slowing.

Through it all, Nicky, clearly in shock, his whole body trembling, neither helped nor hindered what was being done.

Miguel was still in the area outside the cells and Jessica, who had moved to her own cell doorway called to him tearfully. "Please let me go to my son! Please, please, please!"

Miguel shook his head. He said contemptuously, "No mother for a gutless chicken! Let the *mocoso* try to become a man!"

"He's more of a man than you will ever be." The voice was Angus's, filled with rage and loathing; he too had moved to the doorway of his cell to face Miguel. Angus groped for the

Spanish curse Nicky had taught him a week before. "You . . . *¡Maldito hijo de puta!*"

Angus remembered what it meant: *Cursed son of a whore!* Nicky had repeated to Angus what his playground Cuban friends had told him: To bring a man's mother into a Spanish curse was the gravest insult possible.

Slowly, deliberately, Miguel turned his head. He looked directly at Angus with eyes that were glacial, vicious and unforgiving. Then, his face set, his expression unchanged, he turned away.

Gustavo had emerged from Nicky's cell in time to hear the words and observe Miguel's reaction. Shaking his head, Gustavo said to Angus in his halting English, "Old man, you make bad mistake. He not forget."

As the hours passed, Jessica became increasingly concerned about Nicky's mental state. She had tried talking to him, attempting to find some way, through words, to comfort him, but with no success or even a response. Part of the time Nicky lay still, occasionally moaning. Then suddenly his body would jerk several times and sharp cries escape him, followed by a bout of trembling. Jessica was sure that severed nerves caused the movement and accompanying pain. As far as she could tell, most of the time Nicky's eyes were open but his face was blank.

Jessica even pleaded for an answer. "Just a word, Nicky darling! Just a word! Please—say something, anything!" But there was no response. Jessica wondered if perhaps she was going mad herself. The inability to reach out, to touch and hold her son, to try to bring some solace physically, was a frustrating denial of what she craved.

For a while Jessica herself, close to hysteria, tried to empty her head of thoughts and, lying down, shed silent, bitter tears.

Then with a mental chiding . . . *Take hold! Pull yourself together! Don't give in!* . . . she resumed the attempt to talk with Nicky.

Angus joined in but the result was as unproductive as before.

Food arrived and was put into their cells. Not surprisingly, Nicky took no notice. Knowing she should preserve her strength, Jessica tried to eat but found she had no appetite and pushed the food away. She had no idea how Angus fared.

Darkness came. As the night advanced, the guard changed. Vicente came on duty. Sounds from outside grew fainter and, when only the hum of insects could be heard, Socorro arrived. She was carrying the water bowl she had used before, several more gauze pads, a bandage, and a kerosene lamp she took with her into Nicky's cell. Gently she sat Nicky upright and began to change the dressing on his hand.

Nicky seemed easier, less in pain, the jerking of his body more infrequent.

After a while Jessica called out softly, "Socorro, please . . ."

Immediately Socorro swung around. Putting a finger to her lips, she signaled Jessica to be silent. Uncertain about anything, disoriented by strain and anguish, Jessica complied.

When the bandaging was done, Socorro left Nicky's cell but didn't lock it. Instead, she came to Jessica's and opened the padlock with a key. Again, the signal for silence. Then Socorro waved Jessica out from her cell and pointed to the open door of Nicky's.

Jessica's heart lifted.

"You must go back before daylight," Socorro whispered. She nodded in the direction of Vicente. "He will tell you when."

About to move toward Nicky, Jessica stopped and turned. Impulsively, irrationally, she moved to Socorro and kissed the other woman's cheek.

Moments later, Jessica was holding Nicky, careful of his bandaged hand.

"Oh, Mom!" he said.

As best they could, they hugged each other. Soon after, Nicky fell asleep.

7

At CBA News the systematic search of classified advertising placed in local newspapers over the past three months was about to be abandoned.

When the search had begun a little more than two weeks earlier, it seemed important to locate what had been the kidnappers' United States headquarters. At the time it was hoped that even if the kidnap victims were not found, at least some clue might have been left behind as to where they had been taken.

However, now that the Sloane family members were known to be in Peru, though only Sendero Luminoso knew exactly where, the search for the earlier base seemed less important.

Particularly from a TV news point of view, a discovery and pictures of the scene would still be of interest. But as to its being helpful in any important way, the likelihood grew less as days went by.

Still, the effort had not been a failure. Jonathan Mony's search of local papers had produced the Spanish language weekly *Semana,* containing information which led directly to the undertaker Alberto Godoy. Questioning of Godoy revealed his sale of caskets to, and positive identification of, the terrorist Ulises Rodríguez. And later still, pressure on Godoy provided clues leading to the American-Amazonas Bank, the apparent murder of the UN diplomat José Antonio Salaverry and his mistress, Helga Efferen, plus their connection with Peru.

Those developments alone, it was generally agreed, had made the advertising search project worthwhile.

But would further searching be likely to produce anything more?

Don Kettering, now heading the CBA News special kidnap task force, didn't think so. Nor did the task force senior producer, Norman Jaeger. Even Teddy Cooper, who originated the search idea and had supervised it closely from the beginning, had trouble finding reasons to continue.

The matter came up at a task force meeting on Tuesday morning.

It was now four days since Friday's disclosure of all that was known to CBA News about the kidnap, its perpetrators and the victims' presence in Peru, plus the later news on Friday evening which included the videotape of Jessica

Sloane along with Sendero Luminoso's demands.

In the meantime there had been the upsetting revelation of Theodore Elliott's indiscretion, resulting in worldwide knowledge of a CBA decision intended to be kept confidential until—at the earliest—the following Thursday. It was notable that no one at CBA News criticized the *Baltimore Star,* realizing that the *Star*'s reporter and editors had done what any other news organization would in such circumstances, probably including CBA.

Theodore Elliott had neither explained nor apologized for what had occurred.

In Peru, Harry Partridge, Minh van Canh and the sound man, Ken O'Hara, had been joined on Saturday by Rita Abrams and the videotape editor, Bob Watson. Their first combined report was transmitted by satellite from Lima on Monday and led CBA's National Evening News that night.

Partridge's editorial theme had been the drastically deteriorating situation in Peru—economically and in terms of law and order. Sound bites from the Peruvian radio man, Sergio Hurtado, and Manuel León Seminario, owner-editor of *Escena,* made those points, supplemented by pictures of an angry mob from the *barridas* looting a food store and defying police.

In the words of Hurtado, "This was a democratic land full of promise, but we are now on the same grievous voyage of self-destruction as Nicaragua, El Salvador, Venezuela, Colombia and Argentina."

And Seminario had posed the unanswerable question: "What is it in us Latin Americans that makes us chronically incapable of stable government?" He continued, "We are such a sorry contrast to our *prudente* neighbors in the north. While Canada and the U.S. achieve an enlightened concord on free trade, making their nations sturdy and stable for generations to come, we in the south still polarize and slaughter."

In an attempt to balance the report, Rita— at Partridge's suggestion—tried to arrange a recorded interview with President Castañeda. It was refused. Instead, a second-line government minister, Eduardo Loayza, was made available and had taken a placebo line. The problems of Peru were temporary, he claimed through an interpreter. The country's bankrupt economy would be turned around. The power of Sendero Luminoso was diminishing, not growing. And the American prisoners of Sendero would be found and released soon by Peru's military or police.

Loayza's remarks were included in Monday's evening news report, but the man and his message were—as Rita expressed it—"like fly piss in the wind."

Communication between the CBA Lima contingent and CBA New York was frequent, with Partridge and Rita being filled in on stateside developments, including the videotape of Jessica, Sendero's demands and the Elliott snafu. The last left Partridge incredulous and angry that the clandestine approach he was attempting should have been so crudely undermined. Nonetheless, he resolved to continue the tactics he had begun.

It was probably because the initiative within CBA had passed from New York to Lima that at Tuesday's task force meeting so much attention was paid to the relatively minor matter of the classified advertising search.

"I brought it up," Norm Jaeger told Les Chippingham, who had joined the meeting late, "because you were worried about the cost, which is still substantial, though we can stop it any time."

"Touché!" Chippingham acknowledged. "But the rest of you were proven right, so let's make a decision on the merits." What he did not say was that the National Evening News ratings were now so extraordinarily high that being over budget had ceased to alarm him. If Margot Lloyd-Mason made a fuss, he would simply point to the fact that under no other news president had the broadcast audience been as large.

Chippingham asked Teddy Cooper, "What's your feeling, Teddy, about dropping that advertising search?"

From across the conference-room table, the young English researcher grinned. "Smashin' idea as it turned out, eh?"

"Yes. That's why I'm asking you."

"Still could be something comin' out—like turning over cards still hopin' for an ace, then finding one. Not as likely, though. If we drop it, I'll hafta come up with another brilliant notion."

"Which he quite likely will," Norm Jaeger commented—a view one hundred and eighty degrees removed from his original assessment of the pushy Teddy Cooper.

In the end it was decided to terminate the advertising search the following day.

Then, three hours later, as if fate had kittenishly decided to intervene, a breakthrough in the search occurred—the kind hoped for from the beginning.

At 2 P.M. in the task force conference room, Teddy Cooper took a phone call from Jonathan Mony.

Mony, by now, had slipped into a supervisory role and for the past few days had been overseeing all the temporary researchers. An assumption was growing that when Mony's present work concluded, a permanent niche would be offered him in the News Division. On the phone he sounded breathless and excited.

"I think we found it. Can you, and maybe Mr. Kettering, come out?"

"Found what, and where are you?"

"The place the kidnappers used, I'm almost sure. And I'm at Hackensack, New Jersey. There was an ad in the *Record*—that's the local paper—and we followed through."

"Hold it!" Cooper said. Don Kettering and Norman Jaeger had just walked in together. Cooper removed the phone from his ear and waved it. "It's Jonathan. He thinks he found Snatchers City."

A speakerphone was on a desk nearby. Jaeger pressed a button and the speaker came alive.

"Okay, Jonathan," Kettering said. "Tell us what you have."

Mony's amplified voice answered, "There was a classified ad in the *Record*. Seemed to fit what we were looking for. Shall I read it?"

"Go ahead."

The trio in the conference room heard a rustling of paper as Mony continued his report.

The advertisement, they learned, had appeared on August 10—a month and four days before the Sloane kidnap, which put it within

the estimated time frame of the pre-kidnap surveillance.

HACKENSACK—SALE OR LEASE

*Large traditional house in 3 acres, 6 bed, servant
quarters, suit multi-family or convert to nursing
home, etc. Fireplaces, oil heat, air cond. Spacious
outbuildings good for vehicles, workshops, stables.
Secluded location, privacy. Attractive price or
lease. Terms allow for some repairs needed.*
PRANDUS AND PAIGE
Brokers/Developers

One of the young women researchers discovered the ad, buried among many others—the
Record had one of the largest real estate advertising sections in the region. On reading it, she
had contacted Jonathan Mony who was in the
area and now carried a CBA paging device. He
had joined her at the newspaper's business office
from where Mony phoned the real estate brokers, Prandus & Paige.

Initially he had not been optimistic. During
the preceding two weeks there had been many
such alerts. But after quick excitements and fol-
low-throughs including visits to "possible"
premises, all had proven worthless. The likelihood that this latest scrutiny would be different
did not seem great.

In this case, as with most others, on learning

that CBA was making the inquiry, the brokers were cooperative and supplied an address. What was different was some added information: First, that almost at once after the ad appeared, a one-year lease had been taken on the property with full payment in advance. Second: A recent check revealed the house and buildings to be deserted, the lessees apparently having left.

An official at the brokerage firm told Mony, "The tenants were there just over a month, and we haven't heard from them so we have no idea if they're coming back. Right now we're not sure what to do, and if you have any contact with the people, we'd appreciate hearing."

Mony, his interest quickening, promised to keep the real estate firm informed. He then visited the property with the woman researcher.

"I know we weren't supposed to follow up directly," he told Cooper and the others on the phone. "But that was before we heard the kidnappers were in Peru. Anyway, we've found some things we think are important and which made me decide to call you."

He was telephoning from a café, he reported, about a mile from the empty house.

"First, give us the directions," Kettering instructed. "Then go back to the house and wait. We'll be there as fast as we can."

An hour later a CBA courier car pulled into the Hackensack property, bringing Don Kettering, Norm Jaeger, Teddy Cooper and a two-man camera crew.

As Kettering stepped from the car, he surveyed the old decaying buildings and commented, "I can see why that ad mentioned 'repairs needed.'"

Cooper folded a map he had been studying. "This place is twenty-five miles from Larchmont. About what we figured."

"*You* figured," Jaeger said.

Mony introduced the young woman researcher, Cokie Vale, a petite redhead. Cooper recognized her instantly. When the temporary researchers first assembled she had asked whether, at the stage they appeared to have reached now, a camera crew would be on hand.

"I remember your question," he told her and gestured to the crew assembling its equipment. "As you can see, the answer's 'yes.'"

She flashed him a dazzling smile.

"The first thing you should see," Jonathan Mony said, "is on the second floor of the house."

As the others followed, he led the way into the dilapidated main house and up a wide, curving stairway. Near the head of the stairs he opened a door and stood back while others filed in.

The room they entered was in total contrast to what had been seen elsewhere. It was clean, painted a hygienic white and with new pale-green linoleum covering the floor. Mony switched on overhead fluorescent lights, also obviously new, revealing two hospital cots, both with side restraining rails and straps. In contrast to the cots was a narrow, battered metal bed; it, too, had straps attached.

Pointing to the bed, Kettering said, "It looks as if that was an afterthought. The whole place is like a first-aid station."

Jaeger nodded. "Or set up to handle three doped people, one of them unexpected."

Mony opened a cupboard door. "Whoever was here didn't bother to clear out all this stuff before they left."

Facing them were some assorted medical supplies—hypodermic needles, bandages, rolls of cotton batting, gauze pads and two pharmaceutical containers, both unopened.

Jaeger picked up one of the containers and read aloud, " 'Diprivan . . . propofol'—that's the generic name." He peered at fine print on the label. "It says 'for intravenous anesthesia.' " As he and Kettering looked at each other, "It all fits. Doesn't seem much doubt."

"Can I show you downstairs?" Mony prompted.

"Go ahead," Kettering told him. "You're the one who's had time to look around."

Entering a small outbuilding, Mony pointed to an iron stove, choked with ashes. "Somebody did a lot of burning here. Didn't get everything, though." He picked up a partially burned magazine, the name *Caretas* visible.

"That magazine's Peruvian," Jaeger said. "I know it well."

They moved to a larger building. Inside, it was obvious it had been a paint shop. Virtually no attempt had been made to clear the building. Cans of paint—some partially used, others unopened, still remained. Most were labeled AUTO LACQUER.

Teddy Cooper was looking at colors. "Remember when we talked to people who saw the Sloane surveillance? Some reported seeing a green car, yet none of the kinds of motors they mentioned were manufactured in that color. Well, here's green enamel—and yellow too."

"This is the place," Jaeger said. "It has to be."

Kettering nodded. "I agree. So let's get to work. We'll use this on the news tonight."

"There *is* one more thing," Mony said. "Something Cokie spotted outside."

This time the attractive redhead took center stage. She led the group to a cluster of trees away from the house and outbuildings and explained, "Somebody's been digging here—not long ago. Afterward they tried to level the ground but didn't manage it. The grass hasn't grown back either."

Cooper said, "It looks as if earth was taken out and something buried, which is why it hasn't packed down."

Among the group, eyes shifted back and forth. Cooper now seemed uncertain, Jaeger looked away. If something had been buried— what? A body, or bodies? Everyone present knew that it was possible.

Jaeger said doubtfully, "We'll have to call the FBI about this place. Maybe we should wait and let them . . ."

Behind the remark was the fact that after Friday's National Evening News, the FBI Director in Washington had telephoned Margot Lloyd-Mason and strongly protested CBA's failure to inform the FBI immediately of new developments. Surprising some at CBA, the network president did not take the complaint too seriously, perhaps believing the organization could withstand any government pressure and was unlikely to be charged in court. She merely apprised Les Chippingham of the call. The news president, in turn, cautioned the task force to keep law enforcement authorities informed unless there was some compelling reason not to do so.

Obviously, because physical evidence was involved at the Hackensack house, the FBI must be advised of the discovery—certainly before broadcast time tonight.

"Sure we'll tell the FBI," Kettering said. "But first I'd like to take a look at what's under that ground, if anything."

"There are some shovels in the furnace room," Mony said.

"Get them," Kettering told him. "We're all healthy. Let's start digging."

A short time later it became evident that what they were opening was not a grave. Instead it was a repository of discarded items left by the property's recent occupants and presumably intended to stay hidden. Some things were innocuous—food supplies, clothing, toilet objects, newspapers. Others were more significant —additional medical supplies, maps, some Spanish-language paperback books and automotive tools.

"We know they had a fleet of trucks and cars," Jaeger said. "Maybe the FBI will find out what they did with them—if it matters at this point."

"I don't think any of this matters right now," Kettering ruled. "Let's quit."

During the digging, videotaping had been started—initially a sound bite by Cokie Vale describing her search of classified advertising and how it led to the Hackensack house. On camera she was personable, expressed herself clearly and was economical with words. It would be her first appearance on television, she acknowledged afterward. Those watching had an instinct it would not be her last.

Jonathan Mony, it was felt, had earned some camera exposure too and repeated his showing of the upstairs room where the kidnapped trio had almost certainly been held. He also was effective.

"If this endeavor's done nothing else," Jaeger commented to Don Kettering, "it's brought us some new talent."

Mony, having returned from the house, was down in the excavated hole and had resumed digging when Kettering made the decision to quit. About to climb out, Mony felt his foot touch something solid and probed with his shovel. A moment later he had pulled out an object and called, "Hey, look at this!"

It was a cellular phone in a canvas outer cover.

Passing up the phone to Cooper, Mony said, "I think there's another underneath."

Not only was there another, but four more after that. Soon the six were laid out, side by side.

"The people who used this place weren't short of money," Cokie observed.

"Chances are it was drug money; anyway, they had plenty," Don Kettering told her. He regarded the phones thoughtfully. "But maybe —just maybe we're getting somewhere."

Jaeger asked, "Are records kept of all cellular phone calls?"

"Sure are." Kettering, who as business correspondent had recently done a news feature on the booming cellular phone market, answered confidently. "There are also lots of other records including a regular phone user's name and billing address. For these the gang needed a local accomplice." He turned to Cooper. "Teddy, on each phone there'll be an area code followed by a regular number, just as on a house or office line."

"I'm tuned in," Cooper said. "You'd like me to make a list?"

"Please!"

While Cooper worked, they continued videotaping the house and buildings. In a correspondent's standup, Kettering said:

> *"Some may believe discovery of the abandoned American base of the kidnappers is, at this point, too little too late. That may be true. But meanwhile the FBI and others will sift evidence found here while the world watches anxiously, continuing to hope.*

*"Don Kettering, CBA News, Hackensack,
New Jersey."*

Before leaving, they called in the local police, asking them to inform the FBI.

Even before the National Evening News
went on the air, Kettering had telephoned a
friend high in NYNEX Corporation, operators
of the New York and New Jersey telephone systems. Holding in his hand the list of numbers
compiled by Teddy Cooper, Kettering explained
what he needed—the name and address of the
person or persons to whom the six telephones
were registered, plus a list of all calls made to or
from those numbers during the past two
months.

"You realize, of course," his friend—an executive vice president—informed him, "that not
only would giving you that information be a
violation of privacy, but I would be acting illegally and could lose my job. Now, if you were
an investigative agency with a warrant—"

"I'm not and I can't be," Kettering replied.
"However, it's a safe bet the FBI will be asking
for the same information tomorrow and they'll
have one. All I want are those answers first."

"Oh my god! How did I get mixed up with a
character like you?"

"Since you ask, I remember your wanting a

favor from CBA once or twice and I delivered. Come on! We've trusted each other since business school and never regretted it."

At the other end, a sigh. "Give me the damn numbers."

After Kettering had recited the list, his friend continued, "You said the FBI tomorrow. I suppose that means you need to know tonight."

"Yes, but any time this side of midnight. You can call me at home. You have the number?"

"Unfortunately, yes."

The call came at 10:45 P.M., just after Don Kettering arrived at his East Seventy-seventh Street apartment, having stayed late at CBA. His wife, Aimée, answered, then handed him the phone.

"I saw your news this evening," his NYNEX friend said. "I presume those cellular numbers you gave me are those used by the kidnappers."

"It looks that way," Kettering acknowledged.

"In that case, I wish I had more for you. There isn't a lot. First, the phones are all registered to a Helga Efferen. I have an address."

"I doubt if it's current. The lady's dead. Murdered. I hope she didn't owe you money."

"Jesus! You news guys are cold-blooded."
After a pause, the NYNEX man went on,
"About the money, it's actually the reverse.
Right after numbers were issued for those
phones, someone made a deposit of five hundred dollars for each account—three thousand
dollars in all. We didn't ask for it, but it went on
the books as a credit."

Kettering said, "I imagine the people using
the phones didn't want anyone sending bills or
asking awkward questions until they were safely
out of the country."

"Well, for whatever reason, most of the
money's still there. Less than a third was used
and that's because, with one exception, all calls
were solely between the six phones and not to
other numbers. Local interphone calls get
charged, but not all that heavily."

"Everything points to the kidnappers' organization and discipline," Kettering affirmed.
"But you said there was an exception."

"Yes—on September 13, an international di-
rect-dial call to Peru."

"That's the day before the kidnap. Do you
have a number?"

"Of course. It was 011—that's the international access code—51, which is Peru, then 14-
28-9427. My people tell me that '14' is Lima.
Exactly where is something you'll have to find
out."

"I'm sure we will. And thanks!"

"I hope some of that helps. Good luck!"

Moments later, after consulting a notebook, Kettering tapped out a number for another call: 011-51-14-44-1212.

When a voice answered, *"Buenas tardes, Cesar's Hotel,"* Kettering requested, "Mr. Harry Partridge, *por favor."*

8

It had been a discouraging day for Harry Partridge. He was tired and, in his hotel suite, had gone to bed shortly before ten o'clock. But his thoughts were still churning. He was brooding on Peru.

The whole country, he thought, was a paradox—a conflicting mixture of military despotism and free democracy. In much of the republic's remoter regions the military and so-called anti-terrorist police ruled with steel fists and frequent disregard of law. They were apt to kill wantonly, afterward labeling their victims "rebels," even when they were not—as independent inquiry often showed.

A U.S. human rights organization, Americas Watch, had done a creditable job, Partridge believed, in seeking out and recording what it called "a cascade of extrajudicial executions, arbitrary arrests, disappearances and torture," all "central features" in the government's counterinsurgency campaign.

On the other hand, Americas Watch did not spare the rebels. In a recently published report, open beside the bed, it said Sendero Luminoso "systematically murders defenseless people, places explosives that endanger the lives of innocent bystanders and attacks military targets without minimizing the risk to the civilian population"—all "violations of the most fundamental rules of international humanitarian law."

As to the country generally, "Peru now has the sad privilege to be counted among the most violent and dangerous places in South America."

An inescapable conclusion, confirmed by other sources, was that little difference existed between rebel and government forces when it came to random slaughter and other assorted savagery.

Yet, at the same time, strong democratic elements existed in Peru—more real than mere façades, a word sometimes used by critics. Freedom of the press was one, a tradition seemingly ingrained. It was that same freedom which allowed Partridge and other foreign reporters to travel, question, probe, then report however they decided, without fear of expulsion or reprisal. True, there had been exceptions to the principle but so far they were rare and isolated.

Partridge had come close to that subject today during an interview with General Raúl Ortiz, chief of anti-terrorism police. "Does it not concern you," he had asked the erect, unsmiling figure in plain clothes, "that there are so many responsible reports of your men being guilty of brutality and illegal executions?"

"It would concern me more," Ortiz replied in a half-contemptuous tone, "if my men were the ones executed—as they would be if they did not defend themselves from those terrorists which you and others seem to care so much about. As to the untrue reports, if our government tried to suppress them, people like you would raise great howls and keep repeating them. Thus a one-day news trifle, forgotten twenty-four hours later, is usually preferable."

Partridge had requested the interview with Ortiz, believing he should cover the ground, though doubting that much would be gained. Through the Ministry of the Interior the meeting was arranged promptly, though a request to bring a camera crew was denied. Also, when Partridge was searched before being allowed to enter the police general's office, a minitape recorder in his pocket, which he had intended to ask permission to use, was removed outside. Nothing was said, though, about the talk being off the record and the general made no objection to his visitor's taking notes.

General Ortiz's unpretentious wood-paneled office was one of a warren of similar offices in an old, massive raw-cement building in downtown Lima. High walls surrounded the structure, half of which had once been a prison. Getting inside had entailed clearance by a succession of suspicious guards; then, walking across a courtyard within the walls, Partridge had passed rows of armored personnel carriers, as well as trucks with anti-riot water cannon. While talking with the general, Partridge was aware that beneath them in the building's basement were cell blocks where prisoners were often held for two weeks without any outside contact, and other cells where interrogation and torture regularly took place.

At the outset of the Ortiz interview, Partridge asked the question uppermost in his mind: whether the anti-terrorism police had any idea where the three Sloane kidnap victims were being held.

"I thought you might have come to tell *me* that, judging by the many people you have seen since coming here," the General responded. It was an admission and perhaps a not-so-subtle warning, Partridge thought, that his movements were being watched. He guessed, too, that CBA's satellite transmissions to New York, as well as those of other U.S. networks were being monitored and recorded by the Peruvian Government, press freedom notwithstanding.

When Partridge declared he had no information about the location of the American captives despite his efforts, Ortiz said, "Then you are aware how devious and secretive those enemies of the state, Sendero Luminoso, can be. Also that this is a country far different from your own, with vast spaces where it is possible to hide armies. But, yes, we have ideas as to areas where your friends might be and our forces are searching those."

"Will you tell me which areas?" Partridge asked.

"I do not believe that would be wise. In any case it would not be possible to go there yourself. Or do you, perhaps, have some such plan?"

Although Partridge did have a plan, he replied negatively.

The remainder of the interview went much the same way, neither participant trusting the other and playing cat-and-mouse, attempting to obtain information without revealing all of his own. In the end neither succeeded, though in a summary for the National Evening News, Partridge did use two quotes from General Ortiz—

the one about Peru's "vast spaces where it is possible to hide armies" and the cynical observation that alleged human rights violations were "a one-day news trifle, forgotten twenty-four hours later."

Since there was no recording, New York used both quotes in print on-screen, beneath a still photo of the general.

Partridge did not, however, regard his visit as productive.

More satisfying was an interview later in the day with Cesar Acevedo, another longtime friend of Partridge's and a lay leader of the Catholic Church. They met in a private office at the rear of the Archbishop's Palace on the Plaza de Armas, official center of the city.

Acevedo, a small, fast-talking, intense person in his fifties, had deep religious convictions and was a theological scholar. He was involved full-time with church administration and had considerable authority, though he had never taken the ultimate step of becoming a priest. If he had, friends were apt to say, by now he would be a bishop at the very least, and eventually a cardinal.

Cesar Acevedo had never married, though he was a prominent figure socially in Lima.

Partridge liked Acevedo because he was always what he appeared to be, as well as unassuming and totally honest. On an earlier occasion when Partridge asked why he had never entered the priesthood, he replied, "Profoundly as I love God and Jesus Christ, I have never felt willing to surrender my intellectual right to be a skeptic, should that ever happen, though I pray it never will. But if I became a priest I would have surrendered that right. As a young man, and even now, I could never quite bring myself to do it."

Acevedo was executive secretary of the Catholic Social Action Commission and was involved with outreach programs which brought medical help to remote parts of the country where no doctors or nurses were regularly available.

"I believe," Partridge asked early in their meeting, "that from time to time you have to deal with Sendero Luminoso."

Acevedo smiled. " 'Have to deal' is correct. The Church does not, of course, approve of Sendero—either its objectives or methods. But as a practical matter a relationship exists, though a peculiar one."

For reasons of its own, the lay leader explained, Sendero Luminoso did not like antagonizing the Church and rarely attacked it as an institution. Yet the rebel group did not trust individual Church officials, and when some anti-government action or other insurrection was intended, the rebels wanted priests and other church workers out of the area so they could not witness it.

"They will simply tell a priest or our social workers, 'Get out of here! We don't want you around! You will be told when you can return.'"

"And your priests obey that kind of order?"

Acevedo sighed. "It does not sound admirable, does it? But usually yes, because there is little choice. If the order is disobeyed Sendero will not hesitate to kill. A live priest can go back eventually. A dead priest cannot."

A sudden thought occurred to Partridge. "Are there any places, right at this moment, where your people have been told to leave, where Sendero Luminoso doesn't want outside attention?"

"There is one such area and it is creating a considerable problem for us. Come! I will show you on the map." They walked to a wall where, under a plastic cover with crayon markings, a large map of Peru was mounted.

"It's this entire area right here." Acevedo pointed to a section of San Martín Province, ringed in red. "Until about three weeks ago we had a strong medical team in here, performing an assistance program we carry out each year. A lot of what they do is vaccinate and inoculate children. It's important because the area is part of the Selva, where jungle diseases abound and can be fatal. Anyway, about three weeks ago Sendero Luminoso, which controls the area, insisted that our people leave. They protested, but they had to go. Now we want to get our medics back in. Sendero says no."

Partridge studied the encircled section. He had hoped it would be small. Instead it was depressingly large. He read place names, all far apart: Tocache, Uchiza, Sion, Nueva Esperanza, Pachiza. Without much hope he wrote them down. In the unlikely event of the captives being at one of those places, it would do no good to enter the area without knowing which. Effecting a rescue anywhere would be difficult, perhaps impossible. The only slim chance would be total surprise.

"I suspect I know what you are thinking," Acevedo said. "You are wondering if your kidnapped friends are somewhere in that circle."

Partridge nodded without speaking.

"I do not believe so. If it were the case I think there would have been some rumor. I have heard none. But our church has a network of contacts. I will send out word and report to you if anything is learned."

It was the best he could hope for, Partridge realized. But time, he knew, was running out and he was no closer to knowing the whereabouts of the imprisoned Sloane trio than when he had arrived.

The thought had depressed him while in the Archbishop's Palace. Now, in his hotel room, remembering that and the other events of the day, he had a sense of frustration and failure at his lack of progress.

Abruptly, the bedside telephone rang.

"Harry, is that you?" Partridge recognized Don Kettering's voice.

They exchanged greetings, then Kettering said, "Some things have happened that I thought you ought to know about."

Rita, also in Cesar's Hotel, answered her room phone on the second ring.

"I've just had a call from New York," Partridge said. He repeated what Don Kettering had told him about discovery of the Hackensack house and the cellular phones, adding, "Don gave me a Lima number that was called. I want to find out whose it is and where."

"Give it to me," Rita said.

He repeated it: 28-9427.

"I'll try to get that Entel guy, Victor Velasco, and start him working on it. Call you back if there's any news."

She did in fifteen minutes. "I managed to get Velasco at home. He says it isn't something his department handles and he may have a little trouble getting the information, but thinks he can have it by morning."

"Thanks," Partridge said and, soon after, was asleep.

9

It was not until midafternoon on Wednesday that the Lima telephone number relayed through Don Kettering was identified. Entel Peru's international manager was apologetic about the delay. "It is, of course, restricted data," Victor Velasco explained to Partridge and Rita, who were in CBA's Entel editing booth where they had been working with the editor, Bob Watson, on another news spot for New York.

"I had trouble persuading one of my colleagues to release the information," Velasco continued, "but eventually I succeeded."

"With money?" Rita asked and, when he nodded, she said, "We'll reimburse you."

A sheet torn from a memo pad contained the information: *Calderón, G.—547 Huancavelica Street, 10F.*

"We need Fernández," Partridge said.

"He's on his way here," Rita informed him, and the swarthy, energetic stringer-fixer arrived within the next few minutes. He had continued working with Partridge since his and Minh Van Canh's arrival at Lima airport and now assisted Rita in a variety of ways.

Told about the Huancavelica Street address and why it might be important, Fernández Pabur nodded briskly. "I know it. An old apartment building near the intersection with Avenida Tacna, and not what you would call" —he struggled for an English word—"palatial."

"Whatever it is," Partridge told him, "I want to go there now." He turned to Rita. "I'd like you, Minh and Ken to come along, but first let me go inside alone to see what I can find out."

"Not alone," Fernández objected. "You would be attacked and robbed, maybe worse. I will be with you and so will Tomás."

Tomás, they had discovered, was the name of the burly, taciturn bodyguard.

The station wagon Fernández had hired, which they now used regularly, was waiting outside the Entel building. Seven people including the driver made it crowded, but the journey took only ten minutes. "There is the place," Fernández said, pointing out of the window.

Avenida Tacna was a wide, heavily traveled

thoroughfare, Huancavelica Street crossing it at right angles. The district, while not as grim as the *barriadas,* had clearly fallen on bad days. Number 547 Huancavelica was a large, drab building with peeling paint and chipped masonry. A group of men, some seated on ledges near the entrance, others standing idly around, watched while Partridge, Fernández and Tomás stepped out of the station wagon, leaving Rita, Minh Van Canh and the sound man, Ken O'Hara, to wait with the driver.

Aware of unfriendly, calculating expressions among the onlookers, Partridge was glad of Fernández's insistence that he not go inside alone.

Within the building an odor of urine and general decay assaulted them. Garbage was strewn on the floor. Predictably, the elevator wasn't working so the men had no choice but to climb nine flights of grimy cement stairs.

Apartment F was at the end of an uncarpeted, gloomy corridor. At the plain slab door Partridge knocked. He could hear movement inside but no one came to the door and he knocked again. This time the door opened two or three inches only, halted by an inside chain. Simultaneously a woman's high-pitched voice let loose a tirade in Spanish—her speech too fast for Partridge to follow, though he caught the words, *"¡animales! . . . ¡asesinos! . . . ¡diablos!"*

He felt a hand touch his arm as Fernández's heavyset figure moved forward. With his mouth close to the opening, Fernández spoke equally fast, but in reasonable, soothing tones. As he continued, the voice from inside faltered and stopped, then the chain was released and the door opened.

The woman standing before them was probably around age sixty. Long ago she might have been beautiful, but time and hard living had made her blowsy and coarse, her skin blotchy, her hair a mixture of colors and unkempt. Beneath plucked, penciled eyebrows her eyes were red and swollen from crying and her heavy makeup was a mess. Fernández walked in past her and the others followed. After a moment she closed the door, apparently reassured.

Partridge glanced around quickly. The room they had entered was small and simply furnished with some wooden chairs, a sofa with worn upholstery, a plain, cluttered table and a bookcase roughly fashioned out of bricks and planks. Surprisingly, the bookcase was full, mainly with heavy volumes.

Fernández turned to Partridge. "It seems that just a few hours ago the man she lived with here was killed—murdered. She was out and came back to find him dead; the police have taken the body. She thought we were the people who killed him, come back to finish her too. I convinced her we are friends." He spoke to the woman again and her eyes moved to Partridge.

Partridge assured her, "We are truly sorry to hear of your friend's death. Have you any idea who killed him?"

The woman shook her head and murmured something. Fernández said, "She speaks very little English," and translated for her. *"Lo sentimos mucho la muerte de su amigo. ¿Sabe Ud. quién lo mató?"*

The woman nodded energetically, mouthing a stream of words ending with *"Sendero Luminoso."*

It confirmed what Partridge had feared. The person they had hoped to see—whoever he was —had connections to Sendero, but was now beyond reach. The question remained: Did this woman know anything about the kidnap victims? It seemed unlikely.

She spoke again in Spanish, less rapidly, and this time Partridge understood. "Yes," he said to Fernández, "we would like to sit down, and tell her I would be grateful if she will answer some questions."

Fernández repeated the request and the woman replied, after which he translated. "She says yes, if she can. I have told her who you are and, by the way, her name is Dolores. She also asks if you would like a drink."

"No, gracias," Partridge said, at which

Dolores nodded and went to a shelf, clearly intending to get a drink for herself. But when she lifted a gin bottle she saw that it was empty. She seemed about to cry again, then murmured something before sitting down.

Fernández reported, "She says she doesn't know how she will live. She has no money."

Partridge said directly to Dolores, *"Le daré dinero si Ud. tiene la información que estoy buscando."*

The mention of money produced another fast exchange between Dolores and Fernández who reported, "She says ask your questions."

Partridge decided not to rely on his own limited Spanish and continued with Fernández translating. Questions and answers went back and forth.

"Your man friend who was killed—what kind of work did he do?"

"He was a doctor. A special doctor."

"You mean a specialist?"

"He put people to sleep."

"An anesthesiologist?"

Dolores shook her head, not understanding. Then she went to a cupboard, groped inside and produced a small, battered suitcase. Opening the case, she removed a file containing papers and leafed through them. Selecting two, she passed them to Partridge. He saw they were medical diplomas.

The first declared that Hartley Harold Gossage, a graduate of Boston University Medical School, was entitled to practice medicine. The second diploma certified that the same Hartley Harold Gossage was "a properly qualified specialist in Anesthesiology."

With a gesture, Partridge asked if he could look at the other papers. Dolores nodded her approval.

Several documents appeared to concern routine medical matters and were of no interest. The third he picked up was a letter on stationery of the Massachusetts Board of Registration in Medicine. Addressed to "H. H. Gossage, M.D.," it began, "You are hereby notified that your license to practice medicine has been revoked for life . . ."

Partridge put the letter down. A picture was becoming clearer. The man who had lived here, reported to have just been murdered, was presumably Gossage, a disgraced, disbarred American anesthesiologist who had some connection with Sendero Luminoso. As to that connection, Partridge reasoned, the kidnap victims had been spirited out of the United States, presumably drugged or otherwise sedated at the time. In fact when he thought about it, yesterday's discoveries at the Hackensack house, described by Don Kettering, confirmed that. It seemed likely, therefore, that the former doctor,

Gossage, had done the sedating. Partridge's face tightened. He wished he had been able to confront the man while he was alive.

The others were watching him. With Fernández's help he resumed the questioning of Dolores.

"You told us Sendero Luminoso murdered your doctor friend. Why do you believe that?"

"Because he worked for those *bastardos.*" A pause, then a recollection. "Sendero had a name for him—Baudelio."

"How did you know this?"

"He told me."

"Did he tell you other things he did for Sendero?"

"Some." A wan smile which quickly disappeared. "When we got drunk together."

"Did you know about a kidnapping? It was in all the newspapers."

Dolores shook her head. "I do not read newspapers. All they print is lies."

"Was Baudelio away from Lima recently?"

A vigorous series of nods. "For a long time. I missed him." A pause, then, "He phoned me from America."

"Yes, we know." Everything was fitting together, Partridge thought. Baudelio had to have been on the kidnap scene. He asked through Fernández, "When did he come back here?"

Dolores considered before answering. "A

week ago. He was glad to be back. He was also afraid he would be killed."

"Did he say why?"

Dolores considered. "I think he overheard something. About him knowing too much." She began to cry. "We had been together a long time. What shall I do?"

There was one important question left. Partridge deliberately hadn't asked it yet and was almost afraid to. "After Baudelio was in America and before returning here, was he somewhere in Peru?"

Dolores nodded affirmatively.

"Did he tell you where that was?"

"Yes. Nueva Esperanza."

Partridge could scarcely believe what so suddenly and unexpectedly had come his way. His hands were shaking as he turned back pages in his notebook—to the interview with Cesar Acevedo and the list of places where Sendero Luminoso had ordered the Catholic medical teams to stay out. A name leaped out at him: *Nueva Esperanza.*

He had it! He knew at last where Jessica, Nicky and Angus Sloane were being held.

He was still first and foremost a TV news correspondent, Partridge reminded himself as he discussed with Rita, Minh and O'Hara the video shots they needed—of Dolores, the apartment, and the building's exterior. They were all in the tenth-floor apartment, Tomás having been sent down to bring the other three from the station wagon.

Partridge wanted close-ups too of the medical diplomas and the Massachusetts letter consigning Gossage-cum-Baudelio to the medical profession's garbage heap. The American ex-doctor might have gone to his grave, but Partridge would make sure the vileness he had done the Sloane family was forever on record.

However, even though Baudelio's apparent role in the kidnapping was important to the full news story, Partridge knew that releasing it now would be a mistake, leading others to the information that his CBA group possessed exclusively. But he wanted the Baudelio segment prepackaged, ready for use at a moment's notice when the proper time came.

Dolores was videotaped in closeup, the sound recording of her voice in Spanish later to be faded out and a translation dubbed in. At the conclusion of her taping Fernández told Partridge, "She is reminding you that you promised her money."

Partridge conferred with Rita who produced a thousand dollars in U.S. fifty-dollar bills. In the circumstances the payment was generous, but Dolores had provided an important break; also Partridge and Rita felt sorry for her and believed her statement that she knew nothing of the kidnap, despite her association with Baudelio.

Rita instructed Fernández, "Please explain it is against CBA policy to pay for a news appearance; therefore the money is for the use of her apartment and the information she gave us." It was a semantic distinction, often used by networks to do exactly what they said they didn't, but New York liked producers to go through the motions.

Judging by Dolores's gratitude, she neither understood nor cared about the explanation. Partridge was sure that as soon as they had gone the empty gin bottle would be quickly replaced.

Now his mind was free to move on to essentials—planning a rescue expedition to Nueva Esperanza as quickly as he could. At the thought of it his excitement rose, the old addiction to danger, guns and battle stirring within him.

10

Crawford Sloane's instinct during every day of waiting was to telephone Harry Partridge in Peru and ask, "Is there anything new?" But he restrained himself, knowing that any breaking news would come to him speedily enough. Also, he realized, it was important to leave Partridge undistracted and free to work in his own way. Sloane still had more faith in Partridge than anyone else who might have been sent on the Peru assignment.

Another reason for holding back was that Harry Partridge had proved to be considerate, calling Sloane at home in Larchmont during some evenings or early mornings to fill him in on progress and background.

It had been several days, though, since the last call from Peru and while disappointed at not hearing, Crawford Sloane assumed there was nothing to report.

He was wrong.

What Sloane did not and could not know was that Partridge had decided all communication between Lima and New York—telephone, satellite or written—was no longer secure. After the interview with General Ortiz, during which the chief of anti-terrorism police made plain that Partridge's movements were being watched, it seemed possible that telephones were tapped and perhaps even mail examined. Satellite transmissions could be viewed by anyone with the right equipment, and using a different phone line than usual carried no guarantee of privacy.

Another reason for caution was that Lima was now crowded with journalists, including TV crews from other networks, all competing in covering the Sloane kidnap story and searching for new leads. So far, Partridge had managed to avoid the media crowd, but because of CBA's successful coverage already, he knew there was interest in where he went and whom he saw.

For all those reasons Partridge decided not to discuss, especially by telephone, his visit to the Huancavelica Street apartment and what he had learned. He ordered the others in the CBA crew to observe the same rule, also cautioning them that the expedition they were planning to Nueva Esperanza must be veiled in total secrecy. Even CBA in New York would have to wait for word of that.

Therefore, on Thursday morning in New York, knowing nothing of the breakthrough in

Lima the day before, Crawford Sloane went to CBA News headquarters, arriving slightly later than usual at 10:55.

A young FBI agent named Ivan Ungar, who had slept at the Larchmont house the night before, accompanied him. The FBI was still guarding against a possible attempt to kidnap Sloane and there were also rumors that anchor people at other networks were being protected too. However, since the original kidnappers had been heard from the twenty-four-hour listening watch on Crawford Sloane's home and office phones had been discontinued.

FBI Special Agent Otis Havelock was still involved with the case, and after Tuesday's discovery of the kidnappers' Hackensack headquarters had taken charge of FBI search efforts there. Another subject of FBI scrutiny, Sloane had learned, was Teterboro Airport because of its closeness to the Hackensack locale. An examination of outgoing flight records was being made, covering the period from immediately after the kidnap until the day it was known that the kidnap victims were in Peru. But progress was slow because of the large number of flight departures during those thirteen days.

At CBA News, as Sloane entered the main-floor lobby, a uniformed security guard gave a casual salute, but there was no sign of a New York City policeman, as there had been for more than a week after the kidnap. Today the usual stream of people was moving in and out of the building and although those entering were cleared at a reception desk, Sloane wondered if CBA security had slipped back into its old, easygoing ways.

From the lobby, accompanied by agent Ungar, he took an elevator to the fourth floor, then walked to his office adjoining the Horseshoe where several people looked up from their work to greet him. Sloane left the door of his office open. Ungar seated himself on a chair outside.

As Sloane hung up the raincoat he had been wearing, he noticed on his desk a white Styrofoam package of the kind used by takeout restaurants. There were several such establishments in the neighborhood which did a brisk business at CBA, delivering snacks or meals in response to telephone calls. Since Sloane had not ordered anything and usually had lunch in the cafeteria, he assumed the delivery was a mistake.

To his surprise, though, he found that the package, tied neatly with white string, had "C. Sloane" written on it. Without much interest, he took scissors from a drawer and snipped the string, then eased the package open. He pulled out some pieces of folded white paper before the contents were revealed.

After several seconds of staring in dazed disbelief, Crawford Sloane screamed—a tortured, earsplitting scream. Heads shot up among those working nearby. FBI agent Ungar leapt from his chair and raced in, drawing a gun as he moved. But Sloane was alone, screaming again and again, staring down at the package, his eyes wide and crazed, his face ashen.

Others jumped up and ran to Sloane's office. Some went inside, a dozen or more blocked the doorway. A woman producer leaned over Sloane's desk and looked into the white box. "Oh, my god!" she uttered, then, feeling sick, went back outside.

Agent Ungar examined the box, saw two human fingers, flecked with dried blood, and, swallowing his revulsion, swiftly took charge. He shouted to those in the office and crowding the doorway, "Everyone out, please!" Even while speaking, he picked up a phone, pressed the "operator" button and demanded, "Security —fast!" When there was an answer, he rapped out, "This is FBI Special Agent Ungar and I am giving you an order. Advise all guards that no one is to leave this building, as of this moment. There will be no exceptions and if anyone resists, use force. After you've given that order, call the city police for help. I am going to the main lobby now. I want someone from Security to meet me there."

While Ungar had been speaking, Sloane collapsed into his chair. As someone said later, "He looked like death."

The executive producer, Chuck Insen, elbowed his way through the growing throng outside and asked, "What's all this about?"

Recognizing him, Ungar gestured to the white box, then instructed, "Nothing in here must be touched. I suggest you take Mr. Sloane somewhere else and lock the door until I come back."

Insen nodded, by then having seen the contents of the box and noting, as had others, that the fingers were small and delicate, clearly those of a child. Turning to face Sloane, he asked the inevitable question with his eyes. Sloane managed to nod and whisper, "Yes."

"Oh, Jesus!" Insen murmured.

Sloane seemed about to collapse. Insen put his arms around him, then still holding the anchorman, eased him from the room. Those at the doorway quickly cleared a path.

Insen and Sloane went to the executive producer's office; on the way, Insen fired orders. He told a secretary, "Lock Mr. Sloane's office and let no one in except that FBI man. Then talk to the switchboard; there's a doctor on call—get him here. Say Mr. Sloane had a bad shock and may need sedation." To a producer, "Tell Don Kettering what's happened and get him up here; we'll need something for the news tonight." And to others, "The rest of you, get back to work."

Insen's office had a large glass window overlooking the Horseshoe, with a venetian blind for privacy when needed. After helping Sloane into a chair, Insen lowered the blind.

Control was coming back to Sloane, though he was leaning forward, his head in his hands. Speaking half to himself, half to Insen, he agonized, "Those people knew about Nicky and the piano. And how did they know? *I let it out! It was me!* At that press session after the kidnap."

Insen said gently, "I remember that, Crawf. But you were answering a question; you didn't bring it up. In any case, who could have foreseen . . ." He stopped, knowing that reasoning at this moment would do no good.

Afterward Insen would say to others, "I have to hand it to Crawf. He has guts. After that experience most people would have been pleading to do exactly what the kidnappers wanted. But right from the beginning Crawf's known we shouldn't, and couldn't, and has never wavered."

There was a soft knock and the secretary came in. "A doctor's on the way," she said.

The temporary ban on people leaving the building was lifted when everyone inside or about to leave was identified and their presence

accounted for. It seemed likely that the package
with the fingers had been left much earlier, and
since restaurant service people came and left
frequently, no one had seen anything unusual.

The FBI began an investigation at nearby
takeout restaurants in an effort to determine
who might have brought the package in, but
nothing resulted. And while CBA Security was
supposed to check all delivery people's identity,
it was established that they did so irregularly,
and even then in a perfunctory way.

Any doubt about the fingers being Nicky's
was quickly dispelled by an FBI check of
Nicky's bedroom in the Sloanes' Larchmont
house. Plenty of fingerprints remained there
and matched those of the two severed fingers in
the package on Crawford Sloane's desk.

In the midst of the general gloom at CBA
News, another significant delivery occurred,
this one to Stonehenge. Early Thursday afternoon a small package found its way to Margot
Lloyd-Mason's office suite. Inside was a videotape cassette sent by Sendero Luminoso.

Because the tape was expected—Thursday
delivery had been stated in Sendero's "The
Shining Time Has Come" demand received six
days earlier—arrangements had been made by
Margot and Les Chippingham for the tape to be
sent immediately by messenger to the CBA

news president. As soon as Chippingham learned of its arrival, he called in Don Kettering and Norman Jaeger and the trio viewed the tape privately in Chippingham's office.

All three noted at once the recording's high quality, both technically and in presentation. The opening titles, beginning with "World Revolution: Sendero Luminoso Shows the Way," were superimposed over the visual background of some of Peru's most breathtaking scenery—the brooding majesty of high Andes mountains and glaciers, Machu Picchu in awesome splendor, the endless miles of green jungle, the arid coastal desert and surging Pacific ocean. It was Jaeger who recognized the majestic music accompanying the opening: Beethoven's Third Symphony, *Eroica*.

"They had production people who know their business," Kettering murmured. "I'd expected something cruder."

"Not surprising, really," Chippingham said. "Peru's no backwater and they have talent there, the best equipment."

"Which Sendero has big bucks to buy," Jaeger added. "Plus their foxy infiltration everywhere."

Even the extremist spiel that followed was largely over kinetic scenes—of rioting in Lima, industrial strikes, clashes between police and protest marchers, the grisly aftermath of attacks on Andes villages by government forces. "We are the world," an unseen commentator expounded, "and the world is ready for a revolutionary explosion."

Featured at length was an interview, stated to be with Abimael Guzmán, Sendero Luminoso's founder and leader. Some uncertainty existed because the camera focused on the back of a seated person. The commentator explained, "Our leader has many enemies who would like to kill him. To show his face would help their vicious aims."

Guzmán's supposed voice began in Spanish, *"Compañeros revolucionarios, nuestro trabajo y objetivo es unir los creyentes en la filosofía de Marx, Lenin, y Mao . . ."* Then the words faded and a new voice continued, "Comrades, we must destroy worldwide a social order that is not fit to be preserved . . ."

"Doesn't Guzmán speak English?" Kettering queried.

Jaeger answered, "Strangely, he's one of the few educated Peruvians who don't."

What followed was predictable and had been spoken by Guzmán many times before. "Revolution is justified because of imperialist exploitation of all poor people in the world." . . . "False reports blame Sendero Luminoso for inhumanity. Sendero is more humane than the superpowers who are willing to destroy

mankind with nuclear arsenals, which our pro-
letariat revolution will ban forever." . . . "The
United States labor movement, an elite bourgeois class, has cheated and sold out American
workers." . . . "Communists in the Soviet
Union are no better than imperialists. The Sovi-
ets have betrayed the Lenin revolution." . . .
"Cuba's Castro is a clown, an imperialist
lackey."

Guzmán's statements were invariably general. Those seeking specifics searched his
speeches and writings in vain.

"If we were running this instead of the evening news," Chippingham commented, "we'd
have lost our audience by now and ratings
would be in the cellar."

The recorded half hour ended with additional Beethoven, some more scenic beauty and
a rallying cry from the commentator, "Long life
to Marxism-Leninism-Maoism, our guiding
doctrine!"

"All right," Chippingham said at the end,
"as we agreed, I'm putting this tape away in my
safe. Only the three of us have viewed it. I suggest we don't discuss with anyone what we've
seen."

Jaeger asked, "You're still going with Karl
Owens's idea—the story that the cassette was
damaged when we received it?"

"For chrissakes! Do we have anything else?

We're certainly not going to use that tape in place of Monday's news."

"I guess we don't have anything else," Jaeger acknowledged.

"As long as we understand," Kettering said, "that our chances of being believed aren't as good now—not after Theo Elliott's screwup with the *Baltimore Star.*"

"Goddamn, I know that!" The news president's voice reflected the strain of the past few days. He glanced at a clock: 3:53. "At four o'clock, Don, break into the network with a bulletin. Say that we've received a tape from the kidnappers, but it's defective and we haven't been able to fix it. Getting a replacement tape to us is now up to Sendero Luminoso."

"Right!"

"Meanwhile," Chippingham continued, "I'll call in press relations and issue a statement for the wire services, urging them to repeat it to Peru. Now let's move it!"

The misinformation issued by CBA News was circulated promptly and widely. Because Peru was one hour behind New York—the U.S. was still on daylight saving time, Peru wasn't—the CBA statement was available in Lima for evening radio and TV news as well as the following day's newspapers.

Also in the day's news, though circulated

earlier, was a report about the discovery of Nicholas Sloane's severed fingers by his distraught father.

In Ayacucho, Sendero Luminoso leaders noted both reports. As to the second, about a damaged tape, they did not believe it. What was needed immediately, they reasoned, was some action more compelling than a small boy's fingers.

11

Afterward, Jessica remembered, she had a sense of foreboding as soon as she awoke that morning in the half-light of dawn. She had been sleepless through much of the night, mentally tormented, doubting that rescue would ever come. Over the past three days her earlier confidence in eventual freedom had ebbed away, though she tried to conceal from Angus and Nicky her diminishing hope. But *was* it likely, she wondered, that in this obscure portion of an alien, faraway land, some friendly force could find and somehow spirit them home? As more days went by, it seemed increasingly doubtful.

What sent Jessica's morale tumbling had been the brutal dismembering of Nicky's right hand. Even if they got out of here, life could never again be the same for Nicky. His youthful, dearest dream, of becoming a piano maestro, was suddenly, irrevocably . . . *so needlessly!* . . . ended. And what other perils, including death perhaps, awaited them in days ahead?

Nicky's fingers had been removed on Tuesday. Today was Friday. Yesterday Nicky had been less in pain, thanks to Socorro who had changed the dressings and bandage daily, but he was silent and brooding, unresponsive to Jessica's attempts to lift him from his deep despair. And there was always the separation between them—the close-spaced bamboo stalks and strong wire screen. Since the night Socorro had allowed Jessica to join Nicky in his cell, the favor had not been repeated, despite Jessica's pleading.

Today, therefore, the immediate future seemed bleak, with little to hope for and everything to dread. As Jessica became fully awake she understood, as she never had before, a Thomas Hood poem learned in childhood which ended:

> *But now, I often wish the night*
> *Had borne my breath away!*

But she knew that if applied to herself, the wish was selfish and defeatist. Despite everything else she must hang on, remaining the strong staff on which Nicky and Angus leaned.

It was soon after those thoughts, and with the arrival of full daylight, that Jessica could hear activity outside and footsteps approaching the prisoners' shack. The first person to enter was Gustavo, leader of the guards, who went directly to Angus's cell and opened it.

Miguel was immediately behind. He was scowling as he, too, moved toward Angus, carrying something Jessica had not seen him with before—an automatic rifle.

The ominous implication was inescapable. At the sight of the powerful, ugly weapon Jessica's heart beat faster and her breath shortened. *Oh, no! Not Angus!*

Gustavo had entered Angus's cell and roughly pulled the old man to his feet. Now Angus's hands were being tied behind him.

Jessica called out, "Listen to me! What are you doing? Why?"

Angus turned his head toward her, "Jessie dear, don't be distressed. There's nothing you can do. These people are barbarians, they don't understand decency or honor . . ."

Jessica saw Miguel tighten his grip on his gun until his knuckles were white. He commanded Gustavo impatiently, *"¡Dese prisa! ¡No pierdas tiempo!"*

Nicky was on his feet. He too had grasped the significance of the automatic rifle and asked, "Mom, what are they going to do to Gramps?"

Not believing her own words, Jessica answered, "I don't know."

Angus, his hands now tied, straightened his body, squared his shoulders and looked over. "We haven't much time. Both of you—stay strong and keep believing! Remember, somewhere out there Crawford is doing everything he can. Help is coming!"

Tears were streaming down Jessica's face. Her voice choked, she managed to call, "Angus, dearest Angus! We love you so much!"

"I love you too, Jessie . . . Nicky!" Gustavo was pushing Angus forward, propelling him from the cell. They all knew now that he was going to his death.

Stumbling, Angus called again, "Nicky, how about a song? Let's try one." Angus's voice lifted.

> *"I'll be seeing you*
> *In all the old familiar places . . ."*

Jessica saw Nicky open his mouth but, both too choked with tears, neither he nor Jessica could join in.

Angus was outside the shack now, beyond their sight. They could still hear his voice, though it was fading.

"That this heart of mine embraces all day through
In that small café . . ."

The voice faded entirely. There was only silence as they waited.

Seconds passed. The wait seemed longer than it was, then the silence was broken by gunfire—four shots, closely spaced. Another brief silence, then a second burst of gunfire, the shots too fast to count.

Outside, at the edge of the jungle, Miguel stood over the dead figure of Angus Sloane.

The first four shots he fired had killed the old man instantly. Then, remembering the insult of last Tuesday—*"¡Maldito hijo de puta!"* —and the contemptuous reference to "barbarians" only moments earlier, Miguel had stepped forward in a rage and emptied another fusillade from his Soviet-made AK-47 into the recumbent body.

He had fulfilled the instructions received from Ayacucho late last night. Gustavo had also been informed of a distasteful chore which was now expected of him and which, with help from others, he could begin.

A light airplane, operating for Sendero Luminoso, was now on its way to a nearby jungle airstrip which could be reached from Nueva Esperanza by boat. Very soon a boat would leave for the airstrip, after which the airplane would transport to Lima the result of Gustavo's work.

Later that same morning in Lima, a car skidded to a halt outside the American Embassy on Avenida Garcilaso de la Vega. A male figure carrying a substantial cardboard box jumped out. The man deposited the box outside the Embassy's protective railings, near a gate, then ran back to the car, which sped away.

A plainclothes guard who had seen it happen sounded an alarm and all exits from the embassy, which was built like a fortress, were temporarily closed. Meanwhile a bomb disposal squad from the Peruvian armed forces was summoned to help.

When tests revealed that the box contained no explosives, it was opened carefully, revealing the bloodstained, decapitated head of an elderly man, probably in his seventies. Alongside the head was a wallet containing a U.S. Social Security card, a Florida driver's license complete with photo, and other documents that identified the partial remains as those of Angus McMullen Sloane.

At the time the Lima incident occurred, a *Chicago Tribune* reporter happened to be inside the embassy. He stayed close to ensuing developments and was the first to file a story that included the victim's name. The *Tribune* report was quickly picked up by wire services, TV, radio and other newspapers, first in the United States, then throughout the world.

12

The plan to attempt a rescue at Nueva Esperanza was complete.

On Friday afternoon, final details were settled, the last equipment assembled. At dawn on Saturday, Partridge and his crew would fly from Lima, bound for the jungle in San Martín Province, near the Huallaga River.

Since late Wednesday, on learning of the prisoners' location, Partridge had fretted impatiently. His first inclination had been to leave at once, but Fernández Pabur's arguments plus his own experience had persuaded him to delay.

"The jungle can be a friend; it can also be an enemy," Fernández pointed out. "You cannot stroll into it, the way you would visit another part of town. We will be in the jungle at least one night, perhaps two, and there are certain things we must have with us for survival. I must also choose our air transport carefully—using someone reliable we can trust. Flying us in, then returning to take us out will require coordination and good timing. We need two days to prepare; even that is barely enough."

The "we" and "our" made clear from the beginning that the resourceful stringer-fixer intended to be part of the expedition. "You will need me," he stated simply. "I have been in the Selva many times. I know its ways." When Partridge felt obliged to point out there would be danger, Pabur shrugged. "All life is a risk. In my country nowadays, getting up in the morning has become one."

Air transport was their principal concern. After disappearing for part of Thursday morning, Fernández returned and, collecting Partridge and Rita, took them to a one-story brick building not far from Lima's Airport. The building contained several small offices. They approached one which had on its door ALSA— AEROLIBERTAD S.A. Fernández entered first and introduced his companions to the owner of the charter flight service, also its chief pilot, Oswaldo Zileri.

Zileri, in his mid to late thirties, was good-looking and clean-cut, with a trim, athletic build. His attitude was guarded, but business-like and direct. He told Partridge, "I understand you intend to pay a surprise visit to Nueva Esperanza, and that is all I need, or wish, to know."

"That's fine," Partridge said, "except we hope to have three more passengers flying back than we will have going out."

"The airplane you are chartering is a Cheyenne II. There will be two pilots and room for seven passengers. How you fill those seven seats is your affair. Now, may we talk money?"

"Talk it with me," Rita said. "What's your price?"

"You will pay in U.S. dollars?" Zileri queried.

Rita nodded.

"Then the regular price on each round trip will be one thousand four hundred dollars. If there is extra time at destination, required for circling, there will be an additional charge. As well, for each landing in the vicinity of Nueva Esperanza—which is drug country controlled by Sendero Luminoso—there will be a special danger fee of five thousand dollars. Before we leave on Saturday, I would like a six-thousand-dollar cash deposit."

"You'll have it," Rita said, "and if you write

all that out, making two copies, I'll sign, and keep one."

"It will be done before you leave. Do you wish to know some details of my air service?"

"I suppose we should," Partridge said politely.

With a touch of pride, Zileri recited an obviously standard spiel. "The Cheyenne II—we have three—is twin-engined and propeller-driven. It is a remarkably reliable aircraft and can land in a short space—important in the jungle. All our pilots, including myself, are American-trained. We know most regions of Peru well, also the local flight controllers, civil and military, and they are used to us. Incidentally, on this flight I will be piloting you myself."

"All that's fine," Partridge acknowledged. "What we also need is some advice."

"Fernández has told me." Zileri went to a chart table where a large-scale map of the southern portion of San Martín Province was spread open. The others joined him.

"I've assumed you will want to land sufficiently far from Nueva Esperanza so your arrival will not be noted."

Partridge nodded. "Assumption right."

"Then, on the outward journey from Lima, I recommend landing here." With a pencil Zileri indicated a point on the map.

"Isn't that a roadway?"

"Yes, the main jungle highway, but there is little traffic, often none. But at several points like this one it's been widened and resurfaced by drug shippers so that planes can land. I've landed there before."

Partridge wondered for what purpose. Conveying drugs, or people who dealt in them? He had heard there were few Peru air operators who were not involved with the drug trade, even if only in peripheral ways.

"Before we go in to land," Zileri continued, "we will make sure the highway is not in use and there is no one on the ground. From that point a rough trail goes close to Nueva Esperanza."

Fernández interjected, "I have a good map where the trail is marked."

"Now about your return with extra passengers," Zileri said. "Fernández and I have discussed this and have a suggested plan."

"Go ahead," Partridge told him.

The discussion continued, decisions and salient facts emerging.

Three possible pickup points existed for the return journey. First, the highway where the initial landing was intended. Second, Sion airstrip which, after leaving Nueva Esperanza, could be reached by river, plus a three-mile overland journey. Third, a very small landing strip, used by drug traffickers and known to few people, midway between the two; that, too, was reached mainly by river.

The reason for options was, as Fernández explained, "We do not know what will happen at Nueva Esperanza, or which way will be clear, or best, for us to leave by."

The airplane making the pickup could easily pass over all three places and respond to a signal from the ground. Partridge's group would carry a flare gun with green and red flares. A green flare would mean: *Land normally, everything is clear;* a red flare: *Land as quickly as possible, we are in danger!*

If close-in rifle or machine-gun fire was observed from the air, it was agreed that the airplane would not land, but would return to Lima.

Since it was not known exactly when the return flight would be required, an airplane would be sent to fly over the area, first on Sunday morning at 8 A.M. and, failing any contact between ground and air, again on Monday at the same time. After that, any action would be decided by Rita who would remain in Lima during the expedition and in touch with New York, an arrangement Partridge considered essential.

At the end of operational planning, a contract was signed by Rita, on behalf of CBA News, and by Oswaldo Zileri, after which Zileri

and the CBA trio formally shook hands. Looking at Partridge directly, the pilot said, "We
shall keep our part of the agreement and do our
best for you."

Partridge had an instinct that he would.

After making the air arrangements, and returning to Cesar's Hotel, Partridge held a meeting in his suite with all the CBA group members to decide who would make the Nueva
Esperanza journey. Three definite selections
were: Partridge; Minh Van Canh, since some visual record was essential; and Fernández Pabur.
Allowing for three extra passengers returning,
this left a fourth place open.

The choice was between Bob Watson, the
TV-video editor; the sound man, Ken O'Hara;
or Tomás, the mostly silent bodyguard.

Fernández favored Tomás and had argued
earlier, "He is strong and can fight." Bob Watson, smoking one of his pungent cigars, urged,
"Take me, Harry! In a brawl, I kin take care of
myself. Found that out in Miami riots." O'Hara
simply said, "I want to go very much."

In the end, Partridge chose O'Hara because
he was a known quantity, had shown he could
keep his head in a tense situation and was resourceful. Also, while they would not be carrying sound equipment—Minh would use a Betacam incorporating sound—Ken O'Hara had an

instinctive way with anything mechanical, an asset that might prove useful.

Partridge left Fernández to organize equipment and under his direction the items were accumulated in the hotel: lightweight hammocks, mosquito netting and repellent, dried foods sufficient for two days, filled water bottles, water sterilizing tablets, machetes, small compasses, binoculars, some plastic sheeting. Since each person would carry his own requirements, using a backpack, a balance was struck between necessity and weight.

Fernández also urged that each carry a gun and Partridge agreed. It was a fact of TV life that correspondents and crews overseas sometimes went armed, though keeping weapons out of sight. Networks neither condoned nor discouraged the practice, leaving it to the judgment of people on the spot. In this case the need seemed overwhelming and was aided by the fact that all four who would be going had had experience with firearms at various points in their lives.

Partridge decided he would stay with his nine-millimeter Browning, with a silencer. He also had a Fairburn commando "killing" knife, given him by a major in the British SAS.

Minh, who would have camera equipment to carry as well as a weapon, wanted something powerful but light; Fernández announced he could obtain an Israeli UZI submachine gun. O'Hara said he would take whatever was available; it turned out to be a U.S. M-16 automatic rifle. Apparently any weaponry was purchasable in Lima, with no questions asked of those who had the money.

Since Wednesday, when he had learned that Nueva Esperanza was the target, Partridge had asked himself: Should he inform the Peruvian authorities, specifically the anti-terrorism police? On Thursday he had even gone back for advice to Sergio Hurtado, the radio broadcaster who had warned him not to seek help from the armed forces and police. During their meeting on Partridge's first day in Peru, Sergio had said: _"Avoid them as allies because they have ceased to be trustworthy, if they ever were. When it comes to murder and mayhem, they are no better than Sendero and certainly as ruthless."_

Speaking in mutually agreed confidence, Partridge informed Sergio of the latest developments and asked if the advice was still the same?

"If anything, stronger," Sergio answered. "In exactly the kind of situation you are looking at, the government forces are notorious for going in with maximum firepower. They take no chances. They wipe out everyone, innocent as well as guilty, and ask questions after. Then, when accused of killing people wrongfully, they'll say, 'How could we tell the difference? It was kill or be killed.' "

Partridge was reminded that General Raúl Ortiz had said much the same thing.

Sergio added, "At the same time, going in as you plan, you are taking your own life in your hands."

"I know," Partridge admitted. "But I see no other way."

It was early afternoon. For the past few minutes, Sergio had been fidgeting with a paper on his desk. Now he asked, "Before you came here, Harry, had you received any bad news? I mean today."

Partridge shook his head.

"Then I'm sorry to give you some." Picking up the paper, Sergio passed it across. "This came in shortly before you arrived."

"This" was a Reuters news dispatch describing the receipt of Nicholas Sloane's fingers at CBA, New York, and his father's broken-hearted grief.

"Oh, Christ!" Partridge was suddenly overwhelmed by anguish and self-reproach. Why, he grieved, had his own planned action not been undertaken sooner?

"I know what you are thinking," Sergio said. "But there is no way you could have prevented this. Not with limited time and the little information that you had."

Which was true, Partridge acknowledged mentally. But he knew that questions about his own pace of progress would haunt him for a long time.

"While you are here, Harry," Sergio was saying, "there's something else. Isn't your company, CBA, owned by Globanic Industries?"

"Yes, it is."

The broadcaster slid a desk drawer open and from it removed several clipped sheets. "I obtain my information from many sources and it may surprise you that one is Sendero Luminoso. They hate me, but use me. Sendero has sympathizers and informers in many places and one of them sent this recently, hoping I would broadcast it."

Partridge accepted the sheets and began reading.

"As you can see," Sergio said, "it purports to be an agreement between Globanic Financial Services—another subsidiary of Globanic Industries—and the Peruvian Government. The agreement is what's known financially as a debt-to-equity swap."

Partridge shook his head. "Not my specialty, I'm afraid."

"But not all that complicated either. As part of the agreement, Globanic will receive enor-

mous amounts of land, including two major resort locations, for what can only be called a
giveaway price. In return, some of Peru's international debt, which has been 'securitized' by
Globanic will be reduced."

"Is it all honest and legal?"

Sergio shrugged. "Let's say it's borderline,
though probably legal. More significant is that
it's an exceedingly rich deal for Globanic, a
very poor one for the people of Peru."

"If you feel that way," Partridge asked,
"why haven't you broadcast it?"

"So far, two reasons. I never accept anything from Sendero at face value, and wanted to
check how accurate the information is. I have,
and it's okay. Another thing: For Globanic to
get anything as super-sweet as this, someone in
government has been paid off handsomely, or
will be. I'm working on that and intend to do a
broadcast next week."

Partridge touched the pages he was holding.
"Any chance I can have a copy?"

"Keep that one. I have another."

During the next day, Friday, Partridge decided one other matter needed checking before
Saturday's departure. Had anyone else received
the telephone number which had led the CBA
group to the Huancavelica Street apartment,
formerly occupied by the ex-doctor known as

Baudelio, and now by Dolores? If so, it would mean that someone else could know the significance of Nueva Esperanza.

As Don Kettering had explained by phone on Wednesday evening, the FBI had access to the Hackensack cellular telephones immediately after their discovery by CBA News. Therefore it seemed likely the FBI would check the calls made on those phones and learn of the Lima number Kettering had given Partridge. From that point, it was possible the FBI had passed the information to the CIA—though not certain, because rivalry between the two agencies was notorious. Alternatively, the FBI might have asked a Peruvian Government department to have the number checked.

At Partridge's request, Fernández paid a second visit to Dolores on Friday afternoon. He found her drunk, but coherent enough to assure him that no one else had been to the apartment making inquiries. So, for whatever reason, the subject of the phone number had not been pursued by anyone but CBA.

Finally, that same afternoon, through Peruvian radio, they learned the grim and tragic news of Angus Sloane's death and discovery of his severed head at the American Embassy in Lima.

Once the news was known, Partridge was quickly on the scene with Minh Van Canh and sent a report via satellite for the National Evening News that evening. By that time, too, other network crews and print-press reporters had arrived, but Partridge managed to avoid conversation with them.

The fact was, the horrible demise of Crawf's father weighed heavily on his conscience, as had Nicky's severed fingers. To the extent that he had come to Peru hoping to save all three hostages, he had already failed, Partridge told himself.

Later, after doing what was needed, he went back to Cesar's Hotel and spent the evening lying on his bed, awake, lonely and dejected.

Next morning, he was up more than an hour before dawn, his intention to complete two tasks. One was to compose a simple, handwritten will, the other to draft a telegram. Soon after, on the way to the airport in the rented station wagon, he had Rita witness the will and left it with her. He also asked her to send the telegram, which was addressed to Oakland, California.

They also discussed the Globanic-Peru debt-to-equity agreement Partridge had learned about from Sergio Hurtado. He told Rita, "When you've read it, I suppose we should let Les Chippingham see this copy. But it has nothing to do with why we're here and I don't plan to use the information, even though Sergio will next week." He smiled, "I suppose that's the least we can do for Globanic since they butter our bread."

The Cheyenne II aircraft took off from Lima in the still, pre-dawn air without incident. Seventy minutes later the plane reached the portion of jungle highway where Partridge, Minh, O'Hara and Fernández were to disembark.

By now there was ample light to see the ground below. The highway was deserted: no cars, trucks or any other sign of human activity. On either side stretched miles of jungle covering the land like a vast green quilt. Turning briefly away from the controls, the pilot, Oswaldo Zileri, called back to his passengers, "We're going in. Be ready to get out fast. I don't want to stay on the ground for a second longer than necessary."

Then, with a steep, fast-descending turn, he lined up over the highway, touched down on its wider portion, and stopped after a surprisingly short landing run. As quickly as they could, the four passengers tumbled out, taking their backpacks and equipment and, moments later, the Cheyenne II taxied into position and took off.

"Let's get under cover fast!" Partridge urged the others, and they headed for the jungle trail.

13

Unknown to Harry Partridge during his crowded day on Friday, a crisis concerning him erupted in New York.

While breakfasting at home on Friday morning, Margot Lloyd-Mason received a telephone message that Theodore Elliott wished to see her "immediately" at Globanic Industries' Pleasantville headquarters. After inquiry, "immediately" translated to a 10 A.M. appointment. It would be the Globanic chairman's first of the day, a secretary at Pleasantville informed Margot.

Margot then called one of her own two secretaries at home and gave instructions to cancel or reschedule all her morning appointments.

She had no idea what Theo Elliott wanted.

At Globanic headquarters, Margot was kept waiting several minutes in the senior executives' elegant outer lounge where, unknowingly, she occupied the same chair used only four days earlier by the *Baltimore Star* reporter Glen Dawson.

When Margot entered the chairman's office, Elliott wasted no time with preliminaries, but demanded, "Why the hell aren't you keeping better control of your goddamned news people in Peru?"

Startled, Margot asked, "What kind of control? We've been getting compliments about our coverage there. And ratings are . . ."

"I'm talking about dismal, depressing, downbeat reports." Elliott slammed a hand heavily on his desk. "Last night I received a call direct from President Castañeda in Lima. He claims everything CBA has been putting out about Peru is negative and damaging. He's mad as hell with your network, and so am I!"

Margot said reasonably, "The other networks and the *New York Times* have been taking much the same line we have, Theo."

"Don't tell me about others! I'm talking about *us!* Besides, President Castañeda seems to think what's happening right now is that CBA sets the pace and others are following. He told me so."

They were both standing. Elliott, glowering, had not asked Margot to sit down. She asked, "Is there anything specific?"

"You're damn right there is!" The Globanic

chairman pointed to a half-dozen videocassettes on his desk. "After the President's call last night I sent one of my people to get tapes of your evening news programs for this week. Now I've seen them all, I can see what Castañeda means; they're full of doom and gloom —how bad things are in Peru. Nothing positive! Nothing saying Peru has a great future ahead, or that it's a wonderful place to go for a vacation, or that those lousy Shining Path rebels will be beaten very soon!"

"There's a strong consensus they won't be, Theo."

Elliott stormed on as if he had not heard. "I can understand why President Castañeda is furious—something that Globanic *can't afford* to have happen, and you know why. I warned you about that, but you obviously weren't listening. Another thing—Fossie Xenos is fuming too. He even thinks you may be jeopardizing, deliberately, his big debt-to-equity deal."

"That's nonsense, and I'm sure you know it. But perhaps we can do something to improve what's happening." Margot was thinking quickly, realizing the situation was more serious than she had thought at first. Her own future in Globanic, she realized, could easily be at stake.

"I'll tell you *exactly* what you'll do." Elliott's voice had become steely. "I want that meddling reporter—Partridge is his name—brought back on the next airplane and fired."

"We can certainly bring him back. I'm less sure about firing him."

"Fired, I said! Are you having trouble hearing this morning, Margot? I want the bastard out of CBA so that, first thing Monday, I can call the President of Peru and say, 'Look! We threw the troublemaker out. We're sorry we sent him to your country. It was a bad mistake, but won't happen again.' "

Foreseeing difficulties for herself at CBA, Margot said, "Theo, I have to point out that Partridge has been with the network a long time. It must be close to twenty-five years and he has a good record."

Elliott permitted himself a sly smile. "Then give the son of a bitch a gold watch. I don't care. Just get rid of him, so I can make that phone call Monday. And I'll warn you about something else, Margot."

"What's that, Theo?"

Elliott retreated to his desk and sat down behind it. He waved Margot to a chair as he said, "The danger of thinking writers or reporters are something special. They aren't, although they sometimes believe they are and get exaggerated ideas about their own importance. The fact is, there's never a shortage of writers. Cut one down, two more spring up like weeds."

Warming to his theme, Elliott continued, "It's people like me and you who really count in this world, Margot. We are the *doers!*—the ones who make things happen every day. That's why we can buy writers whenever we want and— never forget this!—they're two-a-penny, as the English say. So when you're through with some worn-out hack like Partridge, pick up a new one —some kid fresh out of college—the way you would a cabbage."

Margot smiled; it was evident that the worst of her superior's wrath had passed. "It's an interesting point of view."

"Apply it. And one more thing."

"I'm listening."

"Don't think that people at Globanic, including me, are not aware how you and Leon Ironwood and Fossie Xenos are jockeying for position, each of you hoping one day to sit where I am now. Well, I'll tell you Margot, as between you and Fossie—this morning Fossie is several noses out in front."

The chairman waved a hand dismissingly. "That's all. Call me later today when the Peru thing is all wrapped up."

It was late morning when Margot, back in her office at Stonehenge, sent a message to Leslie Chippingham. The news president was to report to her "immediately."

She had not appreciated being sent for this morning, preferring to do the summoning herself. She found herself pleased at the current reversal of that situation.

Something else Margot had not liked was Elliott's reference to Fossie Xenos as being "several noses out in front." If that relative position was true, she thought, she would revise it promptly. Margot had no intention of having her own career plans disrupted by what she was already regarding as a minor organizational issue, capable of being quickly and decisively resolved.

Therefore, when Chippingham appeared shortly after noon she came as speedily to the point as Theo Elliott had with her.

"I don't want any discussion about this," Margot stated. "I'm simply giving you an order."

She continued, "The employment of Harry Partridge is to be terminated at once. I want him out of CBA by tomorrow. I'm aware he has a contract and you'll do whatever we have to under it. Also, he's to be out of Peru, preferably tomorrow but no later than Sunday. If that means chartering a special flight, so be it."

Chippingham stared at her, open-mouthed and unbelieving. At length, having trouble finding words, he said, "You can't be serious!"

Margot told him firmly, "I *am* serious, and I said no discussion."

"The hell with that!" Chippingham's voice was raised emotionally. "I'm not standing by, seeing one of our best correspondents who's served CBA well for twenty-odd years, thrown out without any reason."

"The reason is none of your concern."

"I'm the news president, aren't I? Margot, I appeal to you! What's Harry done, for chrissakes? Is it something bad? If so, I want to know about it."

"If you must know, it's a question of his type of coverage."

"Which is the absolute best! Honest. Knowledgeable. Unprejudiced. Ask anybody!"

"I don't need to. In any case, not everyone agrees with you."

Chippingham regarded her suspiciously. "This is Globanic's work, isn't it?" Intuition came to him. "It's your friend, that cold-blooded tyrant Theodore Elliott!"

"Be careful!" she warned him, and decided the conversation had gone on long enough.

"I don't plan to do any more explaining," Margot said coldly, "but I'll tell you this: If my order has not been carried out by the end of business today, then you are out of a job yourself, and tomorrow I'll appoint someone else acting news president and have them do it."

"You really would, wouldn't you?" He was looking at her with a mixture of wonder and hatred.

"Make no mistake about it—yes. And if you decide to stay employed, report to me by the end of this afternoon that what I wanted has been done. Now get out of here."

After Chippingham had gone, Margot realized with satisfaction that, when necessary, she could be as tough as Theo Elliott.

Back at CBA News headquarters, knowing he was procrastinating, Les Chippingham attended to several routine matters before instructing his secretary, shortly before 3 P.M., that he was not to be disturbed and to hold telephone calls until further notice. He needed time to think.

Closing his office door from inside, he sat down in the conference area away from his desk, facing one of his favorite paintings—a desolate Andrew Wyeth landscape. But today Chippingham barely saw the painting; all he was aware of was the crucial decision he faced.

He knew he had reached a crisis in his life.

If he did as Margot had ordered and fired Harry Partridge without apparent cause, he would forfeit his self-respect. He would have done something shameful and unjust to a decent, highly skilled and respected human being, a friend and colleague, merely to satisfy another person's whim. Who that other person was and whatever was the whim, Chippingham didn't know, though he was sure that he and others would find out eventually. Meanwhile, all he was certain of was that Theodore Elliott was somehow involved—a thrust which, judging by Margot's reaction, had gone home.

Could Chippingham live with having done all that? Applying the standards he had tried to live his life by, he ought not to be able to.

On the other hand—and there *was* another side—if he, Les Chippingham, didn't do it, someone else would. Margot had made that clear. And she would have no trouble finding someone. There were too many ambitious people around, including some in CBA News, for it not to happen.

So Harry Partridge was going down the drain anyway—at least at CBA.

That was an important point: *at CBA.*

When word got around, as it quickly would, that Harry Partridge was leaving CBA and was available, he need not be unemployed for fifteen minutes. Other networks would fall over themselves vying for his services. Harry was a star, a "Big Foot"—with a reputation as a nice guy, too, which didn't harm him.

Nothing, absolutely nothing, would keep Harry Partridge down. In fact, with a new contract at a fresh network he would probably be better off.

But what about a fired and fallen news president? That was a totally different story, and Chippingham knew what he was facing if Margot kept her word—as he knew she would —assuming he did not do as she wished.

As news president, Chippingham had a contract too, and under it would receive roughly a million dollars in severance payments, which sounded a lot but actually wasn't. A substantial amount would disappear in taxes. After that, because he was deeply in debt, his creditors would attach most of the remainder. And whatever was left, the lawyers handling Stasia's divorce would scrutinize covetously. So in the end, if he was left with enough for dinner for two at the Four Seasons, he would be surprised.

Then there was the question of another job. Unlike Partridge, he would not be sought out by other networks. One reason was, there could only be one news president at a network and he had heard no rumor of an opening anywhere else. Apart from that, networks wanted news presidents who were successes, not someone dismissed in doubtful circumstances; there were enough living ex-news presidents around to make that last point clear.

All of which meant that he would have to settle for a lesser job, almost certainly with a lot less money, and Stasia would still want some of that.

The prospect was daunting.

Unless—*unless* he did what Margot wanted.

If he expressed in dramatic terms what he was now doing, Chippingham thought, he was peeling away the layers of his soul, looking inside and not liking what he saw.

Yet a conclusion was inescapable: There were moments in life when self-preservation came first.

I hate to do this to you, Harry, he attested silently, *but I don't have any choice.*

Fifteen minutes later, Chippingham read over the letter he had typed personally on an old, mechanical Underwood he kept—for old times' sake—on a table in his office.

It began:

> *Dear Harry:*
> *It is with great regret I have to inform you that your employment by CBA News is terminated, effective immediately.*
> *Under the terms of your contract with CBA . . .*

Chippingham knew, because he had had occasion to review it recently, that Partridge's contract had a "pay-or-play" clause, which meant that while the network could terminate employment, it was obligated to pay full benefits until the contract's end. In Partridge's case, this was a year away.

Also in the same contract was a "non-compete" clause under which Partridge, in accepting the "pay-or-play" arrangement, agreed not to work for another network for at least six months.

In his letter, Chippingham waived the "non-compete" clause, leaving Partridge with his benefits intact but free to accept other employment at once. Chippingham believed that in the circumstances, it was the least he could do for Harry.

He intended the letter to go by fax machine to Lima. There was a machine in his outer office and he would use it himself. He had decided earlier that he could not bring himself to telephone.

About to sign what he had written, Chippingham heard a knock at his office door and saw the door open. Instinctively, he turned the letter face down.

Crawford Sloane entered. He was holding a press wire printout in his hand. When he spoke, his voice was choked. Tears were coursing down his cheeks.

"Les," Sloane said, "I had to see you. This just came in."

He proffered the printout which Chippingham took and read. It repeated a *Chicago Tribune* report from Lima describing the finding of Angus Sloane's dismembered head.

"Oh, Christ! Crawf, I'm . . ." Unable to finish the words, Chippingham shook his head, then held out his arms and, in a spontaneous gesture, the two embraced.

As they separated, Sloane said, "Don't say anything more. I'm not sure I can handle it. I can't do the news tonight. I told them outside to call Teresa Toy . . ."

"Forget everything, Crawf!" Chippingham told him. "We'll take care of it."

"No!" Sloane shook his head. "There's something else, something I must do. I want a Learjet to Lima. While there's still a chance . . . for Jessica and Nicky . . . I must be there." Sloane paused, struggling for control, then added, "I'll go to Larchmont first, then to Teterboro."

Chippingham said doubtfully, "Are you sure, Crawf? Is this wise?"

"I'm going, Les," Sloane said. "Don't try to stop me. If CBA won't pay for an airplane, I will."

"That won't be necessary. I'll order the Lear," Chippingham said.

Later, he did. It would leave Teterboro that night and be in Peru by morning.

———

Because of the sudden, tragic news of Angus Sloane, Chippingham's letter to Partridge did not get signed and faxed to Lima until late that afternoon. After his secretary had left, Chippingham sent it to a fax number he had for Entel Peru, from where it would be delivered to the CBA booth in the same building. He added a note to the transmission, asking for the letter to be placed in an envelope addressed to "Mr. Harry Partridge" and marked "Personal."

Chippingham had considered informing Crawford Sloane about the letter, then decided Crawf had had all the shocks he could handle in a single week. He knew the letter would outrage Crawf, as well as Partridge, and expected indignant telephone calls with demands for explanations. But that would be another day and Chippingham would have to cope with it as best he could.

Finally, Chippingham telephoned Margot Lloyd-Mason who was still in her office at 6:15 P.M. He told her first, "I have done what you asked," then gave her the news about Crawford Sloane's father.

"I heard," she said, "and I'm sorry. About the other, you cut it fine and I was beginning to think you wouldn't call. But thank you."

14

Away from the highway where the Cheyenne II had landed, the trek through the jungle for Partridge and the other three was difficult and slow.

The trail—if it could be called that—was often overgrown and frequently disappeared entirely. Faced with a dense and tangled mass of vegetation, it was necessary to hack a way through using machetes, hoping for a clearer space beyond. Tall trees formed a canopy above their heads, under an overcast sky which hinted of rain to come. Many trees had grotesquely twisted trunks, thick bark and leathery leaves; Partridge had read somewhere that eight thousand known species of trees existed in Peru. At lower levels, bamboos, ferns, lianas and parasitic plants were everywhere intertwined—the result described by the same source as "green hell."

"Hell" was appropriate today because of the sweltering, steamy heat from which all four men were already suffering. Sweat streamed from every part of them, their condition made worse by swarms of insects. At the beginning they had soaked themselves with mosquito repellent, applying more along the way, but as Ken O'Hara put it, "The little devils seem to like the stuff."

Fortunately, when contact with the trail was reestablished, there were areas where overhead shade from closely growing trees had made ground growth less prolific, therefore it was easier to move ahead. It was obvious that without the trail, progress would be nil.

"This route isn't used much," Fernández pointed out, "and that's to our advantage."

Their objective was to approach Nueva Esperanza, but to stay well clear of it while locating a position on higher ground. From there, hidden by the jungle, they would observe the hamlet, mainly during daylight hours. Then, depending on what was seen and learned, they would devise a plan.

The entire surrounding area for a hundred or more square miles, broken only by the Huallaga River, was dense jungle over an undulating plain. But the large-scale contour map acquired by Fernández showed several hills near their objective, one of which might work as an observation post. Nueva Esperanza itself was about nine miles from their present position—a formidable distance under these conditions.

One thing Partridge had memorized was the second message Jessica managed to convey while making her videotape recording. As reported to him by Crawford Sloane, in a sealed letter which Rita hand-carried to Peru, Jessica had scratched her left earlobe to mean: *Security here is sometimes lax. An attack from outside might succeed.* Sometime soon that information would be put to the test.

Meanwhile, they labored on through the jungle.

It was well into the afternoon, when everyone was near exhaustion, that Fernández warned them Nueva Esperanza might be near. "I think we have covered about seven miles," he said; then cautioned, "we must not be seen. If we hear sounds of anyone coming, we must melt into the jungle quickly."

Looking at dense brush and thorns on either side, Minh Van Canh said, "Makes sense, but let's hope we don't have to."

Soon after Fernández's warning, the going became easier and several other trails crisscrossed their own. Fernández explained that this whole area of slopes and hills was laced with coca fields, which at other times of the year would be bustling with activity. During a four-to-six-month growing season, coca bushes needed only minor care, so most growers lived elsewhere, coming back and occupying hilltop shacks during harvest time.

Using his contour map and compass, Fernández continued to guide the other three; at the same time, the extra effort now required in walking told them they were gradually moving uphill. After another hour they entered a clearing and, beyond it, could see a shack amid jungle trees.

By now it had become evident to Partridge that Fernández knew the area better than he had admitted earlier. When questioned, the stringer-fixer conceded, "I have been here several times before."

Inwardly, Partridge sighed. Was Fernández one more among the army of pseudo-upright people who benefited in back-door, insidious ways from the ubiquitous cocaine trade? Latin America, and the Caribbean especially, were full of such pretenders, many in high places.

As if sensing the thought, Fernández added, "I was here one time for a 'dog-and-pony show' put on by our government for your State Department. There was a visitor—your Attorney General, I think—and the media were brought along. I was one of them."

Despite his reaction a moment earlier, Partridge smiled at the "dog-and-pony show" description. It was one applied contemptuously by reporters when a foreign government staged an anti-drug performance designed to impress a visiting American delegation. Partridge could imagine the scene here: An "invasion" by heli-copter-borne troops who would uproot and burn a few acres of coca plants and destroy a processing lab or two with dynamite. The visi-tors would praise the host government's anti-drug efforts, either not knowing or ignoring the fact that thousands of coca-growing areas and dozens of other labs nearby remained un-touched.

Next day the visitors' photos would be in U.S. newspapers, accompanied by their approv-ing statements, the process repeated on TV. And reporters—knowing they had been part of a charade, but unable to pass it up because oth-ers were recording it—would swallow hard and nurse their shame.

It had happened in Peru, which was neither a dictatorship nor communist but, Partridge thought, might soon be one or the other.

Fernández inspected the clearing they had reached, including the hut, satisfying himself that no one was there. Then he led the way eastward into the jungle again, but only for a little way, the others halting when Fernández cautioned them with a signal. A moment later he parted a cluster of ferns and motioned the others to look. One by one they did so, observ-ing a collection of dilapidated buildings about half a mile away and two hundred feet below. There were two dozen or so shacks located on a riverbank. A muddy path led from the buildings to a rough wooden jetty and the river, where a motley collection of boats was moored.

Partridge said softly, "Nice going, everybody!" He added with relief, "I guess we found Nueva Esperanza."

After having deferred to Fernández on the trail, Harry Partridge now resumed command.

"We don't have a lot of daylight left," he told the others. The sun was already near the horizon, the journey having taken far longer than expected. "I want to observe as much as possible before dark. Minh, bring the other binoculars and join me forward. Fernández and Ken, pick a sentry post and one of you keep watch to see if we're approached from behind. Work that out between you, and if someone does show, call me quickly."

Approaching the strip of jungle, which prevented them from being seen from below, Partridge dropped to his belly and wriggled forward, carrying the binoculars he had brought. Minh, beside him, did the same, both stopping when they could see clearly but were still shielded by surrounding foliage.

Moving the binoculars slowly, Partridge studied the scene below.

There was almost no activity. At the jetty, two men were working on a boat, stripping an outboard engine. A woman left one shack, emptied a pail of slops behind it, and returned inside. A man emerged from the jungle, walked toward another house and entered. Two scrawny dogs were clawing their way into an open garbage pile. Other garbage littered the area. Viewed overall, Nueva Esperanza appeared to be a jungle slum.

Partridge began studying the buildings individually, letting the binoculars linger several minutes on each. Presumably the prisoners were being held in one of them, but no clue was evident as to which. It was already obvious, he thought, that at least a full day's observation would be needed and any idea of a rescue attempt tonight and departure by air tomorrow morning was clearly out of the question. He settled down, simply to wait and watch while the light diminished.

As always in the tropics when the sun receded, darkness followed quickly. In the houses a few dim lights had come on and now the last vestiges of day were almost gone. Partridge lowered his binoculars and wiped his eyes, which were strained after more than an hour of concentration on the scene below. There was little else, he believed, that they would learn today.

At that moment Minh touched his arm, gesturing toward the huts below. Partridge picked up his binoculars and peered again. At once he saw movement in the now dim light—the figure of a man walking down the path between two groups of houses. In contrast to other movements they had seen, this man's walk seemed purposeful. Something else was different; Partridge strained to see . . . now he had it! The man was carrying a rifle, slung over his shoulder. Partridge and Minh both followed the man's movement with their binoculars.

Away from the other buildings, standing separately, was a single shack. Partridge had seen it earlier, but there had been nothing special to attract attention. Now the man reached the building and disappeared inside. There was an opening in the front wall and dim light filtered through.

Still they continued watching, and for a few minutes nothing happened. Then, from the same shack a figure emerged and walked away. Even in the faded light two things could be distinguished: This was a different man and he, too, was carrying a gun.

Could it be, Partridge wondered excitedly, that what they had just witnessed was a changing of the prisoners' guard? More confirmation was needed and they would have to keep observing. But the probability was strong that the shack standing alone was where Jessica and Nicky Sloane were being held.

He tried not to let his mind dwell on the likelihood that, until a day or two before, Angus Sloane had been confined there too.

The hours passed.

Partridge had advised the others, "What we need to know is how much activity there is at night in Nueva Esperanza, roughly how long it lasts, and what time everything settles down, with most lights out. I'd like a written record kept, with all times noted."

At Partridge's request, Minh stayed another hour alone at the observation point and, later, Ken O'Hara relieved him.

"Everyone get as much rest as you can," Partridge ordered. "But we should man the observation point and the sentry post in the clearing all the time, which means only two people can sleep at once." After discussion it was decided they would alternate duty with sleep, using two-hour shifts.

Earlier, Fernández had rigged hammocks with mosquito netting inside the hut they had found on arrival. The hammocks were less than comfortable, but those using them were too exhausted from the day's activity to care, and quickly fell asleep. The idea of bringing plastic sheeting was justified during the night when rain fell heavily and leaked through the hut roof. Fernández adroitly covered the hammocks so the sleepers were protected. Those outside huddled in their own plastic protection as best they could until the rain stopped half an hour later.

Nothing specific was done about meals. Food and water were handled individually, though they all knew the dried food must be used sparingly. Their water supply, brought from Lima the preceding day, had already been consumed, and several hours earlier Fernández had filled water bottles from a jungle stream, adding sterilizing tablets. He had warned that most local water was contaminated by chemicals used by drug processors. The water in the bottles now tasted awful and everyone drank as little as possible.

By dawn next morning, Partridge had answers to his questions concerning Neuva Esperanza at night: There was very little activity—other than the strumming of a guitar and occasional strident voices and drunken laughter somewhere indoors. Such activity as there was lasted for about three and a half hours after dark. By 1:30 A.M. the entire hamlet was silent and dark.

What they still needed to know—assuming Partridge's surmises about the guards and the prisoners' location were correct—was how often a guard change occurred, and at what times. By morning no clear picture had emerged. If there had been another guard change in the night, it escaped observation.

Their routine continued through the day.

Manning of the sentry post and observation point was maintained, and even during daytime the hammocks were available to those off duty. All took advantage of them, knowing their reserves of endurance might be needed later.

During the afternoon, while it was Harry Partridge's turn in a hammock, he contemplated what he and the others were doing . . . asking himself with a sense of unreality: Is all this really happening? Should their small, unofficial force be attempting a rescue? In a few hours, no more, they would probably have to kill or be killed themselves. Was it all madness? Like that line from *Macbeth, ". . . life's fitful fever . . ."*

He was a professional journalist, wasn't he? A TV correspondent, an observer of wars and conflict, not a participant. Yet suddenly, by his own decision, he had become an adventurer, a mercenary, a would-be soldier. Did this switch in any way make sense?

Whatever the answer, there was another question: If he, Harry Partridge, failed to do what was needed here and now, who would?

And something else: A journalist covering

wars, especially a TV correspondent, was never far from violence, mayhem, ugly wounding, sudden death. He or she lived those perils, shared them, sometimes suffered them, then brought them nightly into the clean and tidy living rooms of urban America, an environment where they were no more than images on a screen and therefore not dangerous to those who watched.

And yet, increasingly, those images *were* becoming dangerous, were moving closer both in time and distance, and soon would be not only pictures on a tube but harsh reality in American cities and streets where crime already prowled. Now the violence and terrorism in the underprivileged, divided, war-torn half-world was moving nearer, ever nearer, to American soil. It was inevitable and had been expected by international scholars for a long time.

The Monroe Doctrine, once thought to be an American protection, no longer worked; nowadays few bothered even speaking of it. The kidnapping of the Sloane family within the United States by foreign agents had demonstrated that international terrorism was already there. There was more, much more, to come— terrorist bombings, hostage taking, shelling in the streets. Tragically, there was no way to avoid it. Equally tragic was that many who were not participants soon would be—like it or not.

So at this moment, Partridge thought, his involvement and that of the other three was *not* unreal. He suspected that Minh Van Canh, especially, saw nothing contradictory in their present situation. Minh, who had lived through and survived a terrible, divisive war within his own country, would find it easier than most to accept this undertaking now.

And, in a personal way, beyond and overshadowing all those thoughts was Jessica. Jessica, who was probably close at hand, somewhere inside that hut. Jessica-Gemma whose memories and personalities, in his mind, were intertwined.

Then . . . fatigue suddenly overwhelming him . . . he fell asleep.

On awakening, some fifteen minutes before his own observation duty, he dropped down from the hammock and went outside to check the general situation.

At the sentry post, as previously, there had been no alarms or action. The observation point, however, had produced specific information and opinions.

- There *was* a regular change of an armed person—presumably a guard—at the same location as on the night before, suggesting that prisoners were indeed housed in the building that stood apart from others. It seemed probable that a guard change was supposed to occur every four hours, but the timing was not exact. A changeover was sometimes as much as twenty minutes late and the imprecision, Partridge believed, showed a casualness on the guards' part, confirming the message conveyed by Jessica: *Security here is sometimes lax.*

- Since morning, what appeared to be food in containers had been delivered twice by women entering what was presumed to be the prisoners' building. The same woman who delivered food made two separate journeys out with pails which she emptied into the bush.

- Within the hamlet, only at the suspected building did any guard or sentry post exist.

- While members of the guard force were armed with automatic rifles, they did not seem to be soldiers or to operate as a trained unit.

- During the day, all comings and goings to and from Nueva Esperanza were by boat. No road vehicle was seen. The engines on boats did not appear to require keys; therefore it would be easy to steal a boat if that line of escape was taken. On the other hand, there were plenty of other boats with which a stolen boat could be pursued. Ken O'Hara, who was familiar with boats, identified the best ones.

- A unanimous view among the observers, though it was only an opinion, was that the people being observed were almost totally relaxed, which seemed to indicate that an aggressive incursion from outside was not expected. "If one was," Fernández pointed out, "they would have patrols out, including up here, looking for people like us."

At dusk, Partridge called the other three together and informed them, "We've watched long enough. We go down tonight."

He told Fernández, "You'll guide us from here. I want to arrive at that hut at 2 A.M. Everyone must be silent all the way. If we need to communicate, whisper."

Minh asked, "Is there an order of battle, Harry?"

"Yes," Partridge answered. "I'll go close up, look in to see what I can, then enter first. I'd like you right behind me, Minh, covering my back. Fernández will hang behind, watch the other houses for anyone appearing, but join us if we need help."

Fernández nodded.

Partridge turned to O'Hara, "Ken, you'll go directly to the jetty. I've decided we'll leave by boat. We don't know what kind of condition Jessica and Nicholas are in, and they may not be up to the journey we had coming here."

"Got it!" O'Hara said. "I assume you want me to grab a boat."

"Yes and, if you can, disable some of the others, but remember—no noise!"

"There'll be noise when we start the motor."

"No," Partridge said. "We'll have to row

away, and when we get to midstream let the current take us. Fortunately it's going in the right direction. Only when we're out of hearing will we start the engine."

Even as he spoke, Partridge knew he was assuming everything would go well. If not, they would improvise as best they could, which included using weapons.

Remembering the planned 8 A.M. rendezvous with AeroLibertad's Cheyenne II, Fernández inquired, "Have you decided which airstrip we'll try for—Sion or the other?"

"I'll make that choice in the boat, depending how everything else goes and how much time we have."

What was necessary now, Partridge concluded, was to check weapons, discard unneeded equipment and make sure they could travel as light and as fast as possible.

A mixture of excitement and apprehension gripped them all.

15

Back in Lima on Saturday morning, after watching the AeroLibertad Cheyenne II depart, Rita Abrams had been taken completely by surprise on two counts.

First, she had not expected an on-the-scene appearance by Crawford Sloane. A message awaiting her at CBA's Entel Peru booth announced that Sloane would be in Lima by early morning, in fact could have arrived already. She promptly called Cesar's Hotel where, according to the message, he would be staying. Crawf had not yet checked in, and she left word advising him where she was and requesting that he phone.

Second, and even more surprising, was the faxed letter from Les Chippingham, sent the previous evening to Harry Partridge. The instruction on the letter to place it in an envelope marked "Personal" had clearly not been noticed by the busy Entel fax operator and it arrived along with other mail, open so that anyone could read it. Rita did, and was incredulous.

Harry had been fired, dismissed by CBA!
"Effective immediately," the letter said, and he
was to leave Peru "preferably" on Saturday—
today!—"definitely" no later than Sunday. If a
commercial flight to the U.S. was not available,
he was authorized to charter. Big deal!

The more Rita thought about it, the more
ridiculous and outrageous it was, especially
now. Could Crawf's arrival in Lima, she wondered, have anything to do with it? She was sure
it did, and waited impatiently to hear from
Sloane, all the while her anger over the abomi-
nable treatment of Harry intensifying.

Meanwhile, there was no way she could
communicate the letter's contents to Partridge
since he was already in the jungle, on his way to
Nueva Esperanza.

Sloane didn't telephone. After arriving at
the hotel and receiving Rita's message, he took
a taxi immediately to Entel. He had worked in
Lima on assignment in the past and knew his
way around.

His first question to Rita was, "Where's
Harry?"

"In the jungle," she answered tersely, "risking his life trying to rescue your wife and boy."
Then she thrust the faxed letter forward. "What
the hell is this?"

"What do you mean?" Crawford Sloane

took the letter and read it as she watched him. He read it twice, then shook his head. "This is a mistake. It has to be."

A sharpness still in Rita's voice, she asked, "Are you telling me you don't know anything about it?"

"Of course not." Sloane shook his head impatiently. "Harry's my friend. Right now I need him more than anyone else in the world. Please tell me what he's doing in the jungle—isn't that what you just said?" Sloane had clearly dismissed the letter as absurd, something he would not waste time on.

Rita swallowed hard. Tears flooded her eyes; she was angry at her own misjudgment and injustice. "Oh, Christ, Crawf! I'm sorry." For the first time she took in the extra lines of strain on the anchorman's face, the anguish in his eyes. He looked far worse than when she had last seen him, eight days earlier. "I thought that somehow you . . . Oh, never mind!"

Rita pulled herself together. "Here's what's happening, what Harry and the others are trying to do." She described the expedition to Nueva Esperanza and what Partridge hoped to achieve. She filled in background, too, explaining Partridge's doubts about telephone security —the reason his plan had not been reported to New York.

At length Sloane said, "I'd like to talk to

that pilot, find out how things were when he left Harry and the others. What's his name?"

"Zileri." Rita looked at her watch. "He's probably not back yet, but I'll phone soon, and then we'll go. Have you had breakfast?"

Sloane shook his head.

"There's a cafeteria in the building. Let's go down."

Over coffee and croissants, Rita said gently, "Crawf, we were all shocked and saddened by the news about your father—Harry especially. I know he blamed himself for not moving faster, but we didn't have the information . . ."

Sloane stopped her with a gesture. "I'll never blame Harry for anything—whatever happens, even now. No one could have done more."

"I agree," Rita said, "which is what makes this so unbelievable." Once more she produced the faxed letter which Les Chippingham had signed. "This is no mistake, Crawf. This was intended. People don't make mistakes like that."

He read it again. "When we get upstairs I'll phone Les in New York."

"Before you do, let's consider this: There's something behind it, something you and I don't know. Yesterday in New York—did anything happen out of the ordinary?"

"You mean at CBA?"

"Yes."

Sloane considered. "I don't think so . . . well, I did hear Les was sent for by Margot Lloyd-Mason—apparently in an all-fired hurry. He was over at Stonehenge. But I've no idea what it was about."

A sudden thought struck Rita. "Could it have been something to do with Globanic? Perhaps this." Opening her purse, she took out the several clipped sheets of paper Harry Partridge had given her this morning.

Sloane took the sheets and read them. "Interesting! A huge debt-to-equity swap. Really big money! Where did you get this?"

"From Harry." She repeated what Partridge had told her on the way to the airport—how he had received the document from the Peru radio commentator, Sergio Hurtado, who intended to broadcast the information during the coming week. Rita added, "Harry told me he didn't plan to use the story. Said it was the least we could do for Globanic which puts butter on our bread."

"There *could* be a linkage between this and Harry's firing," Sloane said thoughtfully. "I see a possibility. Let's go upstairs and call Les now."

"There's something I want to do first, when we get there," Rita said.

The "something" was send for Victor Velasco.

When the international manager of Entel
appeared a few minutes later, Rita told him, "I
want a secure line to New York, with no one
listening."

Velasco looked embarrassed. "Do you have
reason to suppose . . ."

"Yes."

"Please come to my office. You may use a
phone there."

Rita and Crawford Sloane followed the
manager to a pleasant, carpeted office on the
same floor. "Please use my desk." He pointed to
a red phone. "That line is secure. I guarantee it.
You may dial direct."

"Thank you." With Partridge en route to
Nueva Esperanza, Rita had no intention of letting his whereabouts, which might be mentioned in conversation, become known to Peru
authorities.

With a courteous nod, Velasco left the office,
closing the door behind him.

Sloane, seated at the desk, tried Les Chippingham's direct CBA News line first. There
was no answer—not unusual on a Saturday
morning. What *was* unusual was that the news
president had not left with the CBA News
switchboard a number where he could be
reached. Consulting a pocket notebook, Sloane

tried a third number—Chippingham's uptown Manhattan apartment. Again no response. There was a Scarsdale number where Chippingham sometimes spent weekends. He wasn't there either.

"It rather looks," Sloane said, "as if he's deliberately made himself unavailable this morning." He sat at the desk, contemplative, weighing a decision.

"What are you thinking of?" Rita asked.

"Calling Margot Lloyd-Mason." He picked up the red phone. "I will."

Sloane tapped out the U.S. overseas code again and the number of Stonehenge. An operator told him, "Mrs. Lloyd-Mason is not in her office today."

"This is Crawford Sloane. Will you give me her home number, please."

"It's unlisted, Mr. Sloane. I'm not allowed to give it out."

"But you have it?"

The operator hesitated. "Yes, sir."

"What's your name, operator?"

"Noreen."

"A beautiful name; I've always liked that. Now, please listen to me carefully, Noreen. By the way, do you recognize my voice?"

"Oh yes, sir. I watch the news every night. But lately I've been worried . . ."

"Thank you, Noreen. So have I. Now, I'm

calling from Lima, Peru, and I simply have to speak with Mrs. Lloyd-Mason. If you'll give me that number, I promise I will never breathe a word of how I got it, except that next time I'm in Stonehenge I'll come to the switchboard room and thank you personally."

"Oh! Would you really, Mr. Sloane? We'd all love it!"

"I always keep promises. The number, Noreen?"

He wrote it down as she read it out.

This time, the phone was answered on the second ring by a male voice which sounded like a butler's. Sloane identified himself and asked for Mrs. Lloyd-Mason.

He waited several minutes, then Margot's voice, which was unmistakable, said, "Yes?"

"This is Crawf. I'm calling from Lima."

"So I was told, Mr. Sloane. I'm curious why you are calling me, particularly at home. First, though, I'd like to offer my sympathy about your father's death."

"Thank you."

Unusually for someone of his stature, Sloane had never been on a first-name basis with the CBA president and clearly she intended to keep it that way. He also guessed from her tone and aloofness that he would get nowhere with direct questions. He decided to try the timeworn journalist's trick which so often worked, even with sophisticated persons.

"Mrs. Lloyd-Mason, yesterday when you decided to fire Harry Partridge from CBA, I wonder if you realized how much he has accomplished in the whole effort to find and free my wife, son and father."

The reply came back explosively, "Who *told* you that was my decision?"

He was tempted to answer, *You just did!* But restraining himself, he said, "In the TV news business, which is close-knit, almost nothing is secret. That's why I called you."

Margot snapped, "I do not wish to discuss this now."

"That's a pity," Sloane said, speaking quickly, before she could hang up, "because I thought you might want to talk about the connection between Harry's firing and that big debt-to-equity swap Globanic is arranging with Peru. Did Harry's honest reporting offend someone with a stake in that deal?"

At the other end of the line there was a long silence in which he could hear Margot breathing. Then, her voice subdued, she asked, "Where did you hear all that?"

So there was *a connection after all!*

"Well," Sloane said, "the fact is, Harry Partridge learned about the debt-to-equity arrangement. He's a first-class reporter, you know, one of the best in our business, and right now he's out risking his life for CBA. Anyway, Harry decided not to use the information. His words were, I understand, 'That's the least I can do for Globanic, which puts butter on our bread.' "

Again the silence. Then Margot asked, "So it isn't going to be publicized?"

"Aha! That's another matter." In other circumstances, Sloane thought, he might have enjoyed this; as it was, he felt miserably depressed. "There's a radio reporter in Lima who uncovered the story, has a copy of the agreement, and intends to broadcast it next week. I expect it will be picked up outside Peru. Don't you?"

Margot didn't answer. Wondering if she had hung up, he asked, "Are you still there?"

"Yes."

"Are you wishing, by chance, that you hadn't done what you did to Harry Partridge?"

"No." The answer seemed disembodied, as if Margot's mind was far away. "No," she repeated, "I was thinking of other things."

"Mrs. Lloyd-Mason"—Crawford Sloane employed the cutting tone he used occasionally for repulsive items in the news—"has anyone told you lately that you are a cold-hearted bitch?"

He replaced the red phone.

Margot, too, hung up as her phone went silent. One day soon, she decided, she would find her own way to deal with the self-important Mr. Crawford Sloane. But this was not the time. Right now, other things were more important.

The news she had just been given about Globanic and Peru had severely jolted her. But she had been jolted in the past and seldom stayed that way for long. Margot had not climbed as high and fast as she had in the world of business without serious setbacks, and almost always she contrived to turn them to her advantage. Somehow she must do so now. She paused, weighing initiatives she could take.

Without question, she must call Theo Elliott today. He never minded being disturbed about important business matters at any time, weekends included.

She would tell him she had information that word was circulating in Peru about the Globanic deal, that a Peruvian reporter had somehow obtained a copy of the draft agreement and was about to publish it. It had nothing to do with CBA or, for that matter, any other U.S. network or newspaper; it was a local Peruvian leak, though a bad one.

The whole thing was unfortunate, she would tell Theo, and she didn't want to make judgments, though could not help wondering: Had

Fossie Xenos been careless about who he talked to, particularly in Peru? It did seem possible, based on what she had heard, that the enthusiasm Fossie was noted for had made him indiscreet.

She would also tell Theo that because of the activity among the Peruvian press, the matter *had* come to the attention of CBA News. But Margot had given definite orders that CBA would not report it.

With luck, she thought, by early next week any adverse attention would have shifted away from herself and landed on Fossie. Good!

During her ruminations, Margot did give brief thought to Harry Partridge. Should he be reinstated? Then she decided no. Doing that would only confuse things, and Partridge wasn't important, so let the decision stand. Besides, Theo would still want to make his phone call to Peru's President Castañeda on Monday saying that the troublemaker—to use Theo's word—had been dismissed and banished from Peru.

Smiling, confident her strategy would work, she picked up the phone and tapped out the unlisted number of Theo Elliott's home.

The AeroLibertad owner and pilot, Oswaldo Zileri, had heard of Crawford Sloane and was appropriately respectful.

"When your friends arranged their charter, Mr. Sloane, I said I did not wish to know their purpose. Now that I see you here, I can guess it, and I wish you, and them, well."

"Thank you," Sloane said. He and Rita were in Zileri's modest office near Lima's airport. "When you left Mr. Partridge and the others this morning, how did everything look?"

Zileri shrugged. "The way the jungle always looks—green, impenetrable, endless. There was no activity, other than by your friends."

Rita told Zileri, "When we talked about extra passengers coming back, we hoped there would be three. But now it's two."

"I have heard the sad news about Mr. Sloane's father." The pilot shook his head. "We live in savage times."

Sloane began, "I was wondering if now . . ."

Zileri finished for him. ". . . if there might be room for you and Miss Abrams to go on the other trips—one, two, or more—to bring the people back."

"Yes."

"It will be okay. Because one of the expected passengers is a boy, and there will be no freight or baggage, weight will not be a problem. You must be here before dawn tomorrow—and the next day, if we go."

"We will be," Rita said. She turned to

Sloane. "Harry wasn't optimistic about making a rendezvous the first day after going in. The flight is a precaution in case they need it. All along, he thought the second day more likely."

There was one other thing Rita felt she had to do. She did not tell Crawf, but composed a fax message to Les Chippingham, to be waiting for him Monday morning. Deliberately, she did not route the message to the fax machine in the news president's office, but to one at the Horseshoe. There it would be the reverse of private and could be read by others—just as Chippingham's letter dismissing Harry Partridge had been when it arrived at Entel Peru.

Rita addressed her communication:

L. W. Chippingham
President, CBA News
Copies: All Notice Boards

She had no illusions that what she had written would get on *any* notice board. It wouldn't. But it was a signal, which would be understood by fellow producers at the Horseshoe, that she wanted wide circulation. *Someone* would make a copy or copies, to be passed around, read, and probably copied again and again.

The message read:

You sordid, selfish, cowardly son of a bitch!

To fire Harry Partridge the way you did—without cause, warning or even explanation—just to satisfy your cozy crony, the Iceberg-woman, Lloyd-Mason, is a betrayal of everything which used to be fair and decent at CBA.

Harry will come out of this smelling like Chanel No. 5. You already stink like the sewer rat you are.

How I ever let myself go to bed with you regularly is beyond my understanding. But never again! If you had the last erect cock on earth, I wouldn't have it near me.

As for working for you any longer—ugh!

With deep sadness for what you used to be, compared with what you have become,

Your ex-friend, ex-admirer, ex-lover, ex-producer,

Rita Abrams

Obviously, Rita thought, after that was received and digested, Harry was not the only one who would be looking for fresh employment. But she didn't care. She felt a whole lot better as she watched the fax leave Entel, knowing that a moment later it was already in New York.

16

It was 2:10 A.M. in Nueva Esperanza.

Jessica had been restless for the past several hours, drifting in and out of sleep, dreaming at times—the dreams becoming nightmares merging with reality.

Moments earlier, certain she was awake, Jessica had peered through the roughly cut window opening facing her cell, and what she thought she saw in dim light reflected from inside was the face of Harry Partridge. Then the face disappeared as suddenly as it came. *Was she awake?* Or could she still be dreaming? Hallucinating, maybe?

Jessica was shaking her head, trying to clear it, when the face appeared again, rising slowly above the lowest window level, and this time it stayed. A hand made a signal which she didn't understand, but she studied the face again. *Could it be?* Her heart leaped as she decided: *Yes, it could!* It *was* Harry Partridge.

The face was mouthing something silently, the lips making exaggerated movements, attempting to communicate. She concentrated, trying to understand, and managed to grasp the words "the guard." That was it: *Where was the guard?*

The guard at the moment was Vicente. He had come on duty an hour ago—apparently very late—and there had been a heated argument between him and Ramón, who had the earlier duty. Ramón had shouted angrily. Vicente, in arguing back, sounded drunk—at least his speech was slurred. Jessica didn't care about the dispute and, as always, was glad to see Ramón go; he had a vicious streak, was unpredictable, and still insisted on the silence rule for the prisoners which, by now, none of the other guards enforced.

Turning her head, Jessica could see Vicente. He was seated in the chair which all the guards used, beyond the cells and out of sight of the window. She wasn't sure, but his eyes seemed closed. His automatic rifle was propped against the wall alongside him. Nearby a kerosene lamp hung from a beam above, and it was by the lamp's reflected light she had seen the face outside.

Being careful, in case Vicente should suddenly observe her, Jessica answered the silent question by inclining her head toward where he was seated.

At once the mouth on the face at the window—Jessica still had trouble accepting it as Harry Partridge's—began to form words again. Once more, she concentrated. After the third time she understood the message: *"Call him!"*

Jessica nodded slightly, intimating that she understood. Her heart was pounding at the sight of Harry. It could only mean, she thought, that the rescue they had hoped for for so long was finally happening. At the same time, she knew that completing whatever had been started would not be easy.

"Vicente!" She raised her voice no louder than she thought was needed, but it was not enough to penetrate his dozing. A touch more strongly, she tried again. "Vicente!"

This time he stirred. Vicente's eyes opened and met Jessica's. As they did, she beckoned him.

Vicente shifted in his chair. He started to rise and, watching him, Jessica had the impression he was organizing himself mentally, trying to sober up. He stood, started to come toward her, then quickly turned back to collect his rifle. He held it in a businesslike way, she noticed, clearly ready to use it if required.

She had better have an excuse for summoning Vicente, Jessica reasoned, and decided she would ask by gestures if she could go into Nicky's cell. The request would be refused, but at this point that didn't matter.

She had no idea what Harry had in mind. She only knew, while her anxiety and tension grew, that this was the moment she had dreamed about, yet feared might never come.

Crouched low beneath the window, Partridge gripped his nine-millimeter Browning pistol, the silencer extending from the barrel. So far tonight, everything had gone exactly as planned, but he knew the most difficult and crucial part of the action was about to begin.

The next few seconds would offer him limited alternatives, one of which he would have to choose in an instant's decision. The way it looked now, he might be able to hold up the guard, using the Browning as a threat, after which the guard would either be bound securely, gagged and left, or taken with them as a captive. The second choice would be least preferable. There was a third possibility—to kill the guard, but that was something he would prefer not to do.

One thing was working in his favor: Jessica was resourceful, quick to think and understand —exactly as he remembered her.

He listened to her call twice, heard minor noises from somewhere out of sight, then footsteps as the guard walked over. Partridge held his breath, ready to slump below the window level entirely if the guard was looking in his direction.

He wasn't. The man had his back to Partridge and faced Jessica, which gave Partridge an extra second to assess the scene.

The first thing he recognized was that the guard was carrying a Kalashnikov automatic rifle, a weapon Partridge knew well, and from the way it was being handled, the guard knew how to use it. Compared with the Kalashnikov, Partridge's Browning was a peashooter.

The conclusion was inevitable and inescapable: Partridge would have to kill the guard and get his shot in first, which meant surprise.

But there was an obstacle. Jessica. She was now exactly in line with the guard and Partridge. A shot aimed at the guard could hit Jessica too.

Partridge *had* to gamble. There would be no other chance, could be no other choice. And the gamble would be on Jessica's fast thinking and instant action.

Taking a breath, Partridge called out loudly, clearly, "Jessica, drop to the floor—*now!*"

Instantly, the guard spun around, his rifle raised, the safety off. But Partridge already had the Browning raised and sighted. A moment earlier he had remembered the advice of a firearms instructor who taught him to use weapons: *"If you want to kill a person, don't aim for the head. Chances are, no matter how gently you squeeze the trigger, the gun will rise and the bullet will go high, perhaps clear over the head. So aim for the heart, or slightly below. That way, even if the bullet's higher than the heart, it will do a lot of damage, probably kill, and if it doesn't, you'll have time for a second shot."*

Partridge squeezed the trigger and the Browning fired with a near-silent "pfft!" Even though he had had experience with silencers, their quietness always surprised him. He peered down the sights, ready for a second shot, but it wasn't needed. The first had hit the guard in the chest, just about where the heart should be and where blood was beginning to appear. For an instant the man looked surprised, then he fell where he was, dropping the rifle, which created the only noise.

Even before it happened, Partridge had seen Jessica drop flat to the ground, obeying his command instantly. In a crevice of his mind he was relieved and grateful. Now Jessica was scrambling to her feet.

Partridge turned toward the outside doorway to the shack, but a swiftly moving shadow was ahead of him. It was Minh Van Canh, who had stayed positioned at Partridge's rear, as ordered, but now changed places, going forward. Minh went swiftly to the guard, his own UZI at the ready, then confirmed with a nod to Partridge, just entering, that the man was dead. Next, Minh moved to Jessica's cell, inspected the padlock which secured it and asked, "Where is the key?"

Jessica told him, "Somewhere over where the guard was sitting. Nicky's too."

In the adjoining cell, Nicky stirred from sleep. Abruptly, he sat upright. "Mom, what's happening?"

Jessica assured him, "It's good, Nicky. All good!"

Nicky took in the new arrivals—Partridge, approaching and holding the Kalashnikov rifle he had just picked up, and Minh collecting keys which were hanging from a nail. "Who are they, Mom?"

"Friends, dear. *Very* good friends."

Nicky, still sleepy, brightened. Then he saw the fallen, still figure on the ground amid a widening pool of blood and cried out, "It's Vicente! They shot Vicente! Why?"

"Hush, Nicky!" Jessica warned.

Keeping his voice low, Partridge answered. "I didn't like doing it, Nicholas. But he was going to shoot me. If he had, I couldn't have taken you and your mother away from here, which is what we've come to do."

With a flash of recognition, Nicky said, "You're Mr. Partridge, aren't you?"

"Yes, I am."

Jessica said emotionally, "Oh, bless you, Harry! Dear Harry!"

Still speaking softly, Partridge cautioned, "We're not out of this yet, and we've a way to go. We all have to move quickly."

Minh had returned with the keys and was trying them, one by one, in the padlock of Jessica's cell. Suddenly the lock opened. An instant later the door swung wide and Jessica walked out. Minh went to Nicky's cell and tried out keys there. Within seconds Nicky was free too, and he and Jessica embraced briefly in the area between the cells and the outside door.

"Help me!" Partridge told Minh. He had been dragging the body of the guard toward Nicky's cell and together they lifted the dead man onto the low wooden bed. The action would not prevent discovery of the prisoners' escape, Partridge thought, but might delay it slightly. With the same motive, he lowered the light in the kerosene lamp so it was merely a glimmer, the hut interior receding into darkness.

Nicky left Jessica and moved close to Partridge. In a stilted monotone, he said, "It's all right about shooting Vicente, Mr. Partridge. He helped us sometimes, but he was one of *them*. They killed my granddad and cut off two of my fingers, so I can't play the piano anymore." He held up his bandaged hand.

"Call me Harry," Partridge said. "Yes, I knew about your grandfather and the fingers. And I'm terribly sorry."

Again the uptight, rigid voice. "Do you know about the Stockholm syndrome, Harry? My mom does. If you'd like her to, she'll tell you."

Without answering, Partridge looked closely at Nicky. He had encountered shock before—in individuals affected by more exposure to danger or disaster than their minds could handle—and the boy's tone and choice of words within the past few minutes held symptoms of shock. He was going to need help soon. Meanwhile, doing the best he could, Partridge reached out and put his arm around Nicky's shoulders. He felt the boy respond by drawing closer to him.

Partridge saw Jessica watching, her face showing the same concern as his own. She, too, wished the guard could have been someone other than Vicente. If it had been Ramón, she would not have been troubled in the least. Just the same, she was taken aback by Nicky's words and manner.

Partridge shook his head, trying to convey reassurance to Jessica, at the same time ordering, "Let's go."

In his free hand he kept the Kalashnikov; it was a good fighting weapon and might be useful. He had also pocketed two spare magazines he found on the body of the guard.

Minh was ahead of them at the doorway. He had retrieved his camera from outside and now had it raised, recording their departure with the cells as background. Minh was using a special night lens, Partridge noted—infrared didn't work with tape—and he would have passable pictures, even in this dimmest light.

Since yesterday, Minh had been taking pictures from time to time, though selectively and sparingly since there had been limitations on the number of tape cassettes he could bring.

At that moment Fernández, who had been watching the other buildings, burst in. He warned Partridge breathlessly, "Coming here— a woman! By herself. I think she's armed." At the same moment, approaching footsteps were audible and close.

There was no time for orders or dispositions. Everyone froze where they were. Jessica was near the doorway, though off to one side. Minh faced the opening directly, the others were farther back in shadows. Partridge had the Kalashnikov raised. Though he knew that firing it would awaken the hamlet, to get at the Browning with its silencer, he would have to put the rifle down and change hands. There wasn't time.

Socorro walked in briskly. She was wearing

a robe and holding a Smith and Wesson revolver pointed forward, the hammer cocked. Jessica had seen Socorro with a gun before, but it had always been holstered, never in her hand.

Despite the gun, Socorro did not appear to be expecting anything out of the ordinary, and in the almost nonexistent light at first mistook Minh, who was closest, for the guard. She said, *"Pensé que escuché . . ."* Then she realized it *wasn't* the guard and glancing left, saw Jessica. Startled, she exclaimed, *"¿Qué haces . . . ?"* then stopped.

What happened next occurred so swiftly that, later, no one could describe the sequence of events.

Socorro raised the revolver and, with her finger around the trigger, moved swiftly, closing on Jessica. Afterward, it was assumed she intended to seize Jessica and hold her hostage, perhaps with the pistol at her head.

Jessica saw the move coming and, with equal swiftness, remembered CQB—close quarters battle—which she had learned but had not used since capture. While tempted at earlier moments to employ it, she had known that in the long term it would do no good and decided to save her skill for a moment when it really counted.

"When an opponent moves towards you," Brigadier Wade had emphasized during lessons

and demonstrations, *"your human instinct is to move back. The opponent will expect that too. Don't do it! Instead, surprise him and go forward—move in close!"*

With lightning speed, Jessica leapt at Socorro, raising her left arm, braced rigidly, upward and forcefully inside the other woman's right. With a jarring movement as the arms made contact, Socorro's arm flew involuntarily upward, forcing her hand back until the fingers opened in a reflex action and the gun dropped. The entire maneuver took barely a second, Socorro scarcely aware of what had happened.

Without pause, Jessica thrust two fingers hard into the soft flesh under Socorro's chin, the fingers compressing the trachea and impeding breathing. Simultaneously Jessica placed a leg behind Socorro and pushed her backward, throwing her off balance. Jessica then turned Socorro and placed her in a tight stranglehold, making it impossible for her to move. If this had been war—for which CQB was intended— the next step would have been to break Socorro's neck and kill.

Jessica, who had never killed anyone or ever expected to, hesitated. She felt Socorro struggling to speak and slightly eased the pressure of her fingers.

Gasping, Socorro pleaded in a whisper, "Let

me go . . . I will help you . . . go with you
to escape . . . know the way."

Partridge had come close enough to hear.
He asked, "Can you trust her?"

Again, Jessica hesitated. She had a moment
of compassion. Socorro had not been all evil.
All along, Jessica had an instinct that Socorro's
days in America as a nurse had tilted her toward good. She had cared for Nicky after his
burns, and later when his fingers were severed.
There was the incident of the chocolate bar,
tossed by Socorro into the boat when all three
were hungry. Socorro had improved their living
conditions by having openings cut in walls . . .
had disobeyed Miguel's orders in allowing Jessica to join Nicky in his cell . . .

But it was also Socorro who had been part
of the kidnap from the beginning and who,
when Nicky's fingers were being cut, had called
across callously, *"Shut up! There's no way you
can stop what's going to happen."*

And then, in her mind, Jessica heard
Nicky's words, spoken only minutes earlier:
*"It's all right about shooting Vicente, Harry
. . . He helped us sometimes, but he was one of
them . . . Do you know about the Stockholm
syndrome? . . . My mom does . . ."*

Beware the Stockholm syndrome!

Jessica answered Partridge's question. Shaking her head, she told him, "No!"

Their eyes met. Harry had been amazed by
Jessica's demonstration of skill in hand-to-hand
combat. He wondered where she had learned it
and why. At the moment, though, that didn't
matter. What did matter was that she had
reached a point of decision and her eyes were
asking him a question. He nodded briefly. Then,
not wanting to witness what came next, he
turned away.

Shuddering, Jessica tightened her grip,
broke Socorro's neck, then twisted the head
sharply to sunder the spinal cord. There was a
snapping sound, surprisingly faint, and the
body Jessica was holding slumped. She let it
fall.

Led by Partridge, with Jessica, Nicky, Minh
and Fernández following quietly, the group
moved through the darkened hamlet, encoun-
tering no one.

At the jetty Ken O'Hara said, "I thought
you'd never get here."

"We had problems," Partridge told him.
"Let's move fast! Which boat?"

"This one." It was an open wooden
workboat about thirty feet long, with twin outboard motors. Two lines secured it to the jetty.
"I grabbed some extra fuel from other boats."
O'Hara pointed to several plastic containers
near the stern.

"Everybody aboard!" Partridge ordered.

Earlier, a three-quarters moon had been obscured by cloud, but within the past few minutes the cloud had shifted. Now everything was lighter, particularly over the water.

Fernández helped Jessica and Nicky into the boat. Jessica was shaking uncontrollably and feeling sick, both aftereffects of having killed Socorro only minutes earlier. Minh, taking pictures from the jetty, jumped in last as O'Hara, unfastening the lines, used an oar to push out from shore. Fernández grabbed a second oar. Together he and O'Hara rowed toward midstream.

Looking around, Partridge could see that O'Hara had used his waiting time effectively. Several other boats were settling in the water near shore, others drifting away.

"I pulled some plugs." O'Hara gestured to the nearer boats. "Those can be refloated, but it'll cause delay. Threw a couple of good motors in the river."

"Nice going, Ken!" His decision to bring O'Hara, Partridge thought, had been vindicated several times.

There were no proper seats in the boat they were using. As with the one in which Jessica, Nicky and Angus had traveled earlier, passengers sat low on boards running fore and aft above the keel. The two rowers had positioned themselves on opposite sides and were striving hard to reach the Huallaga River's center. As the sight of Nueva Esperanza faded in the moonlight, a strong current was already carrying them downstream.

Partridge had checked his watch as they left the jetty: 2:35 A.M. At 2:50, with the boat moving along well, following the river's generally northwest course, he told Ken O'Hara to start the engines.

O'Hara opened a fuel-tank air vent on the port-side engine, adjusted a choke, pumped a rubber ball and pulled a flywheel rope hard. The engine fired immediately. He adjusted the engine speed to a fast idle, then followed the same procedure with the second engine. As he put both engines in gear, the boat surged forward.

The sky had stayed clear. Bright moonlight, reflected on the water, made navigation relatively easy along the river's winding course.

Fernández asked, "Have you decided which landing strip we'll head for?"

Partridge calculated, visualizing Fernández's large-scale map which, by now, he almost knew by heart.

First, choosing the river for departure had ruled out a rendezvous at the highway landing point where they arrived. That left the intermediate drug traffickers' landing strip, which they might reach in an hour and a half, or the more distant Sion airstrip which could mean three hours on the river, plus a three-mile trek through the jungle on foot—a difficult challenge, as they already knew.

To get to Sion by 8 A.M., when the AeroLibertad Cheyenne II would be overhead, might be cutting things close. On the other hand, at the intermediate strip they would be several hours early, and if a pursuit should catch them there it would mean a firefight which, outnumbered and outgunned, they would almost certainly lose.

Therefore the best and wisest course seemed to continue putting the greatest possible distance between themselves and Nueva Esperanza.

"We aim for Sion," Partridge told the others in the boat. "When we leave the river and go ashore, we'll have to push hard and fast through the jungle, so get whatever rest you can."

As the time passed, Jessica became more composed; her involuntary shaking ceased, the sickness disappeared. She doubted, though, if she would ever have total peace of mind about what she had done. Certainly the memory of Socorro's desperate, pleading whisper would haunt her for a long, long time ahead.

But Nicky was safe—at least for the moment—and that was what mattered most.

She had been watching Nicky, aware that ever since they left the prison shack he had stayed close to Harry Partridge, at moments being almost underfoot. It seemed as if Harry were a magnet to which Nicky sought to attach himself. Even now he had settled beside Harry in the boat, clearly wanting some physical contact, snuggling up close, which Harry seemed not to mind. In fact, as happened earlier, Harry had put his arm around Nicky's shoulders and the two at this moment seemed as one.

Jessica liked that. Part of Nicky's feeling— inevitably, she thought—was that Harry, appearing as he did, represented all that was opposite from the evil gang who engineered the horrors they had been through—Miguel, Baudelio, Gustavo, Ramón . . . the others known and unknown . . . yes, Vicente and Socorro too.

But more than that. Nicky's instincts about people had always been good. Jessica had once loved Harry—in a way still did, especially now when gratitude and love were mingled. Therefore it did not seem strange at all that her son instinctively should share that feeling.

Nicky seemed to be sleeping. Disengaging himself gently, Partridge maneuvered his way across and sat beside her. Fernández, observing the movement, changed sides also, balancing the boat.

Partridge too had been thinking of the past —what he and Jessica had once meant to each other. And even in this short time he could see that essentially she hadn't changed. All the things he had most admired—her quick mind, strong spirit, warmth, intelligent resourcefulness—were still in place. Partridge knew that if he were around Jessica for long, his old love would revive. A provocative thought—except it wasn't going to happen.

She had turned toward him, perhaps reading his mind. He remembered, from the old days, that she often could.

He asked, "Back there, did you ever give up hope?"

"There were times I came close to it, though never entirely," Jessica said. She smiled. "Of course, if I'd known you were in charge of rescue, that would have made a difference."

"We were a team," he told her. "Crawf was part of it. He's gone through hell, but then so have you. When we get back, you'll both need each other."

He sensed she knew what he was saying too: Though he had returned briefly to her life, he would shortly disappear.

"That's a sweet thought, Harry. And what will you do?"

He shrugged. "Go on reporting. Somewhere there'll be another war. There always is."

"And in between wars?"

To some questions there were no answers. He changed the subject. "Your Nicky's fine— the kind of boy I'd liked to have had myself."

It could have happened, Jessica thought. *For both of us, all those years ago.*

Without wanting to, Partridge found himself thinking of Gemma and their unborn baby boy.

Beside him he heard Jessica sigh. "Oh, Harry!"

They were silent, listening to the outboard motors' thrum and the churning river water. Then she reached out and put her hand on his.

"Thank you, Harry," she said. "Thank you for everything . . . the past, the present . . . my dearest love."

17

Miguel fired three shots into the air, shattering the silence.

He knew it was the quickest way to sound an alarm.

Barely a minute ago, he had discovered the bodies of Socorro and Vicente and realized the prisoners were gone.

It was 3:15 A.M. and, though Miguel did not know it, precisely forty minutes since the boat containing Partridge, Jessica, Nicky, Minh, O'Hara and Fernández had left the Nueva Esperanza jetty.

Miguel's anger was instantaneous, savage and explosive. Inside the prisoners' hut he had seized the guards' chair and hurled it against a wall; the chair had broken. Now he wanted to bludgeon, then dismember limb by limb, those responsible for the prisoners' escape.

Unfortunately, two of them were dead already. And Miguel was painfully aware that he also shared some of the blame.

Without question, he had been lax in enforcing discipline. Now that it was too late, he saw that clearly. Since coming here he had relaxed at times when he should have been attentive. At night, he had left others to oversee precautions he should have supervised himself.

The reason had been a weakness—his infatuation with Socorro.

He had wanted her sexually while at the Hackensack house, both before the kidnap and immediately after. Even now he recalled her blatant sexuality on the day of departure when, with a mocking smile she had spoken to him of catheters inserted in the prisoners for the journey: *"That's tubes in the men's cocks and the bitch's cunt. ¿Entiendes?"*

Yes, he had understood. He had also understood that she was taunting him, just as she taunted the others at Hackensack—for example, the night of her sudden, noisy coupling with Carlos, making Rafael, whom she had refused, near-rabid with jealousy.

But at that time Miguel had other things to consider, responsibilities that kept him occupied, and he had been stern and self-disciplined about his own desire for Socorro.

It had not been that way at Nueva Esperanza.

He hated the jungle; he remembered his feelings on their first day here. Compounding that, there had been little to do. He had never taken seriously, for example, the possibility of attempts to rescue the prisoners; Nueva Esperanza, so deep in Sendero territory, had seemed remote and safe. Therefore the days passed slowly, as did the nights—until Socorro, responding to his pleas, opened the doorway to what he quickly discovered was a sexual paradise.

Since then they had had sex together, sometimes in the days, always in the nights, and she had proved the most accomplished and satisfying lover he had ever known. In the end he had become her willing vassal, and like an addict awaiting the next fix had neglected most else.

He was now paying for that addiction.

Earlier tonight, after an exceptionally satisfying orgy, he had slept deeply. Then some twenty minutes ago he awakened with an erection and, wanting Socorro once more, was unhappy to find her gone. For a while he waited for her to return. When she didn't, he had gone to look for her, taking with him the Makarov pistol he always carried.

What he found had returned him—like a harsh, savage blow—to a world of grim reality.

Miguel thought bitterly: He would pay for what had happened, most likely with his life when Sendero Luminoso got word of this, especially if the prisoners were not recaptured.

Therefore the first priority was to recapture them—at any cost!

Now alerted by his shots, with Gustavo in the lead the other guards had emerged from houses and were running toward him.

He flailed them with his tongue. *"¡Maldita escoria, imbéciles inservibles! Por su estupidez . . . ¡Nunca vigilar! ¡Solo dormir y tomar! ¡Sin cuidar! . . . los presos de mierda se escaparon."*

Singling out Gustavo, he tore into him. "You fucking useless moron! A mangy dog would be a better leader! Strangers came here while you slept and you ignored them, helped them! Find out where they came and how they left. There must be traces!"

Gustavo was back within moments. He announced, "They left by the river! Some boats are gone, others sunk!"

In a tearing rage, Miguel hurried to the jetty. The havoc that he found—mooring lines cut, boats and engines missing, some boats sunk in shallow water—was enough to send him into a frenzy. He knew, though, that unless he cooled and took control, nothing would be salvaged from this disaster. With an effort of will, he began to think objectively.

Continuing in Spanish, he told Gustavo, "I want the two best boats that are left, with two motors on each. Not ready in ten minutes, but now! Use everybody! Work fast, fast, fast! Then

I want everyone assembled on dock, with guns and ammunition, ready to leave."

Weighing possibilities, he decided that whoever engineered the prisoners' release almost certainly came by air into the area; it was the fastest, most practical means of transport. Therefore they would leave the same way, though it was unlikely they had done so yet.

Ramón had just reported that he was relieved by Vicente soon after 1 A.M., when all was well and the prisoners safely in their cells. So even if their release occurred immediately after, the maximum head start of the intruders was two hours. Miguel's instincts—aided by the fact that Socorro's and Vicente's bodies were still warm when found—told him it was substantially less.

He continued reasoning: From Nueva Esperanza, a departure by river for rendezvous with an airplane involved a choice between two possible jungle airstrips. One airstrip, the nearer, had no name; it was simply used by drug planes. The other was Sion—almost twice the distance and where the Learjet bringing Miguel, the other conspirators and the prisoners had arrived slightly more than three weeks ago.

There could be reasons for using either airstrip, which was why Miguel decided to send one armed boatload to the nearer strip, a second

to Sion. He decided to go with the Sion-destined
boat.

Even while he had been thinking, activity
around the jetty had speeded up. Two of the
partially sunk boats were now pulled nearer to
shore and being emptied of water. Those in the
Sendero group who were working had been
joined by other hamlet residents. They all knew
that if Sendero Luminoso's leadership became
enraged at Nueva Esperanza, the organization
could wipe out the entire populace without
compunction. Similar acts had happened before.

Despite the haste, getting started took
longer than Miguel would have liked. But a few
minutes before 4 A.M., both boats were under
way, heading northwest with the current, the
twin motors on each opened to full throttle.
Miguel's boat, heading for Sion, was substantially faster and pulled ahead soon after leaving
the Nueva Esperanza jetty. Gustavo was at the
helm.

Miguel, nursing a Beretta submachine gun
which supplemented his Makarov pistol, felt his
anger rise again. He still had no idea who had
released the prisoners. But when he caught
them and brought them back—alive, as he intended—they would suffer slow and horrible
tortures.

18

As the AeroLibertad Cheyenne II lifted off
from Lima airport in the first gray light of
dawn, some words remembered from an earlier
time came back to Crawford Sloane: *If I take
the wings of the morning, and dwell in the utter-
most parts of the sea . . .*

Yesterday, Sunday, they had taken the
wings of morning, not to the sea but inland,
though without result. Today they were heading
inland again—toward the jungle.

Rita was beside Sloane in the aircraft's sec-
ond row of seats. Ahead of them were the pilot,
Oswaldo Zileri and a young second pilot, Felipe
Guerra.

During the preceding day's flight, which
lasted three hours, they had flown over all three
prearranged points. Though Sloane was informed of their arrival at each, he had difficulty
distinguishing one from another, so continuous
and impenetrable did the Selva seem when
viewed from above. "It's like parts of Vietnam,"
he told Rita, "but more tightly knit."

While circling each point, all four aboard scrutinized the area for any signal or sign of movement. But there was no activity of any kind.

Sloane hoped desperately that today would be different.

As dawn changed to full daylight, the Cheyenne II climbed over the Andes peaks of the Cordillera Central Range. Then, on the far side, they began a slow descent toward the Selva and the Upper Huallaga Valley.

19

Partridge knew he had miscalculated. They were seriously late.

What he had not allowed for in choosing Sion over the nearer airstrip was a problem with their boat. It happened about two hours after leaving Nueva Esperanza, with another hour to go before reaching the place where they would abandon the boat and begin their trek to the airstrip.

Both outboard motors had been running noisily but smoothly when an internal, strident horn abruptly sounded on the port-side motor. Ken O'Hara throttled back at once, took the engine out of gear and switched off. As he did, the horn and engine went silent.

The starboard engine continued operating, though the boat was now moving at a noticeably slower speed.

Partridge moved to the stern and asked O'Hara, "Whatever it is, is it fixable?"

"Unlikely, I'm afraid." O'Hara had removed the engine cover and was examining beneath. "The engine's overheated; that's why the horn sounded. The raw water intake is clear, so almost certainly the coolant pump has gone. Even if I had tools to take the engine apart, it would probably need new parts and since we don't have either . . ." He let the words trail off.

"So we positively can't repair it?"

O'Hara shook his head. "Sorry, Harry."

"What happens if we run it?"

"It will run for a short time and go on overheating. Then everything will get so hot, the pistons and cylinder block will fuse together. After that, all an engine's good for is the garbage dump."

"Run it," Partridge said. "If there's nothing else we can do, let's get the most out of it for as long as we can."

"You're the skipper," O'Hara acknowledged, though he hated destroying an engine which, in other circumstances, could be repaired.

Exactly as O'Hara predicted, the engine ran for a few minutes then, with the horn blaring and a smell of burning, it stopped and would not start again. The boat returned to its slower speed and Partridge anxiously checked his watch.

Their speed, as far as could be judged, had been reduced by half. The remainder of their river journey, instead of taking an hour, would take two.

In fact, it took two and a quarter hours and now, at 6:50 A.M., their landing point was coming into sight. Partridge and Fernández had identified it on the large-scale map, also from signs of previous use—soda cans and other debris littering the shore. Now they would have to cover in an hour the three miles of difficult jungle trail to Sion airstrip. This was far less time than they had anticipated. Could they do it?

"We have to do it," Partridge said, explaining their problem to Jessica and Nicky. "It may be exhausting, but there's no time to rest, and if we have to, we'll help each other. Fernández will lead. I'll be in the rear."

Minutes later the boat keel scraped on a sandy beach and they walked ashore through shallow water. An opening in what was otherwise a solid jungle wall was immediately ahead.

If they had had more time, Partridge would have attempted to hide the boat or push it toward midstream and let it drift. As it was, they left it on the beach.

Then, about to enter the jungle, Fernández halted, motioning everyone to silence. Cocking his head to one side, he stood listening in the still morning air. He was more familiar with the jungle than the others, his hearing more finely attuned to its sounds. He asked Partridge softly, "Do you hear?"

Listening, Partridge thought he could hear a distant murmuring sound from the direction they had come, but wasn't sure. He asked, "What is it?"

"Another boat," Fernández answered. "Still a good distance away, but coming fast."

Without further delay they moved into the jungle.

The trail was not nearly as difficult to follow as that from the highway landing point to Nueva Esperanza which Partridge and the others in the rescue team had traversed three days earlier. It was obvious that the trail they were on was used more frequently, because it was only slightly overgrown and not at any point impassable, as the other had been.

Just the same, it was treacherous underfoot. Uneven ground, protruding roots and soft patches where a foot could sink into mud or water were continual hazards.

"Watch very carefully where you step," Fernández warned from in front where he was setting a fast, forced pace.

Partridge echoed, trying to be flippant and keep spirits high, "We don't want to have to carry anyone. I'm sweating enough."

And so they all were. As during the other jungle trek, the heat was sweltering and steamy and would get hotter as the day advanced. The insects, too, were active.

The uppermost question in Partridge's mind was: How long could Jessica and Nicky last under this grueling pressure? After a while he decided Jessica would make it; she had determination and also, apparently, the stamina. Nicky, though, showed signs of flagging.

At the beginning Nicky hung back, clearly wanting to be close to Partridge, as he had earlier. But Partridge insisted that the boy and Jessica be up forward, immediately behind Fernández. "We'll be together later, Nicky," he said. "Right now I want you with your mother." With obvious reluctance, Nicky had complied.

Assuming the boat they had heard was carrying their pursuers, Partridge knew an assault would come from behind. If and when that happened, he would do his best to fight off the attack while the others continued on. He had already checked the Kalashnikov rifle he was carrying over his shoulder and had the two spare magazines in a pocket where he could get to them easily.

Again Partridge checked his watch: 7:35 A.M. They had been on the trail almost forty minutes. Remembering the eight o'clock rendezvous with AeroLibertad, he hoped they had covered three quarters of the way.

Moments later they were forced to stop.

Considered afterward, it seemed ironic that Fernández, who warned the others about stepping carefully, should himself misstep and fall heavily, his foot trapped in a muddy mess of roots. As Partridge hurried toward him, Minh was already holding Fernández while O'Hara struggled to free the foot; at the same time Fernández was grimacing with pain.

"I appear to have done some damage," he told Partridge. "I am sorry. I have let you down."

When the foot was free, Fernández found it impossible to walk without excruciating pain. Clearly his ankle was broken or very badly sprained.

"That's not true; you've never let us down," Partridge said. "You've been our guide and good companion and we'll carry you. We need to make some kind of litter."

Fernández shook his head. "Even if possible, there is not time. I have not spoken of it, Harry, but I have heard sounds behind us. They are following, and not far away. You must go on, and leave me."

Jessica had joined them. She told Partridge, "We *can't* leave him here."

"One of us can take you on his back," O'Hara said. "I'll try it."

"In this heat?" Fernández was impatient. "You would not last a hundred yards and it would slow all of you."

About to add his own protest, Partridge knew it would be an exercise in futility. Fernández was right; there could be no other choice than leaving him. But he added, "If there's help at the airstrip and it can be done, we'll come back for you."

"Do not waste more time, Harry. I need to say some things quickly." Fernández was sitting beside the trail, his back against a tree; the brush was too thick to move him farther in. Partridge knelt beside him. Jessica joined them.

"I have a wife and four children," Fernández said. "I would like to think someone will take care of them."

"You work for CBA," Partridge said, "and CBA will do it. I give you my solemn word, an official promise. The children's education—everything."

Fernández nodded, then motioned to an M-16 rifle he had been carrying and which lay beside him. "You had better take this. You may need it as well as what you have. But I do not intend to be taken alive. I would like a pistol."

Partridge gave him the nine-millimeter Browning, first slipping off the silencer.

"Oh, Fernández!" Jessica's voice was choked, her eyes filled with tears. "Nicky and I owe you so much." She leaned forward and kissed him on the forehead.

"Then go!" Fernández urged her. "Do not squander more time and lose what we have won!"

As Jessica rose, Partridge leaned forward, held Fernández tightly and kissed him on both cheeks. Behind him Minh and O'Hara waited to give a farewell hug.

Rising, Partridge moved forward. He did not look back.

The moment Miguel saw a boat beached at the entrance to the jungle trail, then recognized it as from Nueva Esperanza, he was glad he had made the decision to join the Sion airstrip sortie.

He was even more pleased when Ramón, leaping quickly from their own boat as it nudged into shore, ran to the other boat and announced, *"Un motor está caliente, el otro frio —fundido."*

The hot engine meant their quarry had not been in the jungle very long. The cold, burned-out engine told them the other boat's speed had been reduced, its occupants delayed in getting here.

As well as Miguel, the Sendero group comprised seven well-armed men. Speaking in Spanish, he told them, "The bourgeois scum cannot be far ahead. We'll catch and punish them. Let us move like the wrath of Guzmán!"

There was a ragged cheer as they filed quickly into the jungle.

"We're a few minutes early," Rita Abrams told the Cheyenne II pilot, Oswaldo Zileri, as they approached the Sion airstrip—first point of call on their aerial itinerary. A moment ago she had checked her watch: 7:55.

"We'll circle and watch," he said. "In any case, this is the least likely place for your friends to be."

As they had yesterday, all four in the plane —Rita, Crawford Sloane, Zileri and the copilot, Felipe—peered down at the quilt of green beneath them. They were looking for any sign of movement, particularly around the short, tree-lined airstrip, which was hard to see until they were directly overhead. Again, like yesterday, there was no visible activity of any kind.

Along the jungle trail, Nicky was finding it increasingly difficult to maintain the punishing pace. Jessica and Minh were helping him, each grabbing an arm and partially pulling him, partially lifting him over difficult patches as they continued forward. Eventually Nicky might have to be carried, but for the moment the others husbanded their remaining strength.

It had been about ten minutes since they left Fernández. Ken O'Hara was now up ahead, leading. Partridge had dropped back to his position in the rear, from where he occasionally glanced backward. So far there had been no sign of movement.

Above their heads, the trees appeared to be thinning, more daylight coming through their branches; also the trail had widened. It was a sign, Partridge hoped, that they were nearing the airstrip. At one point he thought he heard the distant sound of an airplane, but could not be sure. Again he checked his watch: nearly 7:55.

At that moment, from somewhere behind, came a short, sharp crack—unmistakably the sound of a single shot. It had to be Fernández, Partridge reasoned. And even in using the Browning, from which Partridge had deliberately removed the silencer, the zealous stringer-fixer provided a final service—a warning that pursuit was close. As if in confirmation, several other shots followed.

Perhaps the pursuers, having seen Fernández—presumably dead—thought they saw others ahead and had fired at random. Then, for whatever reason, the firing ceased.

Partridge himself was near exhaustion. Through the past fifty hours, with scarcely any sleep, he had pushed himself to the limit. Now he was having trouble keeping his attention focused.

In one of those moments, mentally meandering, he decided that what he wanted most was relief from action . . . When this adventure ended he would resume the vacation he had barely started and simply disappear, be unavailable . . . And wherever he went, perhaps he should take Vivien—the only woman left to him whose loving was available . . . Jessica and Gemma had been the past; Vivien could be the future. Perhaps, until now, he had treated her unfairly, should consider marriage after all . . . It was not too late . . . He knew it was something Vivien would like . . . .

With an effort, he snapped back to the present.

Suddenly they had emerged from the jungle. The airstrip was in view! Overhead an airplane was circling—it was a Cheyenne! Ken O'Hara —reliable to the end, Partridge thought—was loading a green-banded cartridge into the flare gun he had carried all this way. Green for *Land normally, everything is clear.*

With equal suddenness, from behind, came the sound of two more shots, this time much closer.

"Send up a red flare, not a green!" Partridge yelled at O'Hara. "And do it fast!"

Red for *Land as quickly as possible, we are in danger!*

It was several minutes past eight o'clock. In the Cheyenne II above Sion airstrip, Zileri turned his head toward Rita and Sloane. He told them, "Nothing's happening here. We'll go to the other two points."

The plane turned away. As it did, Crawford Sloane called out, "Hold it! I think I saw something!"

Zileri aborted the turn and swung the airplane back. He asked, "Where?"

"Somewhere down there." Sloane pointed. "I'm not sure of the exact spot. It was just for a moment . . . I thought . . ." His voice mirrored his own uncertainty.

Zileri flew the plane in a circle. Again they scrutinized as much of the ground as they could. When the circle was complete the pilot said, "I don't see a thing. I think we should go on."

At that moment, a red flare curled upward from the ground.

O'Hara fired a second red flare.

"That'll do. They've seen us," Partridge said. The airplane had already turned toward them. What he needed to know now was which way the plane would land. Then he would pick a position to fight off the pursuers and occupy it while the others boarded first.

The answer quickly became evident. The Cheyenne II was in a tight descending turn, losing height fast, and would come in over their heads. After that, it would land facing away from the jungle trail from where the shooting had been coming.

Looking back, Partridge could still see no one in sight, despite the shots. He could only guess the reason for shooting. Perhaps someone, while advancing, was firing blindly, hoping for a lucky hit.

He told O'Hara, "Get Jessica and Nicky down by the landing strip fast, and stay with them! When the plane gets to the far end, they'll swing around and taxi back. Go forward to meet the airplane, and all of you get aboard. Did you hear that, Minh?"

"I heard." Minh, with an eye glued to his

camera, was imperturbably taking pictures, as he had at various moments throughout the journey. Partridge decided not to worry anymore about Minh. He would take care of himself.

Jessica asked anxiously, "What about you, Harry?"

He told her, "I'm going to cover you by firing down the trail. As soon as you're aboard I'll join you. Now get going!"

O'Hara put an arm around Jessica, who was holding Nicky's good hand, and hurried them away.

Even as they moved, looking back toward the jungle Partridge saw several figures now in sight, advancing on the airstrip, guns pointed forward.

Partridge dropped behind a small hillock nearby. Lying on his belly, he rested the Kalashnikov in front of him, the sights of the automatic rifle directed at the moving figures. He squeezed the trigger, and amid a burst of fire saw one of the figures fall, the others dive for cover. At the same time he heard the Cheyenne II swoop in low above his head. Though he did not turn to watch, he knew it should be landing now.

"There they are!" Crawford Sloane shouted, near-hysterical with excitement. "I see them! It's Jessica and Nicky!" The airplane was still on its landing run, traveling fast on an uneven dirt surface.

The end of the short strip was looming nearer, Zileri braking hard. As the landing run ended, employing brakes and one engine, the pilot swung the airplane around to face the way they had come. Then, using both engines for acceleration, he taxied back down the airstrip, moving fast toward its opposite end.

The Cheyenne II stopped at the point where Jessica, Nicky and O'Hara were waiting. The copilot, Felipe, had already left his seat and moved aft. From inside the fuselage he released and lowered an air-stair door.

Nicky first, then Jessica and O'Hara climbed aboard, outstretched hands, including Sloane's, helping pull them in. Minh appeared and scrambled in behind the others.

As Sloane, Jessica and Nicky emotionally hugged each other, O'Hara called out breathlessly, "Harry's up ahead. We have to get him. He's holding off the terrorists."

"I see him," Zileri said. "Hold on!" He opened the throttles again and the airplane shot forward, taxiing fast.

At the runway's far end he turned the airplane around once more. It was now facing the way it landed, ready for takeoff but with the passenger door still open. Gunfire could be heard through the doorway.

"Your friend will have to make a run for it."
Zileri's voice was urgent. "I want to get the hell
out of here."

"He will," Minh said. "He's seen us and
he'll come."

Partridge had both seen and heard the airplane. Glancing over his shoulder, he knew it
was as close to him as it could come. There was
about a hundred yards between him and the
plane. He would make it at a fast run, keeping
low. First though, he had to spray fire back into
the jungle trail to deter any further advance by
the Sendero force. In the past few minutes he
had seen several more figures appear, had fired
and seen another fall. The others were now hug-
ging the shelter of the trees. A burst of fire
would hold them there, out of sight, long
enough for him to reach the plane.

He had just put a fresh magazine into the
Kalashnikov. Squeezing the trigger, then holding it, he poured a deadly hail of bullets along
both sides of the jungle path. Since the firing
began he had felt his old visceral zest for battle
stir . . . that sensuous thrill; it set adrenaline
running, juices flowing . . . an illogical, crazy
addiction to the sights and sounds of war . . .

When the magazine had emptied, he
dropped the rifle, sprang to his feet and ran,

doubling over to stay low. The airplane was ahead. He knew he'd make it!

Partridge was a third of the way to the plane when a bullet struck his leg. He fell instantly. It was all so fast, it took him several seconds to grasp what had happened.

The bullet had impacted at the back of his right knee, shattering the joint. He could go no farther. A terrible pain, more pain than he had ever believed possible, swept over him. He knew, at that moment, he would never reach the airplane. He knew, too, that there was no time left. The plane must go. And he must do what Fernández had done, barely half an hour earlier.

Summoning a final surge of strength, he raised himself, waving the Cheyenne forward. All that mattered now was that his intention should be clear.

Minh was in the airplane doorway, shooting pictures. He had Partridge in his zoom lens—a closeup—and had captured the moment when the bullet hit. The copilot, Felipe, was beside Minh.

Felipe called in, "He's hit! I think badly. He's waving for us to go."

Inside the airplane, Sloane pushed toward the door. "We have to get him!"

Jessica cried out, "Yes! Oh yes!"

Nicky echoed, "Please don't go without Harry!"

It was Minh, the realist about war, who said, "You can't get him. There isn't time."

Minh had seen through his lens the advancing Sendero force. Several of its members had reached the airstrip perimeter, were running forward and firing their guns. Just then, several bullets hit the plane.

"I'm leaving," Zileri said. He had already lowered flaps for takeoff; now he pushed the throttles forward. Minh, plus camera, tumbled in. Felipe retracted and secured the air-stair door.

As airspeed built, Zileri eased back on the control column. The Cheyenne II left the airstrip and climbed.

Jessica and Nicky were holding each other, weeping. Sloane, his eyes partially closed, was shaking his head slowly, as if not believing what he had just seen.

Minh held his camera against a window, taking final shots of the scene below.

On the ground, Partridge saw the Cheyenne II go.

And saw something else. Through a haze of pain, in the doorway of the departing airplane he saw a smiling figure in Alitalia uniform. She was waving.

Partridge's tears, long held back, began to flow. Then more bullets hit him and he died.

20

Looking down at the body of Harry Partridge, Miguel vowed that never again would he let something like today's fiasco happen.

In the first stage of the kidnap enterprise, which was complex and demanding, he had been fabulously successful. In this second stage, which should have been easy and uncomplicated, he had failed abysmally.

The lesson was clear: *Nothing* was easy and uncomplicated. He should have learned it long ago.

He would remember it, however, from this moment on.

So what came next?

First, he must leave Peru. His life would be forfeit if he stayed; Sendero Luminoso would see to that.

He could not even go back to Nueva Esperanza.

Fortunately, he had no reason to. Before departure, foreseeing the possibility of what actually occurred, he had stowed all of his cash—including most of the fifty thousand dollars he collected from José Antonio Salaverry during his final visit to the United Nations—into a money belt he was wearing. He could feel it now. Uncomfortable but reassuring.

The money was ample to get him out of Peru and into Colombia.

What he intended now was to slip away into the jungle. There was an airstrip twenty-five kilometers away—not either of the two that had been targeted today—where drug-traffic planes flown by Colombian pilots came and went frequently. He knew he could buy passage to Colombia and, once there, would be safe.

If anyone in the group from Nueva Esperanza attempted to stop him, he would kill him. But Miguel doubted if anyone would. Of the seven who had accompanied him here, only four were still alive; Ramón and two others had been killed by this *gringo* who lay at his feet—identity unknown, though a good marksman.

Even back in Colombia, his reputation would suffer a little from the Nueva Esperanza debacle, but that would not last. And unlike Sendero Luminoso, the Colombian drug cartels were not fanatical. Ruthless, yes, but otherwise pragmatic and businesslike. Miguel had eminently salable talents as an anarchist-terrorist. The cartels had need of him.

Miguel had recently learned that a long-term program was under way to convert a series of small and medium-sized countries to the same drug-cartel-dominated status as Colombia. He was certain the project would present an opportunity for his special skills.

As a functioning democracy Colombia was finished. Outwardly, some showcase trappings remained, but even those were disappearing as killings ordered by the cartels' powerful billionaire bosses eliminated the diminishing minority who believed in bygone ways.

What was needed to transform other countries into replicas of Colombia was corruption at or near the top of governments, corruption making it possible for drug cartels to move in and operate. Next, insidiously and quietly, the cartels would become stronger than the governments—after which, as in Colombia, there was never any turning back.

Four countries were mentioned nowadays as potential targets to be "Colombia-ized." They were Bolivia, El Salvador, Guatemala and Jamaica. Later, others could be added to the list.

With his unique experience and ability to survive, Miguel decided, he was likely to be busy for a long time ahead.

21

Aboard the Cheyenne II, several minutes passed before anyone felt capable of speech. Crawford Sloane was holding Jessica and Nicky close to him, the three oblivious to all else.

At length Sloane raised his head and asked Minh Van Canh, "About Harry . . . did you see anything more?"

Minh nodded sadly. "I was focused on him. He was hit again, several times. There isn't any doubt."

Sloane sighed. "He was the best . . ."

Minh corrected him, his voice unusually strong. "The *very* best. As a correspondent. As a human being. I've seen a good many, and there wasn't anyone I knew who came close to Harry in all those years." The words were spoken almost as a challenge. Minh had known Sloane and Partridge for an equal time.

If it *was* a challenge, Sloane did not contest it. He said simply, "I agree."

Jessica and Nicky were listening, both busy with their thoughts.

It was Rita, the professional with responsibilities, who asked Minh, "May I see some of your pictures?" She knew that despite Harry's death, she must put a broadcast together in Lima, barely an hour away.

She also knew they had a world exclusive story.

Minh did some rewinding, then passed his Betacam to Rita. Squinting through the viewfinder, she watched videotape shots: as usual, Minh had captured the essentials of everything. The pictures were superb. Some final shots—of Harry wounded, then falling to the fatal bullets —were stark and moving. As she handed the camera back, Rita's eyes were moist but she wiped them with the back of her hand, knowing there was no time now either to mourn Harry or to cry. Both would come later, probably when she was alone tonight.

Sloane asked, "Did Harry have anybody—a girlfriend? I know he never remarried after Gemma."

"There was—is someone," Rita said. "Her name is Vivien. She's a nurse and lives in a place called Port Credit; that's outside Toronto."

"We should call. I'll talk to her if you like."

"Yes, I would like," Rita said. "And when you do, tell her Harry made a will before leaving and I have it. He left everything to her. Vivien doesn't know it, but she's a millionaire now. It seems Harry salted money away in tax havens all over the world. Along with the will, he left a list."

Minh, unnoticed while they were talking, had been taking video shots of Jessica and Nicky. Now, Rita saw, the camera was directed at Nicky's bandaged right hand. It reminded her of something she had brought from Lima and, reaching into a briefcase, she produced a Teletype message received through Entel Peru.

"Before Harry left," Rita told the others, "he asked me to send a cable to one of his friends—a surgeon in Oakland, California. Harry explained that his friend is among the world's ranking experts on injured hands. The cable asked questions about Nicholas. This is the reply."

She passed the typed sheet to Sloane who read it aloud.

RETEL. HAVE READ INFO YOU SENT ALSO DETAILS IN NEWSPAPERS ABOUT YOUR YOUNG FRIEND'S HAND. PROSTHESES NOT RECOMMENDED. THEY WILL NOT FUNCTION OR HELP HIM PLAY PIANO, MAY EVEN GET IN WAY. IN-

STEAD HE SHOULD AND CAN LEARN TO ROTATE
HAND DOWNWARD UNTIL WHAT REMAINS OF
INDEX AND LITTLE FINGERS COMES IN CON-
TACT WITH PIANO KEYS. INCIDENTALLY IN A
WAY HE'S LUCKY BECAUSE FOREGOING WOULD
NOT BE POSSIBLE IF DIFFERENT FINGERS LOST.
APPLIES ONLY TO THOSE TWO.

LEARNING TO ROTATE HAND WILL TAKE
PATIENCE, PERSEVERANCE. BUT IF ENTHUSIAS-
TIC CAN BE DONE. BEING YOUNG HELPS. HAVE
WOMAN PATIENT WHO LOST SAME FINGERS
NOW PLAYS PIANO. WOULD BE GLAD TO BRING
TWO TOGETHER IF YOU WISH.

TAKE CARE OF YOURSELF HARRY. WARMEST
REGARDS.

JACK TUPPER, M.D.

There was a silence, then Nicky said, "May
I look at that, Dad?" Sloane passed the sheet
across.

"Don't lose that!" Jessica cautioned Nicky.
"It will give you something to remember Harry
by." The instinctive, close companionship of
Harry and Nicky, she thought, had been brief
yet beautiful while it lasted.

She remembered Nicky's early dispirited
words to Harry at Nueva Esperanza: *"They
killed my granddad and cut off two of my fingers, so I can't play the piano anymore."* Obviously Nicky would never be a concert pianist,
which he had dreamed of. But he *would* play

the piano and fulfill his joy in music in other ways.

Nicky was reading the cable, holding it in his left hand while the beginning of a smile appeared on his face. He was turning his bandaged right hand in a rolling motion.

"I guess there will never be a time," Crawford Sloane said, "when there isn't something we'll have reason to thank Harry for."

"Fernández, too," Jessica reminded him. They had already spoken of the stringer-fixer's sacrifice and presumed death. Now she told Crawford and Rita of the promise Harry made before leaving Fernández beside the jungle trail.

Fernández had spoken of his wife and four children, asking if someone would take care of them, and Harry pledged, *"You work for CBA, and CBA will do it. I give you my solemn word, an official promise. The children's education—everything."*

"If Harry said that," Sloane said, "he was speaking for CBA and it's binding like a legal document. When we get back I'll see it's put into effect."

"There's one snag," Rita pointed out. "It happened after Harry was fired, even though he didn't know it."

Minh, who overheard, looked startled—a reminder that only a few people knew about the Chippingham letter of dismissal.

"It makes no difference," Sloane said. "Harry's promise will be honored."

"But it does bring up something we have to decide," Rita pointed out. "Are we going to refer to Harry's firing in what we report today?"

"No," Sloane said emphatically. "That's our internal dirty linen. We won't wash it in public."

But it will come out, Rita thought. *In the end, it always does.*

Crawf still didn't know about the *"You-son-of-a-bitch!"* memo she had faxed to Les Chippingham via the Horseshoe. Probably within a week that would surface in the *Times* or *Washington Post.* And if not there, then later in the *Columbia Journalism Review* or *Washington Journalism Review.* Well, let it happen!

Rita was reminded that, as a result of the memo, she was probably out of a job. Among other things she had signed herself "ex-producer." Well, however it all came out, she would see this present assignment through to its end.

Jessica spoke up. "There's something that's been bothering me. It's about the airstrip we were at, the last one."

"Sion," Rita prompted.

Jessica nodded. "I had the feeling, on the jungle trail and at the airstrip, that I'd been there before. I think it's where we were brought first, when we all came back from unconsciousness. Though I didn't know it was an airstrip then. And there's something else."

"Go on," Rita said. She had reached for a pad and was making notes.

"There was a man in a hut we were held in. I don't know who or what he was, though I'm sure he was American. I pleaded with him to help us, but he didn't. I have this, though."

The day before, Jessica had retrieved from beneath the mattress in her cell the drawing she had made. Since then she had carried it, folded, in her brassiere. She handed it to Rita.

The drawing was of the Learjet pilot, Denis Underhill.

"Tonight," Rita said, "we'll run this on the National Evening News and ask if anyone can identify him. With twenty million people watching, there should be someone."

The Cheyenne II droned on, still climbing, gaining altitude to pass over the peaks of the Andes Cordillera Range, after which they would descend toward sea level and Lima. The time, Rita noted, was a few minutes past 9 A.M. The flight would take another forty minutes.

What was necessary now, she realized, was to make a firm plan for the remainder of the day, in conjunction with Crawf. She had already done some advance work, having anticipated most, though not all, of what had happened.

The dramatic story of the rescue was, at this moment, exclusively CBA's. Therefore, until New York first-feed broadcast time, which was 5:30 P.M. in Peru, Jessica and Nicky must be kept somewhere out of sight, unavailable to the remainder of the media. Crawf, she was sure, would see the need for that.

It meant that Jessica and Nicky could not yet be taken to Cesar's Hotel or Entel Peru, both of which were swarming with reporters and TV crews. The same applied to other hotels in downtown Lima.

So what Rita had arranged was for them to go to the home of the AeroLibertad owner-pilot, Oswaldo Zileri, who lived on the outskirts of Miraflores. They could remain there until 5:30, after which their being seen by others in press or television would no longer matter. In fact, it was an ordeal they would eventually have to face.

In the meantime, working with Bob Watson, the TV-video editor, Rita would put a report together for the National Evening News that night. It would be a long one and use most of Minh's best pictures—of the rescue, the death of Harry Partridge and the sad moment when Fernández had been left beside the jungle trail.

She wouldn't even ask New York for a spe-

cific amount of time. This was one occasion
when she knew she could have whatever time
was needed.

Rita was certain, too, that the network
would want a one-hour news special in prime
time tonight. Well, she had extra ingredients for
that. They included the videotape recording of
Dolores, the drunken companion of the American ex-doctor Hartley Gossage, alias Baudelio,
who so despicably used his medical skills to
transport the three kidnap victims to Peru.
Harry had put that together as a package, with
his own commentary; it was ready to go.

As to everything else, both for the evening
news and later, Crawf would do the narration
and standups. That might be difficult for him.
He would need to speak of the deaths of his
own father, Harry Partridge and Fernández,
and of the mutilation of Nicky's hand. Crawf
was sometimes emotional and might choke up.
No matter, Rita thought. It would make the
story more convincing, and Crawf would recover and go on. He was a professional newsperson, like Rita and the rest.

One item of news, Rita realized, could not
and should not be suppressed throughout the
day. That was the fact that a rescue had occurred and Nicky and Jessica were safe.

There must be a bulletin. When CBA News
received it in New York, they would break in-

stantly into network programming. Once more, CBA would be ahead of the competition.

Again Rita checked her watch: 9:23. Another twenty minutes or so of flying. Allowing time to get from the airport into Lima, the bulletin could be set for 10:30 A.M. They would send just a few pictures, transmitting "quick and dirty"—the way they had from Dallas–Fort Worth airport for the Airbus crash story she, Harry, Minh and Ken O'Hara had worked on less than a month ago.

Was it really only that short a time? It seemed much longer—another world away.

She would need satellite time for the 10:30 bulletin. Rita leaned forward and tapped Zileri on the shoulder. When he turned, she pointed to the aircraft radio. "Can you patch a phone call through? I want to call New York."

"Sure can."

She scribbled a number and passed it forward. In a surprisingly short time a voice on a speaker said, "CBA foreign desk."

The copilot, Felipe, passed back a microphone. "Go ahead," he told her.

She held the transmit button down. "This is Rita Abrams. Get me a bird out of Lima for a bulletin at 10:30 Lima time. Make sure the Horseshoe knows."

A voice replied laconically, "You got it. Will do."

"Thanks. Goodbye." She handed the microphone back.

A script would be needed for the bulletin, also for later. Rita scribbled a few phrases, then decided Crawf would do the rest and find the right words. He always did. He would probably ad-lib in part. He was good at that too.

In what was left of the flight, she and Crawf must work together. Unfortunately, it meant pulling him away from the arms of Jessica and Nicky. But he would accept the need and so would they. Like everyone else in the business, they all understood that the news came first.

"Crawf," Rita said gently, "you and I have work to do. It's time we started."

BOOK MARK

The text of this book was set in the
typeface Times
and the display in Waldbaum
by Berryville Graphics,
Berryville, Virginia.

It was printed and bound by
Berryville Graphics, Berryville, Virginia.

DESIGNED BY CHRIS WELCH